# SPIES OF ROME
*Blood & Honour*
*Blood & Vengeance*
*Blood & Secrets*

Richard Foreman

# Table of Contents

# BLOOD & HONOUR.

# 1.

"She's probably as dry as a bone, and tastes like one too," Rufus Varro joked to his friend, Manius, as he gazed up at the whore on the balcony. She adjusted her dress so that her left breast hung out of it. Varro couldn't quite tell if she'd painted her nipples, or if she had a rash. The ageing prostitute pouted, or mimicked a kiss, at the potential client. Her painted eyebrows must have been put on when she was tipsy, he fancied. A ruddy-cheeked water boy dutifully stood at the top of the stairs, ready to help the whores and customers alike should they want to wash-up afterwards.

It was late. The two men sat in the tavern, *The Golden Lion*, with a jug of wine and a half-eaten plate of ham, cheese and olives on the rickety table in front of them.

"The flower next to her - more thorn than rose - is called Hilaria, if I remember rightly," Varro added. "She was past her shelf-life even when Pompey was alive. I once bedded her younger sister though. She either loved what she did or was a great actress. Some might argue that the two professions are one in the same. I think she's now Nonius Cimber's wife, or mistress. Either way he's probably being unfaithful to her. Although she's doubtless cuckolding him in return. All's fair in love and marriage. If only love and marriage could prove one in the same thing," the poet sardonically remarked, wryly smiling as he drained his cup of honeyed wine. He briefly thought about his own wife, Lucilla, and winced. Marriage hadn't saved his soul. Divorce had.

Manius nodded and grinned in reply, although inside he believed two people could love each other and prove faithful once married. He thought about his parents, long dead. He also thought of Camilla and something inside of him – his heart or another significant organ - yearned to see her. Smell her moreish perfume. Have his fingertips run themselves along her silk dress, or skin. Hear her musical laugh.

Aside from his eyes – bloodshot from a love of good (and indifferent) wine – Rufus Varro appeared younger than his thirty-one years. Glossy black curls hung down over a smooth brow. Pronounced cheekbones and an aquiline nose dominated his classically Roman face. In winter, his unblemished face seemed carved from marble and in summer forged in bronze. A plain tunic covered his slim, well-proportioned figure. It was wise not to dress too ostentatiously in the Subura, for fear of attracting the attention of the robbers and rogues who resided in the infamous neighbourhood. Many joked (and some believed in earnest) that the Subura was the lowest part of Rome, just above the gateway to the underworld.

As well as surveying the languid figures on the balcony Varro cast his eye around the rest of the establishment. It must have been over half a year since he had last walked through the doors of *The Golden Lion*. But it owned the virtue of being open late and the wine on offer was duly tolerable, for the Subura.

The smell of garum and lamp oil infused the air. A bust of Julius Caesar sat on a shelf over the fireplace. Its nose had been clumsily re-attached, having

1

been broken off after a mass brawl. Next to the bust was an old, rust-ridden gladius – purported to have once belonged to Caesar. The landlord often told the story of how a young Julius, who lived in the Subura as a child, came into the tavern and cleared everyone out in a game of dice. "He came, he saw, he conquered," Bassos always exclaimed, when ending the anecdote.

Around half a dozen customers were spread out around the tavern (another patron could be heard from the bed, creaking, upstairs). A couple of men in the corner were conducting some business. A thief was attempting to sell some stolen jewellery to a shop owner. The seller was holding the trinkets up to the light, endeavouring to show-off the craftmanship. The prospective buyer however was pursing his lips, shaking his head and shrugging his shoulders to convey that it was beyond his power to offer a higher price. A couple of grey-bearded sots were asleep in another corner, after having played some dice. A few flies buzzed over them and occasionally landed on their scalps, like they were pieces of dung. Varro couldn't help but notice the mice scurrying along the edges of the room. He was tempted to propose a wager with his friend, as if the two mice were involved in a chariot race at the arena and whichever competitor reached the doorway first would be proclaimed the winner.

Manius let out a yawn. Unlike his friend, he hadn't woken up late nor slept all afternoon. Tiredness was catching up with him. As much as the hulking Briton spent time being Varro's drinking companion, he was also employed by the Roman aristocrat as his attendant and bodyguard.

Though Manius appeared older, the two men were the same age. They had known each other now for a decade. Appius Varro, Rufus' father, had purchased the gladiator's freedom – and adopted him - as a reward for his heroics in the arena. The crowd nicknamed him, somewhat unimaginatively, "The Briton". As well as serving as a bodyguard, Manius was tasked with conditioning the statesman's son and teaching him swordsmanship. In return the poet taught his companion Latin and introduced him to Roman literature and history (as well as to the taverns and brothels of the city).

The Briton had the solid build of the soldier - although he had been brought up in a school for gladiators, rather than in the army. His square jawline was covered with a short beard. He suggested to Camilla that he would shave it off if she wished, but as she said she liked it he kept it. His hazel eyes could harden or soften, depending on his mood. Some might have considered the Briton to be ruggedly handsome. If one moved close enough though they could discern the evidence of several broken noses and small facial scars, earned through doing battle in the arena or fighting in tavern brawls (although Manius was not one to start a fight, he was more than capable of ending one). His tunic stretched across his barrel chest. Brawny arms hung down from the sleeves. And a dagger hung down from his belt.

"Is that a couple of ghosts from the past I see before me?" Bassos, the owner of the establishment, warmly remarked as he walked out from the steam-filled kitchen. Bassos was bald, rotund with bushy eyebrows and a double, if not treble, chin. The apron he wore was even filthier than his whores, Varro

2

mused. And his fingernails were as black as night. The niggarding proprietor, a former sailor from Brundiscium, could often be heard complaining about how little money he earned, but Varro figured that had more to do with his wife's profligacy than his business acumen. The poet recalled how, over the years, Bassos advertised his tavern as being a place filled with good wine and cheap whores. Although he also occasionally argued the establishment was filled with cheap wine and good whores.

"Good to see you again, Rufus," Bassos said. "And you too, Manius." His voice carried a slight sibilance to it, from his mouth missing a few front teeth. The two men got up from their chairs and shook hands with their host, before sitting again. They had spent, or wasted, many a night in the *The Golden Lion* before, over the years. Drinking. Whoring. Gambling. Varro found it difficult to adhere to the Ciceronian "good life", as much as he admired the famed statesman's prose style. As a youth he had carved several quotes into a bench in his garden. *A room without books is like a body without a soul... Honour is the reward of virtue... The greater the difficulty, the greater the glory.*

"I've not seen you both for some time. Have you been travelling?"

"No. I've seen enough of the world not to want to see any more of it," Varro answered, before popping another brackish olive into his mouth. "The best of the provinces, in terms of food, wine and women all come to Rome. I've no need to venture out and encounter the worst they offer too."

"I hope you haven't been ill," Bassos replied, creasing-up his bushy eyebrows in potential sympathy.

"Well Manius here has been sick in one way. Love sick."

"Ignore him. Or better still, poison him," Manius said, rolling his eyes and shaking his head in mild exasperation at his friend. He'd long started to question the wisdom of having told Rufus about Camilla.

"The symptoms are all there. Should Cytheris or Clodia now walk in, in their prime, Manius would not give them a second look. He's not sleeping properly, he's off his food and I may have even caught him singing the other day. Or at the very least humming. I suspect he's even been reading poetry."

"Well if I read any of yours then at least I'd be cured of any difficulties falling asleep," the Briton said, raising his cup to his companion in a mock-toast of getting his own joke in.

"Et tu, Manius?" Varro countered, feigning insult. "You should be more grateful. If it wasn't for my selfish and priapic ways I wouldn't have abandoned you at the party the other month – and left you to discover your intended in the garden."

"It's good to see you haven't changed much in the time I last saw you," the landlord asserted, enjoying the friends' banter. They had been good customers over the years. Varro had plenty of money and purchased his better wines. And Manius had helped Bassos eject more than one troublesome drunk.

"So, how's business been?" Varro asked, having noticed fewer customers, fewer tables, fewer whores and fewer olives on the plate compared to previous visits to the tavern.

"It's been bad. But it's picking up. Soldiers are coming back from the war. Peace encourages prosperity. Octavius finally ran out of rivals and enemies," the landlord said, shrugging his shoulders philosophically – and excavating some wax out of his ear with his little finger. Weariness and optimism seemed to equally chequer his tone.

"This is Rome, remember? Enemies can breed like rats. Everyone wants to be a Caesar. The comedy or tragedy of the course of honours must be played out. Factions in the Senate House will look to curb Octavius' power. Some still view him as an interloper, a boy who inherited a name," Varro argued, unsure about which way he would side, should the Senate attempt to challenge Octavius. Although born to an old patrician family - whose ancestors had served as senators and consuls throughout the history of the Republic – Varro had started to believe in the new Caesar, that he had more chance than the squabbling Senate House of providing stability and prosperity in Rome.

"Well, I'm not sure about Octavius from Velitrae. I'm more excited about Nefertari from Alexandria. I've got a fresh girl coming next week. I remember, Rufus, when you used to try all my new dishes," Bassos remarked, raising his eyebrows and winking suggestively.

"Aye, I had quite an appetite back then. Who's going to be on the menu then?" the nobleman asked, indulging his host and allowing him to deliver his sales pitch.

"Her name means "the most beautiful." Her legs go right up to her breasts and I've got wine that's twice her age. She's exotic looking, being from the East - and as sinuous as the asp which done for Cleopatra. For the right price, I can put your name down for being first on the list to try her out. Invite your friends too," Bassos suggested, licking his lips at the thought of the profits from the girl, rather than picturing the girl herself. Rumour had it that the owner of the establishment didn't sample his own goods because, as a youth, he had contracted a pox and half his manhood fell off. Varro tended to believe however that Bassos behaved himself because, if he didn't, his wife would castrate him completely – if she hadn't done so already.

A crashing sound, emanating from the kitchen, caused the landlord to suddenly break off his sales pitch.

"Stupid bastard! I best see what's gone wrong. Serves me for hiring a cripple as a chef. Thankfully he's cheap and he doesn't mind working through the night."

Bassos marched back into the kitchen, offering up a curse to the world or one more specifically directed towards his cook.

"He's not changed much either, for good or ill," Varro commented, pouring himself another measure of wine. Manius shook his head to indicate that he didn't want anymore. His friend could guess the reason why. "So, are you meeting Camilla tomorrow? Or given the late hour, I should say later today."

"Hopefully. She is now worried her father will find out about us and forbid her from seeing me - or have her followed."

"She's spirited and clever. In my experience, a woman will always find a way to meet her suitor. Of course, the women I see often need to escape the attention of their husbands, rather than fathers," Varro drily said.

Manius raised a half-smile, at best, in response. His stomach churned, dreading that his relationship with the merchant's daughter was doomed to fail. Her father wanted her to marry into the political classes, to advance his own interests as well as his daughter's. The Briton was but a lowly attendant – and a barbaric foreigner. Manius knew what the problem and solution was: money. This was Rome. Respect and influence could be bought, as surely as one of the women up on the balcony could be purchased for the night. More than wine or olive oil, money lubricated Rome. Appius Varro had bequeathed him some capital in his will, but it would not be enough. Manius had been tempted to ask Rufus how much he could lend him, but he had his pride. Camilla professed she loved him for who he was, not for what he did. She argued that she possessed a sufficient income, from her allowance, for both of them to live comfortably. But he had his pride.

Varro subtly observed the tension in his companion's face. The bodyguard's brow was more creased than the ageing whore's dress and his eyes narrowed, as if in physical torment. For once, a satirical or cynical comment wouldn't improve the situation. Camilla was good for his friend, she made him happy (despite his current despondent demeanour). She recognised how honourable, amiable and decent he was. Rufus resolved that he would chat to his friend further, when he was sober, over the next day or so.

But before Varro could address Manius' problem, he would need to deal with his own: Dellius Cinna walked through the doors of *The Golden Lion*.

## 2.

"You owe me money, Rufus Varro... You can either pay in silver, or blood. It's up to you," Cinna issued, standing over Varro, his hand gripping his dagger.

Spittle peppered the air as he spoke, or rather barked. Cinna's deep-set eyes burned as brightly as the flames of the brazier in the corner. As much as his features were scrunched up into a scowl, there was also a sense of satisfaction in his expression and tone. He had finally come across the man who had ruined his life. Perhaps the gods were on his side, he thought. Cinna was drunk enough to feel over confident, but not drunk enough to know he was drunk.

The carpenter was accompanied by three other members of his guild. The first, Porcius, walked, or waddled, forward to stand in front of Manius, with the intention of intimidating his opponents. Wine stained his tunic. Grease stained his plump features. He balled his fleshy hands into two large fists and snorted at the Briton. Porcius had heard the story, on more than one occasion, of how his friend had been cheated out of his money, by the poet, during a game of dice.

The remaining two companions, Nonius and Marcus Ligarius, were brothers. They possessed the same angular jaw, sandy-coloured hair, nut-brown skin, beetle-brow and wiry build. Their eyes glinted, like polished coins, as they recalled Cinna's promise – that, should anyone help retrieve his money, he would give them their fair share.

Manius rose to his feet, towering over Porcius, who gulped but stood his ground. It was the bodyguard's job to intimidate, rather than be intimidated. He yawned, again. Manius had lost count of the amount of times Rufus had caused offence. Usually it was a wronged husband, drunken soldier or a victim of one of the poet's satirical verses who sought recompense. Varro had a gift (almost god given) for antagonising people. His tongue was sharper than a Spanish blade – and he rarely kept it sheathed. His friend was his own worst enemy, the Briton considered. Although Rufus would have argued that no one else was deserving of the role.

The whores on first floor watched on, with more amusement than arousal. They just hoped there wouldn't be too much damage, lest Bassos decided to cut their wages for the month. The water boy widened his eyes in dismay. He had witnessed such scenes before – and was worried that he would have to clean up any mess – although thankfully there was sawdust on the floor to soak up some of the blood.

"I won the money fairly. You would make a liar of me if I paid back the winnings from a just wager. And Rome already has her fair share of liars."

"You ruined my life."

"Why would I do that? When I've every confidence that you'll ruin your life by your own accord, without any help from me."

For as long as he could remember Varro wore a mocking expression, during most of his interactions with people. One couldn't be sure if it was a mask, or his true self. That he married his expression to a sarcastic, or sardonic, tone didn't help his cause to make friends. People should be gently mocked, or virulently condemned, he had long ago concluded. Varro couldn't recall a time when he hadn't laughed at the world. The more earnest and righteous a man got, the more glib and cynical he became in return. Why should he take anyone else seriously, when he thought of himself as a joke?

Varro remembered the night in question, when the two men had first met and played dice. They had been frequenting *The Crooked Plough*, a tavern at the heart of the Subura. Varro had gone there, hoping that the wine would wash away the glutinous boredom which seemed to attach itself to his soul, like tree sap trapping a fly. He had just decided to end his affair with Marcella Laronius. The night before she had declared she loved him – and would divorce her husband to marry him. But Varro had no desire to marry again. Marcella also had children. He did not want to break-up a family, even if it was an unhappy one. Varro knew all too well what it was like to grow-up without a mother and a largely absent father. He decided he would end things by writing a letter to the woman, even if he judged it to be a coward's way out. Or better still he would compose a poem (he could adapt one he had written a year ago for another mistress). The poet would remain fond of the woman, until he forgot about her. Varro had initially seduced Marcella in order to cuckold her husband, the praetor Cornelius Laronius. Cornelius was an odious creature, even for a politician. Snakes would even blush at his sly malpractices. He had changed sides and betrayed his friends in the civil war more times than even Euclid could calculate. The poet had also overheard the statesman criticise his verses. If only Manius could safeguard me from critics, he half-jokingly thought to himself.

And so, to distract himself from any unpleasantness regarding the ill-fated affair, Varro surrendered to a night of drinking and gambling in the *The Crooked Plough*. To further entertain himself Varro goaded the arrogant carpenter into betting money he had put aside for investing in new premises (whilst the aristocrat could afford to stake ten times the amount and not bat an eyelid if he lost). Cinna goaded himself by being intoxicated with wine and the stimulant, or poison, of greed. Varro had toyed with his opponent like a gladiator who could, at any moment, deliver the killing blow to the beast he was combating in the arena.

Cinna snorted on registering Varro's reply. He gripped the handle of his knife more firmly. He wasn't sure where his envy for the handsome nobleman ended and his contempt began. The carpenter judged that Varro had never done an honest day's work in his life. As well-educated as the aristocrat was, he needed to be taught a lesson or two. He recalled the shame and privation he had suffered over the past month, from losing the money. It would take him another year, at least, to save up the necessary capital to expand his business. His shrewish wife had not stopped scalding him too, reminding him of his failure and stupidity.

"We're not afraid of your bodyguard," Cinna announced, baring his rotting teeth, as the vein in his neck throbbed, like a toad's bulging throat.

"More fool you," Varro replied, as he got to his feet. His eyes flitted about the room, taking in the escape routes and possible items he could utilise as a weapon. There wasn't any envy in the Roman's heart. Just contempt.

"How much do you want me to hurt them?" the Briton asked, as he formulated several plans of attack.

"As with when I'm composing a poem, make it up as you go along."

Cinna turned to his companions and gave them a subtle nod, to attack. But Manius was quicker to react. The Briton was agile for his size. He kept himself well-conditioned, setting aside time each month to spar and fence with other former gladiators.

To even the odds Manius attacked three opponents at once by lifting-up the rickety table and thrusting it forward into Porcius, Nonius and Marcus. The muscles in his neck became pronounced, as taut as a ship's rigging. The half-drunk carpenters were forced backwards, shock and fear carved into their features. Nonius lost his footing and fell to the floor. As he walked over him the roaring Briton stamped upon his groin. He lay groaning, doubled-up, dry-retching. Manius put the table down and ripped off one of the legs. He first swung the make-shift club against Marcus' shoulder. He let out a high-pitch scream, like a eunuch, and dropped his dagger. No sooner had the blade clanged upon the stone floor when Manius swung the table leg again and it connected with the side of his opponent's head and knocked him out.

"Bastard!" Porcius spat, holding his dagger aloft. Dark, beady eyes peered out from his flabby face.

Manius dropped the table leg and unsheathed his own dagger. The rasping sound was familiar – but not altogether welcome. Most men enjoyed it when they got to employ their gifts. But Manius' gift was violence. There were times when he would rather have kept his gift wrapped-up, his talent hidden. The ex-gladiator moved forward, rolling his shoulders and balancing his weight. Porcius lunged forward, but with all the speed and grace of a lumbering ox. Manius side-stepped the attack and quick-stabbed his opponent in the thigh. He then, with a deft flick of the wrist, drew the blade across the carpenter's left hamstring. The big man dropped to the floor and whimpered - in pain and disbelief. The sawdust commenced to soak up some of the blood.

Varro owned every confidence that his companion could best three opponents. If only he possessed the same amount of confidence in himself, to defeat his sole assailant. Cinna's dagger swished through the air again – and Varro retreated once more. His back was now to the wall, next to the fireplace. Varro cursed himself, for forgetting to bring his own dagger out.

"You've got nowhere else to go," Cinna remarked. Sneering. Savouring the moment.

But Varro was right where he wanted to be.

As Cinna drew his weapon back, preparing to attack and finally draw blood, Varro reached for Caesar's sword on the mantlepiece. He swung the gladius around with such force that he not only parried Cinna's attack, but knocked his weapon out of his hand. Partly due to fear, partly due to the wine he'd consumed, the disorientated carpenter staggered backwards and tripped over a stool. When he looked up he saw Varro standing over him – and the tip of a blade hovering over his neck.

"You've lost your money. Do you want to lose your life too, over a game of dice? It's up to you," Varro said. A part of him felt sorry for the defeated carpenter. But the poet didn't have that much of a sensitive soul – and duly dismissed any temptation he might have felt to pay back his winnings.

The four men limped and stumbled out of the tavern, bloodied and cowed. Cinna wouldn't be able to recruit them again. They had all learned their lesson – and would wake in the morning suffering from more than just a hangover.

Bassos came out from behind the doorway to the kitchen. If he had hair, he would have begun to pull it out with worry. He tallied up the cost of the broken furniture in his mind and the cost was equal to a day's takings. Another day spent. Another day wasted. But before he had a chance to berate the gods in earnest, Bassos gave thanks to Varro.

"I'll pay for any damages. It's the least I can do. I may not be the most honourable man I know - that title, be it a curse or blessing, belongs to my friend here – but I'd like you to know I did beat that cretin at dice fairly. If you must think ill of me, which you will eventually if you've got any sense, I'd prefer it to be for the right reasons. I should also apologise for damaging your sword, Bassos," the nobleman remarked, holding the weapon aloft so that the tavern owner could see the large new nick in the blade.

"Oh, no need to fret about that. I've got a dozen more just like it out back. I purchased a job lot from a blacksmith, just outside of Ancona, several years ago," Bassos exclaimed, the lustre returning to his eyes, as he recalled the favourable deal he negotiated and the word of mouth he'd generated from the anecdote about Caesar once visiting his establishment.

## 3.

The waxing moon hung in the star-strewn sky like a lantern. Varro envied its stillness and distance. The companions made their way home through the narrow, odorous streets of the Subura, towards their house on the Palatine Hill. Varro had always felt comfortable in his skin, spending time in both districts. The one was home to politicians, the other to common criminals. The residents of both neighbourhoods were more alike than they might concede. Politicians and criminals shared a lust for gold, could go weak at the knees at the sight of a courtesan, would gossip like housewives and pray to avoid the underworld, as much as they belonged there. One group were nasty, self-serving, filthy-minded rogues. And the other group were common criminals.

Varro noticed a piece of graffiti on a wall. Someone had crossed out *"Long Live Caesar"* and written *"Long Live the Republic."* He rolled his eyes and wryly smiled, recalling how, two streets away, someone had crossed out *"Long Live the Republic"* and scrawled *"Long Live Caesar"* in its place.

Octavius Caesar had been declared Augustus – the "Revered One" – in January. Although Varro had recently read some verses which labelled him the "Reviled One".

The Battle of Actium had paved the way for peace – or rather the final victory. Octavius had given thanks to Apollo for his triumph against Antony's fleet, albeit he should have thanked his general, Marcus Agrippa, for ending the war. Instead of framing the battle in terms of Octavius defeating Antony though (and highlight how Rome was divided) the propagandists had trumpeted how Rome had defeated Egypt – and that civilisation had proved victor over barbarism. The gods had been on Caesar's side. Octavius had saved the Republic. At least the god of irony was on his side, Varro fancied.

Octavius still humbly called himself consul, but he was a dictator in all but name. He collected other honorifics too, like a wife collecting reasons to hector her husband. He was "First in the Senate," "Princep" and "Imperator".

Varro remembered witnessing one of Caesar's many Triumphs, when he returned from the East. Magistrates trailed behind Octavius' gilded chariot, like attendants or slaves. The streets were filled with a tangible sense of joy, gratitude and relief. Finally, there would be peace. Rome had endured thirteen long years of civil war – of proscriptions, battles, uprisings, crippling taxation and food shortages. Enough blood had been spilled to wash the Tiber away. But wives would no longer be widowed, children would no longer be orphaned, due to Rome being at war with itself. Caesar's enemies – Marcus and Decimus Brutus, Cassius, Sextus Pompey, Mark Antony and Cleopatra – were all dead. Julius Caesar had instilled the lesson into his heir that it's where one's positioned at the end of the race that matters. There may have still been factions to challenge Octavius' supremacy, but they lacked a figurehead to rally behind. No one desired to put their head above the parapet, for fear of it getting lopped off. As well as the gods, Octavius crucially had the army and populace on his side.

The people had food in their bellies and coins in their pockets once more. Soldiers returning from campaign were resettled. The grain supply was no longer interrupted from the East. Debts were being repaid. A tax system was put in place – which encompassed tax relief and remittances. Each male citizen and soldier was granted a donative, courtesy of the plunder Octavius had brought back from Egypt. Marcus Agrippa, Caesar's chief lieutenant and the architect of many of his victories, became the architect of Rome. Building projects were announced – and completed. Sewer systems and aqueducts provided fresh water and better waste management. Bathhouses and gardens sprung up around the city. Temples were restored to their former glory.

But you cannot please all the people, all the time. Not everyone embraced Caesar's reforms, although they were powerless to stop them. The Senate House was denuded, both of members and authority. Swathes of senators were asked, politely or otherwise, to resign. New men, loyal to Octavius, replaced figures from noble bloodlines which had served in the Senate House for generations. The Republic was restored and reformed at the same time. Augustus allowed the Senate to take of control of half the provinces again. The remaining provinces however, the ones of key strategic importance and home to the majority of the legions, would remain under Caesar's governance. He claimed the Senate had "pressured" him to accept such a settlement.

The law courts were reinstated. Octavius rescinded the edicts which had been enacted under the triumvirate. Elections were re-established – and Octavius and Agrippa were duly voted in as consuls again. The Senate still met to discuss legislation, but they were ultimately just actors on a stage, waiting on their lines and direction from a higher power.

As a courtesan will tell herself she's lost weight, as a Gaulish soldier will consider himself brave, as a politician will call himself honest and a Vestal Virgin will swear that she couldn't possibly have caught the pox – so too Rome believed that it was still a republic, Varro thought. But it was just a façade. If you looked behind the edifice of the state one would have found Octavius Caesar sitting upon a throne, propping it up. Varro remembered another piece of graffiti, which hadn't quite been scrubbed free from the side of a bathhouse: *"We are no longer citizens, but subjects."* How long would it be before Octavius' step-son, Tiberius, was declared his heir? How long would it be before Livia called herself queen? She certainly possessed sufficient outfits and jewels for the role.

Yet the supposed Golden Age of the Roman Republic was, at best, one of half-polished bronze, Varro considered. Rome was always a prize to be won, rather than an idea to be served. Marius, Pompey, Sulla all acted like kings, without crowns. The course of honours was more ruthless and rigged than a chariot race. The great families of the Senate House could little boast that they represented the rest of Rome and had the best interests of the people at heart. Statesmen were as corrupt as tax collectors, as sanctimonious as priests and as rapacious as slave merchants. Uncommon criminals. Varro recalled attending a party, arranged for a senator recently returned from governing a province in Greece. The first question his colleagues asked was, "How much money did you make?"

Whilst Varro mulled over the political state of affairs in Rome, as he wended his way through the Subura, Manius concentrated on the affairs of the heart. His palms grew sweaty and his pulse raced, as if he were about to fight in the arena, as he thought about Camilla. The happy prospect of winning her was matched by the fear of losing her however. Manius knew he would never find another woman like her again or experience such fine feelings.

He recalled the evening they met, a month ago. Varro had been invited to a party, hosted by one of Rome's elder statesmen.

"I'll be turning up with you, but forgive me if I leave with someone else... I may well be indifferent to Rome's senatorial elite – but I'm willing to be charmed by one of their wives or daughters," Varro insisted.

He soon made good on his word and abandoned his attendant, shortly after arriving at the event. Varro encountered a former mistress and either he led her upstairs, or she led him. After sampling some of the food on offer – quail's eggs, asparagus tips, spiced lamprey – and accepting a large cup of Massic from a scantily clad serving girl - Manius retreated into the garden. Such gatherings made the former gladiator uncomfortable. The men peered down their noses at the foreign looking bodyguard. Half the women gazed at him in a spirit of haughtiness, or revulsion. Whilst others leered at the muscular attendant – and he was reminded of his time as a gladiator, when he was whored out to widows or bored, rich wives for the night. There were worse jobs in the world, he argued at the time. And surrendering his will to a mistress was preferable to surrendering in the arena. But only just, in some instances.

The gardens were large and well-kept. Oil lamps hung upon the boughs of fruit trees, bathing the scene in a warm, orange glow. Manicured lawns were bordered by shrubs and vibrant flowerbeds, perfuming the air. Occasionally Manius heard the whispers, moans or laughter of couples. But he pretended not to hear and walked on. He also pretended not to notice a grey-bearded senator grope a serving girl (who was even more scantily clad than usual) behind a statue of Minerva in the garden.

Realising that most of the more amorous guests were secreting themselves along the outskirts of the gardens Manius veered towards the centre. Which is where he discovered Camilla.

Instead of looking down her nose at the attendant she glanced up and politely smiled. Camilla had a round, pretty face – free from artifice or make-up. Her eyes were bright, inquisitive, spirited. Green, like the Tiber. But like the river in summer, sparkling with petals of sunlight. Her skin was as smooth and white as alabaster, but as seemingly soft and lustrous as satin. She was wearing a sky-blue, cotton short-sleeved stola with a ribbon of silk, dyed with saffron, tied around her slender waist. A fan sat on her lap. Her blonde hair, which grew fairer in the summer, had been styled into a matronly bun and was held in place by a pearl-topped silver hairpin. White, round-toed felt slippers peeked out from beneath the hem of her dress as she sat on a stone bench, within the central bower of the garden. A cordon of shrubs and trellis worked its way around in a circle. Bronze statues of Pan and Ceres, on marble plinths, stood at the entrance to the leafy alcove. The boughs of a cypress tree, carrying a brace of oil lamps, illuminated the scene.

"I'm sorry, I apologise if I've disturbed you," Manius remarked, after pausing to take in the beautiful stranger, his mouth slightly agape.

"No need to apologise. Rather I should be thanking you for providing me with some company," Camilla replied, shuffling down the bench to encourage the man to sit down next to her. Despite his size, despite the large dagger hanging from his belt, Camilla didn't feel unnerved or intimidated. He had a friendly face and kind eyes, she judged. It was more likely that she would intimidate him. "Are you not in the mood to join the party too? I wonder why more people haven't come outside to appreciate the gardens and fine night."

"It's because the wine's inside," Manius half-joked.

Camilla let out a short burst of unaffected laughter, as musical as the birdsong and breeze which threaded through the nearby apple and yew trees.

"You must now tell me your name, if only so I can attribute your joke to the right person. I'm Camilla, by the way. Officially I am just taking some air. Unofficially I think such parties are to be endured rather than enjoyed."

Camilla had attended because her father asked her to. Aulus Sanga soon disappeared into the throng however, to gossip and plot with fellow merchants. She soon felt the predatory eyes of would-be suitors upon her, making her skin crawl. They introduced themselves, boasting about the size of their estate (or they enquired about the extent of her father's wealth). Suitors, young and old, buzzed around the unmarried girl like insects. Compliments were offered up as frequently as the canapes. Camilla swallowed neither however and longed to be back home and lose herself in a book. The corners of her mouth began to ache from forcing herself to smile so much. Thankfully her father would not put pressure on her to marry someone she disapproved of (and she disapproved of most men). The widower would have been lonely without his only daughter. He was also willing to wait for the right candidate to come along, someone deserving of his daughter. Someone who could make her happy. Who would prove valuable in terms of his political and mercantile interests. Aulus Sanga loved his daughter, but he also duly thought of her as one of his most prized assets.

"My name is Manius. I am just an attendant. A bodyguard. I needed some air too."

"Where do you come from, if you do not mind me asking?" she said, intrigued by his looks and slightly off-kilter accent.

Her voice was clear, cultured. But not cold, he judged. He felt that no matter how comfortable he was with his Latin his accent would always betray his foreignness. He just hoped that she would not think less of him for not being Roman born.

"Britannia. I am a long way from home, I know. It's a long story."

"Well it's going to be a long night. And I know you enough, Manius, to want to get to know you some more."

And so the Briton sat with Camilla and told her about himself. How, when he was a child, the Romans had attacked his village. His father had been a farmer, his mother a seamstress. "Rome is as much a bastion of brutality, as it is of civilisation… My father was murdered before my eyes… I was only a boy but I attacked the soldier who was about to assault my mother. He turned his sword on me, but I was saved when another soldier, Lucius Oppius, intervened… My mother and I were sold as slaves… She died in Gaul. I was sent to Rome to attend one of Caesar's gladiator schools… I learned my trade and fought well… I survived, which is more than many of my companions did… The arena is a theatre, filled with jeers and cheers. I experienced both… Eventually Appius Varro, the general and senator, bought my freedom and adopted me. He said he won a lot of money betting on me, against the odds, during my last fight. I was a freedman but decided to accept his offer of serving as an attendant to his son – and schooling him in combat," Manius recounted, conveniently leaving out the times spent drinking, whoring and gambling with his employer.

Camilla listened intently and occasionally interrupted Manius' story with a question. She never overtly pitied him. Rather she found herself just being interested in him. Attracted to him. Camilla also found herself telling him things she had not told others before:

"I can only imagine what it is like to be a slave… But I have lived most of my life in a gilded cage. Partly my father locked me away, after my mother passed away. But partly I have locked myself away. My days are spent surrounded by books. They're far cleverer and more entertaining than most people, I find," she said, half-jokingly, her teeth gleaming like coral as she smiled.

"You might want to meet Rufus. He's a poet, although he often calls himself a professional wastrel," Manius said, recalling how, the day before, his companion argued that, "It takes a lot of hard-work and practise to be this idle," whilst a servant poured him another cup of Falernian as he reclined on a couch which had been brought out to the garden (as another slave held a parasol over his head, to shield his eyes from the sun's glare).

"You may have to introduce me to him one day, but I would prefer to just see you again, Manius."

Camilla blushed a little and surprised herself by how forward she was being, in asking a man if she could see him again.

"I'd like that," the Briton answered, his smile shining through his beard - similarly more smitten than shy.

Manius became distracted from his reverie when he came to a familiar turning in the street where, six months ago, he had found Viola. She was a knee-high black and white mongrel. "She's a stray, like me," he had said as he carefully moved towards the dog and fed her a piece of ham. Her ribcage was pronounced from starvation, she seemed to have lost half an ear in a fight with another dog, her claws had nigh-on grown into talons and her fur was mangy. Manius decided to take her home, carrying her most of the way. Viola had a sweet temper and would cower at her own shadow. She would even sit behind Manius' chair in the garden when birds landed upon the lawn. But ferocity was in plentiful supply in Rome. Gentleness was rarer – and therefore more valuable. Manius nursed the mongrel backed to health. He doted on her – and she on him. "The more I get to know people, the more I love my dog," the Briton remarked to Camilla, not even half-jokingly, the last time he saw her.

Manius looked forward to getting home and seeing Viola again. He could never be unhappy in her company. She would jump-up excitedly at him, wag her tail and offer up a couple of throaty growls, by way of chiding him for getting back late. She would then curl-up contentedly at the foot of his bed and occasionally, like her master, snore.

**4.**

When they returned to Varro's house on the Palatine Hill they were met by Fronto in the triclinium, waiting-up for them.

Fronto had, over the years, served as Appius Varro's secretary, accountant, housekeeper and cook. He had also been his son's tutor, schooling him in history, rhetoric and philosophy. The old man still kept himself busy – and served his master's son – by managing Rufus' finances and household. Thankfully income still exceeded outgoings, albeit this had more to do with Fronto's financial acumen than any sense of prudence on Rufus' part.

Wiry white hairs protruded from his nose, ears and chin. His build was slight and his back was hunched but Varro was always pleasantly surprised by Fronto's vitality and robustness. The old man could regularly be found tending to the garden or coming back from the market, laden with produce like a pack mule. He had a shrewd, wrinkled face and kind, grey rheumy eyes. His voice was croaky, sometimes even gruff, but rarely devoid of irony or humour. Varro considered him both sage and sarcastic, in equal measure. He couldn't remember a time when he wasn't fond of Fronto. Or when the old man hadn't taken care of him. Far more than his father, who for long periods of time was absent on campaign, Fronto had been responsible for raising him. As a child he considered Fronto a Mentor to his Telemachos, with his father, Odysseus, away fighting on foreign shores. He had introduced him to Plato, Thucydides and Tacitus. Encouraged him to read and write poetry. Instructed him on how to don a toga and how Roman politics worked (or didn't work). Taught him that the gods could be cruel, comedic or indifferent. That decency - and a sense of humour - matter. He told the child about his mother, who had died a year after his birth. How she was beautiful and pious and her father mourned and missed her every day, even though it might not have seemed like it (Appius had never remarried, though he had courted more than one mistress after his wife's death). Fronto also made sure that, when Manius was adopted, Rufus treated him like a brother rather than rival, or servant.

Viola soon came scampering into the room, her claws tapping across the tiled floor. Manius' smile was nearly as wide as the mongrel's mouth as Viola jumped up at her master and licked his hands and face. She duly greeted Rufus too. Although, at first, he had kept his distance from the mangy and silly dog – and believed it wasn't worth investing time and emotion into a creature that was at death's door – Rufus eventually bonded with Viola. When he was alone with the dog he would play with her – embrace silliness – and feed her treats.

Manius bid his two friends goodnight and went off to bed. Viola followed him out the room, her wagging tail knocking against the furniture, doorframe and walls as she did so.

Varro sat down on one of the three couches in the room. Each had a bronze frame, beneath long, thick cushions and plump goose-feather pillows. He reached over to the marble-topped table next to the couch, where Fronto had left a pitcher of water and plate of dates, figs and slices of apple. The flames from four braziers, in each corner of the room, murmured. Occasionally a tongue of fire would dart upwards, forming dancing shadows against the wall. A large mosaic dominated the floor of the chamber, depicting the Battle of Zama. A brace of intricately woven rugs, brought back from one of Appius Varro's campaigns in the East, also gave the room some colour and character. A frieze, featuring Cincinnatus returning to his plough, hung over the fireplace whilst the walls were home to several paintings – mainly battles scenes. Rufus had lost count of the number of times his father had proudly recounted to party guests how his ancestors had fought for Rome during the Punic, Cimbrian and Mithridatic wars. At the end of his talk he would always exclaim, "And now I just need my son to add to the glory of Rome," in an attempt to goad, inspire or shame his child.

"You have returned earlier than expected. Did you not find a nice young lady to spend the night with?" Fronto asked, raising his eyebrow suggestively, but inwardly pleased that his young master had come back home, safe and sound.

"I would much rather try and find a nice old lady, for you. One that doesn't bleat but likes old goats. You never know, she might light a fire within you," Varro joked, but at the same time hoped that his friend would find a companion in his final years. He worried Fronto had sacrificed too much, in his service to him and his father.

"I would much prefer her to light the stove and cook me a nice meal. Although once she gets to know me I fear she might poison my food. I'd also worry about the strain on my back, should I be called upon to sweep a woman off her feet."

"I just wouldn't mind you being tucked up in bed with a good woman, instead of spending your nights waiting up for me. Why do you still wait up for me? Not that I'm ungrateful for the water and food," Varro remarked, before pouring himself out another cup from the silver pitcher and eating a date.

"Your father asked me to."

"That would have been years ago. Perhaps one day you might follow my instructions, instead of his."

"And what would your instructions be?"

"That you should go to bed instead of waiting up. That you should drink anything but the Falernian when you sneak down into the wine cellar, when you think I don't notice. That you don't overcook the red mullet and that you pluck up the courage to start courting Aelia. I've seen the way you look at our laundry woman, when she's not looking. Similarly, I've seen the way she looks at you, when you're not looking."

"Aelia is a fine woman, endowed with good sense. Which is why she shouldn't look twice at me. I've known for a long time that I'll die alone. We all die alone. It's just that most people, may the gods bless them, don't realise it," Fronto said, almost cheerfully. "But I would be happy to be proved wrong. You should take a leaf out of Manius' book and find someone. Just because your first married failed, it doesn't infer that a second one will. I know you are prone to catching a different kind of pox, but love can be infectious too. I promised your father I would help you make something of yourself and see you settle down. His shade probably visits the house every now and then, in hope that he will see a grandchild to carry on the family name."

Varro forced a smile, as he remembered the two miscarriages Lucilla suffered, whilst he was married to her. She had nearly died each time. The first had somehow brought them closer together, but the second tore them apart. She grew distant, depressed, believing she somehow failed as a woman. That the gods were punishing her. He thought how he was not meant to be a father. He was too faithless and selfish. Varro was frightened that, if Lucilla suffered another miscarriage, he might lose her altogether. He stopped making love to her at certain times in the month. He spent more time with his mistresses and drowned his sorrows with Manius and other companions. It was the beginning of the end for their marriage.

"Once again, you've both depressed me and made me smile," Varro exclaimed, sighing from either exhaustion or melancholy.

"If it's any consolation I've depressed myself, as well as made myself smile. I still can't quite decide whether the wrinkles on my face are laughter or worry lines. They're probably both," the old man posed, before masticating and then yawning.


Varro rested in bed. Tired – but unable to sleep. His eyelids weighed heavy but the words Fronto uttered weighed heavier. He remarked that Varro might soon have plenty of time to find a wife, should Manius leave to marry Camilla. He had yet to confront the reality of his attendant making another life for himself. Perhaps Varro believed the affair was ultimately doomed (like so many others). Aulus Sanga would forbid his daughter from marrying a lowly bodyguard. He had also known plenty of young noblewomen to amuse themselves with a soldier or poet - before committing to marry a relevant cousin or uncle. Manius would be heartbroken - and Varro would not lack a drinking companion again. But what if love somehow conquered all and his proposal was accepted? The house would be emptier without Manius. Varro would miss Viola too, although he might not openly admit it. He would have to find another bodyguard, who could discern and suffer his moods. Varro much preferred interviewing for serving girls.

The words of his father, as well as Fronto, echoed in his ears to keep him awake. What had he done for the glory of Rome? Although he had not wholly failed as a poet, he had hardly succeeded. Most people had judged his first collection of verse, composed nearly a decade ago, to be "promising". Half his friends and fellow poets commented that his poetry was "too original," the other half accused him of being "too conventional." His odes were too joyless, his shepherds too urbane, his extended metaphors too long and his similes were like water, trickling through the minds of his all too few readers. Varro doubted whether he could even afford to live in a tenement building, in the Subura, on a diet of stale bread and sour acetum, from the income he generated as a writer.

He sometimes still felt inspired when he read Horace and Virgil. Their words touched his soul, proving at least that he had a soul. But Horace and Virgil also reminded him of how little talent he possessed. They were Hyperions to his satyr. He spent more time with his mistresses than with his muse. He had lost count of the monumental poems he had started but failed to complete. Varro could still compose short, second-rate, love poems causing female hearts to flutter. But he felt dead inside. He had also fallen out of love with his literary circle. He preferred the company of whores to writers. They were less vain and were more likely to pay their way.

A gentle breeze ushered its way through the shutters - tickling his nostrils with the smell of thyme from Fronto's herb garden beneath his window - but it failed to cool his skin. He turned restlessly, as if suffering a nightmare. *I can't even settle down to a good night's sleep. How am I supposed to settle down to married life again?* Varro remembered however how he had slept peacefully when married to Lucilla – at least during the first few months of their marriage. She would often use his chest as a pillow and her leg would curl around his, like myrtle entwined around ivy.

To sleep.

## 5.

It was closer to midday than dawn when Varro woke up. Or rather when Fronto woke Varro up, by prodding his bony finger into his master's ribcage and yammering in his ear. Varro stirred, his eyes squinting in the light. His forehead throbbed, as if Vulcan himself were hammering upon the anvil of his brow.

"Wake up, you have a visitor!" Fronto exclaimed, either excitedly or in a frenzied panic.

"Tell them I'm out. Or say I'm feeling unwell, which is not altogether untrue. If it's a woman, even Venus herself, explain that I'm unable to raise myself for her. And if it's a man, even the First Man of Rome himself," –

"It's not the First Man of Rome. But it is the Second. Your time may not be valuable, but mine is. Now get up from that bed, before I drag you out of it by the balls," Marcus Vipsanius Agrippa announced, his stentorian voice as hard as iron, as he stood at the door – before retreating back into the triclinium along the hallway.

Despite the sweltering heat a chill ran along Varro's spine. His mouth became even drier, his stomach queasier. He gulped, before turning to Fronto.

"Is it really?" he asked, still hoping that it might be a joke or he was imagining things.

"Yes. I suggest you make a miracle recovery from your non-existent illness."

Varro winced again, either from the light or his aching head, but got out of bed. He plunged his face into a bowl of cold water and donned his tunic from yesternight, which was still sprawled across the floor. Fear vied with confusion. He tried to remember if he had somehow slept with someone he shouldn't have. Varro had no desire to share a mistress with Caesar.

Whilst his master readied himself Fronto quickly hobbled out, with all the grace of a three-legged dog, to attend to their distinguished guest. He hoped to placate the consul by furnishing him with the right vintage or delicacy.

"Would I like anything? I would like my meeting to start," Agrippa replied, testily, to Fronto's offer. Although he swiftly sighed and altered his tone, no longer sounding like a drill master on the parade ground. A servant should not suffer for the sins of his master. "But thank you for your hospitality. Some water will be sufficient."

Fronto poured out a cup of water for Agrippa. Varro finally entered the room, flattening his hair and smoothing down the creases in his tunic. He offered up a respectful bow before speaking:

"My apologies, Consul. I was up late last night, working on a new poem."

"I rather suspect you were working your way through your wine cellar, but no matter. You are here now."

Varro took in the figure before him, whilst trying not to look him directly in the eye. Agrippa was only a few years older than Varro but he had lived ten lifetimes to his one. At nineteen he had accompanied Octavius to Rome, after hearing of the death of Caesar on the Ides of March. Agrippa trained as a soldier and fought at the battles of Mutina and Philippi. When Sextus Pompey – and his fleet of pirate ships – caused havoc on the seas and interrupted the grain supply Octavius called upon his closest friend to defeat his enemy – which he duly did. Caesar may have been the voice of Rome, but his lieutenant turned words into deeds. Bread and circuses were only maintained due to Agrippa's management of the grain supply and his various building projects around the city.

The consul's eyes were as brown and hard as acorns. He was dressed in a plain tunic, as opposed to toga. Whereas some statues can resonate with beauty and elegance Marcus Agrippa projected a sense of authority and competence. Good living had softened some of his muscle definition, but the consul was still powerfully built. His expression often remained impassive, neither smiling nor frowning. His demeanour was serious, but not severe. Indeed, after their meeting Varro thought that the consul had an air of mournfulness, or sorrow, about him. His prominent, corrugated brow hung over his eyes. Years of campaigning – and the death of his wife, Caecilia - had chipped away at his heart and humour.

"Please, take a seat," Agrippa instructed, the guest acting like the master of the house. The consul was used to men following his orders, although he was not afraid to listen to his subordinates, should they proffer helpful advice. Agrippa prized efficiency over self-aggrandisement.

Varro sat on one of his couches and remained silent, nervously turning the ring on his finger. Sweat, from heat and anxiety, glazed his temples.

"I'm not sure if you know but I had cause to meet your father on a number of occasions, several years ago. Although he originally sided against us during the civil war Appius eventually realised that Caesar was Rome's best hope, after Antony surrendered himself to the wiles and ambitions of Cleopatra. Your father was an accomplished commander, not given to sacrificing his men like burnt offerings to the gods. He also behaved with integrity as a statesman, which is easier said than done. I am surprised that you did not try and follow in your father's footsteps and enter the army or submit to the course of honours."

Varro thought how Agrippa was not the first person to posit how surprised, or disappointed, they were in him not living up to his father's legacy. He had flirted with joining the army for all of two seconds as an adolescent. Varro had no desire to die in a foreign field for a cause which he little cared for or understood.

"As adept as I am at lying – and being selfish – I still don't think I have it in me to be a politician. I'm a poet. We write about life, rather than prosaically live it," Varro drily asserted.

Agrippa was unmoved by the reply. Partly he had been distracted by one of the benches outside in the garden. He remembered sitting on a similar bench when he had first met Caecilia, over ten years ago, at Cicero's villa in Puteoli. The view across the valley had been picturesque, but he barely noticed it.

Instead her bright blue eyes and shimmering silk stola burned themselves into his memory and soul. Caecilia had been his first and only love. Agrippa felt like his life was over when she passed away. Time doesn't heal all wounds. Caesar had encouraged his lieutenant to marry his young niece, Claudia Marcella, partly to help take his friend's mind off his grief and partly to strengthen his dynastic ambitions. Agrippa gently shook his head, in regret and remorse, as he recalled the scene. Or he shook his head in chiding himself, for dwelling upon such painful memories when he should be focussed on work.

"I'm pleased you think that you're adept at lying, as you will need to call upon the skill for what I am about to propose. A friend of mine, Quintus Verres, was found dead yesterday morning, having been murdered the night before. His throat was slit. His servants said there hadn't been any sign of a forced entry at the first-floor apartment on the Quirinal Hill. I believe that his murder wasn't committed by someone in his household, though I cannot wholly rule out that possibility. Thankfully his wife and children were spending time at the family villa in Astura, when the killing took place, else they would have been murdered while they slept too, I fear. I was first introduced to Verres years ago, by Cornelius Balbus, Julius Caesar's old ally. Verres was an agent, who ran various informants in Rome and served as a winnowing shovel for who was an enemy or supporter of Caesar's reforms. His services didn't come cheap, but he was a valuable asset. Verres helped recruit several senators to our cause, through bribes or other means, during the war. During our last meeting he informed me that Lucius Scaurus had come to his attention as a possible enemy of the state, without divulging any other details."

Varro had met the affluent and influential senator, Lucius Scaurus, on more than one occasion. He must have now been close to sixty years old, but age had not dulled his appetites or ambitions. His wealth was principally derived from mining interests. The civil war – and the demand for weapons and armour – had been good for business. Scaurus originally made a name for himself as an aedile. He arranged games for the city, which rivalled those of Julius Caesar several years before him. All manner of exotic beasts were slain by teams of gladiators (although sometimes the animals gored their opponents to death, much to the delight of the crowds). Rumour had it that Scaurus made a profit by selling the remains of the beasts – and their victims – to Rome's butchers and gourmets. The senator was a powerful man who could doubtless win – or purchase - the support of several patricians and factions in the Senate. But surely Scaurus would not be so foolhardy as to somehow challenge Caesar and become an enemy of the state, Varro thought.

"Should Scaurus be guilty of any wrongdoing then I'm sure he'll be apprehended. If nothing else Caesar has proved proficient in dealing with – and defeating – his enemies," he remarked, thinking how even if Scaurus was innocent of any wrongdoing he could still be easily prosecuted. Innocence wouldn't get in the way of punishing the senator, should Augustus will it.

"Caesar isn't above the law."

Inside Varro raised his eyebrows and smirked at Agrippa's ability to keep a straight face whist uttering the words.

"Of course."

"Caesar has no desire to open up old wounds, not if he can avoid it. Prosecuting and punishing Scaurus, without any just cause, could create more problems that it would solve. Cutting off one head may cause two others to grow. And you never know, Scaurus may be wholly guiltless of any crimes against the state, although there's more chance of me breeding unicorns. But proscriptions, blood feuds, factionalism in the Senate – all need to be consigned to history. We cannot be seen to be a dictatorship. Yet peace comes at the price of constant vigilance. I hear rumours of plots against Caesar almost every day. I'd be suspicious if there wasn't one. The enemy now is inside the gates. But what the nest of vipers need to realise is that, should any snakes venture outside the nest, or raise their heads too high, then their necks will be wrung. We can all pray to Fortuna – but we cannot rely on the gods to preserve the peace. Which is why I'm relying on you, Rufus Varro. As well as mentioning that you were a good liar, both to others and yourself, your father mentioned that you have a weakness for women – and that crucially they have a weakness for you. He said that women give you their hearts, but you never give yours away in return."

"It seems my father said more to you in a handful of meetings, than he said during a lifetime spent with me," Varro drolly emitted.

"You were once the lover of Cassandra were you not, before she married Lucius? I would like you to re-acquaint yourself with the woman, have her share her husband's secrets. As well as finding your way into her bedroom, find your way into her husband's study and read his correspondence. There is every chance Cassandra will sing like a bird. Should Scaurus be involved in any seditious acts I want to know whether he is the author behind any plot, or just playing a part under someone else's direction. Now you may well be asking yourself - why should you take on such a task? Allow me to furnish you with some answers. Firstly, a good man has died. You can help prevent other innocents from sharing Verres' fate. I do not believe you want to see Rome fall prey to an attempted coup, or to be plunged into civil war again. It is better that any plot is nipped in the bud now, instead of taking root and having the weeds overrun the garden. Would you like another figure such as Sextus Pompey to emerge and starve Rome, have it bend to his will again? But if I cannot appeal to your sense of duty, perhaps I can tempt you by appealing to your self-interest and self-preservation. I can happily put in a good word for you to Maecenas, should you have want of a patron to turn your career as a poet around. Conversely, I could put in a word at the treasury and have your estate undergo a tax audit. You surely have no desire to earn Caesar's displeasure, especially as you have already noted how poorly his enemies fare. The last person you should want to say no to, I imagine, is the most powerful man in the world," Agrippa remarked, with the faintest of smiles on his lips.

"Do I have any choice in the matter?"

Varro realised he would need to surrender to events now. But events can change, and he nursed a hope that he could somehow extricate himself from his fate, once he had time to think. He was willing to work hard to maintain his life of leisure.

"You could say yes, but you would be lying to yourself. But do not consider yourself trapped, Rufus. Rather I am giving you an opportunity, to climb out of the hole you have dug for yourself. You may live comfortably, but wealth isn't worth. You may enjoy writing, but words aren't deeds. Rome still needs honourable men to protect her, it's just that sometimes they need to work in the shadows. And all I am asking you to do is to continue to be a gossip. You are a poet, which means you have little immunity against vanity. But whereas you may desire a certain clique of people to gossip about you, your brief now will be to ensure that people gossip to you."

"Flattery will get you everywhere."

Agrippa continued to brief Varro on the job at hand, providing him with further intelligence on Scaurus and his allies. The senator was also hosting a party that evening, which Varro would attend and re-introduce himself to Cassandra and her husband.

"I will leave it to you to judge the lay of the land... Subtly imply that you have little love for Caesar when you talk to Scaurus. But make haste slowly," Agrippa advised, borrowing a maxim from his friend, Octavius. "Eventually we can bait the hook and catch him... Do not underestimate Lucius however. He's intelligent and ruthless. Rumour has it that he poisoned his brother-in-law when he discovered he was indebted too much – and a business partner offered to marry his sister in return for signing a contract for mining rights. As much as you seem to have a love for staying in bed, I do not want you dying in your sleep... I much prefer the honesty of an open battle to the back-stabbing games played-out by ignoble politicians. But we are where we are."

Agrippa also instructed his new agent that his assignment must remain a secret. Varro countered however that he would need the help and council of his bodyguard and his elderly attendant, Fronto.

"You can trust Manius more than you can me."

"He is the Briton and former gladiator is he not? I believe I saw him fight once, in the arena. His technique was matched by his brute strength. Every Briton I know drinks more than what's good for him, but what they lack in acumen they more than make up for in courage."

"Fronto can be trusted too. He's so old that, whatever I tell him, he'll forget by morning."

Agrippa finished his debriefing and, without ceremony, took his leave. He believed Varro had it in him to prove equal to his task. The consul was just unsure whether Varro believed it too.

Fronto entered the triclinium, his wizened countenance more wrinkled than usual. His master was sitting on the couch, with his head in his hands. Either in despair or mourning, for his past life.

"What happened? At least we can be thankful that you're not being hauled away in chains," Fronto remarked, curious and worried.

"I'm not so sure. It might be a preferable fate. My father might be pleased though. I've been called upon to work for the good of Rome. Unfortunately."

## 6.

A brace of butterflies danced across the scene, either in a courtship ritual or one desired to escape the other's advances. A few ambling clouds smudged the sky, to take the sting out of the midday sun.

Manius and Camilla sat side by side, overlooking the undulating Tiber, on a blanket of grass. The gardens, which had once belonged to the Clodii family, were now open to the public, by order of Caesar. Several plumes of smoke, from houses and bakeries on the opposite side of the river, drifted upwards and melted into the warm air. The clatter of wooden swords sounded in the background, as a couple of children played at being soldiers. A rake-thin mime appeared from nowhere and stood in front of the couple but Manius gave him a look, which intimated an obscenity or three, to communicate that they did not want to be disturbed.

"So, did you go out last night with Rufus?" Camilla asked, casually but curious.

"Yes, he wanted to visit the Subura. I thought it best I accompany him, as it was late and he had a few drinks," Manius replied, hoping that he wouldn't be forced to lie to her about how events unfolded towards the end of the evening.

"Is the Subura as bad as they say?"

"It's probably worse, in some respects. I wouldn't recommend you travel there by night, or even by day. But the district is home to decent, hard-working people too – trying to survive or better their lot."

"My father has forbidden me from going there. I'm occasionally tempted to don a disguise and have a few of my attendants accompany me though. I've been locked up, like a Vestal Virgin, for too long. My father too often treats me like a priceless statue, forever fearing that I might break, if exposed to the weather or people."

Manius imagined how Aulus Sanga might crack, or even explode, when his daughter revealed how she was being courted by a suitor from somewhere even worse than the Subura. Britannia.

He breathed in her jasmine infused perfume, as if storing up the fragrance to re-live it later. He also drunk in her good looks. The sun brought out the freckles on her rounded cheeks. Her hair was pinned-up, but two tendrils on either side of her head hung down, framing her pretty features. Her snub nose would scrunch up slightly just before she laughed, Manius noticed. Her startling eyes, bordered by innocent and coquettish lashes, could probe and yet make someone feel at ease at the same time. Did he think she was beautiful because he loved her, or did he love her because she was beautiful?

"Your father is just trying to keep you safe."

"But the truth must out. I'm intending to tell him about you – and how I feel – this afternoon. I have asked our cook to prepare his favourite food."

Camilla had been preparing some of her arguments too. Her father always said he wanted her to be happy. Manius made her happy. Therefore, he should allow them to be together. Unlike other suitors Manius wasn't motivated by money. He would not ask for a dowry.

Manius hoped Sanga wouldn't end up choking on his favourite food after he heard what his daughter had to say.

He reached over and clasped his hand in hers, to comfort her. The rough with the smooth.


Varro made his way across the Palatine. He occasionally nodded his head and smiled politely at an acquaintance, but he was in no mood to stop and chat. He wended his way through the human traffic, scurrying to and from the Forum: merchants, messengers, slaves, officials and shoppers.

He thought how it had been a while since he had walked so quickly and determinedly. *Should I give thanks to the almighty Augustus for my new-found purpose?* Varro thought about all the honours conferred upon Caesar in January. A laurel wreath was hung on one of the Princep's properties to indicate how he had saved the lives of Roman citizens (no mention was made of the lives he had taken however). An ornate, golden shield was also mounted on one of the walls of the Senate House, with Caesar's chief virtues inscribed around the rim: clemency, justice, valour and piety. Varro considered how he could select some other choice words to describe the dictator.

Rumour had it that Octavius wished to re-name himself Romulus, as opposed to Augustus. But Maecenas warned that Romulus conjured up thoughts of a king. Romulus had also murdered his brother and, so one version of his life ran, was killed at the hands of the Senate.

Varro avoided an oncoming litter – and mound of dung - on the street whilst wondering how much he was working for the good of Rome and how much he was working for the good of Caesar. Agrippa would have loyally pronounced that they were one in the same thing.

Caesar would soon be departing from Rome to lead a campaign in Spain which was why, when the Princep turned his back on the city, Agrippa needed to ensure that no one stabbed Octavius in the back and attempted a grab for power. Caesar's chief lieutenant didn't want any trouble on his watch, lest he found himself being replaced by the likes of Maecenas as the Second Man of Rome.

It was not unreasonable to think how Agrippa might be paranoid in speculating that Lucius Scaurus was an enemy of the state. Quintus Verres could have been killed by a burglar. He could have been having an affair, or an old enemy could have exacted revenge on him. Varro decided to collect more intelligence and evidence, before the party that evening, to ascertain how guilty or innocent Scaurus might be.

As such Varro would swallow his pride and talk to one of the last people in Rome he wished to be indebted to. His ex-wife, Lucilla.

*Desperate times call for desperate measures.*

27

Camilla had only been out of his company for a few moments and already she missed him. She still felt the sensation of his lips on hers and her skin still tingled from where his beard had brushed against her cheek. Camilla wasn't sure how long her last embrace with Manius had been – she just knew that it hadn't been long enough.

She owned a spring in her step when entering the gardens to meet with Manius but now Camilla's footsteps seemed leaden as she trudged up the grassy slope to meet with her litter bearers, to take her home. To her father. She sensed he already knew something was different about her. Perhaps a litter bearer had said something, or he could have ordered an attendant to follow her. She knew her father could be secretive and ruthless when it came to business matters. But she had faith that he loved her and would want what was best for his daughter. And nothing felt better than the thought of being with the man she loved. Camilla would effusively tell her father that Manius was the noblest and bravest man she knew. He also loved Rome, more than his homeland. He was still awestruck when he visited the Senien baths or Circus Maximus. He respected Roman law, customs and prayed to the gods. She would assure her father that there was no danger of Manius taking her away from the city. Although she would subtly hint that she would be willing to run away with him, if he forbade her from seeing him. Her pulse raced faster than her feet. Camilla felt breathless. Partly she was frightened about how her father might react. And partly she was in love. She had never seriously thought about having children, until now. She took more time over what to wear whenever she saw him. She felt safe with him – and he loved her in return, for who she was rather than for how much she stood to inherit.

Camilla told herself, unconvincingly, that she could be worrying about nothing. Her father would give her his blessing, in the same way Rufus Varro had. She didn't quite know what to think of the nobleman, who had a reputation. Everything seemed to be a joke for the satirist. He also needed to dilute his wine more. She had read some of his poetry and judged that he modelled himself too much on Catullus. His wit could be too abrasive and his language too bawdy. Too much irony can be a double-edged sword. But if Manius trusted him then she would too. And he never prevented his bodyguard from taking time off to see her.

*He doesn't seem to have a care in the world... That's sad rather than enviable.*

Diana, Lucilla's attendant, instructed Varro to wait in the triclinium while her mistress was getting ready. Diana couldn't, or wouldn't, disguise her discomfort and distaste. The Greek maid had served Lucilla during her marriage to Varro. She dried her mistress' tears too many times to mention and heard too many stories of his callousness and infidelity. Diana could neither forgive nor forget his behaviour.

Varro sat on a couch. The maid said her mistress would be free at any moment, but he knew from experience that Lucilla would keep him waiting. He looked around the tastefully decorated room, admiring various pieces of sculpture and art. He then remembered how much each piece cost him and he pursed his lips. Out of guilt for the way he had treated his wife – and from desiring a quick divorce – Varro had been generous with his settlement. He purchased a house for Lucilla on the Palatine (a suitable distance away from his own) and provided her with an allowance each month. Lucilla made some wise investments – and could now afford to support herself, if she chose to. Her financial independence also meant she could choose not to marry, although she was not wanting for wealthy suitors and young lovers claiming her attention.

Varro still visited his former wife once or twice a month. They were, just about, on amicable terms. They had even slept with one another one evening, a year after the divorce. Come the morning after though Lucilla said she wanted him to leave – and to forget about the night before.

"We will only end up despising each other again," the woman gravely remarked.

"I'm not sure I ever despised you, Lucilla."

"But I did you. And I didn't like the person I became."

Lucilla was the only woman who he had ever genuinely admired, respected and loved. During their courtship and early days of being married she had inspired him to write his finest love poems. Sweetness sours though and during the divorce Varro composed nothing but cynical, acerbic satires. Yet still she was his muse, inspiring him.

He heard a burst of laughter out in the hallway between the maid and her mistress (no doubt one of the two women had directed a barb at him) before Lucilla finally entered.

As many disagreements as Varro had while they were married he could never argue against how beautiful his wife was, almost painfully so. Her body was as lithe and graceful as a dancer's. Lucilla had always appeared older than her years in her youth but now she seemed miraculously younger than her twenty-eight years (despite the anguish he had caused her), Varro thought. Her almond-shaped eyes were perpetually smiling - whether joyfully, sensually or slyly. Her skin was pale but radiated like a pearl. If she went out Diana was always by her side, holding a parasol over her mistress. Her high cheekbones and slender jawline could have been sculptured by Praxiteles himself.

Varro heard the rustle of silk behind him and turned to face her. Her lustrous, kohl-black tresses were artfully pinned up on her head, held in place by silver, gem-encrusted clips which glinted in the sunlight. She wore a long, sleeveless, pleated dress of Tyrian purple, with a narrow slit up one side. Occasionally Varro would catch a glimpse of her smooth, contoured calf and he'd need to redouble his efforts to concentrate on the conversation. Her leather sandals, with straps that disappeared up the hem of her dress, were painted gold.

If Lucilla wanted to have reminded her former husband about what he was missing, she succeeded. Yet Varro didn't just esteem her for her beauty. Lucilla, who had largely educated herself, was considered as well as considerate. She had always treated his staff with kindness and generosity, calling out doctors for them if they were sick and making sure that they ate well. Fronto and Manius were suitably devoted to her too and regularly sided with his wife when he would go to them with grievances against her. But he knew that those soft lips, which could kiss him so lovingly, and those rows of gleaming teeth, guarded a tongue shaped like a scorpion's sting.

"You've given up one of the rarest and most desired blooms in Rome," Fronto asserted, on the day their divorce was settled.

"But the most beautiful flowers can also be the most poisonous," Varro replied, trying to convince his attendant – and himself – that he had done the right thing.

Yet Varro often missed her scornful wit and wisdom. They shared the same black and dry sense of humour. He missed trading quotes from Horace, Aristotle and Aeschylus with her – and her critical comments after a performance at the theatre:

"It was a tragedy, but not in the way they intended... The Trojan Horse gave a less wooden performance than the protagonist... I've never known someone to try their best and fail so much at the same time..."

Varro had to concede that Lucilla had flourished after she left him. She had become one of the great social lionesses of Rome. She threw parties which were attended by all manner of statesmen, artists and figures of influence. Lucilla was regularly consulted, by men and women alike, on business matters, the latest fashions and trends in the art world. She was a favourite of the Princep's wife, Livia – and rumour had it that her son, Tiberius, had recently declared that she was the most beautiful woman in the empire.

"What an unexpected pleasure. Would you care for some refreshments?" Lucilla remarked. Her voice was the soul of politeness rather than warmth. As much as she might have been pleased to see him, she didn't wish to show it. He noticed the ornate glass pendant around her neck, a gift from an ex-lover from when they were married (who had once been a friend of Varro's).

"I'm fine, thank you. I'm also worried that Diana might poison any dish she served me. Although she may be out of poison, having whispered it all in your ear since my arrival."

The veneer of Lucilla's formality cracked a little and an amused smile shone through. She reined herself in though, when tempted to laugh.

"You are too hard on Diana. Or perhaps not hard enough, given how much she, rightly or wrongly, has cause to dislike you. But I hope all is well. Are Fronto and Manius in good health?" Lucilla asked, as she noticed something amiss in his aspect (although his careworn expression may have just been the result of another long night spent in the Subura).

"They are both well. Fronto still quotes my father's maxims and nags me," Varro replied, resisting the temptation to add, *like a wife*. "And Manius is, of all things, in love. He's even ignoring Viola, to spend time with the woman."

"I have heard. Her name is Camilla I believe. I met her once. She's pretty. Much lovelier than her father, although he's no benchmark for any competition, I warrant. But I hope Manius is not falling too deeply in love,

30

lest he's unable to climb out of the hole when the affair ends. Aulus Sanga will never allow his precious daughter to stoop to marrying someone of such a base rank. It's a shame. Manius deserves some happiness. He can't stay married to you – and live under your roof – forever."

Varro was slightly taken back by Lucilla's knowledge of Manius' affair, although he endeavoured not to show his surprise. And in a way, it wasn't such great a surprise. If gossip was currency in Rome then Lucilla was as rich as Croesus. People trusted her, either to keep their secrets or, more so, spread stories which they wanted to disseminate. She knew everyone. Her nobility and beauty opened doors. Doubtless she still had spies in his own household.

"Well I thought I'd come and speak to you regarding another affair, so to speak. I am due to attend a party this evening, hosted by Lucius Scaurus. I'm keen to know what you think of him, seeing as his wife and I were once intimate. I don't want to arrive at his house and be set upon by his hunting hounds or, worse, be served any second-rate wine."

"Lucius certainly approves of affairs himself, given the number of mistresses he's courted since being married. He even cast his glassy eye over me at one point. But he's far too old - and poor - for my taste, of course. The greatest love affair Lucius has conducted has always been, like most men, with himself. He owns aspirations of obtaining a consulship, but even he must have woken-up to the fact that the dream is over... He is forever listing the achievements of his noble ancestors, but it only serves to highlight how little he has achieved... I heard he is spending more time lately with a troupe of actors at a theatre, situated just outside the city, than he is with his senatorial colleagues. Not that our statesmen couldn't teach the performers a thing or two about putting on an act... Apparently, he was once a victim of Cicero's wit, in the Senate House. Lucius exclaimed that he was "a modest man". Cicero chirped in with the reply, "Aye, with a lot to be modest about." The laughter that followed made him shrivel up like a salted slug... I knew one of his mistresses. She shall remain nameless, but she revealed how, when making love, she couldn't quite tell if it was the bed, or his bones, creaking... Perhaps I am being slightly unfair. Lucius can be charming in a vague way. But he is best summed up by saying he's a senator. His most distinguishing feature is his mediocrity. He's like Crassus, but not as wealthy. He's like Brutus, but not as noble. He's like Pompey, but far from great. And like Caesar, but without the courage."

"And what do you think Lucius thinks of Caesar's heir?"

"His only son died at the Battle of Philippi and his father perished at Pharsalus, so I'm not sure the name of any Caesar is particularly welcome in his house. Yet I suspect you will be welcome, despite your previous dalliance with his wife. Lucius is always looking to recruit men of wealth and noble blood to his faction. He knew your father well, I believe. Although I imagine that he liked your father more than your father liked him. Lucius may even encourage you enter into office, unless he's already been briefed that you would rather suffer the underworld than ever countenance the thought of working for a living. You will soon work him out for yourself though, once introduced to him this evening. As dense as Lucius can be, you'll see through him."

"Would you consider him dangerous?"

"I wouldn't want him as an enemy. I wouldn't much like him as a friend either. You may want to think twice about re-igniting any flames of passion with his wife. The last time I saw Cassandra she was wearing a bruise on her cheek, which no amount of make-up could quite conceal. I was told that he beat her for having flirted with a soldier. But be careful, for both your sakes. You seem to have more on your mind that just the party however, Rufus," she said, seemingly genuinely concerned.

Lucilla looked up, gazing fixedly into his eyes – or what was left of his threadbare soul. His semblance seemed to burn with shame - and he buried his chin in his chest. Varro noticed the bold, cherry-red colour of her fingernails as she placed her hand on his. He remembered how she would stroke her nails along his back and the inside of his thighs. He also recalled however how he had described her long fingernails as being akin to cat-like claws in a poem he wrote, after they were married. The poem recounted an incident of how Varro had come home late, drunk, to his wife. He blearily, yet spitefully, confessed to having slept with one of her best friends – and she slapped him around the face. Her nails broke the skin and drew blood – although, partly because of the drink, he barely felt anything.

He thought how, even more than Fronto or Manius, she could read his moods. More than anyone else Lucilla also had the ability to alter his mood. She could make him grin and laugh or, by reminding him of his past, cause him to feel guilty or miserable.

"It's nothing. I'll be fine. Once I've had a drink, of course," he replied, forcing an unconvincing smile.

"Are you writing anything at the moment?" Lucilla knew how listless – and worthless – Varro felt when he wasn't working on something.

"No."

He wanted to tell her that nothing inspired him anymore. He found it harder to laugh in the face of an absurd world. The joke of life, with its punchline of death, was no longer funny. His poems were forged from lead, not gold. Horace and Virgil would rightly live forever. But anything he had written would be lost, like footprints blown away in the sand. He wanted to tell her how someone had recently scrawled one of his couplets on the inside of the Servian wall. But come the following day it had been replaced with a lewd piece of graffiti and the picture of a giant phallus.

"I don't want you to squander your life," Lucilla said softly, almost in a whisper, her voice now infused with warmth and meaningfulness. For all that had happened between them – and that she couldn't forgive or forget – Lucilla still cared for him.

Varro was going to reply how he had already done so, by squandering his marriage to her. But he desisted. A sigh came out, and then some brittle words.

"I'm more concerned about squandering my estate."

"Oh, you needn't worry about that. I intend to bankrupt you far quicker than you can do so yourself. On that subject I must show you a new piece I purchased last month, off a dealer over from Alexandria."

"I suppose I should see it. After all, I probably paid for it."

"I remember you once telling me that what's yours is mine."

"It must have been the wine talking."

"I think you also said at the time that you gave me your heart too. But this piece I'm about to show you is far more valuable than that."

## 7.

Sunlight still burned in the sky, like embers. It had been a long day. For Varro it seemed even longer. And it was still far from over. He sat, along with Manius, in the triclinium of his house. Fronto had put out some fried squid, olives and grapes on the table but neither man felt hungry. Varro recounted the morning's events to his friend.

"It appears that you don't just have to be in the Subura to get screwed, when you're in Rome," the Briton commented, in response to Varro's predicament. "So, are you going to attend the party this evening?"

"Am I going to drink the night away and seduce a former mistress? Yes. Duty calls," Varro joked, holding his cup of wine up in a toast. There was little good humour in his strained expression however. "I suppose my best hope is that I fail to find any evidence of possible treachery – and I report back to Agrippa that Scaurus is not worth investigating any further."

"And if you do find any evidence?"

"Then I'll just have to drink and fuck some more, for the good of Rome and pursuit of truth."

Varro raised a corner of his mouth, in a gesture towards a half-smile, as he took in Viola, curled-up contentedly at Manius' feet. The mongrel had sat attentively when he first began discussing Agrippa's unexpected appearance that morning. But her yawning soon turned into a bout of gentle snoring.

"I may have to ask for a pay rise, given the newfound peril you're placing yourself in," the bodyguard half-joked.

"You may well end up deserving one. I'm caught between Scylla and Charybdis – Caesar and Scaurus. But I'm depressing myself, talking about me. How was your day?"

"More pleasant – and less dramatic - than yours. Although it may increase in drama by nightfall. Camilla said she would tell her father about us today," Manius divulged, with more anxiety in his voice than relief and elation. He pictured the scene of Camilla talking to her father over dinner – and the various outcomes of the conversation. Come morning she could be his intended, with her father's blessing. Or come morning she could be forbidden from leaving the house or sent away to the countryside. Perhaps Sanga wouldn't make a quick decision, either way. He could reserve judgement and ask to meet with the man his daughter professed to love. Should her father ask him about his estate and prospects though the conversation could prove a short one. He possessed neither. Manius had thought about cobbling together his money and wagering it all on a chariot race. Or he could ask Varro to use the sum as stake money in a game of dice. But neither idea appealed to the Briton. Camilla had said that she would pray to Venus. Yet Manius knew he couldn't just hope that the gods would favour his suite. It was always prudent to rely on a plan which didn't depend on divine intervention.

"You may well have to hire me as your bodyguard when Aulus finds out. I'll tell Fronto to make sure the doors are double-bolted. Enough people have been murdered in their beds this month. If I was capable of praying, my friend, I'd make an offering to Fortuna for you this evening. But I hope all will be well. You deserve some happiness. You certainly deserve more than me."

"Your lot doesn't seem so bad. After all, you've just been given a commission from the semi-divine Caesar, to drink and screw. You've been in training half of your life for this role. But do you have a plan for tonight?"

"I'm intending to make it up as I go along, as usual. It may even be the case that Lucius and Cassandra have no time for me. Not that Agrippa would accept such a scenario. If you could see what you can find out from the other attendants and bodyguards."

"Hopefully we'll be permitted wine and it'll loosen some tongues," Manius remarked. The task would help distract him from his thoughts concerning Camilla and her meeting with her father.

Camilla ran out of the room, sobbing like a child. Aulus Sanga had been unmoved by his daughter's pleas and arguments.

"You have brought shame on yourself and this house. Did you honestly believe I would permit you to marry a lowly attendant – a slave turned freedman? You may think me a tyrant right now, but other fathers would whip their daughters for such disgraceful and disobedient behaviour... I have no intention of you making me a laughing stock. How do you think my business associates will react when I tell them that my daughter has become infatuated with a barbarian? And a barbarian will always be a barbarian, no matter how finely woven a tunic he wears. You cannot put in what the gods have left out. Sooner or later, if you stayed with him, he would show his true colours and raise a hand to you. I am just trying to protect you. I have loved you since the day you were born - and I cradled you in my arms. This ape and gold-digger has loved you since he found out about your wealth and name... If you are lonely and wish to now marry, then I will arrange something. You have never lacked for suitors. Gaius Pansa's son has come of age. He is handsome and is training to be an advocate. Our two families would prosper from the match."

Camilla breathlessly tried to argue back that she only wanted Manius. He was one of the most decent men she had ever known. He loved her for who she was. And he had left his violent past behind him. But Aulus responded:

"The past is never the past. His violent nature lays simmering in the blood – it will eventually come to the boil. You just wait and see. Trust me, you will forget about him. First loves never last. Life is not like one of those poetry books you read. It's best that you find these things out now, before you are hurt even more... You cannot marry him. Or even see him again. That is the end of the matter."

Aulus Sanga seethed rather than breathed when Camilla rushed into her bedroom. His pallid complexion grew ruddier as blood rushed to his face. His bony hand shook slightly as he picked up his goblet of wine. His bony finger had jabbed the air whilst admonishing his errant child. It was the first time that he and his daughter had raised their voices to one another. Already the scurrilous foreigner was coming between them. But Aulus had been determined to win the argument, although he didn't wish to do so at the cost of losing his daughter. He was struck by her defiance – and devotion to the Briton. Little did Camilla know that, as she had prepared her arguments beforehand, her father had prepared his also. The respectable merchant knew about her daughter's new friend, as he had instructed his secretary, Milo, to follow her one afternoon. Milo proved diligent and reported back to his master, providing him with further information about Rufus Varro's bodyguard. Aulus had hoped that his daughter would submit to his authority and desist from seeing the rogue. But he was worried about the strength of her feeling and that Camilla might attempt to run away. At the very least his relationship with her could sour. Aside from his business interests, she was all he had. He hadn't been lying when he declared how much he loved and wanted to protect his daughter.

Sanga's coffin-shaped head faced the fireplace. The flames flickered in his black eyes. He bared his sharp, yellow teeth in a grin, or grimace, as he decided to proceed with a different plan to dispose of the Briton.

## 8.

The guests were ushered in, accompanied by the sound of a lulling harp. Lamps hung from the trees like giant fireflies. The scene was awash with freshly laundered togas and tunics, as well as vibrantly dyed dresses and glimmering pieces of jewellery. The sound of whispers, laughter and polite conversation swirled about in the air like the cinders from the braziers.

Varro took a couple of deep breaths, like an actor waiting to go on stage, and entered the party. He told himself he had no need to be nervous. He was in familiar territory. One party had blurred into another for as long as he could remember. Varro decided he would introduce himself to his host first, as opposed to hostess. Hopefully husband and wife would not be joined at the hip throughout the evening.

Varro surveyed the crowd. The good and the great were in attendance: politicians, merchants and financiers. Favours and promises would be traded between them throughout the evening. Later he would realise how many of the elder statesmen present could have been considered members of the old optimate party, which had put itself in opposition to Julius Caesar. Many would still declare, in hushed tones, that they were still adherents to the faction's cause, given their love of tradition and commitment to patrician bloodlines. He also spotted several courtesans working the party. Either they were accompanying their latest paramours – or they were on the hunt for a new one. The ageing, noble Romans were low hanging fruit – rich pickings. The women smiled and fingered their hair – and were quick to laugh or seem impressed, entertained. Varro imagined them asking their potential suitors if they liked their dress, or they might ask where they were going after the party. They were well practised at telling prospective partners what they wanted to hear. One or two of the women winked at Varro as he moved through the throng. He couldn't quite decide if they were attempting to generate business or if he had slept with them previously.

Before he could make up his mind Varro was distracted by a voice calling his name.

"Rufus. How have you been?" Gaius Macro asked, delight animating his features for having encountered his old drinking companion. Varro thought the philosophy student turned property investor was tolerable company. He thankfully knew how to laugh at himself and knew how to hold his drink and a conversation.

"Drunk, most of the time. I think," Varro drily replied, warmly clasping his friend's hand.

"I envy you your freedom – and wine cellar. I used to crave the married life at one point. But now I'm married, I crave a more carefree existence."

"Is your wife here tonight?"

"No, thankfully. She's at home. Hopefully she's taken a lover. I dare say I'm no longer capable of putting a smile on her face."

"You do yourself down."

"No, that's her job," Macro flatly replied, before his deadpan expression broke into an infectious, wine-fuelled grin.

Varro smiled too, before he excused himself by saying he needed to meet someone - but hopefully he would see Macro later in the evening. Varro continued to make his way into the house. He had glimpsed Scaurus inside. He wryly smirked as he noticed how several people peered over the shoulder of those they were speaking to, in the hope of catching the eye of someone more important or attractive. Women superciliously cast their eye over other women too, critically surveying their garments and make-up, hoping to find flaws.

Varro walked through the colonnaded portico into the house. The triclinium was bustling with guests, but he briefly took in the décor. Expensive pieces of cedarwood furniture, inlaid with tortoiseshell, were dotted around the chamber. Greek frescos, depicting pastoral scenes and images of the gods, decorated the walls. Varro noted busts of Pericles, Cato and Lucius Junius Brutus, who overthrew Tarquin the Great to establish Rome as a republic. A large, elaborate mosaic, portraying a scene from the Battle of Marathon, covered most of the floor. The craftsmanship was breath taking, as must have been the cost.

Varro suitably re-focused his efforts on locating his host however. A flat-faced secretary, carrying a polished bronze stylus and wax tablet, stood next to the senator, like a statue waiting to come to life at its owner's command. Throughout the evening the secretary would shadow his master and take notes on anything that was said – and arrange future appointments with clients and colleagues. Perhaps he was also charged, like Tiro assisting Cicero, with remembering the names of people. If he was so employed, then he would have been at pains to reveal the name of the handsome aristocrat who now stood before them.

"Good evening, Senator Scaurus," Varro remarked, respectfully bowing before his venerated host.

"And you are?" Lucius Scaurus replied, somewhat confused and decidedly unimpressed. His thin, blade-like nose became pinched and his eyebrows contorted themselves into a pronounced V-shape. The patrician was cleanshaven and healthy-looking for his age. His mouth occasionally smiled – but his dark, deep-set eyes rarely did. His oiled hair was black, with wolfish grey patches around the temples. A few liver spots could be seen on his hands and brow. The senator was getting old, Varro judged – and he knew that time was growing short in regards to achieving something and adding to the honour of his family name.

"I am Rufus Varro, son of Appius Varro. You knew my father. We met some time ago too."

"Ah, yes, forgive me. In trying to remember everyone, I end up remembering no one at these parties. But I recall you now," Scaurus amiably uttered. His features turned a scowl into a smile in the blink of an eye – partly as he remembered the extent of Appius Varro's wealth. He had become a rich man off the back of the slave trade. Blood money was still money. "I admired your father greatly. Tell me, do you still live on the Palatine?"

"Yes, I retained our family home. Not many can say that, given the extent of proscriptions and appropriations during the civil war. Occasionally, I will holiday at one of my villas in the country too."

"And you are a poet, are you not, if memory serves?"

Scaurus fastidiously adjusted his closefitting toga as he spoke. His hooded, hawkish eyes also flitted around the room, whilst always seemingly giving Varro his close attention. The young man was beginning to be of interest to the senator.

"I used to be. It was fun, but folly. I am now searching for a new venture and calling. I want to write a fresh chapter into my life. Either to invest in a business or to campaign to serve as a quaestor. I would greatly value your advice and guidance, although I appreciate we cannot talk in earnest now at your party. But I admire what my father – and you - did – and do - for Rome. I celebrated when Caesar restored the powers of the Senate House. Rome finally became Rome again, I believe," Varro exclaimed, exuding enthusiasm and civic duty. He was far from proud of the fact - but lying came as easily as breathing. He may have imagined it, but he thought that the patrician bristled when he mentioned the name "Caesar".

"I but met you as a boy before. Now you are a man. You must let me help you, should you decide to run for office. Your father would be pleased. He was the best of men," the charming senator said, with a lump in his throat, lying. Scaurus lost respect for Appius Varro the day he chose to side with Octavius Caesar. It would prove a welcome piece of irony however if Scaurus could recruit and convert his son – and have him serve his cause. He needed his capital. As Cicero once posited, "The sinews of war are infinite wealth." He also might be able to put the young man's writing talents to use too. He would need propagandists, to aid him in his campaign when the time came.

"I believe Rome stands at the crossroads. Caesar's reforms were welcome, but more must be done I warrant. Not that I am questioning the wisdom of Caesar."

"You shouldn't be afraid to question anything. It's a politician's duty to never settle. One must always be open to fresh ideas. You are amongst friends here too. People old enough to remember the Republic before Caesar crossed the Rubicon. We must talk further, Rufus. Rome needs good men like you, who have a respect for the past and want to build a better future. Are you a lover of drama, as you once were poetry? I have recently purchased a theatre, not far from the outskirts of Rome, on the road to Ostia. I have a troupe of players there, rehearsing. Would you like to travel out and see them on my next visit? We can discuss your future there. I will send a messenger to your house, to make arrangements."

"I would like that very much," Varro replied, offering his host a polite bow once more. He puffed out his cheeks and breathed a sigh of relief once the two men were out of each other's company. The first act was now over in a drama which he didn't know if it would ultimately prove a comedy or tragedy.

## 9.

Having been unable to locate Cassandra in the house Varro retreated out into the garden (after extricating himself from a conversation about Rome's rising property prices with one of his father's former acquaintances; Appius Varro seemed to be more than just a shade in his son's life sometimes). He grabbed a cup of wine from a serving girl. It was Falernian. Nothing but the best for the best of men, Varro fancied.

The night sky was even more bejewelled than the guests at the party, but only just. A burst of balmy air – and the smell of perfume – hit him as he walked onto the well-kept lawn. Varro noticed a shooting star dart across the ink-black firmament but was surprised when no one else seemed to observe the would-be omen. Maybe the sight was meant for him alone, although he couldn't judge whether it presaged his doom or ascendency.

The moreish smells first drew Varro to the banqueting table, where all manner of dishes, decoratively set on silver trays, glistened and steamed. The centrepiece was a succulent Trojan Pig. Fish dishes – included lamprey flavoured with garlic, spiced red mullet and poached mackerel – made-up one end of the table. At the other end were various vegetables and delicacies: leeks, oysters, radishes, baked pear slices, honey-drizzled sausages and peacocks' feet fried in breadcrumbs, among others.

As he partook of some food at a table in the garden Varro's thoughts turned to Cassandra. She knew how to catch a man's eye, both consciously and unconsciously, he recalled. She was vibrant, good-hearted and alluring. His affair with her had burned bright. And had perhaps burned out too quickly. It was lust rather than love. But that was fine.

Cassandra was the daughter of a quaestor, who traded a career in politics for running a construction company. He also headed-up one of the largest stonemason's guilds in the city. The famed beauty was young but far from inexperienced when he first courted her. She had seduced him as much as he had seduced her. It was only a couple of months after they met when her father took her away to Baiae for a holiday. Little did she realise though Cassandra had been whisked away to be introduced to Lucius Scaurus. The senator gained a wife and Cassandra's father was granted tax relief on building a new tenement block on the Aventine Hill. Just before she took her leave for the famous holiday resort the lovers met-up one final time.

"I wish you could come," she whispered, or whined imploringly. Cassandra had long been indulged by her father – and others – and was accustomed to getting what she wanted.

"I wish you could stay," Varro replied, both feigning and experiencing a sense of loss.

The poet gifted her a silver brooch, in the shape of dove, as a love token (having had a previous mistress give the piece of jewellery back to him a few weeks earlier).

Cassandra wrote him a letter when she returned to Rome and her marriage had been announced, having obeyed her father and consented to the match. He was a powerful nobleman – and she would consequently be a powerful woman. Her affection for Lucius increased too after witnessing his house and gardens for the first time. He was older than her, but that was the Roman way. Varro had already found another mistress by then, but he duly wrote back and, out of good form, confessed he was heartbroken and would cherish her memory like a precious stone.

"Rufus?" an astounded but not unelated voice sounded out, distracting him from his reverie. "It's been an age – and not a golden one."

When Cassandra first spotted him from across the other side of the lawn she doubted her eyes, thinking that she had imbibed too much wine already. But it was him. He hadn't changed. Still handsome. Still virile, most likely. Still happy to sit by himself – and still happy, hopefully, to be disturbed by an attractive woman. Her heart beat faster as she tried to count the tears and months between when they had last spoken. It had been too long. When she first realised her marriage was an unhappy one Cassandra wanted to send him a letter. Meet. But she thought how she must have hurt him – and she didn't want to now be hurt, even more, in return if he spurned her. It was better to just retain the fun, fond memories. He knew how and where to touch her. Satisfy her. They had been a gilded, feted couple but even more so they enjoyed their own company, she remembered. Nights in by the fire. The memories of them making love. She wanted to hear his voice, feel his fingertips against her thighs. She waited before approaching him however. She needed to catch her breath, compose herself. Cassandra tried to recall if it was because or despite of his reputation that she first became attracted to him. They had met at a dinner party. They arrived with different partners but left together. Her friends warned her that the rakish poet would break her heart. Had she broken his in the end though? But most of all, because of him, the young woman (who could be shallow and selfish at times) discovered that she had a heart.

"Cassandra. How lovely to see you," Varro replied, genuinely pleased to finally encounter her, for several reasons. The surprise was a pleasant one. The poet didn't need to spout any florid words to convey how beautiful he thought she looked. Admiration and desire shaped his expression. His mouth was slightly agape, and his eyes were stapled wide – drunkenly drinking in the sight of her. Varro usually affected such a pose, but with Cassandra the reaction came (almost) naturally.

Her face was thinner, having shed the last of her youthful puppy fat. Even the make-up couldn't hide the tiredness, or weariness, around her eyes if one looked close enough. They were wine-filled eyes (he knew, from looking at himself in the mirror each day). Her skin had lost some of its lustre and her posture wasn't quite the same. But Cassandra was still arrestingly attractive, worthy of being any artist's model. Her countenance was classically beautiful, unblemished and symmetrical. In the first blush of youth Cassandra grew used to brushing away the admirers like flies. The host's wife was wearing a crimson cloak over a sapphire-blue stola, made from the finest Chinese silk. The cut enhanced her already enviable figure. Her jewellery was tasteful and complimented her appearance, unlike others at the party who seemed weighed down like pack animals in gold baubles, coloured glass necklaces and semi-precious gems.

"Are you here with anyone?" she tentatively asked, ardently hoping that the answer would be no. Partly she had delayed speaking to him in order to discover if had come unaccompanied to the party. If he was alone, was it because he wanted to freely speak to her?

"I came with Manius. As you know he's not the most alluring companion, but it's one of the longest relationships I've been in."

Cassandra laughed, for the first time in days. Varro could always make her giggle. He was the wittiest and most sarcastic person she knew. He was a breath of fresh air, when they met. Cassandra recalled how she could forget and find herself at the same time when they were talking – and making love. Passionately. Experimentally. Frequently.

"Are you free to walk with me awhile?" she asked, or almost pleaded, glancing around to see if anyone was watching them. "The gardens this way will be quiet. We can talk freely. You can have me all to yourself. If you want."

Varro observed the subtle or otherwise hint of suggestion in her tone.

"Won't I be keeping you away from your guests?"

"Have you not seen them? I would like to be kept away from my guests. Or rather they are Lucius' guests. His tribe or pack," she said, little masking her disdain. It was if she had just tasted a bad olive.

"Will your husband not come looking for you? I met him earlier in the evening. I would prefer not to upset him," Varro remarked, as a sop towards propriety.

"I am the last person here he would want to spend the evening with," she issued. A grin broke forth, like sunlight peeping through clouds.

The couple covertly glanced around them to ensure they were not anyone's centre of attention and disappeared off into the far reaches of the garden, as if the wife of the host were giving the honoured guest a tour. Cassandra led him into a small grove - swaying her hips as she walked, to draw attention to her lissom figure. A marble fountain and old statue of Sextus Scaurus, a consul in the time of the Punic War, stood in the middle of the grotto. Lucius' ancestor bore the same pointed chin and bat-like ears as his descendent. Varro broke the ears off the head, citing that he didn't need to worry about him listening to their conversation now. Cassandra's reaction was a picture of shock and mischievous satisfaction. The sound of the babbling water thankfully drowned out the sound of the distant babbling voices from the party.

They first discussed what they had been doing since they last saw each other. After sharing commonplace news Varro revealed, with a pained expression, he had been lonely – even when he had been cavorting with mistresses and drinking companions. Or especially when he had been cavorting with mistresses and drinking companions. Varro had delivered the lines and played the role of the tortured poet so many times he was almost bored with the routine performance. But Cassandra believed the act – and confessed she was lonely too. Varro lied and said he was half-way through writing an epic poem, based on the labours of Hercules – adding that he would be grateful if Cassandra could be one of the first people to read the draft once it was completed. She was touched and said she would be honoured, her voice breaking a little with emotion. The cynic in Varro wondered if she was playing a part too.

Cassandra's voice shook further still when she told Varro she was unable to have children:

"It could be him and his blood has grown tamer. But he says that he already fathered a son and therefore I am to blame. I'm unnatural - or being punished by the gods."

Varro deftly moved towards his former lover as she bowed her head and leaned towards him, breaking down in tears against his shoulder. The harmonious coming together almost seemed choreographed. He curled a strong but tender arm around her, stroking her back. He breathed in her perfume and the fragrant smell of her glossy hair.

"You're not to blame. He is... And I'm here now."

"At least divorce is just a matter of time. He will choose someone soon from a suitable noble family, who can present him with a child and a dowry."

"I'm sorry for you," he said, gently kissing her upon the top of her head and then her brow. Her arm curled around his body and pulled him even closer.

"I'm not. The day I divorce him will prove to be a far happier day to that of when we married."

Varro paused briefly in his comforting, or seduction, of the young woman as he considered whether he was happier on the day he divorced Lucilla, to when he married her. He knew the answer.

"Do you ever dwell upon what would have happened to us, if I had remained in Rome and we stayed together?"

Cassandra pulled away from him a little and gazed into his eyes - in an attempt to divine how honest he was being in his answer. She always had her doubts - a pea beneath her mattress - that she loved him more than he loved her. She never wanted to be just another conquest to the poet. Yet Cassandra suspected that, although he was no longer in love with Lucilla, no one would ever be able to take her place.

"We both know I would be lying if I declared I missed you every day. But I do spare you a thought every now and then and think what could have been – and remember that red dress which clung to your body even more than I did."

She laughed and blushed – and realised how much she missed him. Cassandra adjusted the cloak around her shoulders. Varro noticed the silver brooch he had given her, all those years ago, pinned to her breast. His heart didn't know whether to lift or sink. He pretended not to notice the love token. Maybe Cassandra had forgotten she was wearing it too. Or had she deliberately adjusted her cloak, so he would see it? He experienced a swelling affection for the woman. But it was succeeded by a swelling guilt. Varro was using a woman who had already been long abused by her wretched husband.

When Varro suddenly kissed her, hungrily and meaningfully, she felt pregnant with desire. Cassandra surrendered her lips and wished to surrender more. They had made love in a garden in the past, but she could not risk being discovered now, for her sake or his. She had wanted to take other lovers out of revenge or boredom before. But this was something different, deeper.

"Come and see me tomorrow," she said, breathlessly, arching her back in exquisite pleasure and lifting one foot off the ground. "He is visiting his precious theatre again. He's probably infatuated with an actress. He spends half his days there... We sleep in different quarters. My room is on the ground floor, next to his study. Close to the eastern wall. I can arrange for a couple of maids to be posted outside my room and window to warn us if we are going to be disturbed. Lucius will be accompanied by most of his staff, when he leaves the city. And I know the routines for the ones who will be remaining behind."

Varro was unconcerned by the fact that Cassandra had her instructions too readily to hand. She wouldn't be the first wife in Rome to invite a lover into her chamber and order her maids to act as sentries.

Varro promised he would meet Cassandra tomorrow evening, as he cradled her in his arms. As they walked back towards the party he asked her what her husband thought about Caesar:

"He curses his name, which makes me celebrate Caesar's. He says it's because of Caesar that the dream of Rome has turned into a nightmare. That he is a dictator, far worse than the tyrant who came before him... Only the other day he railed that, "the gods would not countenance Caesar ruling Rome like a king. And more importantly, I will not countenance it either.""

So as not to cause any suspicion the couple took their leave of one another once in sight of the party. They were discreet. Her make-up was retouched. Garments were smoothed back into place. Cassandra dared to hope that fate had brought her former lover back into her life – and that she would soon come out of the shadow of her husband. The word "divorce" was tantamount to a prayer. Varro dared to hope that he would find some incriminating evidence come the following evening - and his work would be done. Even better than a divorcee, Cassandra deserved to be a widow.

Before Varro left the party altogether he made sure to reconnoitre the location of Scaurus' study, in relation to his wife's bedroom.

A weight was lifted as soon as Varro left the grounds of the house. He felt as relieved as a soldier who had come through his first battle. Although the war still wasn't over. He still felt drained, wrung out like a sponge, and yearned for his bed. To sleep. He was an actor who had remained on stage for too long. Varro had been tempted to tell Cassandra the truth. Such was her enmity towards her husband that she could prove a greater asset if she knew that he was being investigated. She could, quite literally, open doors. But when he discussed the possibility with Agrippa during their initial meeting the consul was resolute:

"As much faith as I have in a woman's capacity to lie to her husband, it's too great a risk. The truth would place the young woman in too much peril – and will compromise you as well."

Varro met with Manius and the two companions made their way home. It had been a long night.

"Did you get to speak to Scaurus?" the Briton asked.

"Yes. I would say that he's a typical senator - fuelled by conceit and ambition - but for the fact that he's more wretched than most... I can understand how the recently departed Verres thought he was worthy of his interest. Scaurus certainly has no love for Caesar... I just need to put more flesh on the bone and investigate further. I'll be meeting with him again soon. I think he views me as a possible recruit or ally... I was also able to discreetly meet with Cassandra. Scaurus will be leaving the city tomorrow and she has asked me to come to her room once it gets dark... I should be able to search his study, once she falls asleep. Maybe I'll read her one of my poems."

"And how was she?"

"Beautiful but broken. Marriage is a prison – and the man is always the jailor. He's squeezed most of the life out of her. Most, but not all. Cassandra is young and spirited enough to write a second act into her life. I hope. The sooner he divorces her the better... How was your night? Learn anything interesting?"

"I've learned that attendants and bodyguards can be more gossipy than a bunch of housewives. I also learned that he serves acetum to his staff and the finest vintages to his guests, which is cause enough for Caesar to execute him as far as I'm concerned. Before I start I should warn you that, to encourage others to loosen their tongues, I was dutifully disloyal to you. I mentioned you deserved your reputation as a drunk, but not as a lover. And if not for Fronto you would be in penury... A year ago, Scaurus liquidated numerous assets. He sold off some mining rights and a couple of villas he owned in Baeie and Pompeii. Scaurus used the money to purchase several gladiator schools, as well as the theatre you mentioned... The bastard beats his wife – and is even callous enough to invite his mistresses around and parade them in front of Cassandra. He is fond of personally whipping his slaves... As much as he spent on the lavish gathering tonight, he was spending to invest. Many of the guests were clients or potential donors to his campaign to run for the consulship next year. I'm not sure how safe a bet that will be for his supporters though. Even if they ran as corpses, Caesar and Agrippa would still garner the votes at present."

"The plot thickens," Varro replied, before yawning.

**10.**

Partly as an act of defiance, because he knew Marcus Agrippa would disapprove, Varro woke-up late the next day and remained in bed until close to midday. He felt he deserved the rest.

In contrast Manius woke early, waiting on a message from Camilla. Any news would have been better than no news, he decided. The Briton restlessly paced around the house, as if he were a man on trial, waiting to hear back from a jury about the verdict. His stomach churned. He couldn't sleep, despite being awake for half the night before. He sharpened his dagger and sword to keep himself occupied. But his thoughts prickled and his tunic scratched like a hair shirt. Viola followed him in close attendance, either confused or worried about her master's erratic behaviour.

Manius was in two minds whether to visit the house and confront her father or not. He could end up causing a rift where one, at present, didn't exist. But he didn't want to just do nothing. More than anything Manius just needed to know Camilla was well. He imagined her locked in her room, her hair dishevelled – tears streaming down her distraught features. The nervous energy was akin to that of when he was a gladiator, prowling around like a caged animal, waiting to enter the arena and get on with the fight. Fronto advised patience however, when he spoke to the bodyguard:

"He's her father. Whether you respect his decision or not, the law will… Just give it a bit of time. Wait a couple of days. Will it not be worth sacrificing a couple of days for a possible lifetime with the woman you love? She will also still feel the same about you, Manius, no matter what her father decrees."

The Briton thanked the old man for his advice and resolved to wait a couple of days, before attempting to see Camilla. Hopefully he would receive a message from her by then. In order to take his mind off things Manius agreed to run an errand for Fronto.

"If you could pass on this note to Albanus, in the market. Stress the need to deliver the item as urgently as possible. Tomorrow will be too late."

Varro woke with a start, from a nightmare. The disturbing images from which were still branded in his waking mind. In the dream he had woken up in his bedroom too – but with a ribbon of blood around his neck from where his throat had been slit. His chest was also drenched in blood, as if he had spilled a jug of wine down himself. Varro was dead, a ghost. A shade of himself. He stumbled out of bed, trembling from the cold (despite it being a summer's day outside). He stood uneasily, like a sailor trying to regain his sea legs. His legs gave way completely however at seeing Fronto and Manius on the floor, murdered. His old tutor had been strangled with a harp string and Manius had been stabbed in the breast, with his own sword. Viola stood and whimpered by his side, licking his face in a futile attempt to revive her master. He knew with certainly that Scaurus had entered his home and slaughtered his companions. Grief and revenge chequered what was left of his soul. A terrifying presentiment scythed through his being, like a lightning bolt. He believed Scaurus was now making his way across the Palatine to torture and kill Lucilla.

Sweat covered his chest, as much as blood had during the nightmare, when Varro woke. It took him several moments to re-orientate himself and catch his breath. As much as he was relieved to know it was all just a dream Varro realised it was likely that Verres died by Scaurus' hand. And it was likely that his own life – and those of his loved ones – were now in danger. Spying no longer felt like a game.

"Manius! By Ares, it's you!" Felix Dio chirped above the cacophony of noise in the marketplace. The Briton turned to take in the former lanista at his ludus, as he was making his way home from delivering Fronto's note.

The market square was situated on the Esquiline Hill. Various shops – clothiers, fishmongers, silversmiths, barbers and shoemakers, among others – bordered a central network of stalls, selling foodstuffs and other goods. Rival costermongers bellowed out their prices and pithy one-liners to attract attention. Heads were vigorously shaken, or nodded with approval, as shoppers haggled. The haggling would increase to fever pitch at the end of the afternoon, as certain customers looked to beat down the prices on produce that would perish, unless sold by the close of day. Buyers and sellers would gesticulate more than bad actors. Slaves attended on their masters and mistresses, swelling the motley crowd, and carried their owner's purchases like beasts of burden. People were dressed in silks and sack cloths. The market was a melting pot of languages, accents and classes which only occasionally boiled over into bouts of trouble. Gossip and lewd jokes were traded. People shouted, rather than politely spoke, to be heard above the ritual clamour. Some customers beamed with satisfaction from their purchases, whilst some stallholders looked like they had the world on their shoulders, from having another bad day. Yet they forced an obsequious smile for their next potential customer. The wine sellers proved the most popular vendors – and due to competition, they kept prices low. As such the market square contained more than a few drunks. "All human life is contained in the market, unfortunately. Rome lives to shop, and shops to live," Varro had once written, as part of a satire, the Briton recalled earlier, when he had first entered the square.

Manius took in the squat, mole-faced man making a bee-line towards him. Tufts of dirty grey hair protruded out from a red, felt hat, which rested on his head at a jaunty angle. Despite the fine weather Dio still wore woollen stockings beneath his tunic. Thankfully he still had an aversion from showing off his fat, hairy legs in public, Manius thought. He had suffered worse lanistas during his career as a gladiator. Dio fed his charges well and would call for surgeons whenever they were needed. He also seemed to enjoy his work when acting as a pimp - and renting out gladiators for the night to wealthy Roman women (and sometimes men). Manius recalled a joke he heard at the ludus, about the overseer. "Felix would sell his own mother, if the price was right. Or rather he'd lease her out, to make more of an income over a longer period."

He was accompanied by two burly bodyguards wearing impassive, or bored, expressions. From his clothes, new found staff and the gold rings on his stubby fingers it appeared that Dio had done well for himself, since the last time they met.

"Stay there. Let me look at you, my old friend," Dio remarked. "No, better still come this way where we have room to breathe. The tide of people might wash us away here. We also need to watch out for filthy pickpockets. Rome breeds them, like cockroaches."

Manius was slightly taken back. It was the first time the lanista had ever described him as a "friend". Dio grabbed the Briton by the elbow and ushered him to one side, with more force than one might have expected.

"It's good to see you, Felix. You are looking well," Manius calmly remarked, in contrast to his excited and excitable companion.

"I am perhaps looking too well, eh? You have kept yourself in better shape than I have," Dio replied, affectionately patting his pot-belly. "I eat so much suckling pig that I fear I may turn into one in the future. But tell me, are you still part of Rufus Varro's household? Does he pay well? Or does most of his money go on mistresses and his wine cellar? It was a gift from the gods was it not, that day, when Appius Varro saw you fight and bought your freedom?"

"Maybe the gods owed me some good fortune," Manius said, by way of an explanation.

"Indeed. The gods have smiled on me these past few years too. I left the ludus after meeting up with Faustus Bursa. Bursa saw a gap in the market, which I widened when he died, and I took over the operation. The war may be over, but Rome still has an appetite for blood sports, no? But who wants to sit next to a sweaty Gaul or Ethiop at the Circus Maximus? And drink the swill they call wine there? Or sit so far away you couldn't even recognise your own brother, if he was one of the combatants? And so I provide an experience, for those willing to pay, of a more intimate arena dedicated to gladiatorial combat. I have converted an old grain warehouse, installing seating and other amenities. No matter how much I put the prices of the seats and wine up we are always full to the rafters with an audience. Women attend as much as men, almost. But as we know Roman noblewomen always did enjoy seeing a bit of gladiatorial flesh. May the gods bless them. You should come along one day. Or better still you should take part. You still know how to swing a sword, I imagine. I will pay you handsomely. Winning pays a lot more than losing, of course - and the fights are not to the death. You will just need to knock your opponent out or have them yield. We have our own surgeons too. C'mon, what do you say? It's the best kind of money. Easy money!" Dio exclaimed, fraternally clasping the Briton by the shoulders, all but standing on tip-toe to do so.

"It's kind of you to offer and I'm glad you are doing so well for yourself Felix but it's not for me," Manius replied, equitably. His fighting days in the arena were over. He made a promise to himself – and Camilla. Appius Varro had given him a second chance in life – and Manius had grasped it.

Dio was not one to take no for an answer however. He made a face, as if to suggest that he was at war with himself, and finally spoke:

"It's against my better judgement. Yet I'll do it. Because it's you. And hopefully some people will remember "The Briton", as you were called. But not only will I give you a small cut of the ticket revenues, but I'll let you keep a modest percentage of what I make from all the wagers taken at the event. I can't say fairer than that, can I?"

Whether he put it down to divine intervention or not, a kernel of an idea began to form in Manius' head. If marrying Camilla was a question of money for Aulus Sanga, he may have found the answer.

Varro spent part of the afternoon composing his report to Marcus Agrippa. The poet had written more lyrical and philosophical lines before – but none so important, he reasoned. His work – and words – could now change lives. Hopefully for the better. Should he even just help save Cassandra from her abusive husband then the action would be worth more than all his poems put together. His father might even be proud of him. Varro felt purposeful. It was a strange but not unwelcome sensation.

Varro reported he had introduced himself to Scaurus at the party – and the senator had taken a liking to him. He relayed their conversation and said he was due to meet Scaurus again soon, at his theatre outside of Rome.

*"I have but suspicions rather than proof that Scaurus is an enemy of the state. He certainly cannot be relied upon to be a friend to Caesar."*

When he relayed how Scaurus was selling assets to fund his candidacy for a consulship Varro fleetingly thought he could be being used by Agrippa to scupper Scaurus' ambitions, in order to cement his own position.

Varro made a list of the senators and other influential guests who attended the party. Finally, he mentioned his meeting with Cassandra – and that he was seeing her again this evening.

A trusted slave delivered the sealed message to the consul's residence. As Mark Antony appropriated Pompey the Great's house after his death, Agrippa similarly moved into the extensive property after Mark Antony's demise.

## 11.

The muggy weather hung in the air like a piece of spiced ham hung out to dry, outside a butcher's shop. Varro and Manius sat in the garden, sharing a jug of wine, having just finished their lunch of sea bass, served on a bed of mushrooms, cabbage and onions. Fronto had just excused himself, saying he already looked like a prune and therefore had no desire to sit out in the sun.

"It sounds risky," Varro warned, after hearing his companion explain his plan. "You could be seriously injured or killed."

Manius had agreed with Felix Dio to take part in a gladiatorial bout, the day after tomorrow. The fee from the contest would not change his circumstances, but should he stake all he owned on winning the bout he could then raise sufficient capital to prove to Sanga that he could provide for his daughter. Especially if, like he planned, he fought on the back foot during the opening of the fight. Once the odds were long enough Varro would place a bet on Manius – and he would change tack and win the contest. The Briton told himself he wasn't being dishonourable and throwing the fight.

"Camilla is worth it. I need the money."

"I can loan you the money. Or I'm even happy to just give it to you," Varro stressed, no longer being able to sit comfortably on his reclining wicker chair.

"No, this is something I have to do for myself. Call me proud and stupid."

"I have. And I will. But this is madness," he asserted, though Varro could see the method in his madness.

"Besides, you will need all your money to keep paying for Lucilla's dressmakers and decorators."

"That's only funny because it's true. But I'll probably be murdered in my sleep by Lucius Scaurus, or exiled by Marcus Agrippa, before Lucilla ever ruins me," Varro remarked, grimly. Yet grinningly. "But I'll arrange the stake money and put the wager on during the fight. You know that I'll never forgive myself if something happens to you. Worse than that, Viola would never forgive me," he said. The mongrel briefly raised her head at the sound of her name, but then reverted to just lazily laying back down on the grass, sprawling herself out in the afternoon sun.

"I am grateful for you helping me solve my problems, when you have plenty of your own. I take it you're still intending to see Cassandra this evening?"

"It's going to be a late night. Not even Fronto will be able wait up for me this time. I will need your help. Once it gets darker than Erebus' arse, you can lift me over the wall of the house. You will need to remain in the vicinity in case I'm discovered - and I call for help. Should you somehow hear the odd moan coming from the house though there's no need to be alarmed. There should be few staff however – and they will be asleep for the most part. My only problem is that I will only be able to leave the room once Cassandra is asleep too. She might take offence if she thinks I've seduced her to gain access to her husband's study. She might panic - and fear retribution should I be absent for too long a time. I'm not sure what to do. I don't think hoping she falls asleep quite cuts it as a sufficient plan," Varro said, as his mental unease and lack of comfort in his chair grew worse.

"You seem to have forgotten one of the first Latin phrases I taught you, when you were a boy. Nil desperandum," Fronto said, as he stood before Varro and held up a small glass phial filled with a light blue liquid. "This is a sleeping draught, which I ordered from the Albanus Pollio, the apothecary. His attendant has just delivered it. Should Cassandra not doze off from your conversation, or more amorous activities, then you need only pour this into her wine and she should fall asleep shortly after."

"What would I do without you Fronto? Perhaps it's best not to imagine that scenario. I am grateful though," Varro warmly expressed, thinking how the old man could be as garrulous as Nestor – but as wily as Odysseus too.

Fronto handed over the phial and recalled how he used to provide a similar theriac for Lucilla. After her second miscarriage she had problems sleeping. "I want to be dead to the world, like my baby," she tearfully confessed to Fronto one evening. The attendant also noticed how Lucilla liked to fall asleep before her husband returned from spending time with his mistresses or drinking companions. Fronto always made sure he acted as an intermediary between the distraught woman and apothecary, just in case Lucilla ever desired something more potent and poisonous than a sleeping draught.

Before Fronto could reply he was interrupted by the arrival of one of Marcus Agrippa's lictors, who was being shown out into the garden by a whey-faced slave – who decided it best not to keep the fearsome official waiting outside the house.

"Rufus Varro, I have a message for you from Marcus Agrippa. I am to wait here until you have both read and destroyed this letter," the lictor said, the soul of formality, his voice as flat as the back of a sword.

Varro broke the seal and read the scroll.

*"Thank you for your update, Rufus. Good work. But the field is barely half ploughed. There's more to be done. I am already aware of Scaurus' financial activities over the past year or so – and the ambitions he harbours to win a consulship. I am also aware of his cruel streak and the abuse of his wife and slaves. But that is not our concern.*

*Our quarry has started to take an interest in you, it seems. Hopefully your success was down to your performance, as opposed to being genuinely cut from the same cloth as the backward-looking patrician. Your name, or the respected name of your father, is of value to him. More so your wealth is worth something. He will doubtless encourage you at some point to donate to his campaign fund – and in return he will promise to look after you when in office. Politics is the second oldest profession. Should you need a sum of money to buy his trust then let me know... His small army of gladiators isn't sufficient to overwhelm the Praetorian Guard and attempt a coup. But his numbers may swell according to campaign funding... The theatre must be a cover for something. Scaurus is far too much in love with himself to be overly enamoured with an actress... Keep digging, so as to put him in his grave...*

*We are still not seeing the whole picture. Something, or someone, remains in the shadows.*

    *M."*

## 12.

Pinkish-grey clouds moved slowly across the sky like a smack of jellyfish drifting across the ocean. It was late. Even most of the drunks had wended their way home. Varro and Manius made sure to avoid the pools of urine and vomit in the streets of the Palatine. Young noblemen shared the same vices and bodily functions as their less scrubbed cousins in the Subura.

The two men wore dark tunics and even darker cloaks.

"Let's just hope she's still awake, when you tap upon her shutters," Manius quietly remarked as they came to the spot along the wall which stood close to the window of Cassandra's bedroom.

"She's deluded enough to think I'm worth the wait."

"I know you want to take the opportunity to search Scaurus' study – but take care too, Rufus. Ensure you leave everything in its place. Flee as fast as Cleopatra at Actium if you're caught, rather than attempt to fight your way out. Try to keep your face concealed. Work out your exits and escape routes beforehand. I'll just be here too."

Manius first lifted his friend so Varro could check if anyone was patrolling the grounds of the house.

"Are you ready?" the Briton asked. He couldn't help but observe the anxiety etched into his companion's features. It was a new look for the carefree poet.

Varro nodded.

"Thankfully this is not the first time I've snuck into the bedroom of a senator's wife."

*Let's just hope it's not the last time.*

The attendant let Varro stand on his shoulders. He climbed over the wall and dropped down on the other side with little fuss or noise. Thankfully a bench was positioned on the other side of the wall, which would allow him to climb back over later in the night. His pulse raced, but not for any amorous reason. The shutters on the window were already spread outwards, welcoming him with open arms. Cassandra was in view, the window operating as a frame to a vision of wanton beauty. She had been waiting, calmly or otherwise, for him. Moments before she had stared up at the moon and offered a prayer to Diana that he would come. With every ten beats of her heart the woman had experienced different, alternating, feelings: fear of being caught; the satisfaction of taking another lover – and defying her husband; the hope of rekindling her relationship with Varro; the anticipation of sex; the crippling doubt and sorrow that Varro would reject her - and leave her alone for the evening and the rest of her life.

But he was here. Standing in front of her. He cupped a hand around her buttock. His mouth pressed against hers. His tongue flicking and then fencing against her own. Varro drunk in her perfume and tasted the wine on her satin lips.

They eventually paused and caught their breath. Beaming. Cassandra gazed up at him, in a spirit of desire and disbelief. She had started to consider that he wouldn't come. That the night before had been a passing fancy, a dream she misinterpreted. But he was here. Part of her felt nervous. Butterflies fluttered in her stomach, like she was about to be intimate with a man for the first time.

"Would you like some wine?" Cassandra asked, already moving towards the silver ewer containing one of her husband's vintages. She wanted a cup herself and expected Varro to say yes.

He quickly took in his surroundings as her back was turned. Polished bronze braziers murmured in the corners of the room. Scented candles and figurines of Vesta, Venus and Helen of Troy were dotted all around. A large dressing table, replete with a silver mirror, was positioned along one side of the room. A few paintings, depicting scenes from Horace's Georgics, hung on the wall. A large bed, with Indian cotton sheets and ornate scroll work along its sides and posts, dominated the chamber. A walk-in closet caught the eye, housing a treasure trove of bold colours, luxurious materials and differing styles of garments. Along the bottom of the dresses Varro noticed an equally extensive collection of sandals, slippers and boots.

As Cassandra swivelled back around his eyes rightly feasted on her instead of the room. That morning she asked her maid to dye her hair red, with henna. She wanted the same colour hair to that of when they first met, at the dinner party. She also put braids in her hair, like she wore that evening. Her autumnal red tresses hung down, a cascade of rubies. Cassandra was dressed in a black silk gown, with nothing beneath. The plunging neckline revealed a sapphire pendant on a fine gold chain – and the glimpse, promise, of greater treasure. An inverted V-shape hung down at the bottom of the garment too, her shapely legs as smooth and bronze as the statue of Helen of Troy which adorned her bedside table. The dress clung to her achingly alluring figure like a second skin and shimmered in the mellow candlelight. The garment was fastened in a bow at the front, but Varro knew from experience that just one slight tug of the silk belt would cause the entire gown to slip from her body.

He thanked her for the drink, savouring the vintage – whilst wanting to also devour the banquet before him. He complimented her new hair colour – and referenced when they first met. Both recalled sitting next to each other at dinner, making polite conversation. She rubbed her calf against his leg, as the dish of some asparagus tips dipped in a honey sauce was served. Varro slipped his hand through the slip in her stola and caressed the inside of her thighs beneath the table.

They took a further half-step towards one another in unison, as if they were about to dance. He cupped her cheek in his hand, as her sinewy arms snaked themselves around his body like vines around a tree. He led her onto the bed and they lay next to each other, their breathing and heartbeats in sync.

"Can we talk first? I don't want this, us, just to be about sex," she said, yearning for him. "You mean more to me than that."

"You mean more to me than that too," Varro replied, not without a modicum of honesty. He was about to pull the woman towards him – onto him – but he merely let his hand rest upon her hip.

"I am sorry how we left things years ago. You must believe me when I say that I did not know the real reason why my father wanted to take me away from Rome. I sometimes wonder, if I would have delayed things, or feigned illness, Lucius would have married someone else and my life would have been different. Better. Or maybe I deserve to be unhappy. I was spoiled when I was a child. I often made fools of men. I wanted to be the centre of attention. If I didn't feel like I was the lead actress, then I didn't want to take part... I ignored the gods and made few offerings to them in my youth, believing I was the author of my own fate. Should I blame them now when, after all my recent offerings, they ignore me?"

"You shouldn't be so hard on yourself. Any man you've known would have eventually made a fool of himself, with or without your encouragement. It's what we do. And I regularly thank the gods for ignoring me. Much like officials in Rome, who make promises to make your life better - and tax your time and wealth when doing so – it's best if they don't bother with you. You deserve to be happy Cassandra – and once you're free of your husband you will be," Varro argued, as he ran his fingers up and down her spine, which arched slightly at the thrill of his touch. Her eyes purred.

"You always knew how to make me smile. You taught me how to laugh at myself and that I was greater than just the sum of my wardrobe. Perhaps I forgot those lessons over the years, but I am willing to learn them again."

"I am glad the past caught up with me too and I met you again, whether it was by accident or fate. If nothing else, I can get to tell you that what we shared was special. Real. Precious. It may be a double-edged compliment, which praises you but rightly paints me in a dim light, but I was always faithful to you when we were together, Cassandra. I cannot say the same for when I courted other mistresses. Perhaps it was because you tired me out so much. If it was too much about sex when we were younger, I want you to know I realised it meant more to me when the affair was over... The wounds from my marriage – and divorce - were still tender. I wasn't ready to commit back then, but I think I am now. I won't run or duck should I see Cupid shoot an arrow in my direction... I was conceited. Narcissus was less vain. I thought I had to play the lusty but lovelorn poet. But poetry is but a shadow of life. Life is life. I vainly thought, through writing, I might live forever. But I could no more achieve immortal fame composing poetry, than Sisyphus could complete his task of rolling his stone up the hill... My father was right. I owe a duty - to Rome and my family name - to have children. A man's legacy should be his offspring, not some hastily written epodes, which even the author can't remember and recite," Varro soulfully declared.

Cassandra stared with wonder and pity at her former lover. She had never known anyone to be so achingly honest with her. He had bared his heart. How could she now callously break it?

Varro cobbled his speech together from past confessions, spouted out in bed to previous mistresses. He realised, many years ago, that women wanted to save him – so he let them believe they could. He had refined his act and script over the years. He furrowed his brow, paused for effect and forced a pained smile when a line called for it. A subtle awkwardness and vulnerability abounded. Some of the words stuck in his throat, emphasising the impression that he had never uttered them before. Varro's performance was convincing because he believed in what he was saying, from a certain point of view. Long before lying to Cassandra, he had deceived himself about his sins. When Varro first artfully seduced a woman, claiming her body and soul, he felt as proud as a painter, who had created a masterwork. But the price the artist paid for his success was to be condemned to paint the same picture over – and over - again. As much as life might amuse Varro, he was still painfully bored – like a gourmet who has yet to discover a dish which truly satisfies him.

"Did you not want to have children with Lucilla?"

"It's a long story," Varro replied, feeling genuinely awkward and vulnerable. Some truths and lies were best left buried. "And we're already halfway through the evening. I don't want to think about Lucilla now. I want to think about you. Be with you. I don't want to waste another moment."

"Nor do I."

"I have been thinking about you all day. Half the time I dressed you with my eyes, imagining what you'd wear and how you'd look. And the rest of the time I spent undressing you. But I fear I'm babbling now. The cure of course will be to stop my mouth with a -"

Cassandra kissed Varro deeply and straddled him, sweetly surrendering to her desires. She emitted a small sigh, or moan, as she rhythmically gyrated – arousing him and herself. Varro pulled the bow of her gown and the garment slid off, revealing her taut, burnished body. The sapphire pendant glinted in the light of the glowing brazier, as did her eyes.

The solitary candle flickered as it grew close to burning itself out. Camilla lay curled-up in a ball, her eyes as puffed-up as the goose feather pillow which she clung to. Her stomach fizzed with hunger. But the young woman no longer had any appetite. Food tasted like ash and she had been sick the last two times she attempted to eat something, since her father had forbidden her from seeing Manius. Camilla had similarly lay curled-up in a ball and cried after her mother passed away – and when her father had put her pony, Hector, to sleep after it had injured its shin in a fall.

She felt helpless.

But not quite hopeless. In the same way the candle fed itself on every drop of wax, Camilla sustained herself on the hope that she would see Manius again. She could and should be his wife. It was meant to be. Her father had called her in to him earlier. She didn't know whether to appear resentful or piteous. He said he would be willing to compromise and countenance a match, depending on certain conditions:

"You must understand how I need to feel satisfied about his character and prospects, that he has left his life as a gladiator and ruffian behind. The attendant needs to own genuine ambitions. I need to be sure he is not seeking to marry you for financial gain. I must protect your reputation, as well as mine... In the meantime, promise me that you will not attempt to contact him. If he tries to send you a message or dares to intrude upon this house, you must ignore his entreaties... Do we have an agreement?" Aulus Sanga posed, as if he were finalising a business deal. "I am only asking you to wait a few days, while I carry out my enquiries. I am being reasonable, am I not?"

Initially Camilla thought her father was asking a rhetorical question. But the pause which hung in the air signified otherwise and finally she deferentially – and dolefully – replied:

"Yes, father."

Camilla suspected her father was just pretending to give Manius a chance. She would honour her promise however and not endeavour to contact Manius, despite her ardent desire to do so. She believed there was still hope. She had to. The alternative was too dreadful.

*Hope.*

Had Pandora kept the vilest evil – the disease of hope - in the jar on purpose, out of compassion? Or, should she have released hope too, did she realise it would have helped to cure all the other plagues she set free?

The candle finally died out, leaving Camilla in darkness.

## 13.

Varro crept along the tiled corridor towards Scaurus' study, located next to Cassandra's bedroom. After making love he poured her a cup of diluted wine, with the sleeping draught mixed in. It had not taken long for the already tired woman to drift off to sleep. Before she did so Cassandra drowsily expressed to Varro how she did not want him to compose any poetry for her:

"You are right. Poetry doesn't capture life. Real life. Words mean nothing – and the more one says the less one means anything. You were not the only suitor to send me poems, all those years ago... They would always compare me to a flower, whether it be a rose, violet or amaranth. I yawned more then, than I am doing now. I was, apparently, always in bloom – but they never mentioned how flowers also wither and die. But everything is born to die, even – or especially – love."

Any sense of pride or purpose which Varro experienced working for the good of Rome was eclipsed by a wave of shame he felt, at seducing and using the woman. She was innocent – as innocent as a Roman noblewoman could be. He had taken advantage of her, in more ways than one. There was a stain on his conscience. Over time such stains can fade, but they can never disappear altogether, he considered. Varro told himself he was doing what he was doing for Cassandra's benefit. Investigating Scaurus would lead to her being free. But he knew he was lying to himself, again.

As the would-be spy slowly turned the handle to the door of the study Varro fleetingly thought about what he might be doing now, if Agrippa had not called on him. He might be staggering home, as merry as Bacchus, or in bed with a whore – who cared as little for him as he cared for her. As much as he might pay lip-service to Epicurus' philosophy, Varro knew, deep down in his soul, that pleasure was not the beginning and goal of a happy life.

A solitary oil lamp, hanging from the ceiling, still burned, gifting the room some light. A large cedarwood desk, inlaid with ivory and gold, sat towards the back of the chamber, in front of a line of cabinets. Portraits and death masks, of Scaurus' sour looking antecedents, lined the walls. Opposite the desk, at the other end of the room, stood a display case filled with a dozen or so daggers. Marble busts of Cato the Elder and Younger were positioned on either side of the desk and seemingly looked at Varro disapprovingly, or accusingly, as he checked the correspondence in view on the table. The letters just dealt with the senator's clients and business partners. Next Varro checked the draws. The only thing he found worthy of interest was a list of names of various officials and merchants, with numbers attached. The figures could have related to campaign donations, or the cost of bribes Scaurus was going to pay to buy their support. One name stuck out in particular. Varro made a mental note of the list, to pass on to Agrippa.

Varro's heart froze – and then beat like a war drum – on hearing a couple of voices outside of the closed shutters. Although it was unlikely anyone could see inside he still quickly ducked behind the desk and breathed as calmly as possible (which wasn't altogether easy) before he was sure that the slaves patrolling the grounds had disappeared. Varro turned his attention to the four large cabinets against the wall. Thankfully they were unlocked. The cabinets contained various scrolls. The first was dedicated to housing business contracts and accounts. The second contained a collection of speeches - by the likes of Cicero, Marcus Brutus and Cato - praising the Republic and denouncing Caesar. The third was home to Scaurus' personal correspondence, which proved as potent as a theriac in nearly sending Varro to sleep, such was the mundane contents of the letters. The fourth cabinet contained documents relating to the running of Scaurus' household and his personal finances. The only thing of interest which seemed curious or out of place was a map on the inside door of one of the cabinets. The map was neither overly detailed or to scale, but it traced a route from Alexandria to Ethiopia and then from Ethiopia to Rome. The map also marked stop-off points and dates along the route, going back three years. Again, Varro made a note of the information and hoped that Marcus Agrippa would be able to cast more light on things.

As per instructed by Agrippa, Varro made sure to leave everything back in its place. He also checked the furniture for any secret compartments – and peeked behind each painting for a strongbox concealed in the wall.

The spy pursed his lips in frustration. He felt like a courtesan who had attended a party for the evening and was travelling home alone. Or he was a fisherman, sailing back to shore with an empty net. He was still no wiser as to Scaurus' intentions or plans. Varro reasoned however that it was always unlikely he would uncover a clear, damning piece of evidence which would seal the senator's fate. Scaurus was too careful to leave any compromising documents in an unlocked cabinet in his unlocked study, which is not to say that there wasn't a hidden strongbox located somewhere else in the house. The thought struck Varro again that, rather than being too careful, could it not be the case that he was unable to find any evidence of wrongdoing because Scaurus was too innocent? As unpleasant a character as the vain-glorious senator was he should not be tried and executed just for whipping his slaves, collecting speeches which lauded the old Republic and purchasing a gladiator school. Not even Cicero or Hortensius in their pomp could have secured a conviction based on such scant proof. No matter how much a hound Varro might prove, was he ultimately barking up the wrong tree? Was he being used by Marcus Agrippa to scupper a possible rival?

Manius kept his eyes closed but ears open as he sat in the street by the house and pretended to be a sleeping drunk. He poured some pungent wine down his tunic and an empty jug stood between his legs. A few passers-by noted him but understandably thought better about disturbing the large, fearsome looking figure. The beast might stir and turn on them.

Anxiety about Camilla, more than dutiful concern for his friend, kept Manius awake. Thoughts prickled like stinging nettles. He shivered, from fear more than the cold, as he imagined losing her. He mustered himself however and told himself that all would be well. He would soon generate the necessary capital to gain her father's blessing for the union. Manius would tell Camilla that the money had come from a provision in Appius Varro's will, to grant his adopted son additional money for when he married. He would feel uncomfortable lying to her, but he didn't want to lose Camilla or have her worry that he was about to return to his old life. His thoughts naturally turned to the imminent bout. The Briton was confident of winning the contest. Dio had hinted that his opponent would be inexperienced. The match-ups were used to blood new fighters. Manius wryly smiled to himself as he pictured the scene of when new recruits joined the ludus – and they used their swords against the training posts. In some instances, the posts nearly won the duels.

Varro returned to the woman's room and bed. The first thing she saw when Cassandra opened her eyes was the statue of Helen of Troy – and her first thought was that Varro, her Paris, might whisk her away. No matter how dire the consequences might be.

The couple made love again – and Varro had to stop Cassandra's mouth with a kiss when her screams became too pronounced.

Afterwards, catching their breath once more, Varro subtly steered the conversation towards the subject of her husband, despite the ire and discomfort it caused.

"I am not sure how much more I can endure… I sometimes think that, if he beats me again, I will grab one of his precious daggers from his study and murder him in his sleep," the distraught woman confessed, talking to herself as much as Varro, as she coldly stared up at the ceiling.

"Daggers?"

"Lucius is obsessively tracking down the daggers which the libertores used to kill Caesar on the Ides of March. He has also been obsessed with Mark Antony over the past six months or so. He has invited many of his officers and attendants for lunch and dinner. I have been present a few times and he quizzes them on what Antony was like – and did – during his time with Cleopatra in the East. He asks for details about their life at court and Antony's relationship with the child, Caesarion, Cleopatra conceived with Caesar. Lucius tells them that he is planning to commission a book on the last days of Antony and Cleopatra. He also probes Antony's officers as to where their soldiers' loyalties now rest, with Antony or Augustus."

The chirping of crickets outside had long since rescinded – to be replaced by thrill birdsong. The brazier of the dawn had been ignited on the horizon and a blood-red sky oozed towards the bedroom.

## 14.

Rome was already wide awake and stretching its limbs. Bakeries coughed out smoke. Officials and merchants were making use of the long summer days and commenced to do business, or idly gossiped, whilst twiddling their styluses. Slaves briskly ran errands – shopping and delivering messages, sweat pouring off their brows, their stomachs rumbling. Sandals slapped against flagstones. Litters criss-crossed one another. Carters traded ribald obscenities, claiming right of way. Attendants lifted the hem of the skirts of their mistresses as, dressed in their finery, they made their offerings in the temples, before visiting their beauticians and dressmakers. The smell of horse dung and refuge festered in the air, along with the acrid odour of smoke from chimneys. Wine and food stalls were set-up and generated immediate queues. Freshly scrubbed boys, accompanied by attendants (and occasionally a parent), made their way to school. The business of Rome was business.

Varro barely noticed the hive of activity though as he made his way home, with Manius. He bowed his head, in fatigue and thought, and appeared sheepish – despite having just played the fox and entered and exited the hen house. Varro had barely touched a drop all night, but he felt hungover, nauseous.

When he reached his house, the agent, as he now began to label himself, scrawled down some notes while his thoughts were still fresh concerning the events of the night before. The asset would write up a full report for Agrippa later in the day.

As soon as he walked through the door Manius asked Fronto if there had been any messages. The old man ruefully shook his head and creased his face in sympathy with the Briton, who felt like tearing his hair out in despair. Or at least drinking a jug of wine and breaking Aulus Sanga's front door down in an attempt to see his daughter.

"Be patient. Have faith," Fronto said, philosophically.

"It's easier said than done," Manius replied, not without a little despair, as if already in mourning for his relationship.

Varro and Manius took to their beds to catch up on some sleep. They were exhausted.

Varro only reached the stage of being half-exhausted before Fronto woke him with the news that a messenger, sent by Scaurus, was waiting for him in the atrium. The nobleman yawned – and wished he could close his eyes and go back to sleep – but replied that he would attend to the messenger, as much as he was inclined to send him away.

"Senator Scaurus requests your presence for lunch – and to grant you a tour of his theatre," the attendant announced, in a grating, nasal tone. Marcellus, who served as a secretary to the statesman, adopted a measure of his master's haughty manner. He owned a pronounced, upturned nose and his features seemed permanently pinched. His back was as straight as a pilum, his chin jutted out like the prow of a ship. Varro had encountered the type before. Marcellus was far from the only petty official in Rome who believed he carried the same authority as his employer – and thought that officiousness equated to virtue. "The senator has arranged a carriage to take you to him, which is currently waiting outside the city gates for you," he added. The secretary ended the message by forcing a smile - which looked like he was sucking on a lemon.

Varro was aware that Scaurus' request was tantamount to an order. He was setting the parameters of their future relationship. Despite Varro's wealth and noble name, the senator would lead, and the would-be aedile would have to follow. No matter what his plans were for the day he would have to cancel them. Scaurus was testing his loyalty and commitment. If he turned down this invitation, Varro knew he might not see another.

The nobleman replied that he would be ready to leave shortly and that his bodyguard would be accompanying him on the journey.

"I think I preferred things when you were a wastrel," Manius remarked, when Varro woke him. "At least I got to sleep in then." The Briton sighed and rolled his eyes but nevertheless got washed and dressed as quickly as he could. Although he wanted to remain at home, in case Camilla sent a message, Manius would welcome the distraction of joining Varro. He was also aware of how his friend might need his protection in earnest soon, in light of the events the night before.

Varro briefed Fronto. He asked him to send a message to Marcus Agrippa, informing him about his imminent meeting with Scaurus – and that he would update the consul when he returned.

*If I return.*

## 15.

With not a little spite Varro instructed Marcellus to ride up next to the wagoner during their journey, as he would be discussing some personal matters with his bodyguard in the carriage. He wanted to remind the official of his station and class.

The lemon Marcellus seemed to be sucking on momentarily grew sourer, but he nodded and assented to the order. He duly ignored the plebeian wagoner when he tried to engage him in small talk.

The carriage, which was comfortable and covered, moved slowly at first along the congested road outside the city gates. As they passed the army of graves which lined the road Varro noted some of the inscriptions on the tombstones:

*"A father, much missed."*

*"I hope you find more peace in the next life than you did in this one, my dear soldiering son. You dedicated your life to protecting Rome."*

*"To my darling wife, who meant the earth to me."*

Varro cynically thought how the widower husband had made a mistake and he had meant to inscribe, "cost the earth."

Some of the tombs were tasteful and inscriptions heartfelt, but too many of the monuments to grief resembled edifices dedicated to vanity and vulgarity. It was not uncommon for tombs to loom as large as a house, with architecture worthy of any temple or palace. Varro remembered a time when he had broken into one such structure and made love to a mistress. *Nothing is sacred.* Strangely he remembered the name of the person whose resting place he had violated, but he had forgotten the name of the woman he made love to.

Varro pensively stared out the window, his chin propped up on his hand, and wondered how many of his former lovers would attend his own funeral. *I might be being generous by saying none... More would doubtless wish to attend any reading of my will... At least Lucilla would come, if only to make sure I was put in the ground. She has probably already bought a suitable funeral dress, on my account."*

Varro turned to his companion. He was about to ask him how he was feeling, in regards to not hearing from Camilla, but the Briton was gently snoring. Varro would be happy for his friend if he married the woman, but he also had to admit that he would be happy, for himself, if the marriage was forbidden and Manius remained within his household. He could barely remember a time when the good-hearted and good-humoured Briton wasn't there, nor did he want to imagine a future where the two men didn't go drinking together. Perhaps the fear of losing his best friend had been behind his reluctance to support him in his plan to fight again in the arena.

They soon began to make good time and entered the countryside. The carriage glided over the smooth Roman road like a ship's prow sailing with a fair wind across a calm sea. Sunlight poured between the clouds like honey.

Wild flowers speckled the golden-green fields. Varro filled his lungs with the fresh air. Rome was stuffed full of people – and therefore full of vanity and folly. Choking him. The change in scenery was welcome. Contoured hills and valleys housed orchards, olive groves and small farms, teeming with crops and pens of livestock. Varro couldn't help but lick his lips as he surveyed the ripening vines, stretching over the horizon. He thought of Horace.

*"Happy the man who, far from business concerns, works his ancestral acres with his oxen like the men of yore, free from every kind of debt; he is not wakened, like a soldier, by the harsh bray of the bugle, and has no fear of the angry sea; he avoids both the city centre and the lofty doorways of powerful citizens…"*

Varro remembered his countryside retreats, with Lucilla, just outside Arretium. The villa he owned was relatively modest but met their needs. A silvery stream bordered one side of the property. He would eat fresh fruit for breakfast and share pleasantries with his neighbours. Varro would read and write in the morning but then spend the afternoon walking with his wife or making love to her. Lucilla even suggested they move to the countryside permanently, perhaps to lead him away from the temptations of the city. But Rome was in the nobleman's blood, for better or worse.

"It's peaceful here," Lucilla argued, whilst tending to her flower garden at the villa.

"But it'll become boring eventually, if we stay. You can have too much of a good thing."

"You will be able to write more here, there are fewer distractions, aside from me of course," she said, raising her eyebrow in a humorous manner.

"The more I write, the more I realise I'm not a writer," Varro posited, before draining his wine cup.

"I sometimes worry about you, Rufus. You may never be happy."

"I'm not sure I was put on this planet to be happy. Drunk, maybe. But not happy," he glibly replied, hoping to head-off having a serious conversation with his wife. And put an end to the idea of moving away from Rome.

Varro eventually fell asleep, as the carriage rocked him like a cradle. Occasionally he heard the odd hawker, trying to sell his produce from a handcart by the side of the road. Or fellow carters, carrying amphorae of wine and olive oil, swapped dirty jokes, that might even have made the whores blush in *The Golden Lion*.

Both Varro and Manius stirred when they stopped at a small village and inn, so that the wagoner could feed and water his sweat-streaked team of horses. Varro blearily recalled visiting the inn, *The Ancient Forrester*, several years ago. He had been travelling back to Rome with Lucilla. The light was fading - and they needed feeding and watering themselves - so they decided to stay overnight and leave for Rome in the morning. Lucilla finished her supper and retired early. Varro continued drinking and then slept with one of the serving girls, before returning to his own room. His hair was unkempt, and he smelled of wine and cheap perfume. Husband and wife lay with their backs to one another in bed. The chill in the air wasn't caused from the draught alone.

Lucilla was doubled-up, as if in physical pain, and quietly sobbed. Varro pretended not to hear her. He wanted to say he still loved her, but the words would have seemed hollow, or sarcastic, given his actions earlier in the evening. He hated himself, to the point of crying too – and wasn't sure if the wine was quelling or fuelling his self-loathing. Varro was as guilty of vanity and folly as the next Roman. Eventually Lucilla spoke, her brittle voice draped in resignation and remorse:

"I'm not sure why you like punishing me so much. But in the end, you will punish yourself more. I used to think that you were different, decent. That you had so much to offer the world. I still do, sometimes."

"Unfortunately, I think so little of this world that I don't want to offer it anything, except my contempt."

Varro calculated it was after that night when Lucilla began to conduct her own affairs – either to punish him or satisfy a need to be loved. He pretended not to care when he uncovered her infidelities (not that Lucilla tried hard to keep her affairs particularly clandestine). At times, Varro even hoped that she would find someone who made her happy. He also felt her behaviour gave him greater licence too, although the nobleman felt he was always entitled to do as he pleased. Aside from his father, there wasn't a married aristocrat in Rome who hadn't, at some point, taken a mistress, Varro judged.

There was a distinct absence of fondness in his expression as Varro surveyed the inn. The painted sign hanging over the door had faded. He hoped that his memory of the place would one-day fade – and disappear – too. It was like returning to the scene of a crime. Manius had not been present during his last visit. Perhaps he would have checked his friend and prevented him from getting drunk and sleeping with the serving girl (Varro could neither picture her face nor recall her name). He realised that he seldom needed to get drunk when in Lucilla's company. She intoxicated him in different ways.

"Are you not coming in, for a drink?" Manius asked, slightly puzzled by his companion's hesitation and the discordant look on his face.

"No. You can have too much of a good thing. I'll stay here. I need some air. If you buy the wagoner a drink though. He deserves one, having sat next to that pompous prick all morning."

To pass the time – and potentially gain some additional intelligence on Scaurus – Varro approached a tradesman, travelling to Rome. His cart was filled with small wooden tables and iron lampstands. One of his dapple mounts whinnied – and Varro calmed it by stroking the horse's neck.

"Good day," the nobleman remarked.

"It will be if I can get a fair price for this lot," Marcus Tarius amiably replied, nodding his head in the direction of his cart. Tarius had an honest face, which may or may not have been an asset in his business dealings with Rome.

"You have some nice pieces to sell, it seems. All should be well. But tell me, I am due to visit a theatre soon, up the road, between here and Ostia. Do you know of it? Is it far?"

"I live in the village, close to the theatre. I hope you're not expecting to see a performance there this afternoon though. The theatre has not put on a single play in months, ever since it changed hands. All they seem to do there is rehearse. My son often sneaks in and watches them. He enjoys the sword practise. As well as actors they transport in gladiators, from the nearby ludus. If they had more dancing girls taking part in rehearsals, I'd sneak in too. Occasionally some of the troupe - its acrobats, singers and, unfortunately, mimes - visit the village and perform in the taverns and market square. Whoever owns the theatre must have more money than sense. Even if the place opened again I'm not sure how full the theatre would be. Few people around here know their Aeschylus from their elbow – and I'm not sure how many theatre lovers will make the trip from Rome, when they have all that they need there. If they use the theatre for some gladiator contests, then the owner could make some money. But at the moment the bugger can afford to make a loss it seems. Unfortunately, I can't afford to do the same and I need to be on my way."

Varro thanked the tradesman for his time and purchased one of his lampstands, giving him the money there and then, as well as the address to deliver the piece of furniture to.

Thankfully, after setting off from the inn, it was only a short time before the theatre came into view. The distinctive concrete, semi-circular structure dominated the horizon, like a ship's sail vaunting upwards from the sea. Villas and farmhouses were also scattered across the landscape, which surrounded the theatre. The carriage soon turned off onto a road which would lead them to their destination. As they grew closer the number of houses and buildings increased. The area was blessed with wealth and industry. Varro noticed a blacksmith's, butchery, stonemason's and bakery, among other shops, along the side of the road. He craned his head out the window and observed a camp, full of tents and wooden huts, to the side of the theatre where, doubtless, Scaurus housed his actors. The senator was either investing for the future or throwing good money after bad.

Varro couldn't help but observe the small procession of a dozen or so carriages travelling in the opposite direction as he approached the theatre. Unfortunately, the curtains were drawn across most of the windows, but he caught a glimpse of a few of the occupants. First up was Julius Fabius, a former ally of Lucius Antony. Octavius had confiscated his property and exiled him from Rome after Lucius Antony's failed revolt. Fabius had settled in the East and now controlled various shipping and slave trading companies. Varro also briefly witnessed the sallow face of Sextus Plancus stare wanly out from his carriage window. The financier's mouth was habitually downturned, his eyes as black as a shark's. Rumour had it that Octavius had taken his young wife, Cassia, as a mistress. She divorced her elderly husband, who doted on her, in the hope that Caesar would leave Livia and marry her. But Augustus soon lost interest in Cassia. His garden was populated by other blooms worth plucking. Some said that the young woman fell ill and died, others that she took her own life. Finally, Varro took in the sharp, aristocratic features of Publius Carrinas. Carrinas was from one of the oldest and most influential patrician families in Rome. Octavius had compelled the senator to give up his place in the Senate House however, during his reforms. Varro was torn as to guess who, out of the three figures, harboured the greatest animus towards Caesar. He also suspected that the other, unseen, occupants in the line of carriages were staunch enemies of Augustus.

Manius remained a picture of stoicism but Varro commenced to tap his foot in nervousness. Scaurus had potentially exposed Quintus Verres, and he was an experienced agent. At any moment Varro imagined that the politician, who had dealt with lies and lying throughout his career, would see through his act. Varro wondered again how he should play things, when he confronted Scaurus. He would be wise not to show too much zeal in responding to anything the statesman proposed, but at the same time he should not prevaricate too much. "Find Aristotle's "golden mean" in your approach and response," Agrippa had sententiously advised, which was little or no help.

Varro told himself he could play on Scaurus' greed. Agrippa was right in that his name and influence meant little to the statesman, compared to his wealth. The senator was deigning to entertain him today not because he enjoyed his ebullient company. Scaurus wanted his money, even more than his loyalty. And Varro could afford to be generous with Caesar's wealth when making a donation to the would-be consul's campaign fund. Greed would blind the statesman and buy his trust. Scaurus needed to seduce him, as much as he needed to seduce Scaurus, Varro considered.

The carriage came to a stop. They reached their destination. Marcellus opened the door and fawningly ushered the nobleman out. Manius was all but ignored. The display was more for the benefit of impressing his master, than his guest. Varro briefly smirked, witnessing the secretary's beetroot-red face. Believing that he would sit inside the carriage during the journey, the attendant had chosen not to bring his wide-brimmed sunhat with him. When Marcellus forced a smile now for Varro it hurt a little.

Scaurus' smile was wider – reptilian-like – than either his guest's or secretary's though when he saw Varro arrive. He adjusted his toga and smoothed down his already oiled hair.

"Welcome to my modest theatre, Rufus Varro. I am glad and grateful that you could accept my invitation. We have much to discuss. Today could be the first day of the rest of your life," the venerated Lucius Scaurus cordially exclaimed, opening his arms up like the wings of an eagle – or harpy.

Varro just hoped that today wouldn't be the last day of his life.

## 16.

Scaurus stood at the vanguard of a small group of people, outside the theatre. Manius surveyed the scene while Varro greeted his host. To the left of the building was a sun-baked yellowing field, where a couple of dozen gladiators were being drilled. Wooden swords clacked against one another as instructions were barked out. The sweat-glazed men looked well-fed and well-disciplined. The gladiators were hemmed in by a steep bank, which curved around them. Manius peered through the large, arched entrance to the theatre and glimpsed part of the circular, sand-covered stage. It reminded him of the many arenas he had fought in. Rows of concrete seats curved around. A number of plush pillows littered one level, from where Scaurus' previous guests, who Manius had just seen journeying home, had sat. To the right of the theatre was the main camp. Wooden huts and tents were dotted all over the sloping field, like mushrooms sprouting up across a garden lawn. Groups of actors – as well as set builders, costumers, dancers and slaves – mulled around campfires and steaming cooking pots. The chirr and crackle of their conversation and laughter seeped into the air, like the smoke billowing up from their fires. Theatre folk were an incessantly cheerful bunch, perhaps annoyingly so.

Manius took in the party of people in front of his friend, as Scaurus introduced them. There was a colourfully dressed, pot-bellied bald man and, next to him, stood the senator's bodyguard, a man-mountain of a man who briefly nodded at the Briton, out of professional courtesy. Behind them were two provocatively dressed women (actresses or courtesans) who simpered and giggled as they looked to catch the handsome nobleman's eye. Which of course they did.

"Rufus Varro, this is Sharek, my theatre manager. He is responsible for our troupe and forthcoming production. There is very little Sharek doesn't know about his trade. Or rather I should say craft."

"Pleased to meet you," Sharek said, bowing a little too flamboyantly as he did so, as if part of him were mocking the aristocrat. "Lucius tells me you are an accomplished poet." Sharek head was hairless, save for a triangular strip of beard on his chin, which resembled a pyramid and was worn as a symbol and reminder of his Egyptian homeland. The actor wore a layer of make-up, to smooth over his pock-marked skin. Sharek simpered almost as much as the women behind him, Varro thought. As the theatre manager smiled his servile, beatific smile and his plump cheeks rose on his face, narrowing his kohl-rimmed eyes. His fingernails were long and painted silver, his skin was tawny-gold. He wore several bangles around his wrists, which jangled like the sound of a tambourine, each time he gesticulated with his hands (which admittedly was often). The Egyptian wore a Tyrian purple skirt, brocaded at the hem, and a loose-fitting, patterned blouse which shimmered in the breeze.

For as long as he could remember Sharek had been part of a theatre company. As a boy no older than seven he was sold, as a slave, to a troupe which performed in and around Alexandria. At first, he served as a kitchen hand and cup bearer, but then he worked as a set-painter, carpenter and costumer. He soon took to the stage as well. Sharek fell in love with playing a part, telling a story and garnering applause. Within the space of a couple of hours he felt that he could make a group of complete strangers fall in love with him. Several lead actors and patrons fell in love with the boy in a far more intimate way too, as he served as their catamite. A wealthy merchant was so taken with the youth that he bought his freedom. Sharek remained a slave to his profession however. After working as an actor, writer and choreographer, he set up his own company of travelling performers. Hearing about Rome's increasing prosperity under Augustus the shrewd Egyptian decided to follow the money and venture west. Business was good – especially since being in the exclusive employ of the Roman senator. The former catamite could now afford his own string of young, virile lovers. The senator granted him use of his villa, as Sharek worked on writing the tragedy he was commissioned to put on. The play was slowly but surely taking shape, despite or because of his patron's suggestions. The gourmand in Sharek instructed the cook – and the sybarite in him instructed the slave boys at the house.

"I fear he is using some poetic licence to describe me as accomplished," Varro replied, squinting in the afternoon sun. Or he was part-blinded by the theatre manager's garb. Varro couldn't help but notice Sharek wearing a pair of glass earrings and an accompanying necklace, which he had also seen Lucilla wear. He didn't know whether to smirk or cringe.

"Sharek will give you a tour of our theatre and introduce you to some of our actors, should you wish. I can also arrange for Vedius here to have our gladiators give you a demonstration of their skill. As well as serving as my bodyguard, Vedius oversees the local ludus," Scaurus remarked, briefly turning to the hulking figure beside him.

Vedius appeared formidable – and Varro had no doubt that the granite-faced attendant was formidable. He was dressed in fine pieces of armour and his weaponry – a gladius, hand axe and dagger – were of the highest quality. Vedius nodded at his master's guest, but otherwise gave off an air of being indifferent or unimpressed by the supposedly distinguished visitor. Varro couldn't quite tell if his blubbery mouth was curled into a permanent sneer, or he suffered from a slight harelip. His nostrils were as wide as a bull's. His arms were knotted with muscle, his skin as tough and leathery as animal hide. Vedius' chest and shoulders were even more pronounced than Manius'. Varro imagined the bodyguard could easily thrust a spearhead through a man's torso, even if he was clad in armour. The former gladiator gave off an air of knowing about pain, both absorbing it and, more so, inflicting it.

"I'd be delighted to take a tour and be introduced to some of the actors. Whilst doing so you might like to have your gladiators give a demonstration to my attendant, Manius. He can then duly report back to me."

"Excellent. Once you are finished I will have Sharek bring you to my villa, where we can have lunch. I can provide you with a carriage to take you back home, but should you not need to return to Rome urgently you will be welcome to stay the night. We can lodge your bodyguard in our slave quarters too," Scaurus suggested, without even glancing at Manius. Slaves were little more than cattle to the senator. They were unable to vote and unable to contribute to his campaign fund.

Varro resisted the temptation to correct his host, by stating that his attendant was a freedman – and his adopted brother even. Perhaps he was being tested again. Manius was also sufficiently thick-skinned to shrug off the insult.

"I am afraid I will have to travel back after our lunch but thank you for your kind offer. You must allow me to invite you to lunch or dinner, to repay your hospitality. I can even arrange a party in your honour," Varro warmly issued, greasing the wheels of his burgeoning relationship as much as his host.

"I have never been one to decline an invite to a party, especially one organised in my honour. Before we proceed I should just also introduce you to Tabiry and Salassi, two of the lead dancers in our company. They will be joining us for dessert at lunch. You can see more of them then, if you wish. I should mention beforehand that they barely speak a word of Latin, but less is often more when it comes to female conversation, wouldn't you agree?"

Varro grinned in reply – and then turned to smile at the two dancers standing a dozen paces behind his host. They were equally alluring and wore similar, diaphanous dresses which left little – or a lot – to the imagination. They eyed the nobleman up, as if he were a feast. Varro was twice as handsome – and half the age – of Scaurus' previous guests. Tabiry pouted and Salassi seemed to mouth a couple of words - or kiss the air. She then let out a burst of laughter and poked the tip of her tongue through her gleaming teeth as she did so. The woman on the left, who Varro took to be Tabiry, was dusky-skinned. Her almond eyes and thick black hair suggested she was from the East. Salassi had paler skin and auburn hair. Perhaps she was from Gaul, or a barbarian tribe north of the Rhine. Her eyes were dark yet playful, kittenish. As Scaurus beckoned them to come closer their less than subtle oeillades grew even more suggestive. The myrrh and jasmine of their perfumes wafted through the air and nearly overpowered and intoxicated his senses. Nearly.

Sharek clapped his hands three times, as if to break the spell of the women - and focus the nobleman's attention back on himself.

"Shall we proceed? I have much to show you."

The dancers scowled momentarily at their impresario - or bawd - but then turned their smiles back on, as if they were closing and opening shutters. They knew they would be centre stage later. The attractive and wealthy Roman could have one - or both of them - for dessert. They could all feast on each other.

"I am in your hands, Sharek," Varro said, after offering the women a bow and an equally suggestive look.

*If only*, the decadent ageing actor desirously thought.

RICHARD FOREMAN

## 17.

Manius was all too familiar with the sights, scents and sounds before him. An oval-shaped blanket of sand, spread over concrete, covered part of the field. Sword posts sprung-up from the ground like saplings. Steaming bowls of barley sat over campfires. Slaves ladled out rations of watered-down wine. He winced not at the fetid smell of sweat, as he was led towards the make-shift arena. Whilst some men wore armour, some walked around shirtless – and Manius was at least pleased to see how Vedius spared the use of the vine-staff. The Briton had seen enough warriors, whipped like livestock, to last a lifetime. *Tirones* – beginners – practised their sword strokes or were drilled to improve their strength and conditioning. Thankfully clouds began to marble the sky, tempering the searing sun. A cacophony of grunts, roars, orders, howls, curses and clangs galloped through the air. The gnarled, swarthy expressions, surrounded by long, lank hair had little changed since his time as a gladiator. No doubt some of the men were condemned criminals, who had chosen to enter the ludus rather than be sentenced to death immediately. Some might have been slaves, who had turned on their masters and were suffering the consequences. Or some were impoverished young men from the countryside, who had ventured to Rome in search of fortune and glory. Others would have once been destitute and desperate soldiers. The arena was a source of hope, as well as dread – reward as well as punishment. Some of the figures before him would end up as fodder, for beasts and veteran gladiators alike. But a few might win fame and freedom – and eventually work as bodyguards or debt collectors.

"You were a gladiator too were you not, some time ago?" Vedius asked, in his low, rasping voice.

Manius nodded, not quite knowing if his tone was more sinister or suspicious.

"I would say you fought honourably in the arena, but if you did you'd be dead. There was only one rule for me: kill or be killed. I fought as if my life was at stake even when the contest wasn't a fight to the death. And I still train as if my life depends on it. Every now and then I need to bloody my blade, like a wagoner needs to grease his wheels to keep them turning. I was trained as a *provocator* – but I also trained myself to fight as a *retiarius* and *eques*. I was undefeated. The people chanted my name."

Vedius puffed out his chest, like an umbo protruding from a shield, as he spoke.

Manius had heard many a soldier and gladiator tell old war stories and sing their praises before. He was tempted to yawn but he appeared interested and impressed.

"This all takes me back," Manius replied, affecting a sense of nostalgia. But the Briton had scant fondness for his time as a gladiator. He still suffered occasional nightmares. If he concentrated he could still feel the prick of the surgeon's needle, from when he sewed-up his wounds. Manius remembered how his arm would often feel like a slab of lead at the end of a day's training. He would often wake-up, with a companion dying from a fever or his injuries, in the bed next him. The smell of death – both real and metaphorical – would fester in his cramped quarters. A slave's lot seemed more enviable. The crowd would applaud him, especially if they had placed a winning wager. But gladiators were still creatures to be fettered, rather than feted. The memory of Spartacus lingered. The notorious gladiator, who led a rebellion against Rome, was a monster, a tale to scare children with. The crowd might cheer but it was more likely they would curse his name and call for his death, Manius remembered. He could still picture them spewing spittle and gnashing their rotten, crooked teeth. And that was just the women in the arena.

"Well I intend to get your blood racing some more, instead of just stirring some memories. Should your master be taken under our wing then you may one day serve under my command. I wish to test your mettle, and have you fight one of my men. Call it a bit of friendly sport if you like. Let us hope that you fare better than the bodyguards who faced my men this morning. As much as it's dog eat dog for most men, whether they be a beggar or senator in Rome, the city can also make a man grow soft. He can attend too many parties or catch a pox. You are more likely to have to protect your master from a nagging wife or scornful mistress than from a bandit nowadays."

"Serve under your command? I didn't know we were at war," Manius replied. He started to notice he had attracted the attention of several gladiators. They eyed him suspiciously, although a few smirked in amusement when Vedius mentioned the previous bodyguards, who had attended to Scaurus' senatorial party earlier. It seemed that their mettle had been tested – and found wanting. Manius gazed back at the various fighters, neither defiantly nor timidly.

"We all possess enemies, it's just that some don't always know who they are. War is as inevitable as death," Vedius decreed, before snorting a gob of phlegm out of his broken nose. "If you want to head over there and see our quartermaster, Amatius, you can choose your preferred weapons and armour. In the meantime, I'll select a fitting opponent for you."

Manius felt like he was being ambushed or bullied into accepting the challenge. But he agreed to take part in the contest. He needed to earn Vedius' respect and trust – not for his own sake but for Varro's. Scaurus might have entrusted his plans to the lanista. And perhaps Vedius would entrust his plans to his newest recruit. The more intelligence he could gather the better. Also, Manius viewed the contest as a training exercise for his more important bout tomorrow. As he walked across the lip of the oval the Briton observed various spots of blood marking the sand. He also heard Vedius sound out some instructions to two gladiators practising nearby:

"Plant yourself like a tree, otherwise be chopped down. Good footwork can finish an opponent off, or save your life… Don't just thrust with your arm, like some limp-wristed eunuch, but thrust forward with your whole body…"

The ageing quartermaster had a sage – or grizzled - air. He stood in front of a table and a brace of wagons containing all manner of weaponry and armour: greaves, tridents, axes, swords, breastplates, helmets, knives and spears. Either due to the sunlight, or poor eyesight, Amatius squinted as he took in the bodyguard, whilst gnawing on a ham bone.

Manius instantly dismissed fighting as a *retiarius*. He had seen more men enmesh themselves in their own nets than he cared to remember. He picked up a few practise swords, their points rounded off and edges blunted, to gauge their weight and balance. Manius also thought intently about how much armour he should wear - and asked for the quartermaster's advice. Protection and mobility needed to be taken into consideration. It would have helped if he knew the type of gladiator he would be facing. In the end Manius donned the short sword and large shield of a *provocator*. As the Briton readied himself he observed the crowd – audience – surrounding the practise arena.

"How do you rate my chances?" the bodyguard remarked, as he tightened the strap on his manica.

"Unfortunately, for you, Vidius won't pit you against one of the tirones. I see he's lining up Bulla. He'll snarl and bark like a cur but don't underestimate him. He's sly as well vicious. He won't treat things like a practise bout either. The edge on that sword may be as dull as a German's wit but it can still do some damage. I once saw Bulla bludgeon a man to death in the arena with just the pommel of his gladius. But if you are Manius "The Briton", who bested more than a dozen similarly sly and vicious curs in his time, then your chances are far from dire," Amatius replied, having recognised the former gladiator. The sage quartermaster had seen and assessed many a fighter in the arena over the years – and the Briton could stand toe to toe with most of them, in his prime.

"And what if I'm not that Manius?"

"Then you may want to find him and ask if he can take your place."

Both men offered each other a wry smile and respectful nod. Manius swished the sword around to loosen up his wrist – and went through a few more stretching exercises – before making his way back towards Vedius, who was waiting in the middle of the oval, beside his opponent.

Amatius was right. He was no tirone. The leather-faced veteran grinned, as if he was already triumphant. Vedius had chosen to match him up with a *Hoplocanus* – a Hoplite fighter. The seasoned combatant wore a padded jacket for protection, as well as greaves and armguards. His build was solid and stocky, an alloy of strength and speed. His helmet sat on the ground in front of him. In his right hand the fighter carried a thrusting spear, with its tip rounded off instead of coming to a point. The weapon wouldn't be able to penetrate Manius' armour, but it could still crack bone or leave him with some nasty bruises. In his left he held a polished bronze shield, which the experienced fighter would try and use to deflect the light and temporarily blind his opponent. The crowd started to chant their champion's name. He was either famous, or infamous, Manius judged. Bulla's furtive expression bespoke of his former profession, as a bandit. Until he was captured. But the ferocious – and wily – criminal had flourished in the arena.

The plan would be to avoid the tip of the spear and move inside. His opponent would then be vulnerable. But no doubt his opponent already knew this. Manius reasoned that he needed to end the bout as early as possible. The longer he fought the shorter the odds would be on him suffering an injury. And he needed to be in good condition for his bout the next day. He filled his lungs and gripped his sword and shield in determination. Manius was now fighting for Varro and Camilla, as well as for himself.

Vedius called for quiet as he introduced the combatants and explained the rules. The gladiators could yield at any time. Victory could also come from one of the opponents putting the other on his back.

"Let us hope that our bodyguard fares better than his predecessors. He certainly couldn't fare any worse," Vedius announced, to a chorus of cackling laughter.

Bulla slowly, ceremoniously, donned his helmet – as if it were a crown. Another cheer went up from the throng. Swords clanged upon shields as a form of applause. The fighters stood half a dozen paces apart. Vedius stood between them, with his right arm aloft. Once he lowered it the bout would begin. Bulla licked his lips, as if he were about to savour a mound of roasted meat. He also briefly clasped a small iron amulet around his neck and offered up a silent prayer to Mars. Gladiators were even more superstitious than soldiers, Manius fancied. The hoplite fighter then addressed his opponent, in a guttural rather than Greek accent:

"You won't be the first Briton I've bested. I even killed one of your bastard countryman a few years back. He pissed himself as I stood over him. He died a lonely death, a long way from home."

This time Manius gave in to the temptation to yawn. The reaction riled his opponent. Bulla's eyes widened - ablaze - with ire. His grimace transformed itself into a grin again though as the sun broke through the clouds. He could now use his burnished shield to its full effect.

Manius planted his right foot forward, digging his toe in the sand. Bulla scuffed the ground with his left foot, as if he were a bull about to charge. The two men barely blinked as they glowered at each other, whist also noting the position of Vedius' arm.

The lanista paused, enjoying the attention and power he wielded. He didn't quite know whether to be impressed or disconcerted by the Briton's air of calm and confidence. But Bulla would do his job. Vedius had briefed his gladiator to toy with his opponent: "Sap his strength and probe any weaknesses. I want to know if he'll prove an asset or not, should Scaurus recruit his master to the cause. We need durable men, who can follow orders."

The crowd ceased their chanting and waited, with baited breath, for the contest to commence. The men leaned forward or peered over the shoulders of those in front of them, to gain a better vantage point. They welcomed the break from training – and looked forward to the Briton being humiliated. Bulla was one of the most accomplished fighters in the camp.

Bulla's eyes burned hotter than Vulcan's forge. He bared his yellow teeth and snorted, pointing his spear in his opponent's direction. Ready and willing to hurt - or kill - the man in front of him.

Vedius took two steps back but kept his arm raised, prolonging the tension. He decided he would step in and halt proceedings if the Briton was in danger of serious injury.

Manius pictured Camilla, to remind him what he was fighting for, before observing the light reflect off the rim of his adversary's shield. Sooner or later Bulla would look to blind him. But Manius had his own tactic to blind his opponent first. No sooner did Vedius lower his arm than the Briton flicked up his right foot, sending the portion of sand kept between his toes into Bulla's eyes. The gladiator was momentarily unsighted. But a moment was more than enough for Manius to exploit his advantage. He quickly moved forward, swatting the loosely held spear out of his way with his gladius. Bulla's eyes stung, his vision was blurred, and coordination addled. Before the gladiator could shift his shield into the correct defensive position Manius used his own scutum as a weapon, powerfully punching it forward into his opponent's chest – knocking him to the ground.

The crowd were stunned and slack-jawed, having been cheated out of their sport. Many hadn't even had the chance to place a wager on the outcome of the bout. Some murmured in discontent at the Briton's underhand tactics. Few were more shocked or surprised than Vedius, who eventually managed to offer a gracious, or at least neutral, expression. He took the defeat of one of his most skilled gladiators personally.

## 18.

*Actors.*

Varro forced a smile, whilst sighing from the bottom of his bedraggled heart. Their company was to be endured rather than enjoyed, for the most part, he judged, as Sharek introduced him to some of the leading players in his troupe. Varro once thought how poets could be as self-absorbed as Narcissus, until he met theatre folk. A few of them could be witty, well-rounded beings with a sense of perspective. But only a few, unfortunately.

Actors fed on attention, like leeches feed on blood. If an actor wasn't being seen or heard, then he didn't exist. Varro remembered Alba, an actress he had once courted. She had a remarkable talent - or disease - for always turning the conversation back towards the subject of her. And when - on the rare occasion when someone else held court (especially a rival actress) – she would appear bored, pout or sigh until she regained the floor again. Varro had yet to encounter a performer who was concerned more for the whole play than he was for his own part in it.

The large tent, made from waxed goat-hide, was filled with a number of couches and tables. Plates of empty oyster shells and stems left over from asparagus tips were strewn around the floor. Incense burned in each corner. Sharek argued it was a source of courage, to remind his actors to be bold and tell the truth – although more so he kept it burning to take the edge of the smell of cheap perfume and body odour which pervaded the tent. Whether the troupe had gone through a dress rehearsal or not that morning they all seemed to be in costume, or they naturally dressed flamboyantly. Varro almost cringed at some of the brightly patterned garments and garish items of jewellery.

Thankfully the entrance was kept open, letting in some air and light. A couple of slaves pulled upon ceiling fans to keep the occupants cool too.

The actors – four men and one woman – lounged on sofas and worked their way through more than one jug of wine. Sharek introduced Varro to the group.

"This here is one of our veteran performers, Pawah. He will be playing the ghost of Cicero in our play."

The well-groomed actor offered Sharek a tart expression, for calling him a "veteran" but then turned to the young nobleman. His expression was appreciative, suggestive, lurid. As well as competing for lead parts over the years the two men had stolen lovers from one another. But their rivalry was friendly, for the most part. The two cats may have hissed at each other, but they rarely showed their claws and drew blood.

"It's nice to see the senator widen his circle of acquaintances. Youth should have its head, no? I am surprised that Sharek is deciding to share you however – and he is not keeping you all to himself," Pawah exclaimed, after re-positioning his hairpiece, which Varro couldn't work out if he wore for personal or professional reasons. His voice was rich and refined, like someone mimicking a member of the patrician class. Pawah had possessed chiselled good looks and a fine figure, once. "You have had the tour, it seems. I expect Sharek spent most of the time talking about himself. But for whatever his successes, he has stood on the shoulders of giants."

"This is news to me, Pawah. I always thought you preferred to lie rather than stand," Sharek replied in good, or waspish, humour. A couple of the other actors in the room sniggered.

"And how are you finding the role of Cicero?" Varro remarked, wishing to cool rather than fuel any heated argument between the two ageing, bristling players.

"Did you ever meet the great statesman?"

"No," Varro answered, lying. He had no desire to become side-tracked and be asked to share any thoughts or anecdotes.

"He bestrode the age like a colossus. Cicero invented words and framed how a Roman politician should behave. I should really receive a bigger part. Not that my part isn't big enough. But art should mirror nature should it not? Cicero was one to deliver great speeches in life, so he should do so on stage. I believe Cicero is the conscience of our play. In some ways the story is more about Cicero than Antony or Octavius."

"Well Cicero himself would surely applaud your theory, if no one else would," Sharek iterated, arching his plucked, serpentine eyebrow. "Certainly, Cicero's love affair with himself was as legendary as Antony's and Cleopatra's."

"Let the greybeards come out and clap for Cicero. But the play is the tragedy of Antony and Cleopatra," Lycus asserted, who Varro surmised was playing the part of the chief protagonist. The tanned Athenian puffed out his chest and ran his hand through his thick, black hair – before gulping down the dregs of his wine. "I have been doing my research. Getting into my role. 'Twas Antony who bestrode the world like a colossus. Antony was a soldier, who turned the tide at the battles of Alesia and Pharsalus. He was a great orator and statesman, whose words at Caesar's funeral changed everything. He was also a great lover and descendant of Hercules. We should not condemn a man who is ruled by his heart as well as head. Antony should have our admiration and pity. "These bronze shoulders alone can bear the heavy burden of the fate of the world," to quote one of my lines from the play. 'Tis a just line Sharek, and I and Rome thank you for it."

Sharek smiled and nodded his head in graciousness and gratitude. At least one of his cast members was happy with his part and line count.

"And I take it, Myron, that you are playing Octavius?" Varro asked, turning to the young actor who was studiously sitting in the corner, going over his lines. His finger traced the words along the page and his lips moved in sync. Sharek had already told the youth to dye his hair blond. "Are you the villain of the piece?" he added, fishing for any extra morsel of intelligence about the prospective play or potential plot.

"That he is," Sharek answered. "He may appear sweet-faced now, but he will lose his puppy-fat and innocence by the time the play is performed in earnest. Myron is already a fine actor, but he still has much to learn. Yet I have a will to teach him things. His Octavius will be as cold as a winter's night. He will be as ruthless as a haggling Jew and as hypocritical as a lecherous priest. You will observe a young man experiencing power going to his head, like a heavy wine. I just need to make sure that none of us lose our heads, by offending Caesar too much and alienating some of our audience. Our Agrippa over there will also be a source of comedy and satire," Sharek remarked, pointing towards Hilarion.

At the mention of his name the tipsy actor put down the olive he was about to eat and sprang to his feet.

"I live to serve and serve to live. At the start of the play I am seen peeling Octavius' grapes and agreeing with everything he says. In each scene I'm in I also mention a new statue of Octavius that I've commissioned. I may even pant and beg for approval like a dog. I have two expressions for the most part - dutiful and serious. I am going to give our consul a yokel's accent too," Hilarion breathlessly exclaimed, champing at the bit to perform on stage and make the audience laugh.

Varro grinned, as he pictured Agrippa's reaction to seeing the play. It was unlikely he would see the funny side.

As if giving herself her own cue Helena rose to her slippered feet and walked towards their honoured, monied guest. Lustrous blonde curls hung down over her shoulders. She was young – but far from innocent, Varro surmised. The actress' skirt and hips swayed in harmony as she moved. Partly due to her sculpted eyeliner, Helena's narrow eyes seemed to curl up and smile at him. Before coming out from behind one of the tent's stanchions the Greek actress had undone another button upon her blouse. One of the slave boys next to her, working the fan, feasted on the sight of the actress' two greatest assets and unconsciously began to tug on his contraption more vigorously.

"Last, but not least, this is Helena, who will be playing Octavia," Sharek remarked, pursing his lips and rolling his eyes at his actress' lack of subtlety in making a play for the nobleman. She seemed to have deftly moistened her lips and touched-up her make-up during the short time Varro had been present in the tent. Her bracelets, necklace, anklet and brooch glinted as much as the glassy look in her eye. Helena could sometimes prove more trouble than she was worth, but the comely actress was popular with certain segments of their audience. She also proved to be a valuable chit when negotiating for patrons to invest in past productions. The singer/dancer/artist's model was one of his prized assets – and the theatre impresario milked her like a cow. And she could behave like a cow in return, Sharek tartly judged.

"I am barely playing Octavia, given the paucity of lines I have been given. Wouldn't you like to see more of me, Rufus Varro?" she remarked, teasingly.

"If less is more then you may be revealing too much already, my dear. Although as it is the height of summer you may wish to cover your chest up, lest you catch a cold," Pawah joked, to a smattering of laughter.

"You're just jealous. The only thing you have to show under your tunic are some sad old dugs and wiry grey hairs. If you ever had a prime Pawah, you are now past it. But, unlike yourself, there is more in front of me than behind me, which is why I should be granted a proper role. I want to make the audience believe I'm Octavia," she said passionately, raising her chin up – and thrusting her chest out even more, if it was at all possible.

"You are certainly equal in beauty to Caesar's lauded sister, although you understandably lack her sense of modesty and virtue. As to giving you a greater part, I will quote our patron. "Women should be seen and not heard." Just act contented – you can act, I hope, my dear – to be on stage when you are, even if you are only a piece of scenery. Take consolation from the fact that you have plenty of costume changes, to compensate for any lack of dialogue. Now let that be an end to your latest tantrum," Sharek said firmly, holding up his flabby hand to her mouth, to emphasise that it was her cue to stop talking. His soft, fleshy features hardened - and a menacing scowl briefly replaced his beatific smile. The mask slipped. But only briefly. "It is unfortunate, Rufus Varro, that we do not have any time to act out a scene or two from the play, to give you a feel for our humble tragedy."

"I know enough to sense that you may only get to perform your play once in Rome, before the authorities close you down for its satirical portrayal of our leading statesmen," Varro asserted.

"Scaurus has said that once will be enough. Rome may never be the same again after our performance and final, revealing, scene," Sharek said, with pride and trepidation in his voice. It seemed he was excited - as well as fearful - about giving birth to his new creation. "But we should not keep Scaurus waiting. I will take you to his villa shortly. We will need to collect your bodyguard, or what's left of him. I dare say Vedius and his barbarian horde have had their fun with your attendant," Sharek said, wrinkling his nose up as he mentioned the gladiators. The theatre manager considered the spectacle of gladiatorial combat to be savage and detestable. He had lost count of the number of times that arenas had chosen to host bouts, at the expense of cancelling a performance of a play. As much as Sharek might have despised the sport however he could often be found watching the young recruits on the training ground, the sweat glistening on their cobblestone-like muscles.

Before Varro had the chance to worry about the fate of his friend Manius appeared at the entrance to the tent, wary of entering for fear of being caught up in the conversation of actors.

"All well?" Varro remarked to his companion.

"I'm fine. I don't think I can say the same for the gladiator who Vedius matched me up with."

"It seems I have to take my leave," Varro warmly and regretfully expressed, turning to the small band of actors. "Thank you for your company and for giving me an insight into the play."

"It has been our pleasure. You have been a breath of fresh air, compared to the previous gaggle of guests we had to host. You would think that politicians would show a professional interest in our craft, given their life of posturing and deceit. But most wouldn't know good acting if it jumped up and bit them on their walking stick. Apollo and Venus protect us from another toothless frown, coughing fit and the constant interruption of someone getting up and leaving to take a piss," Sharek proclaimed, sighing more loudly than a coastal breeze.

"Well I imagine that I will see you all again, soon. I have the feeling that Senator Scaurus is keen to recruit me for something. But I am in the dark as to what for. Unless you can enlighten me," Varro asked, innocently.

For once the gaggle of actors fell strangely silent, just when he would have preferred them not to.

## 19.

Scaurus' villa was modest compared to his house on the Palatine, but the property was the most lavish he had seen in the area. Varro squinted as the light reflected off the sun-bleached walls. It had been a short carriage journey from the theatre, during which Sharek briefed the nobleman about Berenice, his lead actress. As indiscreet as Sharek could sometimes seem however, Varro sensed he was a keeper of secrets and never divulged the entire story unless it was in his interest to do so.

"Our Cleopatra lives with our would-be Caesar. Even before securing the role however Berenice deemed herself a queen, although she was just a slave girl when I first encountered her. She was Galatea - and I was Pygmalion. I taught her how to seduce men – when to act submissively and when to dominate her suitors. One must stoop to conquer. I replaced her guttural accent with a refined, cut-glass voice which could also purr and lisp. I cut away her sackcloth cloths and dressed her in silk. I even used to spy on her through a hole in the wall – and give her directions – when a patron spent the night with her. Yet she is self-taught too, both as an actress and woman – as much as one might argue there is little difference between those two roles. My Berenice is a natural. She possesses a singing voice to rival a siren – and can writhe better than any nereid. She is my Calypso, or Circe. Cleopatra herself could have learned a thing or two from our wily succubus. Men will howl, pant and drop to their knees when she takes to the stage in Rome. I am even worried that, when the asp goes to bite her in the closing act, the snake will instead bow its head in subjugation to its queen. Aye, I fear I have created a monster, albeit a beautiful one. Berenice attends rehearsals late and whispers in Scaurus' ear to enlarge her part. And crocodile tears gush from her eyes whenever I try to bring the bitch to heel. Sooner or later Scaurus will tire of his Cleopatra. The ripest of fruits will eventually rot. Her company will grow stale and he will look to sample another dish, one which I will lay before him if needs be… Even despite all my warnings though, Berenice will turn your head. And you may well turn hers, should she find out that you possess a house on the Palatine."

Varro nodded his head in receipt of Sharek's words as they walked through the colonnaded garden of the property. Undernourished slaves sweated in the afternoon sun, pruning back fruit trees, removing weeds and drawing water from the well. The theatre manager accompanied Varro as far as the atrium. The pair waited a short while, standing on a lavish mosaic of a peacock, surrounded by trellis work and painted wooden panels, before being greeted by a simpering, sun-blushed Marcellus. Sharek offered up his serene smile one last time, trying to suppress the lust in his heart, as he took his leave of the handsome nobleman. The two men clasped one another's arms whilst parting – and Sharek stroked his fingertips along Varro's surprisingly soft skin as he did so.

"I look forward to seeing you again. Perhaps next time I could tempt you into my tent to share a vintage when you visit," the honey-tongued Egyptian suggested, hoping that he could arrange an aphrodisiac to lace the wine with if the opportunity arose.

"I would very much like that, Sharek. Thank you for your hospitality this afternoon. I understand your desire to return to your troupe. I suspect that, should you leave them alone for too long, they might try to kill each other. Or at the very least steal each other's lines. I wish you well for the play. Please do write to me and keep me abreast of developments – and if you are ever in the capital you must come to the house for lunch."

Sharek bowed and beamed. One could almost hear the cogs in his brain begin to turn, trying to invent an excuse for Scaurus to permit him to travel to Rome.

Marcellus ushered Varro into a tastefully decorated dining room. The smell of spices and roasted pork wafted in from the nearby kitchen. A brace of dull-faced slaves finished-off laying the table. The secretary shooed them out of the room like a couple of whipped curs.

"Senator Scaurus will join you soon. Can I get you a measure of wine while you wait?"

"No, I will be fine for now. I am happy to be left alone, until the senator arrives," Varro replied, hoping that the ingratiating secretary would take the hint.

Thankfully he did. Part of Varro wanted time and space to process the events of the day so far. To what extent were Sharek and the other actors complicit in Scaurus' plans? Was Vedius training an army, or a company of gladiators? How would the tragedy end? *And how will the drama end that I've been written into?*

He sighed as he plopped himself onto the sofa and wearily gazed out onto the freshly cut lawn, his eyes half-closed. Varro also wanted to empty his head of various competing thoughts. He was a like a juggler who had taken one too many balls – and was in danger of dropping them all. Varro briefly wished how he could have joined Manius in the staff quarters. He could now be sharing a jug of wine and a joke with his friend, over a bowl of chicken stew. Varro was exhausted. There were still more questions than answers. He wouldn't feel aggrieved should Agrippa give up on him and want to re-cast his role. If Caesar had to rely on Rufus Varro, then perhaps Octavius deserved to be usurped, he blithely considered.

For a few sweet, reposeful moments Varro closed his eyes, forgot his mission and let the amber rays of the afternoon sun wash over him. He wanted his old life back – full of wine, women and song - free from the likes of Lucius Scaurus, Vedius, Marcus Agrippa and Caesar. He even wanted to be free of Cassandra. How far did he want to travel back? To when he was married to Lucilla? He had been happy then - for a few, sweet, reposeful months. Until the gods ruined things.

*No. Until I ruined things.*

Varro was distracted from his thoughts by the sound of sonorous laughter. He rose and turned towards the bewitching figure of Berenice, entering the room. She tossed her head back when she laughed, shaking her ebony tresses away from her face so the Roman nobleman could see her in all her glory. The actress feigned surprise at seeing Varro, having pretended not to have noticed him when coming through the door – but then gifted him a smile. Her teeth gleamed all the more, for being set against her tawny skin and lustrous, dark hair. Varro thought her exotic looking and couldn't quite place her heritage. She possessed almond, Indian eyes and full, Persian lips. Her high cheekbones and slender jawline were Egyptian – strong yet sensual.

Berenice wore a ruby red dress, tailored to accentuate her voluptuous chest and slender waist. A bejewelled headband, which resembled a crown, kept her hair in place. The obligatory slit in the gown ran down the front, rather than the side, of her burnished, unblemished thigh. The straps from her sandals clung to her calves, almost lovingly.

The actress was accompanied by a youth, aged around twenty, as she walked into the chamber. The adolescent, dressed in a sky-blue tunic, appeared strangely familiar to Varro, as though he had seen him before but couldn't quite remember where or when. His complexion was dusky, but his features were hard, haughty, Roman. He appeared too old to be the woman's son, yet too young to be her lover. He briefly scrutinised Varro, as if he were a sentry assessing whether a camp visitor was a friend of foe, before Berenice said something into his ear. For a moment he drew breath and puffed out his chest, as if he was going to defy the woman, but he duly nodded his head in assent after her features became taut with displeasure and she firmly whispered something else in his ear. The youth bowed and took his leave, without offering Varro a second glance.

"You must be Rufus Varro. I am Berenice. Or Cleopatra," the actress remarked, casting an appreciative eye over the attractive aristocrat. She almost leered at one point. Her voice was clear yet soft, like the breeze sweeping through the shutters. Before Varro had a chance to reply however Berenice clapped her hands, twice, and a slave quickly appeared carrying a tray, containing a jug of wine and two golden cups. With a subtle nod of her head she ordered the slave to pour out the wine and scurry back to the kitchen. "Do you mind if we sit?"

Berenice sauntered across the room – her hips seemingly moving up and down to the beat of a drum that only she could hear – and sat down on the sofa without waiting for Varro's reply or permission. Alba was but her understudy, Varro thought to himself. As he sat down opposite her the alluring woman crossed her legs, giving him a glimpse of what she wore beneath her dress. The faintest of amused smiles flickered on her lips. The actress enjoyed shocking men, as well as seducing them. There was both candour and character in her expression – or expressions. Beneath the make-up, hers was a face which had known hardship and hedonism. Varro later thought how sometimes she seemed biddable and sometimes wilful. Perhaps she was gauging which role the nobleman preferred. Berenice wanted to please him, in order to control him. Varro had encountered similarly brazen women in the past however – and he pretended to be shocked and entranced, out of politeness. He breathed in her musky perfume and let his gaze fall upon her bare leg, for a little longer than was necessary.

"I suspect that Sharek, the old queen, has told you all about me. He probably left out the best, or worst, bits though."

"He spoke well of you."

"Ha! Sharek is an actor – and I learned long ago never to trust an actor. Or any man. Lies bind a man together, as much as skin and bone. I imagine he reeled off the story of how he made me what I am today. Trained me. But Sharek was more pimp than mentor. I made me, for good or ill. I suppose he introduced you to the rest of his company. Allow me to introduce you to them also. Pawah is a veteran – but no matter how long his career he will always be destined to play a supporting part rather than the lead... Myron is a sweet boy. Unfortunately, his voice is as weak as a Jew's measure of wine and it's doubtful his voice will project beyond the front row of the amphitheatre. Even the other actors may not hear his lines. But his performances for Sharek in bed have secured his part, as opposed to any talent... Did you stay awake long enough to hear from Lycus? He fervently believes he is Antony re-born. Yet he is more likely to die on stage, in more ways than one... Poor Hilarion lives to make people laugh. The joke is on him however, as more people laugh at him than with him... And did you meet our semi-precious jewel in the crown? There is nothing, or no one, Alba wouldn't do to add an extra line or three to her role. But I should not be too harsh on her. I was once in her position. Do you think my tongue too sharp, or blunt, Rufus Varro? I am but having some fun, of course. I am only half - or twice – as cruel as you think. They are my fellow players and I love them dearly. I certainly love them more than they love me, which is not particularly difficult. But tell me, are you married Rufus Varro?"

"No."

"Are you still hoping to find love?

"I am divorced. Love is the last thing I'm hoping or expecting to find."

Berenice pouted - her full lips grew even fuller - and thought how it was a shame that the nobleman was unmarried. Married men tended to succumb to her charms more than most. Faithfulness was rarely in fashion, in Rome or Alexandria.

"And what are you hoping or expecting to find here, if you do not mind me asking? The senator is not usually one for bringing in new blood. You must be talented, or wealthy."

"I warrant it is the latter. And I suspect I am about to find out why I am here, over lunch. But Lucius believes in the Republic, as do I. What Rome witnessed in January was tantamount to a coronation – a sly piece of theatre that not even Sharek could script. If Lucius is an enemy of tyranny, then I will call him a friend. Do you have any insight as to how I may be able to make a favourable impression on my host?"

Varro wondered if Scaurus was hiding in the wings, listening in on his conversation. He would instruct the courtesan to report back to him, at the very least.

"Lucius values loyalty. If you help him achieve his ambitions he will help you achieve yours. Should you lose his trust however, you will be dead to him."

Manius slowly chewed his food, like a cow chewing on grass. He sat in a wooden outbuilding, away from the villa, having lunch with a few of Scaurus' slaves. He kept an ear open for any valuable gossip, but his mind replayed the scene from when he had he had parted with Vedius.

"There is more to you than meets the eye, Manius. You have put Britannia on the map for some of my men. I hope your loyalty will be to Rome and Scaurus when the time comes though. Ultimately you must know that Rome will wipe Britannia off the map, one day. We will civilise the savage island, beat it like a dog until it obeys its master. Servitude will become second nature, as your people are brought to heel by the empire," Vedius goadingly remarked.

But Manius remained unmoved. He had long felt comfortable being both a son of Rome and Britannia.

"Every dog has its day," Manius wryly, cryptically, replied.

"The next time we meet, we should arrange a practise bout between ourselves," Vedius suggested, forcing an unconvincing smile. His hand tightened around his sword, as he ground his teeth too.

As much as Manius was willing to wipe the smile off his face should they meet once more, in combat or otherwise, the Briton hoped that he wouldn't have any cause to encounter the gladiator again. Scaurus would soon be Agrippa's problem.

Berenice stretched herself out across the couch – languidly and enticingly. More of her body seemed outside, rather than inside, her dress. She laughed - again - in reply to something Varro said. She couldn't, or didn't, disguise how much she liked the insouciant Roman poet. He was urbane, modest, could quote Menander and often asked her what she thought. He was a refreshing tonic, compared to Scaurus' previous guests. She still wore the bruises from where one drunken, boorish senator had pinched her breasts and posterior from the night before.

Was her laughter affected or genuine? Varro fancied that not even she could tell the difference anymore. Berenice took another sip of wine and ran her tongue around her glistening lips. He wondered if the wine, or her perfume, was making him feel slightly light-headed. Her beauty was fierce, aggressive, unrelenting. It could bludgeon a man into submission, as well as slip a blade through a weak spot in any man's armour, Varro mused. He also thought of Manius - and envied his friend. He wouldn't have been tempted at all by the low-hanging fruit in front of him, at least not until he had been married for a year or so.

"I must insist that you stay the night with us. You can return to Rome in the morning. I will dance for you – and more – this evening. We can share more wine too. Or are you worried that I might take advantage of you?" the lead actress remarked, humorously yet seductively.

"I'd be more worried that you wouldn't take advantage of me," Varro half-jokingly countered. "But it would be rude - and stupid - of me to abuse my host's hospitality by bedding his mistress under his own roof."

"Lucius would want you to enjoy yourself while you are here," the woman replied, thinking how Scaurus - and Sharek - had pimped her out before. "Lucius will no doubt offer up the company of Tabiry and Salissa after lunch. But why court a slave girl when you can have a queen? I may even inspire you to compose a poem for me."

"I have started writing something already, would you believe? How about I offer a trade? I will recite the opening of the poem if you can tell me how your play ends."

"Rome may never be the same again after our revelatory final act. The world will be turned upside down," Berenice exclaimed, as the actress shifted on the couch, her skin and eyes tingling with excitement.

"But the world will have to wait. Few will come and see our production, my dear, if they already know how it ends," Lucius Scaurus instructed, as he made his way, unseen, into the room. "Welcome Rufus. My apologies for keeping you waiting. I had some urgent correspondence to attend to. I trust our Cleopatra has kept you suitably distracted. Rome will take her to its heart more than the real queen ever did. Even eunuchs and blind men throw themselves at her feet. But life cannot be all fun and games. Let us get down to business."

## 20.

Petals of sunlight, shining through the cypress tree outside the window, scattered themselves across the marble flooring. The warm air massaged his neck and cold water quenched his thirst as Marcus Agrippa sat at his desk. The consul had just dealt with a procession of messengers, who attempted to pull him in a dozen different directions. Everyone wanted a piece of him, on behalf of their masters, to the point where there was little left of himself.

An intimidating mound of work sat on his large oak desk. Tenders for building contracts. Correspondence from clients and friends. Sketches for proposed statues of Augustus. Plans for a public garden at the foot of the Caelian Hill. Intelligence reports from agents in Capua and Massilia. A begging letter from the governor of a province in Gaul requesting urgent additional funds and resources to defeat a group of bandits. Next to the document was a note from a desperate merchant in the province, who claimed that the governor was the real bandit in the region – who had raised taxes four times in a year and orchestrated a culture of bribery and extortion. Agrippa would prioritise the issue. Corruption and complacency were the former soldier's enemies now. A piece of Senate legislation, which Caesar had re-drafted, also needed to be signed-off on by the end of the day. Some in the Senate House would not like his amendments, but they would accept them.

As much as the stoical statesman was tempted to sigh at his role and workload, he remembered a time when his desk was filled with maps and quartermaster reports and butcher bills from being at war with Antony.

Agrippa put his stylus down and stood up. He needed to stretch his legs. He soon paced around the room, frustrated that he hadn't received a message from Rufus Varro. Part of him worried that the frivolous aristocrat was out of his depth - but Agrippa also had to concede how valuable an agent the wastrel might prove. *Finally, a poet might make something of his life.* Varro was comfortable in high and low society alike. He knew how to keep a secret - and extract secrets from others. Varro had made progress in gathering intelligence on Scaurus - but there was more work to be done. Sooner or later he would need to go in for the kill, Agrippa considered - although he hoped that his new agent wouldn't end up dying in the attempt.

Agrippa was distracted by the sound of footsteps and voices outside, as his wife, Claudia Marcella, and her unctuous astrologist, Toranius, strolled towards the atrium. The practically minded consul pursed his lips and furrowed his brow at the sight of his wife in thrall to the soothsayer. He shook his head in objection - and contempt - at the "science" of astrology. He would have laughed, with scorn, if his wife didn't take things so seriously. Agrippa mused how Caecilia would have laughed too, if offered to have her fate told by the failed priest, who would read a bird's entrails as if interpreting a passage from Plato.

Yet Marcella hung on the charlatan's every word, as if he were the Delphic Oracle. She saw the astrologist twice a week. Maybe more. At least she had stopped passing on his pronouncements and wisdom to her sceptical husband. Agrippa knew why she put her faith in Toranius however. He advised her - and gave her hope - on conceiving a child. She wanted a baby, preferably a son. A child would make her, her husband - and her uncle - happy. She would be fulfilling her purpose. When Toranius recommended she dye her pubic hair and drink goat's milk when the moon was full, she did so. When he advised her to rub bat dung on her stomach after sex, whilst offering up a prayer to Venus, she willingly assented. The astrologist drew up a schedule each month as well, citing the optimum times she could conceive. "It is written in the stars," as to when the baby would be born, his wife earnestly, stupidly, believed. Agrippa wondered that if the soothsayer augured that Marcella should divorce him to find happiness, would she do so? It was likely however that instead of the dictates of fate his wife would listen to an even greater power, her uncle.

Agrippa wryly smiled to himself as he recalled the time when, whilst growing up on Apollonia, he and Octavius had visited the famed astrologer, Theogenes. The wizened sophist had first asked Agrippa for the time and date of his birth. After offering up other pieces of information the astrologer stroked his beard and retreated into his study, to construct his horoscope. He came back, with wine and a pronouncement on his lips. Agrippa was destined for greatness. At this point a cloud appeared over Octavius' head - and the trip to see the soothsayer no longer felt like a joke. Agrippa sensed that his friend was worried his fate would eclipse his companion's – or that Theogenes would pronounce that their paths would diverge. Octavius rarely lost his composure, but he did a little that day, as he paced around the room, agitated, whilst the astrologer disappeared to interpret his horoscope. He was absent for some time. Agrippa imagined he was working his way through a jug of wine in the next room. When the old man returned however he fell to his knees and exclaimed that Octavius would be "master of the world".

Did people now regard him as great? Agrippa experienced little anxiety about his friend being considered greater. The prophesy had come true, albeit their success had been written in blood rather than the stars. Agrippa now lived in a house so vast that one could, quite literally, get lost in it. He possessed so many slaves that he could no longer remember all their names. He could no longer keep track on how many properties he owned. He had more riches than he could possibly spend, in ten life times. Yet Agrippa would have given all his wealth up, in a heartbeat, if it meant he could spend one more day with Caecilia. There was still a hole in his life, which no amount of work could fill. Caecilia was his everything – and it is mathematically impossible to give your everything twice. He wanted to tell her he missed her, loved her. He needed to say he was sorry. During the final couple of years of their marriage they had grown apart - because they had lived so much apart. Caesar would not have been able to win the war without him. Agrippa promised his wife that they would spend time together, once they had triumphed. Once Rome was safe. But the war dragged on, like a funeral oration. He argued that he needed to finish the job and defeat Antony, else Antony would take everything from them.

"He will take our home," he warned.

"This hasn't been your home for some time. You're only at home now when you're on the battlefield," Caecilia mournfully countered, tears glistening in her eyes as they endured another fight. "Octavius can live without you at his side. And you need to realise that you have a life - and a family - autonomous of him… Duty should be ennobling, not enslaving. You say he is your oldest friend and you owe him a debt. But Octavius needs to repay his debt to you. Free you."

As Marcella passed by the doorway she glanced and briefly caught her husband's eye. She raised the corners of her tight mouth but only her lips, as opposed to face, smiled. Her features were plump but pretty. Her silk dress seemed a size too big and she wore too much jewellery. She moved stiffly, as if still only halfway through a course of deportment classes. Marcella was barely into her womanhood. She was not unintelligent or without her virtues, yet she lacked the wit and character of her mother. When they were first married she tried her best to please her new husband - but she realised he was happier when she left him alone. Agrippa lamented how there was just one thing wrong with her. She wasn't Caecilia. He hoped that Marcella would make someone else a good wife, someone closer to her age who appreciated her. There was a hint of an apology in her expression, as Marcella knew that today was one of their days when they would try and conceive. Usually they slept apart. Augustus was keen to secure his bloodline and legacy - and it was tantamount to an order, rather than a request, that Agrippa should marry again and present him with a possible heir. "Marcella will grow into a fine woman, like her mother… You will thank me for my decision, one day. Caecilia would want you to be happy too, my friend," Caesar suggested. Agrippa did not like the proposal. But he accepted it. He would still honour the promise he had made to his companion all those years ago, on Apollonia, upon hearing the news of Caesar's death. The two friends committed themselves to one fate.

"You have my sword," Agrippa had told a stricken Octavius. And how he had been made to use it. It was difficult to tell where the rust started on the blade and the blood ended.

Agrippa forced a polite or pained smile in reply, although he couldn't help but roll his eyes in dismay when he glanced at Marcella. He determined to close his eyes again - and picture his first wife later - when in bed with the second.

## 21.

Scaurus quickly dismissed his mistress after greeting his guest. For a moment she drew breath and puffed out her chest, as if she was going to defy the senator, but she duly and demurely nodded her head in assent when his expression grew taut with displeasure. Her features dropped but, as if by magic, her default, beguiling smile blossomed on her face once more as she said goodbye to Varro - promising she would see him again soon (with the promise of something else sown into her countenance). Scaurus smiled too, after his lover affectionately kissed him on the cheek, but the smile fell from his face as rapidly as shit sliding off a shovel.

Scaurus invited his guest to join him in a private dining room. The corner room was well lit by the afternoon sun. The large, long table could seat half a dozen. The two men sat at either end. The host's chair was wider and higher than the others in the room and anyone sitting near Scaurus would have been made to look up to him.

Wine - Falernian - was served in elegant silver goblets. A tray of steamed red mullet, with spiced scallops and honey-glazed carrots, was also laid on the table. Once the slaves had transferred the food onto their plates Scaurus ordered them to leave, without a thank you. As the food was being served Varro couldn't help but take note of the large stone statue in the garden of Hercules strangling the Nemean lion. The Greek hero bared his fang-like teeth more than the animal - and appeared more savage. The defeated and distraught creature, his eyes bulging, was stretching out a sinewy front leg - in a plea of surrender. Varro felt more pity for the lion than admiration for the famed hero.

"I always remember something your father once told me. "The safety of the people shall be the highest law." He regularly visited our home in Rome when I was a young man. He was a great friend of my father. They were both ardent republicans, servants of the people. We are, or should be, keepers of the flame for our parents. The torch of their wisdom and traditions should be passed on, from generation to generation. New men may come and go – but the best men should remain. One need only breed horses to appreciate the importance of a bloodline. Leaves fall and scatter. It's the roots and branches that matter, is it not?"

Varro nodded his head in solemn agreement, ignoring the fact that Scaurus had borrowed a quote from Cicero and attributed it to his father.

"I cannot confess to always feeling that I owe a duty to my family name and to Rome. I squandered many days - and more so nights - throughout my youth. But I am now ready to make a name for myself, instead of living in the shadow of my father's."

"Let us not lie or pretend. We are both good Romans. Good republicans. Which is why we know that Rome has become an autocracy. Rome is a monarchy, lacking an official king. And Caesar is a king, lacking an official crown. How long before, like Sulla, Octavius lines the walls of the Forum with the heads of his enemies? For those who argue that Caesar has defeated all his enemies, I would counter that he will create new ones. Blood begets blood. Caesar even craves enemies, in order to sow fear and act as Rome's guardian. His forthcoming Spanish campaign is a piece of theatre, to win the applause of the army and the mob. And whilst away on campaign his dullard co-consul - a glorified stone mason - will use your taxes to build a legion of statues to honour, or deify, his vile master. But all is not lost. Not every senator and soldier will serve under the pretend king's yoke. Caesar has his fellow victors, but he has also created an army of victims, willing to rise-up and overthrow the tyrant. I will give the people a new hero to cheer for, whilst re-establishing the authority of the Senate. Our supporters are preparing themselves. But we are not wholly ready yet, to strike. I must continue to build-up my war chest. But my intention to invite you here today is not to extract a donation from you. Rather look at it as an investment. And I am not just asking for you to invest in me, but rather to invest in yourself. You possess the name and means to progress through the course of honours - to climb the ladder. I can help you get your foot on the first rung. My allies will not go unrewarded. Doors will be open to you, even before I become consul. I can also furnish you with an able secretary, so you will you not be burdened with any day-to-day duties in your role as quaestor."

"I appreciate your candour. Which is why I feel compelled to be candid in return. I believe in your cause. Rome is being defiled. Caesar is making a mockery of the Senate and the old order needs to be re-established. My horse has more noble blood running through its vein than the likes of Marcus Agrippa. But I will need assurances in regards to a return on any donation, or investment, I make. I will want to know where my money is being spent. You will have to flesh out your plans. I can also assist you in securing additional support. I have friends, sons of noblemen who were dispossessed or killed by Caesar in the civil war, who would be willing to fund your campaign too. I would however ask for a modest finder's fee, for recruiting them to the cause."

It was Scaurus' turn to nod in agreement and approval. The senator would have been wary if the young man was solely motivated by his convictions. Greed made him seem more human, genuine.

Lucilla relaxed out upon her portico, with an awning protecting her from the citrus rays of the sun. Her legs were tucked up beneath her as she sat on a cushioned chair, pensively staring out into her garden. She wore a silk dress, which was dark blue beneath her breasts and pearl coloured above. She had owned a similar garment when married to Varro. It was one of his favourites, she idly recalled.

"It's tasteful and I like the colours," he had commented. "I'm also fond of the cut of the dress, as it accentuates your figure and, more importantly, the swell of your breasts," he had half-jokingly added.

Lucilla wrinkled her nose a little as she heard some recently bought silver wind chimes sound in the breeze and realised that the noise irritated her. Similarly, a barely half-eaten plate of sliced fruit rested on a table beside her.

She had wanted nothing more a short time ago but after Diana had prepared and served the dish Lucilla apologised to her maid for her loss of appetite.

*Does anyone know what they truly want in this world, especially when their wishes come true?*

Two messages sat on her lap. Both contained invitations. From potential suitors. Potential husbands. The first was from Quintus Leochares. The merchant was twice her age, but that could be viewed as a blessing rather than a curse, Lucilla reflected. He was courteous and intelligent. Quintus was too tired to be passionate and let lust control his life. His face was craggy and brown, like bark. Perhaps he had been attractive and athletic, some time ago. The merchant owned a fleet of ships and had trading concerns throughout the empire. Quintus had recently allowed his eldest son, from his first marriage, to manage his business so his father could spend more time enjoying the fruits of his labour. Despite their age gap Lucilla considered that she had plenty in common with Quintus. They both enjoyed the theatre, the countryside and discussing literature. The merchant was also one of Rome's most connected and knowledgeable art collectors. She liked quizzing him on his friendship and correspondence with Cicero and Atticus. The latter had bequeathed him a number of statues and artworks when he passed away. Quintus kept the collection in a special room in his villa. Lucilla had all but swooned on viewing the unique, beautiful pieces. He was happy to see her happy. The couple enjoyed each other's company and conversation. She always learned something after spending time with him. Lucilla considered how he rarely made her laugh - but he would never make her cry. Perhaps he did or could love her, but it would be a love akin to the way he appreciated a fine piece of sculpture. He enjoyed it when others appreciated her beauty.

Lucilla realised that she could - but did not want to - marry Quintus. Sooner rather than later however he would offer a proposal and want to possess her. But she was already drafting a polite refusal. Hopefully they could just be friends.

And hopefully she and Marcus Sosius could just be lovers. Lucilla ran her fingers over the letter from the young, besotted aristocrat and raised the corner of her mouth in a wistful and satisfied smile. He was virile, fun and attractive. If only he was wise, witty and capable of melancholy too. Lucilla was over ten years older than her admirer. Marcus was fresh-faced and enviably - or exhaustingly - energetic. His bright blue eyes were child-like. They sparkled with a sense of being pleased or wanting to please. He lived off an allowance that his father gave him each month, although he was keen to boast to Lucilla that his income would be substantially greater once his father died. She had first encountered Marcus at a party. The slightly tipsy youth quite literally fell into the woman's lap, although it was as much by accident as by design. He gave the older, but stylish and demure woman his best smile. He laughed at her witticisms and pretended to be fascinated by her conversation (Lucilla didn't know whether to laugh or cry when he thought that Plautus and Terence were the names of a gladiator and charioteer). Perhaps the lustful Roman thought that he would seduce the woman and teach her a few new things in the bedchamber - but it was Lucilla who took on the role of teacher and seducer. Sosius wrote sweet - but risible - poems to "his goddess" and "swan". He declared his love for her too, after their second night together. "I looked at past affairs as conquests. But now I want to be conquered by you." Lucilla smiled - the soul of irony - in reply, as the line has been lifted from one of Rufus' early poems.

Lucilla knew that, sooner rather than later, Marcus would fall out of love with her, especially if his love was returned. If they married, he would soon seek a mistress. If married, he would take ownership of her estate and income. It was unlikely now that they would even remain just lovers. Lucilla was largely bored by the sweet - but foolish - youth. She also felt guilty in unwittingly, or not, seducing him. She sighed and wrinkled her nose once more. But this time reproving herself - realising that Marcus' greatest attraction and virtue was that he made her first husband jealous.

Diana re-appeared and glanced at the letters on her mistress' lap, awaiting instruction. Lucilla decided to tell both suitors that she was already engaged for the evening. In truth she would remain at home, share a cup of wine or two with her maid and retire early to read a book. Lucilla also knew that, for better or for worse, she would spend, or waste, part of the evening thinking about Varro.


Lucius Scaurus nodded in agreement once again - and slightly more vigorously - when Varro revealed the amount of money he was willing to donate to the senator's campaign fund. The young aristocrat could also raise and transfer the sum by the end of the month. Scaurus licked his lips - and not just because he wished to clean the mushroom sauce off the corner of his mouth.

Varro thought how his host possessed the grin and untrustworthiness of a crocodile. He noted how far apart Scaurus' eyes were. Lizard-like. As though he needed eyes on the side of his head, to watch for both predators and prey all around him.

The two men convivially spoke about numerous subjects (chariot racing, recent court cases and the rising property prices in Pompeii) over various dishes (seabass with cucumber, game pie, beef sausages in an oyster sauce). And the conversation and food continued to be washed down with a selection of vintages from Scaurus' cellar. Varro was keen to keep as clear a head as possible however. He made sure to dilute his wine, even to the detriment of its taste. A lifetime of drinking had also strengthened his tolerance for wine. Perhaps he had been unwittingly training as a spy all these years, he idly reflected.

"Tell me Rufus, are you married?" Scaurus asked, already knowing the answer.

"I was married, which is now why I'm divorced. I cannot quite recall if I got bored with her or she grew tired of me," Varro wryly answered. "I am conscious however of the fact that, should I wish to harbour an ambition to succeed in politics, I should take another wife. I would welcome your counsel on the matter."

"I would be happy to help arrange a suitable match for you, from a noble family, who will be able to pay a suitable dowry. Their clients can become your clients. A wife will be able to manage your household, to free-up valuable time so you can manage Rome. Like a moth to a flame, a beautiful wife will attract attention and widen your circle of friends and supporters. The daughter of an old friend, Publius Laronius, has just come of age. I can broach a proposal for you, when you're ready," Scaurus suggested. *Publius used a horsewhip on the girl to discipline her, so a husband won't have to.* "From what I have heard about you though, Rufus, you will have little trouble in arranging a mistress or two to keep you entertained."

"I am not averse to getting married - and divorced - again should circumstances require it. Women can be as changeable and as harsh as the weather. It is only right that we are afforded the opportunity to change them every now and then."

Scaurus hummed in harmony and even raised his cup, to toast his guest's comment.

"I will soon be taking another wife myself. My current one is barren and has grown dull. I have no intention of waiting around for her to grow ugly too. Of course, it is an open secret that Caesar conducts more than just affairs of state. Despite his propaganda and policies promoting wholesome family life there doesn't seem to be a wife in Rome safe from his roving eye. And it is rumoured his she-wolf of a spouse encourages his infidelity - and even selects certain mistresses who lack the guile and ambition to rival her. Livia is a bawd. As much as Caesar considers himself a king, Livia deems herself a queen. In some respects, she is more co-consul than Agrippa. She never misses an opportunity to promote her son, Tiberius, over more worthy candidates. As well as whispering poison in Caesar's ear she is rumoured to have put poison in the food of her enemies as well. The pair deserve to rot in the underworld together. They are a blight on Rome," Scaurus judged, clutching his knife in his hand. Scowling. Varro noticed how, whenever he mentioned the name Caesar, his upper lip receded over his radish coloured gums.

"Their time will come," Varro re-assuredly replied.

"But not soon enough. I feel more wedded to Rome than I do my wife. And the people of Rome are my children. We must mould them into being dutiful citizens rather than slavish subjects to a Princep. Everything I do, I do for the people of Rome. Not for myself... And sometimes we must punish our children, for their own good... Rome must be won from within and the rest of the empire will duly fall into line. Pompey should have never abandoned the city to Caesar. It was his first and greatest mistake. Antony was a fool too if he believed he could capture Rome from the East. Octavius will shortly be leaving Rome as well. If all goes according to plan, the dictator will return in chains. Or as a corpse."

## 22.

"We promise to give you a night to remember," Berenice said, suggestively, with an even more suggestive look on her face, as she attempted to persuade Varro not to return to Rome. Varro wasn't sure who she meant by "we", whether she was speaking for her and Lucius Scaurus, or her and Salissa, who was enticingly positioned by her side, her arm coiled around the actress' waist.

Berenice's expression conveyed she was crestfallen, or even insulted, when Varro insisted he had to leave. He told himself that her disappointment was borne from the personal as well as the professional. Varro was understandably tempted to prolong his stay, to further sample his host's - and hostess' – hospitality. He could glean more intelligence. But he thought it best to take his leave. He was exhausted, from the oppressive heat and stomach-bloating lunch. Varro also didn't want to try his luck too hard. His head was in the jaws of a lion and one wrong word could arouse his host's suspicions or ire. At any moment a messenger could appear with news that he was cuckolding him or conspiring with his enemies. As with playing dice, one should always quit while ahead. Varro spared a thought for his companion as well. He knew Manius would be keen to return to Rome. A reply from Camilla could be waiting for him. He also needed to properly prepare for his fight.

"I will be in contact soon," Varro warmly remarked to his host, as he stood between the front of the house and waiting carriage. "I will raise the necessary capital as soon as I can. You have my word. And I am as much of a man of honour as yourself."

"I am pleased to hear it. I can trust you, I hope. The gods may be on our side, but our ambitions will need funding too... I want you to think about which rung of the political ladder you would like to place your foot upon. If I need to unseat a supporter of Caesar's to get you into office, then that's more to the good."

It was late afternoon, or early evening, but waves of heat still hit him like a woman slapping his face (a sensation not unfamiliar to Varro). The golden-green fields glowed, the sky was ablaze. Varro thought how it seemed that the world was about to catch fire. Or it was already on fire.

He couldn't help but hear the constant singing of the increasingly tipsy wagoner:

"The soldier sharpened his sword
Every day and every night.
Until the edge wore away
And he couldn't kill, for all his might...

The fisherman kept on catching fish
Praying to the gods to fill his net.
Until the sea ran as dry as a bone

And only his tears were left as something wet."

The driver, whose withered arm meant he held the reins in just one hand, was different from the one who had brought him from Rome. At first Varro fancied that he might be a spy, whose brief was to report any conversation he caught between his two passengers. But it was more likely that the man possessed the same wit as his beasts of burden, than he was a master-spy.

"So how was your lunch?" Manius asked his friend, leaning forward and lowering his voice. "Did he give you food for thought?"

"He certainly did. After I write my report Agrippa will surely take some action, which hopefully will no longer involve me. He will be able to interrogate one of the co-conspirators and they will implicate Scaurus in the plot. Should he question Sharek too, the difficulty won't be getting him to start talking but getting him to stop. There will be a trial, or a punishment will be meted out secretly. I'll then be free to return to a life of idleness or, better still, debasement. I think this whole experience has made me realise that I haven't got the will to save myself, let alone save Rome. But how did you fare and feel when you returned to the make-shift ludus?

"Unlike you, I have no desire to return to my old life - as much as I will have to draw my sword one last time tomorrow. But it's for a worthy cause. I'm breaking an oath once, in order to be faithful for the rest of my days," the Briton remarked, smiling as he thought once more of a shared future with Camilla.

For a moment his friend's sense of fidelity and hope reminded him of his younger self, just before and after his marriage to Lucilla. He was a better person back then, although he didn't quite know whether that was due to himself or his wife's influence.

"Let's just hope that I've broken my oath to Scaurus in the name of a worthy cause."

"How serious a threat do you think he is to Rome and Augustus?"

"Well you know how loath I am to take anything seriously. He may well have the means and will to challenge Caesar in some way, but I cannot envision him succeeding. He will bite off more than he can chew. I've known poets who are less conceited. I could give him ten times my fortune and he still would not have enough gold to purchase the number of troops he would need to take on his opponent. Scaurus won't be able to win over the people either. He's the wrong figurehead. He's a patriarch rather than populist. They will see the old, privileged senator as part of the problem, not the solution. A Caesar will serve as the first man of Rome for some time yet, I imagine."

As the carriage departed Berenice slotted herself next to the senator and stroked his cheek, in a signal that she was ready to make love if he wished. She soon retreated however upon witnessing the admonishing look on his face. For some reason he was angry with her. She had failed to entice the young aristocrat to stay the night. Had she been too forward, or not forward enough, with him? Scaurus would not be a slave to pleasure and let a woman weaken his devotion to duty. He needed to think, not fuck.

As soon as Varro had turned his back on the senator to enter the carriage the cordial smile on his countenance was crushed as his lips compressed together and his eyes bored into the aristocrat's soul. The son of Appius Varro had said all the right things, but he couldn't help but feel that something was amiss. Doubts about his character flitted in and out of his mind like sprites flitting in and out of view in a haunted forest. Perhaps it was because he had said all the right things. But nobody's perfect. His guest had not displayed the slightest flicker of surprise or distress, after hearing about his treasonous intentions. He was almost expecting to hear them. The senator had liked Varro (and he would like his money even more) but better to be paranoid than betrayed, Scaurus reasoned. He had made the mistake of inviting Quintus Verres into his circle too quickly, although he had corrected the fault by disposing of the agent before he could betray his plans.

Varro woke with a start as Manius snorted, or snored, heavily. His friend seemed dead to the world. He envied his ability to fall asleep at will, shut out everything. The vanity. The ignorance. The beastliness. Perhaps he had developed the skill out of necessity, during his time as a slave or gladiator, to take advantage of any rest while he could.

The aristocrat yawned, and then rolled his eyes, as the carriage travelled over a gash in the road and Varro spilled some of his wine. As he wiped his hand he noticed a coin on the seat next to him and picked it up, peering at the words upon it as if he were reading them for the first time.

*"Imperator Caesar, son of the Deified, in his sixth consulship."*

And on the reverse...

*"He restores the laws and rights of the Roman people."*

Varro recalled how a number of statues of the gods had been melted down in the past six months. Statues of Augustus took their place. Blink and you may have missed the transition. It was also recently decreed that Caesar's name should be added to the names of the gods within public hymns. Man may be the paragon of animals, but he should not play god. Gods are seldom merciful or fair - indeed they often inhabit the flaws and foibles of men. Perhaps Scaurus had a point and Augustus needed to be checked, else his appetite for power could consume Rome.

The wagon travelled over another hole in the road and at that moment Varro became more concerned for his reserves of wine than he did for the fate of the empire.

Varro recognised the scenery and realised they were close to home. He craned his neck out of the window and saw Rome in the distance. He who is tired of Rome is tired of life. He looked forward to opening the door and being welcomed by Fronto - and Viola. Should he have stayed away from the capital any longer he would have soon missed its taverns, theatres and women. Its colourful streets, heaving with variety and inanity. He would have even missed its smells, albeit not all of them. Varro thought to himself however what he would miss most about Rome, should he have to live in exile - hoping that he would drift off back to sleep before the wine ran out.

Manius stirred, as Varro sighed. The spy felt like a sprinter, coming into the home straight. His assignment would soon be over. Agrippa would surely be pleased. The consul might even smile, though Varro would not necessarily place a wager on it.

The sun beat down like a molten fist. The blazing heat fired the senator's resolve. It was time to return to Rome, a day before scheduled. He would task one of his agents to shadow his newest recruit and find out more about his character and allegiances. He could re-direct the agent who was currently following his wife, to report on Varro's movements. What did he care if his wife proved unfaithful? He would divorce, or dispose of her soon, anyway. Scaurus also needed to return to the capital to cement the loyalty of the pack of senators who had recently pledged their support. Most believed in his campaign and plan, but some would have to be bribed, or blackmailed, to commit to the cause. The coup.

## 23.

Cassandra fell into Varro's arms as soon as he walked through the door. Shock and surprise grabbed him by the throat, causing the poet to be lost for words. The long day was about to get longer. Varro was exhausted and couldn't quite tell if he was holding her up, or she was supporting him. Tears cut streaks through her make-up and strands of her hair clung to her face like seaweed clinging to rocks. She was dressed modestly, matronly, in a plain stola. She knew that Varro saw her as an alluring lover - but she also wanted to prove that she could act the good Roman wife also. Or at the very least dress the part.

Fronto had looked after their unexpected guest for most of the day. Fortunately, or not, the senator's wife was not the first woman to ever turn up at the front door of the house in tears (albeit most times the tears sprung from regret or rage). Occasionally she quizzed the old servant as to the whereabouts of his master - and if he was currently courting any other women. Fronto wisely pleaded ignorance, whilst trying to cast his master in a positive light.

"I cannot stay with him another night," Cassandra sobbed, her despair as potent as her perfume.

Varro hoped that the sigh he emitted would be interpreted as one of relief or gratitude, rather than weariness. He had wanted to come home to his bed, or a long bath. Towards the end of his coach ride he planned on inviting one - or two - of his slaves (Aspasia and Sophia) to bathe and massage him. He imagined Aspasia's soft but strong hands rubbing oil into his shoulders and kneading the tension out of his back, having taken off his sweat and mud stained tunic. He would invite them both into his bath with him. At the end the dextrous Sophia would run her strigil along his enlivened skin, scraping the grime and his cares away.

"You can stay here this evening," Varro replied, soothingly, stroking the back of her head - akin to the way he stroked Viola. He rested his head on the distraught woman's shoulder, so she was unable to witness the subtle, or not, distress on his own countenance. If he had loved her he would have declared that she could have stayed with him for a lifetime. But he didn't.

Fronto raised a single, grey, wiry eyebrow at the scene before retreating into the kitchen. His expression conveyed a thousand words. If Varro had not already made an enemy of Lucius Scaurus, he soon would. Manius also took his leave, with Viola loyally following behind, as happy as any soul in Rome.

"Thank you for helping me take care of business today. I'll duly help you take care of your business in the morning," Varro remarked to his friend, before he retreated to his room to dwell upon Camilla - and his forthcoming gladiatorial contest. By this time tomorrow the Briton could have everything he ever wanted. Or be slain.

Fronto retired too, torn between worrying for his master and being hopeful of the prospect of Varro having finally found himself another wife. If she was just half the woman Lucilla was then she would still be twice as virtuous as most brides, Fronto mused.

Varro sat next to Cassandra on the couch and held her hand. He tried to be attentive but there were moments when he struggled to keep his eyes open. He promised himself that he would tell her everything in the morning. Where he had been. What his mission was. How he felt about her. Secrets were beginning to weigh like giant gallstones throughout his innards. The dam would need to break. Varro wryly, tiredly, mused how lying to women had been second nature to him, for years. He justified his behaviour by believing that lying came second nature to women too. But the truth would set him free. Varro judged that Cassandra would help condemn Scaurus. Damn him. Crucify him.

The evening drew in. Darkness was thickening, congealing like a scab. Cassandra's devoted maid stood sentry-like in the corner of the room, eyes down as if deep in prayer. Praying for the handsome, noble Roman aristocrat to deliver her mistress.

Varro had no desire to play god, but he would try to save the woman. He would arrange for her to stay at his villa, just outside Arretium. Fronto could take her there tomorrow. She might protest and demand she wanted to stay with him, in Rome. But he would be firm, even in the face of any histrionics or tears - crocodile or otherwise. Once Scaurus' fate was sealed Cassandra could return to the capital. He would break it to her gently how, although he cared for her, it was best if she found someone else. He would dust off some old lines. How she deserved someone better than him. More faithful. Less selfish. He was incapable of love. "You cannot put in what the gods have left out." Varro consoled himself with the thought that Cassandra would not be lacking for suitors when she returned to Rome, such was her beauty (and potential wealth, should she inherit her husband's estate). She was a flower - and the world was full of bees.

Varro led Cassandra into the bedroom, but his desire to sleep overpowered any urge to make love. He drifted off as soon as his leaden head sunk into the pillow.

The loud trill of birds and crickets, seemingly conversing with one another, woke him up in the dead of night. Cassandra was also awake. Her cheek rested on his chest and her foot gently rubbed up and down his shin. But Varro pretended to remain asleep and planned his day ahead. He would unburden himself in the morning. He would confess that he was working as an agent, under the instruction of Agrippa. But it had not all been an act when he had slept with her. He would still protect her from her baleful husband and would join her as soon as he could at his villa on the outskirts of Arretium. He started to compose, in his mind, the lines he would deliver: "I know you have no reason to do so, but you need to make a leap of faith and trust me... Our night together was real. The way we feel about each other is real... I do not believe in fate, but I believe in friendship... With your help I can prove that Lucius is an enemy of the state. Rather than a divorcee, you will be a widow - once

Caesar issues his judgement. He is not known for his clemency." After speaking to Cassandra, Varro would instruct Fronto to make the arrangements for her to journey from Rome to his country villa. The sooner she departed the better, for various reasons. Varro wanted the woman safe and out of his hair. He also aimed to write to Agrippa by midday, or better still deliver his report in person. He wanted to be sure that Scaurus and his co-conspirators would be apprehended. He would duly devote part of his day to Manius as well - and place his wager.

*It's going to be a busy day. I will need a drink at the end of it all.*

Cassandra slept fitfully, at best. Her heart pounded, with dread and hope. She trembled at the thought of seeing her husband once more, his rancorous face contorted in wrath and violence. Her marriage had scarred her, inside and out. But there wouldn't now be any fresh wounds. Perhaps Lucius would be pleased that he could divorce her quickly - and in marrying someone who could provide him with a child he would forgive and forget her for defying him. But such a hope seemed as flimsy as a butterfly's wing.

At least she could be sure of the way Varro felt about her. *He loves me.* And the way she felt about him. *And I love him.*

"I knew we would be together again, as soon as I saw you at the party, in the garden. Something fell into place in my heart, like a key fitting into a lock. And after the night we spent together I knew that I could never go back to my old, stale existence. Something inside of me changed. Or needs to change. I am beginning to believe in fate. Admit it, you came to the party because you wanted to see me again, did you not? We're fated to be together," Cassandra excitedly, almost hysterically, exclaimed, as they sat on the couch together earlier.

Varro kissed her in reply, to save himself from deceiving the wronged woman again.

She sensed he was awake and the couple stirred. They made love. She straddled him and did most of the work - her arms spread out, as if she were being crucified. She closed her eyes and arched her back, surrendering to pleasure or fate. Her supple torso glowed, like hot coals, in the candlelight.

"I love you so much," she breathlessly issued, her heart and loins almost bursting.

Again, instead of words, Varro offered up a kiss to serve as his reply. He glanced at the portraits of his mother and father on the wall and a wave of shame crashed against his soul. He couldn't bear to have them glare at him any longer and buried his head in the woman's chest. He nuzzled and kissed the v-shaped space between her breasts, passionately proclaiming that it was one of the most beautiful features of her beautiful - divine - body. Varro had lost count of the number of women he had used the line with. He would have grown tired of saying it, but for the fact that his mistresses never grew tired of hearing about how "unique" they were.

After making love they rested on their sides, facing one another - their noses almost touching. Varro tenderly tucked a tendril of her long hair behind her ear. Cassandra caught her breath whilst smiling. Varro attempted a similar expression but the strain on his heart - and facial muscles - grew too much. His fingers caressed her shoulders, arms, stomach and thighs. But with an artfulness, borne from several years' worth of practice, Varro pretended to fall asleep. He soon rolled over, so his back was to his lover and he didn't feel obliged to smile anymore. Part of him never wanted to seduce - use - a woman in such a fashion again. He felt limed in guilt, or fatigue. Or worthlessness.

*I don't want to go back to my old, stale existence. Something inside of me has changed. Or needs to change.*

Viola lay curled-up, cat-like, at the end of his bed. Occasionally she whimpered, perhaps dreaming about her time living on the streets. Friendless. Starving. The sound of her whimpering, or snoring, would then wake her and she would wag her tail at the sight of Manius. The corners of her mouth would even raise themselves in a contented smile.

Manius stirred at the sound of the dog, or himself, snoring too. He immediately thought of Camilla but whereas the image of her in his mind's eye was once as sharp and familiar as his own reflection her features seemed blurred. The Briton appeared even more mournful as he thought how time had worn away the picture of his parents over the years. He tried his best to recall them every day, clenching his eyes shut, but the wind and rain can erode the hardest of stone. Yet their faces were all too clear when he saw them during a re-occurring nightmare he suffered.

Lightening stabbed the horizon. The rain slashed down. Manius was trapped in the body of his child self again. Enfeebled. Terrified. The village had just finished sharing a feast, having made an offering to its gods. But the gods must have been sleeping, or ungrateful - as they did little to protect the tribe from the attack. The Romans came out of nowhere, encircling their prey, their spear tips glinting in the moonlight.

Women and children were skewered, like the pieces of roasted meat offered up to their deities. Huts were set alight, whether the soldiers knew there were people in them or not. Horses whinnied in the background, but the screeching sound couldn't drown out the blood-curdling human screams. The Romans were methodical and savage at the same time, fuelled by wine, bloodlust and a will to loot and rape.

Tears mingled with raindrops across his cheeks as Manius splashed his way through the mud towards his home and, hopefully, parents. A few of the men from the village fought back, but in vain. One warrior staggered around, cradling his intestines in his hands. It looked like his stomach was full of adders. One of the village dogs soughed louder than the wind, from being pinned to the ground by a pilum having pierced its chest. Manius was fleetingly tempted to put the animal out of its misery - but he had his own miseries to deal with first.

Manius darted in between clumps of soldiers fighting and made it back to his family's hut. His father, along with a few of his kinsman, stood guard at the door. As he entered his mother, Minura, clutched the child to her bosom - to the point of almost suffocating him. She then grabbed a basket, filled with what food and valuables she could muster. There would be no escape however. His father entered the hut, doubled over from a stab wound to his stomach. A brace of snarling Roman soldiers also entered, their swords dripping with fresh blood. A smirk, like a gash, lined the lead solder's countenance as he caught sight of his mother. Attractive. Defeated.

The legionary first ran his gladius across his father's throat, as though his hand was pulling a curtain across a window, before striding towards his mother. Drool ran down his stubbled chin. The Roman stood as large an oak tree - and Manius was but a sapling then. Scrawny and unaccomplished. He had joined his father on more than one hunting party, but he had yet to make his first kill.

Manius stood between the soldier, Tarius, and his trembling mother. The legionary laughed at the defiant looking child. But his laughter was cut short when the boy attempted to stab him with a small knife he had swiped off a table.

"Little bastard," Tarius barked, as he grabbed Manius by the wrist and nearly yanked his arm out of the socket. The second soldier, Corvinus, restrained the boy, as he waited his turn to be with the woman. In the meantime, he glanced around the barbarian's hut, in the hope of locating something valuable.

Tarius stood over Minura. Her gaze flitted between her husband, son and the man about to rape her. She wailed, in anger or grief, whilst retreating into the corner. Minura tucked her knees under her chin and shook her head as the soldier grew closer. Her head then shook from the invader striking her around her face. Blood dripped from her quivering lips. The soldier said something in a strange tongue. If he was striking a deal whereby he would let her son live if she submitted - then Minura would have submitted.

Thunder rumbled, or growled, in the background. His breath reeked of acetum. She noticed how black his fingernails were too as Tarius clawed open the woman's dress and his eyes ogled her naked breasts. He licked his lips and slavered. Minura wanted to die.

"Stop."

The voice was clear, forceful. His expression was unyielding, like his will.

Tarius turned around, gnashed his teeth and responded to his fellow soldier, who had stormed into the hut:

"Fuck off. Find your own piece of meat," he barked. The legionary considered the barbarian woman to be a legitimate spoil of war. Even more than being rough with a whore, he enjoyed having his way with Rome's enemies. The terror and submission in their eyes aroused him. He had tasted the women of Gaul. Now he wanted a Briton. It was his right. Part of his pay for being a Roman soldier.

Lucius Oppius was a man of few words at the best of times - and he wasn't about to waste his breath on the two wayward soldiers in front of him. Oppius first swung a bolder-like fist into the face of the legionary restraining the boy. Corvinus lost consciousness before his head even touched the ground. Tarius let out a curse and rushed forward, thrusting the point of his gladius at his opponent's chest. Oppius swatted the blade away, using the bronze bracer on his forearm. He then moved inside and buried his sword into Tarius' groin.

Oppius dragged the two bodies into the corner with little ceremony. Minura hugged her son and observed the Roman with a sense of wariness and confusion. He proceeded to instruct a man mountain of a soldier, one Roscius, to invite other villagers into the hut and keep them safe whilst Oppius continued to try and restore discipline to the bloodthirsty pack of soldiers outside.

Manius never discovered whether the raid on the village was ordered by Caesar. Some said the general let his soldiers of the leash, breaking a peace treaty, to send a message out to neighbouring tribes. Others argued Caesar put a stop to the bloodletting, after hearing about the mutinous behaviour. When all the guilty legionaries were rounded up Caesar decimated the group. One in ten soldiers were slaughtered. But, in terms of the villagers, only one in ten survived.

The following afternoon Caesar made an appearance at the village. Manius had already heard the stories about the great Roman who had, against all odds, landed his army on the south-east coast. Some argued he had come to trade, rather than conquer. Manius would later realise that Rome conquered, in order to trade. Some claimed that Caesar would create the same rivers of blood that ran through Gaul. The Roman bribed or threatened a number of tribes in the region to prevent them from uniting against him.

Manius peeped through the throng and stood on tip-toe to catch sight of Caesar. His red cloak billowed in the wind. The general's hawkish eyes took everything in. He was quick to smile, or frown, depending on whether he was pleased or displeased. Caesar briefly stood before the villagers and nodded his head, impassively, as a clerk presented him with a wax tablet, which tallied up their value as slaves. The bloody and bowed souls before him were, at best, livestock to Caesar. If the Roman mourned his father and others in the village, he mourned the profit he had missed out on even more.

Manius would wake, soaked in sweat, from the nightmare - his mind trapped in a vice of grief and trauma. As he lay in bed now the Briton wondered whether, in years to come, if he would similarly have re-occurring nightmares about losing Camilla. Would she be a fond or painful memory? A dream or nightmare?

Dawn. Bars of tawny light shunted themselves through the shutters and reflected off the pair of swords, hung diagonally in a cross-shape, on the wall opposite his bed. The weapons were a legacy from his days as a gladiator. Manius couldn't remember the last time he had held them in his hands, or even given them a second thought. Perhaps he always knew he would somehow use them again however, as every six months he would oil and polish the weapons. Hopefully he would not have to use them again for too long. Manius recalled his conversation with Felix Dio:

"It is likely you will be matched with a beardless wonder. The lanistas like to use us to blood new fighters… We are seldom able to attract veterans or gladiators in their prime, as they want to fight in the big arenas... The gore on your tunic at the end of any contest should not be your own..."

Manius was confident of victory. He had no reason to distrust the fight promoter.

## 24.

Whilst Cassandra's maid attended to her mistress' hair and make-up in a guest bedroom Varro briefed Fronto about his plan to parcel the woman off to his villa in Arretium. Their bones creaked, for different reasons, as they sat on a stone bench in the garden. A fountain, depicting Orpheus dying at the hands of a trio of maenads, murmured in the background. Lucilla had designed and overseen the construction of the fountain years ago. Perhaps the piece was her way of warning Varro not to allow the Bacchante in him to triumph over the poet.

"Have you told the lady of your intentions yet? She seems to be under the impression she will be remaining here," the old man remarked, scribbling away on a wax tablet with a speed and neatness worthy of Tiro, Cicero's famed secretary.

"I will talk to her this morning. Hopefully she will understand. Self-preservation should, quite rightly, eclipse any amorous feelings she harbours for me," Varro argued, as he anxiously played with some dice in his hand and shuffled a little, in an attempt to sit more comfortably on the bench. He often carried the ivory, gold-spotted dice in his hands when he went out into the garden, read in the library or drank in the house. Sometimes he would practise rolling them, as he tried to devise a system of securing the score he desired. Just when he thought he had mastered a technique he would then throw several scores counter to his wishes. Good luck runs through one's hands quicker than sand or water. The corners were becoming rounded and the gold was beginning to fade on the dice. But still he played on.

"Do you think it's for the best, to send her away?"

"I dare say you have known me long enough to conclude that I never know what's for the best. I just want Cassandra to be safe. Even if I break her heart, that will be nothing compared to the pain her husband might inflict upon her, should he find her."

"Should Augustus choose to prosecute the senator, or dispense with justice in some other fashion, then she will be a free woman again," Fronto said, raising a suggestive eyebrow. The old attendant was still optimistic that he could see his master become a husband and father before he died.

"Well you know how I prefer to pay for my women," Varro joked, deflecting any talk of him remarrying. "Now have you secured the funds I will need for later, for Manius?"

"Yes. Hopefully you will return with even more gold than both of you can carry."

"It's unfortunate Manius will have to pay for his woman too. Should his plan somehow fail however, and Camilla's merchant father still doesn't wish to sell his daughter, then I will have to come up with a different approach."

A sly smile enlivened Fronto's features.

"And why, pray tell, are you grinning like an idiot?"

"It's nice to see you thinking of others for a change."

"Enjoy it while you can, because I'm sure it won't last. But if I can have a slight - and temporary - change of heart by thinking of others then you should start thinking of yourself, my friend. I would prefer it if Aelia put a smile on your face, rather than me. The gods only know why, but she likes you. Perhaps I could come out of retirement and compose a love poem, which you could send to her."

"That would be a bold and clever plan, if Aelia were able to read."

"I am determined to make a match for you Fronto, more than even you are determined to see me married I warrant. If needs be I'll drug you with some of Albanus Pollio's theriac, wait till you fall asleep, carry you across the house and leave you in Aelia's bed. She can have her wicked way with you, whether you like it or not. But before that we need to put a stop to Lucius Scaurus' wickedness. After I talk to Cassandra and we finalise arrangements for her departure, I will dictate my report to Agrippa. If the gods are willing, I will then be able to start thinking of myself again and things will be back to normal."

Varro felt a sudden cramp in his hands and the dice dropped to the ground. He noted how they fell.

The Dog throw. The lowest score one could get.

*Just as well I'm not superstitious, thank the gods... At least things can't get any worse.*

The morning sun beat down, like a drum. Rome was sweating. The smell of seafood, freshly baked bread and sweetened wine assaulted his nostrils. The sound of competing hawkers, selling their wares, assaulted his ears. Varro and Cassandra made their way down towards the Forum. Varro wracked his brains for suitably quiet locations where he could tell Cassandra that she needed to leave Rome. Leave him. He was tempted to delay the scene and wait till they got back to the house. There was a corner of the garden he had used before to tell other lovers that their affair should end. But no, he had put off the conversation for too long already. He should tell her before they returned.

Cassandra cast another sidelong glance at Varro. Sometimes he clenched his teeth. Sometimes his features dropped, as if they were about to fall to the ground. She knew something was wrong but didn't want to ask. They had made polite conversation on their walk. But one of the virtues of a good Roman wife was to know when to speak and when to remain patient and silent.

Varro breathed in the hot, dirty air and sucked in the scene. A jaundiced plaster wall was home to a patchwork of graffiti, scrawled by various hands. Although dominated by curse words and insults there was the odd, worthy, satirical comment. Varro was pleased to note quotes from Aristotle and Euripides, among the literary vomit staining the side of the building: *There is no great genius without some touch of madness... Ten soldiers wisely led will defeat a hundred without a head.*

A couple of pot-bellied government officials shuffled past him. Their togas and faces had seen better days. Varro caught a snippet of their bleating conversation:

"We're now overworked and underpaid. Caesar is rooting out corruption against his enemies but turning a blind eye to the greed of his supporters... Thankfully I put some money aside when the going was good, when I was in a position to grease the wheels."

"Aye, I felt more courted than a whore, when I was involved in auctioning off the licences to collect taxes."

Varro passed by his local bookseller and he remembered he had a couple of books on order. He thought about popping in and asking if the copyists had finished their work. The shop's owner, Novius, had been a keen supporter of his poetry over the years (although he couldn't remember the last time the bookseller had sold any of his works). Perhaps he championed me more out of a sense of pity than profit, Varro half-joked to himself. Varro grinned too as he remembered how Novius would always mention if a female fan came in to order a book or ask about the author. *Bless him. In some ways he was my pimp.*

A gaggle of women, accompanied by an army of slaves, entered the marketplace as if they owned it. Their garish stolas, and oversized pieces of foreign made jewellery, scalded the eyes more than the summer sun. Their make-up was applied like cement, covering over the cracks. Some wittered on, or feigned moral outrage, about the latest scandal or affair to come to the attention of their social circle: "She only has herself to blame... She should have kept one eye on her appearance in the mirror and the other eye on her straying husband... Senator Haterius groped me again the other evening. We should band together and say time's up on such appalling behaviour. He is the most beastly man I know. Although hopefully I will see you at the party Haterius is throwing tomorrow. He has contacts with merchants, who will be attending, who import Chinese silks." Others complained about the rising price of avocados, as if the world was coming to an end.

Varro quickened his pace to escape the increasingly vapid and dinful market. He winced slightly as a blister on his left foot burst. He had been on his feet, rushing around, far too much lately. He looked forward to catching up on a week's worth of afternoon naps. Before he had a chance to lament his minor injury anymore he was distracted by Bassos walking towards him. The landlord of the *The Golden Lion* appeared harassed and in a hurry. His nose was beetroot red (in summer he was unable to blame the phenomenon on the cold weather) and his hair was mussed up more than one of his whores, after a busy night up against the headrest.

"Morning, unfortunately I cannot stop to talk," Bassos said, breathlessly, carrying a sack of vegetables over his shoulder. "My wife is minding the tavern. If I'm away for too long my life won't be worth living. Although, once I'm back and suffering her company then my life won't be worth living even more. Remember, we have that new wine coming in from Alexandria soon, which I thought you might like to be the first to try."

The landlord offered his patron a wink, just in case he didn't quite understand his meaning, that the new wine was code for his new whore, Nefertari.

Bassos rushed off before Varro had a chance to reply. His attention was also diverted towards Cassandra, who leaned into him, nestling her head against his arm. Her maid had doused her hair in too much perfume this morning, he noted. Didn't she know how he preferred her natural fragrance? Varro recalled how he enjoyed waking up next to Lucilla - and the first thing he would smell would be the moreish scent of her hair and skin. He missed the fragrance all the more, now that it was gone.

"May we visit the temple? I would like to make an offering to the gods. Either I feel my fortunes have changed and the gods are on my side - or I should offer up some prayers to the gods to secure their blessing and support. Do you pray to the gods too, to win their favour?" Cassandra remarked, hoping that Varro might find her sudden sense of piety attractive.

"I suspect that I'd think even less of the gods, if they were ever on my side," he glibly replied.

"You are all too willing to castigate yourself, even if you do so behind a veil of humour. Ever since I've known you Rufus there has been someone good inside you, trying to get out."

"I've not been trying that hard, it seems. I have certainly come to the realisation that there isn't a great poet inside of me," Varro asserted, less glibly.

Having concluded that the pair were lovers (they were probably being too affectionate towards one another to be married) and wealthy, due to the quality of their clothing, a street performer accosted the couple. He jumped out in front of them as if he were about to rob them.

"Good day to you both. And what a day! The sun is shining up in the sky and in our hearts is it not? The whole world can see that you are in love. Please, would you allow me to sing a song for you, or recite a love poem?"

Varro rolled his eyes and just about prevented himself from yawning. He had encountered such performers before. Their familiarity and enthusiasm for life, whether feigned or genuine, was utterly nauseating.

"How about I pay you twice, not to do either of those things?" Varro said, as he retrieved a couple of coins from his purse and paid the youth.

The slightly bewildered performer gladly accepted the money.

"Are you sure? I am no beggar. I can still perform for you."

"You have done enough, just by not being a mime," Varro proffered, sincerely. He then clasped Cassandra by the hand and led her out of the marketplace.

The couple soon found themselves on a quiet side street - at the other end of which was a temple. Varro resolved that he would tell Cassandra the truth there. He pondered whether it was morally good - or cruel - to tell her the truth. He would tell her that he didn't love her a much as she loved him - if indeed she loved him at all. More so she loved the idea of him, or the idealised portrait she painted in her head of them together. But the image would fade.

Reality is a form of rust. Everything is born to die. The death of his father - and the death of his unborn children - had brought that truth home to him some time ago. Perhaps it is, along with two plus two equalling four, the only truth life has to offer, Varro mournfully judged. Love is born to die, like anything else. No matter how much one invests in any relationship the returns diminish. If the way he felt about Lucilla changed, not even the gods could save them. Varro imagined Cassandra would protest, cry or attempt to seduce him upon hearing what he had to say. Her histrionics, or his sense of guilt, may even provide a stay of execution. But for how long? A week? A month? If she argued that they could and should carry on from where they left off years ago he would agree - and confess how he did not love her before. It was all an act.

*Nothing is real, except death.*

Varro noticed a litter appear out the corner of his eye, carried by a team of brawny, uniformed bearers - their expressions as stern as lictors. The wooden poles, decorated with intricate scroll work, were painted gold. The purple curtains were richly dyed and patterned, replete with tassels. Varro hoped that the occupant wasn't a former, aggrieved, mistress.

The litter slowed to a halt. They were close to the sanctuary of the temple. But not close enough. Varro traded a glance with Cassandra. At first, she smiled - as serenely as a vestal virgin. But then her expression shattered like glass, into shrill distress. The hairs on his neck stood up as Varro heard a shuffling sound behind him. Cassandra opened her mouth. She was about to scream or say something to him. But Varro never found out which. Instead he felt a sharp blow from a cudgel on the back of his head. Darkness enveloped him, like a hood being put over his eyes.

## 25.

"Are you ready?" Felix Dio asked, as he rhythmically squeezed the bulging purse hanging down from his belt. In the other hand Dio carried a rolled-up scroll, containing an account of the profit he was making on the event.

"I'm ready," Manius replied, unceremoniously. He was wearing a leather breastplate with polished bronze bracers and greaves covering his forearms and shins. A gladius hung on his left hip and, behind him, a dagger was sheathed in a metal scabbard. A large, rectangular shield, containing an image of a prancing horse, was propped up against the wall. Manius would be billed as a *secutor*. A chaser. The Briton wryly smiled at the irony, as he planned for his opponent to commit to most of the chasing. He needed to stay on the backfoot – in order to lengthen his odds.

*But is Rufus ready?*

Manius hadn't seen Varro since the morning, when he had left the house with Cassandra. He promised he would be back in time for the contest and to place the wager. But Varro had let him down plenty of times before - being either late, or absent, when they were due to meet. Oftentimes his friend could be found drunk, taking part in one last game of dice or asleep in his mistress' bed. Oblivious to the world. Did he not appreciate the importance of today? It would break the Briton's heart if Varro broke his word. Without the winnings, he couldn't win Camilla.

"Excellent. Excellent. I'll be back soon. The crowd are growing restless but it's good when they start baying for blood. Also, the more wine they drink the more they'll bet on proceedings. We're making a fortune on selling water too, because of the weather. I've doubled the price and no one's complaining. We have a full house out there. I've not even had to tell my men to go out into the streets and sell cheap tickets to the plebs. I'm sure you will give them a good show. You are the climax. I remember your bout with Urbicus. The blood soaked the sand in the arena that day. Just repeat that performance and everyone will go home will a smile on their face."

Dio left, with a jaunty spring in his step, followed by a brace of lumbering bodyguards. Manius started to pace around the windowless room again. He was aware something was wrong - and equally aware that there was nothing he could do about it. He tightened the straps on his armour again, swished his sword around to loosen his arm and cracked his knuckles. The room was growing even hotter, like he was trapped in an oven. A pungent odour of blood and rotting flesh still permeated the air. Manius noted the crimson stains on the wooden table in the corner. A gladiator had recently been treated in the room. Maybe even had died in the room.

He heard the crowd in the background. Occasionally they had erupted in a crescendo of noise - doubtless when an opponent had triumphed or drawn blood. Manius also suspected, given the bursts of laughter and applause he heard, that Dio had arranged for two or more *andabatae* to give battle in the arena. The contest involved two or more gladiators wearing helmets, with their eyes covered, engaging one another blindly and bloodily

Manius recalled the scene outside of the venue, as the spectators entered. A sea of coloured silks and linens, like a polished mosaic, filled the area. Many arrived in litters. Manius was and wasn't surprised at the number of women attending the gory event. Slaves frantically walked beside their masters and mistresses, fanning their faces or filling their wine cups. A couple even tripped up, concentrating more on their duties than their footing. Manius recognised a few faces - sons of senators and aristocrats. Varro had attended the same parties as them, shared the same mistresses. Dio rushed out to greet one or two esteemed invitees. No sooner had they clambered out of their litters than the promoter was bowing and vigorously clasping their hands, as if he were shaking a purse to ensure all the money was falling out. A pack of usurers also accosted some of the young, gaudily dressed young men in the crowd. They were easy prey - and they knew that their fathers would cover their debts. Some considered that it didn't matter in Rome how much money you had, it only mattered how much money you were able to borrow.

The best of civil society eventually entered and took their seats, squawking and braying, as they yearned for one man to butcher another in the name of entertainment.

*A pox on Rome.*

His anger towards his friend slowly but surely turned into worry. Varro knew where Manius was and what was at stake. *He would at least send a message.* Perhaps Agrippa had summoned him. But that still wouldn't prevent him from sending a messenger. Fear suddenly gripped the Briton's being, like talons clutching his shoulders, as he imagined his friend being taken by Lucius Scaurus. But the senator was absent from Rome. Or had the irate Cinna caught up with him again, having not learned his lesson from the other night? Manius felt guilty, having spent half the morning cursing Varro - when he should have insisted on accompanying him on his walk with Cassandra. It was his job to protect his friend.

A trumpet sounded in the background, signalling that the final contest was about to commence.

Honey-coloured sunlight poured in through the open roof. A blast of heat hit him, as though he was back in the ludus again and his trainers were shunting him backwards with army issue scutums. Manius strode out onto the sand covered flooring of the warehouse. The blast of noise from the animated crowd nearly knocked him off his feet too.

Some sat on the rows of wooden benches and stamped their feet, causing the entire structure to shake and grains of sand to shift. Women who would have acted primly outside the arena bared their teeth and licked the lips, either in anticipation of the blood that was about to be spilled or to wipe the wine from their chins. Wagers were made, either hastily or with painstaking forethought. Faces were flushed, either from sunburn or from the copious amounts of wine consumed. People were expecting or demanding a good show.

Manius recalled the last time he had stood in the arena. Afterwards, Appius Varro had changed his life. Manius just hoped that his son was present this time and would similarly change his fortune. He glanced around the sea of people, in a vain attempt to spot Varro. But it was like looking for a needle in a haystack. Even so, out of hope or desperation, Manius also surveyed the crowd, believing that he might recognise Fronto's wizened features. Varro might have sent word for him to place the wager in his absence.

But the gladiator had to shake such thoughts out of his head. He needed to concentrate on his opponent and the task at hand, rather than dwell on Varro, Fronto or even Camilla. *Distractions cause deaths in the arena.*

His palms were slick with sweat, but Manius was pleased to see a converted brazier, filled with chalk. As the gladiator wondered again about who his opponent might be, the crowd provided him with the answer.

"Flamma… Flamma… Flamma," they rhythmically chanted. Raucous cheers, and whistles, pierced the air as, from the other side of the arena, Manius' opponent made his entrance.

*Valerius Flamma.* The swarthy Etruscan had earned his nickname from his custom of heating the blade of his sword beforehand, so the tip glowed. On one occasion he had set fire to the clothes his opponent had been wearing, after he had wounded him, and watched on, in neither triumph nor regret, as the defeated gladiator was burned alive.

Manius issued a cursory glance around the front row of the arena. Dio was nowhere to be seen. The promoter had deceived the fighter, although Dio could and would argue otherwise. Manius realised how Dio had selected his words as carefully, as connivingly, as any advocate. He said it was only "likely" he would fight a novice. But Manius couldn't now cry foul and back out of the contest. The die was cast. He would act honourably, even if others didn't. Manius recalled something Camilla had said to him, during their last encounter:

"You are too trusting sometimes. I worry that you may be too good."

"There are worse things I could be," he responded, shrugging his shoulders.

Camilla replied by smiling and kissing him sweetly on his cheek. She realised he was truer, more real, than any character from Virgil or Homer. She was already proud of him, akin to how a wife should be proud of her husband.

The bug-eyed announcer's bombast words were largely drowned out by the excited crowd as the two imposing figures marched towards each other. Manius had heard of the undefeated gladiator. Flamma was celebrated by the good people of Rome for the entertainment he had provided them with over the years. He was also understandably much loved for money he had earned them, from the winning bets they had placed on the fighter, over the course of his career.

Manius took his opponent in. He was dressed as a *dimachaerus*. His face was gnarled and bony. His eyes were bloodshot, or bloodthirsty, beneath a pair of bushy, russet eyebrows. The hint of a lopsided, disdainful smirk was chiselled into his expression. His large grey teeth resembled small flagstones. The Briton was an insect he had to swat, or a piece of meat he needed to tenderise. Flamma's blubbery bottom lip protruded like an ape's. His pronounced veins ran across his body like rivers marked out on a map. And those were not faded wine stains on his tunic, Manius considered. He briefly recalled a former gladiator in his ludus, Massa – "The Butcher." Massa used to deliberately smear his tunic and weapons with pig's blood in order to intimidate his opponents and live-up to his nickname.

When Manius entered the arena and surveyed the crowd Felix Dio had ducked down in his seat, located in the far top corner, believing that the fighter was searching for him. All had gone to plan, so far. There was no reason why he wouldn't receive his full fee from Aulus Sanga. The merchant had approached him, made him an offer he couldn't refuse, at the beginning of the week. His brief was to persuade Manius to return to the arena.

"Look at it as an opportunity for both you and him to make some money. The principal task is that he fights again, though I would you match him up with an experienced, skilful opponent - one that he is no match for... My reasons are my own for engaging your services... All you need to know is that I will pay you handsomely, should you succeed," Sanga remarked, unable to mask his resentment towards Manius. It was enough that he suppressed his disdain for the unseemly, vulgar fight promoter as he negotiated the terms of the deal with him. Dio would comply, partly because it was his dream to gain enough capital and influence to one day order senators and equestrians about, like servants. He kept a mental record of those who had sneered at him – so that he could one day wipe the smile off their face and wear a satisfied, triumphant expression himself, like a laurel wreath.

Felix Dio told himself he had not acted wholly dishonourably towards the fighter. He had always said there was a possibility that his opponent could be a veteran. Was he not compensating the Briton by paying more than he was to the other gladiators involved in the event (aside from Flamma – whose fee he would recoup from Sanga)? Did he not ensure a competent surgeon was at hand, in case Manius suffered a serious injury? Had he not instructed Flamma to spare his life? Still, Dio shifted uncomfortably in his seat, at having deceived Manius. He told himself he would offer the Briton a second fight - and he would promise Manius he could handpick his opponent. He would even offer him a contract in writing, to guarantee he kept his word. The Briton was an honest fighter and had never give him any trouble, back in the ludus. Surely there was a part of Manius however which realised there were no honest fight promoters? He only had himself to blame, for his greed and naivete.

Dio tried to distract himself from thinking about the Briton by revelling in the success of the event. The crowd was enjoying the spectacle. The wine and blood were flowing. Even the new food menu had been a success. He had come a long way from cleaning out the dormitories at the ludus. *Not bad for a boy from the Subura.* His mentor, Faustus Bursa, would have been proud of him. Although given his behaviour towards Manius, Dio couldn't quite say if he was proud of himself. But he would be compensated for his troubles. Dio would collect his remaining fee from Sanga later in the week. He didn't like the haughty merchant, but if he only dealt with people he liked then the promoter would have been a poor man. When Dio returned home he would make sure to keep his additional income secret from his wife, otherwise she would spend the sum faster than he could count it. *How many pairs of shoes does just one woman need?* He intended to build a new, larger koi carp pond in his garden. His wife despised the creatures and thought them ugly. But the fish relaxed him - and his wife seldom disturbed him while he sat next to the pond. Dio would also use the additional profits from the event to buy a small rhinoceros. The crowd enjoyed it when the fighters took down an exotic animal or two. Maybe he could engineer things however, so the rhinoceros lived to fight another day - and he could get a second payday out of the beast.

"Don't die Briton, otherwise I'll lose my wager. And if that happens my wife will kill me," someone shouted out in the crowd at Manius. A few people who heard the comment laughed, although the gladiator couldn't be sure how much the man who had addressed him was joking or being serious.

Manius plunged his hands into the chalk, wistfully consoling himself with the thought that, given the quality of his opponent, the odds on him winning would lengthen. His heart pounded. His throat was dry, as though he had just swallowed a cupful of the chalk in front of him. In a few short moments he might be wounded, or worse. He couldn't help but note the collection of scars on the back of his hands and knuckles. He remembered how Camilla had kissed them once. Healing him.

The two men stood a spear's length or so away from each other, tightening their grip on their weapons.

"I saw you fight once. You could handle yourself in your day. But your day has past. Even in your prime, you wouldn't be a match for me now. You've come out of retirement, but I'll retire you for good if I have to… Listen to the crowd call my name. They know a winner when they see one… Don't yield too quickly. We need to put on a show. You're just lucky there's not any bonus on the table for if I kill you," Valerius Flamma stated, matter-of-factly. His voice was as hard as obsidian, his stare as baleful and black as an Ethiop's armpit.

Manius remained impassive, as though his opponent were addressing a block of stone. He needed to concentrate - remember all the old tricks of the trade and be on the lookout for any new ones invented during his absence from the arena.

Flamma played to the crowd. He lifted his swords up to them and then pointed them at his opponent. They applauded - and some even howled - in delight. In some respects, they worshipped gladiators like gods when they were in the arena. But others viewed them as little more than slaves. Less than men.

*He's just a man, like you. Not some god… And every man bleeds.*

Varro came to, although on balance he might have wished to remain unconscious. He winced, both at the light screeching through the carriage window and the throbbing pain at the back of his skull. He could feel the breeze kiss the open wound. A radish-sized lump had formed and his hair was matted with blood. Varro felt groggy, like he was suffering with a hangover from Hades. His heart sank but he felt bile rise-up into his throat. Lucius Scaurus sat opposite, a picture of cold malice. Imperious. Reptilian. Cassandra sat opposite too, hunched in the corner away from her husband. Trembling. Blood dribbled down her petal-soft chin from her busted, quivering bottom lip. Her eyes seemed more deep-set in her head, couched in her swollen, bruised and lacerated cheeks. To avoid injuring his hands, Scaurus had instructed Vedius to administer an initial beating to his wife.

As much as Varro might have wanted to roar like a lion he felt as meek as a lamb. Enervated. Drained, as though the world had wrung him out, like a damp cloth. He didn't have the energy to beg for mercy or try to explain himself to Scaurus. His captor would get the truth out of him, sooner or later. Yet Varro desperately wanted to tell Cassandra he was sorry, for everything. He wanted to tell her the truth. And then he wanted to tell her that all would be well, which would have been one last lie.

But before any words could pass through his bone-dry lips Scaurus nodded to Vedius. The grimacing gladiator, sitting next to Varro, curled one of his brawny arms around the prisoner's neck in a choke hold. Varro struggled, for a moment, in vain, before darkness swallowed him once more as if he were caught in the belly of a whale.


Flamma attacked once again. He moved with the fluidity of a dancer. For the *dimachaerus* - armed with two swords rather than a shield - attack was the best form of defence. The Etruscan had already drawn blood. The Briton had suffered a glancing cut on his right arm. Flamma taunted and toyed with his adversary.

Manius just about parried his opponent's flurry of sword strokes. The metallic clash of blades set more than one audience member's teeth on edge. Before the contest it was Manius' intent to pretend to be bested, make his breathing laboured and hide behind his shield whenever possible – with the intent of lengthening his odds. But, ironically, there was no need to pretend. He had to concede that the younger man was slightly faster and slightly stronger than him. Sooner or later he would be in more than a slight amount of trouble.

Flamma's crooked - cruel - grin widened, as he strutted towards his quarry again, believing he could defeat his opponent at will. He conceded that his opponent was good.

*But not good enough.*

"I know what move you're going to make even before you do, Briton."

The dimarchaerus feinted, at twice the speed he had before, and moved inside. The two men came together like stags, about to butt and lock antlers. Manius punched his shield forward but Flamma raised his bracer and not only blocked the blow but forced his opponent backwards. As he retreated the Etruscan roared and slashed one of his blades against Manius' sword. Such was the force of the blow that the weapon spun out of the Briton's hand and the blade snapped in half. The crowd, who often acted as a chorus to proceedings, let out a collective gasp of shock or adulation. Out of the corner of his eye Manius saw one spectator point at him and then run his finger across his neck. The lugubrious fellow next to him shook his head dismissively, as if he were looking at a condemned man. Or a walking corpse.

Flamma raised his swords up above his head and turned to the crowd, celebrating his imminent victory. The gladiator basked in the crowd's veneration, revelling in another triumph.

Sweat dripped down Manius' corrugated brow and stung his eyes. His muscles felt like they were on the cusp of cramping up. It was the first time in his career than an opponent had disarmed him. For a moment he became defeatist. But it was just for a moment. Manius retained a fighting stance and adjusted his shield so he was standing - hiding - behind it. Perhaps he somehow intuited he would be injured - or suffer a worse fate - today. He had clasped Fronto's hand more vigorously than normal - and embraced him fondly - when saying goodbye. He had also given Violet an extra treat or two. But this surely couldn't be the end, the fighter reasoned, because he had yet to say goodbye to Camilla.

*I love her.*

Those three words strengthened his resolve and stiffened his tired sinews. Manius would give himself one last role of the dice. He pulled his arm out of his shield and tossed it on the ground. A few members of the crowd jeered and spat out insults, but most remained eerily quiet, gripped by the drama unfolding before them. The Briton took a few calm, deep breaths – in contrast to his opponent, who panted or seethed.

The two fighters were around a dozen paces apart. Manius eyed Flamma. For once the Briton had the appearance of a man who knew something that his opponent didn't. He even smiled at the ferocious, swarthy Etruscan, as he placed his hands around his back. Flamma scoffed and shook his head dismissively. He had already noticed how his opponent - victim - had a dagger hanging from the back of his belt. He was going to repeat that he knew what his opponent's next move would be before he knew it himself, but instead asked:

"Do you yield, Briton?"

A brace of crows, perched on the beams criss-crossing the roof of the warehouse, cawed, as if asking the same question or looking forward to stripping a carcass.

"No retreat, no surrender," Manius stoically replied, before he whipped his hand round from behind his back and launched a metallic missile at his opponent. Flamma predicted the move however and casually, yet skilfully, swiped his swords across his body and deflected the attack. Yet something felt wrong and the sound was weaker, tinnier to what he expected. A clink, rather than clang, rang out. The gladiator furrowed his forehead and glanced down at the ground at what he thought was a dagger. But it was only a metal scabbard. The blade it housed was currently swishing through the air. It buried itself in the Etruscan's thigh. Flamma cursed and seethed in pain. When he looked up from surveying the wound Manius slammed his forearm guard against his adversary's face, smashing the bridge of his nose. The hulking gladiator crashed to the ground, like a tree being felled. Winded. His eyes were now blood-soaked. One of Flamma's swords slipped out of his hands. His opponent stole the other. Manius pinned the man down by sitting on his chest – and twisted the blade sticking out of his thigh for good measure.

Aside from a few pockets of cheers, no doubt emanating from spectators who had placed a wager on the Briton, the arena fell largely silent. Mouths were agape from shock, or lips were compressed in resentment. They barely blinked, as they sucked in the unexpected scene of the Briton holding the veteran's own sword to his throat.

"Do *you* yield?"

The crows cawed, or laughed, once more.

## 26.

After being informed about who was waiting at his door Marcus Agrippa instructed his attendant to show the bodyguard into his study. Manius couldn't help but note the reception room, outside the study, filled with all manner of petitioners wishing to claw out a moment of the consul's time. He also observed the mound of parchments and work piled-up on the desk. Agrippa had a thousand and one things to attend to but Manius needed to compel the mighty statesman to help him locate and rescue his friend.

Manius breathlessly told the consul everything he knew, trying to marry a sense of urgency with a sense of accuracy. Blood still trickled a little through the stitches of his wound, on his upper arm. After defeating Valerius, Manius did not wait to bask in any applause. He didn't seek out Varro in the crowd or think to confront Dio about collecting his fee. He did however think he recognised a familiar woman's face in the audience but then she was gone - and he thought nothing more of it. A voice, as clear as his own, told him that Varro had been abducted. Scaurus had, or would, torture and kill his friend. That his only hope in saving him was to enlist the help of the man who had put him in danger in the first place. Manius was willing to break down the consul's door and leave a pile of groaning lictors on his tiled floor in order to say his piece.

A thick silence hung in the humid air after Manius finished speaking. A pensive Agrippa commenced to slowly walk around the room. Varro was missing. The Briton had forcefully argued that the new agent had been abducted and that his life was in peril. Agrippa would have preferred hard evidence to supposition however. Varro could just as easily be holed up in a tavern in the Subura, or in bed next to Scaurus' wife, extracting pillow talk out of the woman.

My job is to attend to the fate of Rome, rather than just one man, Agrippa posited to himself as he turned his attention to the intelligence Manius had presented him with. Varro's trip to the senator's residence just outside of Rome had been productive. Insightful. The senator was possessed with motive. Every statesman in the capital seemingly wanted to be the First Man of Rome, aside from perhaps himself. Agrippa had always been content to be the Octavius' lieutenant. Scaurus wouldn't be the first politician in Rome to be consumed by envy, ambition and greed, although no doubt he dressed his desire for power up in the robes of idealism. Scaurus would tell himself that he was Brutus reborn, compelled to defend the Republic against the tyranny of Caesar. But Agrippa was more concerned about the possible tyranny of Lucius Scaurus. He wouldn't be the only statesman to buy a ludus or two, to use as a front whilst building a private army. Clearly the ambitious aristocrat was on manoeuvres too, either buying or selling favours in regards to his senatorial colleagues. Was the money for campaign funds, or a war chest? Yet there seemed to be much more to pick at, if Agrippa was to unravel the full extent of Scaurus' prospective coup. How many senators had he recruited to his cause? And who were they? What was the purpose of staging a play in the capital? Do we not already know how the story of Antony and Cleopatra ended? Tragedy turned to triumph, as Caesar returned a hero – bringing peace and prosperity to all. Questions still needed to be answered too in relation to Varro's belief that Scaurus was intending to put forward another candidate, as opposed to himself, to challenge Caesar.

*But who?*

Agrippa felt like he possessed four fifths of a map, which would lead him to his destination. His head hurt. The careworn consul briefly closed his eyes to shut out the world or focus on the problem. His hair was unkempt and stuck up at the back from where sleep had finally got the better of him and he slept for an hour at midday, after suffering another sleepless night. He knew how impractical and inefficient it was to worry. But worries still plagued him. He had worked on through the night by candlelight, continuing with the arrangements for Octavius' campaign in Spain. It was right that people sometimes recognised that Caesar carried the weight of the world on his shoulders. But few observed how Agrippa often carried Caesar.

The Briton stared at the Roman in hope or expectation, clutching his sword and tapping his left foot. He was akin to a charioteer's horse, champing at the bit to unleash himself. He took in the weapons and armour mounted on the wall, flanked by portraits of the consul's late wife. Pictures of Agrippa's current wife were conspicuous by their absence. Manius licked his dry lips - and his stomach rumbled - as his gaze also lingered on a half-eaten plate of salted ham, soft cheese, ripened dates and succulent grapes.

"I must try and save him," the Briton stated, with a mixture of purpose and desperation. "Because he would do the same for me."

"I know what you would ask of me, Manius. Varro is fortunate to have you as a friend. It is my hope that you will return home and Rufus will be there, sleeping or half-drunk, from having a lost afternoon," Agrippa remarked, sympathetic but not swayed by the bodyguard's plea. Varro would have to be sacrificed for the greater good. For the good of Rome. Agrippa occasionally thought how much blood he had on his hands, from the civil war. One more death would not damn his soul, as a one more cup of water added to the oceans would not cause them to overflow. Also, if there was one thing which Rome had a surplus of, aside from corrupt politicians and unfaithful husbands, it was aristocratic poets. If Scaurus had abducted Varro – *if* – then it was already too late. He would have been tortured and killed by now, surely. His body may already have been buried - or burned. Even if he were to quickly muster a detachment of soldiers, recruited from Caesar's personal Praetorian Guard, he had little chance of finding Varro. Or what if he confronted Scaurus about his suspicions? The senator would be aware of his interest in him - and he and his confederates might retreat further into the shadows. And what if he discovered his agent at the mercy of Scaurus and tried to apprehend the enemy of the state? He had no idea of the size and quality of the senator's forces. He could be outnumbered and outmatched. It was a foolish general who rode into battle without reconnoitring the strength of his enemy and the lay of the land beforehand. *Fail to prepare. Prepare to fail.* Caesar would be displeased, to say the least, if he suffered a defeat in his name. Both consuls would lose a portion of their *dignitas* and *auctoritas* should Scaurus score a victory over them. No, Varro must be sacrificed. He would not die in vain though. If nothing else his death confirmed his suspicions. Scaurus was indeed plotting against Augustus. He was responsible for Verres' murder. He would face justice. Retribution.

It would be too much, too soon, to send out a contingent of soldiers to apprehend Scaurus now. He needed to collect more evidence and extract testimonies from fellow conspirators first. Any charge against Scaurus must be proven beyond a reasonable doubt. It would not do to turn the senator into a martyr. Scaurus should not become a *Gracchus* for the old optimate party, which was buried but not quite dead, to rally around. *Make haste slowly.* In a few days' time he could also arrange for half a legion to descend upon the senator, as opposed to a detachment of Caesar's personal guard. Octavius would also want to be consulted, before moving against his enemy. Agrippa wondered whether he would be surprised by the aristocrat's boldness, after having once dismissed Scaurus as a possible threat: "Lucius will not even merit a footnote in history. He may not even merit a footnote in his own family's history... Self-importance should not be mistaken for importance... The old guard are dying out, or dead. Those that hark back to the old Republic are but speaking in an ever-diminishing echo chamber... Lucius Scaurus will come and go out of this world having barely been noticed, like a flitting shadow." Perhaps Octavius would have a mind to punish Scaurus more for having proven him wrong.

Agrippa was looking forward to having supper with his co-consul that evening. It may have been another reason why he had no yearning to drop everything in order to locate his missing agent. Not only did he need to brief Caesar on some of the logistics and tactics he should employ, during his imminent campaign, but it had been some months since the two men had sat down to dinner alone. Like old times, without the voices of Maecenas and Livia interceding.

Agrippa became slightly distracted from his thoughts by the sound of his wife outside, taking a tour of their grounds with their head gardener. Marcella was asking Helvius whether he could still plant several species of flowers which she thought were pretty - but were either out of season or unable to flourish in the climate.

"I am afraid they will not grow," the gardener courteously, but firmly, explained.

"Plant them anyway," the young woman replied, less courteously but more firmly. Marcella was used to people doing her bidding, without question. After all, she was a Caesar.

Agrippa rolled his eyes, in exasperation or embarrassment, at his young wife. He couldn't quite decide whether she was displaying faith, or stupidity, in believing that the plants would take root and flower. Was Varro's bodyguard embodying a similar sense of faith, or stupidity, believing he could save his friend? He pictured Marcella's expression. Petulant or gormless. Two traits that one could never have accused his first wife of inhabiting.

Agrippa sighed. The world is as it is, not as it should be, the sigh implied. As powerful as the consul was he wasn't all-powerful. Agrippa recalled Theogenes' words again. The astrologer had predicted he would be great but, tellingly, not good or happy. "Perhaps they are incompatible," Octavius had once plaintively argued, shortly after hearing the news that the order to kill Cicero had been carried out. It was one of those rare occasions where Caesar's imperious mask slipped.

Manius' strong chin, which had jutted out in determination when petitioning the consul to find his friend, now buried itself into his chest. Resignation replaced righteousness. He felt scared, helpless, defeated – similar to when, as a boy, he had tried to protect his mother from Tarius. Lucius Oppius had saved him then. *Lucius Oppius.* Or the *Sword of Rome*, as he had been named when he fought in the arena. A spark, lit by a dying ember, appeared, as if god-sent, in the Briton's soul. Manius gave himself one last throw of the dice, again.

"You fought alongside Lucius Oppius, did you not?"

Agrippa's aspect narrowed as he heard the words and wondered why Manius had mentioned the name. Oppius had been more than just a comrade in arms. The centurion had encouraged Agrippa to be a soldier - and mentored him - back in Apollonia. Oppius had taught him swordsmanship, archery, tactics, the burden of command and so much more. The consul was yet to meet a man who could rival his old friend for courage and loyalty. Oppius had first served under Julius Caesar - from his invasion of Britannia to the Battle of Pharsalus. He had then kept his oath to Caesar to keep Octavius safe. Octavius and Agrippa owed Oppius their lives.

"I did," he laconically replied, swaying a little on the balls of his feet, not wishing to reveal how much the veteran soldier had meant to him.

"Lucius Oppius was one of the first Romans I ever encountered. During Caesar's invasion of my homeland our village was attacked by a mutinous group of legionaries. Oppius helped restore order and was responsible for saving my mother and me. The light shines in the darkness - and I can remember his kindness towards me, as if it were yesterday. The following morning, after the attack, during which my father had been murdered, Oppius checked upon my mother and I and spoke to us through a translator. I asked him what would happen to us now? He said that he was too tired to lie to me. That we would be sold as slaves. "But do not despair," he said. "Just because you may be a slave tomorrow that does not mean that you will serve as a slave forever. And even if you are a slave you can still be the noblest thing a man can ever be. You can be honourable." I believe that you still value duty and honour, otherwise you would be conspiring with, not against, the likes of Lucius Scaurus. I have not just come to you because there is no one else to turn to. You are wearing the tunic of a soldier, instead of donning the toga of a politician. Your sword and armour hang on the wall, not some portrait of some pompous ancestor, who was quick to claim glory but slow to join the battle. Honour and hope still, just about, exist in Rome. Rufus can be saved."

Manius let his, or rather Lucius Oppius' words, hang in the air. He knew he was in no position to bribe or threaten the consul. The only option left to him was to try and inspire, or shame, Agrippa into action.

*Be honourable.*

He doesn't give up easily, in or outside the arena, Agrippa thought to himself. He remembered watching the gladiator fight, many years ago. He was both dogged and skilful. He kept moving forward, like a boxer. Bloodied but unbowed. Agrippa suspected that part of the bodyguard's dogged determination now stemmed from the guilt he felt at having been absent from his friend's side, when he was taken. When, not if.

Agrippa turned his back on the desperate man standing before him, either through shame or from wishing to signal to Manius that their meeting had come to a close. Sunlight glinted off his sword on the wall and caught his eye. Agrippa also found himself staring at a portrait of Caecilia. He knew what she would have wanted, expected, him to do.

*Be honourable.*

Agrippa remembered sitting by the fire with his wife one evening, after she had dismissed the servants and cooked him a meal. His features were as taut as a bowstring, as he dwelled upon the death of Cicero and Octavius' assertion - that it was impossible to be both good and happy in this world. Caecilia, noticing that her husband was troubled, asked him what was wrong. Agrippa recounted his friend's words to her.

"Octavius has got it wrong, as much as you may think I'm blaspheming to say such a thing," Caecilia replied, as the light from the purring fire danced in her eyes and gilded her sage expression. "It is not a question of either/or. Goodness *is* happiness. To be good is to be happy... And even if to be good means to be unhappy, it is a price worth paying."

The tension fell from his features and his heart lightened as he kissed his wife and they made love.

Manius was halfway out of the door. But he glanced back after hearing the scraping sound of the consul retrieving his sword from the wall. Agrippa may not have been all-powerful. But he wasn't powerless.

Aulus Sanga gripped his stylus and caressed it with his thumb as he scrutinised a roll of parchment containing his accounts for the month. Costs could always be cut. Margins could always be widened. The consummate merchant ceased working however when he noticed that Milo had entered the room.

The attendant breathlessly made his report. Sanga breathed a sigh of relief. The Briton had taken the bait. He had fought as a gladiator again.

*Once a brute, always a brute.*

A self-satisfied blade-thin grin appeared across his face - wider than what it seemed was natural or possible, as if his face were being stretched out on a rack.

"I am a happy man, Milo. My daughter will now come to her senses and see the Briton for who, or what, he truly is. We can put this unseemly episode behind us. Instruct the cook to prepare some of Camilla's favourite dishes tonight. You can also accompany her to the dressmakers tomorrow. Treat her to whatever she wants, within reason… Do you know the result of the match by the way, not that it matters much? Once he stepped out to fight, he lost. I beat him. Ah, this news pleases me greatly. She may still pine for him for a week or so, although once she has heard how he has betrayed her, lied to her, her sentiments may end as quickly as the affair started. Perhaps we should visit our villa in Etruria, until she is fully cured. This Manius may attempt to contact her one last time. He could prove desperate or violent - so it will be best if we are away from the city… I have no wish to meet with the grubby promoter again. If you could arrange to pay Dio the remainder of his fee. When he shook my hand, to secure our arrangement, I duly washed it, thoroughly, afterwards… The beauty of this outcome is that Camilla cannot hold me responsible for ending or forbidding the relationship. She will spurn the undesirable of his own accord. I cannot be blamed for his faults and barbarous nature. He made his choice to fight again - and will have to respect her choice not to see him. That said, if you ensure you intercept any mail or messengers who arrive at our door. Do not let her out of your sight tomorrow either. I am about to get my little girl back. I do not want to lose her again," Aulus Sanga remarked, pouring himself a measure of wine, to celebrate the good news. His authority would be re-established. Time spent at their villa in the countryside would restore his daughter's health and humour too. She could press flowers, sew and bake honey bread, like she used to.

Sanga rubbed his hands together and thought, for once, that his accounts could wait. He ascended the stairs, up to his daughter's room, mindful of removing the smile from his face and donning an air of sympathy and regret. He started to compose his lines too. He would try and soften the blow. He needed to resist the urge to say, "I told you so." *She needs love, not a lecture.* Sanga didn't want to see his daughter hurt, too much.

"It gives me no pleasure to tell you this Camilla, but…"

## 27.

The air rippled with heat. An unforgiving sun beat down on Varro as he sat, ironically in a birthing chair, waiting to die. It was an even more unforgiving Lucius Scaurus who instructed an all too willing Vedius to beat his prisoner again. The gladiator had targeted the pretty poet's mouth before, busting his lip. The second blow cracked open his nose like an egg. Blood gushed. Tears welled in his eyes. His throat was parched. It hurt when he spoke or swallowed. His eyelids felt leaden, like he was suffering a hangover. The back of his head still ached, like a giant throbbing bee sting.

Scaurus hadn't even begun to interrogate his prisoner yet. The senator just took pleasure in seeing the younger man suffer. Scaurus didn't want to confine the experience to himself however. Varro sat in the birthing chair in the middle of the theatre, surrounded by dozens of gladiators enjoying the spectacle. Some appreciated the respite in their day's training, some enjoyed the raw cruelty on display.

Sharek was also present. He winced at each blow the brutal Vedius inflicted on the man he had, yesterday, called his friend. The theatre director thought to himself what a waste of an attractive face, as opposed to mourning the imminent potential loss of life.

Berenice stood next to Sharek, leaning into him, dressed in a sky blue linen dress which showed off the top of her shoulders - and breasts. The actress was flattered and repulsed by the attention she received from the ogling gladiators clustered around her.

"I liked him. I believed him," she remarked, wistfully.

"I suppose I was right, in saying he would have made a fine actor," Sharek replied, sighing ruefully whilst deciding which vintage he would liberate from his employer's wine cellar that evening - and take into Myron's tent.

A delectable smile danced across Berenice's red, glossy lips. Although tinged with sadness, concerning the fate of the likeable and handsome poet, she couldn't help but be pleased when Sharek told her the news: Scaurus' wife was dead. Berenice knew she would ever play the mistress, never the wife. But with the other woman out of the way she could command more of his attention. Scaurus might even assign some of his late wife's staff to her and grant her first refusal on items from her wardrobe and jewellery box.

Varro remained unconscious whilst Scaurus questioned and tortured his wife in a basement chamber at his villa. She remained in the dank, mold-ridden room still. Her throat cut, using the same ritual dagger Cassius Longinus had used to murder Caesar. Part of her tongue hung out of her mouth, like a dog. Flies began to buzz around the dead woman and landed on her still glistening wounds. Her hand still cradled the silver dove-shaped brooch Varro had given her, when they had first met. The more they tortured her, the tighter she had clasped it.

As soon as the carriage pulled up at the residence Vedius dragged his master's wife down into the basement. Cassandra's appeals for her husband to forgive her, to act mercifully, fell upon deaf ears.

"You must have loved me once," she protested, as Vedius bound her to a chair.

"I loved you like a whore, that I didn't have to pay for. Your only task in life was to become the mother of my children, which you failed miserably at. I blame myself, in part. I should have chosen someone with more noble blood to serve as my wife. You have slop running through your veins," Scaurus responded - telling himself that his wife was already dead to him, before he killed her.

Vedius first beat her, disfiguring her. On more than one occasion, during his time torturing the terrified woman, the gladiator revived her with smelling salts when she blacked out. He stuck hairpins through several parts of her body, including her cheeks and breasts. He cut open her dress and seared her thighs with a branding iron. Scaurus grinned as her skin sizzled. He seemed fascinated by her reactions to different forms of pain, like a scientist conducting an experiment.

Both Scaurus and Vedius interrogated the woman. Cassandra revealed everything she knew, which was enough to condemn her and yet leave her husband unsatisfied too. She told him the details about her affair, how when Rufus had stayed the night she noticed him leave the room and enter his study. How, when she had visited Varro at his home, she had overheard him talking about delivering a message to Marcus Agrippa. Words tumbled out of her bloody mouth like broken teeth.

Once Scaurus had extracted as much information out of his wife as he could he passed the dagger to Vedius and gave the order to kill her, not wanting to do the deed himself and stain his recently laundered toga.

"Where's Camilla?" were Varro's first words to his captor, as he blearily took in his surroundings and attempted to wipe away the blood pouring from his nose.

"It's touching and futile that your first thoughts should be for her, especially when you have enough to worry about yourself. I thought I would widow myself, rather than suffer the ignominy and expense of a divorce. Should you miss your whore though you will see her again anon, in the next life."

Anger welled up in Varro's hobbled heart, but he was too weak, despondent, to leap out of his chair and attack his enemy - although the temptation to grab the knife on the table by the senator and plunge it into his throat was tempting. Unfortunately, Vedius remained close by, wearing a gore-stained tunic and cruel, rictus grin. His odious face was also freckled with blood. Her blood, Varro surmised. No one is wholly innocent in this world - but Cassandra was more innocent than most. He couldn't quite decide whether he felt more guilt than sorrow. All Varro knew was that her death just added to the pain of life. The next world can't help but be preferable to this one, he wryly considered.

"At least Cassandra can take comfort that in the next life that she'll never see you again," Varro asserted.

"She may not be as fond of you, as you think, should you see each other again. You used her, to get closer to me. You were responsible for her torture and death. But she talked, betrayed you, before she died. She told me about your spying - and how you report to Marcus Agrippa. It is a crime against nature for you to turn on your class and the bloodline of your family - and support Caesar, a man intent on destroying the thing that your ancestors held most sacred, the Republic. Your father would disown you. In his absence however, I will disown you," Scaurus remarked, smirking - as he thought again of his plan to have Varro sign over his estate to him, before his death.

The knuckle-faced gladiators around him were legion. Doubtless a number of them welcomed the fact that, for once, it was a member of the aristocracy who was being tortured for the enjoyment of gladiators, rather than vice-versa. If only the audiences to his evenings performing his poetry were as well attended. There were few members of Sharek's company present however (although Varro put that down to their squeamishness and propensity to gossip). It wasn't even worth thinking of a plan to escape. There was none among the crowd who would not put a knife in his back, Varro judged. Even if Manius had worked out what had happened and where he was, he would perish in any attempt to save him. *Manius. May he - and the gods - forgive me for not placing his wager.* At least his friend would inherit a large portion of his estate and he could afford to then marry Camilla, he consolingly thought. Varro closed his eyes and offered up some brief, but heartfelt prayers, for his bodyguard, Fronto and even Viola. He wished them well and asked Jupiter to watch over them. He couldn't remember the last time he had prayed in such a way. Jupiter had probably forgotten all about him. It could be argued that the gods seemed somewhat indifferent to his fate, given his current predicament. But had not Varro been indifferent to the gods, in return, for so many years?

Varro also spared more than one thought for Lucilla. If he could compose one last poem, he would dedicate it to her. He wanted to visit Arretium again with her, even if it was just as friends. He remembered his Horace. *Happy is the man who...* If he could make love one last time, he would make love to her. If the gods did, or could, play matchmaker to their charges then he hoped Lucilla would be granted someone who was worthy of her. He hoped she would marry again. Lucilla had been a wonderful wife. She would make an even more wonderful mother. The world would somehow be a finer place, if she could live on through her children. When Varro had asked himself, during the carriage ride home the day before, what he would miss most about Rome should he be sent into exile - the answer had been pure and simple: Lucilla.

"As you may already be aware, you are not the first agent to attempt to ingratiate himself into my confidence," Scaurus pointedly remarked, standing over Varro. The prisoner welcomed the old man standing in front of him however. He was in the shade and no longer had to squint. "Know that you will suffer the same fate as your predecessor. I got close to Quintus Verres before he could get close to me. I had him followed, as I had my wife followed too. One of our actors here is a trained acrobat and he was able to scale the wall of Verres' building. He let down a rope and Vedius made him wake to a nightmare. Verres died ignobly, blubbing like a child and emptying his bowels in fear. What do you think of that?"

"Shit happens," Varro replied, drolly. Even beneath the blood, swelling and bruising he still retained the remnants of his mocking expression.

The corner of his mouth twitched in anger and he balled his hand into a tight fist but Scaurus' temper simmered rather than boiled over. He wanted to remain calm and collected, superior - and not show any weakness in front of his men or give Varro the satisfaction of riling him.

"You will not be laughing soon. Rather you'll be screaming in agony."

"Then you must be about to bring out a mime act."

Varro told himself that he would try and die with a smile on his face, as an act of defiance towards Scaurus and life itself. Life, which couldn't help but be tragic - because it was so comic.

Varro tasted the metallic tang of blood on his tongue. Out of the corner of his right eye he could see the glowing brazier, containing a branding iron. He also noticed a pair of tongs. His heart shuddered at the thought of being forced to swallow a searing coal and burning to death from inside out. Beneath the blood, swelling and bruising Varro was scared. Pride, rather than courage, prevented him from weeping and begging for his life. His plan was to try and keep Scaurus talking. But all he would be doing was delaying the inevitable. But isn't all life just a process of delaying the inevitable and trying to avoid death?

Vedius moved towards the brazier - perhaps having seen that it had attracted the prisoner's attention - and pushed the branding iron and tongs deeper into the pile of hissing coals. On their carriage ride back to Rome the day before Manius judged that the gladiator was unstintingly loyal to his master. And cruel for cruelty's sake. "Sometimes the arena attracts such animals, and sometimes it rears them."

Lucius Scaurus retrieved his dagger, which had once belonged to the famed and infamous libertore, from the folds of his tunic and wordlessly ran the blade across the top of Varro's brow. His face briefly twisted in spite - and he gnashed his teeth like Cerberus - as the senator lashed out at his adversary. The young nobleman had cuckolded him, pretended to believe in him and his cause. The spy - Agrippa's lapdog - had tried to undermine his dignity and authority. He deserved to die, along with the ungrateful, unfaithful, whore.

Varro clamped his jaw together, suppressing the urge to whimper or scream. He didn't want to give his antagonist the satisfaction. He remained silent, albeit he cursed his torturer with aplomb beneath his breath.

Scaurus handed his weapon to the lanista, who wiped the blood off the blade with his tunic before returning it. The senator seethed for a few moments but then smoothed down his oiled hair, adjusted his toga and forced a polite smile. He wished to give the impression he was still fully in control.

"For as much as you think you may be aware of my plans, you still know very little. I can assure you that I will have the last laugh. Berenice and Sharek told me that you were eager to know how our play ends. The tragedy of Anthony and Cleopatra will end with the revelation that Caesarion escaped his captors. And made his way to Rome. Our "Revered One" will be ensconced in Spain when I make the pronouncement. I will give tickets away for free to the play. Come the night and morning after of the proclamation graffiti artists and posters will have spread the news like wild fire. My men will enter taverns, from the Subura to the Capitoline, to buy drinks and toast the return of the true Caesar. Rumours will abound that Caesarion will offer a donative to every citizen and soldier who swears an oath of loyalty to him. Offerings will be made in temples and people will rejoice at the news that Julius Caesar's son - his true heir - lives. Guarded by his own personal retinue of gladiators, he will stand up and tell his story in every market square and public forum in the city. Prominent statesmen will support his claim. The narrative will be that he has only revealed himself now because he feels it safe enough to do so, with Octavius absent from Rome. Women will want to mother him or offer their daughters to him. He will promise lower taxes (except for the Jews of course) and ban foreigners from leeching off the state. Our slogan will be "For the many, not the few." We will be for the people - and the army - but behind closed doors I will ensure that the nobility will be rewarded. Supporters will be promised favours and given their seats back in the Senate. And at the same time as Rome welcomes its new favourite son I will form a grand alliance, of all Octavius' enemies. Loyal supporters of Antony, Brutus and Sextus Pompey will flock to my banner. Soldiers can be bought like whores, as when Octavius purchased their loyal support from Antony. When he returns from Spain it will be too late. I will win the propaganda war - and any other war. I will tear his statues down, grind them into dust or re-cast them into monuments to Cicero and Cato. Caesar's defence, that Caesarion is an imposter, will involve him confessing to the crime that he murdered an innocent boy. Such villainy will not engender him to the people. His crown will slip somewhat. But by then I would have circulated evidence, timelines and testimony that Caesarion is who he says he is. If the gods are willing I would have Octavius stand - or kneel - before me. I will remind him of my father, who died fighting for the Republic at Pharsalus - and my son who fell at Phillipi. And then, clasping the same dagger Brutus used to slay Julius Caesar, I will look my enemy in the eye and plunge it into the would-be king's breast. Rome and history will remember my name."

Lucius Scaurus puffed out his chest as he finished speaking, perhaps envisioning the sight of a defeated Augustus beneath him, or the Senate House granting him an ovation. He was a little breathless, as if sexually excited by his machinations.

Varro was silenced from disbelief, or dread. The old, embittered senator was either mad or a genius. He imagined rioting in the streets or another civil war. The new dawn of peace and prosperity in Rome could prove a false dawn. It was possible that he had failed in his assignment. His father's shade would still not witness him doing something for the good of Rome. The asset had proved a liability. The truth had even been staring him in the face at one point, as he realised that the adolescent accompanying Berenice had been the pretend Caesarion. He had even reminded Varro of busts of the young Caesar, but he had been distracted, blinded, by the actress' beauty. What was between his legs had addled what should have been in his head yet again. Only now, when it was too late, did the virgin spy conclude that the map he discovered in Scaurus' study traced the timeline and journey of Caesarion's route from Alexandria to Rome. Only now did he realise that the interviews Scarus conducted with Antony's attendants had been an intelligence gathering exercise, so as to make his actor's performance all the more convincing. If he could have only put all the pieces together earlier. He could have prevented a catastrophe. Agrippa could have strangled the coup before it had a chance to draw breath. Octavius would have murdered Caesarion behind closed doors, again. Augustus had intimated on more than one occasion how he wanted a Caesar to succeed him. How right he could be, but not in the way he imagined.

"You underestimate Marcus Agrippa," Varro muttered, croaked - his voice becoming as broken as his body and spirit.

"No, Agrippa underestimates me," Scaurus countered, more forcefully. "Sharek has created his masterpiece. He has schooled our prized actor daily. Groomed him. Cleopatra herself would not be able to tell the difference between her own son and our Caesarion. We have familiarised him with his history, made him read the right books and endowed him with the right customs and clothes. I have spent the past year procuring certain documents and possessions that will further authenticate our narrative. I concede that not all the people will believe or embrace our story. But enough will. The world wants to be deceived, Rufus. So let it. I have faith in my plan."

"Man plans. The gods laugh," Varro asserted, not quite altogether broken yet.

## 28.

Beads of sweat ran down his mulched-up countenance, causing the blood trickling into his mouth to taste even more brackish. He trembled every time Vedius came near him and tried to escape out of his chair. But he was held down by two of the lanista's cohorts. He writhed in utter agony as Vedius cut open his tunic and rested the red-hot branding iron upon his stomach. His flesh melted like butter. A filthy rag was stuffed in his mouth to muffle the screaming.

Varro welcomed death. Life had already felt like it had been prolonged for too long. He wanted the torture to be over. Life was cruel. Life was an exhausting act. *Nothing is real, except death.* Death would be a relief. Death was peace. It would allow him to catch up on all the sleep he'd missed. Varro recalled a quote from Socrates and clung to the words like a rock in a storm.

*"Death may be the greatest of all human blessings."*

"I gave you the opportunity to honour your bloodline and support our cause. But you chose to side with Caesar. You will understand that I will need to know what information you have passed on. Vedius would prefer it if you resisted somewhat, as it means he will get to enjoy himself even more, but I would prefer it if I spilled as little as your noble blood as possible. I also promise I will be merciful, once I am satisfied," Lucius Scaurus cordially remarked.

"You're too kind," Varro replied. A scab opened-up on his lip as he wryly smiled at his own joke.

A vexed Scaurus screwed his face up in displeasure. He still hadn't quite broken the doomed spy. But he would.

"Take his eye. Turn it to jelly. The traitor won't see the funny side of things then."

Vedius didn't wait to be asked twice. He removed his knife from the brazier. Varro's terror seemed to feed the torturer's sense of amusement. If he was a dog the gladiator would have wagged his tail and panted in response to his master's command to fetch out the prisoner's eye. It was at the point where the tip of the blade touched the skin that the spy would confess everything, sell-out his own mother. Everyone talked in the end. But Vedius would finish the job, even if Varro babbled out the truth like a gushing fountain. The lanista gave a nod and the two gladiators, either side of the captive, held Varro down. The poet struggled in vain, wriggling like a worm on a hook. Varro knew that he had no chance of begging for his life. He promised himself that he would kill Scaurus if he somehow got the opportunity. Not for the good of Rome. But for himself. Or for Cassandra.

The blood-stained blade, glowing at its tip, loomed large in his vision. Varro could smell the garum on his torturer's breath and feel the heat of the weapon close to his skin. He turned his head away, clenched his teeth shut his eyes. Courage had gone. Faith gone. Pride gone. Sense of humour gone. He wanted to die rather than live, before the heated blade scooped out his eye like an oyster from its shell. He shuddered, as though a snake made-out of ice was slithering along his spine.

Vedius' grin grew wider as the knife slowly but edged towards its target. The torturer was enjoying himself. He would wait until his victim had recovered somewhat - and then squeeze the eyeball between his fingers in front of him. Varro heard a couple of gladiators snigger and mock him in the background. Trauma vice-lie gripped his bones. Varro was now more fear than flesh.

His heart pounded in his chest, as if trying to escape. The pain would break him. Perhaps just the thought of the pain had broken him. The sensation of the blade slicing through the delicate skin. The eyeball being cut or wrenched from its socket. And that would only just be the beginning of the interrogation. What could he do or say to end things? He could no longer picture Fronto or Lucilla in his mind's eye.

But the skin beneath his eye remained unbroken. Whether other parts of him remained unbroken was another matter. A feint breeze cooled his cheek, as the heated blade seemed to withdraw. Varro heard a number of the surrounding gladiators murmur and mutter, their weapons and armour clinking as they moved, en masse. He dared to open his eyes.

It's always darkest before the dawn.

Varro was not the only occupant of the theatre who stared, squinted, at the solitary figure entering their midst – his gladius drawn. All eyes were on Manius. The crowd of gladiators had parted so that Scaurus and Vedius could observe and address the Briton. If he thought his voice would have been strong enough Varro would have instructed his friend to save himself, although he would have welcomed a drinking companion to join him in the next life.

Manius pointed his weapon at Vedius. Challenging him. Goading him.

"I'm here for our practise bout. If I win then I get to take my friend home. But if I lose then you get to wipe this Briton off the map," Manius issued in a voice wrought in iron.

Vedius nostrils flared, like a dragon about to snort fire. He first turned to his employer. Scaurus gave him permission to reply. The rancorous senator gave the warrior the nod, to approach and butcher their unwanted guest. The patrician thought the bodyguard a fool, or drunk. He had complete confidence in Vedius to defeat the Briton but should he somehow best his opponent Scaurus had no intention of honouring his word and letting him - and Varro - leave the theatre alive.

Vedius drew his sword and purposefully strode towards his adversary. He had no intention of losing face in front of his men and shirking from the challenge. He would brutally dismember his opponent - cleave his arms off his torso - and then finish him off. Perhaps he would force him to witness the torture and demise of his friend first. A few of his men offered him words of encourage but Vedius didn't need their support to help gut the man in front him. The dead man walking.

Sharek's eyes were stapled wide open, as he took in the unfolding drama. Along with the lascivious actress beside him, he duly admired the muscular forms on display. Berenice called for her wine cup from her slave boy again and applauded the spectacle, as though the two combatants were about to fight over her.

Manius checked his advance, not wanting to wholly enter the belly of the beast and be enveloped by his enemies. He wanted to be out of range of a *hoplomachus* stabbing him with his spear, or a *retiarius* entrapping him in his net.

Manius couldn't help but notice the sour-faced Bulla within the congregation of gladiators giving him looks like daggers. His eyes bulged in unadulterated malice, as he looked forward to Vedius filleting the man who had unfairly defeated him. It would be revenge by proxy. Which would be satisfying enough.

*Keep your distance. Let him come to you.*

The two guards who had held Varro down had let go of their prisoner. They had shifted their attention towards the imminent contest. Scaurus too had turned his back on his captive. Varro was too weak to try and escape however. All he could do was pray for his companion - and hope that he could defeat as many of the enemy before they could kill him. Manius shouldn't have come. He was too honourable.

Vedius sliced his sword through the whistling air and launched a gobbet of phlegm into the sand. He filled his lungs and puffed out his barrelled chest, a picture of confidence. Or arrogance. Yet victory was assured. Even if his opponent somehow got the better of him his men would intervene and cut the Briton down.

Manius' sword weighed heavy in his hand. His mobility was limited. His thighs burned and were stiff from the long journey on horseback. The bout earlier, against the formidable Flamma, had taken a lot out of him. Blood and puss still oozed from the wound in his shoulder, which further stifled his movement. But he couldn't afford to show fear or weakness - and stifle his performance.

"You know you can't save your friend," Vedius raspingly issued, as the two men stood around half a dozen paces from one another.

"Maybe this is not about saving my friend - but about damning you."

"And how will you do that?"

"By taking your advice. You can't fight honourably in the arena and expect to live," Manius coolly remarked, and knowingly smiled.

Should Vedius have now had an inkling of his opponent's plan he had no time to prevent the springing of the trap. The arrowhead punched through his back, punctured his heart and protruded out of his chest. Blood flooded his lungs. It was a testament to his strength and will that he remained standing. But not for long. For good measure Manius quickly jabbed his sword into his throat, as if he were back in the ludus again and stabbing the head of a wooden sword post.

Further arrows - and pilums - swished through the air, scything down the enemy. The diversion worked. Whilst the gladiators concentrated on the scene of Manius challenging Vedius to a fight Agrippa's small force climbed the walls of the rear of the theatre and stealthily took up their positions. Agrippa was to give the signal to attack by shooting the first arrow.

The consul briefly thought to himself that Oppius would have been proud of the shot, which had skewered the gladiator closing in on Manius, having first introduced Agrippa to a bow many years ago. *The harder you practise, the luckier you get.*

Manius had been impressed by the speed with which Agrippa formed his plan and the proficiency of the way he mobilised the Praetorian Guard. His orders were clear and forceful, albeit Manius had his doubts that he would be able to pull off his ruse.

"What about if I walk out before them and I am cut down straightaway?"

"That's a risk I'm willing to take," Agrippa drily replied.

Every one of the soldiers knew their job, whether he was armed with a bow, gladius or spear. The first volley of missiles decimated the enemy and caused havoc in their ranks, scattering them like a colony of insects under attack. Or they ran around, like cats with torches attached to their tails. Groans and shouts clotted up the air. Not only did Agrippa utilise the advantage of surprise, but he instructed his men to resist engaging the gladiators in close combat. They needed to retain the higher ground, rather than play to their opponents' strengths. Those with spears and swords were directed to protect the bowmen should the enemy attempt to storm their high positions.

Arrows and spearheads rained down and thudded into torsos. After the second volley the gladiators no longer outnumbered the Roman soldiers (veteran fighters from the civil war). After the third, the living tripped over the dead. With Vedius gone - their head cut off - the body of gladiators lacked purpose and cohesiveness. No orders were given to form defensive positions or coordinate a counterattack. The battle became a massacre. The first instinct of a gladiator is just to survive and live to fight another day, by any means necessary. Some lay down their weapons and surrendered, some routed and scurried past Manius through the entrance to the theatre.

A few of the veteran fighters managed to muster themselves - and launch a spear into the enemy - but not many.

A cluster of arrows poked out of the pot-bellied Sharek, as if he were a pincushion. A confused, contorted expression shaped his features. One of the last things that had gone through his mind was a sense of outrage, that the soldiers could have mistaken his person for a brutish gladiator. He was a genius. He should be spared, he considered - as the first arrow lodged itself in his sternum.

Berenice took better possession of herself than her shrill director as she ran towards a group of the enemy occupying the right side of the theatre. She raised her hands and projected her voice as powerfully as she ever had done in the past, on stage.

"Please help me. I am being held captive."

Suffice to say the actress was not short of soldiers who volunteered to break-off the fighting to protect the beautiful woman in distress.

Scaurus wanted to call to his men to protect him, but he couldn't remember their names. They were little more than slaves. He felt like running too but he knew his legs would give way if he did. Or perhaps naked fear rooted him to the spot. Scaurus' world was crumbling around him. Turning to ash. His features - and chest - tightened. He felt the air thin - or choke him with the sand kicked-up from the fighting. The senator could always re-group in the future. Self-preservation was sovereign now. He would surrender. He would be treated honourably. He would survive.

As Scaurus turned to surrender himself to the closest group of soldiers he found himself face-to-face with his prisoner, having raised himself from the birthing chair. He winced and recoiled from the crimson countenance in front of him. Varro could hear Agrippa calling his name in the background, ordering him to stand down. To run to safety. But another voice called to him. His own. Reminding him of his promise. Varro mustered what strength and speed he could. With one hand he grabbed his enemy by the folds of his toga, with the other he snatched Scaurus' dagger away from him.

"History won't remember your name. No one will. You don't even have a wife to mourn you. But who's to blame for that?" Varro exclaimed, before plunging the ritual blade into the senator's chest and letting him fall to the ground. The reign of Lucius Scaurus - and Caesarion - was over before it began.

Agrippa sighed, as he watched Varro stab the enemy of the state. He would have liked to question Scaurus, extract from him all the information and names linked to the conspiracy. He believed he had worked out the nub of his plot though. When Manius asked who he thought the senator would put forward as a candidate to challenge Caesar, Agrippa replied that "only a Caesar could challenge Caesar". At the same time, he recalled the map, in Scaurus' study, which Varro had flagged up to him. The only other map he had come across, tracing the same wayward route from Egypt to Rome, had been found in Alexandria, amongst the possessions of Caesarion. Octavius had tasked Agrippa personally to carry out the murder of the boy who could one day grow-up to oppose him. For once however Agrippa could not bring himself to carry out his duty - and he paid a loyal centurion to kill the child. When he returned to Rome Caecilia asked her husband if he had any knowledge of or involvement in the dreadful crime to murder the innocent boy. "No," he steadfastly remarked. Lying. Again.

Perhaps Octavius was now being punished for his sins. Caesarion was coming back to haunt him. Rome might be split in two, should Scaurus be able to convince enough of the empire that the son of Julius Caesar and Cleopatra lived. Both old and new wounds would open-up. After confronting such a scenario Agrippa kicked his heels into the flanks of his chestnut mare and drove his men on to reach the theatre in time.

Agrippa sighed in relief more than sorrow. The battle, if it called be as such, was over. Corpses littered the stage, like the final act of a Greek tragedy.

Thankfully only a few of his own men appeared injured or slain. But a few was still too many.

Agrippa managed a semblance of a smile however as he noticed Varro and his bodyguard greet one another. He couldn't quite be sure if they had embraced, or if Varro had collapsed into his friend.

Tears welled in Varro's eyes, but tears of gratitude rather than trauma. He was still in shock. Despite the oppressive heat, a chill hung around his shoulders like a shroud. But Varro hadn't been completely broken. When Manius asked him if he needed anything, he replied:

"I could use a drink."

Manius couldn't quite tell if his friend's eye had closed because of the swelling, or because he winked.

## 29. Epilogue

Agrippa was still able to meet his co-consul for dinner that evening, albeit slightly later than scheduled. Supper was at Caesar's residence. It was a modest sized house as opposed to palace, which sometimes surprised people. Agrippa thought to himself how he could have been having dinner at a farmer's cottage, such was the lack of ostentatiousness and simple cuisine (grilled sea bass with fresh vegetables) on show. Caesar was comfortably the richest man in Rome. So he felt no need to prove it.

Agrippa couldn't be quite sure if the First Man of Rome was "happy" or led "the good life" (perhaps he had too much blood on his hands as well for that), but Octavius seemed content of late. The civil war was over. Work was rewarding rather than irksome. Caesar was devoted to the glory of Rome – or the cynics might say, the glory of Caesar. But to his mind the two things were indistinguishable. Octavius also enjoyed family life, as much as he could with the family he'd been given. "I have the love of a good woman," he had remarked to Agrippa the other month. "Thankfully I have the love of several mistresses too."

The two friends sat around the dinner table. A small fire hummed in the background and half a dozen candles further illuminated the scene.

Agrippa noticed how Octavius' hair had grown a little fairer during the summer but was still darker to that of when he had first encountered him as a clever but slightly diffident youth. Caesar's complexion was smooth and paler than most, as he was still in the habit of wearing a wide-brimmed sunhat when out during the afternoon. His eyes were blue, but more cordial than cold nowadays. His nails were manicured but stained with ink, from where he had been working all evening, answering correspondence and signing official documents. His tunic was plain and freshly laundered. The garment had been woven by his sister, Octavia.

Agrippa didn't believe in Caesar because he was a demi-god, but rather because he was a man. Agrippa had known his friend to be both unsure of himself and too sure of himself. He had stood by him when Caesar exhibited moral courage as well as physical cowardice. He read widely but wore his learning lightly. He was earnest in his ambition, to turn Rome into a city of marble, where once it had been a city of rubble. Agrippa had never regretted the oath he made to his companion, many years ago, on Apollonia. He gave Octavius his sword. Caecilia had warned him, a year afterwards however, that Caesar would never allow him to sheathe it again. "He will never stop asking you to do your duty. And you will never stop offering to do so, even if duty means dishonour." His wife had been right, again, of course. Both men had committed crimes during the civil war which they would have liked to see erased from history - and their conscience.

Agrippa spent most of the evening briefing Caesar about the events of the afternoon - and the conspiracy his agent had uncovered. His co-consul remained calm and collected in response to the dramatic news. He only interjected occasionally on certain points of interest.

Perhaps Octavius was becoming a man at peace, Agrippa judged, as Caesar decided to spare the life of the actor who was due to play Caesarion.

"We already silenced him in Alexandria. It would be over-kill to execute Caesarion again... As to the rest of the company of actors you can provide them with the necessary funds to travel back to Egypt. Their passage should be one way. It won't be just the critics who have their knives out for them if they return. Some performers die on stage. If you warn them that they will die before they even complete rehearsals, should we hear wind of them putting on the "Tragedy of the Antony and Cleopatra," Caesar drily remarked, his voice as clear and sharp as glass. "Scaurus bit off. more than he could chew, which still won't put off other candidates who long to eat at our table, Marcus... It was a calculated risk to confront Lucius as soon as you did, but you had your reasons. If you continue to investigate and gather intelligence. We must unweed our garden, root out any co-conspirators... As for Varro and his bodyguard please pass on our sincerest thanks. We are in their debt. Varro has been a victim of his own success however. We may have use of him again, in the future. Livia is friends with his ex-wife, Lucilla. Despite her divorce to him she considers Varro capable of great things. He just doesn't know it yet, she said... At the very least he has good taste in women. What do you think of the man?"

"He has potential. He has become a better agent than he is a poet, which admittedly was not too difficult."

"Let us just allow him to rest and recuperate. For now... You must get some rest too, my friend. You will have an even greater workload once I leave for Spain. But Rome is in safe hands, I warrant. If anyone else attempts a coup in my absence make sure it turns out to be a bloody one, for them," Caesar half-joked.

The following morning Augustus instructed his personal surgeon and doctor to call on the patient. Aside from his nose being a little out of joint and suffering the legacy of a scar on his forehead (which would be largely concealed by his fringe) time would heal most of Varro's wounds.

He slept for most of the rest of the day. When he woke his nostrils were filled with the once familiar fragrance of Lucilla's hair and skin. For a fleeting moment, Varro believed he had woken to a dream. She was a sight for sore eyes. Ringlets of hair hung down, framing an elegant yet concerned countenance. She had been crying. Lucilla was sitting on a chair next to his bed, her hand gently clutching his. A pair of onyx inlaid gold earrings, which he had gifted to her when they first met, glinted in the lustrous afternoon sun. Varro had forced a smile for other visitors, but not her.

"Thank you for coming. I didn't know you cared," he said, his voice more playful than croaky.

"You still don't. I came to call on Manius to give him his winnings, from the wager I placed yesterday. Fronto sent me a message yesterday morning. I thought Manius was worth investing in. I even attended the bout. And I thought women could be cruel to one another! I have just given him his share of our winnings. I thought the money should go to a good cause, if love is a good cause."

His smile widened, even though parts of his face ached as a result. Varro wanted to tell the woman that he still loved her. But didn't.

"I didn't know you considered love to be a good cause."

"You still don't," Lucilla replied, unable to suppress a sly, or even flirtatious, smirk. "I made sure I won some money myself though. I cannot go on spending yours indefinitely."

"Now that's a cause that I could get behind."

"I just hope the sum is sufficient to win, or buy, Aulus Sanga's blessing. I suspect Manius may still have more chance of finding an honest politician - or an honest poet - than of Sanga permitting his daughter to marry him."

"Don't worry, I have a plan. I'm going to make Sanga an offer he can't refuse."

"It seems you are turning into quite the hero. I would be wary of making too positive an impression on Caesar however. You may live to regret it."

"I warrant I am already regretting it. I may have to ask you to denigrate me in front of him, take the lustre off my achievements."

"How do you know that I haven't done so already?"

Varro emitted a laugh, despite it hurting to do so. A poignant, tender expression then replaced the usual mocking one which shaped his features.

"I'm grateful for you calling on me, Lucilla. Thank you. And I'm sorry."

He wasn't sure if she squeezed his hand first or he squeezed hers.

"For what?" she answered, slightly confused.

"For everything," he replied, meaningfully. "I'm intending to travel to the villa outside Arretium soon. I could use some peace and quiet. I thought you might like to join me. Just as a friend," Varro tentatively remarked, wanting to lift her hand to his lips and kiss it. But he thought better of it. He didn't want to ruin the moment or their friendship.

"Well it seems you have made someone else an offer they can't refuse."

Later in the day, while there was still a slither of daylight remaining, Varro mustered the strength to arrange for a litter to take him to Aulus Sanga's house. He snuck out as Manius lay asleep.

Sanga first paused but then agreed to meet with his unexpected guest when a slave told him who was at his door. No doubt Varro wanted to petition him to allow his bodyguard to meet with his daughter. He would, politely or otherwise, refuse the request. The merchant decided to neither pander nor be overtly rude to the nobleman. He would merely tolerate him and greet him with a face that looked like he was chewing a wasp. Should Varro have somehow uncovered his involvement with Felix Dio then he would feign offence and ask him to leave.

Varro entered his host's reception room. A quick glance around at the décor made Varro conclude that the merchant had more money than taste (a common occurrence in Rome). Sanga was understandably taken back by his visitor's countenance, mottled with bruises and laced with cuts. He couldn't help but stare.

"Excuse my appearance. If you think I look bad, you wouldn't want to wake to the fate of who did this to me."

Aulus Sanga was caught between being curious and not caring about his guest's well-being - and the story behind his injuries.

"Would you like some wine?"

"No thank you, I am afraid I cannot stay too long."

"Should you be here to intercede for your bodyguard, then I am afraid you have had a wasted journey," Sanga remarked, with a thin veneer of civility. "I knew your father – and I will duly respect your rank Rufus Varro. But I hope however that you will duly respect my position - and allow me to forbid my daughter to see your attendant, who has proved himself to be little more than a savage. The law is on my side in this matter, as I am sure you will concede."

Varro sighed a little, after yawning, as he took the weight off his feet and sat down. Or he offered up a sigh in response to his host's attitude.

"From what I have experienced of noblemen in the past few days, I might prefer to be courted by a savage. But to the matter at hand. News travels fast in Rome, as you know. People will soon hear rumours of a failed coup, involving Lucius Scaurus."

Sanga held his nerve upon hearing the name of the senator. He tried his best to convey that the name and news meant nothing to him. But he tried too hard. The shrug was too pronounced, the lips were too pursed.

"I am pleased to hear that any coup was hindered. I fail to understand why you are giving me forewarning of this news though," the merchant replied, his heart beginning to canter and then gallop as he worried that Scaurus or an ally might have implicated him in the conspiracy. All he did was contribute to the senator's campaign fund, in return for favours and contacts to help him in his business dealings. Sanga was going to ask his guest again if he wanted a cup of wine, mainly because he now craved one himself.

"Forewarned is forearmed. I am in possession of certain information and evidence linking you to the coup. I also have the ear of Marcus Agrippa, who will be keen to prosecute anyone who called Scaurus a friend. You are a successful merchant and are well versed in negotiating - and knowing whether you are in an advantageous position, or otherwise. I wish to make a trade. Marcus Agrippa will not hear of your name, in connection with the coup, but in return you must give your blessing should Manius and Camilla decide to marry."

The colour drained from Sanga's pinched expression, either from dread or from the shock of suffering such insult.

"Are you attempting to blackmail me, Rufus Varro?"

"No. I like to think I'm succeeding in blackmailing you. I have no qualms about informing the authorities that Scaurus confessed you were an ardent supporter of his - and resided at the heart of the conspiracy. You may hire the most expensive advocate in Rome and cite that you have the law on your side.

But I will have Caesar on mine. You well may be wondering whether Caesar, not known for his clemency, will take your life or your capital. I suggest he will take both. I have little doubt that you wish to here protest your innocence. But I am too tired, weary, to listen. What isn't in dispute, as far as I'm concerned, is that you are guilty of wronging my friend."

Aulus Sanga looked like he was chewing on two wasps. Anger was rising-up in his throat, like bile. But the thought of suffering Caesar's displeasure tempered his reaction. He would have to swallow it.

"You have no honour," the merchant asserted, albeit his tone already conveyed a sense of capitulation. The merchant didn't want to countenance being tortured and executed, or no longer being able to balance his books.

"That may well be the case. But you will be pleased to know that your future son-in-law is the most honourable man I know."


The following night Marcus Agrippa called upon Varro. He was sitting out in the garden, along with Manius, and he invited the consul to join him. Varro had also asked his estate manager to join him earlier too. But Fronto had other plans.

"I have arranged to have supper with Aelia. If you can write a second act into your life, I figure I can too. Suffice to say, please don't wait up for me."

Agrippa took a seat, after handing his host a jug of wine.

"A gift from Caesar."

"Thank you."

As fine as the vintage is, I hope Caesar doesn't now think we are somehow even, Varro mused.

The evening air was balmy and fragrant with flowers - and the even more welcome aroma of garlic infused roasted pork. A cloudless sky was studded with stars and, aside from the sound of a man vomiting behind the garden wall, Rome seemed at peace.

Viola nuzzled Manius' leg as a prompt to feed her another piece of meat. The dog had spent the previous evening sleeping in Varro's room. Partly because she was worried about him. But more so Manius had spent the night with Camilla - and they locked his bedroom door. Aulus Sanga had a change of heart and it had nothing to do with Manius' change in fortune. The gods do work in mysterious way, the bodyguard thought to himself.

"Are you healing well?" Agrippa asked his agent.

"I've felt better. As a poet I played the tortured soul. But now I know what it really feels like however, I wouldn't wish the experience on anyone."

"Your father would be proud of you, Rufus. But I would rather you were proud of yourself."

"Maybe I will feel proud of myself later, after another measure or two of this vintage. But thank you."

## End Note

It was fun to write Blood & Honour. I hope readers enjoy the book, at least half as much as I enjoyed writing it. The book came about because I wanted to write something slightly different, with a new set of characters. But at the same time I was drawn to writing about Augustus Caesar and Marcus Agrippa once more. I hope I have satisfied fans of the *Augustus* books and *Sword of Rome* series. But I similarly hope I have pulled in some new readers.

Should you be interested in some further reading, both fiction and non-fiction, I can recommend the following. *The Roman Revolution*, by Ronald Syme. *Augustus: The Life of Rome's First Emperor*, by Anthony Everitt. Caesar's Spies, by Peter Tonkin. And Steven Saylor's *Roma Sub Rosa* series.

Should you have enjoyed this book, or others written by myself, please do get in touch via richard@sharpebooks.com

Rufus Varro and Manius will return in *Spies of Rome: Blood & Vengeance* https://www.amazon.co.uk/dp/B07L4XY6NW

Richard Foreman.

**Blood & Vengeance**

**Richard Foreman**

RICHARD FOREMAN

First published in 2018 by Sharpe Books.

*"Nothing exists except atoms and empty space; everything else is opinion."*
Democritus.

*"Death is the only water to wash away this dirt."*
Euripides.

## 1.

A platinum moon hung in the sky like a polished brooch pinned upon a black, silk dress, studded with diamonds. It was the dead of night. The taverns had long turfed out their drunks and the early morning shift-workers of bakers and tanners had yet to stir. Even Rome slept for a couple of hours each night.

But Rufus Varro and his mistress, Cornelia, were still awake. A film of sweat covered her smooth skin, like a glaze on porcelain. The sheets on the bed were crumpled. A smell of wine and perfume fluttered around in the air like moths in a courtship dance. The lovers lay in bed, tired and satisfied in equal measure.

Nestled so close to him, Cornelia could see the long, thin horizontal scar which ran across the top of his forehead, beneath the black curls of his fringe. She had noticed the scar before and was curious as to what caused it but had been too hesitant to ask. Now Cornelia believed she was close enough to him to pose the question. The scar was part of him. She would duly accept and love it, like every other part of him.

"Tell me, how did you get your scar? You don't have to say anything, if you don't want to. I don't mean to pry," the woman remarked, prying, as she sensually ran her long fingernails down his chest.

"A year ago, in a fit of boredom, I decided to test my mettle by fighting as a gladiator. I trained for several months and a lanista arranged a bout for me - sufficed to say the contest wasn't to the death - at a small arena just outside of Capua. I won the fight, but not before my opponent left me with a memento of the experience. Whether due to my near miss, or that I scratched the itch of testing my courage, I refrained from stepping foot in the arena again... Obviously you get my blood pumping, but there are times when a man needs to lose and find himself at the same time - bleed or draw blood... It was only after the tip of his sword wounded me on the forehead that I became bold and went on the attack," Varro remarked, before sensuously kissing Cornelia on the lips, throat and breasts.

She hummed in pleasure, opening-up her body and heart. Her eyes had widened as his confession unfolded and she pictured him combating and defeating a brutish gladiator. Varro was even braver than her centurion husband. She had never met anyone like him. No one had ever made her feel this way, in or out of bed. Every time she met him, Cornelia discovered something new and admirable about the nobleman and poet.

In truth, Varro received his scar whilst being tortured by Lucius Scaurus, a senator who nursed ambitions of leading a coup against Caesar. Instead of being bold, after being bloodied, something inside of Varro broke (and as much as one can try and put a cracked statue back together, it is never quite the same again). In many respects, the story of Varro's torture - and defeat of Lucius Scaurus - was more heroic than any victory over an opponent in the arena. But he decided not to divulge it.

In truth, Rufus Varro was a nobleman, poet and spy. He met Cornelia at a party around ten days ago. His brief, given to him by the consul Marcus Agrippa, was to seduce the woman in order to gain intelligence on her husband, Flavius Hispo. Hispo, a centurion posted on the Spanish frontier, was suspected of corruption and taking payments from an enemy warlord - in exchange for turning a blind eye to smuggling and betraying the positions and strength of the legions posted in the region. Agrippa had no wish to punish an innocent man, however. The morale of the legions would also suffer if Hispo was arbitrarily executed. He consequently instructed one of his agents to uncover evidence of the centurion's guilt.

Varro's eyes softened, and he smiled appreciatively, as he gazed into his lover's eyes, feigning adoration. The scar didn't detract from the handsomeness of the rest of his countenance. His sculptured cheekbones, playful aspect and strong jawline. Sometimes his face shaped itself into a mocking expression ("Life is a joke - and death is the punchline", the poet had once written) but not now. Now his features were artfully positioned to project a sincere affection for the woman beside him. He wanted Cornelia to trust him.

Her hum turned into a contented sigh. The past week had been akin to a dream - or a poem. A chance meeting at a party was now becoming something resembling fate. Cornelia was aware of the nobleman's reputation, but she was still suitably flattered when he spoke to her throughout the night. He asked her about her upbringing and the books she enjoyed. When realising how well read she was, Varro asked Cornelia if she would do him the honour of being one of the first people to appraise his latest work. She nodded so vigorously in reply, her earrings jangled. She liked it when other women paraded themselves, subtly or otherwise, in front of Varro but he only had eyes for her. Not once was he lewd with her. Not once did he proposition or try to take advantage of her, though later that night she mused that she would not have spurned such an advance. She had proved faithful in her marriage so far. But her husband couldn't have said the same. Cornelia was bored and wanted to test her own mettle. Could she attract someone like Rufus Varro, rather than just settle for a centurion who was unable to put a sentence or outfit together? Even if nothing came of having an affair with the handsome stranger, she would still have fun and revel in being courted by the nobleman. The following day, Cornelia woke to a messenger, carrying a love token from Varro (a silver necklace, inlaid with orange carnelian). The piece of jewellery was accompanied by a poem he had composed just for her. Her heartbeat discovered a new cadence and she thought about him all day, fingering the necklace or clutching the poem to her breast. The messenger also asked if "the lady" would be free to have dinner with his master the following night. "Yes," she said, beaming as brightly as the morning sun. Her only unhappiness came from having to wait an entire day to see him again.

The way he looked - and perhaps more so the size of his house on the Palatine Hill - took Cornelia's breath away. His charming conversation - and vintages - made her feel lightheaded. She loved the way Varro doted on his dog, Viola. And the way the black and white mongrel doted upon him. They made love and spent the night together, after their exquisite meal. Cornelia thought to herself about how the nobleman could have had any woman he wanted. But he wanted her. During the next few days Varro took Cornelia to the theatre, introduced her to one of the finest dressmakers in Rome, and invited her to a dinner party, where the guests included senators and celebrated artisans.

The married woman glanced at her bedside table. She had turned her father's death mask away from her, to face the wall. The former stonemason would have judged her current behaviour to be un-Roman. But there were perhaps few things more common in Rome than a wife - or certainly a husband - being unfaithful. For a man, it was almost a badge of honour or rite of passage to retain a mistress. At first, Cornelia felt awkward at the attention, but now she enjoyed walking into a room with her lover and turning heads.

Tonight was the first time she had invited Varro back to her own home. Cornelia felt a little uneasy and embarrassed, at first. The Viminal Hill was far from the Palatine, in more ways than one, and she hoped that her slaves would be discreet and not tell her husband about her dinner guest. Thankfully, her home looked far nicer than it had a year ago. Many pieces of furniture were new and expensive, along with recently purchased paintings and ornaments. The property was also well-kept due to the additional staff she had taken on, over the past six months.

Varro couldn't help but observe how the interior of the house was beyond the pay of a centurion. There was of course a chance that Flavius Hispo was borrowing the money to finance their new lifestyle. If debt was a crime, then over half of Rome was guilty of the offence. Both soldiers and senators alike owed more than they could afford. But, the more likely explanation for Flavius' change in fortune over the past year, was due to him receiving illicit payments.

Varro surveyed the paintings on the bedroom wall and fine, bronze figurines of Aurora and Spes on a rosewood dressing table.

"You have a good eye. I am even tempted to buy some of your artworks from you. I worry that your husband may be overextending himself however, to pay for your recent purchases. I wouldn't want to see you impoverished or having to flee Rome to escape your creditors," Varro remarked, concern replacing lust on his semblance.

"Everything has already been paid for. My husband has one of his legionaries bring back money and valuables for me, when he also brings back official correspondence. He says they are a gift from a local warlord. When Flavius next comes to Rome, on leave, he has promised to buy us a new house, on the Quirinal Hill. So as far as I know we shouldn't have any debt collectors knocking on our door. You won't be able to get rid of me that easily," Cornelia joked, although a sense of worry, from Varro suddenly getting bored with her, had laced her otherwise amorous thoughts over the past few days.

Cornelia had now unwittingly betrayed her husband in a different - and far more damaging - way, Varro judged. Once he made his report to Marcus

Agrippa, the consul would have confirmation of his suspicions. The legionary, who was complicit in Flavius' crimes, would be tracked down and compelled to give evidence. Both men would be condemned. Varro would petition Agrippa, so Cornelia would not be left bankrupt. She should not suffer for her husband's transgressions. She was young enough to attract another husband. She was pretty and not without a modicum of good sense. As much as Varro may have wished her well, he knew that he would soon forget about her, whether he took on another lover or not. Cornelia was just another mistress - who wasn't Lucilla.

Varro let out a sigh, which was borne more from relief than contentment. He was keen to extricate himself immediately, though he didn't wish to appear rude. He didn't want to steal himself away, like a thief in the night, as soon as his mistress fell asleep either. He had done that enough for more than one lifetime. The nobleman would talk to Cornelia in a day or two about why it was best that they no longer saw each other. He had rehearsed and acted out the scene on more than one occasion. Varro could tell her that he was still in love with someone else. That he didn't want to ruin her marriage or put her in danger, should her husband discover their affair. He would also pedal out the line that he wasn't good enough for her, that he didn't want to hurt her. Or a sense of weariness - and cowardice - could grip his heart and Varro would tell his mistress that the affair was over by sending a letter. To avoid any additional scenes Varro would take himself off to his villa, in Arretium, for a month, until the dust settled. The villa, hidden in the heart of the countryside, had become a sanctuary for the spy.

Eventually Cornelia drifted off to sleep. Varro turned his back on the woman and the lover's smile fell from his face, as quickly as a mask falling to the floor. His features became as hard as the stone statue of Augustus in the nearby market square (one of many commissioned by Agrippa, in honour of the demi-god). He felt as dead inside as the statue, as empty as the wine jug on the bedside table. He wanted to be back in his own bed, or in *hers*.

*Lucilla.* His ex-wife had helped nurse him back to health, in more ways than one, after Scaurus had tortured him a year ago. They had lived together at his country villa for a few months, just as friends. There had been more than one moment and opportunity for him to make an advance towards Lucilla. He had stood outside her door at night - but always refrained from knocking and retreated to his room. But, even more so than rejecting his advance, he was worried that she might surrender to it. Varro was afraid of hurting her again. Scared of them losing another child - or bringing a child into such an iniquitous world. Scared of giving himself to her again, fear had paralysed Varro and, after returning to Rome, he realised he was in the same boat as when he left. Afloat, but longing for a port to call home. He loved her, but knew Lucilla was better off without him.

As well as being oppressed by a poet's melancholy, Varro felt burdened by guilt. He had used Cornelia, as he had used other women in the past, whether for pleasure or work. He had lied to the young woman, barely out of her teens, from the start. He pretended to be interested in her at the party. The love token he had given her the following morning had been one of many, part of a bulk order. Sooner or later a rash might appear on her throat, betraying the fact that the necklace wasn't made of pure silver. The love poem he had composed, especially for her, had been written over a decade ago. He just inserted a different name, as to the dedicatee, when the occasion called for it. He had purchased an aphrodisiac from the apothecary, Albanus Pollio, and poured it into Cornelia's wine to encourage her to stay the night. Even Viola didn't belong to him, but rather he had borrowed the dog from his bodyguard and friend, Manius. Everything had been a lie. An act.

*Nothing is sacred. Nothing is real.*

Varro sometimes told himself that he was doing his duty and working for the good of Rome, or Caesar. But he knew he was lying to himself, as much as he had lied to Cornelia. The nobleman, or wastrel, had fallen into the role of a spy. He had spent most of his life in a hole, as deep as a grave, and he wasn't quite sure if he could ever climb out of it.

Birdsong began to thrill from the roof. The rays of the morning sun moved slowly towards them, like honey dripping down a hive. He felt Cornelia stir. He would don his enamoured expression one more time and make love to her. Their play, whether a comedy or tragedy, was now in its final act.

"I could get used to waking up to you. It's like waking up to a dream."

## 2.

Cornelia asked if he would like breakfast in bed, but Varro already felt like the walls were closing in on him and the air was growing thinner. One more lie, one more kiss, and he might be sick. Varro duly took his leave and walked off stage.

As he closed the door to the house behind him Varro experienced a mixture of exhaustion and exhilaration. His assignment was all but over. He just needed to make his report to Agrippa. He resolved to leave Rome for Arretium the following day. Varro already started to picture the view outside his bedroom window. A luscious valley, seemingly sculptured by a higher power, was home to olive groves and vineyards. Sheep ambled in the pasture - and clouds ambled across the blue skies above. He wanted to feel the quilt of his lawn beneath his bare feet, pick fresh apples off the trees for breakfast. Feel a sea breeze against his skin. He would sleep and read for most of the day. He would invite his neighbours over for lunch or dinner. He enjoyed the company of an old married couple, Sergius and Miyria. They had been together for fifty years yet still doted on one another and laughed at each other's jokes. He realised they were an antidote to his scepticism and cynicism concerning love and marriage. He craved fresh air. The smoke and sins of Rome were choking him.

Before Varro had a chance to breathe out, however, he was accosted by two men walking towards him on a narrow, cobblestoned street around the corner from the house he had just escaped from. He heard footsteps behind him too and when Varro turned his head he was greeted by an equally inhospitable figure.

The eldest of the trio stood closest to Varro, to the point where he could smell the vinegary wine and garum on his breath. The man's creased, leathery skin betrayed his fifty plus years. Yet his frame was still broad and knotted with muscle. When he made two fists his brawny arms hung down like mallets. His short, cropped brown hair, dusted with grey, meant that Varro couldn't help but notice the man's left ear lobe, which had been half sliced off. His black eyes were narrow, accusatory. His pronounced brow was large and bony, like a cliff jutting out over the sea. A large dogtooth, housed in swollen gums, turned his smile into a sneer. Varro took the two younger men accompanying him to be his sons, given their similar features. Their tunics were as dirty as the looks they gave the nobleman.

"You don't know me, but I know you Rufus Varro. Or the likes of you. I fought under cowards and reprobates like you during the civil war. You think you're entitled to take what you want and damn the consequences. You think the blood running through your veins makes you superior to everyone else. But the only thing your blood is good for is being spilled. My name is Valerius Hispo, brother to the man whose wife you've corrupted. These are my sons, Vibius and Macro," Hispo stated, in a voice as rough as sack cloth, nodding to the stout youth behind him and then the sour-faced figure breathing down Varro's neck. "I want you to know the names of the men who are about to teach you a lesson - beat some sense into you."

Varro refused to give his enemies the satisfaction of appearing unnerved, which he duly was. Rather he appeared mildly amused. A mocking expression still shaped his features, as if chiselled by the gods. He recalled how Agrippa had warned him about Flavius' brother - and to avoid encountering him at all costs. Valerius was a veteran legionary turned debt collector. Even though he employed plenty of thugs to collect for him, Valerius still enjoyed the hands-on part of his business.

Vibius Hispo sniggered, like a hyena. The youth had a pronounced squint, to the point where his left eye seemed half-closed. Macro tapped his cudgel against his leg, eager to get on with the task at hand. He had a lean, flinty expression which bespoke a man who hated for hate's sake. Mercy was not a prized virtue in the debt collecting trade.

"I was just keeping your brother's wife warm for him. You should be thanking me, not threatening me," Varro replied, his voice limed in civility - and sardonicism. His sarcastic wit had got Varro into trouble more times than it had got him out of it over the years.

"So, you want to play the joker?" Valerius replied, cracking his knuckles. The debt collector had experienced all manner of responses when going about his business. Some begged for forgiveness or one more day to pay the sum. Some accepted their beating, being as bold as a lion or meek as a lamb. Some tried to run. Some tried to fight. The outcome was always the same though. The debt was paid, in blood and then gold.

"Surely playing the joker is preferable to playing the mime? I don't suppose you would accept a bribe to make all this unpleasantness go away?"

Varro was tempted to comment that he hoped the act of receiving a bribe ran in the family, but for once he considered it wise to hold his tongue.

"Family honour is more important than gold."

"Now who's playing the joker?"

Flight was preferable to fight, Varro judged. His best hope was to get past the rogue to his rear and run as fast as his legs could carry him, as if the hound of Hades were on his heels. He would try and reach the nearby tavern, *The Water Hole*. Varro was friends with the landlord and he could duly offer payment to various patrons there to keep him safe.

Varro glanced around at the vicious looking adolescent edging closer towards him, chewing a piece of dried goat and clutching his cudgel, stained with dried blood. Vibius was already anticipating his prey running. He altered his stance and stretched out his arms, to form a human cordon. Vibius would be able to grapple with his victim, long enough for his father to weigh-in and haul him to the ground, where Varro would be helpless. Doomed.

It would have to be fight, not flight. He shivered, despite the heat, as the spy experienced a flashback to being tortured last year. The beating had come first. And then a branding iron had been placed on his stomach. Time doesn't heal all wounds. His only hope was that the gods might intervene, but Varro thought it unlikely that the gods were awake this early in the morning. He slowly but surely twisted his body and stood with his back to the wall in the alleyway, so at least he could see any attack coming. His fingertips rested on the handle of his dagger. Sweat glazed his skin.

"You deserve to be punished. My brother can do as he will with his whorish wife, but I'm here now to take care of you," Valerius decreed. His word was used to being law.

"I have an ex-wife who I still pay a monthly allowance to. Haven't I been punished enough? Despite her drain on my estate I still have sufficient capital to pay you a handsome bribe, if you'd like to reconsider."

A splinter of fear lodged itself into Varro's playful tone and he experienced a catch in his throat as he spoke. The three men moved one step closer to their prey, in unison. It was as though a noose was tightening around his neck.

"Instead of a bribe, how about I offer you a new deal? Walk away, or limp away. It's up to you."

The calm but resolute voice came from behind Valerius.

Manius. The bodyguard's broad frame and square shoulders made the Briton resemble a legionary's scutum. Not for the first time, the former gladiator needed to act as a shield and protect his friend. Usually Varro needed protection from himself - from sore losing gamblers, irate husbands and fellow drunks Varro would insult. Manius was never one to start trouble, but he often proved the last man standing to end it.

The two men had known one another for over a decade. Varro's father had watched the Briton fight valiantly in the arena and purchased his freedom. Appius Varro invited Manius into his household. In return for teaching Varro swordsmanship and serving as his bodyguard (and drinking companion) the young poet instructed the Briton on learning his letters. Manius' build was as solid as his sense of loyalty and the Briton had, on more than one occasion, risked his life to save Varro's. Not because the nobleman was his employer, but because he was his friend.

Manius' usually open, friendly features became taut, tightening like the tunic across his torso as the bodyguard puffed out his barrel chest.

Valerius Hispo grunted and eyed-up the newcomer in the alley.

"And who are you?"

"Someone who's carrying a bigger stick than you," Manius replied, brandishing a large club in one hand and a dagger in the other.

Valerius screwed-up his leathery countenance and grunted again. Unimpressed. The ex-soldier had never been one to back down from a fight, especially when his force outnumbered his opponent. It would be two against one, in terms of bringing the big man down. The gods are on the side of the biggest legions. Valerius had faced down and collected debts from enough noblemen to know that Varro wouldn't put up much of a fight. Soon it would be three against one.

The air seemed to thicken with tension and violence. There would be blood. Manius just needed to make sure that the father and son turned on him, rather than Varro.

"Enough talk!" Valerius snapped, his tone akin to a drill master.

"Aye, I've no desire to stand around here and chew your ear off. Especially since someone has got there before me it seems," Manius goadingly replied.

It was the final insult, for Valerius. It was time for action, not words. His blood was up. Frothing. Valerius let out a roar and, along with his youngest son Macro, advanced towards Manius.

Vibius breathed a sigh of relief, internally, as it would be his job to deal with the debauched poet rather than formidable bodyguard. He barked out a curse, accompanied by no small amount of spittle, and menacingly raised his cudgel - with the intention of bringing it down upon Varro's skull.

Valerius and Macro rushed Manius at the same time. The ex-gladiator deftly shifted his body so that his opponents got in the way of each other as they attacked. Valerius lost his footing on the cobblestones as his bloodlust got the better of him. Manius sidestepped Macro's nail-studded cudgel and sliced his forearm, disarming his assailant. Before the youth had a chance to react the Briton moved inside and butted his enemy. His flinty expression cracked, in shock and agony, and Macro dropped to the ground.

Varro reached up and caught hold of the young man's wrist. Holding his dagger in his free hand the nobleman flinched not in skewering the blade into his shoulder. The hyena yelped and howled, before Varro whipped his elbow around and struck Vibius' cheek, flooring him quicker than a boxer taking a fall and throwing a fight. The poet had learned to cut someone down, over the past year, using more than just a witticism or satirical verse.

Cudgel struck cudgel. The sound resembled the clop of a horse's hoof. The was no second clop, however. Manius was too quick. Too purposeful. Too powerful. The bodyguard swiped low to connect with his opponent's kneecap, felling the old soldier. Before he could recover Manius kicked the debt collector in the side, cracking a couple of ribs, and then broke a finger on each of his hands. When you put someone down, make sure they stay down, a veteran gladiator had once advised. To further immobilise Macro the stony-faced bodyguard stamped on his groin. Macro groaned, doubled-up on the ground - dry retching as if he had just eaten a plate of bad oysters.

The two friends left Valerius and his sons for dead - and tramped home. Rufus Varro wanted nothing more than to climb into his bed, whilst others in Rome rose from theirs. The city was coming to life. Shutters were being slammed open. Carters hollered out, demanding right of way. Slops were being poured out of windows, splashing on the flagstones beneath. The smell of fresh bread wafted through the streets, although unfortunately it couldn't quite wholly flush away the odours of stale wine and ordure pervading the air. Slaves, some scurrying like mice and some as leaden-footed as oxen, carried out errands. Shrewish housewives harried their husbands out the door to go to work - and then traded gossip with their neighbours whilst hanging out the washing.

Manius acted on the instructions of Agrippa - and his own brief - and shadowed Varro the previous evening. After stealing a few hours of sleep, the

Briton woke before dawn to be ready for when Varro re-appeared the next morning. He duly noticed the trio following his friend and tracked them all accordingly. He wondered if Varro was of interest to the men for being a spy, as opposed to cuckolder.

"I am grateful to you Manius. One day I will get to save you, I'm sure of it. In the meantime, I really should grant you a pay rise," Varro amiably remarked, breathing normally again after the breathlessness of the ambush.

"I would normally say that's the drink talking, but not even you drink this early in the day. How was your night with Cornelia? Did she say anything to implicate her husband?"

"She said enough. Flavius will soon be waking up to a fate that's worse than just a bad hangover. I just need to make my report to Agrippa, but then the assignment will be over. I am looking forward to catching up on some sleep and reading. I will be staying in Arretium for a few weeks. You and Camilla will be welcome to join me. I need some time away from Rome, some peace and quiet to make some plans," Varro expressed, with a mixture of palpable relief and fatigue - albeit he forgot one of his own maxims:

*Man plans, and the gods laugh.*

## 3.

Fronto woke his master around midday. The wizened estate manager had first loyally served Rufus' father, Appius Varro. Fronto kept watch over the young nobleman and his finances. Due to some shrewd investing, income still, just about, exceeded outgoings for the estate. Thankfully, during the past year, Varro had courted fewer mistresses, thrown fewer parties and gambled fewer nights away.

"I have just received a messenger from Marcus Agrippa, summoning you to his house immediately. No rest for the wicked, or idle, it seems," Fronto remarked. "It's a glorious day outside."

"It'd be even more glorious if I was left to sleep and only saw the end of it. Does Agrippa never sleep? He oversees an entire network of spies, from Alesia to Alexandria, yet why does he only seem to bother me?"

Varro yawned and ran a hand through his mussed-up hair. His eyes were ringed with tiredness, or despair. As much as he whispered a curse directed at Agrippa under his breath he would duly submit to his request. Or order. It wasn't wise to keep a consul waiting, whose best friend and co-consul was a demi-god, he wryly considered.

After washing himself Varro went to put on his tunic, the one he wore the day before but, upon smelling Cornelia's scent on the garment, he chose another. Before leaving he checked himself in the large silver plate mirror on his wall, as he smoothed down his hair and tightened a belt around his slim waist. Varro appeared younger than his thirty plus years, as much as his face had grown leaner and harder over the past year. "Yet your eyes are kinder," Lucilla had judged recently, intrigued or impressed. A few grey hairs marked his temples. Staining them. Varro grinned and chided himself after, for a moment or two, he was tempted to pluck them.

*I would rather have tenfold grey hairs than be as vain as a courtesan - or poet... I've wasted time. Now time wastes me.*

If Varro was still a poet, he was an old rather than young one he concluded. Perhaps part of the attraction of being a writer was the conceit that he could cheat time - and death - by living forever through his work. Agrippa had offered him a lifeline a year ago, by arranging for Gaius Cilnius Maecenas to act as his patron and promote his poetry.

"If Maecenas takes you under his wing, you will soar," a fellow poet, Quintus Perilla, had enthused. "He knows everyone worth knowing. He has the ear of Augustus. Your verses could be read throughout the empire. You could be famous!"

"I've suffered from enough poxes during my life. I have no wish to add "fame" to the list," Varro had drily replied to his companion. Agrippa was keen for the nobleman to continue to play the poet, however. The cover helped him infiltrate the best households in Rome - and the bedchambers of the best, or worst, women in the capital. Varro had lost count of the amount of times that noblewomen had drunk down his verses like wine and he had taken advantage of them. Or they had taken advantage of him.

Varro's life as a poet had not only led him into the finest houses on the Palatine. He had also regularly caroused with his fellow versifiers in various venues of ill-repute in the Subura. He gambled and whored as if inspired by a muse to do so. Sucking the marrow out of life. Washing it down with a cellar's worth of Falernian. He wasted his time and talent. Poems were started but seldom completed. Instead of challenging himself to write an epic poem he found himself composing second-rate couplets, to leave on the pillows of his mistresses before he crept out of their beds in the middle of the night.

Yet there were times in his youth when Varro felt he was but acting the epicurean - and his heart wasn't really in it. There was a hole in his soul, which even poetry couldn't feel. He grew tired of the company of preening authors. They were self-regarding rather than self-aware. Their only virtue seemed to be that they were not actors or, worse, mimes. When he looked into the mirror back then Varro witnessed a figure worthy of loathing. Life was a tragedy rather than comedy. There were no happy endings.

Lucilla had saved him. Ironically, they had met at a poetry reading. Varro no longer needed to play the lovelorn poet because he was in love. He didn't need to be Catullus. He yearned not for a Lesbia to inspire him. She taught him how to smile and laugh again, when sober. Varro had never met a woman who he had admired so much. He still hadn't. During their courtship and the early years of their marriage Varro was content, at peace. Boredom and contempt, directed towards himself or the dung-heap of the world, no longer gnawed at his soul. Yet life has a tendency to get in the way of happiness. Lucilla nearly died giving birth, twice. The babies were stillborn. A doctor warned him that, should his wife become pregnant again, she might die. He stopped making love to her. Lucilla felt diminished, depressed. The divine spark dimmed in her fine eyes. Varro tried to lose himself again in drinking - and whoring. He proved serially unfaithful, seducing mistress after mistress with little regard for whether his wife knew or not. He told himself it was in his, or man's nature, to be unfaithful. Dishonourable. A scorpion must sting, a magpie must steal. It was man's lot to be weak - or wicked. Lucilla, out of revenge or a desire to be loved, eventually took lovers too. They divorced. Out of guilt, or from a sense of decency and devotion, Varro granted Lucilla a generous allowance each month.

The nobleman reverted to a life of debauchery. The hole in his soul throbbed once again. Swelled. Varro was a ship, caught in a storm, not knowing when he was going to reach port. *If* he was going to reach port. He was a wastrel, who occasionally wrote the odd half-lauded verse. Varro hoped wine would wash away his sins. He hoped that an endless procession of courtesans and mistresses would make him forget about his wife.

*You can have a noble face but an ignoble heart* -Varro considered, as he continued to take in his reflection. *Especially when living in Rome.* He flicked his hair away from his forehead and ran a finger along the serpentine scar on his brow. He winced, as if experiencing physical pain, as he touched the film of skin and remembered Cassandra. Lucius Scaurus had brutally murdered his own wife, but Varro had blood on his hands too. The spy had been the one who had seduced the woman and used her to glean intelligence on her husband. Varro had been the one to promise her false hope, that they would live happily ever after. Varro had been the one unable to protect her from her husband, when he slit her throat. Guilt now filled the hole in the soul. But guilt was good. Because it was better than nothing.

When he was a child Varro was precociously intelligent, gifted. He read voraciously and dreamed of being Hector reborn - heroically fighting for a cause - even if he and the cause were doomed. Or he pictured himself as Aeneas, pious and courageous. Goodness, not glory, mattered. Perhaps there was still something of that boy in the careworn man framed in the mirror.

*Perhaps…*

Varro stroked his jaw and chin. He would arrange for Aspasia to shave him this evening. He liked to be clean shaven and equally he liked the way the slave girl felt on his skin. He would close his eyes and breathe out, forget himself, as she straddled him on the chair and ran her fingers down his back. The comely, fawning girl would give him a massage too, knead out the tension in his shoulders. Aromatic oils would glisten on their burnished skin. He would kiss her, taste the sweet grapes on her soft lips. She would laugh at his jokes, even if she didn't wholly understand them. The dusky beauty knew that it would be an act of lust, not love. If only more of his mistresses over the years had been as wise as the slave girl, it would have prevented a myriad of awkward scenes and broken hearts.

Varro brushed his fringe to cover the scar and tore himself away from his reflection. His gaze was distracted by a portrait of his father, which hung on the wall next to the mirror. For many years, Varro could barely bring himself to look at the image of his father in the eye. Disapproval shot out from his painted aspect. The Medusa turned fewer people into stone, Varro half-joked. His painted lips even seemed more pursed sometimes, in shame, as Varro came home late from another night in the tavern. His father, an esteemed general and senator, loomed large in his early life - albeit Appius Varro was also largely absent, away on campaign or attending to diplomatic assignments in far-flung lands. His father returned every now and them, to deliver a lecture to his errant son. He would listen avidly as Appius Varro told him about the history of Rome and the importance of honour. "Rather fail with honour than succeed with fraud," his father would speciously preach, quoting Sophocles. But there were times when the boy wanted to know more about his late mother, rather than Cato the Elder and Aristotle. Varro never knew his mother and barely knew his father. So, the young man was drawn to the Socratic lesson, to *know thyself*.

Rufus Varro knew himself, more than most. Which was why he didn't particularly like himself, at times.

## 4.

"Good work," Marcus Agrippa laconically remarked after hearing the agent issue his report. If less was more then the consul sometimes said too much, Varro fancied.

Agrippa sat upright in his chair, his back as straight as a column. His expression was often serious, but seldom severe. His aspect, beneath a heavy brow, was often hard but seldom callous. The statesman still exhibited a soldier's build and he was dressed in a plain tunic rather than finely woven toga. Varro had grown to admire the consul over the past year. He was a man of action - but a man of forethought too. Agrippa was comfortable talking to legionaries and legislators alike (although Varro noticed he, quite rightly, preferred the former). When Agrippa gave his word, he liked to keep it - which was not altogether in keeping with usual political practise. More than the gods, Augustus Caesar had reason to give thanks to Agrippa for his gilded fate. Caesar's ancient had first defeated his enemies – Marcus Brutus, Sextus Pompey and Mark Antony - and now he was helping to re-build Rome after the ruinous civil war. The general had won the war for his friend. Now as co-consul he was winning the peace. Agrippa's aqueducts quenched the thirst of Rome and his management of the grain supply fed the city. The re-designed circus maximus entertained the capital and his public gardens and statues were helping to turn a city filled with rubble into one clothed in marble. Temples had been restored to their former glory. The second man of Rome had, quite literally, got his hands dirty too by improving the sewerage in the city. The "new man" was worth ten times the amount of "best men", including himself, who belonged to old patrician families. The soldier and son of a common farmer had come a long way, which bred as much opprobrium as admiration in Rome, unfortunately. "Success breeds as many enemies as friends," the co-consul had once philosophically remarked to his agent. Yet Agrippa ploughed on regardless. He worked tirelessly for the good of Rome. But Varro sensed that duty - and a devotion to his old schoolfriend - was not his sole motivation. Agrippa buried himself in his work to help him forget that he had buried his first wife, Caecilia. More than Octavius, soldiering, the dream and ideals of Rome, she was the love of his life. Although he had re-married (Caesar had prompted his co-consul to marry his niece, Claudia Marcella, to further his dynastic ambitions), Agrippa seemed to resemble a grieving widower more than loving husband at times. Yet still he ploughed on, either doing his duty in public or working in the shadows, through a network of agents, to defeat Caesar's enemies.

"I will deal with Flavius Hispo from hereon in. As for Cornelia, I will ensure that she is not unduly punished for her husband's wrongdoing. Nor will she be rewarded, however. Should she have twenty slaves in her household, she will soon have two. If she currently wears diamonds and silks, she will soon wear coloured glass and linen... You have helped to swat a gadfly on the

Spanish frontier, Rufus. As much as it is the lot of an agent for his work to go un-lauded, Caesar will be pleased and grateful for your service... But I have not just invited you here to give your report. I have another important assignment for you."

Varro shifted uncomfortably in his seat. His skin prickled, his scar itched as though his stitches had just been taken out again. Over the past year he had done his duty, worked for the glory of Caesar and Rome. But he was bone tired. Weary of seducing - and hurting - the women he was ordered to spy on. Varro was beginning to feel akin to a common whore, with Agrippa acting as his pimp. Enough was enough.

"I was intending to spend time away from Rome. Not only am I concerned that Cornelia or Valerius might knock on my door - and I am far more worried about the former doing so than the latter - but I also suffered some injuries during my encounter with Valerius," Varro argued, feigning a slight shot of pain in his ribs and wincing as he did so.

"If would you hear me out, Rufus. I warrant that I will have no need to compel you to take on the assignment. Rather you will choose to," the consul said confidently, knowingly. Varro didn't know whether to be curious or alarmed.

"Tell me, have you heard of the name Herennius of late?"

"He was the soldier who, along with Popilius, hunted down and murdered Cicero. Antony and Fulvia rewarded him for his service and he grew wealthy through investing in the slave trade. Rumour has it that he was also a partner in a smuggling ring, which controlled a small fleet of pirate ships. Herennius recently bought a house on the Palatine, but I never met the man. He died last month, after being robbed in his own home."

"Herennius was stabbed with a thin-bladed dagger through the chest. Few mourned his passing. Rome's loss is not exactly the underworld's gain. I cared little for the man when I barely knew him. I care less now, since I have got to know him more. By all accounts Herennius was an odious, ignoble brute. After attending slave auctions, he would arrange for the "stock" he didn't sell to be thrown into a pit - and the men and women would be ordered to fight for their lives whilst Herennius and his fellow slave traders placed bets on the contests. "They lack value in life. Perhaps I can extract some money out of their deaths," he once told me at a party, making a boast of his enterprise... He was known to be abusive towards whores - as well as his wife... His wealth funded and fuelled his corrupt and boorish behaviour. He once bought up the debts of his neighbour, in order to force him out of his home so Herennius could take over his house and build a swimming pool... I also remember the time he tried to buy his way into the Senate House. Octavius replied that he didn't need his money and that even the Senate House demanded a minimum requirement of wit and morality... I have little doubt that Herennius developed numerous enemies over the years, both for personal and professional reasons. He collected them, like my wife collects hairpins or astrologers. But I believe Herennius was murdered by someone he knew, rather than a random intruder. There was no sign of a struggle in the triclinium, where he was found. He also appeared to be carrying a goblet of wine and a few dates in his hands, when he fell to the floor after being stabbed... I am confident his murderer has a connection to one of the guests at the dinner that night, or indeed the culprit was one of his guests."

"Do you know the people present?" Varro asked, before yawning.

"Firstly, there was Herennius' wife, Corinna. She has yet to reach twenty. Corinna is a sweet girl, by all accounts. I sent a trusted attendant over to question the servants in the house. But she was a woman scorned. Such sweetness can sour, and Corinna could have murdered her husband in order to be free of him. At that point she might have also considered she would inherit his estate. Also, in attendance was Lentulus Nerva - Herennius' father-in-law - and his wife, Lucretia."

"The advocate?" Varro remarked, somewhat surprised.

"The very same. I have met Lentulus and seen him perform at trial. He is an accomplished advocate. He would claim he was second to none, but lawyers have been known to massage the truth. He is wonderfully fawning towards anyone equal or higher in social status. And wonderfully dismissive of anyone he considers beneath him - unless they are potential clients, with sufficient capital to buy his time and favour. You may question why Lentulus permitted his daughter to marry an ex-soldier and son of a swineherd. The answer is the cause and solution to all of life's problems: money. Herennius took a fancy to Corinna and found out that Lentulus owed considerable debts. The advocate hadn't built-up debts from gambling or poor investments. But rather Lentulus suffers from pride and envy. He desires to live the life of his wealthiest clients. So, he purchased a villa on the Palatine, which he could ill afford. His wife also burned through money, whilst decorating the house, quicker than the great fire of Alexandria engulfed the library. Much to their resentment, Herennius saved them. It was a choice between the shame of financial ruin, or the shame of having their family name linked to that of the slave trader. "To know him is to despise him," Lentulus once said of his son-in-law. But like most lawyers, he decided to take money from a far from innocent man. We could look at the crime as a murder of convenience. Lentulus wanted to be free of Herennius, as much as his daughter did."

Varro nodded his head to convey he was taking Agrippa's words in, but he still wondered what this all had to do with him. He wanted to get back home, to a choice vintage and the equally intoxicating Aspasia.

"So far I'm not regretting having missed out on an invitation to the gathering."

"Marcus Sestius was also present, Herennius' long-term business partner," Agrippa added, ignoring Varro's glib comment. "Sestius had served with Herennius in the army, before they started their slave trading venture. Such was the closeness of the pair - or his lack of affection for his wife - that Herennius bequeathed the bulk of his estate to Sestius, when his will was unsealed after his demise."

"Did Sestius know about the contents of the will beforehand?"

"I'm not sure. It's now going to be somewhat difficult to ask him too, as I was informed that he had been murdered himself yesterday afternoon. Sestius was found, in his bedroom, with his throat slit from ear to ear."

"Blood begets blood, it seems. I could always feign concern or curiosity, should you ask me to, but I still fail to see why I should be compelled to be interested in any assignment linked to these murders," Varro asserted, thinking that Agrippa must have other agents at his disposal who could investigate the crimes.

"There were three more guests at the dinner party. The first was a young poet who, at the invitation of Herennius' wife, gave a reading half-way through the night. I will pass on his name and address to you later. You will be familiar with the name of the second guest however: Licinius Omerus Pulcher."

Agrippa's face betrayed a flicker of irritation or portent as he said the name.
"The nobleman?"

"You could call him that. You could also call him a propagandist, diplomat, blackmailer and patron of the arts - as well as a spy and assassin. As you know Pulcher serves the higher power of Maecenas. He first came to my attention during the civil war. He was rumoured to be Maecenas' lover, but that did not prevent him from seducing a Vestal Virgin, in order to steal a copy of Mark Antony's will, which proved invaluable in the propaganda war against the enemy. Pulcher further worked under Maecenas, blackmailing or bribing senators who wavered in their support of Caesar during the Actium campaign... Like Maecenas, Pulcher is unfailingly polite and unfailingly duplicitous. I would trust him about as much as I would a priest or Parthian. On the surface of things, he is cultured, charming and dedicated to his duty. But if ever Pulcher whispers flattery in your ear, he will more than likely be pouring poison into your wine cup while you're distracted... He spends half his time in Rome and half his time abroad, tending to the political and business interests of his paymaster... Licinius Pulcher did not attend Herennius' dinner party by accident, or for the quality of the cuisine and conversation."

"Well it seems that you have your prime suspect."

"I thought that too, until I discovered Pulcher has a cast iron alibi. On the night of Herennius' murder, he spent the evening with your ex-wife, Lucilla."

## 5.

Varro felt winded, as if punched in the stomach by a hulking gladiator, on hearing her name being linked to the gruesome murders. Lucilla was the last person he would have expected to attend a party hosted by Herennius. She had also never mentioned Pulcher before. Varro was shocked and confused, light-headed. He called for some wine and took a seat, else he feared his legs might give way. It was one of the rare occasions when the nobleman was incapable of insouciance.

"Are you sure?" Varro asked, after downing his first cup of wine.

"Sure about what, exactly?"

"About everything. Was Lucilla really present that night, with Pulcher? And did she really spend the night with him?"

Varro would have genuinely preferred to be hit in the stomach by a gladiator than to find out the answer was "yes" to his questions.

"I am sure. I even spoke to Lucilla myself. I consider her an honourable woman, which thankfully isn't quite an oxymoron in Rome yet; like honourable politician. I do not believe she was lying to me, to gift Pulcher an alibi. I am confident Lucilla has nothing to do with either of the deaths, but she may have been unwittingly drawn into someone else's plot. There is a slim - but real - chance that someone may be targeting the guests at the party. Lucilla might be in danger. For that reason alone, I thought you might want to take on the assignment."

Raw jealously began to bubble-up in his guts, like lava in a volcano - ousting or incinerating the feelings of shock and confusion. His nostrils widened as he breathed out. Heavily. Wearily. Although he was no longer married to Lucilla, he still felt like he had been betrayed. She had been unfaithful. She had taken lovers before, even when they were married. But somehow this was different. Pulcher was dangerous. He could be using her. He was somehow his rival as an agent.

Varro unconsciously clasped his dagger and pictured Pulcher's face. He had met his fellow nobleman countless times, both before and after he had discovered he was a spy, working in Gaius Maecenas' employ. They had attended the same parties over the years, read the same books and slept with the same women. Like a courtesan slapping on make-up, Pulcher always plastered a blithe - or self-satisfied - grin on his countenance. He smiled too much, to the point of it being unnatural - or certainly annoying. Or his smirk was more akin to a leer. Pulcher acted the life and soul of the party - generous and gregarious. But it was all just an act. He was but playing a part. Like himself.

Varro told himself Lucilla was her own woman and he was not responsible for her. That he didn't care who she took as a lover. If she needed protection, Pulcher could provide it. But what if the man protecting her was the same man who she needed to be protected from?

"What do you want me to do?" Varro said, resigned to his fate, as he accepted his new assignment.

"I need you to investigate Herennius' murder. But, as well as finding his killer, I need you to find something else too," Agrippa replied, ominously.

The sun's massaging rays spread themselves over the scene, like butter across bread. The flowers in the garden were in bloom, freckling the air with colour and tickling the nostrils with their varied fragrances.

They laughed together, again. In harmony.

Lucilla had been rapt, enamoured, as Licinius told her a story about Horace. He was visiting his poet friend at his estate near Licenza. They were taking a walk around his grounds and Horace was extolling the virtues of nature and the quiet life - when he accidently stepped in a mound of horse dung, wearing open-toed sandals.

"Suffice to say he let out a string of obscenities which were far from poetic, or extolled the virtues of nature… You must accompany me when I next visit him however."

"I would like that," Lucilla replied, her eyes widening with delight and anticipation. She had been introduced to numerous poets before, by Varro. She couldn't help but be unimpressed. They were often drunk, vain - telling each other they were talented. They each thought themselves Homer or Catullus re-born but were blind to the truth. Yet, Horace was Horace. To meet the author of *The Satires*, one of her most beloved books, would be tantamount to a dream. She would be happy to listen to him recite his verse or see him step in more dung. Just to hear his voice. Meet a genius.

Pulcher smiled - his mouth crescent-shaped, like a Persian blade. He was happy that she was happy. The nobleman had stayed the night, again. The couple had talked long into the evening, about literature, art, the theatre and politics. He valued her opinion. Men seldom encouraged women to speak their mind in Rome. But he was different, she judged.

She had first met him at a party at Maecenas' house. Their host had introduced them.

"As long as you promise not to tell me if I have overpaid for certain pieces Lucilla, I will let Licinius show you my collection of Greek bronze figurines in the atrium towards the back of the house. The tour will give you a chance to escape some of my less engaging guests. Worse than being fantastically dull, some of them have committed the unforgivable crime of being ill-dressed."

The couple spent most of the night in one another's company. Pulcher arranged to have some food and wine brought out into the garden. She was more intelligent - and wittier - than he expected. He was more self-effacing and candid than she predicted.

"You are a diplomat, are you not?" Lucilla asked, sitting on a marble bench opposite a statue of Voluptas.

"You're being wonderfully diplomatic in saying so, when we both know that I am a spy," he replied, making a face whilst whispering the last word in the sentence. "I have recently been attached to a trade delegation. Our official brief was to improve the trade between ourselves and certain chieftains in the south-east region of Britannia. My unofficial brief however was to gather intelligence on their military strengths and natural resources... The people there are not as drunk as reported. They're drunker... The height of cuisine there is to trim the mould off the bread before they eat it... But we have whipped barbarians into shape before... As much as travel may have widened my sympathies and knowledge, I have arrived at a point in my life where I want to settle again in Rome. It's my home. I missed the capital all the more for suffering Gaulish conversation, Spanish theatre, Greek financial advice and the wine from Britannia. Or, as they should call it, vinegar..."

At the end of the evening they agreed to attend the theatre together the next day. Lucilla often went with her maid, Diana, but the uneducated servant frequently screwed her already sour countenance up in confusion and disappointment, in response to the unfolding drama. Part of the enjoyment of the theatre for Lucilla stemmed from discussing the play afterwards, which she found she could do with Licinius: "The lead actor seemed to take pride in his regional accent. He shouldn't... Her voice set the audience's teeth on edge and one could hear dogs bark in response to her shrill tone, as if serving as her chorus. Hopefully she will go far in her career, as far away from Rome as possible... A playwright should aim to produce some form of conflict in his work, and then resolve the drama. Unfortunately, after that showing, I am only resolved to never see another one of his plays."

She saw him again, and again. He made her laugh. He was unfailingly courteous - yet passionate when aroused. She knew he had a past, with other women. *But the past is the past.* They wrote letters on the days when they were unable to see one another. Licinius invited Lucilla to his house. He tenderly held her hand as he showed her his art collection.

"You have excellent taste," the fellow collector exclaimed in earnest, smiling to herself as she noticed how she had bid on a couple of the landscapes herself.

"I know," Pulcher replied, gazing at the woman appreciatively - and amorously.

The nobleman and spy similarly gazed at Lucilla now, appreciatively and amorously, as he sat next to her in the garden. She was wearing a summer stola of cream linen, with a border of turquoise silk along the hem and sleeves. The silver earrings he had bought her - which had once belonged to Julius Caesar's daughter, Julia - glinted in the pristine sunlight.

Lucilla returned his gaze. His build was athletic and the lines of his figure and face were as clean and striking as any sculpture she owned. His emerald eyes could be playful or piercing. The breeze teased itself through his black, curly hair.

"I hope I am not keeping you from your work today," Lucilla said, reclining in a wicker chair in the shade of a cherry tree.

"You have no need to apologise. Rather I should be thanking you. Work can wait. I warrant my hands might become calloused soon, if I keep spending my time grasping a stylus and writing reports. I have spent a memorable evening with you, Lucilla. It would be rude and stupid of me not to want to spend the day with you also."

"You may regret saying that. I will be leaving soon to visit my dressmaker, should you wish to join me. But I wouldn't envy anyone who spent their morning shopping for clothes with a woman, especially when she has plenty of money in her purse and doesn't quite know what she wants."

"I will risk it. As a diplomat I have had plenty of experience in being patient and nodding my head in agreement. The only condition I have in accompanying you is that I buy you something."

"I hope you are a tougher negotiator when the interests of Rome are at stake. What do you think I will look good in?"

"Well as a diplomat I should assert that you will look good in everything. But especially I'd like to see you in my bed."

Lucilla grinned and hoped that the shade concealed her blushes. There was a part of her that wanted to make love again.

"That can of course be arranged. But later. After visiting my dressmaker, I am due to call upon Tiro. He has some pieces, from Cicero's collection of marble garden statues, he wishes to sell before he departs from Rome to live permanently at his villa in Puteoli."

"It's always a pleasure to see Tiro. He's a true gentleman. You may regret inviting me along however, as I may be tempted to bid for some of the pieces myself."

"Hopefully I will be able to distract you in the new outfit you would have bought for me."

"I am hoping to be distracted too."

"I must then attend a meeting with my estate manager, to go over my accounts for the month. You might get to find out how much I am worth."

"I already know how much you're worth - and it's even more than your weight in gold."

"I hope you are not going to flatter me like this during our day together, or else I will need a litter to carry me, lest I swoon. We have quite a bit of ground to cover today. I also need to pay a visit to Antonia Tillius. She has not been well of late. I want to make sure she is taking her rest and eating well. I also need to ensure that she is listening to her doctor more than Toranius, the soothsayer. It's always difficult to predict favourable futures for those who put their faith in silver-tongued augurs and astrologists."

"The longer the day with you, the better," Pulcher said, in earnest. Smiling again.

Lucilla briefly bathed in his handsome, burnished features. And her smile reflected the light back. The woman had been hurt in the past, by Varro, and was wary of giving her heart again. But the past was the past. It struck Lucilla that she couldn't remember the last time she had been this happy. She was looking forward to spending the day with the nobleman. She might even be able to spend the rest of her life with him.

Agrippa recounted the events of Herennius' party to Varro. The guests arrived early in the evening. Halfway through the night there was a break in the courses of the dinner and the poet gave his reading.

"Can you remember the name of the poet?"

"I've forgotten it, unfortunately. But the reason I cannot recall it is because he's a no one. You will need to interview the youth, however. One of the slaves mentioned that, after the poet left, he spotted someone who had a similar build - and was wearing what could have been the same black cloak - on the street opposite the house... There was a discordant, or strained, atmosphere throughout the evening, according to Lucilla," Agrippa posited.

"You have spoken with her?" Varro asked, slightly vexed that Agrippa had kept things from him. It's almost a natural state of affairs for a spy to become paranoid. He felt he could no longer wholly trust the consul, who had become a friend over the past year. But it cut even deeper to think that he could no longer wholly trust Lucilla. That he had lost her.

"Yes, she was most helpful."

Agrippa had been impressed by the woman's memory and perceptiveness. He even flirted with the idea of trying to recruit her as an asset. The consul knew a little of her history. Varro once confessed how the woman had lost a child in the womb when they were married. He blamed the tragedy for being the beginning of the end to their marriage. He shortly afterwards confessed however, whether immersed in wine truth or not, that he was to blame for ruining their marriage. Agrippa concluded how the best of Varro had won the esteemed lady, but the worst of him had lost her.

"It's nice that she told someone about her night with Herennius and Pulcher. She may even deign to get around to telling me one day too," Varro waspishly said, unable to suppress his grievance.

"There was little warmth and gratitude between Lentulus and his son-in-law. Herennius spent most of the evening gorging on food and getting drunk with Sestius. They dictated the conversation by sharing old war stories and boasting about their wealth... Towards the end of the evening Lucilla heard raised words between Herennius and Lentulus out in the garden. Our advocate marched rather than walked out of the house. His blood was up. There is no reason why the advocate couldn't have returned to the house and put an end to their argument by putting a knife in his son-in-law's chest... Lucilla mentioned that Corinna seemed ill at ease for most of the night, cowed by her husband. He curtly ordered her about, like a slave, and silenced her when she attempted to join in the conversation... Lucilla noticed a possible intimacy between Corinna and the poet, if you bait your hook accordingly when you go fishing and question them both."

"And how did Lucilla report upon Pulcher's behaviour throughout the evening? Do we even know why Maecenas' agent was in attendance?"

"She said that he tried to placate people and change the subject when the atmosphere grew too heated. Although the arch diplomat failed in his brief it seems. As to the question of whether Lucilla knew why Pulcher was there I believe she remains in the dark. I can enlighten you, however. He had been instructed by Maecenas, on the orders of Caesar, to meet with Herennius. His assignment was, or is, to acquire the gift Mark Antony and Fulvia gave the soldier as a reward for murdering Cicero. As you know Antony issued a handsome reward to Popilius Laenas, who led the small contingent of soldiers which tracked down Cicero. But what you may not know is that Fulvia made a gift of a dagger to the man who carried out the deed. It was perhaps the only time I ever saw the woman happy, when she talked about the death of Cicero. She probably hated Cicero with a greater passion than which she loved Antony. When Popilius brought the head of Cicero back to her she arranged to have it nailed onto the speaker's platform in the Forum. She gleefully then spat in its face and repeatedly stabbed the tongue, which had been used to defame both her and her husband, with a hairpin. Fulvia was cruel, even for a woman. I warrant that even Antony was cowed by her at times. First, he was led by Fulvia. And then by Cleopatra. He was a great leader of men, but a follower of women... But as to the dagger. It is made of gold, with a ruby encrusted pommel. Fulvia reportedly chose rubies to symbolise Cicero's blood. Now it appears that Pulcher left Herennius' house empty-handed. Yet somebody entered the house that night and stole the knife, as well as a few other choice valuables. Or it could well be the case that the dagger still resides at the property - and my attendant missed it during his search. Your first port of call should be to visit the house and double-check the dagger's not there. After hearing of Herennius' death - and Maecenas' inability to secure the trophy - Caesar sent me a message, instructing me to locate the knife and find Herennius' killer. In that order. But if we find one, we should find the other. Although the death of Sestius has made things murkier. Bloodier... You should pay a visit to each of the guests at the party. You are a keen reader of people, as well as poetry, Rufus. One of them must surely know more than they have so far admitted. I have a letter from Caesar, decreeing that any and everyone should assist you with your investigation. Fear may shake some fruit free from the tree. If you have any problems with people cooperating, let me know."

"Should I question Lucilla too?"

"Question, but do not interrogate. I imagine you must be worried about her dalliance with Pulcher, Rufus. But Lucilla will eventually see through his act, or Licinius will show his true colours and prove inconstant. Don't try and force the issue. If there's one thing that being the second most powerful man in Rome has taught me, it's that you can't control everything. The heart has a mind of its own."

**6.**

The blue skies turned grey. Clouds poured across the horizon, like smoke. Varro walked from Agrippa's home towards Herennius' house. The scene of the crime. The streets were teeming with all manner of people: slaves and senators, jewellers and jugglers, actors and aediles, dyers and drunks. Some dawdled but most scurried, like ants. Or vermin, Varro darkly - and admittedly unkindly - thought. Rome was a river, he mused - with foaming and, occasionally, tranquil eddies. No one knew where the river sprung from and no one knew where it flowed to.

"Rufus, my dear friend," Novius, the bookseller, exclaimed as he caught sight of one of his best customers. It's fate, or more likely good luck, that I have ran into you. My copyist has finished the edition of *The Last Days of Socrates* you wanted. You will be free to collect it at any time, or I can have my assistant run it round to you."

Novius stood before him, with his stoop and squint on full display, his knees gnarled and knobbly beneath his worn tunic. Varro liked the amiable and knowledgeable bookseller. He had always tried to champion his poetry - and always noted down the name of any young woman who came in to buy one of collections of verse.

"It's nice to see you Novius. I trust you are well. I will pick the book up over the coming days," Varro replied, figuring that he would be passing by the shop during the course of his enquiries. He liked to visit the store every now and then, just in case he spotted something new. He looked forward to reading the book. He remembered his father recommending it to him many years ago.

"I also had a customer come in and buy a couple of your books recently. It wasn't a fetching young lady, alas. But rather a well-read and most charming gentleman, one Licinius Pulcher."

Varro briefly made a face and bit his bottom lip but thankfully the bookseller failed to notice, or his eyesight had grown even poorer. The poet was far from grateful for the additional sales, for once. Why was Pulcher buying his poetry? Was he intending to criticise and ridicule his verse in front of Lucilla? Was the agent's assignment to get close to him, rather than her? As per usual the spy had more questions than answers.

"Well, if nothing else, it seems he has superior taste. As ever, thank you for promoting my work Novius."

"And can we expect any new works soon? It has been some time. People sometimes ask if you will be releasing any new verses."

"I've just begun working on something new, actually. 'Tis a tale of murder, seduction, greed and a rare, bejewelled dagger."

"I'm intrigued. Have you figured out how it will end yet?"

"No, unfortunately I have no idea about how things will turn out at the moment. From experience, things seldom turn out well though," Varro half-joked, straining his facial muscles to force a smile.

Manius stared into space, his features frozen. Pained. He looked like he had just heard the news that a good friend had died. A bee buzzed around his head, but he didn't flinch or notice it at all. Usually her husband was alert and attentive. But he had been distracted for most of the morning, Camilla judged. Yet she was at least comforted by the thought that she knew why her husband appeared anxious. He was due to take on another client. Whilst Manius still occasionally worked for Varro as a bodyguard he had recently taken on work as a tutor, teaching swordsmanship to the sons of aristocrats, wealthy merchants and politicians.

Business was good. He had several clients. She was proud of him. The past year had been even better than she dreamed it would be, she considered. Because it had been real. There was a moment when her future had been as black as the river Styx. Her father had forbidden any talk of marriage to the lowly bodyguard and foreigner. He even kept her housebound, so she could no longer see him. Yet her father underwent a change of heart and Manius experienced a change in his fortunes when he came into some money. They married and bought a house on the Caelian Hill. Camilla spent her days cooking, sewing and reading. Varro kindly allowed the couple use of his villa in the countryside. Her maid, Decima, had become her best friend. She had little interest in parties or making a name for herself, or her husband, in Roman society. The household was happy and in good health, including - or especially - Viola.

She loved him, more and more each day. Camilla believed that her husband would never prove unfaithful or lie to her. His heart was nobler, for having endured so much misfortune. As a boy, Manius had watched his father die when a group of Roman soldiers attacked and burned his village. Along with his mother, he was sold into slavery in Gaul. His mother died soon after. "She just wasted away, like ice melting on a mountaintop in Spring," he had once confessed to Camilla, tears welling in his eyes. It was rare for the Briton to share much of his past however, yet his silence spoke volumes. After his mother passed away Manius was sent off to train as a gladiator. His body became work-hardened, like a piece of metal, and he began to make a name for himself as a young gladiator. The crowds called him, somewhat prosaically, "The Briton". He remained undefeated, but not untouched during his time in the arena. When she first saw Manius naked, Camilla did well not to recoil from the scars, which marked his torso like features on a map. The Briton had enough blood on his hands for two lifetimes, from gladiatorial contests and tavern brawls.

Appius Varro had saved him, taking him in as a young man. He bought his freedom and cut short his career as a gladiator (before his career as a gladiator cut short his life). Rufus Varro taught his new companion how to read and write and Manius taught him swordsmanship in return. The Briton proved the more diligent student, by some margin.

Manius' life had been good, serving as Varro's bodyguard. But it became even better, after meeting Camilla.

Varro was invited into the atrium and met by the household's head slave, Fabullus. He explained that the lady of the house was out shopping for the day. Like many slaves in Rome, Fabullus was sallow-faced and lank-haired with an expression of submissiveness and apprehension on his countenance - as though at any moment Varro might admonish or strike him. When the nobleman informed the slave how he was investigating the murder of his master, under the authority of Caesar himself, Fabullus' anxiety increased. His eyes blinked more than a coquette's. Varro attempted to put the man at ease, however. He just wanted to ask some questions and look around the house.

Varro first asked what had been stolen. Fabullus confirmed that the gold dagger, which usually hung, pride of place, in the triclinium was missing. A few other pieces of jewellery - and some gold coins - had also been taken. The intruder had not ventured up to the first floor during the robbery. The staff and lady of the house had all been asleep during the incident too, although Fabullus confirmed that one of the slaves, Dio, had noticed a figure wearing a dark cloak standing across from the front of the property on the night of the murder. "He seemed to be waiting for something." Fabullus also told Varro about a piece of black wool which had been found by the front gate in the morning. To his mind, it hadn't been there when he had shown the guests out earlier in the evening.

"Thank you, this is all helpful," Varro remarked, as he interviewed the slave on a bench in the atrium. "But tell me, were you party to the heated discussion your master and his father-in-law had after dinner? I was told that there were raised voices. You seem a conscientious servant Fabullus. One who would remain within earshot of his master, in case you were summoned."

"I do not want to speak ill of the dead," the slave said, sheepishly, unable to look Varro in the eye.

"On the contrary, the dead are the best people to speak ill of. They cannot take you to court or answer you back, to prove you wrong. And the more I get to know your old master, the more I am inclined to speak ill of him. Whatever you tell me I will keep in the strictest confidence. Rather than protect the reputation of the dead, you owe a duty to the living. As you know, Sestius has also been killed. I am here to ensure that no one else is murdered. So, did you overhear what was said?" the investigator asked, firmly and fairly.

"Yes. He claimed that my master owed him money. He said that his son-in-law needed to pay the second instalment for what he owed for his daughter. That he was reneging on their arrangement. My master replied that possession was nine tenths of the law and his daughter was now his property. He would pay the remaining money once his daughter had fulfilled her wifely duty to bear him a child. A son. My master would withhold the second payment until then."

"And how then did Lentulus react?"

"He grew angrier."

"Did he threaten Herennius?"

"Yes. He said my master would pay, one way or another. He then left with his wife to go home."

Varro considered how Lentulus' words were far from a confession, but the finger of suspicion was pointing towards the advocate. He had sufficient motive it seemed to kill Herennius. It was also conceivable that, after killing his son-in-law, he then might murder Sestius to make sure that Herennius' estate passed to his daughter. Any financial difficulties he was suffering would be over - and his daughter would be rid of an undesirable husband."

"Tell me, was your master abusive towards his slaves and wife?" Varro asked, already knowing the answer to his question.

Fabullus nodded his head in reply, appearing pained - perhaps reliving an incident of his master punishing him or the mistress of the house. Corinna had motive too, even more motive than her father. Varro also thought how Fabullus, or another long-suffering slave, could easily be put on the suspect list. It was not uncommon in Rome for a slave to turn on a cruel master out of revenge, or to defend himself. Manius had spoken of many a fellow gladiator who had chosen to fight in the arena to avoid a death sentence, in punishment for killing his employer. Could the whey-faced slave in front of him be the murderer? Again, annoyingly, Varro had more questions than answers.

"Thank you for your time and candour Fabullus. Is there anything you would like to add?"

"Yes, my master may have been cruel, but my mistress is kind. Although she may have had reason to do him harm, she did not kill him. She is an innocent woman."

*Another potential oxymoron. Is he trying to exonerate his mistress because she is guiltless, or protect her because she's guilty?*

"I will heed your words… I would like to now look around the house. I imagine you have duties to attend to, Fabullus, so I will be fine to do so unaccompanied."

Manius cleared away his weapons and armour - the tools of his trade - having finished sharpening and oiling them. Again, he became distracted, not quite knowing what to do with himself. He bit his nails and failed to notice Viola, nuzzling his shins. She was perhaps keen to go out in the garden or, more likely, craved a treat. The knee-high mongrel could eat like a horse. Manius smoothed down his hair and removed a couple of pieces of fluff from his tunic. He was due to meet his new client soon. The tutor needed to be presentable, even more than he needed to be skilled in swordsmanship.

Yet Manius wasn't anxious due to his forthcoming appointment as a tutor. He was used to taking on new business. Rather he was on edge because he was about to take on his first assignment for Agrippa, as his agent. The consul summoned Manius to his house several months ago. Agrippa had greeted him in a familiar and friendly manner, which immediately made the Briton wary.

"I want to grant you an opportunity, Manius," the consul remarked, after having a slave re-fill his guest's cup. "I have a business proposition for you. How would you like to be employed as a tutor, in swordsmanship, by Rome's elite? The sons of senators, plutocrats and aristocrats need instruction, whether they will be serving in the army or not. You will not run short of clients, I can assure you. Partly because many of the chinless wonders will prove so inept, your tenure of employment will likely be long-term. I would be happy to invest in you and your burgeoning brand, but the beauty of the business is that it is low-cost. I cannot imagine that you wish to work as Rufus' bodyguard forever, although I appreciate that he may still have need of you from time to time due to his work for me... But this is Rome, Manius. One does not get something for nothing. In return for my support I would ask you to take on a client or two for my benefit, or rather for the good of Rome... You will eventually become part of the furniture in a household. One of your greatest virtues, Manius, is that people underestimate you. Your brief will just be to keep your eyes and ears open and collect information, intelligence. I will need you to report on who visits the house, be they a politician or mistress. It's in our nature to be indiscreet and gossip after a measure of wine... The peace and prosperity of Rome must be maintained through eternal vigilance. You duly helped foil Lucius Scaurus' attempted coup last year. As many lives were lost on that day, you helped save thousands. Because you - and Rufus - kept your ears and eyes open... Rome and Caesar will always have their enemies, who operate in the shadows. It's why we must operate in the shadows too... I first thought that you may be too honourable, or honest, to be an effective agent. But it is because you are honourable that you will work to protect Rome from its enemies inside its gates. It's because you have an honest and earnest face that people will trust you. But I have confidence that you will be able to play a part. You were once a performer, as a gladiator, were you not? Rome needs good men, Manius. You have a wife. You will soon have children, I warrant. Help me create a future for your children, one where they will be free from privation or civil war."

The Briton ended the meeting by agreeing to Agrippa's proposal. He felt he had little choice. Few people could say no to the consul. And no one could say no to Caesar. The spymaster argued that it might prove the case that he would have no need to call upon the fencing teacher. But both men knew that was a lie.

A few days ago, Agrippa had summoned his agent. The consul had arranged, through an intermediary, for Manius to take on a new student. The boy's father had been making a name for himself. It was time for his first assignment.

"Just note who he meets with and, if possible, find out what is being said. I have heard rumours of a planned political rally, which means there could be a riot. People may get injured or killed. Unless we prevent it, by priming the Praetorian Guard to dispel the mob before it can cause harm... He is a danger to Rome. You may not think it now, but if he remains unchecked then he could become another Catiline. Anyone who exclaims, "Power to the people," is usually pursuing power for his own ends... If you gain his son's trust, you may gain the trust of his father. Keep note of who he meets. I need to know his prospective allies, in and out of the Senate House. He may have a weakness for women or wine, or something else. Any intelligence which could provide a chink in his armour may prove invaluable... I must ask you to keep your assignment secret, from your wife and Rufus... Secrecy often equates to survival in your new trade."

Manius sighed, as though he had the weight the world on his shoulders. For once he didn't quite know whether he was acting honourably or dishonourably. He couldn't help but feel uncomfortable lying to Camilla, although that could prove the least of his problems. After the thick, rich sigh, however, Manius smiled, as he noticed Viola at his feet. Wagging her tail, without a care in the world. She jumped up and placed her front paws on his knees and licked his left hand as his right stroked her behind the ear. The Briton had found the dog on the streets and taken her in. Saving her. Had Agrippa taken him in, with an eye to saving him? Manius wasn't so sure. He recalled a conversation he recently had with Varro, as the two men shared a jug of wine and sat in his garden, taking shelter beneath an awning during a heavy storm. The rain stung like needles. Forked lightning stabbed repeatedly upon the horizon, like a trident. The thunder claps reverberated through the air, as if Jupiter himself was stamping upon the drear clouds above. Viola scampered inside and took sanctuary beneath his bed.

"My career as a spy may not even last as long, or be as unsuccessful, as that of a poet, my friend. I'm losing myself or becoming bored. The lines are blurring between who I am and the roles I play. Even the greatest actors need to spend time offstage... I tell myself that I am being honourable, working to protect Rome, but it's all such a grubby business. I feel like a whore - and Agrippa is my bawd. I spend half my time lying and exploiting people. I have little doubt that the intelligence I've passed on has caused women to be widowed and children to be orphaned. I all but hammered the nails into the crosses, for the so-called enemies of the state who have been crucified. I have told myself that the means justify the ends. But what justifies the ends? A small nod of gratitude from Caesar, a man who pretends he is a demi-god? I have to laugh, otherwise I'd cry... And what of my fellow agents? Some are zealots for a cause, whilst others are as mercenary as politicians. Some will cannily just tell their paymasters what they want to hear, or pedal lies instead of truth - if lies pay more. Agents will bribe, blackmail and extort like common criminals. Yet because they are somehow working for a great cause they are exonerated - and venerated... Any relationship I now have will be founded on a lie, because I will be unable to tell them what I do. Who I am. Deception becomes second nature, to the point where you no longer realise you are fooling yourself. Though perhaps that is the lot of everyone, not just spies... Although I informed Lucilla about my work. I told her enough lies whilst we were married. I didn't want to tell her another one. I do not want her thinking less of me, even if I think less of myself..."

Varro also mentioned periods when he found it difficult to sleep, since he had become an agent. Manius had seldom slept himself over the past few days. When he woke, he would remain dead still however, since he did not want to wake his wife. He had welcomed the task of keeping watch over his friend, during his seduction of Cornelia. It had helped take his mind off his own imminent assignment.

Camilla walked in the room. Manius smiled, not knowing how forced or genuine his expression was. Somehow, he felt that his "honest face" wasn't so honest anymore. Yet he loved his wife. That much, which was almost everything, was true.

Camilla wore an apron, dusted with various ingredients from baking a fresh batch of honey cakes. The pendant around her neck glistened. Her eyes gleamed too, with intelligence and fondness. He never tired of kissing her tender lips. She wanted to wrap her arms around him, nestle her head in his chest, but she didn't want to stain his tunic. She wanted to make love to him, both as a thing in itself and because she desperately wanted a child. But there was no time.

"Are you feeling better? You seemed distracted earlier," Camilla remarked, trying to fend Violet off from licking the hem of her apron. The well-read young woman thought earlier how her husband possessed the build of Ajax, the courage of Hector and the faithfulness of Odysseus. He would never cheat on her. He would never lie.

"I'm fine," Manius replied, lying.


Varro went through the house, from top to bottom, in more than just a cursory manner. The agent searched through every potential hiding place in hope of finding the dagger. It would save Varro an uncommon amount of time and energy if the knife was still in the house. He could be in Arretium by the following evening. Free. At peace. Or as much as at peace as he could be, knowing that Lucilla had fallen under the spell of Pulcher.

Varro was decidedly unimpressed by the garish décor of the property. He could hear the waspish voice of Lucilla inside his head, commenting on some of the modern pieces of art scattered throughout the house:

*He has more money than sense, or taste… The resale values would have bankrupted him, as Herennius would have had to pay people to take the vulgar pieces away.*

Varro was dogged in his search, to the point of picking open the lock on Corinna's large jewellery box with a hairpin he found in her room. Unfortunately, he did not find the dagger, but the spy did finally discover a something of interest. Love letters. The notes heaved with affection, passion and eroticism. Varro had composed similar missives in his youth, either to get into the heart or bedchamber of his mistresses. It seemed that Corinna was conducting an affair. The letters made no mention of her husband however - or a plot to do away with him. Varro couldn't help but admire certain turns of phrase in the notes. The author was witty, well-read and lusty. And anonymous, as he hadn't inserted his name in the correspondence. Although at the bottom of the first note he had signed off with the letter "O". It suddenly struck Varro that Licinius Omerus Pulcher could be the mysterious author and lover. The spy certainly owned the motive and skills to seduce the young wife. Perhaps his goal was to encourage her to steal the dagger for him. Or had Pulcher manipulated Corinna to such an extent that she had murdered Herennius, in order to be with her lover? There was a part of Varro which craved for the rival agent to be responsible for the crime. And he craved to provide evidence of the fact to duly condemn him. But just because Varro wanted something to be true, it didn't infer that it was true.

He continued his search. When Varro came to the wine cellar, he again found something which piqued his interest. At the far wall he noticed a design of wine rack which he owned too. The spy licked his lips and raised his hopes once more as he approached the custom-made piece of furniture. Instead of reaching for one of the vintages however Varro reached around the wine rack, unhooked a couple of catches and carefully swung open the item like a door. Behind the rack in his own cellar Varro kept a number of vintages which he didn't wish guests to see and sample. Could Herennius have kept valuables or private papers in the alcove behind this piece of furniture? Sweat glazed his palms and the back of his neck tingled. Varro suddenly experienced a premonition that he was about to find the dagger. Were the gods being kind to him, for once? He pictured the gold blade in his mind's eye, gleaming in the darkness. But in reality, there was nothing to be found, except an empty wooden shelf. Varro emitted a small sigh and muttered an obscenity beneath his breath for being so optimistic. Foolish.

Varro was tempted to wait for the lady of the house to confront her about her affair. Uncovering one secret could lead him to uncover another. But Varro was tired, weary - as though the strigil of life had scraped away at him too much. He wanted to process things and discuss the day's events with Manius. He resolved to meet his friend later that night, for a drink in the Subura. As much as Varro wanted to collect his thoughts, he also wanted to forget his troubles, wash the image of Lucilla and Pulcher out of his mind with a jug of wine. Or two.

## 7.

Such was his absorption in Varro's account of the day's events that Manius barely touched his drink. The two men sat at their usual table in the tavern, *The Golden Lion*. Varro did his best not to miss anything of importance out:

"Agrippa is keen to succeed, where Maecenas failed, and retrieve the dagger for Caesar. Perhaps, like Herennius, he wants to hang the trophy on his wall. If I had to place a wager on who the culprit was the smart money would be on Lentulus Nerva at present. He all but vowed to kill him on the night of the party. His wife would of course supply him with an alibi, as he went back to the house after everyone else departed. Herennius would have invited him in and would have poured out a cup of wine and ate an olive, as the advocate drew a knife and stabbed him in the chest. Lentulus then stole the dagger and a few other valuables to make it look like a robbery. And when he discovered that Sestius would inherit Herennius' wealth he murdered him also, so the estate would pass to his daughter. Or, more realistically, he could have paid an assassin to kill Sestius. Nerva certainly possesses the necessary contacts with the criminal underworld. One of the first things an investigator should ask himself is, who benefits? The answer is Lentulus... But has not Corinna benefited too? Women break hearts every day. They are surely not beyond skewering them with a blade too, if suitably provoked... Or could "Omerus" be our "O" - and have seduced Corinna into murdering her husband and giving him the dagger? But then that doesn't explain Sestius' death... Lucilla has also provided Maecenas' attack dog, or lap-dog, with an alibi... In conclusion, I do not know what to think. If the height of intelligence is Socratic ignorance, then I feel like the wisest man in the empire... I will talk to Lucilla tomorrow. She doesn't seem to be acting like the wisest woman in the empire at the moment, given her involvement with Pulcher."

"Do not look to judge her too harshly, partly because that may be what Pulcher wants. Let him be the one to fall on his sword, not you," Manius advised his friend, imagining the slight Varro was suffering. Lucilla was breaking his heart, again - and seemingly stabbing him in the back by courting the rival agent. "Remember that you are her friend now, rather than her husband. You will be unable to lay down the law. Hear what she has to say. It may be the case that Pulcher is using Lucilla to get to you, or someone else. You need to keep the door open with Lucilla. If nothing else, you may need to use her to spy on Pulcher... There's no need to despair."

"As ever, you are right. Annoyingly. There are worse fates I could be enduring, than getting drunk with an old friend. I have reasons to be cheerful, do I not? There are fewer maggots in the bread than usual. I actually found a sizeable piece of meat in the stew tonight and I'm not wincing or retching from the wine," Varro drily remarked, as he cast an eye around the tavern.

It was late, but early in the evening for *The Golden Lion*. Old and fresh cobwebs hung down from the lamps on the creaking ceiling. An ashen-faced sot coughed-up blood in one corner, before amorously staring at a whore on the first floor. She returned his gaze. Varro fancied that her make-up had been slapped on by a heavy-handed house painter rather than a fine portrait artist. The prostitute was past her prime. *But aren't we all?* The drunk wiped the blood away from his mouth with a phlegm-stained rag. The pair gave each other a nod and the old man shuffled upstairs, his bones creaking more than the bannister. Words and coins were exchanged, and they disappeared into a backroom. Lust, rather than love, was in the air as a virginal student, his eyes blood-shot with desire and wine, was led away by Nefertari, a beguiling Egyptian beauty the landlord, Bassos, had imported into the tavern a year ago.

A few patrons began to rest their weary, heady heads in their arms and fell asleep on the tables, whilst others laughed and talked animatedly, putting the world to rights. People were drinking their troubles away, with their love of drink perhaps being the chief cause of their troubles.

A blanket of damp sawdust covered the uneven floor. A sword hung on the wall, which the landlord boasted - lied - had once belonged to Julius Caesar. Smoke poured out of the kitchen. The smell of watery stew, body odour and pungent acetum filled his nostrils. Motes of dusts - and flies - swirled about in the air.

Varro pricked his ears up on hearing dice rattling across a table. A trio of customers sat in the corner. It was a familiar sight. One chewed his nails and glanced at his dwindling pile of coins in front of him. Another tapped his foot and mouthed a prayer. And another kissed his dice and threw. Varro used to find the sound even more welcoming than the pouring of wine, sizzling meat and the rustling of silk. There was a time when the poet was more addicted to gambling than he was women. Gambling was a remedy for the malady of boredom. He loved winning and equally, or more so, Varro loved defeating his opponents. Gambling made him feel alive, whether it was dice, wagering on a chariot race or even betting on the toss of the coin. The nobleman could be more stoical about his losses than most. Thankfully the bets Fronto made, in terms of investments, compensated for any losing streaks. If fortune was indifferent to him, he could afford to be indifferent to it. Everything was meat to place a wager on. Perhaps his life as a spy had helped replace the rush and risk he gleaned from gambling, to wean him off his addiction. Gambling had certainly proved as dangerous as espionage at times. He had lost more friends than he had made over games of dice. Not everyone took to losing with good grace and, on more than one occasion, Manius had needed to escort Varro from the table.

Varro could feel his heart beat faster just watching the game in the corner of the tavern. He tapped his foot in rhythm with the player who had just offered up a whispered prayer. Varro had once sought out games in the Subura and in the houses of noblemen. He would lie to himself, that he was in control of his habit. But his habit had been in control of him. He would spend hours practising his throw and willing the right outcome. But the dice, like women or the weather, were only constant in their inconstancy.

Varro was distracted from his thoughts by a familiar voice.

"Evening. How was your food?" Bassos amiably asked. The plump, balding landlord was always happy to welcome the aristocrat and bodyguard into his establishment. Varro spent plenty of money and Manius was one to end rather than start a brawl.

"Well you didn't poison me, for once," Varro joked, sincerely hoping that his meal wouldn't repeat on him. He had no wish to relive the taste.

"I am sorry about the milk curdling earlier. My wife must have stared at it," Bassos replied, not joking as much as one might expect. Fausta, his formidable wife, drained her husband's soul and capital. When she deigned to show her face in the tavern, she would scold Bassos like a child. Fear of his wife, rather than any devotion to her, kept Bassos from having an affair with one of the whores. "But I have just arranged for a more welcome sight than my wife to come to the tavern. I am importing a whore from your homeland, Manius. She's well endowed. I've been told that her breasts are as large as those on the statue of Venus at the foot of the Capitoline Hill. Her hair is as red as the dawn and she's as clean as one of Agrippa's aqueducts. Nessa will give you a chance to speak in your native tongue, although she can use her tongue for more than just talking, if you know what I mean. Being from that wild island, she will probably be able to drink most of my customers under the table. But she'll take you on the table too. She's young as well. Fresh meat. Tender meat. I recommend that you book her early as she'll be as popular in here as the house wine, and taste as sweet too," Bassos exclaimed, winking and nudging the Briton, causing him to spill his drink.

"Thank you, but no thank you. I'm married, remember?" Manius replied.

Bassos was about to respond that married men were more likely to say yes when it came to his girls, but the landlord checked himself. He consoled himself with the thought that, with or without Manius succumbing to temptation, Nessa would be worth the money he was paying for her. His wife had said he had overpaid. But Bassos wanted to prove her wrong, as much as Fausta might make him pay for doing so, he fancied.

The landlord's attention was diverted away from his friends however as he heard laughter and insults sounding out behind him. Bassos turned around to see a quartet of youths - students, no doubt - harassing one of his regular customers, Benjamin. The adolescents were hurling food and abuse at the elderly Jew, who was doing his best to ignore his tormentors, in the hope that they would then leave him alone.

"Go home Jew. You think you're a porcupine, who can't be touched. But Publius Carbo is showing us the way. Your time is nearly up in this city. We'll drive you out, like rats."

Bassos grunted on hearing the name. Carbo was a former senator, who had been forced to resign his position by Augustus. He rarely attended the Senate House to vote. And when Carbo did contribute to a debate, he more often than not raised the subject of the Jews in Rome. He argued they were the cause for any and all of the city's problems. Julius Caesar and Augustus had decreed that the Jewish community should be free to practise their religion without persecution. But there was not space for Romans and Jews in the city.

Having lost his position in the Senate House, Carbo had recently taken to the streets, as a demagogue, to spread his message. He called it a "new kind of politics". He gave speeches in market squares and had his followers daub graffiti in the Subura. He wanted the Jews to first be taxed of their wealth and then banished from Rome. Their religion should be prohibited once more. Rome cannot serve two gods, he argued. It was rumoured that he desired to ban religion altogether, although one suspected he would have allowed the cult of Publius Carbo to continue and flourish. Jews should be prohibited from practising usury, he demanded. Any debts owed to them should be cancelled (a policy which proved especially popular among students). Carbo's principle political slogan was that "Rome is for the many, not the Jew". He further fomented resentment towards the Jews by claiming that they had caused the civil war between Octavius and Antony, by whispering poison in their ears. They had encouraged the triumvirs to commit to war, in order to lend them the money to do so, and profit from the interest they earned. Jews had too much influence in the Senate House. Their tentacles had a hold over too many political and economic institutions. Those who spoke out against Carbo and his lies were threatened with violence or shouted down by his army of zealous supporters. And his army was gaining recruits by the day. The Jews were a scapegoat for all manner of aggrieved citizens. Tutors spoke-up for Carbo and parroted his message, hoping to encourage students to study with them. The heads of a number of guilds pledged their support for Carbo, as he promised them that the taxes extracted from the Jews would be distributed to their members. Rather than claiming that they belonged to a political faction, his followers called themselves a "progressive movement". And they had momentum. Bassos had recently read, with shame, a new slogan painted across various locations in the Subura: "The only good Jew is a dead Jew". Trouble was brewing and boiling over. Jewish shop owners had recently had their premises set fire to. His more fervent supporters had also vandalised places of worship and broken-up Jewish religious services. A number of Jews had been injured - and died - fighting back against his followers. When the authorities asked Carbo to give up the names of those who had committed the acts of anti-Semitism, he refused. The demagogue was becoming a law unto himself.

But Bassos was determined not to allow Carbo's followers to become a law unto themselves in his tavern. Benjamin was his friend, as well as his customer. He excused himself to Varro and Manius and approached the youths.

"I'd like you all to leave, gentlemen," the landlord said, firmly, wishing that his voice could be just half as harsh as his wife's tone. "Are you well Benjamin?"

The Jew nodded, unconvincingly, as his eyes warily flitted between Bassos and his tormentors. The silversmith had often been the victim of ridicule and abuse by Romans, but he was now all too conscious of the stories of his fellow Jews being physically attacked, or even murdered, since the rise in popularity of Carbo. The former senator had emboldened his supporters, given them licence to turn prejudice into persecution.

"And I'd like you to fuck off," one of the youths, Tarquin Gellius, exclaimed. His language may have been coarse, but his accent was aristocratic. Gellius was educated, monied. A wisp of a beard covered his chin. The student had straw-coloured hair and a pasty complexion. He needed to get out in the sun more and, from his rake-thin build, he needed to eat a few hearty meals. There was nothing of him, Bassos thought. His face was sharp, angular. He wore a pinched expression, patterned tunic and a few items of jewellery. His eyes were bloodshot, beady, vindictive.

Gellius' words were accompanied by a chorus of sniggers, from his three friends. The students had been brought up to consider themselves, in education and manners, to be superior to the likes of the landlord. Their parents and tutors had told them so many times that they were special and entitled that they believed them.

"Would you rather serve this animal, than us?" Gellius added. "He should be the one to go home, not us. We will spend more than him too. And from the look of things here you could do with earning some extra money," the student exclaimed, sneering as he surveyed the old tavern.

As little as he thought of them Bassos knew that the half-drunk youths could cause plenty of trouble - and damage. Each had a small dagger hanging down from his belt. If he tried to forcibly eject them on his own, he could easily cause a greater disturbance or suffer an injury. Thankfully Bassos was not alone in wanting to see the back of the group.

"You've been asked to leave, politely. Should my friend here have to ask you he may not be so civil. If he needs to chuck you out of here, he's likely to throw you all into the Tiber too," Varro remarked, as the former gladiator stood next to him, cutting an imposing figure.

"You would side with him, over your own kind?" Gellius replied, confused and contemptuous. His tone became shrill, as if his voice hadn't broken yet. He was young, but as pompous as a politician, Varro thought.

"You're not my kind," the nobleman countered, less than cordially.

"Believe it or not but we are here for your benefit, to spread the good word about our leader, Publius Carbo, and his enlightened policies. If you listen to him and follow his ways your lives will be better. You will drink less wine, eat a healthier, vegetable-based diet, ban the barbaric sport of hunting, the unwanted will be driven out of Rome. Your debts will be cancelled, and everyone will work for the good of the state, directed by a council of elders, led by Publius Carbo. Ordinary working people will be live better lives. Our leader has a five-year plan," Gellius preached.

Varro, amused and saddened, considered that he had known poets less conceited than the addled student.

"My plan is not so long-term, unfortunately for you. I just want to be rid of you from my sight and, more importantly, have you out of earshot too."

"I'm not scared of you," Gellius countered, unconvincingly, as his large Adam's apple bobbed up and down in his throat.

"But if you're half as clever as you think you are you should fear me. Benjamin here is far more welcome here than you are," Manius posited, as he amiably and respectfully nodded to the silversmith, who had recently crafted a ring for him, which he had given to his wife as a present. The Jew nodded back, in thanks to the Briton. Benjamin also appeared awkward - and even apologetic - for somehow causing a fuss. It was not the first time he had been mocked. But he was all too aware of the growing animosity towards his people. Carbo was stoking the fires of resentment. He had a friend, Abraham, whose beard had been singed, by a group of students, after they had beaten him to the ground. His neighbour had a brick thrown through his window. His own wife and daughter had been spat upon in the market.

The Briton's expression was far from amiable and respectful when he turned towards the irksome youth.

Varro could no longer hear the sound of rattling dice. Instead the noise of scraping chairs filled the room, as customers moved to obtain a better view of the unfolding spectacle.

Gellius and his confederates offered each other a nervous stare. They gulped in unison. They were all used to intimidating elderly Jews - or abusing their opponents at a distance, anonymous within a mob - as opposed to facing brutal-looking bodyguards. Tarquin Gellius' friends were willing to drink with him (especially as he usually paid for their wine), but they had little desire to spill blood for their comrade.

As Manius stepped forward, the three ashen companions stepped back. Gellius' eyes widened, and he recoiled a little. The adolescent also began to hold his hands up. The Briton was unconcerned whether he was doing so in a gesture of surrender, or if he was about to throw a limp-wristed punch. Manius was agile for his size. His arm darted forward, as swiftly as a ballista bolt, and grabbed Gellius' right hand, twisting it so that the student bent down and contorted his body to alleviate the pain. Gellius whimpered and was about to snivel. Manius' face remained impassive as he bent back his little finger and then broke it. A couple of regulars, sitting nearby, winced slightly at the clicking sound. The bodyguard neither enjoyed the action, nor felt any remorse. It just needed to be done, like a carpenter has to hammer in nails.

"If you come back, or if I witness you tormenting another of my friends, or even a complete stranger, I'll break your arm. Do you understand?"

Gellius' lip quivered and his injured hand trembled, like a leaf half hanging from a branch. He scrunched his face up, as if he were about to sob, and nodded. Although the petrified youth would have agreed with the bodyguard even if Manius said that two plus two equalled five, just to be free of him.

"Now you fuck off, before I further injure you with a barbed comment," Varro remarked, unable to suppress a grin in response to seeing the bullies retreat, with their tails between their legs, as they nearly tripped over one another when scrambling out the tavern.

To celebrate, or ease the tension in the room, Varro bought a round of drinks for everyone. It was Manius' turn to appear awkward - and blush - as a number of regulars applauded him for despatching the unwelcome youths. People offered to buy him drinks but he politely declined. Manius had to wake early in the morning to give a fencing lesson to the son of Publius Carbo.

## 8.

Any twinge of guilt was decidedly absent, in regard to his behaviour towards Publius Carbo's followers, as Varro made his way home later that evening. He did however suffer a rare twinge of envy as Varro parted from his friend. The nobleman was heading home to an empty bed (unless he summoned one of his serving girls to attend to him). Whilst Manius was walking in a different direction, towards a loving wife and an equally devoted dog.

"We're trying for a child... Camilla is being both scientific and amorous in relation to conceiving. I've known lanistas who were less demanding of my time and energy," Manius half-joked, as they trundled up the hill, out of the Subura. He thought how his wife might be waiting up for him, expecting him to sober up enough - or be drunk enough - to perform his husbandly duties. "But there are worse fates to endure, than a man having to make love to his wife."

"Aye, a man divorcing his wife is a far more painful - and expensive - experience," Varro replied. He clasped his friend by the forearm and wished him well as they went their separate ways. The bodyguard did offer to accompany his employer to his door, but Varro remarked that the Briton needed to save his strength.

"It's Camilla's job, not mine, to wear you out tonight. I'll be fine. All the husbands I've cuckolded, who'll be baying for my blood, will be tucked up in bed by now."

Although he never expressed his feelings on the subject Varro sometimes felt vulnerable, naked, without his bodyguard and friend by his side. They had naturally spent less time together, since Manius had married and moved in with Camilla. Varro couldn't blame his wife for seeing less of his drinking companion, as she actively encouraged Manius to spend time with him. *Perhaps she feels sorry for me. She knows how few true friends I possess.* He would never admit it but, as well as missing his drinking partner, he missed seeing Viola every day. Varro was at pains to think of more than a handful of women who he had loved more than the sweet-tempered mongrel. *But life must move on.* The nobleman comforted himself with the fact that he had seen more of Lucilla over the past year, since Manius had married - which was no mean fate. He had not seen so much of her lately however - though he now realised why.

*Life moves on. For other people.*

Whereas he would have preferred to be greeted by Aspasia when he walked through the door, Varro was met by his wizened estate manager, Fronto, when he returned home. Fronto had served his father for decades. Now the attendant served Varro, overseeing his staff and capital. His aged countenance was weathered, rather than defeated. There was still an occasional twinkle in his rheumy eye, especially since Fronto had started to court the laundrywoman, Aelia.

Fronto had served as Varro's tutor throughout his youth, and the nobleman still sought his elder's counsel. The old man could be cynical, but it was a cynical world Varro reasoned. Yet, in the face of such a cynical and even wicked world, Varro admired his friend's determination to retain his sense of decency and sense of humour. His frame may have been hunched, but the stoic was unbowed. He still gardened, cooked and kept his promise to Appius Varro, that he would wait up for his son and keep watch over him. Fronto still nursed hope that his young master would find someone and bear a son to carry on the family name. Have a future. Or, in the form of Lucilla, the old man hoped that the nobleman's future lay in the past.

Fronto poured out a couple of cups of diluted wine as Varro recounted the events of the evening. He frowned, with his skin resembling creased-up parchment, when Varro spoke about the attack on the silversmith. It was rare for Fronto to raise his voice or lose his even-temper, but he did so after hearing Carbo's name. He even began to down his wine quicker than Varro, which was perhaps a first.

"This Carbo could prove to be another Clodius, given the chance, inciting mob rule. I had the misfortune to hear him pontificate once, in the market. He affects the air of a priest. But he possesses a black soul. Beneath the smell of his perfume I warrant that there is something which smells rotten, gangrenous. Caesar should douse the spark before it turns into a conflagration. Carbo would happily see everything turn to ash, so he could volunteer to rebuild things... His thuggish followers will first come for the Jews. But then they will come for the nobility and the educated... The demagogue may even harbour ambitions of challenging Caesar. I would like to see him try. Caesar knows how defeat an enemy. Any enemy. He fears no man, though he might be wise to fear his wife... I've witnessed the fool's followers first hand. I saw one of their mobs drag a Jewess out of her litter the other month. The vile dogs urinated on her, claiming that the wife of a banker should suffer for her husband's sins. Bankers were to blame for all of Rome's ills, they pronounced. The imbeciles also blurted out various trite slogans, force fed to them by Carbo and his propagandists. I'm not usually one to trouble the gods, as it's often best not to bring oneself to their attention, but I feel compelled to pray to them. To blight the demagogue and his odious ilk. I'm not sure how much my prayers will help, but they probably can't do any harm... So, what are your plans for tomorrow?"

"To keep digging, even if I start digging a hole for myself. I will interview Lentulus tomorrow. I will also grab the bull by the horns and visit Lucilla in the morning," Varro remarked, although he planned not to leave too early. He wanted it to be late enough for Pulcher to have departed, should he have spent the evening with her.

*He can crawl into his own bed, or someone else's. Maecenas', if the rumours are to be believed.*

"You must be patient with Lucilla. She will be innocent of any wrongdoing. You must tread carefully with Lentulus Nerva too. The advocate is a powerful man, with even more powerful friends, both amongst the Senate House and criminal fraternity in Rome. Agrippa may be able to afford to make an enemy of Lentulus, but you can't. Choose your words wisely when speaking to him, as if you were selecting the right word for each line in a poem. Ask rather than accuse. Even if you suspect Lentulus is guilty, the advocate will have carefully covered his tracks. Your case will need to have stronger foundations than the Servian wall. I have seen Lentulus perform at trial. He puts on quite a show. I have seen him tie defendants up in Gordian knots. I will do some digging myself. I will visit your father's old advocate, Gabinius, and see what he has to say about his counterpart."

The cup weighed heavy in his leaden arm, but Varro nevertheless raised it in gratitude.

"Thanks. I would be lost without you."

"Worse. You would be bankrupt without me. Which is a fate worse than death in Rome," Fronto playfully remarked.

"Or, in the case of Lentulus, bankruptcy could be a crime more heinous than murder," Varro replied, less playfully.

Moonlight, as gentle as a whisper, poured through the open shutters of the room. The sheets were half on the bed, half on the floor, as Manius and Camilla lay next to one another. The only thing between their warm bodies was a glistening film of sweat. His bulging arms cradled her. Her back was pressed up against his large chest. His chin rested on her shoulder, as he breathed in the scent of her hair and silken skin.

Their hearts beat in time and they breathed in unison, coming down from the high of their lovemaking. Camilla closed her eyes and wore a satisfied, dreamy smile, on her comely face as she let out a brief hum of pleasure. Although she had noticed how tired he was after coming home from the tavern she wanted him. And wanted a baby. She kissed him hungrily, after Viola had greeted him, and they made love. Passionately. Meaningfully. Breathlessly.

"How was your day?" she asked, having not given them the chance to make small talk earlier.

"It ended well, when I came home," Manius answered, planting a kiss on his wife's neck and caressing her sun burnished thigh.

"How was Rufus? I am beginning to worry about him."

"That worry may last a lifetime. He was both distracted and focussed tonight. I used to think that his work for Agrippa was good for him. It gave him some purpose - and helped him to fend off boredom, and certain vices. His work added something to his life. But now I fear his work may be diminishing him. Each assignment eats away at his soul, like a bird pecking away at a piece of bread. And he has just taken on a mission for the wrong and right reason. Lucilla."

"Should I worry about Lucilla too then?" Camilla replied, her body tensing in anxiety. Goosebumps appeared on her forearms, borne not from the draught coming through the window. She had grown to like Varro's former wife over the past year, albeit she was initially intimidated by her beauty and intelligence. Lucilla could match Varro's wit and seemed as accomplished as any man, when discussing politics, literature – and even financial matters!

"No, I believe she will be fine… Rufus probably loves her more now than when he was married to her. He realises what he lost."

"It seems Rufus had quite an eventful day. But what about this evening? Did you have a quiet night?"

"Nothing happened of note," he replied, casually, before affecting a yawn. Yet his body tensed, and Camilla could feel his pulse quicken. She said nothing, telling herself it was nothing. Manius told himself he was lying to his wife for her own good. Ignorance was bliss. She would only overly fret if she knew about the altercation this evening. It was also best she didn't know how Agrippa was employing him to spy on Carbo. Should the demagogue and his followers uncover the truth then the agent - and his wife - could be in danger.

Manius recalled the afternoon of his wedding. He had told his friend that he "didn't feel married". Varro told him not to worry: "You will know soon enough when you will feel married, like other people. It will be when you start lying to your wife and keeping secrets from her."

Had Varro been, annoyingly, right again? Manius shifted uncomfortably in his bed and slept fitfully that evening, like a loving husband who had been unfaithful to his wife for the first time.

**9.**

The streets dripped with a thick, sticky heat and screeching light.

Varro walked across the Palatine towards Lucilla's home as if he were wading through glutinous mud. He was in no rush to confront his former wife. His head was bowed down in thought, or grief. He prepared his lines and the wording of his questions. He resolved to treat her politely, professionally, even if he had to do so through gritted teeth. She was a witness and interviewee, that was all. Not his first wife. Not the woman he loved.

A splash of colour in the corner of his eye caught his attention. The smell of perfume also sliced through the odorous air to prickle his nostrils. A mother and daughter, dressed in their finest garments and jewellery, were about to enter a temple. A brace of slaves trailed behind them, carrying the offering they were about to make. Both mother and daughter were tantalisingly attractive, sparkling. Varro feared that some onlookers might suffer a crick in their neck, as they quickly turned their heads to catch a better view. Varro also wryly smiled as he remembered a similar looking mother and daughter, who he had courted and seduced - at the same time - several years ago. He even dedicated the same love poem to them both, but just changed the name in the first line. When they discovered his infidelity, which he knew they would eventually, their outrage was succeeded by declarations of devotion. Did they love him, or did they just want to win him like a prize and defeat their rival? The mother and daughter ended up despising one another, more than they did him. Amusement was succeeded by shame. The wry smile fell from his face, like an axeman felling an old, diseased tree.

Varro wondered what each woman might pray for in the temple. The mother might pray to Venus, for a young lover to cross her path. Or she may make an offering to Nemesis, for her husband's mistress to catch a pox. The daughter would doubtless be praying for a suitor. A rich, faithful, virile and virtuous husband. But not even the gods could provide such a man who possessed all those traits, Varro conjectured. Sunlight glinted off their necklaces, brooches and colourfully dyed silk dresses. They were hopeful perhaps of attracting the gods' attention, as they were the men in the marketplace. Yet, Varro mused, they were surely more likely to provoke pity from the gods if they dressed humbly.

*And what would I pray for, if I entered a temple again?*

Varro certainly wouldn't offer up a prayer for Caesar, as if he were a god himself. Caesar possessed half the world. He didn't need anyone wishing him well. Yet it seemed he needed Herennius' dagger - and may even be willing to give up half the world to secure it. Should he pray for the world as a whole? But Varro knew too well how the world - or Man – didn't deserve his blessing. Prayers were but empty words, as meaningful as a politician's promise or harlot's wedding vow. The mother and daughter would light some incense and their sense of the sacred and virtuous would last no longer than it took for the incense to burn away. The gods wouldn't answer their prayers. But at least they could be considered fair and just, as they would turn a deaf ear to all.

Varro let out a strong yawn, or feeble roar, as he came to Lucilla's house and knocked on the oak door. He flinched, twice, with each knock - from the sound and his hangover. Varro flinched slightly again upon being greeted by the grim expression he received from Diana, Lucilla's knuckle-hard maid. As usual Diana didn't pretend to be pleased to see her mistress' former husband. The maid had served under Lucilla whilst she was married to the dissolute nobleman. Diana had been the one to try and comfort her mistress late at night, when her husband hadn't come home again. Or when he came home drunk, smelling of perfume. Diana would never be able to forgive Varro for his hurtful behaviour, during his marriage, towards Lucilla. But should she have known how Varro couldn't forgive himself either, she may have forgiven him a little.

Her face was wrinkled, like a prune. Her hair was as dry as straw, her tunic as grey as her complexion. Her shins were as veiny as marble and her spindly hands resembled talons. Varro sometimes pictured the maid spitting in his food, before she brought it out to him in the garden. Or clawing at his portrait when Lucilla came to visit him.

"Good morning Diana. You are looking well," Varro remarked, greeting her like a dear friend, amusing himself rather than her.

The sniff cum grunt which the old woman issued in reply expressed a thousand words. Few, if any out of the thousand, were cordial, however. She still thought him as frivolous as he was selfish. A spoiled aristocrat, who was nowhere near as charming as he thought he was.

The maid led Varro through the house, as though she were a drill master marching an errant legionary out towards a punishment square. He noticed, as he came to the garden, how Lucilla had planted the same flowers around her lawn as could be found at his villa in Arretium. Lucilla put down the book she was reading and rose to her feet, to greet her guest.

Out of interest, rather than due to his brief as a spy, he caught a glimpse of what she was reading. *On the Nature of the Gods*. He recalled the moment, many years ago, when the poet realised that she could quote more of Cicero than him. It was another one of those moments when Varro was compelled to conclude that he loved the vibrant young woman lying in bed next to him. She was different, special. They would often ask each other what they were reading, back when they were courting. Lucilla devoured books, even more than him - and she fed his mind and soul. He became a better poet, inspired by her fine feelings and recommended reading. Varro remembered how, when they were first married, he would write couplets of love poetry on her stomach and kiss her naval when finished. Lucilla would crane her head to read the lines and laugh or beam, joyously. He thought such joy might last forever. Unlike when he had courted other women, Varro always cited the quote if he borrowed one from other poets. Not only would Lucilla be familiar with the work but, more so, he didn't want to deceive her. But that was all in the past.

He had more chance of bottling his own shadow than re-capturing those days again now.

Lucilla was still achingly beautiful, however. That much hadn't changed. Her glossy black hair hung down her shoulders. A dusting of make-up coloured her smooth, porcelain cheeks. She always possessed the right expression for the right moment - but, unlike several of his former lovers, Lucilla was no actress. Part of him wanted to reach out and touch her - or articulate his feelings. But he knew if he tried, he might, like Icarus, fly too close to the sun and damn himself. For better, or worse, marriage had taught Varro that it was best to leave some things unsaid.

The garden was awash with a festival of colour, textures and floral fragrances. Clouds marked the blue sky above, like wisps of foam floating across a vast ocean. A couple of pink finches chirped in a wicker cage. Varro couldn't quite tell if they were serenading one another or bickering.

The nobleman offered up not the best half-smile he had ever presented to the world, but it wasn't his worst either. It seemed to take all his strength however to raise one corner of his mouth. He willed himself to try and breathe normally, as much as Lucilla nearly took his breath away. She was wearing one of his favourite dresses. She had a glow about her. Varro told himself it was due to the mellow sunshine and her inner spark, rather than Pulcher.

Her bright, kind eyes probed his aspect, as if searching his soul. Varro averted his gaze. Her smile was fuller than his, exuding beauty and concern. She noted the rings around his eyes due to sleepless, or drunken, nights. He could still affect a boyish twinkle, but it was just an affectation. His heart was old, weary. There had been too many women. Too many jugs of wine. Too many unfinished poems. No man was an island, as much as her former husband sometimes attempted to dispel the theory. The picture he presented to the world was an attractive façade. He revered and reviled his father. Only she knew how lonely, cut-off he could be when pretending to be the life and soul of a party. When she first met Varro, she mentioned how different he was to the rest of his set.

"By different, do you mean better?" Varro asked, as he gestured to a slave to fill Lucilla's cup.

"No, by different I mean sadder."

Perhaps, in an attempt to make himself feel less lonely, Varro eventually caused Lucilla to be sad. He was walking proof of his own philosophical outlook, that Man is a selfish and faithless creature. They were happily married, for a while. Life - and the deaths of their unborn children - got in the way of marital bliss. Where he once believed that marriage had delivered him, from a solitary and depraved existence, Varro determined that divorce would save him - and more so her.

A long winter eventually thawed. Friendship blossomed between them. They were now older - and perhaps even wiser. Lucilla still knew and cared for Varro like no one else. When she had agreed to accompany him to Arretium a year ago Lucilla thought that something, other than friendship, might flourish between them. On more than one occasion she woke in the night, walked along the hallway and stood by his door, ready to knock. But she knew he would, sooner or later, hurt her again. He would prove as constant as Cressida. It was preferable that they remained good friends. Or perhaps they were even best friends, Lucilla considered. Divorce hadn't quite wholly dissolved their bond.

Had he called upon her as Marcus Agrippa's agent, rather than as a friend? It was likely that Varro knew about Licinius - and she had been the cause of sleepless, drunken nights.

"I thought you might cross my threshold today," she remarked.

Varro had wondered, since yesterday, how much she knew. And how much she thought he knew.

"There are times when people have little need of an augur to predict what will occur."

"I can predict that I will not allow any augur to cross my threshold in the near future, given that one spilled bird entrails over my Persian rug last year. Would you like some refreshments? Water or wine?"

"Some wine, please."

"Wonders will never cease," Diana murmured, albeit loud enough for Varro to hear, as she rolled her eyes and left, to fetch a jug. She would further dilute the vintage, just to vex her mistress' guest.

"Are you visiting at the request of Marcus Agrippa? Or have you come for yourself?"

"Does it matter?"

"It might."

Tension entwined itself, like briars, around their playful tone. Lucilla's smile tightened, like a garotte. Varro's nostrils subtly flared. They were akin to two warriors, each waiting for the other to draw his sword. Or two gamblers, each waiting for their moment to roll the dice. Not knowing the outcome.

"I am not here for myself," Varro replied, lying. "Agrippa asked me to come. I have a letter from Caesar himself, granting me the authority to investigate Herennius' murder. I can show you the document, should you wish."

"No, I believe you Rufus. I will also be honest with you and answer any questions - and not just because Caesar is asking me to cooperate."

As much as Lucilla's tone was placating, Varro didn't feel placated.

"An honest woman in Rome. Wonders will never cease."

"I would prefer it if we did not argue as much as Herennius and Lentulus, on the night of the murder. I would like us to remain friends," Lucilla said, her voice pleading as much as placating now.

"You have another friend to call upon now, do you not?"

Varro briefly creased his face in resentment and sneered. He noticed the new earrings Lucilla was wearing and suspected they were a gift from Pulcher. His stomach knotted. Although unmarried, Varro felt as cuckolded as Flavius Hispo.

"Is this Agrippa, or you, asking?"

"Does it matter?"

"Yes. I am grateful for your concern, but as I told Marcus I am confident I will be safe from any killer."

"It's not the killer I'm worried about, but rather the man who invited you to the party as his guest."

"Even an augur could have predicted you would say that."

Varro seldom raised his voice or lost his composure, partly due to his ability not to care enough about anything, but his innards struggled to keep his temper in check, as if he were a man attempting to grasp an eel, swimming in a barrel of oil.

"I have never thought to offer you any advice as to who you should court before, Lucilla, which is why I hope that you will take note of me now and think me sincere. Licinius is wrong for you," Varro exclaimed, trying to imbue his words with reason rather than emotion. Finally saying his name to her, out loud, made things more real. Worse. Bitterer.


The sound of the wooden practice swords smacking against each other reminded Manius of his time as a young gladiator. He had arrived, along with a batch of other slaves, as a scrawny teenager at the ramshackle ludus. Yet he soon bulked-up and learned to fight in practice bouts as if his life depended on it. He forged a few friendships with his fellow trainees, but eventually sickness, or opponents in the arena, cut them down. Manius had been lucky, as much as it may not have felt like it at the time. He still often spared a thought for those who were less fortunate than him, however.

The Briton allowed his new student, Calvus, to force him backwards as they fenced on the freshly cut lawn. The teenager was trying his best, exerting himself. But Manius feared he would be but a tryer, rather than a success. The studious youth lacked a killer instinct. He held his weapon with too little conviction. Manius noticed how the boy often glanced at his father, for approval or praise. But the former senator ignored his son, immersed as he was in conversation with his guest, the tribune Paulus Labeo.

Publius Carbo didn't give the fencing tutor a second look, when he was briefly introduced to the Briton, but Manius duly took in his new employer. His previously neatly trimmed beard was now longer and unkempt, styled to resemble the kind of beards his supporters donned. His hair was a dull silver, or polished iron. His build was average. His features often appeared tired and ageing, yet a certain vigour returned when the former senator was speaking at the rostrum. Although in public he wore a plain tunic, similar to a common citizen, in private he still liked to wear a toga - a garment befitting his patrician rank. Carbo projected an air of both superiority and sanctimony. Agrippa was right to describe him as "more priest than politician". When called upon his obsidian eyes could soften and his dour, downturned mouth could hoist itself into a mild, knowing smile. Over the past year Carbo had tried to school himself out of it, but the demagogue still possessed an aristocratic rather than plebeian accent.

"I am still not sure if he is a wolf in sheep's clothing, or a sheep in wolf's clothing," Agrippa commented to Manius, during his briefing. "I am hoping that you will shepherd me towards the truth, so to speak... There are many in the Senate who consider Carbo a joke. Unfortunately, I cannot afford to be so dismissive. I warrant that he would happily see Rome invoke mob rule, so long as he ruled the mob in question. But the city does not need another Clodius. Its walls have been scorched by fire enough, its streets filled with blood."

Manius also subtly observed Paulus Labeo. Agrippa described the tribune as being even more radical - and potentially even more dangerous - than his master. During his early years as a student - and as a disciple of Catiline - Labeo campaigned for the release of several foreign terrorists, who had attempted to assassinate a number of senators. He artfully judged them "freedom fighters". His initial attempts to engage with the course of honours had ended in failure. His philosophy subsequently was, if you can't join them - beat them. Labeo worked as Carbo's chief propagandist and served as an intermediary between his paymaster and a number of guilds. He encouraged strike action and was the author behind political pamphlets, which "revealed" Jewish conspiracies and agitated for the populace to rise-up. The merchant and political classes were enemies of the people. Whenever Labeo was challenged about his propagandist claims, or reminded of past contradictory and mendacious remarks, he would deny and obfuscate, arguing that his enemies were misquoting him, or the parchments were forgeries. Fake news.

Labeo had a flat, thuggish face. His build was somewhat portly, to put it politely. It was difficult to tell where his chin ended, and neck began. A large, radish-red nose dominated his face. His hair was as black as the inside of Viola's nose. When he smiled it seemed an unnatural act. Forced. False. He was notably younger than Carbo and was willing to bide his time for his ally to die or retire. The tribune's plan was to eventually inherit the movement - and eventually seize power. He would turn the Senate House into a theatre. Not that he enjoyed literature or frivolity. Rome would be made anew. It was fate, his destiny, historically inevitable, the former philosophy student believed. The old order would collapse - and the "man of the people" would be waiting in the wings, ready to save the city. Or, if needs be, cause the old order's collapse. "Labeo would be content to see Rome burn, providing he could rule over the ash-heap afterwards," Agrippa remarked to Manius.

The tutor congratulated his pupil on his progress, but he decided that Calvus should practice his strokes in the air, as opposed to against another sword. The lack of noise, from the weapons clacking against each other, would enable Manius to better hear the conversation.

Carbo and Labeo sat on a stone terrace, which protruded out into the garden like a pier in a sea of green. The propagandist consumed another cake and sat with one of his fleshy hands, or paws, resting on his pot-belly. The tribune often proclaimed that Rome was starving (as a result of merchants and Jews fixing the price of grain) but it was clear that at least one of its citizens was well-fed each day.

Both men gesticulated and raised their voices as they spoke, as if in competition with one another to prove who was more passionate about their cause. They paid no heed to the nearby ex-gladiator. As per Agrippa's instruction, the Briton nodded his head slowly and pretended not to understand every word which was said when he was introduced to Carbo.

"They will think you a half-wit or brute. A nobody. They will feel comfortable being indiscreet in front of you. People who are their own worst enemy are my favourite kind of enemy," Agrippa remarked, quoting his friend and co-consul.

The sun beat down relentlessly, as if the air might catch fire.

Varro finished his second cup of wine, but his thirst remained unquenched and his argument remained un-won. Lucilla stood her ground, defiant and mocking.

"Life is rich with irony enough, without having you lecture me on matters of the heart," Lucilla asserted, her voice caked in sarcasm. She imagined that Varro would not take the news of her relationship with Licinius well, but she was still disappointed and angry at his reaction. He should be happy for her. She would have been happy for him if he found someone, Lucilla told herself.

"I need to be honest with you," he replied, his voice a mixture of desperation and plaintiveness. Beads of sweat hung on his temples. His face was flush from the sun - and a stinging frustration.

"An honest man in Rome. Wonders will never cease."

"Has Pulcher been honest with you? He is no more a diplomat than Viola is a wood pigeon. He is a spy. He may not have murdered Herennius, but he has plenty of blood on his hands. He could bathe in the stuff. Maecenas has used him as a weapon, to bully, seduce and corrupt across the empire. If Pulcher has told you he loves you for your intelligence, he is indeed being honest."

"Licinius has already been candid with me about his past. I am not sure I can say the same about you, concerning your exploits as an agent for Marcus Agrippa. He has told me about some of his assignments. Some of his targets were innocent, some less so. But, unlike you, Licinius wants his past to remain in the past. Once he completes his task to secure Caesar's dagger, he will cease to be an agent. Should you find the dagger and murderer, will you be able to say the same? Licinius wants to begin a new life," Lucilla argued, resisting the temptation to add, "with me."

Varro compressed his lips and shook his head, either in disbelief or because he didn't want to hear any more. The breeze passed through the nearby leafy trees, as if making a shushing sound to admonish the quarrelling couple.

"He has only told you what you want to hear."

"He has told me about his past, with other women. Can you make claim to the same? At least he was unmarried, during his time seducing other women. Can you make claim to the same? There is little that you can accuse Licinius of, that he couldn't conversely accuse you of."

Her features became harder, her voice colder.

"I'm not like him," Varro steadfastly - and agitatedly - countered. Her words were as sharp as the knife used to slice through Sestius' throat. Such was their growing animus he fancied that the pair of them could have been married again. She was the only woman who had ever truly hurt him.

"That could prove a blessing rather than a curse for him."

Her barb hung in the air, like a rain cloud ready to spit out a bolt of lightning. Varro wore a storm on his brow too. But the sound of his laughter, as opposed to any thunder, broke the silence.

"I deserved that. And worse. I preferred it when we remained repressed and didn't share our feelings. I think it may be best if we agree to disagree for now. We have the rest of our lives to argue like an old married couple, I hope. It will be easier that way. And we both know how much I enjoy the easy life."

Lucilla's icy gaze melted. Her features softened. The sun peeped through the clouds once more.

"You would test the patience of the gods," she remarked, sighing and gently shaking her head. But she was pleased they were no longer arguing. That they would not say something they might regret.

"Personally, I find the gods to be impatient. They are ever quick to punish, fall in love or turn into some rutting animal."

"The gods will condemn you for such blasphemy."

"The gods condemned me a long time ago."

*Or I condemned myself.*

## 10.

Thankfully a breeze swept through the door and tempered the needling heat. Varro and Lucilla sat on adjoining couches. He diluted his wine, whilst admiring a new painting on the wall, depicting a scene from Horace's *Odes*. Varro remembered how he had always promised his wife that he would introduce her to the poet. But he never did. It was perhaps the least significant of his broken promises over the years.

Varro decided it was best to cease discussing Pulcher. What was the good of trying to win an argument, if it meant losing something far more valuable? *Her*. Her friendship. The agent told himself he was here in a professional, rather than personal, capacity and brought up the evening of Herennius' murder.

Lucilla was relieved at the change of subject. She was worried Varro might ask her to choose between the two men. Or try to order her from seeing Licinius. If he did so, she would have asked Varro to leave. And he may have never come back. But there was peace between the former married couple, for now. An unspoken accord. Hostilities could, or would, break out again in the future. It was a matter of when, not if, she lamentably thought. She knew it was difficult for him to be happy for himself, but why couldn't he be happy for her?

She sat close enough to him for Varro to subtly breathe in her perfume and the natural fragrance of her skin and hair. As much as it was a sweet sensation, it was also bittersweet.

"I am not quite sure which proved to be the most unpalatable, the atmosphere or overdone venison… Our host had a good enough time for all of us - eating, drinking and singing his own praises - but that may have been his plan all along. His language was coarse, his manner boorish, particularly when he addressed his wife. At one point, after a particularly lewd comment, Lucretia tried to upbraid him and called him rude. If looks could kill, then she would have murdered him then and there. Herennius replied that it was ruder still to try and tell a man how to behave in his own home."

"Did Herennius or any other guest mention the dagger during proceedings?" Varro asked, as he started to paint a more detailed picture of the dinner party and its participants.

"He spoke briefly, or boasted, about how Cicero's demise had been the making of him. Apparently, he did Rome a "great service" by silencing the troublemaker. "The only good advocate is a dead advocate," he added, but one suspects he said this for Lentulus' benefit. He went on to recount how he was invited to meet Fulvia, after she heard about his heroic deed. "She was a fine-looking lady. They rarely make Roman women like that anymore… Her dark eyes bulged with spite and she coloured the air with insults as she stabbed her hairpin into the severed head's lolling tongue and face. Blood freckled her cheeks. "Where's your wit now? Where are your vile lies? Who's laughing now?" she said. Maybe it was her time of the month." I am just surprised that Herennius wasn't murdered ten years ago. He knew he was being obnoxious - but didn't seem to care. Or he revelled in his tasteless behaviour, like a pig rolling in mud. He said, "When you're as rich as I am you don't need to worry about what people think of you. They need to worry about what I think of them." Again, he turned to Lentulus when he spoke. Goading him. As he regaled us with his stories and philosophy, he held the dagger in his hands. Stroking it. He talked about its value. "It's very dear to me. Caesar said he would be in my debt if I sold it to him, which is worth more than any sum of gold I know. Mark Antony is said to have designed the knife himself." The irony is he could have sown the seed of his murder and the theft of the dagger there and then. What do you think?"

"I've had too many thoughts on the matter. I'm clouding my own judgement. I keep returning to the notion that Lentulus is the likeliest suspect, whether the killing was pre-meditated or he decided on the crime that night, after his argument with Herennius in the garden," Varro posed, as he stared at a small figurine of Apollo on the cedarwood table in front of him, briefly fancying that the statue might come alive and mouth who the murderer was. "But tell me about Sestius. Could he be guilty of murdering his friend and business partner?"

"It's doubtful. The two men seemed close. They certainly shared the same colourful vocabulary and table manners. It could be possible they shared the same enemies too. They were considered callous, even for slave traders. Families were broken up in their camps. People were branded and tortured. Half-starved. The weak and infirm were left to die," Lucilla revealed, whilst failing to name the source of her information. Pulcher had spoken to her about their host's business practices, with indignation and pity brimming over in his eyes.

"Do you think Sestius could have known about the contents of his friend's will, that he would be the chief beneficiary?"

"I'm not sure. But Sestius had little need to kill for money, as a motive, given how wealthy he was in his own right."

"Did he engage you in conversation during the party?"

"He tried to. But I gave him such a withering look he duly kept his distance."

Varro briefly smiled, picturing the likely expression Lucilla must have offered the slave trader. He would have been akin to a slug - and his ex-wife would have been the salt.

"And what of the poet who was present for part of the evening?"

"Publius? He was sweet and fun. And talented. He reminded me of you, when you were younger. But do not let that prejudice you, either way. Corinna invited him to perform. He didn't eat with us, but he drank as if playing catch-up with some of the guests. His poetry flowed like the wine - and could be as fruity too. It was witty, lyrical and at times remarkably insightful, given his tender age. I couldn't help but notice the subtle, or not so subtle, looks Corinna offered him from across the room. Either she is his mistress, or she longs to be so."

"And do you believe Publius has returned her advances?" Varro asked, a little crestfallen that Publius would probably not have signed his name as "O", in relation to the love letters in Corinna's jewellery box.

"It's likely. Although I sense it's likely he has returned the advances of women from across the city. As I said, he reminded me of you somewhat. In the same way that a sailor has a girl in every port, I suspect Publius has a mistress living on every one of Rome's seven hills... He was mercurial. I noted how he could at one-point sit in the corner of the room and quietly observe everyone - and then within the blink of an eye he could come to life and demand to be the centre of attention at the party. Again, like you, he could say something, and one couldn't quite be sure if he was being sarcastic or not. His poetry could capture a fine feeling and, within the next line, ridicule that same fine feeling."

"It seems you are smitten. But did the amorous young poet make a play for you? I of course would have done so, when I was his age," Varro remarked, curious to now meet the precocious teenager.

"No. And I am not sure if I should feel relieved or insulted. Perhaps he sensed that I have had enough of being courted by poets for one lifetime... He knew I was once married to you, would you believe? And he was familiar with your verses. He quoted you in our conversation, more than once."

"Did you notice if he stole any of my lines during his readings?"

"No, his work was refreshingly original."

"I should almost feel insulted rather than relieved."

"He hoped your best years were not behind you, that you were working on an epic. Publius preferred your satirical verses to your love poems. He admired you, in that the only thing you took seriously was your propensity to laugh at the world. Yet he also asked if there had been tears behind the laughter."

"And how did you reply?"

"I said there was certainly copious amounts of wine behind any laughter."

"How seriously should I consider him a suspect?"

Lucilla let out a little laugh, at the thought of the sweet-faced teenage poet murdering the odious slave trader.

"Not very, would be my answer. Publius would be happy to cut Herennius down with a jibe, but I cannot picture him wielding a knife."

Varro nodded his head, taking Lucilla's words into consideration. But he could not exonerate the youth yet. If he was in love with Herennius' wife, then Publius would be judged a serious suspect. As insane as the idea of the poet killing Herennius was for Lucilla, love fosters madness. Could Corinna be Circe - and have turned her lover into a beast, one wild enough to commit murder?

"Leave us," Gaius Maecenas ordered, with a mixture of terseness and civility. The handsome slave bowed his head and departed, leaving his master to converse in private with Licinius Pulcher, a regular visitor at the house. Although Maecenas trusted his staff, he made it a rule never to trust anyone completely. If a man cannot wholly trust himself, why should he wholly trust another?

Maecenas still lay on his massage table, his fleshy body glistening and fragrant with the special blend of oils he instructed his staff to apply. A towel covered his buttocks. But Pulcher had seen everything before. His skin, burnished like polished oak, still tingled from when he instructed the slave to be vigorous with the strigil. He wanted every dead fleck of skin scraped off, every piece of dust removed so his flesh was as smooth as marble. "Cleanliness is even better than godliness," he had recently advised Propertius, having encouraged the poet to install a bathhouse at his villa in the country.

His slightly round face could not altogether bury his prominent cheekbones and aquiline nose. His eyes could be piercing, playful - or as black as a shark's. A tonsor clean-shaved him and cut - or sculptured - his hair every morning.

Blades of light slanted through the shutters. Maecenas used the tip of a manicured finger to remove a bead of sweat from his temple. He gently closed his eyes and breathed out - carving out a moment of repose - before addressing his agent.

Maecenas smiled at his friend. It was difficult for him to tell anymore how sincere or contrived his expression was.

Licinius Pulcher sat in a chair, opposite his employer. His semblance was attentive, dutiful - although his thoughts turned to Lucilla. They were due to have dinner that evening. She was even going to cook for him. They would make love afterwards. Pulcher grinned, inside.

"What do you think of Restio's food?" Maecenas asked. The gourmand had just employed a new cook. The old one had been caught in a compromising position, in the kitchen, with a serving girl. Maecenas did not condemn the cook for his appetites, but the thought of him using his kitchen as a bedchamber couldn't be countenanced. The cook was dismissed immediately, and the serving girl was sold to a slave trader. It was nothing personal. He needed to make an example of the girl, to dissuade others from such depraved - and unhygienic - behaviour.

"It's excellent. Restio's meals will be worth any complaint Quintus Cinna dishes up, in reference to you poaching his prized cook from him," Pulcher replied, after sampling another bite of the dish - salted sea perch, drizzled over with spiced olive oil and lemon. Pulcher was careful not to eat too much of the delicious fish however, lest he spoil his appetite for the evening. He would rather offend the cook and Maecenas, by not finishing the plate, than upset Lucilla through not eating her meal this evening.

Pulcher went on to give his report, which essentially amounted to there being nothing to report. The trail was running cold. Finding the dagger would be a problem.

"Do not bring me problems. Bring me solutions."

His voice was rich and smooth, like a fine wine. Maecenas pursed his lips a little, to convey his displeasure. "Perhaps you should have tortured Sestius more, before killing him," the spymaster added.

"I believe Sestius was telling the truth, when he said that he wasn't in possession of the knife. Nor did he have any idea who might have murdered his friend. I have known oxen more guileful. It is as we suspected. Sestius did not inherit the dagger."

"Then perhaps we should turn our attention to Lentulus. There are few more guileful creatures in Rome than the lawyer. Though I would count myself as one of them," Maecenas argued. A flicker of a smile, but no more than that, danced across his lips as he spoke. "Most lawyers are guilty of more crimes than the felons they defend. I know you have your doubts as to whether Lentulus would want to get blood on his hands, but in my experience all men are willing to wash their hands in blood, if it means they can shower themselves in riches afterwards. It is because of - and not in spite of - his distinguished character that we should treat the advocate as a suspect, whether it was a crime of passion, after his heated argument with his son-in-law, or a more mindful act. Lentulus would have believed that by wielding the knife against Herennius he would be wiping away his debts. He could have then taken the jewelled dagger, out of greed or to convince us that the crime was a mere robbery… I am convinced the killer was one of his guests that evening. You should pay another visit to his wife. She already yielded up the secret that she lost a child, after her husband beat her. Perhaps, with a little more persuading, she might let slip something even more revealing. Damning. And what of the poet? Should I grant him an audience? I could promise him patronage in return for information. Is he handsome, or some pock-marked, moon-faced, stripling?"

Pulcher was tempted to reply that, although Publius may have been Maecenas' type, the attraction would not be reciprocated. He was also struck by an absence of any pang of jealousy, of his mentor taking an interest in the young poet. He had Lucilla now and no longer craved Maecenas' favour, or anyone else's.

"He is indeed handsome. His verses are accomplished - lyrical and rich with sly humour. I believe he already possesses a patron however, in Marcus Messalla."

"Messalla is a good man, but a weak man. The two are far too often one in same thing. Should this Publius impress me, in one way or another, then I will duly take him under my wing. Let us hope he first proves useful as an informer, rather than poet, however. Our attention must be focussed on finding that dagger, before Agrippa does. There will be no prizes for second place, in Caesar's eyes. I have grown accustomed to winning. There are some habits one can get tired of - but not that one," Maecenas asserted, his features and tone growing tauter.

"Have you heard any news, or rumours, from your network of spies in the city?" Pulcher asked, whilst further diluting his wine. He wanted to have a clear head when he called upon Lucilla later.

"No, unfortunately. The silence has been deafening. I have briefed my agents, who have briefed their contacts, to alert me should the knife come up for sale. If the killer has no need or intention of selling the dagger - or the other valuables stolen - it gives credence to the idea that the murder was a based upon a personal grievance, as opposed to common robbery. I will of course inform you should I hear anything. My web is stretched across the entire city, but no insect has landed on it yet."

"At least Agrippa must be suffering the same fate, in relation to his investigation."

"I would equally celebrate his failure over my success. I understand he has instructed Rufus Varro to retrieve the knife. His father was an impressive and annoyingly uncorruptible. I am torn as to whether to underestimate or overestimate his son. Did you know Varro was once granted the opportunity to accept my patronage? I am not sure I can wholly admire a man who tells me "no". For years he remained idle, on an almost industrious scale. He could have been a praetor, should he have engaged with the course of honours. His poetry was not without merit too. His verse was pithy, when it wasn't being prosaic. His passion wasn't poetry however, but other peoples' wives. Agrippa has done well to exploit Varro's talents. Women understandably have a weakness for the attractive, wealthy aristocrat. One could argue that his weakness is women. It is a shame I didn't get my hands on him at a younger age. Rufus would now be a more successful agent and poet as a result of my influence. He was one of many poets who tried to emulate Catullus, in their appetites and verse. It was a pity they never shared Catullus' talent, however. I suppose Varro was the best of a bad bunch, in terms of his literary set. I can recall some of his contemporaries. There was Lucius Ligarius. I could forgive him for sleeping with his sister, but not for butchering a classical hexameter. Then there was the prize fop Quintus Decidius. He once offered me his wife in return for my patronage. I told him that his wife was more elegant than his verses - but that his wife was as ugly as a mule, who had been kicked in the face several times. Too many young poets want to enjoy the garlands, without putting in the graft. Poetry is one percent inspiration and a hundred percent blood, toil and tears. It is easier to prize a stone out of one's cock, or have a woman tell the truth, than it is to write a good poem... Too many poems nowadays may be blessedly short, but they are still overlong. They use colloquial language, due to their authors possessing a limited vocabulary. I would rather contract a pox than write a poem for "the people". Populism. It's worse than wicked - it's vulgar," Maecenas stated, shuddering at the thought of a poet pretending to give voice to the great unwashed of Rome.

"I intend to finish the assignment and find the knife. Even if I have to go through Rufus Varro to do so," Pulcher replied, determinedly, thinking that it would be his pleasure to confront and subdue his rival, should certain circumstances prevail. He thought it prudent not to address any issues regarding Maecenas' digression, concerning poets and poetry. He could end up listening to a lecture on literature and aesthetics all evening.

"I have every confidence in you, Licinius. It may be the case that you will have to go through, or around Varro, to complete your other assignment too. What is the state of the affair, so to speak, with Lucilla? Has your fruit ripened yet and she is ready to be plucked? She is a rare beauty, the definition of statuesque. Although I hope she doesn't behave like a statue in bed. The woman is also not without education or a refined sensibility. I cannot ever recall Lucilla boring me, which makes her rare indeed. I am given to understand that she is also blessed with sound business acumen. Livia often consults Lucilla about her investments. Unlike other partners she may even make you some money, rather than just spend it - which would make her rarer still as a wife. Seducing and marrying Lucilla is far from the most unpleasant assignment I have ever given you, I warrant. She is such a fine woman that it may take up to six months or more before you feel compelled to take a mistress," Maecenas playfully remarked, before running his tongue over his teeth to assess if they needed polishing once more.

Pulcher forced as smile. Maecenas thought he knew Lucilla, but he didn't. The agent conceded he didn't wholly know her either. But he wanted to get to know her - and not just for the sake of gleaning intelligence. Maecenas had allowed his asset to return to Rome, on the condition that he take a wife of his choosing. Due to her intimacy with Livia - and relationships with other prominent figures in Rome - Maecenas instructed Pulcher to seduce and wed Lucilla. "I do not want your talents going completely to waste. That would be a greater crime than the murder of Herennius," the spymaster remarked recently. Pulcher remembered the night Maecenas had wined and dined him. They had made love - or rather Maecenas instructed Pulcher to make love to him. There was little shared pleasure, unlike when he was with Lucilla.

Pulcher would honour his agreement and marry Lucilla. He would also report back on any correspondence between Lucilla and Livia. But it felt good, right, keeping at least one secret from the spymaster. He would be marrying Lucilla, because he loved her. What he would feel less comfortable about was keeping the truth from her. Their marriage would, from a certain point of view, be built on a lie. Pulcher consoled himself with the thought however that he had yet to meet a husband and wife who didn't lie to one another or themselves.

"As you know I am hosting a modest party tomorrow night. Invite Lucilla. My home will always have room for one more beautiful object. I will also invite the young poet and speak to him. Our guest of honour however shall be Rufus Varro. In the same way that I will entice this Publius away from his patron Marcus Messalla, should I see fit to do so, I will also lure Varro away from Agrippa. Everyone has a price, an Achilles heel... If finding the dagger is a race between you both then I will form a plan to duly hobble your opponent."

Wheels were already in motion in his mind. Maecenas was as inspired as an author, conjuring up a story for his latest work. Plotting an enemy's downfall was one of the few things which made him genuinely happy. It mattered little if his victim was innocent or guilty. His narrative involved a love triangle, jealousy, betrayal, violence and poetic justice. Maecenas would welcome his guest with open arms but stab him in the back while departing. And how ironic, delicious, that Varro would be the author of his own demise.

*Not discounting my role in the scheme of things. Not that he will ever realise I played a part in the drama.*

Manius sat on the lawn and showed Calvus how to sharpen a sword, but he ran the stone along the razor-like edge less vigorously than normal to lessen the sound it made.

Paulus Labeo talked. And Manius listened. Occasionally he thumped a fist upon the table to hammer home his point. His eyes were ablaze, with zeal and ambition. Carbo often stroked his beard and nodded, sagely, in reply.

"We must grasp the nettle now, make a show of strength in order to grow stronger. We need more people to flock to our banner. We have the numbers to march on the Jewish quarter - and drive them out like vermin. I can also task some of our men to enter houses and appropriate gold and valuables. We can always use more money in the campaign coffers. Eventually we will need a war chest, to pay for an army. We will spread the word afterwards that the Jews started to agitate and riot. We can be viewed as the peacemakers, who brought order to chaos... We need to go back to a time when Jews were seen as enemies of the people. Julius Caesar should have never handed out an olive branch to them. No doubt he did so because he owed them money. Augustus is continuing a policy of integration. But the Jews need to be our scapegoats. We need to keep feeding ordinary working people with grievances... Let Augustus win glory in Spain. We need to win support and power in Rome while he gallivants in foreign lands... The purge of the Jewish quarter will act as a statement of intent. Might is right... Our long-term strategy should be to de-stabilise the state, so people look to a new Rome with a new form of government. We must work within the Senate House, but our ambition should be to demolish it. We need an uprising, revolution. Power must be given to the people and placed in our hands - for the good of the people. The state must control agriculture and industry, so it works efficiently. I am working on a five-year plan for the economy. It cannot possibly fail. If it does, then the people will be to blame, rather than us... All property is theft, so private property will be confiscated and bequeathed to the state... This raid will be the spark that lights the fire."

Labeo often reached for his cup whilst he spoke (in contrast to Carbo, who remained abstemious). Wine stained his lips and chin. It was as if the tribune had been spitting blood. Labeo's capacity to hold his drink was the only thing Manius found remotely admirable about his character. He briefly fancied how he would have liked to witness a drinking contest between Labeo and Rufus. He had seen his friend outdrink poets, priests and sailors over the years. He always managed to keep his head and wits about him, whilst others lost theirs.

"Let us not get too far ahead of ourselves, as much as I believe in a new Rome too. I am willing to take a lead, for the good of ordinary people. Our first task should be to set a date to purify the Jewish quarter. Rome should be for the Romans. Any immigrants we invite in should serve as a cheap labour force. One half of our forces should re-claim the streets, whilst the other half enters properties and secures valuables. Make sure the latter are sufficiently trustworthy. We need to fatten our purse, not theirs... Now tell me, how are we faring with recruitment?"

"Recruitment is up, especially among students. The young have wonderful, mouldable minds. They believe in hope and change and are not afraid to tear down the old world to build a new one. The policy of cancelling their debts - funded by tax rises to the wealthy and elderly - is proving extremely popular... Molon, the charioteer, is willing to be an advocate for our cause. Numerous actors have also agreed to endorse you, although in return some would like you to mention their latest play in the next speech you give."

"That can be arranged. Perhaps we should organise a dinner party for some of our more distinguished supporters. But ultimately, we need to recruit from the guilds and the army to properly swell our ranks. Students and actors will disappear, faster than water runs down a drain, when the real fighting starts. They're as capricious - and witless - as women. The mob and the army need to be won over. Caesar knew this. We just need to come up with the right promises and rewards," Carbo remarked, as he began to tug, rather than just stroke, his beard in thought.

Or the right lies, Manius mused. He suspected the reason why the demagogue hadn't won as much support among soldiers and the working classes was because they had heard it all before. They had older, more cynical heads on their shoulders. "Beware of politicians bearing gifts," Fronto had told the Briton, on more than one occasion over the years.

"I am currently drafting some new literature, which will be posted up and given to our supporters to spread the word. I have re-worked some old propaganda I found, originally penned by Gaius Gracchus and Catiline. The mob will hopefully lap it up like wine. Free wine. I also wanted to present you with some new slogans, for your approval. What do you think of the following? "Forward, Not Back", "Workers of Rome Unite" and "Things Can Only Get Better". I think they suitably convey our message. I am even looking into producing tunics, which we can sell to our student followers, with the slogans dyed into the material."

"The slogans are fine. But this is not a time for soundbites. I feel the hand of history upon my shoulder. What we need now are deeds, not words," Carbo proclaimed, as if speaking to an audience of thousands and hearing a rapturous applause inside his head.

Manius rolled his eyes and pursed his lips, envisioning a hand upon the agitator's shoulder, apprehending him.


"The only way in which I'll know if I am closing in on Herennius' killer is if he endeavours to murder me," Varro joked.

For once however Lucilla failed to appreciate his black humour and the smile fell from her face. There may have been scores of people in Rome -

women and men - who wanted Varro dead but, ironically or not, his ex-wife wasn't among them.

The awkward pause was thankfully cut short by Diana walking into the room, to remind her mistress that one of her dressmakers had arrived for their appointment. The servant offered Varro a pert, accusatory look.

Diana retreated. Varro rose to his feet, as did Lucilla. He didn't know whether to bow politely, embrace her as a friend or kiss the woman. In the end Lucilla saved him from any awkwardness by embracing him and kissing Varro on each cheek. He breathed in her perfume once more and exhaled in the subtlest of sighs. The kiss lingered, tingling on his skin, for longer than he expected.

As he reached the doorway Varro turned to face Lucilla. For once his expression was devoid of irony or playfulness.

"Why didn't you tell me about Pulcher?" he asked, more forlorn than angry.

Lucilla paused before answering:

"Would you believe me if I said I didn't want to hurt you?"

Varro paused and then answered:

"Yes."

## 11.

Agrippa looked upon Manius with something resembling paternal pride, after the Briton delivered his report. He didn't doubt the veracity of Manius' words. Agrippa recalled Varro's assertion, that his bodyguard was one of the most honourable men in Rome. Even taking into account his career change - of becoming a duplicitous spy - he was still one of the most honourable men in the capital. Although there may have been a distinct lack of competition from others in the city, which handed Manius an advantage.

Agrippa even permitted himself a smile, his granite expression cracking.

"Should the gods be willing - and you can find out the day and location of when Carbo will assemble his followers - we may be able to wipe them off the map in a single action. Stamp out the fire, before it even becomes a spark. As much as they will be doing our job for us, by rounding themselves up, we cannot allow them to disperse and run riot in the Jewish quarter. It would be a massacre. Timing will be key. I can ready the Praetorian Guard, but we will still need to know when and where the mob will congregate. If you are unable to gain the intelligence beforehand you must shadow Carbo over the coming weeks. Send word once you are sure our opponents are assembling. My men will be ready," Agrippa instructed. He heard the words of his mentor, Lucius Oppius, echo in his head: *Fail to prepare, prepare to fail.*

Manius nodded. He couldn't help but be pleased with his initial success as an agent, during his first assignment. When the consul recruited him, the guileless Briton was worried that he would be unable to play the part and live a lie. Yet, as Agrippa argued, "Man can take to lying like a duck to water. Lies hold a man up, as much as his skin and bones. We deceive ourselves and others every day, so much so that we barely notice it. To work as an effective spy, you just need to raise your quota of lies each day - to something resembling a politician or courtesan."

As much as Manius felt comfortable in deceiving the likes of Carbo and Labeo he still felt uneasy about lying to his wife. But he was lying to Camilla out of good intentions, he believed. He needed to protect her. And she would surely only worry if she knew the truth.

*But the road to Hades is filled with good intentions.*

Manius shuffled a little on his feet and his proud expression faltered. To distract himself from thinking about Camilla he took in his surroundings. As usual a mountain of correspondence, from the four corners of the empire, was piled up on the consul's desk. Agrippa would, sooner or later, reply to each letter personally. As much as he may be wedded to an attractive young wife, Agrippa was still married to his work. A tower of wax tablets was balanced precariously on the edge of the table and, if added to, would likely lurch over and fall onto the floor. A special corner of the desk was devoted to architectural plans - for temples, theatres and aqueducts - and designs for various statues which would honour the gods and, more importantly, his co-consul. A living god.

Ironically, Manius dared not stare too intently at the correspondence lest Agrippa thought he might be spying. So, his eyes flitted around at the walls. To his left hung a new portrait of his late wife. Next to it was a sword, once belonging to Lucius Oppius, a centurion who had fought bravely under Julius and Octavius Caesar. The centurion had a connection with Manius too. During an attack on his village as a boy, the Roman soldier had saved him and his mother from being slaughtered by a brace of mutinous legionaries. To his right was a map of Rome and, next to it, a map of the Spanish frontier, marked with the latest details of Caesar's campaign.

When Manius had entered the room earlier he had caught the consul staring wistfully up at the map, as if Agrippa were wishing he could be leading an army again or with his friend. Or both. Yet part of the reason why Caesar had decided to lead the campaign was to prove to himself - and Rome - that he could win military glory without the help of his friend.

Agrippa kept himself in good condition and rode when he could. He wanted to be ready to answer the call, should Caesar fall ill or find himself in difficulty.

"Should all go according to plan then Caesar will doubtless reward you, Manius, for your service. Is there anything particularly you desire?"

"My wife would like a child, but not even Caesar can bestow that," Manius replied.

Agrippa thought to himself how, given the attractiveness of the Briton's wife, it could be the case that his priapic friend would be willing to try to grant Manius his prize.

"Indeed. But what about you? Are you so annoyingly content that you do not want for anything yourself?"

Manius first appeared awkward - and the words stuck in his throat - but then thought how fortune favours the brave. All he could do was ask.

"It would be an honour, Consul, if I could receive a fencing lesson from yourself," Manius said, sheepishly. He wanted to test himself against the best - and it would be a tale to tell his unborn child, that he had once fought (or even bested) the legendary general.

"Such a reward is cheap at half the price Manius - and will not impact on Rome's treasury. Caesar would approve. It would also be my honour and pleasure. Either you will teach me a thing or two, or I will give you a lesson in swordsmanship. I hope that you won't go easy on me however, as I can assure you, I will not go easy on you. If I win then I will permit you to buy me dinner. Should you get the better of me though you will have another secret to keep as an agent of Rome. We cannot have news spreading around the capital that a Briton conquered a Roman," Agrippa said, in good humour. He suddenly became keen to test himself against the skilled gladiator. It was important he still exerted himself. Swords which remain too long in their scabbards can become stuck. The consul was growing increasingly appreciative of the Briton, both as a man and now as an agent. He thought how Caecilia would have liked him. She was always an astute judge of character. The Briton had come from nothing. Or, in regard to being a slave and foreigner, less than nothing in some eyes. Agrippa too had been scorned in front of his face years ago (and doubtless behind his back now by the self-proclaimed elite) for coming from a humble background. His father was farmer. But he was a good man. "Goodness is not the province of those who have read moral philosophy, nor is honour the province of the Roman nobility," his wife had rightly once argued.

Agrippa instructed his agent to take care when spying on Carbo and his confederates. "Don't let the hunter become the prey… Your wife would never forgive me if something happened to you, Manius," the consul remarked, missing out how he would unable to forgive himself too.

The Briton took his leave and started to prepare various responses for when Camilla would ask him about his day. Agrippa called in a servant and asked for some food - olives, bread and ham - to be brought in. Thankfully his wife was away for the afternoon. She had one of her appointments with Toranius, the augur. Another husband might have worried that his wife was spending so much time with another man. But Agrippa was pleased to have the girl out of his way. He could even forgive her for being unfaithful, just so long as the affair was kept secret. He had been tempted, on more than one occasion, to take a mistress himself. It was even expected of him. Somehow Agrippa felt he would be being unfaithful to his first wife, rather than second, if he took a lover. Agrippa felt confident Marcella would remain faithful, however. It would not be due to any affection she felt for her husband, but rather she feared her uncle's disapproval should she commit adultery.

Agrippa sighed, with the hoarse weariness of a water carrier in the hot sun. The correspondence in front of him loomed large, like a mosaic made up of pieces which, no matter how many times one tried, the pieces would never tesselate. He reached for Caesar's most recent letter again and took in its contents.

*"… The army is Rome's most invaluable asset, but I suspect that there will come a time when the army might prove too costly. At present Rome is a state with an army attached, but such is the growth in numbers and influence of the legions that I fear Rome will, at some point, become an army with a state attached. It is another reason why I must secure my succession. I do not wish my legacy to be a civil war, with the victor being decided by who controls the most legions. Or which statesman the legion controls. To that end, once I conclude this campaign, I will be wary of extending the bounds of the empire and therefore extending the size of the army. The Rhine should be a Rubicon we should not cross. Let the channel between Gaul and Britannia serve as a natural barrier too. The island is filled with more tin than gold and their idea of culture is to sing a drinking song and tell a lewd joke. Spain has little more to offer, aside from the fact that the women are prettier - and they produce wine, as opposed to just consume it. Unfortunately, our opponents here are more adept at hiding than fighting. The landscape is littered with mountains, trees and shrubs - behind which lurk swarthy barbarians who, although they*

*may not know how to bathe and dress, know how to kill... But too much talk of war will bring me little peace. Tell me, how is my niece? Forgive her any acts of childishness or conceit. She will grow into a woman and the role of wife soon enough. I predict that one day she will become less obsessed with augury. Time is accustomed to revealing the error of our ways. I will forgive you of course should you choose to take a mistress. Fruit exists to be plucked, after all. You need to relax and enjoy the company of a good woman, in and out of the bedchamber. Sober I'd be if I only tasted Livia's wine. The decision of a husband to take a mistress has saved more marriages that it has ruined over the years, I warrant... 'Tis a rare occurrence, but I found myself drinking the other evening. I cannot quite recall whether the bout of drinking was the cause or effect of it all, but my mind's eye started to witness a macabre procession of the dead, of fallen friends. My great-uncle. My mother. Cleanthes. Roscius and Teucer. Oppius. Cicero. They gazed upon me with a mixture of pride, fondness and mournfulness. I nodded my head in gratitude and respect for each - and downed a measure of wine to honour them. I decided to down two measures of wine for Cicero however, as something inside of me died on the day Herennius took his life. Or rather something in me died on the day I capitulated to Antony's demands and signed his death warrant. He was a friend, mentor. Even when we disagreed, I still valued his company and counsel. Caesar would have never agreed to such a deed, deal. But I was young, ambitious and unwise. I also felt betrayed, when I heard Cicero say I should be, "Praised, honoured and removed." I told myself I needed to be rid of him, before he got rid of me. He taught me much. I am not sure how much of his teachings I have remembered, however. Not enough, some might argue. I find it difficult to re-read his books. Waves of shame and guilt crash against me, like a foaming tide will crash against the shore. Eventually such a tide will wear me down and wash me away. I have also started to hide from view his cherished letters. Yet we should not altogether hide from our sins. They are part of us. We should remember them, so they prompt us to pay restitution and better ourselves. The ghost of Cicero cannot make me un-sign his death warrant, but it can stay my hand when I am due to sign the next one. I am told that the knife reminded Herennius of his finest hour, his greatest achievement. Yet, for me, the dagger will serve as a reminder of my greatest infamy, ignominy. When my divine spark dimmed - or was extinguished. Perhaps one can never properly ignite it again after such a black crime. I would happily give up half the riches in the treasury to have the old man back just for one day, to have dinner with him, after giving a thunderous speech at court or oration in the Senate House. Rome would cheer his name, which he would enjoy even more than dinner... When I pass into the next life, I will of course possess enough riches to bribe the ferryman and hire him for the day. I would first instruct the boatman to take me to see Caesar and my mother. I would drop in on Oppius and Roscius. No doubt they will be sharing old war stories and a jug of acetum around a campfire. But at the end of the long day I would much like to visit Cicero. I would bow down before him and ask for forgiveness. I would show him my neck, as he showed*

*Herennius' his, and hand him the gold dagger. Perhaps the gesture might lack an air of self-sacrifice however, given that I would already be dead... I am not overly concerned with finding out who murdered Herennius, indeed there is an argument that I should reward the culprit, but I would like you to still prioritise locating the dagger. My wish may sound absurd - but I have found that most of the important things in life have an element of the comic or absurd about them. It's what makes life so tragic... We cannot rely on Maecenas to secure the item. His agent had the knife in his sights at the beginning of the party. Unfortunately, he did not have it within his grasp by the end... I will endeavour to return to Rome soon, my friend. I agree with Cicero, when he said that Rome resembled a cesspool more than it did Plato's Republic. But home is home. I miss the city, as I still miss the old man..."*

Agrippa's head hung over the parchment. He closed his eyes and pinched his nose. Parts of the letter brought back memories and made for uncomfortable reading. He had been present when his friend signed Cicero's death warrant. He should have advised him not to do it, to defy Antony. Antony was always the real enemy, not Cicero. But Agrippa had been young, ambitious and unwise too.

## 12.

Varro weaved his way through the sweltering streets and heaving marketplaces. The nobleman used to pride himself of never having to draw sweat, rush around or be purposeful. He thought how, a year ago, he would have stayed home during the afternoon heat and slept.

"You are missing out on life," Fronto would argue, or nag.

"Life is worth missing out on. Life can be as unpleasant as people, partly because people make life unpleasant. The only thing which keeps me going is the certainty that it will all be over one day," Varro replied, before yawning.

But his afternoon naps were currently few and far between. He occasionally, wistfully, missed them. Duty now called, annoyingly. He missed Lucilla too, even on the days he saw her. Or especially on the days he saw her. But Varro couldn't afford to dwell on what might have been - or what might be. He needed to concentrate on the task at hand. Somewhere out there a dagger was waiting, yearning, to be found.

He arrived at Lentulus Nerva's house. The exterior had recently been scrubbed clean of any grime or graffiti. There was not a single cracked tile on the roof. Manicured, pollarded trees peeped over the garden walls. It was a house worthy of a corrupt senator, rather than an overworked lawyer.

As much as Varro considered that the advocate might be his strongest suspect, he would also be the most difficult to trip up. Nerva would possess a water tight defence and alibi. He was more likely to extract a promise from a politician than a confession from the lawyer. Most of the clients Nerva represented over the years had turned up guilty at court - but left as innocent men. Few knew how to game the system better than the seasoned advocate. At least Augustus' letter would permit him to question him. Nerva wouldn't think twice about deceiving Varro, but he wouldn't want to be found guilty of lying to Caesar.

His reputation preceded him, like a growling dog strutting in front of its master. Nerva first made a name for himself when prosecuting Sextus Silanus, a senior official in Gaul. Silanus was corrupt, at the lowest and highest levels. He used the province's treasury as an interest free loan, which he had every intention of not paying back, and he raised taxes to such an extent that even the tax collectors blanched at the increases. Nerva took the time to travel to the region and investigate the allegations against Silanus personally. Evidence and testimonies were collected. At the trial Nerva skewered the defendant like a piece of meat. The arrogant official shrivelled up, like a slug, with the young advocate relentlessly pouring salt upon him. Silanus was found guilty and sent into exile for five years. On his return Silanus, due to his family's influence within the Senate House, secured another post. When he was accused of corruption again Silanus hired Nerva to defend him - and the official was acquitted of all charges.

Lentulus Nerva was as feted, in some quarters, as much as any actor or charioteer. A rival lawyer called him "an intellectual gladiator." The advocate promised that, if a client's money was good, then his defence would be too. It was rare for Nerva to lose a trial. His performances were often entertaining, as well as edifying, as "the new Cicero" ridiculed his opponents, whilst condemning them. No barb was too sharp, no insinuation too outrageous. If the law was an ass, then Nerva rode it like a thoroughbred. The advocate had made plenty of enemies over the years, but more so he had made plenty of powerful friends. Varro mused if it had got to the point where Nerva considered that he was a law unto himself.

He knocked on the thick, iron-bracketed door. A haughty looking slave first peered through a shutter, before opening the heavily bolted entrance to address the uninvited caller.

"My master is a busy official. He only receives people by appointment," the slave pronounced, thrusting his chin out and holding his blade of a nose up in the air.

"No doubt your master might be tempted not to see me, when you pass on my name. I can't honestly blame him for that, as sometimes I grow tired of my own company. But in shunning me the author of this letter may also feel shunned, which would prove un-wise."

The slave squinted, taking in the signature and contents of the document, before his eyes were stapled wide in alarm. His hand trembled as he handed the letter back to its bearer. The slave's supercilious air quickly turned into a model of obsequiousness. He bowed and invited Varro in. The caller was ushered into a reception room and offered refreshments, whilst being asked to briefly wait while the servant convened with his master.

The slave soon returned, in a mood of barely suppressed anxiety, and asked Varro to follow him. Varro was hastily led through the house, to the sound of the slave's sandals slapping against the polished marble floors. Varro noted a large library, which would have rivalled Cicero's. Freshly painted artworks were housed in golden frames. Bronze and marble statues - of Janus, Justitia, Victoria and Lucifer - populated the atrium. Not a flower, or blade of grass, was bent out of shape. A small army of slaves were deployed around the house, to clean and maintain the property. Varro thought to himself how Nerva was likely to be one of those people who liked to be seen to be rich. Perception was reality. Most of the house and its contents had been purchased with "borrowed money", Agrippa had explained. Or Nerva and his wife could be described as being "new money". New money was often the worse kind of money. Certainly, it was the most vulgar kind of money, the aristocrat judged.

Lentulus Nerva sat in his study. He pursed his thin lips, in response to the inconvenience of the visit, but he had also expected a call from an official, sooner or later. The distinguished advocate would let Caesar's investigator come to him. A hierarchy, authority, needed to be established. He would project an air of calm and confidence. And his guest would be an opponent, whether he knew it or not. Nerva straightened his toga and covered up certain correspondence on his lavish, silver inlaid desk. He instructed a slave to open the shutters behind him, so that the sun would shine in his appointment's eyes, causing him no little discomfort and displeasure. Every advantage helped, no matter how seemingly insignificant. Nerva briefly closed his eyes and summoned from his mind every fact, or rumour, about Rufus Varro.

*Know your enemy.*

Varro entered the chamber. With a nod of his head Nerva dismissed the slave who had shown his guest in. The lawyer's expression, in and out of court, could oscillate between being accusatory or suspicious. He briefly smiled at his guest - although if Varro would have blinked, he might have missed it. Nerva wanted to communicate to Caesar's lap-dog that he was being unnecessarily bothered. Yet he would assist the official in his enquiries, if the mood took him to do so. A narrow, triangular nose - like a shark's dorsal fin - dominated the advocate's coffin-shaped head. Although unrelated to the once libertore, it had been commentated upon how Lentulus Nerva resembled Cassius Longinus. He was clean-shaven and smartly attired. His gaze was probing - but ready and willing to be darkly playful at any moment. Varro sensed that the advocate was not just assessing him - but judging him. Even condemning him. His figure was lean, but Varro considered he would have been strong enough to plunge the knife through Herennius' chest, especially if spurred on by rage. Although he suspected that Nerva would have been cold, clinical, with any attack.

The room, like the rest of the house, was newly and expensively furnished. A bust of Hortensius sat on the desk. Nerva would publicly - and modestly - state how he was but an apprentice compared to the celebrated orator and advocate. But privately he believed he was, at least, the great man's equal.

"Please, sit down," Nerva remarked, in a tone more akin to an instruction than invitation. "Would you like some wine?"

Nerva had briefed his slave not to dilute his guest's wine too much should he require a cup. Hopefully the wine would addle his wits or cause him to feel tired and depart.

"No, thank you," Varro replied. Before taking a seat, he glanced at the shelves of scrolls peering out like dozens of black eyes. He noticed how, rather than works of poetry or philosophy, the labelled scrolls contained copies of the advocate's own speeches.

"I knew your father. He was far too incorruptible to ever have use of my services. He was a good Roman. Whether or not I judge him to be a good father will depend upon how this conversation goes. I am of course happy to assist Caesar in any way he sees fit. But, as you can appreciate, my time is valuable, and I may have to cut short our appointment and have us reconvene at a later date. I have innocent men to condemn and guilty ones to liberate. Only joking, of course," Nerva remarked, with little humour.

"I will try not to impinge upon your day too much."

"Thank you. I will save both of us some time by being candid. Although I may have wished my wretched son-in-law dead, I did not kill him. You may have already discovered, during your investigation, that Herennius and I had a heated argument on the night of his death. We raised our voices, whilst raising certain issues. But have you never raised your voice to someone, Rufus Varro?"

"Given the surfeit of hangovers I suffer from, I try not to raise my voice too much. But it would be strange if someone didn't have a disagreement during a family gathering. Can you recall what you argued about?"

"Unfortunately not, which would signify that the argument was of little importance."

"I have received testimony that you threatened your son-in-law during your exchange."

Varro probed, but the lawyer parried.

"I can neither confirm nor refute such testimony. Deeds, not words, matter in life - and the law. I could have even threatened to murder my host. But it means nothing. If we were all punished for the crimes we threaten to commit then half of Rome, particularly warring spouses, would be incarcerated. Did you know or ever meet my son-in-law perchance?"

"No," Varro replied, neutrally. He observed, with an inner smile, how Nerva often groomed himself while he spoke. He would scratch away flecks of dirt from his toga, smooth down his oiled hair and clean his fingernails. The advocate believed in being immaculate and precise - in his actions and words.

"May the gods continue to grant you such good fortune. He was a vile caitiff. Even Circe kept tamer and more refined beasts in her pen. I will be open with you - and Caesar. I am pleased my son-in-law is dead, and my daughter is free of her husband - tormentor. I had cause to kill him myself - and not for any trivial reason, like money. Herennius regularly beat my daughter, even when she was pregnant - and due to one such beating she lost her unborn child, as well as nearly losing her own life," the advocate bluntly remarked. Anger towards Herennius creased his features, rather than pity for his daughter.

Varro felt a twinge of sympathy for the woman, shooting up his side like a man suffering a heart attack, as he recalled the time when Lucilla lost their child and nearly died. His sympathy didn't quite extend to Nerva - and he didn't quite believe that money was a trivial matter for the lawyer.

"I can refer you to her doctor to corroborate my testimony," he added.

"That won't be necessary. I am aware of your son-in-law's temper and character, or rather lack of character. I will not grieve for him either, but that will not prevent me from finding his killer. From discovering the truth."

"The truth? I do not know whether to laugh or weep at your naivete. The truth is a facade. Poets and philosophers seek the truth. Investigators and advocates seek outcomes. The truth can be moulded like clay, worn like the robes of a king or the costume of a clown. I have known the truth to be bought and sold more times than an antique bulla, or a whore's favour. Even if, by the gods, you ever discovered the truth it might prove the case that no one would recognise it. People are used to lies, Rufus Varro. The truth, about anything, would spoil their day, like some stale wine rotting their stomach. The mob only really cares about the appearance of things. The surface of things. You should do yourself a favour and become a lotus-eater. Even the gods forget, so it's perfectly pardonable for mortals to do so too. Forget about finding out the truth - or pursuing its bastard offspring of justice. No one else is bothered about honouring my son-in-law. Why should you? Do you believe that you should be diligent in your investigation, in the name of Rome? Trust me, Rome would rather see an innocent man crucified than a guilty one escape punishment, such is its bloodlust. The heinous crime is not even a memory for most people. The surface is clear, clean. But break through the surface and things become a blur – and one is in danger of being pulled under by the tide. Yet perhaps I am being too cynical and glib - and lying to you. There is one truth which I cling to. That I love my daughter. It is a father's duty to protect his child. But I failed in my duty. Yet I am also a child of the law - and Roman law decrees that a husband is his wife's master. I felt as helpless as a child, as I watched my precious, sweet-natured girl be abused during her marriage to that brute," Nerva exclaimed, holding his head and hands up to the gods in despair, before burying his head in his hands on the desk. Varro had witnessed the advocate perform the same gesture during summations at trial. Varro also observed how the seasoned orator took frequent sips of his wine, whilst he spoke. Not because of any enjoyment he derived from the vintage, but because he didn't want his mouth to dry-out and voice to dry-up.

Varro was tempted to ask if ever Nerva thought about buying his daughter back to keep her safe, after mercilessly selling her like a slave to pay for his marble flooring.

"I would like to take you back to the evening of your son-in-law's death. How was his mood?"

"Unpleasant, as usual. He was inebriated, as usual. And when he got drunk, he grew garrulous. He liked the sound of his own voice," the advocate asserted, without irony. "Along with his equally unpleasant and drunk business partner, Sestius, we had to listen to old war stories. I was rudely cut off, at more than one juncture, when someone asked me about my previous trials. I wish I could say that our host was only discourteous to me. Perhaps everyone around the dinner table, or in the staff quarters, wanted to kill him that night. I imagine it is proving difficult to narrow down your list of suspects. I have seldom encountered a murder where so many of the great unwashed - and the great and the good - cared so little for the victim. That should perhaps tell you to let sleeping dogs lie. I heard about the demise of Sestius too. News travels fast in Rome, especially bad news. Or good news. How will the slave trade cope with the loss of so much cruelty and ineptitude? Perhaps you wish to now posit how Sestius was the victim's benefactor and as a consequence of his death my daughter will inherit her late husband's estate. You might then insinuate, or be plainer in your language, that such a chain of events makes her a suspect. An investigator should always ask the question, who benefits? But I can assure you Rufus Varro that my daughter did not murder my son-in-law. Nor did she murder his business partner. I would not look on you too kindly, if you considered her a suspect and tarnished her good name."

There was more than a hint of warning in the advocate's countenance. The mask of soup-thin cordiality slipped. His eyes somehow seemed blacker, caustic. The skin tightened across his face, like someone was pulling his hair back. Varro considered at that moment how Nerva seemed wholly capable of murder, whether from the cause of protecting his daughter or preserving his own interests. Nerva wagged a bony, talon-like, finger at the investigator, as a warning. Varro had seen him unsheathe the same finger before, in court - either admonishing a witness for telling a lie or stabbing the air to hammer a point home and condemn a man. Or the advocate would flick the finger up when recounting a list of reasons why a jury should judge a man guilty or innocent.

"I am afraid I must consider everyone a suspect at present."

"Except your former wife. Surely, she, like Caesar's wife, must be above suspicion?"

"If I had more time, I could reveal to you the details of our divorce settlement. You might then appreciate what my former wife is capable of. The poet, who gave a reading that evening, is even a suspect. A slave mentioned that they saw a figure, similar in build to the young writer, in the shadows, across the street, later that night. Can you tell me if you witnessed any such figure when you left? Also, what are your thoughts concerning the poet? I understand that he is a friend of your daughter and she invited him to the dinner party."

"I have very few thoughts concerning poets. I have no idea how close my daughter is to him. I did not observe anyone loitering across the street either when I departed. But that is not to say there wasn't someone present. Allow me to impart some advice. I have probably investigated and prosecuted more murders than you have had affairs with married women. Yes, that many. It is tempting to try and construct an elaborate story, or shadowy conspiracy, to explain a crime. But the real world is far more mundane - yet, admittedly, not without wickedness. The likely explanation of Herennius's death is that a robber invaded his house, slew him and stole what valuables were to hand. Or I have a suspicion Herennius' past came back to haunt him - and a maltreated slave finally took his revenge. I hope you are sufficiently sensible to believe in a dull, but credible, story. Now you may wish to question my wife and daughter at some point, but they will not be able to shed any additional light on your investigation. They will say the same as me."

Varro was tempted to reply that their story might be exactly the same, as if they were reading from a script which had been given to them.

Before Varro spoke, he noted a black cloak, draped over a chair in the corner of the room. He briefly scrutinised the garment, to check whether it had been torn, but he couldn't rightly tell, either way.

"You will appreciate that I will still need to speak to your daughter at some point," Varro said, once she had ceased grieving through the act of shopping, he thought.

"Yes, I understand," Nerva conceded, through all but gritted teeth.

"Instead of awkwardly broaching the subject with your daughter, perhaps you could help me? I do not have to be a seer to know that Corinna had an unhappy marriage, but can you tell me if she ever found solace in the arms of another man?"

"My daughter possesses more virtues that you and I will ever have, Rufus Varro. To my knowledge she was faithful," he calmly replied. Varro noticed a growing, seething, tension in his voice, however. The advocate was not accustomed to being questioned, investigated, himself. It impinged upon his dignity and authority. He bristled, like a sophist who had just been corrected by a clever, upstart student. "Could you say the same for your wife, while you were married? I do not say this to rile you, but Lucilla and Licinius Pulcher did seem to make a fitting couple. Licinius seems as interested as you are in who murdered Herennius. He came to speak to me too, on behalf of Maecenas no doubt. Now there's a man who can shape the truth like a god. Black can become white and white can become black, should he decree it. Licinius appeared to be more interested in locating my son-in-law's dagger, than he was in finding the fool's gold of the truth. Please do not take offense, but if I had to place a wager on you both then I would back Licinius to find what he is looking for, before you. And not just because he has the love of a good woman behind him. Ironically, the more you attempt to uncover the truth, the more the truth may remain buried. The culprit will catch wind of your investigation and abscond. He will choose not to sell the dagger, for fear of being apprehended. My counsel would be to cease your enquiries. Make your report to Caesar. Fill it with endeavour and earnestness. But then go back to chasing married women. The sport will provide you with far more meaning and pleasure than any search for the truth."

Varro began to grow a little irritated with his suspect offering him advice, on how best to conduct his investigation - partly because there was a certain degree of wisdom in his words.

"I am grateful for your words," the investigator remarked, not without a hint of sarcasm. But just a hint. Yet Varro would have conceded that the lawyer had knocked him off his stride somewhat, during the interview. Nerva had driven the conversation and second-guessed his lines of enquiry. Varro regretted not having any notes to refer to. He was sure he had more questions to ask; he just didn't know what they were. Already he was turning into a lotus-eater.

"I can only offer you so much advice and expertise however, else I might have to start charging for my time. I am afraid I must ask you to leave now, as duty calls once more. Time is money to a humble lawyer. Thankfully Rome is a wonderful font of crime and corruption. Much like the whores in the Subura, which you may or may not be familiar with, I am never short of work. Should you have any questions in the future I would be happy to answer them, but I must ask that you make an appointment to see me through my secretary first. Please forgive me if I allow you to show yourself out," Lentulus Nerva issued, not without a hint of politeness. But just a hint. Either the advocate forced the briefest of smiles, or the corner of his mouth twitched. He then picked up his stylus, bowed his head and turned to a document on his desk to further indicate to Varro that their meeting was over.

The investigator stood with his mouth open for a moment or two, slightly dumb struck. He felt akin to an actor who had forgotten his lines - and there was no one to prompt him from the wings. Varro was lost for words. He took his leave, with his tail between his legs somewhat. He later thought how Nerva had acted with the confidence an innocent man, or a guilty one who knew he would never be punished. As well as murdering his son-in-law he had it in him to kill Sestius too. Although, surely, he would have hired assassins for the task? Nerva wouldn't want to get any blood beneath his manicured fingernails. Varro didn't quite know whether to deem the lawyer immoral or amoral. People probably wondered the same about him, he imagined, over the years.

As Varro made his way back through the house, he attracted the attention of a number of slaves, who seemed to eye him with suspicion or disapproval - as if they had been ordered to do so by their master. Or perhaps he was just being paranoid. The agent recalled Agrippa's words, from a year ago - advising him that one of the maladies of being a spy meant that he would trust people less. "Everyone will become a possible enemy, or asset to exploit... But just because you're paranoid, that doesn't mean that people won't be out to get you." Certainly, since becoming a spy, Varro thought less of people, which he might not have believed he was capable of a year ago. "If trust comes naturally now, it won't do soon. Or shouldn't do. You must cultivate trust in others, but not yourself. If ever you start to ask, who can I trust? The answer is no one." Yet, against the advice of Agrippa, Varro still trusted Manius, Fronto and even Lucilla. If he didn't, then life would have been even lonelier for the spy.

He gulped down the fresh-ish air when he left the house and let what little breeze there was brush against his clammy skin. His back was stiff. He wryly smiled as he mused whether he had been sitting down too much of late, or not sitting down enough. He briefly closed his eyes and imagined opening them to a view from his country villa.

Varro trudged home, no wiser or closer to the truth. Indeed, the truth seemed even further away. He might as well try and grasp the morning mist. The investigator knew he was walking across flagstones, but he felt like he was wading through mud.

## 13.

Varro developed a new-found affection for the broken tiles on his roof and his unkempt trees and shrubs in his garden as he returned home.

"You seem to be going up in the world," Fronto remarked, as he told his master about the party invitation from Gaius Maecenas.

"Or down," Varro replied, pursing his lips and rolling his eyes.

On another day, particularly in his youth, he would have been pleased to have received such an invite. Given the quantity - and quality - of young wives on display he would have been as happy as, to borrow an expression from Manius, "a pig in shit" to rub shoulders with Rome's gilded elite. He would attend now however out of duty, rather than for pleasure. His time - and life - were no longer his own. He knew Maecenas owned an ulterior motive for inviting him. But even if it was a trap, Varro would walk into it.

As he yawned and stretched, he felt the bones in his spine crack into, or out of, place. His shoulders slumped, as if they might fall to the floor. His eyelids felt leaden. He exhaled - or groaned. He still needed to question Corinna. He still needed to track down and interview the young poet, Publius. He still needed to visit and search Sestius' house, just in case the dagger was hidden there. Albeit he believed he had more chance of discovering the Shield of Achilles, wrapped in the Golden Fleece.

"The messenger also mentioned you could invite a guest," the old attendant added, after masticating, like a cow chewing cud, and running his tongue around his mouth as if counting how many teeth he had left.

A plethora of women's name and faces appeared, like shades, in Varro's mind's eye. Or they were presented before him, like the scrolls mounted along the wall in Lentulus Nerva's study. Before his dalliance with Cornelia he had courted, or been courted by, Hypatia. Hypatia was the wife of the general, Livius Galba. She possessed plenty of virtues. She was Greek - and the poet could practise his second language on her. She appreciated his dry sense of humour and never needed to explain, or defend, any barbed comments. Her thighs were as smooth and burnished as new leather. She was older than most of his lovers, but that was a blessing as much as a curse. He wasn't her first affair. She was experienced in being discreet, as well as amorous. Hypatia, a former actress, still looked good for her age - although she had a tendency to wear too much make-up. "I've grown used to fending off suitors over the years, but now I need to fend off time... My husband still finds me attractive and likes fucking me, which I suppose makes me a rarity in Rome... I like you Rufus. You make me laugh, which might not be good for my make-up cracking, but laughter is good for the soul. You also don't get jealous, or possessive. Most women like a man to be jealous. But you will learn that I am not like most women. I know certain friends who, for want of a better word, have called me a trophy wife. But I must be won and earned, instead of just merely bought - like them."

No sooner had Varro felt an inkling to see Hypatia, however, than he remembered he would be unable to do so. Her husband had recently returned to Rome. Like most Roman men he considered it fine for a husband to conduct an affair, but a wife should be forbidden from doing so. "I have no wish to have you both fight over me like stags, when Livius comes back. Partly because he would probably beat you half to death should he find out about the affair. I wouldn't want him disfiguring your boyish looks, would I?" Hypatia remarked, before promising that she would send a message once her husband left the city again. "At the same time as the gates of Rome close behind him I'll open my door to you once more."

Varro easily shrugged off any disappointment he might have felt however. He knew who he had to invite instead. It was the same person who had accompanied him to more parties than any mistress before. Manius.

"How was your day?" Fronto asked, hoping that his meeting with Lucilla had gone well.

"Long."

"Would you like me to arrange dinner for you?"

"No, I'll just have some kitchen scraps later. I have been feeding off scraps of information all day, so it seems fitting. I feel more tired than hungry anyway," Varro said, as he noticed Aspasia walk across the room. The comely slave girl wore an inviting, enticing, expression on her face. But for once the nobleman desired an empty bed. As much as it may have been worth it, he didn't want to put his back out any more. He didn't want to just wrap a blanket around his body. He wanted to wrap sleep itself around him. Cocoon himself.

"I also received a message from Manius and Camilla. They have invited you over to their home for drinks this evening."

Ever since their wedding they had invited Varro over to their house once a week. More often than not he accepted the invitation. Perhaps they did so out of pity, he considered, as much as they enjoyed each other's company. For as many mistresses as Varro courted, the nobleman had few true friends. He also enjoyed seeing Viola too. She would loyally and lovingly sit by his side - although hopefully not just because he would covertly feed her treats.

"If you send a messenger to convey, I will be free to join them. Thank you. But please forgive me now Fronto, bed beckons, as if Venus herself was waiting in my chamber for me."

Varro retreated to his room, his eyes already half-closed. The shutters were open, but the light was becoming weak. *Honey has turned into piss* - he thought, quoting from one of his own poems, composed over a decade ago. Clouds hung over his head too. He regretted not closely checking Nerva's cloak on the back of the chair, in his study, to see if it had been torn. He regretted not asserting his authority and right question the advocate's wife. He regretted not confronting his suspect more on the issue of him threatening to his son-in-law, during their exchange in the garden. He regretted being unable to warn Lucilla off seeing Pulcher. But everyone has regrets.

*I've more regrets than unfinished poems.*

222

Ultimately Varro knew he would be able to brush away the clouds hanging over his head. Only two regrets mattered. Shadowed him. One was not being able to save Cassandra, from Lucius Scaurus murdering her.

Evening.

Clouds smothered the sky, like too much mould-ridden honey spread across a slice of bread. A few drunks could be heard on the street outside, slurring their words and scuffing their feet across the ground.

An oil lamp hung from the ceiling, as bright and mellow as a sunset. The smell of oatcakes and freshly cut flowers filled the rooms. The walls were adorned with bucolic scenes, painted by the mistress of the house. The furniture and furnishings were well put together and attractive, but not gaudy. It was a home, replete with laughter. The only thing which was missing was the sound of children. But that might soon be remedied, Varro thought. Rather than being envious of his friend for the home he had created, he was happy for him. Thankfully he didn't need to pretend to like Camilla too, for the sake of his friendship. She was sweet-natured, smart and would never knowingly hurt Manius. Camilla was also the one woman in Rome who he would never attempt to have an affair with, which was a goodly minority to be in, Varro considered. Perhaps he wasn't so immoral or amoral after all.

For most of the evening the trio enjoyed some good conversation, over some ruby-red wine which warmed their stomachs and the atmosphere. They sat around a cedarwood table, which Varro had given the couple as a wedding present (among other things), in a small dining room. Braziers hummed in the background. Varro and Manius shared some old stories about each other, ones which they considered fit for their hostess' ears. Laughter is good for the soul. For the most part the two men forgot their present troubles by reminiscing about the past. But Varro could not altogether escape his present as eventually the conversation turned towards his ill-fated investigation.

"As much as it vexes me to say so, I am tempted to take Nerva's advice and report that it was likely that Herennius was murdered by a common robber. And that our best hope in recovering the knife will be to purchase it when it comes onto the market," Varro explained, after recounting his day and the progress, or lack of, of his enquiries.

"Caesar won't be happy," Manius warned.

"Caesar is master over half the known world. It would be churlish of him to be unhappy, for want of a garish dagger," Varro replied, as he bent down and stroked Viola behind the ear. The black and white mongrel rested against his leg. Every now and then she would yawn or pad over to her water bowl. On her return she would jump-up, so her paws were perched on Varro's knees - in order to encourage him to stroke her, or survey if there were any leftovers on the dinner table. "I would also like to think I am still in credit with Caesar, having, according to Agrippa last year, "potentially saved the empire". Granted he had worked his way through half a jug of Falernian, before making the claim."

"Well, before I have as much to drink as Agrippa, I should take myself off to bed. I will leave you both to reminisce over the stories which were not fit for my ears. Thank you again for the book, Rufus," Camilla remarked, as she got to her feet and picked up the scroll Varro had bought her, containing the latest verses by Propertius.

"I look forward to you heavily criticising them and casting them in an unfavourable light, next to my works," the poet joked, before thanking his sister-in-law for a wonderful evening. Varro was truly grateful for the distraction, more than she knew.

Camilla then gently kissed her husband on the top of his head and covertly whispered in his ear:

"I'll be waiting up for you. Don't drink too much."

Manius nodded his head to affirm he would duly perform his husbandly duties this evening. As soon as Camilla disappeared down the hall however the Briton filled both the cups left on the table. Varro had observed how, once or twice, his friend had been distracted. He wasn't quite his good-humoured self. Manius clasped his cup, as if it might break in his hand, and took a couple of deep breaths. He was briefly torn between his loyalty towards his employer and his friend. The latter soon won out and Manius filled Varro in on his mission and meeting with Agrippa. Although a problem shared is never a problem halved Manius did feel better for unburdening himself to his friend.

"And there I was thinking that Caesar was only making my life miserable," Varro commented, after the bodyguard, now spy, finished speaking. His features remained largely impassive, as usual, but disquiet filled his heart, like a gathering storm, in reaction to the news that Agrippa had recruited his friend as an agent. Varro felt like Agrippa had somehow taken advantage of Manius' good nature and honourable character. He was too honest to be a spy. Sooner or later Manius' life would be in danger. Varro knew all too well how an assignment could suddenly go from bad to worse. The life of an agent had already taken bites out of his soul. It could well swallow Manius up whole. "You will need to be careful in front of Carbo and Labeo. Politicians are even less trusting than spies. As much as you need to keep eyes on your quarry, do so from a distance if possible. His retinue doesn't consist of just pox-ridden students and oafish guild members. He also employs a group of bodyguards to keep him company, who would be happy to tear you limb from limb, like a pack of bacchants, if he gave the order... Agrippa may play the plain-speaking Roman, but he can be as sly as a Persian when the fancy takes him. He'll be recruiting Fronto next, or Viola... Can I help in any way?"

"It's doubtful. Carbo is not a great lover of noblemen, especially ones allied to Caesar. You won't be able to get close to him. And I haven't the heart to ask you to seduce his wife. She's frostier than the Alps - and with craggier features. I am hoping for some good luck and that someone will be indiscreet and let slip the details of the plan."

"Well if you are blessed with some good fortune then bottle up a measure of it for me. I'm going nowhere, fast, in my enquiries."

"How was your meeting with Lucilla this morning?"

"Awkward, at best, at first. But it could have gone worse. I drew back from the edge, and didn't throw myself off the Tarpeian Rock, to completely damn myself. I would rather she had killed Herennius, than see her courted by Pulcher. He has worked her well, I warrant. Played the gentleman. I would have hoped she would be able to see through such acts by now, having been married to me. Something is amiss though. Maecenas introduced them for a reason. Perhaps it's not about warning Lucilla off Pulcher, but convincing Maecenas to warn his agent off Lucilla. I formed an idea on my walk over here. It would prove fruitless to try and pay off Maecenas or threaten him. But he may be open to bribery. If I can find Caesar's dagger - and promise it to him, instead of Agrippa - then I may possess the leverage to have him order Pulcher to end the affair."

"Agrippa will not be happy."

"What he doesn't know can't hurt him. At least Caesar will be happy, which is all that matters of course," Varro drolly remarked. Any guilt he felt would be assuaged by his grievance towards Agrippa, for recruiting Manius as an agent behind his back. "My plan is predicated on finding the knife however, which at present seems like no plan at all. If I knew what the dagger looked like, I would commission Benjamin to make a copy. I will still present my offer to Maecenas tomorrow evening. If he agrees to the arrangement, then at least I will be spurred on to find the dagger."

"What are your plans during the day, before the party?"

"To continue my lacklustre investigation. I will visit Sestius' house in the morning and search the property for the knife, as well as conduct an interview with his estate manager. I will then pay my respects to the ungrieving widow and question her, although I suspect that her father has already provided Corinna with all the answers she needs. Should there be time I will track down the poet, Publius. Lucilla mentioned that he reminded her of me, when I was younger," the agent remarked, raising a sceptical eyebrow. The vain poet still inside of Varro thought that he was one of a kind.

"If that's the case then you will need more than just a measure of good luck for Publius to cooperate and provide you with some sage responses," Manius joked.

Varro grinned and raised his cup, before downing its contents. As he glanced up, he noticed a new painting on the wall, slightly different from the others around the house. The scene was of a village, populated by mud huts with thatched roofs. The sky was leaden. A few campfires, like clusters of wildflowers in a field, furnished the picture with some colour. The painting depicted the Briton's old home. Varro imagined how there was an alternative image Camilla could have produced. That of Manius' village in flames, with the villagers being slaughtered by Roman soldiers. A father dead at his son's feet, a mother beaten and nearly raped. Varro briefly thought about what his friend had endured. Had Manius become the man he was because, or despite of, his traumatic experiences. Whilst the orphaned slave was fighting for his life in the arena, as a young gladiator, Varro was merely suffering from melancholy and fighting off boredom (as well as recovering from the odd dose of the pox). There had been a couple of occasions when Varro had suggested to his friend that they travel to his homeland. But perhaps the Briton had little appetite to visit his past. Rather than re-live the past, he wished to bury it.

"The wine will be as sour as most of the women. Your spirits will be as damp as the climate. You won't enjoy yourself. It's a long way to travel to be underwhelmed," Manius had argued, to dissuade his friend from making good on his proposal.

Varro, using the example of his friend, considered that a man could overcome his past. *It doesn't have to cling to you, like your shadow.* One should not make a shrine to one's past, presenting it with offerings each day. For too long Varro had felt guilty, thinking about his father - trying to live up to his expectations, or defy them. For too long he had looked back to Catullus and his era, in attempt to re-live the past. Yet at the same time Varro considered it fitting that the past could, or did, define you. Regrets can be beneficial, if they prevent you making the same mistakes again. He needed to remember Cassandra, to honour her.

"Sweet is the memory of past troubles," Cicero once stated. But Varro wasn't so sure.


A blend of sweat and perfume filled the chamber, like threads woven into a tapestry. The whites of eyes, teeth and glistening flesh could be glimpsed in the darkness.

The couple finally began to catch their breath. Lucilla still held his hand, as she had done so throughout their lovemaking. Licinius brushed his shin against her leg. Her entire body still tingled.

Lucilla finished off her cup of water, resting on the bedside table. Beside the cup and jug was an ivory figurine, of Pomona. A present from Varro, when they were first married. She thirsted for more but was too exhausted to get up. The woman felt her legs might give way, should she stand. Her body was singing, elated, but part of her heart was still mired in thinking about *him*. *Rufus.* The name was tantamount to a sigh. He was part of her life, like grain running through timber. But she was with Licinius now. And she wanted to be honest with him.

"Rufus came to see me today. Principally because he has been asked to investigate Herennius' murder," Lucilla casually remarked, as if she had been visited by an elderly uncle. Not only did she need to be careful with Varro, in regard to any feeling of jealousy - but she needed to take Licinius' feelings into consideration. *Men.* The word could be tantamount to a sigh too. A more exasperated sigh.

"What did you tell him, if you do not mind me asking?" Licinius replied, as he involuntarily squeezed her hand.

"The truth. I said that I had no idea who killed Herennius. I also finally told Rufus about us, although he already knew."

"How did he react? I hope he wasn't too unhappy," the agent said, hoping that he was.

"Unfortunately, I imagine that Rufus will remain unhappy, no matter what my situation," Lucilla suggested, her voice tinged with sorrow or, at best, wistfulness. She pictured his face. Her eyes softened. She may have even raised one corner of her mouth. She moved her leg, so it no longer brushed against his.

"Maecenas has invited us to a party tomorrow evening. I should warn you that Rufus may be attending too. I know it will not be a problem for you, but I pray he will not cause a scene," Licinius said, praying that he would. "If he causes you any distress, you must tell me Lucilla. He will then answer to me. You are no longer responsible for his happiness."

*He is your former husband. But I will be your future one.*

"I know I am no longer responsible for him," Lucilla answered, feeling that she was, partly, lying to the man next to her. And herself. "Rufus will be fine seeing us together, because he will have to be."

"How was the rest of your day, after he left?"

"It was fine. I caught up on some correspondence."

"Did you write back to Livia?" the agent asked. He had been able to search Lucilla's room earlier in the evening but, frustratingly, could find no trace of the letter from Caesar's wife.

"I am planning to do so soon. But I fear the contents would bore you to sleep. And I would prefer to keep you awake for a little while longer," the woman sensuously expressed, whilst rolling over and kissing his parched, parting lips.

The spy could no longer rightly judge where his assignment ended, and feelings began.

## 14.

Varro woke early the next morning. Or rather early for him. A greasy drizzle swirled around in the air, like a plague of insects. His expression was one of disgruntlement - with the weather, his assignment and, perhaps, life. He had drunk too much the night before - or needed a drink now. The nobleman was tempted to use a litter but considered it was better that just one person got wet, as opposed to six. Fronto needed the slaves for chores around the property too. His home was in a state of perpetual maintenance.

He travelled, with his head bowed down and rain spitting his face, to Sestius' house. Varro showed the estate manager, Milo, his letter from Caesar. Milo appeared nearly as old as Fronto, although he must have been at least a decade younger. The slave shuffled, more than walked, and led the investigator into the triclinium. His back was arched, and Varro had encountered corpses less pale and gaunt. Milo spoke slowly, but thankfully because he was considered in his answers rather than dim-witted.

Could his master have had anything to do with his business partner's murder? No, they were close companions and never had a falling out. Herennius would visit his friend at least every week, the estate manager reported. They would sometimes stay up late and drink by themselves - or arrange for prostitutes to join them. Was Sestius an abusive master, towards his slaves? No more than most Milo replied, either mournfully or philosophically. It was difficult to tell. On the evening of Herennius' murder, how was his master's mood when he returned? He was drunk, but that was normal. Was his master wearing a black cloak on the night? No. Did his master have many enemies. Milo couldn't say, but Sestius seldom went anywhere unless accompanied by a bodyguard. Had he seen Sestius in possession of a golden dagger? No. Had a man, called Licinius Pulcher, visited the house after the murder and enquired about the knife? Yes. Did Sestius have any dealings with the advocate, Lentulus Nerva? No. Did he, or any of the other slaves, notice anyone or anything strange before Sestius was murdered? No.

After questioning the estate manager Varro conducted a search of the house. The only thing he discovered of note was that Sestius owned an appalling (or impressive) amount of pornography. Some might have called it art, but most, quite rightly, wouldn't have.

Varro took his leave. The investigation had more dead ends than King Minos' labyrinth, he joked to himself. But he didn't feel like laughing. Failure's not good for the soul. Even if he could hammer out some cast-iron theories concerning who murdered Herennius - involving Nerva, his widow or even Pulcher - he still lacked any cast-iron proof.

The rain persisted, as did his enquiries. Varro made his way across the city towards Herennius' house again. He still needed to interview the victim's wife. Every step seemed to take a gnat's bite out of his soul, like a grain of sand slipping through an hourglass. He darkly mused how, even if all the grains of sand had fallen through, the hourglass would be turned over and the process would start all over again.

*Life diminishes.*

Fabullus instructed Varro that his mistress was out shopping once more, when he called at the house. He wondered if shopping might be an unofficial code – and Corinna was meeting her lover. "O". Perhaps the widow was avoiding the investigator however, because she was concealing something. Before Varro left however Fabullus did mention an incident of possible interest.

"I forgot to mention this during our previous conversation, but six months ago my master was briefly harassed by an old soldier comrade. He claimed that he had been there when my master apprehended Cicero - and this soldier wanted his fair share of the reward that he received."

"Can you remember the name of this man?"

"No. But he was distinctive looking. He had long, grey hair. Pitted skin. He walked with a limp and had a scar, in the shape of a forked serpent's tongue, on his neck… He hounded my master for several days and threatened him, but, after my master's bodyguards attacked him one evening, he disappeared… There have been other incidents of aggrieved merchants, women and employees over the years. But they are almost too numerous to mention."

Chinks of light shone through the sodden air as he left the house and a chink of optimism dimly glowed in his heart as he thought how he might have a solid suspect in the shape of the old soldier. Solid, as in a shadowy figure who he could point the finger towards, to satisfy Agrippa and Caesar. He may not be finding out the truth, but he wouldn't be wholly lying either. Perhaps he could serve as an advocate after all, if he cultivated such a viewpoint.

As much as Varro yearned for a hot bath - and massage - he decided to plough on and interview the poet. At the very least he hoped he could eliminate him as a suspect. The agent was temporarily delayed however, when he walked through a main thoroughfare, by Gaius Macro, an old drinking companion. The former philosophy student was now a property developer. Macro was one of the few friends he had kept in touch with from his dissolute youth. They attended the same parties and bath houses. Macro was good humoured. Unlike too many from their class, he knew how to laugh at himself. The two men stopped to talk with one another. The throng of people moved around them, like water bending around a rock in a river.

"Rufus, what a pleasant surprise. I'm not sure I've ever seen you out and about this early - and in such foul weather. Has someone's husband come home early and a mistress has kicked you out of bed?"

"Ask me no questions and I'll tell you no lies," Rufus replied, warmly clasping his friend's arm. He noticed how Macro's pot belly had grown more pronounced since he had last seen him, and his complexion had grown more florid, roseate. "And how comes you are not at home?"

"Because the wife is. I would say she kicked me out of bed, but happily we no longer sleep in the same room. I finally feel like I have a marriage similar to my parents. I missed you at Ligarius' party last month. He hired both a fire eater and sword swallower. I envied their diet - given the quality, or lack of, of the food the rest of us had to consume throughout the evening."

Varro laughed. Seeing Macro was often a tonic. He always wondered how his friend managed to be so cheerful in the face of such a drear and wicked world. He once asked Macro how he managed to marry his contented disposition with being a philosophy student.

"I was a bad philosophy student. Or perhaps I was an average one - and therefore attained Aristotle's golden mean... I would say that having a surfeit of money has caused me to be happy, far more than passages from Plato and Lucretius ever did."

The rain started to abate. The showers had turned the excrement on the streets into a slick film of grime. Varro mused how even the greatest storm would never be able to wash all the filth away from Rome. More would just turn up.

"Let's hope the food will be better at Maecenas' party tonight. I take it you have been invited?"

"No, this is the first I've heard of it. I don't know anyone else who has been invited either. Seems it's a somewhat exclusive gathering. I'm not sure whether to be relieved or offended at being snubbed. If you let me know the quality of the serving girls, I'll make my decision then. I would be careful of getting too close to Maecenas and letting him do you a favour. You could end up in his debt for the rest of your days. As much as he may wear a toga, he still seems to have plenty of pockets to put people in."

"I will be mindful. Thanks. Tell me though, have you ever had any dealings with Lentulus Nerva, the advocate?" Varro asked, innocently. As well as being an inveterate drinker, Macro was an inveterate gossip. On more than one occasion the agent had used his friend as a source of information for an assignment.

"My father once hired him to settle a legal matter, which he did so effectively. I have heard that he has generated debts which no honest man can pay. Thankfully Nerva is a lawyer though. He already knows that honesty doesn't pay... He has ambitions of entering the Senate House. He moves in rarefied circles, which is why he needs a rare amount of money. Why do you ask?"

"His daughter has recently become a widow. I thought I might pay my respects to her."

"Indeed. Nerva sold his daughter once. I doubt if he will have any qualms about re-selling her. Although I dare say you could do better, my friend. Corinna may be considered a beauty, but not a great one. I'm not sure she's quite marriage material. Then again nor are you. But feel free to blissfully ignore any advice I might offer. It's somewhat difficult for me to sing the praises of married life, what with me being a husband."

Varro grinned and gently shook his head in bafflement.

"I am always amazed by how much you malign marriage - and your wife - Gaius."

"I should invite you to dinner soon. Meeting my wife will help clarify my attitude for you. I should mention, in relation to any bid to court Nerva's daughter, that he has a formidable enforcer working for him. His nephew, Titus Sura. A nasty piece of work, by all accounts. He killed a fellow officer in the army, stabbed him in the throat. His uncle defended him however and Sura was found innocent. He owes Nerva his life. And Sura would probably take yours away if ordered to do so, should you wrong the fair Corinna."

"I'm grateful for the information. It's all food for thought."

The poet's address was in a smart neighbourhood on the Quirinal Hill. Although his name was unfamiliar to Varro, he suspected that Publius was from a respectable, affluent family. His father had probably bought the house for his son to put a roof over his head, as well as for investment purposes. The more Caesar's reign promoted peace and prosperity, the more property prices soared in the capital. Far more importantly than any military glory, the people loved Augustus for their increased wealth - and the tax cuts he introduced. Given that the poet seemed financially secure, it was unlikely that greed would motivate Publius to murder Herennius and rob him. Although should someone tell the writer how much money he would make throughout his career, he might be tempted to supplicate his income through more practical and profitable means.

As Varro approached the poet's house, he could hear a voice bellow over the hissing rain, in the nearby square. A soldier was delivering the latest news from the front.

"Caesar's glory is your glory. He fights in your name - and triumphs in your name. He puts himself at the vanguard, battling the enemies of Rome and civilisation, so you do not have to... His military prowess and courage are unmatched. He is his father's son..."

Varro wryly smiled. He thought he might suggest to Agrippa to employ a new propagandist, but then considered that the consul might order him to fill the position.

A burst of laughter drowned out the sound of the rain and soldier's proclamation. A young woman stood outside the doorway of the poet's house, as the lovers said their goodbyes. Her dress was creased, her hair hastily pinned up. Varro paused, not wishing to disturb the couple. Parting is such sweet sorrow.

A hand reached out from the house and grasped the woman's buttock, as if it were squeezing a piece of fruit to check how ripe it was. He heard a voice - playful and amorous - recite a few lines of poetry:

"None but you shall be sung

In my verses, you and you alone

Shall give my creative spirit its form and theme."

The woman sighed, her legs even gave way a little, before she launched herself upwards and hungrily stole another barrage of kisses. The poet continued to whisper verses in her ear, when they came up for air from kissing.

"Honestly, all I desire is to care for you

Till death do us part - for the two of us to live together."

Finally, they parted. Her expression was a picture of adoration and satisfaction as she sauntered away, her coquettish eyes gleaming like semi-precious stones. Her cheeks sat on her face like two plump, rosy apples when she smiled.

Varro nearly laughed to himself, observing the scene, although part of him also wanted to cringe. Already, he could see why the poet had reminded Lucilla of his younger self.

The investigator put on a stern expression, as cold as the rain. He intended to establish his authority straightaway. Fear, rather than civic duty, would motivate the adolescent to tell the truth, he reasoned. He banged, rather than just knocked, on the door. Twice.

The young man opened the door himself, as opposed to instructing a slave to do so. If he was disappointed that it wasn't his mistress returning to his threshold the youth didn't show it. He couldn't have been more than eighteen years old, albeit he would soon learn that the adolescent was wiser - and wittier - than his years suggested. The fresh-faced poet smiled, easily and amiably. His features were not so dissimilar to Varro's, although the older man's face looked more "lived-in", one could say. His frame was slender, his hair and complexion fair. He wore a clean, plain, light blue tunic with a smart, leather belt. Its gold buckle glinted in what little light the day afforded. His skin was smooth. When Varro clasped his hand, later, he guessed that the poet had never done a proper day's work in his life. It takes one to know one, he judged. The youth's sea-green eyes shone with verve, intelligence and amusement. Varro found it difficult to maintain his stern gaze - and his voice wasn't as stentorian as he would have liked, as he spoke to his suspect for the first time. The words were as much of a statement as a question.

"Publius Ovidius Naso?"

"Yes. But, please, call me Ovid."

## 15.

The young man's grin grew broader and the light in his eyes shone brighter when his visitor introduced himself. He briefly blinked, repeatedly, and his mouth was agape. Varro didn't need to show Ovid his document, signed by Caesar. He was invited in straightaway and offered refreshments (which Varro discourteously declined, conveying that he was here for business rather than pleasure). When the investigator mentioned the purpose of his visit his host said that he would assist him in any way he could. His bubble didn't burst.

As Ovid led his guest through to the back of his house and small garden, Varro couldn't help but notice various scraps of parchment containing poems, in varying states of completion, pinned against the walls and resting on pieces of furniture. Scrolls, books and wax tablets also populated the otherwise tidy and well-furnished property. Varro was compelled stop and take in some of the poet's works in progress. He was impressed - very impressed - by what he read. His tone could be tawdry in one couplet and yet tender in the next. The adolescent possessed genuine talent and wit - and seemed dedicated to his craft. Love and poetry were all that mattered.

*"Love is a warfare: sluggards be dismissed,*
*No faint-heart 'neath this banner may enlist.*
*Storms, darkness, anguish, weary trails you'll find*
*On love's campaign, and toil of every kind."*

Ovid avidly watched on, as proud as a mother when a stranger admires her children, as he noted flickers of reactions on Varro's face, whilst he absorbed different poems and lines. The investigator's features softened - and a smile was carved into his previously stony expression. Varro even looked like he was going to laugh on more than one occasion.

*"Youth tempts me. So do riper years. Youth's prettier,*
*Yet older women's ways have me in thrall;*
*Yes, every worthwhile girl in Rome's great city,*
*My love's a candidate to win them all."*

The nobleman was handsome, as Ovid imagined (it couldn't solely have been his wealth which captured so many hearts). The rain caused Varro's fringe to be parted and Ovid noticed the scar on his forehead. Varro would later explain to the young man that his scar was a result of a cuckolded husband catching him with his wife - "so let my error serve as a lesson to you."

An enthralled Ovid had been an admirer of his guest for as long as he could remember, as he first started to compile his poetry library in his home town of Sulmo. As well as learning technical and stylistic lessons from Varro, his works also taught him that writing poetry was a way for the youth to attract women. Virgil and Horace had offered no such guidance or encouragement.

"I hoped to meet you one day. I was even tempted just to knock on your door when I first came to Rome, to continue my education. I was scared that you would slam the door in my face, however, and my appreciation of your poetry would be somehow lessened and tainted. For me, whilst growing up, you were a star in poetry's firmament," Ovid remarked, with a catch in his throat before speaking. As they reached the garden, with the rain abating, Ovid wiped a chair down and offered it to his guest.

"I suspect that I am a dying star, at best, now. I haven't penned anything of substance for some time, that's worth offering up to the world. Especially as the world may just chew it up and spit it out - or worse, blissfully ignore it," Varro wryly replied, staring at his callow host with no little amount of wonder and curiosity. Did he genuinely know and admire his poetry? Or was he just flattering the investigator, in an attempt to win his favour? Varro decided, partly due to Lucilla's comments, to give the youth - or suspect - the benefit of the doubt.

Light began to eke through the leaden clouds. Varro fancied that a rainbow might even soon decorate the sky. Some people might interpret it as a good omen, a sign of hope.

*Let them.*

"You would have at least one book sale, if you penned another volume of verse. But I understand that you are on official business of the state," Ovid said, looking at his guest with not a little wonder and curiosity. Why was a nobleman and poet now working as an investigator? Did he volunteer, because of his former wife's involvement? Or had Caesar given him a direct order? Ovid had more questions than answers.

Varro soon realised that, unlike Nerva, getting a straight answer out of the adolescent would not be like getting blood out of a stone. The poet didn't ration his words or opinions.

"… I arrived halfway through the evening. The atmosphere was as stale as the cheese in the Subura. To call the gathering a "party" is using more poetic licence than I am comfortable with. The host was having a good time, often at his guests' expense. He drank, like a camel at a wadi. Wine is a gift from the gods - along with poetry, red mullet and women. Wine should make a man pleasant, not pernicious. But Herennius was the latter. He seemed particularly abusive towards Nerva and Corinna… He rudely spoke over everyone and, along with Sestius, bored his audience with stories about the campaigns he had taken part in – although, I have faith in my scepticism that Herennius didn't take part in half the engagements he mentioned. I was even glad when he belched, at least it meant that I didn't have to suffer his conversation. I think a few of the guests were grateful for my arrival, as my readings provided a fire break during proceedings," Ovid explained, frequently flicking his head as he spoke or brushing his long fringe out of his eyes. Apparently, it was the fashion for Rome's youth to wear their hair in such a style. Yet, after recently finding out that he was unwittingly following a trend, Ovid vowed to trim his hair back.

"Did you notice a particular enmity between Herennius and his father-in-law?"

"Well, other than I overheard Nerva threaten to kill his host, no," the poet drily posited, arching an eyebrow. "I left shortly after that, as much as I was asked to stay. Thankfully I was able to converse with your former wife before I took my leave."

Ovid was about to launch into a paragraph or two of praise for Lucilla - and how attracted he was to her - but he thought wiser of it. He pictured the elegant woman in his mind's eye again however, her slender yet strong limbs. Her figure was not dissimilar to a statue of Athena that his father had bought for his garden, back in Sulmo. He was as surprised as he was enamoured by how well-read Lucilla was. She had good taste in literature, evidenced by her admiration for his verses, he judged. Ovid had seduced several older women before, but none like Lucilla he reckoned. She was both demure and steely. Being married to a poet had doubtlessly put her off writers. And quite rightly too. It wasn't that she was too old for him - but too wise.

"Lucilla mentioned she chatted with you."

"Really. What did she say?" the youth asked, as fleetingly lusty-eyed as a sailor, fresh into port.

"I can't remember," Varro answered, lying.

"I spoke with Licinius Pulcher for a short while too, which was long enough. His manner was oily as his slicked-back hair. He showered me with compliments for my verses, but I somehow felt akin to a swan, having radishes and fruit shoved up its arse before being roasted. No, I didn't take to him," the poet opined, making a face when he mentioned the man's name, as if he had swallowed a bitter olive.

"I have changed my mind. I will join you in a measure or two of wine," Varro remarked, as he appreciated the poet for being a source of information and amusement.

Ovid called for one of his slaves to serve some wine. Neither man diluted their measures. They let out a satisfying "ah" - almost in unison - after savouring their first mouthful.

"Tell me more about Nerva. How black and bloody do you think his mood was at the end of the evening? Do you believe him capable of murder?"

"Capable, yes. Culpable, maybe. There is perhaps a volcano, waiting to erupt, beneath the veneer of his civilised temper. Or distemper. But Nerva is one for being cold, scheming. On one hand the advocate loves the sound of his own voice," the poet remarked, without irony. "But as garrulous as Nerva can be he doesn't give anything away. He keeps his own counsel and he has more secrets than Cupid owns arrows… During the afternoon, before the night of the party, I saw the advocate in conference with his bodyguard, Titus Sura. Now, Sura could have easily stabbed Herennius, as a farmer could wring the neck of a bird. Have you seen the man? His mirthless stare could curdle milk at a hundred paces. His hands seem permanently balled up into fists. And if you examine those hands closely enough, you'll see them marked with numerous scars from brawling. Or, they are pitted from the ape draggling his knuckles along the ground, when he walks. Should Sura ever enter the arena, he would be billed as more beast than man, I warrant. If snorts, snarls and grunts could serve as epigrams he would be one of Rome's foremost poets. Rumour has it that the brute used to volunteer to torture prisoners on the front, as well as discipline his fellow soldiers. Lucretia is one of the few wives in Rome I would never be tempted to touch, lest Carbo unleashed his enforcer on me."

If Titus Sura wasn't already a person of interest to Varro, he was now. He could prove the missing piece of the puzzle. Alternatively, it was not beyond the realms of possibility that Ovid was pointing the finger of suspicion away from his guilty self. Herennius' death would allow the youth to marry the potential object of his affection, as well as provide him with enough capital to have no need of a patron.

"Yet, you are not afraid, it appears, of getting your hands on Herennius' wife, Corinna. You understand how I must treat you as a suspect too and ask you a number of questions?"

Varro proceeded to pose a series questions to the youth, which Ovid answered plainly and, seemingly, honestly. Was he wearing a black cloak on the night of the murder? Yes. Did he loiter outside the house after he left the party, perhaps waiting for a message from his mistress? No. Did he see anyone else loitering across the street? No. But it was dark. There could have been someone there. "I am often in a world of my own - filled with heroes from the Iliad and mistresses more interested in Horace than shopping - when walking the streets of Rome." Did he have an alibi, as to his whereabouts after the party? Yes. He visited his patron, Messalla. Did he notice the gold dagger at the house? Yes. It was a shiny yet vulgar object. "One didn't need the eye and insight of a poet to notice how much Licinius coveted the item."

"And how much have you coveted the item of Herennius' wife? Is the relationship serious between you both?" Varro asked, his eyes probing as much as his words.

"A serious relationship? I must note that down as an oxymoron, to use in one of my poems. Corinna let me into her heart, and more importantly her bed chamber. I met her at a reading I gave one evening. It wasn't only my words which touched her that night, if you can forgive my crudity. We exchanged a series of letters. But our affair is drawing to a close, as the smell of perfume on those letters is fading. All love is vanquished by a succeeding love."

"You are not intending to marry her?" Varro asked, in an attempt confirm that the poet had no desire to secure Corinna's hand in marriage - or money. Part of the investigator was keen to exclude the likeable youth from his suspect list.

Ovid offered up an infectious laugh in reply, nearly spitting out his wine as he did so.

"You of all people must know that there's no such thing as a married poet, or rather a faithful one. I love women. I adore them, even when they are being beautifully stupid. Or especially when they are being beautifully stupid. But I couldn't ever envisage loving just one woman for the rest of my days. It would be selfish of me - and her. Look at how faithful the gods are! They are as monogamous as vermin. Fidelity is unnatural. Women know that their partners are unfaithful. But at the hint of thinking she possesses a rival a woman will raise her game. In my experience a mistress will be devoted to you more, not less, for desiring someone else. Corinna may well still be in love with me. But the affair is over. She just doesn't know it yet... I am akin to a honeybee, trying to be fair and visit all flowers. Penelope remained faithful to Odysseus only in literature. In the real world she would have married the first attractive, or wealthy, suitor who came knocking on her door. Corinna's complaints about her husband at first were a signal to pursue my quarry. Yet her complaints about her husband remained, even when I satisfied her... She probably tells herself that she still loves me. Women are the only creatures on earth who lie more to themselves than men do. But no love can endure more than a month's exposure to the real world, as no sword is immune from rust once pulled from its scabbard. Absence may make the heart grow fonder, but familiarity breeds contempt," Ovid yammered, only pausing to re-fill the two cups on the table.

Varro was slightly taken back, or even slightly in awe, of the young poet's ebullience and energy - amorous or otherwise. Ovid spoke, breathlessly, as if he had just been saved from drowning and wanted to impart all the half-truths his soul could hold. He didn't quite know what to do with his hands too. Sometimes they sawed the air or nervously fingered the stem of his cup. What Ovid's hands really wanted to do was write, as if they had a mind, or muse, of their own. This was one of the times of the day when the poet usually locked himself away and wrote.

"But you know these truths only too well. You were a honeybee too! I am not quite sure which inspired me more, your poetry or your conquests. Each inspired the other. And when women read your verse - and they knew who you were and what you were after - the flowers still opened-up to you. Some probably thought that they could save you from yourself. But men do not want to be saved, they want to be satisfied, to quote a line from one of your poems. Your work served as a guidebook for me. I felt like I had a teacher, in the arts of seduction. As you instructed in your first collection of verse, I narrowed and softened my eyes to project sincerity. My eyebrows can send wordless messages across a crowded room. I gently and briefly squeezed the hands of my mistresses to convey support sympathy and devotion. The first kiss is always akin to a light breeze, but it is the prologue to a maelstrom of passion. Each gesture and word should be a musical note that, when played in the correct order, creates a harmony between two souls. I cherish each lithe body which stretches out before me, unravelling like a scroll, ready to be written upon. Surely you felt the same way too?"

Ovid gazed at his guest with conviction, gratitude and a desire for approval. A speechless Varro downed his wine. He was understandably flattered that the young author had studied his work. Every writer wishes to be an inspiration. Yet Varro also felt that he had somehow helped create a monster. He wondered how similar or different he was to the talented, or turgid, poet. He made a half-promise that he would think about it some more at a future juncture. He had enough to investigate at the moment, after all.

"My question is, why did you stop writing?" Ovid added.

"I got married," Varro replied.

*I loved her. I was faithful. For a time, I felt saved.*

"A married poet? May the gods preserve him. Rather than a source of inspiration, I fear that a wife will be a source of worry, mistrust and expenditure... No, my current contract with women benefits both parties. I use them as a source of inspiration and in return I immortalise them in verse. Rumour has it that Pompey would leave his lovers an impression of his teeth upon their buttocks. I prefer to leave an even longer-lasting legacy. Beauty is a fragile thing, but my poems frame my mistresses at their best, like a fine portrait. Whilst their husbands age them."

Ovid raised his cup in a toast to Varro again and grinned, seemingly without a care in the world. But was he somehow too carefree? He lacked a sense of despair, grief. *The last thing a poet should be is happy.* Romans often grew their beards long to mark a period of mourning. Ovid would be lucky to grow a convincing stubble. Yet sooner or later his host would suffer from melancholy, experience a sense of exile from the world. It is how one reacts to misfortune, rather than happiness, which shapes a man's character. Varro recalled one of the few times when Agrippa quoted a piece of verse. And it was one of the few times when Varro wanted to turn words into deeds.

*"Easy is the descent into Hell; night and day, the gates of Hades stand wide open; but to climb back again, to re-trace one's steps to the upper air – there's the task and there's the labour."*

"You have a promising future ahead of you as a poet, if age - or a number of husbands - do not catch up with you first. There are far worse patrons in Rome then Messalla too."

"And one of them has invited me to a party tonight. Maecenas recently lured Propertius away from Messalla. But as much as I am willing to eat from Maecenas' table - and be introduced to the desserts of the wives and daughters of his inner circle - I will remain loyal. He is a good patron and a good friend. My ambition is to one day attract the attention of Caesar however," the young man remarked. The gleam in his eye suggested he was imagining his own immortal fame, spreading out across the empire like a forest fire.

"Just make sure that, when you attract the Caesar's attention, it's for the right reasons," Varro warned, although he was unsure whether Ovid was listening.

## 16.

Varro and Ovid spoke for a little longer, enjoying the clement weather and conversation.

"While I am trying to figure out whether I have had too much or too little wine, let's fetch another jug," Ovid half-joked. "Every day I permit myself one or two solemn statements, just to ensure that irony and sarcasm do not completely rule my being. You should be careful in your dealings with Lentulus Nerva. Be as certain as death, or taxes, should you accuse him of any wrongdoing. He will not think twice in ruining your reputation in court - and starting a whispering campaign outside of it too. Titus Sura is not to be underestimated either. He will break your bones, rather than your spirit, without batting an eyelid should Nerva instruct him to do so."

"And should I take care in my dealings with his daughter? If she was involved in her husband's death, she will not be beyond killing again to escape prosecution," Varro remarked.

"I sincerely hope Corinna isn't capable of revenge and murder, as I am about to end our affair... But she is innocent. I wish her well. Hopefully Corinna will find a portion of happiness, now she is free of her despicable husband."

Varro took his leave. As much as he wanted to fit in a nap before Maecenas' party that evening, he decided to take a slight detour and visit Novius, to pick-up and pay for his books.

The bruise coloured skies had lightened. The smell of damp in the air receded, like a sluggish tide. Rome bustled and bellowed once more. Litters criss-crossed one another, containing finely dressed women who would shop until exhausted. Some of them walked together too, their entourages following like the train of a gown.

Varro found himself walking alongside a couple of women, who appeared to be the wives of politicians. He had encountered their kind before. Pinched expressions. Clipped, haughty tones. Plucked eyebrows. Coiffured hair. Their stolas barely granted them room to breathe. They would be members of various salons, literary or otherwise, in Rome's more fashionable neighbourhoods. They would be married to husbands, who would be devoted to infidelity. Their shrill voices cut through the air like shards of glass, as they gossiped to the point of becoming breathless. Varro couldn't help but catch snatches of their conversation as he strolled along the crowded, narrow street. His ears pricked up upon hearing Nerva mentioned too.

"Flavia is as brazen as a courtesan. She considers herself a new Servilia. She is working her way through the Senate House, like a pox working its way through a tavern in the Subura... I hear she has her eye on Lentulus Nerva, or Flavia has her eye on him. If he thought it expensive to keep his wife happy and buy a new house on the Palatine, then he will be in for an unpleasant surprise when he finds out how much it will cost him to keep Flavia in the style she's grown accustomed to. Money makes money, but loans breed loans. And lust breeds lust."

Varro had thought how love, or lust, could have driven Corinna to murder Herennius. But could Nerva have been motivated by passion to secure this Flavia as a mistress? Love can drive a man to do many a foolish, or vicious, thing.

As Varro turned into the market square, where the bookstore was located, he felt the hairs on the back of his neck tingle. He turned and thought he saw a grey-haired man with a limp in the corner of his eye. But he believed it was just his imagination playing tricks on him.

The musty smell of parchment and books were as welcome and familiar to Varro's nose as freshly baked bread. He greeted Novius warmly and offered up a few half-nods of recognition to a number of other authors currently populating the store. Few of them had any interest in buying anything, but rather they were there to ask the owner to display their books more prominently and ask about the sales of rival authors.

Novius was not the best bookseller in Rome, nor its worst. He worked his copyists like miners in the basement of his shop, but he paid a fair-ish wage and owned genuine good taste in the form of championing talented writers. Although, quite a few authors took it for granted that they should be championed and lauded. They often titled themselves as being the new Horace or Virgil. Varro wryly smiled to himself, remembering how he used to call himself the new Catullus. He considered how Ovid was either too vain, or filled with too much integrity, to desire such reflected glory. He wanted to make a name for himself - and may the gods bless him for it.

Varro made sure to mention the young poet to Novius, as a possible rising star.

"I have not heard of him, I'm afraid. But I will be happy to meet with the young man should you recommend I do so," the bookseller remarked, as he eyed a couple of customers who frequently came into the shop, but only browsed through his stock, instead of buying anything.

"He's prodigiously talented. Sooner or later Rome will hear of Ovid. He may well offend the old and prudish, but that will only mean he will appeal to the young. I have only read a small sample of his work but he's satirical, without being malicious, and has mastered rhythm and rhyme. Should all his former lovers buy a book, to see if they are featured in his verses, then you will already have a captive market," Varro enthused.

Novius promised he would mention the young poet when he next had dinner with Messalla.

"Oh, I forgot to mention that Lucilla came in the other day."

The bookseller couldn't help but smile when uttering the name of one of his most valued customers. His smile widened as he pictured the elegant woman. The old man's blood was now tame, but he would have been duly enamoured with the well-read lady in his prime, he thought.

*If I ever had a prime.*

"Did she say much, or mention me?" Varro replied, casually.

"She enquired about the books you have ordered this year."

Varro raised a corner of his mouth in a knowing, amused half-smile as he recalled a snippet of conversation between himself and his former wife a month ago.

"You always say you are "fine" when I ask how you are. But I know you feel less than fine most of the time. And sometimes, when drinking, you feel better than fine. It would be easier to ask which books you are reading at any given time, to gage your mood. You are what you read."

As well as paying for his copy of *The Last Days of Socrates*, he also purchased, on Novius' recommendation, a comedy by Plautus. *The Chaste Husband.* The bookseller then offered to have one of his slaves deliver the order to Varro's house by the end of the day.

When Varro left the shop, he immediately encountered a familiar face, sitting on one of the wooden benches outside the store. A torrent of clacking people passed by, but the old man appeared like an ocean of calm. Owlish. Content. Tiro's aged countenance, as creased as the folds in a toga, broke out into an even kinder, brighter smile on seeing Varro. Silvery-grey wisps of hair covered his scalp. A large head sat upon spindly shoulders and appeared like they might not support it. But they did. Bat-like ears protruded, as if still pricked to attention to catch the gossip in the Senate House. Varro noted how Tiro now carried a walking stick. He wore a cream tunic, along with a tatty, brown cloak. His legs resembled white marble, replete with pronounced blue veins. Tiro had also lost weight. His body appeared shrivelled-up, like a piece of fruit drying out in the sun. The skin on his neck hung looser. His cheeks were hollowed out, as if a sculptor had re-chiselled his face. Yet there was still life, intelligence and kindness in his aspect. Tiro was still Tiro.

Cicero's former secretary motioned to stand, but Varro gestured for his friend to remain seated. There were few people he admired more, or was fonder of, in Rome. Despite the trials he had endured, from standing by Cicero in his hours of need, and the anguish he experienced at his master's demise and death, Tiro always remained courteous and cheerful.

"Please, there is no need to stand on ceremony, or stand on the cracks in the pavement, for my sake," Varro remarked, as he sat down and warmly greeted his friend.

Originally, Tiro had been Varro's father's friend, through his relationship with Cicero over the years. Appius Varro would often invite the pro-consul over for dinner. As a child Rufus would perch himself at the top of the stairs and listen to his father, Cicero and Tiro converse. They would gossip and talk late into the night about literature, philosophy and the politics. He remembered how Tiro would often take the heat out of any argument, if - or when - his father and Cicero disagreed. He knew when to be witty and when to be wise - and that the two were not mutually exclusive.

Tiro had first been Cicero's slave but the advocate soon rewarded his diligent secretary with his freedom. Tiro remained in the Cicero's service however (despite generous offers of employment from Crassus and Pompey).

Impressed by the system of shorthand Tiro invented, Caesar also invited him to join his staff. Tiro politely declined the offer.

Tiro's duties were many and varied for his employer. Cicero would dictate to his secretary - and he regularly asked Tiro for his thoughts, when composing his speeches or writing his books. He helped to temper his master's bombast and overly acerbic wit. As much as Cicero was famed for his ability to remember everyone he met, Tiro would often whisper the name in his ear before the politician engaged the voter or client. The advocate's secretary would also play a difficult witness, or produce counter arguments to accusations, when Cicero was involved in a trial. Tiro oversaw Cicero's meals as well - as he was as particular about his food as he was the words he used in his oratory.

"You're the only person I trust, other than my daughter, who I know won't poison me," Cicero once confessed to his secretary.

"But what about your wife?" Tiro asked.

"My statement still stands," Cicero replied, half-joking at best.

Tiro remained devoted to his master, even after his death. He collated and published Cicero's correspondence and commenced to write his biography (which he was close to finishing). "I want his name to echo through history, even more than Caesar's," Tiro ardently argued. "Julius may have given Rome many a victory on the battlefield. But any pride we feel will eventually turn to shame. He was a butcher and a bully. Rome's legacy should be its language, literature and laws - the things Cicero mobilised and sent into battle."

The secretary was still married to his master's cause, even when Cicero could no longer give breath to it, to the point where Tiro sacrificed any notion of marrying and having a family himself. He would have felt he was being unfaithful, disloyal. Varro suspected that Tiro hadn't turned himself into a eunuch, however. On more than one occasion he had noticed Tiro gaze, tellingly, at one of his servants. Lust was mixed in with fondness for the woman, like spice mixed in with flour to liven up the taste of bread. "Fine minded men are still men," Tiro had himself once conceded.

The old man smiled at his young friend. It was a fulsome, toothy smile. "The gods may have taken away most of my hair and eyesight but maybe they took pity on me - or were forgetful - as they have thankfully left me with most of my teeth," Tiro once drily said to Varro.

The secretary, or the historian as he was also now called, bent down and pulled up the weeds that were growing between the cracks in the paving stones outside of the shop. It was another tiny, kind act in a life filled with inestimable kind acts, Varro thought. Should Cicero prove to be a chapter in the history of Rome, then he hoped that Tiro wouldn't serve as a mere footnote to the story.

"I just thought I would take the weight off my feet, before I meet Novius and ask him about my underwhelming book sales. My bones grow easily tired nowadays, although they don't yet feel too wearisome, I'm pleased to say," the old man remarked, smiling as if sharing a private joke with himself. "As you can see, I've succumbed to the inevitable and bought myself a walking stick. I am finally the punchline to the Sphinx's joke, or riddle. What has four legs in the morning, two in the afternoon and three in the evening? It has been too long, Rufus. I will look to call in on you before I leave. If nothing else, you can listen to Fronto and I compare ailments... You are looking well, although that may be due to the fact that my eyes are deteriorating again. A lifetime spent reading has strained my sight. But the price has been one worth paying. The streets of Rome are now often just a blur, fortunately. Unfortunately, the smells and sounds of Rome are as sharp as ever. Even when I start to breathe the country air in Puteoli I feel I may still be able to smell Rome in my nostrils. I have lived here for too long. Cicero never much liked his time in exile, but I did. Roman politics is an endless drama and each act seems to finish on a greater tragedy. A thunderclap from Rome plunges the whole world into a storm. How long before Mars stirs and craves to amuse himself again by starting a war? It will prove an unrivalled achievement, should Augustus live a long life and die in his bed... I want to feel the grass beneath my feet, gaze out across a sapphire sea and try to mirror its calm. People should just listen to the ocean more and allow it to shush them. After I finish writing Cicero's biography my only jobs will be to feed the birds, water the plants and read. But I must finish his life, before life finishes me," he sighed, philosophically. "You will of course be welcome to visit, Rufus. Bring a vintage or two with you, although there will be no need to bring any gossip from Rome. You can keep that unpacked."

His voice had grown croakier, Varro considered, as if flecks of granite tiled the inside of his throat. He observed how his hands seemed stiff and arthritic, shaped like he was permanently holding a stylus. Varro did his best to ward off any expression of pity on his face. He forced a smile through the thick-ribbed sorrowfulness of his thoughts.

"And should you travel to Rome again you are more than welcome to stay at our house. I remember how my father offered to provide you with protection and hospitality if ever you needed it, after Cicero's death. I am happy to honour his promise."

"Your father was prouder of you than you might think, Rufus. Don't mistake not showing an emotion for not possessing it. I know he may not have seemed a good father at times, but Appius tried - and often succeeded - in being a decent man. Even the gods have their flaws, so it is only natural that man should prove eminently fallible too. Nobody's perfect. None of us is without sin," Tiro proffered, as much to himself as to his younger companion.

"Perhaps Herennius finally is, now he's dead."

"Yes. I heard about his end - although one person told me he was stabbed and the other mentioned he was bludgeoned to death in his own house, by an intruder. I do not believe they have apprehended the culprit. I will not consider it a travesty of justice should they never find him. I must confess I wished him dead, many years ago. But Herennius is a ghost from the past, already dead to me. I cannot say I ever forgave him, but I certainly forgot about the vile man. The soldier would have argued that he was only following orders, when he struck down my friend. But the past is the past. What of the present and the future? Tell me, are you still writing?"

"No. I realised that one has to give one's heart and soul when writing poetry - and I cannot impart that which I do not possess," Varro replied, glibly or otherwise.

"You are hard on yourself, although I will not say you are too hard on yourself. Laziness eclipsed application, where your writing career was concerned. You diluted your talent all those years ago, as surely as you didn't dilute your wine. But just because you fell victim to a certain indolence - and dissoluteness - in the past, it doesn't mean that you cannot write a new chapter into your future. Similarly, just because you're unmarried now, it doesn't mean that you should remain unmarried. When I saw Lucilla the other day, I gifted her the same advice," the old man remarked, raising a knowing and suggestive eyebrow as he spoke.

"The last person that Lucilla would want to marry - would be the first person she married," Varro said jokingly, or forlornly.

"I wouldn't be so sure. The past is the past. Ask yourself how you feel about her now - and how she might feel about you?"

### 17.

Tiro's words hung in Varro's mind, like a body nailed to a crucifix, later that evening as he prepared for the party. He had bathed, shaved and combed his hair. He wanted to look his best or, at the very least, better than Pulcher. He positioned his fringe to cover his scar - although Lucilla would still know it was there.

Varro asked himself, how much can we consider ourselves the sum of our pasts? Or how much do our pasts leave us misshaped, hamstrung?

*Can we free ourselves from our past, cut the anchor? Or rather does the past serve as the wind in our sails, to inspire and drive us forward? If we constantly look back will we not have eyes on where we're going? But if we constantly look forward, will we be fated to fall for the same traps which snared us in the past? When she looks to the past, does she remember the days spent at Arretium? Love-making. Planning for a family. Or does she just remember the affairs, drunkenness and distance I put between us after we lost our child?*

Manius called upon his friend and the two men made their way through the balmy night towards the party. Maecenas' house loomed large on the Esquiline Hill. Varro had oft taken in the lavish, imposing property but he had never been inside. Maecenas' art collection was the envy of Rome. His furniture was produced by Rome's - and the empire's - finest craftsmen. His gardens were reported to be attended to on a twice-daily basis. During the evening, lamps were hung in windows, even if the rooms were empty, so the house lit up the night sky.

"So here we are, about to enter the lion's den again, my friend. At least we can be sure that the wine will be agreeable, even if the company won't necessarily be so. And at least you can be sure Publius Carbo won't be an honoured guest. How was your day?" Varro asked his companion, as he negotiated walking along a cobbled-stone street, mindful that he wouldn't be able to do so on the way home should he drink too much throughout the evening.

"Duller than a mime show. Carbo went about his business and I duly followed him. He met with Labeo but, rather than inspect any would-be army, they just lunched together. He didn't even take to the streets to give a rabble-rousing speech. I am due to visit the house and give another fencing lesson on the day after tomorrow. Perhaps I will be fortunate enough to learn more then. If only I could be in two places at once and track Labeo's movement's too. But I would prefer not to re-live my uneventful day. Fronto mentioned that you encountered Tiro this afternoon," Manius remarked. The bodyguard had long been fond of Cicero's secretary. The Briton remembered staying up late one night with him, discussing his homeland. Manius couldn't ever recall Tiro ill-treating a slave, glowering or raising his voice. He was the soul of decency, in a slough of turpitude.

"He's looking good for his age, would be the polite thing to say, given how decrepit others are. I hope the country air will be of benefit. He may then yet live another ten years or more," Varro asserted, thinking how he must still possess a hidden robustness to have walked across Rome this afternoon, when he could easily afford to travel in a litter. "He could outlive us both, but that may not be saying much given that we could easily say the wrong thing tonight and not see the dawn."

Varro's words took on a dark air of prophecy when he observed Livius Galba and his wife, Hypatia, enter the house to attend the party. The general possessed a flat, adamantine expression. A beetle brow hung over black, unforgiving and unimpressed eyes. The career soldier puffed out his broad chest, as if to challenge or defy all the world - or warn off anyone who looked at his young wife inappropriately. Galba locked his grey yet muscular arm around his wife, like a fetter, to keep her close. In an unspoken agreement Varro and Hypatia pretended not to notice one another. Varro told himself not to venture over to any corner of the room where his mistress stood during the party.

*Better to be safe than sorry.*

A procession of litters snaked around the side of the house. Many occupants took their time in disembarking, as though the more time they took the more important they must be.

Brawny, well-attired slaves held torches, either side of the entrance, to welcome guests into the palatial property. As impressive as the colonnaded front of the house was it still did not prepare guests for the unrivalled opulence of the interior, once one passed by the surrogate guard of honour. Even those guests who had witnessed the entrance hall before emitted small gasps and coos of admiration as they crossed the threshold.

Manius peered around, his mouth agape. Varro's house seemed pauper-like in comparison. Agrippa's estate equalled the property in size, but not in expense or decadence. A large, oval mosaic, taken from Cleopatra's palace in Alexandria, had been reassembled in Maecenas' entrance hall, an island of colour in a sea of polished Carraran marble. Every seat and sofa came with plump, silk-covered cushions. The entire house was swathed in light, from candles, lamps and braziers. And every shining surface seemed to reflect and increase the light: ivory figurines, gems, bronze statues. Many squinted in reaction to the coruscating brightness. Various ornate silver mirrors adorned the entrance hall, framed in gold. Opulence dripped from the walls and vaunted ceiling, like molten lava pouring down the side of a volcano. Golden candlesticks. Gold-painted scroll work and cornicing. Gold-plated steps and bannisters. Every piece of marble seemed flecked with gold too. Such was the bright scene that more than one guest noted how Maecenas had the power to turn night into day.

Varro thought to himself, how much of his wealth had his host earned and how much had he stolen? He wondered whether Maecenas would recognise if there was any difference between the two.

Varro and Manius followed a stream of people towards an even greater sized hall at the rear of the house, where the majority of guests congregated. Two expansive friezes, depicting the battles of Mutina and Actium, decorated the walls of the corridor which funnelled the party goers towards the food and drink. Occasionally, over the years, a visitor would ask their host if he had taken part in the monumental, bloody campaigns. Maecenas would merely cryptically reply,

"What do you think?"

Caesar's close confidant was on the verge of changing the friezes however, as the victories at Mutina and Actium belonged too much to Marcus Agrippa. They were a reminder of his success and close relationship with their master.

Their munificent host stood beneath an arch, which served as the main entrance to the great hall. Maecenas greeted each guest personally and effusively. He would also make a mental note of anyone who snubbed his invitation. A black mark would be put next to anyone's name who was absent. And it would be difficult - but by no means impossible - to erase the mark. Everyone was a cherished, special guest. Everyone received a hearty handshake, kiss or smile. His teeth gleamed, having been polished throughout the afternoon, as much as the gilt-inwrought marble archway which surrounded him like a picture frame, or garland. His toga was coral white, bordered with purple silk, embroidered with golden thread. His skin was oiled and perfumed - and Varro noticed that his host was even wearing a little make-up. He had probably taken longer to get ready than many of the women at the party.

Maecenas greeted the nobleman and poet with open arms, like an old, familiar friend. The act of Varro spurning Maecenas' offer of patronage for his poetry had been forgotten. It was water under the bridge. What mattered now was the present and their potential future relationship. Varro smiled back. They were all smiles now, although both also briefly narrowed their eyes in scrutiny, to try and divine what was behind the perfectly civil masks they wore.

"Ah, Rufus. I am so glad you could attend. I am keen to introduce you to Propertius, who is here tonight, along with some other poets I am patron to. He is a great admirer of you and your work. As am I. Together we can hopefully persuade you to come out of retirement. I will make you an offer you can't refuse," Maecenas remarked. His voice was smooth, equitable and even playful. The host took in his guest. He would have made a handsome addition to his stable of writers, Maecenas thought. And he would have improved Varro as a writer, as well as instructed him in other ways. Maecenas licked his lips and smirked once more. Perhaps he could still induce him to accept his offer of patronage, as a poet - and agent.

"The planets must be aligned, as I came here tonight hoping to make you an offer you couldn't refuse too."

"I am intrigued - and it is not often I can say that. It appears that an accord between us may be written in the stars. Please, allow me to greet my guests and I will seek you out later. We can discuss matters in private. In the interim, enjoy my hospitality. Should you desire a particular dish or vintage then do ask one of the serving girls. I am auditioning a new chef this evening. Do let me know what you think of the food. You can be as pointed as a literary critic with your comments."

"I am not sure that even I can be that cruel, though I am willing to give it a try," Varro grinningly replied.

"Ha! You have a healthy, wicked sense of humour. Of course, should there be a particular serving girl you desire then I can happily furnish you with an introduction. And you must be the famed Manius? Gladiator, bodyguard and teacher of swordsmanship," Maecenas remarked, congenially turning towards the Briton.

Manius tried his best to suppress his surprise - and trepidation – at being known to his host. Despite his imposing figure he had always been pleased with his ability to stay in the background. Anonymous. Maecenas smiled - but his oppressive gaze made Manius feel slightly uncomfortable in his skin. The host always prided himself on knowing more about his guests than they knew about him. He preferred to inspire fear rather than love, as a rule. Things worked much more efficiently that way.

Varro noted that the host's wife was conspicuous by her absence from the party. It was one of Rome's worst kept secrets that Caesar had taken Tarentia as a mistress. Although some argued that Maecenas had freely given his wife to the princeps, in order to spy on his master.

Manius and Varro made a couple of token pleasantries before entering the main hall, which was already over half full. Varro surveyed the marble chamber, like a general surveying the lay of the land on the eve of a battle. As well as smelling of perfume and wine, the air reeked of wealth and privilege. He had attended similar parties before. Too many. Many of the guests would be faithful supporters of Caesar. They would have backed him, with capital or political support, during the civil war. Caesar in turn showed them favour now. Preferential treatment would be given when awarding government contracts. Tax collectors and the courts would turn a blind eye to misdemeanours (and more serious crimes). But corruption and cronyism were ever thus - and ever would be. Varro was too tired to feel indignant or self-righteous, but many of the people present made him feel nauseous.

Most of the men wore togas, young and old. The domed foreheads of the latter proved another surface for the light to reflect off. Their sharp, aristocratic features matched their sharp business practices. They were part of Rome's elite - prosperous in times of war and peace. Varro noticed that most of the guests had invited their wives, as opposed to mistresses. Perhaps they did not want to provide Maecenas with more material to blackmail them with. Word could get back to Caesar too. Despite his own indiscretions and infidelity, Augustus frowned on others replicating his behaviour. Some argued he wasn't displaying hypocrisy, but fine leadership. Varro fancied how he was inhabiting a gilded cage. Rather than thinking how they were imprisoned, the good and the great believed that they were protecting themselves from the outside world. From the stench and the plebs.

Some of the older women wore traditional, matronly stolas and often glanced with disapproval and distaste at a number of younger women wearing revealing, diaphanous dresses which clung to them as if the material or their bodies were damp. The silks shimmered. Jewels sparkled. Bulbous earrings hung down, elongating lobes. Hairstyles resembled edifices, which defied gravity. Make-up was applied with the same gusto that artists had applied to the paintings on the wall.

Varro attended similar gatherings almost every night. The sight of so many people often reminded him of a menagerie. His stomach could only cope with so much rich food and folly. The yoke of melancholy sat too often on his shoulders. Wine lessoned the load. Drink made him happy, but one can't be drunk all the time in society. Too many people in one place bred too much misanthropy. Varro lost count of the amount of times he had accompanied someone's wife or daughter to a glittering party. His mistresses wanted to give him everything - their time, wealth, hearts and bodies. They would offer to leave their husbands and face estrangement from their families. But all Varro wanted to offer them in return was some half-decent sex and a half-decent poem to remember him by. Until Lucilla. All he needed was her society.

"I can see a few familiar faces," Manius issued, arching an eyebrow, as he also glanced around the room. "A couple of your former mistresses and at least one cuckolded husband."

Perhaps tonight would be the night when the past would catch up with the priapic nobleman. A woman scorned can become quite scornful. The bodyguard took comfort from the fact that it was unlikely someone would want to cause a scene and earn their host's displeasure.

Varro nodded and rolled his eyes a little. He had already observed Calpurnia in the far corner, with her husband. The affair had ended some time ago, but the woman had just glowered at him, as if he had wronged her only yesterday. Varro extricated himself from their affair by explaining to the enamoured lady that he needed time to himself, due to his father recently passing away. In truth he had grown tired of the shipbuilder's wife. She constantly talked about her days spent shopping and had the annoying habit of biting her nails, before and after sex. Once he broke off the affair, he immediately courted another mistress, Scribonia, who it turned out was a cousin of Calpurnia's - who she shared news of all her affairs with. Varro made a mental note to avoid any corner of the room where his past and present mistresses resided.

Varro caught the sound of a melodious harp. Maecenas had hired Cornelius Rullus to play for him. Rullus was a peerless musician. And he knew it. His cheekbones were as high as some of the notes he played, and more than one satirist had commented that Rullus was as highly strung as his instrument. He nodded sagely in agreement whenever someone praised his talent and boasted how he had the ability to touch a woman, without laying a finger on her. "My notes pluck her heartstrings and she doesn't quite know whether to give herself over to the music or the musician." As sweet as the melody was, unfurling from the harp, the harpist's expression strangely remained impassive, joyless. Perhaps at another time, during another mood, Varro would have approached Rullus and confessed how he seduced his wife over a year ago. He would have been curious to see whether the musician would still be able to strike all the right notes.

Unfortunately, the sound of the melody was drowned out by the shrill conversation emanating from various party guests. It sounded like a menagerie, as well as looked like one, Varro fancied. Snorts of derision, braying laughter, cooing compliments and roaring opinions swirled around the room, as if in competition with one another. He overheard people talk about the weather, the success of the war on the Spanish front and the beauty of their host's home. A few guests artfully admired the paintings on the wall and raised their voices when complimenting the pieces, hoping that Maecenas might catch their flattering comments.

Thankfully, a breeze continued to waft through the room - via the row of doors, which opened-up and looked out onto the garden. It cooled his skin and ire. Varro cursed Agrippa under his breath. Now, more than ever, at the heart of Roman society, he longed to be in Arretium.

Varro caught the eye of a lissom serving girl, wearing a dress which could intoxicate more than the wine she was carrying, and grabbed his second cup. As he did so he also noticed Lentulus Nerva enter the hall. The advocate was accompanied by his wife, Lucretia, who was wearing a dress which was far too expensive and far too revealing. The garment displayed what little the wearer had to offer, Varro judged. Sura was also accompanying Nerva. He was equal, if not larger than Manius, in size. The shape of his muscular frame could be seen beneath his tunic. Tooth-shaped scars gleamed, like pieces of ivory, on his shaven head. A dour, downturned mouth was housed within a square, charmless jaw. A billy-goat beard sat on his chin, above his ram-like neck and shoulders. Every face tells a story. Sura's was a violent one. Varro had little doubt that he could have killed Herennius in cold blood, if called upon to do so. The former soldier appeared slightly ill at ease in the rarefied atmosphere, among the rarefied company. Sweat glazed his skin. Varro was tempted to approach the bodyguard and try to goad him into making a confession.

He was distracted from doing so, however, by another temptation entering the hall. It was time for Varro's mouth to become slack. He knew that she would be attending but that still didn't temper the shock - and hurt - of seeing Lucilla with Licinius. She was wearing an elegant sea-blue silk dress. High-necked. Belted. Sleeveless. The material clung to her slender legs but then trumpeted out at her feet. Through an unassuming slit at the bottom one could catch a glimpse of her snow-white felt sippers and pretty, sun-kissed ankles. She was somehow more attractive to him than she had been ten years ago. He wanted to reach out and clasp Manius' arm, to help steady him, lest his legs gave way.

Varro instantly recalled three other occasions when Lucilla wore the same dress. He also remembered how much he desired her - and how Diana did her best to stand sentry alongside her mistress and remind her that she had an early start in the morning.

"I think that she's trying to protect you from me," Varro had whispered to Lucilla, wryly smiling.

"More so you need protection from you," she replied, half-joking.

"You know me too well."

"I do, unfortunately. But still you are welcome around my dinner table."

Licinius spotted Varro, before Lucilla, but pretended not to notice him. He slid his arm inside hers and gently pulled her close, whispering something in her ear. She tilted her head back, flashed an unrivalled smile, and laughed.

Varro tried to remain impassive, stoical, but something gnawed at his being. His pupils burned, like hot coals. His innards rumbled, as if starving. But the poet knew that, even if he ate, he wouldn't be satisfied. Or be able to keep any food down. Jealousy, grief, resentment, misery, powerlessness - all jabbed the points of their swords at him. Death by a thousand cuts. Varro told himself he was experiencing despair because of his rival. He was wrong for her. Using her. Deceiving her. Sooner or later Licinius would hurt her (admittedly not as much as he had once hurt her). If it was anyone else courting her, he could stomach it. If she married the agent, Varro knew that he could no longer bear seeing her. They could no longer have dinner together. Laugh together. Discuss the books they were reading and satirise Rome's finest citizens. He couldn't quite tell if his heart was beating wildly out of hatred for him, or love for her.

Perhaps if he could reconcile himself to Lucilla turning the page, he could move on too. Write another chapter. He wanted to at least get to the point where he could pretend to love someone else - to fool his would-be wife and himself. He wanted someone else to know which wine he liked, which translation of Homer he preferred. When he needed to be alone and when he needed company. When he was joking. How much and how little his poetry meant to him. But it felt like it would take a lifetime for someone else to learn those things which Lucilla already knew by heart.

She finally saw him from across the room, glimpsing him between the throng of guests. But one glance was enough for Lucilla to observe the anguish on his face. She knew that it would hurt him to see them together. But sooner or later he would have to. Her heart went out to him, although Lucilla felt it would be inappropriate to abandon her current lover to talk to her former husband. There had been times in the past when she had dreamed of inflicting such torment upon him. How many times had she witnessed him attend a party with a mistress? Yet Lucilla knew that he was the last person she wanted to hurt now. He looked like he was about to cry, she thought - a scared and lonely child, too traumatised to put on a brave face. Manius was next to him, but there was nothing the bodyguard could do to protect him from the pain he was enduring. Why couldn't he be happy for her? She had her doubts about Licinius too. Even if she thought Licinius was somehow second best, second best was still good enough for her. She wasn't getting any younger. And Lucilla wanted to be a wife, to then be a mother. Even if it killed her.

Varro craned his head a little, so he could still see her - as if he believed that if he lost sight of her now, he might never lay eyes on her again. She was achingly beautiful. Lucilla offered him a consoling smile and appeared as if she wanted to mouth something to him. He wanted to smile back but the corners of his own mouth - and soul - lacked the strength to do so. Varro could never quite resolve, during this past year or so, if he would make her happy, should he confess how he felt. Yet, he knew for certain that Licinius wouldn't make her happy. Something inside of him - fuelled by the wine - told Varro that he could not leave Lucilla to her fate. He needed deeds, not words. Though words were all he had. Varro was suddenly determined to work his way through the forest of people between them and tell Lucilla how he felt, give air to his emotions. He recalled Tiro's advice, again. Even if he failed, he had to try. Varro needed to tell her that he was a different man to the one she married, or rather divorced. He was a better man, partly because of her. If he didn't tell her how he felt now, he feared he might lose her forever. Licinius would get his claws into her, pour poison into her ear.

Varro drained his cup and wiped his perspiring palms against his tunic. Even at night, Rome could be a furnace. He took a deep breath. He would take her by the hand and lead Lucilla off into the garden, into the fresh air and quiet. Away from Licinius.

*It's now or never.*

"My master is ready to see you now. If you would like to accompany me out into the side garden," a fastidious attendant remarked. His nasally tone was courteous yet firm. Maecenas was not accustomed to waiting. Duty called. Varro was about to speak, defy his host - assert that he had something to attend to beforehand. But didn't.

## 18.

Varro was led out into a small, secluded garden. Gaius Maecenas sat on a marble bench, flanked by oil lamps and twin statues of Veritas. A bodyguard stood, as mute and still as the statues, by the door. His head was as square as the small shield he carried. His face had endured a thousand scouring winds and a dozen tavern brawls. Varro couldn't quite decide if the attendant was the soul of duty or dullness.

Birdsong out-sounded the trill of conversation from the party. A manicured lawn, bordered by recently pruned shrubs and rose bushes, sat in front of Maecenas. The scent of jasmine tickled his nostrils and the white flowers pin-pricked the inky background. Ironically Varro pictured a similar scene, when he envisioned taking Lucilla off to talk to her. To open-up his heart.

Varro fancied that a dozen dark thoughts and machinations might well be preoccupying his host right now - who appeared content, at peace. Or perhaps he was composing a poem in his head, as the celebrated funder of the arts also dabbled in writing himself. Maecenas had to swat away praise for his verses, like flies - as any and everyone looked to ingratiate themselves with the munificent patron. Thankfully Maecenas knew the merit of his work and he endeavoured to champion Virgil and Horace more than himself. At least, in that, Gaius Maecenas could be considered just.

The agent recalled Agrippa's words, as he approached his host:

*"Do not underestimate him. Gaius can charm the wick out of a wax candle - and talk the leaves off the trees. Work from the premise that he knows more than you think he knows... Gaius can delve into a man's soul and divine what he wants before he even realises it himself."*

"Please, join me Rufus," Maecenas blithely remarked, as he courteously stood up and allowed his guest to sit beside him. His manners could be impeccable, even to a torture victim. The host dismissed his attendant and poured Varro a cup of wine from an ornate, silver jug. The handle was in the shape of a dolphin, the spout in the shape of a serpent.

"Thank you."

"Are you happy with the wine? It's one of my favourite vintages. It's from a small vineyard, just outside of Asculum."

"The wine is excellent," Varro replied, thinking that he was happy with most wine. "I import some of my stock in from that region too."

"I knew you were a man of good taste, literary or otherwise, Rufus. I should take you on a tour of my library and cellar one day. I think it's best we do so in that order too. I have an uncommon respect for you, both as a nobleman and poet. The blood which courses through your veins is as ancient as the waters of the Tiber. Which is why I will afford you the courtesy of being honest and candid."

Varro merely offered an unassuming, non-committal nod in reply. At the same time as wishing to appear relaxed, unimpressed and unintimated - he willed his mind to be as sharp as a blade, fresh from the lave.

"We are both men of the world, Rufus, in that we know how tawdry and pernicious this world can be. We know that the gods do not always have their hand in the tiller, in steering this ship of fate. I will not treat you like a fool. In return I expect you not to take me for a fool either. I am aware that you work as an agent for Marcus Agrippa. I know that you uncovered Lucius Scaurus' treachery last year and that your role in bringing him to justice remains unsung. I have also been apprised of several other assignments you have carried out over the past year, for the benefit of Rome. Either Marcus has schooled you well as a spy, or you possess a natural talent for being an agent. I am inclined to consider it more the latter than former," Maecenas asserted.

"I am not sure if I would be much of a spy, if I admitted to being a spy," Varro answered.

"Indeed. But should you work as an agent for Agrippa, he would have doubtless mentioned me. If he does not consider me a close friend, we are still strong allies. We both serve Caesar and have his best interests at heart. Whereas Marcus builds aqueducts, I build alliances and support in the Senate House. I also wish to create a cultural legacy for Caesar. The works of Virgil should far outlive any temple which Agrippa has laid the foundations for. Rome should honour its poets, as well as its soldiers. My greatest achievement was not to serve as steward to Rome, in Caesar's absence, during the civil war. But rather I am prouder of bringing Horace to the attention of Caesar, who then brought him to the attention of the world... I do not wish to put you in a compromising position, or betray any confidence, by asking you what Agrippa said, or didn't say. I like to think of myself as a problem solver. I fix things. I arrange marriages, or divorces. I help merchants avoid bankruptcy - or compel them to pay their debts. I arrange praetorships and senatorial positions - or sometimes encourage others in office to retire. I ensure that our esteemed governors refrain from collecting too much, or too little, tax. I often work in the shadows, because our enemies work in the shadows. There has been more than one Scaurus in the past few years - and there will be more than one Scaurus in the future, hoping to tear down what we have built... When a senator has been found guilty of embezzlement, or a general of cowardice, they do not pray to the gods to spare them, they pray to me... Some people may paint me as a villain, but I blackmail, bribe, extort and torture - all for the good of Rome and Caesar," Maecenas said in earnest, whilst placing his palm over his heart to emphasise his sincerity.

Varro often performed the same gesture when declaring his love to a mistress, so he remained unconvinced by his host's performance.

"I do what little I can for the good of Rome and Caesar too, but I suspect you have invited me here this evening to find out what I can do for the good of Gaius Maecenas," Varro remarked, with more playfulness than cynicism.

"I am aware of your current assignment for Agrippa. You have been asked to find Herennius' killer and retrieve a certain dagger, which was in his possession. I have been asked to find the item too."

"All of Rome is keen to possess the knife it seems. We have as many suspects as you have guests at your party. I wonder however, why is Caesar so determined to recover the dagger?"

"I only have my orders, not explanations. I am willing to offer you a deal. Should you find the dagger, I would like you to hand it over to me rather than Agrippa. I can assure you it will still find its way back to Caesar, who, after all, is your ultimate employer."

"I owe a duty to Agrippa. A Roman who lacks honour can scarce call himself a Roman," Varro replied, somewhat sententiously.

Maecenas remained unconvinced by his guest's performance.

"Duty?" the political agent said, screwing his face up in either confusion or contempt. "Duty is just habit. Duty is fear. Duty is a conceit. It is a commodity, which can be bought or sold. Senators talk about "duty". That should be enough to tell you all you need to know about its worth. The gods will forgive you - and I am sure you can forgive yourself - if you put yourself in front of your duty. Duty, like celibacy, is an almost unnatural state. Did you not owe a duty to be faithful to your former wife? Do you not owe a duty to your family name, to produce an heir? Do you not owe a duty to your muse, to write an epic poem? No man has the energy, or sense of honour, to be duteous all the time. What an unconscionable bore he would be! Trying to do one's duty and the right thing sometimes resembles a man standing in a bucket, trying to lift himself up by the handle. Yet, should you still wish to cling to the conceit of duty, that is all well and good - for you will still be fulfilling your duty to Caesar by handing over the knife to me. Agrippa need never know of any dishonour. And what he doesn't know, cannot hurt him," Maecenas persuasively argued, whilst also thinking that he could one day blackmail Varro over betraying Agrippa.

"And should I hand the dagger over to you - and I am only suggesting if rather than when at present - what will you offer me in return?"

Varro was determined to remain coy, non-committal. People who sell their soul too easily are rarely able to command a high price, he thought.

"Immortality - and a consignment of this vintage. I can arrange for Caesar to become a patron of your poetry. You will be lauded in this age and in eras yet to come. Your verses will be taken to heart by every child in school. Women will call your name and sigh. Your work will be distributed throughout the empire. And when you die, you will live on through your words."

"Immortality sounds like torture. I am not sure if my life is worth living now. Death is about the only thing I am looking forward to," Varro remarked, glibly.

"What are you most passionate about in life?" Maecenas asked. Every man has a passion and every man has a weakness, he judged.

"My indifference," Varro replied, with a knowing, nonchalant shrug. "But I would ask one favour in return, which is in your power to grant, should I be able to retrieve the dagger for you. Call off your dog. Licinius needs to stop courting my former wife, Lucilla."

"I was unaware that he was seeing her," Maecenas countered, nonchalantly. Innocently. "But I can speak with my agent. I cannot make any promises, however. This is a matter of the heart, rather than the state."

"I am confident you will do your duty - to yourself."

"You can be sure of it, as night follows day. Of course, this will all prove to be supposition, unless you can deliver the aforementioned dagger. I will not be averse to employing your services in the future though, should I have need of them. Agrippa may have been a young lion during the civil war and we should all be grateful for his service to Rome. But young lions turn into old lions. There are no more great battles to fight, thankfully. We have need of men with political prowess, as opposed to military prowess. Agrippa is a man of honour. But the enemies of Rome possess no such code. I would have nailed Scaurus to the highest crucifix in the land, before he had time to recruit a single gladiator and plot to overthrow Caesar."

"I can make no promises either. You wouldn't wish to make a liar out of me. Rome already has a surfeit of them, as you know."

Varro made his way back through the house and re-joined the party. A dazzling brightness still glistened across the chamber, like petals of sunlight strewn across a lake. The guests chirruped even louder, like crickets. Yet the words of Maecenas chimed in his ears even more. Varro had shared some of his thoughts - those which were next to worthless - about his ongoing investigation. Maecenas repeated how he looked forward "to doing business together" with the patriotic nobleman and agent.

When he returned to the great hall, he was unable to find Manius, but he did spot Ovid. His back was against the wall. Varro grinned to himself as he witnessed the poet subtly, yet lustfully, take stock of the women present. His eyes feasted on the beauty and flesh on show. Surely his expression could not have been too dissimilar to his own, when he was that age? There was a blend of discernment, as well as desire, in his features. His expression would artfully change once he caught someone's eye, or they caught his. Perhaps he was deducing which women were unattached and ripe to be approached. Who would stray from the herd? Ovid licked his lips a couple of times and sipped his wine. No doubt he wanted the timing - and prey - to be right for when he entered the fray. The adolescent displayed a palpable relief and pleasure at encountering his new friend, however, and temporarily postponed his hunt.

"Evening Ovid, I hope I am not disturbing you," Varro amiably issued. He was genuinely pleased to see the young poet again.

"I welcome your company. I arrived alone, although that does not mean that I would wish to leave alone. It's quite a party. The jewels in the room could buy a small palace, or a dozen senators... I overheard Gaius Statius, the poet, if you can call him such, earlier. He pronounced, in a voice as high as a eunuch's, that he owed everything to his muse. I was tempted to remark that he should hire an advocate to prosecute his muse, for crimes against humanity. His verses are sentimental trite. Steaming piles of perfumed shit! He has a dedicated following it seems though. Hopefully they will follow him off the Tarpeian Rock one day... There's more than one woman in the room, worthy of dedicating a poem to. If only I could somehow make their husbands disappear. Most would then doubly thank me. I had one pigeon earlier glance at me demurely, as she prettily tucked a tendril of hair behind her sparkling ear. She batted her eyes so much, I could veritably feel a breeze emanate from them. But then her husband, or it could have been her father, distracted her and my pigeon flew away. But there's sport to be had, no matter what," the eagle-eyed youth pronounced, as much attracted to the verses he might write as to any potential mistress. "Wish me luck."

"I am sure that you won't need it," Varro replied.

"Every man needs a portion of luck in his endeavours, whether he be Caesar or a nameless beggar. Luck affects everything. Let your hook always be cast; in the stream where you least expect it, there is sometimes a fish. In love one must cultivate perseverance, as well as good fortune. Love is a kind of warfare. Seduction is a campaign. One must fight the good fight. Every lover is a soldier," Ovid said with relish, quoting one of his own verses. "Women seem to enjoy the fight too, as well as surrendering. Whether they give or refuse, it delights woman the same just to be asked."

It struck Varro how he had shared some of Ovid's sentiments and philosophy when he was in the first flush of manhood. But he was different now. Either wiser, or wearier. Lucilla needed to be won, but not conquered. Love should engender a state of peace, not war.

"And have you been the hunted, as well as the hunter, this evening? Has Maecenas approached you about recruiting you to his army of authors?"

"He tried to make me an offer I couldn't refuse earlier. He quoted Horace, advising that I should "seize the day" and allow me to him to recruit me. He would have been wiser to have read some of my poetry and quoted me. But I said I was tempted by his offer to leave Messalla and accept his patronage. It's important to let powerful men think they have triumphed. From some of his expressions, facial and verbal, it seems that Maecenas was keen to get me into his bedroom, as well as his stable. But I have no desire to succumb to his advances, on any front. Messalla has done right by me so far. Also, Maecenas already possesses enough stars in his firmament. I do not want to forever be eclipsed by Horace and Virgil and live in their shadow. I want my star to burn just as brightly one day," Ovid remarked, empyreal-eyed.

If anyone else would have uttered the same words Varro would have thought them full of bombast and foolishness. But, somehow, he believed Ovid's name might one day be mentioned in the same breath as Virgil and Horace. He wished him good luck in his vaunting ambition.

"Of course, our host also invited me this evening to ask about the night Herennius died. I was courted and interrogated at the same time."

"What did you tell him?"

"I told him almost as much as I told you, which amounts to very little. I said that not only would the gods think it worthy of punishing Herennius but plenty of mortals owned a grievance against him too. He is, like you, suspicious of Nerva. He asked questions about Corinna, albeit I'm not so sure he knows how close to her I got. I had nothing to say when he quizzed me about Sestius, as thankfully I didn't get to know the oaf... The questions came thick and fast, but the answers didn't. I've been less breathless during poetry readings though."

Varro took heart that Licinius appeared even less advanced in his investigation as he was. *No wonder Maecenas is eager to recruit me.*

His agent was proving to be a disappointment. Hopefully he would prove a disappointment for Lucilla too.

"You have already had a busy evening it seems, and the night is still young."

"Not quite as young as the redhead over your shoulder. She may have just dyed her hair, however. I would be willing to dedicate ten or twenty love poems to her to find out if she is a natural redhead. Her nose is a little too pronounced and sharp for my taste though. It cuts through the air like the prow of a ship. The milky-skinned specimen behind her has a perfect nose. It's just that the rest of her features are fantastically bland... But I sense that you only have eyes for one woman in the room, Rufus."

For the first time, in a long time, Varro blushed slightly. Even while Ovid was speaking, he was casting a glance around the hall, searching for a glimpse of Lucilla, like a sailor desperately looking for land. Even Ovid thought it best to bite his tongue when he was tempted to confess that, out of all the beauty on show at the party, he would wish to possess Lucilla. Or have Lucilla possess him. Clearly there was still something between the former husband and wife. They both still loved each other. The tragedy would be that they would be the last ones to realise it.

## 19.

She was nowhere to be seen. But out of sight was not out of mind. Varro pictured Lucilla being led away by him. Captivating her, like some male Calypso. He was smirking. Simpering. The amount of oil in his hair was equal to the amount contained in the lamps overhead. Her smile was so thin as to barely exist. Varro thought how she could be on the other side of the room - but she may as well be as far away as the stars. His love for her was a curse. Cassandra was fated to always tell the truth but never be believed. Varro was fated to love Lucilla but never be with her.

"She's gone," Manius stated, plainly, after his friend met up with him again. "I was speaking to her out in the garden, while you met with Maecenas."

Lucilla had observed Manius across the room, alone and not a little awkward looking, and decided to keep him company. Licinius had frowned upon his lady wanting to converse with someone who was barely more than a servant, but she ignored him. Manius and Lucilla spoke for some time. He provided her with some advice, in relation to an issue which needed resolving. Lucilla said she would talk to some friends and spread the word about his new business. It would be best if he didn't have to spy on all his clients, the Briton thought.

"I am afraid I need to leave now. I have another engagement to attend, before the end of the night. Marcus Trainus is having a party to celebrate his wedding anniversary. Everyone is going to be there apparently, including his mistress and illegitimate sons. Give my regards to Camilla. And Viola, of course."

"Would you like me to give any message to Rufus?"

Lucilla felt a twinge of pain on hearing his name - and took a breath before replying.

"Yes. No. I will write to him soon," she pensively murmured, although not even the gods knew would what she would include in the letter, Lucilla thought.

They left the party, shortly after finding one another. As much as his fellow guests might have been similar in rank and wealth, Varro felt like he didn't belong. Or he didn't want to belong. He shuddered in revulsion too, that he might be being dragged into Maecenas' orbit. *My world shouldn't revolve around his.* Perhaps he hadn't had enough to drink. He didn't want to talk to any of the men around him and he would somehow feel unfaithful talking to any of the women, as though Lucilla was still watching him from a vantage point in the room.

Varro's eyes were heavy-lidded, and he felt heavy-limbed as he left the party. He didn't even feel the inclination to finish off the evening in the Subura, as he was accustomed to do. He wanted to retain a clear head, to mull over Maecenas' offer and then interview Corinna in the morning. *No rest for the wicked.* He also needed to make a decision about Lucilla.

Maecenas enjoyed the quietude of the garden and collected his thoughts. He was surprised that Varro's ex-wife had proved to be his weakness. He didn't even love his current wife, let alone previous partners. The patron believed he would be able to entice the poet to do his bidding by promising him fame and immortality. He would have offered the nobleman riches, but his wealth was already substantial. Maecenas was confident, however, that if he had not already secured Varro's loyalty, he soon would. *Agrippa's loss will be my gain.* It felt good. He had narrowed his odds in finding the dagger, which is all he could hope for at present. Maecenas's gentle, sumptuous smile faltered however when he thought how he had lost faith in Licinius. Perhaps the woman was proving too great a distraction. His agent had failed to locate the dagger and was yet to secure any intelligence from Lucilla, about Livia or Caesar. He hadn't prised out one secret or stolen one letter. Maecenas weighed up the benefit of ordering Licinius to end his affair with Lucilla, even if Varro could not fulfil his part of the deal. He would select another suitable wife for his agent, one which would bear more fruit.

It was likely that Varro would not be able to fulfil his part of the deal, especially as by the end of the evening he would be temporarily unable to continue his investigation. He still had time to call off the attack on Varro. But he wouldn't. Cruelty for cruelty's sake was still as valid a philosophy as any other, he posed. Maecenas' offer of employment should hopefully annul any suspicions the agent might have that he was the author behind his misfortune. Perhaps if Varro had unequivocally declared his loyalty this evening. he might have spared him.

Maecenas yawned and then picked up another oyster and slid it down his throat. It felt as warm and slippery as a kiss. He imagined the young poet on his knees, looking up at him. Sooner or later Ovid would submit to him. Everybody else did.

They tramped home in silence. Rain spat down. Darkness swelled, like a bruise. Manius occasionally cast sidelong glances at Varro, who seemed buried in thought. The Briton was worried for his friend. He recognised the mournful expression. He knew he was thinking about her.

The past isn't always the past, Ovid had argued when Varro had remarked that Lucilla was no longer a meaningful part of his life. Varro said that he did have eyes for at least one other woman in the room, by subtly pointing out Hypatia and revealing that they were conducting an affair. But the young, uncommonly wise, poet was right. Lucilla was with him, even when she wasn't there. She was like a shade, haunting him. Judging him. His love for her was like a blessing, as well as a curse. Lucilla still inspired him. Varro wanted to be worthy of her. Noble. He sometimes found himself thinking whether she would approve of his actions or not. When he read certain poems, he thought of her. He smelled her perfume on other women and was compelled, or condemned, to recall too many fond memories. He avoided ordering her favourite foods. He dreamed of her, constantly. Of making love to her. But a legion of nightmares came too. Reliving past sins. She was a ghost at Arretium, as much as she was ever present in Rome. Varro couldn't step out into the villa's garden without picturing Lucilla there too. When he heard the wheels of a carriage outside, he always hoped that it was her, paying him a surprise visit. He did his best not to picture her with Licinius now. But failed. Someone was reaching into his chest and rinsing out his heart, like a mouldy sponge. He may as well try to outrun his shadow than forget about her. For good or ill, Lucilla was as much a part of Varro as himself.

He breathed out, in resignation or exhaustion, and told himself that things might look different in the morning. That is, if he made it through the night.

"Are you Rufus Varro?"

Even through the drizzle and stygian evening Varro immediately recognised the livid features of Galba, standing before him in the alleyway. His voice was rough, hoarse, from a lifetime of bellowing out orders. A brace of bodyguards flanked him, like columns, wearing similar gnarled expressions. They were doubtless ex-soldiers. Seasoned brawlers. Both carried cudgels. Both would be more than happy to use them, he thought.

A plump, bark-brown rat scurried along the alleyway and squealed in alarm - or excitement perhaps, at the potential feast of a corpse.

"Yes, providing of course you're not a tax collector," Varro drily replied.

"Do you know who I am?"

"No, fortunately not," he said, feeling guiltless about the lie and insult. "Would I be being impertinent if I asked how you know me?"

"Because you have been impertinent enough to come to know my wife, Hypatia, you insolent cur," Galba asserted, his hands balled into two fists.

Maecenas had told the general about his wife's affair with the infamous nobleman that afternoon. At first Galba refuted the accusations, arguing that his wife would not dare behave improperly. But soon after he was gnashing his teeth and vowing to disembowel the aristocrat - or castrate him. Galba viewed Varro's seduction of his wife as an act of theft. Hypatia was his property. The general told himself that the degenerate poet led his wife astray, that he had promised her the world. Maecenas sympathised and agreed with his friend's arguments. Varro should be punished.

"He will be attending the party this evening. You can confront him afterwards. You will not approach him during the party and cause a scene... I have no desire to see him killed however, so temper your ire... You shouldn't also underestimate his bodyguard. There is strength in numbers... I recommend that you do not reveal to your wife that you know about the affair, lest she tries to warn him."

Galba said he would comply with his instructions. Such was the soldier's anger and anguish at his wife's infidelity that he little concerned himself with Maecenas' motivation, behind him revealing the affair. Knowing Maecenas, it had nothing to do with friendship or honour. After leaving the meeting Galba resolved to confront his wife the following morning. He would put on an act for the party this evening. He would give her a chance to explain herself and then punish her accordingly. She was a woman. Weak. His wife, like the soldiers under his charge, needed to be loyal. The general would ensure his wife wouldn't stray again while he was on campaign, by having a slave accompany her at all times when she left the house. It would be a form of guard duty. He would not risk her impinging upon his dignity again. Should word get out about the affair, which Maecenas assured him it wouldn't, then he would be a laughing stock. He would lose his authority with his soldiers. Should Hypatia not give him a son within the next two years, or should her beauty begin to fade, then Galba vowed that he would divorce her. Aye, he would deal with his wife in good time. But first he would deal with the vice-ridden poet.

Manius glanced behind him to witness two more of the general's men, carrying cudgels, positioning themselves to attack. Rather than Varro's past catching up with him, his present had, the Briton thought. It was unlikely Varro could talk his way out his predicament. Galba was baying for blood.

"Can I ask who my accuser is? It seems that somebody is wronging both myself and your wife. You must allow me to defend myself."

Galba's grimace, or rictus, widened as he snorted.

"You can defend yourself. But it won't do much good."

The snarling general - cuckolded husband - launched himself forward to attack, his sandals scraping along the ground. Manius swiftly stepped across in front of his friend and kicked out a long leg, striking Galba's kneecap. The general stumbled back and fell to the ground, in shock and pain. The cudgel he was carrying dropped out of his hand and Manius quickly retrieved it. Violence had become second nature to the ex-gladiator. Although he sometimes thought about his nature after a fight, he always surrendered to his instincts during one.

Varro turned to the two men behind him. He didn't want Manius, or himself, to be assaulted from the rear. A stocky, craggy-faced bodyguard closed in on him. Varro instinctively remembered one of the first lessons Manius had taught him, when defending himself. His foot buried itself in his opponent's groin. The air rushed out from his lungs and he doubled-over in pain.

Manius raised his arm and the cudgel struck him on his bicep. He had suffered far worse hits in the arena. The sheets of bulging muscle, like layers of leather, tempered the blow. In reply the Briton punched the tip of his own cudgel into his attacker's throat. He retreated, half-choking.

The second opponent, behind Varro, ran forward, spitting out a curse, and slammed the nobleman up against a wall. Varro reached up in time however to grab the bodyguard's wrist, before he could bring the thick, wooden cudgel down on his head. They grappled, equal in strength and determination. Varro could smell the garum and wine on the ex-soldier's breath. The stalemate was ended by Varro unsheathing the knife, which hung from his attacker's belt. He stabbed him in the stomach. He spat out another curse, as blood was added to other stains on his tunic. He soon spat out blood too. Instead of punching his opponent - and run the risk of injuring his hand - Varro whipped his elbow around and struck him square in the face. The bodyguard dropped to the ground, like a bleary-eyed drunk in the early hours of the morning.

Varro scarcely had time to feel triumphant, however. His first assailant was about to recover and attack again. Varro reasoned what worked perfectly well once could work again - and so he took two quick steps and buried his foot in his opponent's groin once more. The man writhed on the floor, dry heaving.

Manius grunted, twice, as he suffered two blows to his ribs in quick succession. His blood-lust dulled the pain however and he turned to confront the last bodyguard left standing. Manius grabbed the man's lose fitting tunic and pulled his opponent towards him. At the same time the Briton thrust his head forward and butted the bodyguard, squashing and splitting open his nose like an overripe piece of fruit.

Groans reverberated throughout the alleyway. Manius and Varro easily disarmed their prostrate attackers. Varro seethed, as he also tried to catch his breath, whilst crouching down and holding a knife to Galba's leathery throat. He demanded to know who had "wrongfully" accused him of having an affair with his wife.

"One of my slaves told me," he replied, through gritted teeth, on the instructions of Maecenas. "If somehow Varro gets the upper hand and presses for the truth, lie and tell him a slave was responsible," Maecenas advised. Varro was unsure whether to believe Galba or not. He sensed there were other powers at play. But he was too tired to torture his enemy for further information.

"You have the wrong Rufus Varro," he asserted, half-convincingly. Right then he wished he could be someone else. He told himself it was best not to see Hypatia again, for her sake as much as his. He also vowed to himself that he would never seduce a married woman again. But he had made and broken such a promise, more than once, before.

The two men continued to venture homewards, even more wearily than before. Manius walked a little gingerly. Unfortunately, he had all too much experience at knowing what cracked ribs felt like. He sat on the horns of a dilemma too, of whether to tell his wife that he had been involved in another fight. Could he grin and bear the pain of his injuries until the pain receded and bruising faded? He didn't want Camilla to think less of him, or his friend. One more secret, lie, couldn't hurt.

Varro desired his bed - more than even for a woman to be in it, waiting for him when he reached home. He didn't know, or even much care, who was behind Livius Galba being unleashed. The wronged husband had every right to be angry. Perhaps Varro deserved to be punished too. He felt like the very air of Rome was poisoning him. Arretium seemed further away than ever. But he would interview Herennius' wife in the morning and write up his report for Agrippa. The evidence may point towards Nerva, but he had more chance of proving the existence of the gods than finding the lawyer guilty. Or he would argue that Herennius was murdered by an unknown intruder. Or he could point the finger at the aggrieved soldier, who Fabullus mentioned. Agrippa - and Caesar - could believe what they wanted to believe and act accordingly.

## RICHARD FOREMAN

*I feel like a step, leading-up to a cheap brothel, worn out from the sun and constant traffic.*

## 20.

Morning.

Manius crept into bed the night before, feeding Viola a number of treats to keep her quiet. He didn't want to wake Camilla. He was in no fit condition to make love or explain himself. The injured bodyguard lay on his side, facing the wall rather than his wife. When she woke at dawn, he pretended to be asleep. When he was sure Camilla was busy in the kitchen Manius tended to himself. Cold water didn't quite numb the pain. Two star-shaped bruises, mottled in purple and black, coloured his ribs like birthmarks.

Manius explained that he might be out for most of the day and night again as he grabbed his sword. He stole a kiss from Camilla whilst, for once, avoiding her embrace. He tried to behave as normally as possible, whilst incessant stabbing pains plagued his torso every time he moved. He doubted his ability to keep up the act over the next few days. He was minded to pretend to his wife that he needed to work for Varro full-time, until his ribs sufficiently healed. If not, sooner or later, Camilla would find out that he was trying to deceive her. He would lose her trust. But still Manius thought it best to keep the truth from his wife.

"When will you be back?" Camilla asked, as he readied to leave.

"I'm not sure," Manius replied, with the hint of an apology in his tone, before he closed the door behind him. The Briton expected another uneventful day, spent following Publius Carbo.


Fronto ordered his master to sit down and eat the breakfast he prepared. Steam wafted up from the eggs and bacon on his plate.

"You need to put some food inside you, to help soak up all the wine. You don't just want your troubles weighing you down. You can afford to put on some weight in the more traditional way," Fronto argued, as he placed some cold ham and fruit in front of Varro too.

"I have of late encouraged you to marry. You have need of a wife. But maybe you have more need of a husband, so as to nag him like a wife."

For once Varro was not hungover. But he felt hungover. His mouth was dry, and his tongue felt like a slab of old leather. His brain pounded against the front of his skull, like a blacksmith's hammer pounding on an anvil. As much as he experienced a good night's rest, sleep had not acquitted him of all his exhaustion, melancholy and troubles.

After finishing his breakfast, Fronto spoke about his meeting with Aulus Gabinus, his father's advocate. Although retired, Gabinus still kept abreast of the gossip and careers of his fellow lawyers.

"It seems that Lentulus Nerva may be a more unpleasant and unscrupulous character than we first thought. And we didn't think much of him initially. Gabinus disclosed that Nerva had arranged for witnesses to be bought or intimidated, in order to win trials, over the years... A poor fellow named

Sertorius was also conveniently murdered, just before he was due to give testimony against the head of a smuggling ring. Gabinus said Nerva was not only complicit in his murder - but suggested the idea in the first place... The advocate is still burdened with considerable debts but apparently assured his creditors recently that he is in a position to pay the money back. Now of course he could be lying - lawyers have been found guilty of not telling the entire truth before - or Nerva has taken control of his daughter's estate and is using it for his own needs. Or he has come into new capital through selling off the possible valuables he stole from his son-in-law, after killing him."

Again, fuel was being added to the fire that Nerva was behind Herennius' murder. Again, Varro constructed a case against the advocate. He had motive, or motives. He had killed his son-in-law to save his daughter from an abusive husband. And/or he had killed the slave trader for financial gain. If one followed the money then, it stood to reason, Nerva was behind Sestius' murder too. Sura could have been involved in both deaths. After the party, Herennius could have let in both Nerva and his bodyguard, innocent of their intentions. Yet, Varro still only possessed a suspect, not evidence. His sole hope now, to convict Nerva, seemed to be Corinna's testimony. If his daughter was involved in the murder - and if she could be tricked or pressured into implicating her father - then Varro could secure the dagger and deliver it to Agrippa. Or Maecenas.

Today would be the day, Licinius Pulcher told himself. He would ask Lucilla to marry him. Once married he could defy Maecenas, should he instruct him to change assignment. It would be too late, appear too suspicious. Maecenas feared very little in the world, but he did fear death and Caesar. If it came to a choice between Maecenas and Lucilla, he vowed to choose the latter. Maecenas could not risk him confessing his sin to Caesar, that he had been ordered to spy on Lucilla to gain intelligence about Livia.

*Today will be the day.*

Licinius had just finished washing and grooming himself. He stood before the mirror, in his intended's bedroom. Lucilla had woken early to catch up on some correspondence. She mentioned she had received a letter from Livia, among others.

The agent felt a little giddy, nervous. Strange. Perhaps, for the first time in his life, he realised that he was happy. Or that happiness was on the horizon. Lucilla would make him a fine wife, in the domestic as well as public sphere. He smiled mercurially, considering how she had unwittingly seduced him, as much as he had consciously seduced her.

Light oozed through the window, like massage oil. The garden was in bloom. Bees hopped from flower to flower. It was a beautiful day. It would be a memorable day. He looked handsome. She would look beautiful. He ran through his lines, again. She would say yes. Licinius didn't care where they made their home. He would wait until lunch, after she had come out of her study. The agent had picked out a bench and bower in the garden. Perhaps he would commission Horace to compose a poem for their wedding. If he was unable to do so Licinius would contact Propertius. Failing that, he would approach the youth Publius Ovidius. Lucilla seemed fond of the poet, although the agent was not so approving of his overly satirical character.

Licinius would also aim to fulfil his brief to Maecenas today and enter Lucilla's study. As well as reading Livia's correspondence, for any valuable intelligence, he looked forward to reading Lucilla's reply - to see if she mentioned him.

Yes, today would be the day. The suitor was determined to make Lucilla happy. Varro would be a memory - a bad memory. Licinius had been slightly irritated by her determination to speak to Varro's bodyguard the night before. But she had duly come back to him and not made any attempt to seek out her former husband.

*He is her past. I am her future. She will accept my proposal. I want to make up for all his lies - and mine - by being true to her… The only codicil to my offer will be that she never sees him again.*

Lucilla sat in her study and stared up at the painting above her desk. The landscape depicted a contoured, fertile valley. A soothing blue sky crowned a tapestry of rich greens and warm brown hues, speckled with figures, flowers and animals populating the scene. The colours had barely faded over the years. The painting had been a gift from Caecilia, Agrippa's wife. Over the course of one summer Lucilla had accompanied her mother and visited the esteemed woman several times. Agrippa was away, on campaign. Although Lucilla sensed that she enjoyed her own company, the wife of the soldier still welcomed visitors.

Lucilla considered that Caecilia was unlike any other woman she had known. She was witty, opinionated and, despite her power, always kind and courteous, whether dealing with patricians or paupers. She was effortlessly elegant and wise, without ever wanting to show-off her learning - like some women like to flaunt a new outfit. Grace abounded in her aspect and actions. More than even the heroines in the books she read, Lucilla wanted to be like Caecilia. The daughter of Atticus sparked an interest in painting and sculpture in the young woman.

One afternoon, whilst waiting for her mother to arrive, Lucilla sat alone with Caecilia and expressed an admiration for the landscape on the wall, which still glistened with fresh paint. Not only did Caecilia reveal that she was the artist, but she also spoke about the inspiration behind the work.

"I have painted this scene more than once, I must confess, whether when present or in my mind's eye. The valley is close to Puteoli. It's where I first met my husband… Marcus is faithful, decent and doesn't just expect me to follow all his orders, like one of his soldiers… He makes me laugh, which may be a sovereign quality above all others… Marcus is my best friend. I think of him every day - and miss him every day. As lonely as I may sometimes feel, I do not feel alone in the world. Apologies if I am making about as much sense as one of our devoutly hypocritical politicians… Lucretius wrote, "We are each of us angels with only one wing, and we can only fly when embracing one another." I only really understood that line after falling in love… Love is good for the soul. It may be the only proof that we possess a soul. A divine spark. You will hopefully fall in love one day too, Lucilla. One's first love is perhaps one's only true love, for if you find a second then the first might not have been true after all."

Lucilla remembered Caecilia's words once more and thought about Rufus and Licinius. Two letters sat in front of her on the desk. One was in her hand, the other in another's, signed - "Livia". Lucilla read the letters once more. Satisfied. Resolved.

## 21.

The air was heavy with heat - strength sapping - and littered with flies. Rats were legion. A smell of rotting flesh pervaded the packed streets. It felt like Rome might soon suffer an Egyptian-like plague. Perhaps it deserved to, Varro judged. His throat was parched, his skin strewn with sweat and dust, as he entered Herennius' house once more. The agent had sent a messenger the day before, to arrange for the widow to be home when he called. She needed to answer some questions, by order of Caesar.

Varro requested for the slave, who answered the door, to bring him some wine, water and a plate of grapes and figs. When he asked after Fabullus the slave replied that he was attending to their mistress. She was unwell, yet she would still honour the appointment. Varro was led into a chamber which Herennius had called his "trophy room".

Several animal skins and pelts hung on the walls - or served as rugs. A shelf laden with strange-shaped, polished bones and pieces of ivory sat over a shelf filled with phallic-shaped ornaments. Various pieces of weaponry and armour, both Roman and foreign, also decorated the chamber: swords, spears, knives, clubs, shields, breastplates. A couple of coiled whips, side by side, hung on the wall, opposite the doorway. They looked out like two empty, sinister eyes. Varro couldn't help but notice the pieces of dried blood caked upon the whips and on the wall behind them. He wondered if the blood belonged to Herennius' slaves, or his wife. Most likely it was both.

Books were conspicuous by their absence in the chamber - and throughout the property. Varro recalled a quote from Cicero. "A room without books is like a body without a soul." When the slave brought his wine and refreshments Varro also requested a towel. He wiped his perspiring face and hands. He didn't want to somehow appear desperate or nervous in front of his interviewee. Suspect. Varro sat on a couch and waited patiently. When he heard voices outside the room, he altered his expression. The agent flared his nostrils and compressed his jaw to make his countenance seem squarer, more determined. He narrowed his eyes and creased his forehead, creating an inverted V-shape along his brow. He wouldn't enjoy the process, but the agent knew that he might have to intimidate the woman in order to extract information. Varro just wanted the truth. Was it so much to ask?

A fretful looking Fabullus entered first and nodded to the investigator. Corinna followed, shuffling her feet, her eyes downcast. Even more fretful, seemingly as delicate as the most fragile of ornaments. She was petite and woebegone. Her eyes were puffy, from lack of sleep and from recently crying. The widow was perhaps grieving for having lost Ovid, rather than her husband, however.

The widow wore a matronly black stola, yet her semblance was youthful. Her jewellery was new and expensive. Corinna was no great beauty - but far from plain. Her cheeks were freckled, and dimples appeared when she forced even the slightest of smiles. There was a softness and vulnerability sown into her countenance, in stark contrast to her parents' faces. Few would have guessed that she was the advocate's daughter, from their contrasting demeanours. Varro recalled how Ovid said he was attracted to her vulnerability - perhaps because it made it easier for him to take advantage of the mistreated girl.

Corinna dismissed Fabullus - but asked him to wait outside the door. She politely but diffidently greeted Varro, before offering up a snivel and a cough - to prove our ill she was. But the agent wasn't convinced. Varro suspected Corinna would recover enough to go shopping come the afternoon. He reminded himself that women were not altogether wedded to telling the truth, when dealing with themselves or others. In that sense, women had achieved a certain parity with men.

She sat down and stared intently into her lap, as if the answers to life's most profound questions might be there. Varro was intending to offer his condolences and say how sorry he was for the woman losing her husband. He was going to remark how much of a trying and terrible time it must be. But he didn't. He needed to be as hard as obsidian. Intimidate. Bully and threaten if required.

"Before you address any questions today, you need to consider that, rather than me, you are answering to Caesar. A report will be sent to him. Caesar will expect you to tell the truth - and there will be consequences, that not even your father will be able to protect you from, should he discover that you are attempting to deceive him. Do you understand?" Varro asked, or demanded, as he retrieved a wax tablet and stylus from his bag.

"Yes."

Corinna nodded her head. Her features tightened. Her skin grew paler, her expression more stricken. "As an agent, a sense of distrust and determination must overrule any feelings of pity," Agrippa had advised his agent.

"On the evening of the party, was there an altercation between your father and husband out in the garden? Did you hear raised voices?"

"No," the woman - or girl - replied, quietly.

"Can you speak up."

"No."

"Are you sure? I have received testimonies from others which contradict you."

"No. I don't know. I'm not sure."

Varro pretended to write something down on his tablet.

"I would remind you that this report will be read by Caesar."

Each time he said the name a ball of fear inflated in the young woman's innards. She was fearful - of Caesar and her father - of saying the wrong thing. She felt flustered and forgot some of the advice her father gave her, to help answer the investigator's questions. Varro regretted not inviting Manius, to further intimidate his suspect.

"Yes, I think my father did raise his voice against my husband that night. But that doesn't mean that he wanted to kill him. My husband was a difficult man."

Her hands and voice trembled a little as she spoke. Perhaps she was reliving a moment from her past, with her difficult husband. She was clearly distressed. Varro thought he might be getting somewhere. A chink of light was showing, through the dense forest he had been stumbling through. He felt uncomfortable interrogating the distraught woman. But needs must.

"Did your father ever ask you about the contents of your husband's will?"Corinna gulped and then reached for a glass of water. Her breathing became irregular.

"No, not to my recollection," she said, remembering the response her father had provided her with. That the advocate had prepared the witness told him everything and nothing.

"Are you aware of your father's debts?"

"No. He does not talk to me about his business affairs."

"And how about his love affairs? Are you aware that he keeps a mistress? An expensive one, by all accounts."

"No, please. I do not want to know," Corinna tremulously said, shaking her head - as if she were being physically tortured. She suffered a genuine coughing fit - and snivelled.

"But I need to know everything. On the night of your husband's murder did you see Titus Sura, your father's bodyguard, at any point?"

Corinna swallowed, again. Clearly neither she, nor her father, had been expecting the question. She fanned herself and sipped her watered-down wine. The girl was unsure of what to say. Varro's stylus hung over the wax tablet, like the Sword of Damocles.

"I do not remember," she replied, half-defeated. The young widow was akin to a quivering leaf, about to be blown from a tree.

Varro didn't need any advice from Agrippa to know the woman was lying. He decided to keep pressing home any advantage. The agent needed her wholly defeated. His features and voice remained as flat and hard as the head of a hammer.

"You can understand how things may appear to Caesar and others. My worry is that, should you be innocent of any crime, you will still be implicated and found guilty, because you concealed the truth. Caesar will ask himself, who benefitted from your husband's murder? Similarly, he will ask, who benefitted from the murder of Sestius?"

"I didn't have anything to do with my husband's murder."

She initially looked Varro in the eye as she spoke, but then tucked her chin into her chest and stared into her lap again. Tears wended their way down her flushed cheeks. The agent couldn't quite divine whether the tears sprung from anger, guilt, fear or pretence.

"But did your father? You should not have to answer for crimes you didn't commit."

Corinna drew in a breath, as if she were on the cusp of making a confession or preventing one from spilling out. Varro imagined receiving a name and retrieving the dagger. He thought how, when he succeeded in his assignment in thwarting Scaurus' coup, Agrippa drew him into his orbit even more. Should Varro serve Caesar well again, he may never win his life back. The agent would become too valuable an asset, a victim of his own success. His assignments - duties - would increase rather than diminish. Perhaps, if he did find the dagger, he should give it to Maecenas. As much as he may owe a duty to Agrippa, Varro owed a greater and longer-lasting one to Lucilla. He made a solemn promise to his wife to love and protect her all those years ago. Neither the gods, nor himself, could absolve him of such a vow, because they were now divorced. And how much of a duty did he owe towards Agrippa, after recruiting Manius and meeting with Lucilla behind his back? Agrippa would probably not even be beyond recruiting his former wife, Varro considered, if Maecenas didn't get his claws into her first.

"No. No. He had nothing to do with my husband's murder."

Corinna buried her head in her hands and sobbed. Varro felt like burying his head in his hands too, albeit he was seldom one for tears. He found that he had drawn in a large breath - but he suddenly exhaled. Sighed. He never felt proud of himself, after making a woman cry. He had broken too many hearts. That his own heart had been broken was no justification.

He still felt no wiser as to whether Nerva was guilty or not. Varro allowed Corinna to dry her eyes and recover her composure. He continued to question her, but less sternly. As much as it may have made her feel uncomfortable again, Varro asked about her relationship with Ovid. She said she had invited him to the party to give a reading - but she no longer wanted anything to do with the poet. "He used me," she dolefully remarked, hoping the three words would explain the entirety of the affair. Varro didn't think highly of Ovid, or himself, at that moment.

By the end of their interview pity wormed its way into the agent's heart, ousting out some, but not all, distrust. The young woman had been a victim. Her father, husband and lover had all mistreated her. He was tempted to offer her some advice and encouragement. She now had an opportunity - and the funds - to start over. She might feel alone and helpless now, but she would attract plenty of friends and suitors soon. The people of Rome were drawn to money, like flies are drawn to shit. She should choose someone decent, even if it meant someone dull. "Just try not to marry a poet," he would have counselled.

Perhaps something inside of the widow thawed in relation to the investigator by the end of their interview too. Corinna offered up at least one half-smile, which was not altogether forced. She thought the nobleman handsome and she had heard about his reputation. But she hoped she would never see him again.

Varro was mindful to leave the door open, however.

"Please do get in touch should you remember anything else. Also, if you come into possession of the dagger, or know who may be able to retrieve it, I can arrange for immunity from prosecution. The person who took the dagger will remain anonymous. I can even arrange a reward, a finder's fee if you like, for its return. You will earn Caesar's favour, as opposed to displeasure."

The agent probed for a telling reaction in the woman's expression on hearing his tempting offer. But she was either an accomplished actress, or genuinely ignorant - innocent - as to where the knife might be.

Corinna coughed and snivelled once more, before instructing Fabullus to show their guest out. Lentulus Nerva had asked his daughter to report back to him immediately, once her meeting with the investigator was over. The advocate would perhaps interrogate her more than the agent. Corinna felt drained, however. She decided to take to her bed again, before visiting her dressmaker and then calling on her father.

Varro puffed out his cheeks. The agent was almost as relieved as the young widow that their interview was over. There was little point in continuing the investigation, he judged. His race was run - and Varro didn't much care if he had come first or last. He resolved to write-up his report that afternoon. Caesar would have to console himself with being the richest and most powerful man in the world, to offset the disappointment of not possessing the dagger. Again, Varro briefly closed his eyes and pictured Arretium. But the image didn't hold, it slipped out of his mind like water running through his fingers. Agrippa could choose to investigate Nerva further, or anyone else, without him.

"I am not sure if it's of any importance, but I just thought I would correct something I said before, or rather what one of the staff said. The scrap of material we found on the morning of our master's murder was not black, but dark brown. Here, please, take it," Fabullus remarked, handing over the frayed square of cloth, as they stood on the street, just outside the house.

*The missing piece.*

"Rufus Varro?"

The voice was a blend of formality and breathlessness. The stern-faced praetorian, Aelius Vulso, stood to attention and addressed the nobleman. The soldier was awash with sweat and quivering from exhaustion. Stubble dusted his strong jaw. His hair was matted to his brow. Vulso had first raced across Rome, to Varro's property on the Palatine Hill. The aged estate manager had informed the soldier that his master was absent, but it was likely he could be found at the address which Vulso stood outside now.

"Yes," Varro answered, not knowing whether to be confused or curious.

"I must ask you to accompany me, by order of our most venerable Consul, Marcus Agrippa. I regret to inform you that your bodyguard, Manius, is in peril. Indeed, he may already be dead."

273

## 22.

Carbo winced, as the vine stick slapped against the Briton's bare back once more. The prisoner's skin was criss-crossed with lacerations and welts. The former senator would have preferred to keep his hands clean, but he had no inclination to call-off torturing the man. The aristocrat may have been squeamish, but he wasn't weak. Carbo needed to know what the spy knew - and who he was working for. Nothing could prevent his progress, ascendency. Not a man's death. Not a thousand deaths.

The warehouse had been vacant for a month, but the pungent smell of salt and rotting fish still hung in the air like a hundred broken promises. Spots of blood marked the dusty, warped floorboards and cracked walls. The former overseer's office was situated at the back of the building, at the end of a narrow corridor. The door was shut. Light slanted down from two open shutters positioned half-way up the wall. But they were too high for anyone to see through. Labeo didn't want the small army of men, congregating in the main part of the warehouse, to know they had captured - and were torturing - a spy.

Manius arched his back on receiving another vicious blow. He felt like his arms might come out of their sockets. His bound wrists bled from where the rope had worn through his skin, like a warm knife through butter. The piece of rope hung over a hook, which was attached to the main beam on the ceiling. A pulley system meant that a couple of Labeo's foot soldiers could easily raise the Briton up - and let go of the rope when ordered, to leave him to drop to the floor. His bottom lip was split open, his nose was broken - and his right eye and cheek had swelled to such an extent that his vision was blurred. The world was growing dimmer.

They may have broken his nose, but they were yet to break the man. The only words Manius uttered so far were, "I am a Roman citizen". The first time he spoke there was a measure of defiance, or irony, in his tone. He soon mumbled the sentence however, not quite knowing why he was doing so. Under his breath however Manius cursed his captors and ill fortune.

The new agent had duly followed Carbo that morning, making sure to keep his distance, adopting the tradecraft he had learned from Agrippa. Manius expected another routine day, as Carbo met with his friend. He was wrong. Along with a larger retinue than usual the two men purposefully walked through Rome, towards a district situated between the river and Jewish quarter. They entered the warehouse and soon after a steady stream of others joined them. Realising that the attack upon the Jewish district was imminent Manius resolved to get word to Agrippa. The demagogue needed to be stopped. Some may have considered Carbo and his policies to be foolish - the cancelling of debts, the state appropriating private capital and industry, the persecution of Jews - but Carbo was dangerous. His promises and propaganda were proving popular among the gilds and students. This attack could just be the start of things. Weeds grow quicker than flowers. But Agrippa would soon cut the rabble-rouser down to size, Manius thought.

Unfortunately, the agent was being spied upon. Tarquin Gellius had caught sight of the man who had attacked him at the tavern. It was surely more than a coincidence that he was present. At first Gellius merely observed Manius, before he suspected that the brute was surveilling the warehouse and his comrades. The student rushed to alert Paulus Labeo, who instructed his chief enforcer, Gnaeus Piso, to muster some men and apprehend their uninvited guest.

Manius was injured and outnumbered. He was able to fend off the first couple of attackers but then he was brought to the ground. The Briton suffered blows to the face and hobnailed boots stamped upon already cracked ribs. Gellius was sufficiently wise, or cowardly, not to enter the fray until he was sure his enemy had been knocked unconscious.

Gnaeus Piso used smelling salts to arouse his prisoner. Or his acetum-drenched breath may have been considered just as potent. Piso was a soldier, who had served out his twenty-five years in the army. He had been given a plot of land near Cosa, after his retirement, but Piso had been a better fighter than farmer. His wife passed away and his sons left to join the army. He sold his farm, to pay off his debts, and travelled to Rome to find employment, as a tanner. He blamed the Jews for his fate. They had loaned him the money, at a crippling interest rate, to cover his gambling debts. But the Jews were not content just to ruin his life. He believed that they had bled Rome dry, during the civil wars, as they loaned money to Caesar, Pompey, Antony and Augustus over the years. They worshipped false gods and stole Roman women. When he heard Publius Carbo giving a speech in the marketplace, the demagogue was preaching to the converted. He met with Paulus Labeo and soon became his enforcer. The ex-soldier helped to recruit men in the taverns and gilds and break-up rallies by opponents. Piso was loyal and believed in Labeo and their cause. He had yet to refuse an order, including that of setting fire to a Jewish temple, abusing Jewish women - and torturing a suspected spy.

A square head sat on even squarer shoulders. His eyes were bloodshot, his nose veiny, as if it were a map of all the tributaries of the Rhine. Piso was the wrong side of fifty but his frame was still brawny, his mind a patchwork of bitterness, courage, duty and rage. He would not bat an eyelid at continuing to torture the man, hanging up like a slab of meat in front of him. And he would not bat an eyelid at then killing him. He was a spy, an enemy of the cause and a foreigner.

Piso bared his yellow teeth, in a seething smile, as he thrashed the captive's back once more. His hand ached from clutching the cane too tightly, for too long. The malice he bore the Briton still easily eclipsed the begrudging respect he gave him, for his ability to endure his blows.

"I'll break the bastard. He'll be squealing, like a pig about to be slaughtered, soon. I'll wring the Briton's neck, like a chicken, if I have to. I'll beat him so hard that even his own mother won't recognise him," Piso remarked to Labeo, who had been tapping his foot impatiently, waiting for the prisoner to confess.

The propagandist was keen to know who his enemy was. Once Piso had compelled the Briton to talk, he would silence him. A dead witness was no witness at all.

*Death is the solution to all problems. No man - no problem.*

"We must still proceed with the plan," Paulus Labeo ordered, taking charge of the matter. He knew that his aristocratic friend had little stomach for some of the decisions that needed to be made. "You can have your fun with him later. The men have assembled. We cannot afford to call the raid off and lose face or followers. We may never get this opportunity again. Publius, you should give your speech - put iron in their souls. And then, Gnaeus, lead our forces off. You have your instructions."

"Yes, Sir," Piso replied, as if he were back in the army. He would direct select groups of trusted men to enter properties and steal valuables. Coinage and jewellery should be prioritised. Many of the younger Jewish men would be away, at work. Most of the inhabitants would be women or elderly men. There would be little resistance and Piso had the numbers to subdue the enemy. Properties would be ransacked or torched. Temples would be desecrated. Their holy men would be abused and beaten. Women defiled. It would be a joyous day - one Rome would remember. Carbo could deny responsibility. But new recruits would flock to his banner and support the cause. They would no longer be an idealistic movement, but a force to be reckoned with.

"You can leave two of your men with us. We will be here, if the dog decides to talk. Should he be encouraged to loosen his tongue we can then release him. Set him down for now. He has suffered enough," the tribune said, lying. He hoped that the prisoner had heard and believed in his offer of freedom, in return for a confession.

The rope slackened and Manius slumped to the floor, like a puppet with his strings cut. He heard Labeo's words but believed them not. He knew that a full confession was tantamount to a death sentence. "Better to trust an augur than politician," Fronto had always advised.

The prisoner let out a groan. He hoped that his captors would hear and believe that he was a broken man. Frightened. Enfeebled. The hulking bodyguard lay curled up like a baby. His arms and shoulders felt like they were on fire. His bounds still bit into his wrists, like a bracelet of serpent's teeth. His ribs were a slab of agony. Every breath caused him pain. But where there is life there is hope, Cicero had consoled. His plan was to convince his enemies that he was weaker than he was. He had employed the tactic in the arena, on more than one occasion, of convincing his opponent that he was injured or defeated. And then suddenly fighting back. Sooner or later they might move him. Or they might leave him alone. Left for dead. Manius had already surveyed the room, for weapons. There was a hammer and rust-ridden chisel on a large chest by the door. A heavy, clay jug sat on a nearby table, along with a bronze stylus. Labeo had called the Briton a "dog".

*But every dog has its day.*

The determination to find and save his friend overruled the fear Varro felt at entering the lion's den. He was not sure he had ever experienced such breathlessness as he ran through the streets of Rome, following Vulso. His thighs and throat burned. The praetorian finally led him up to a rooftop, where Agrippa was waiting. The roof overlooked an anonymous looking warehouse, albeit the crowd assembling there were far from inconspicuous. Many were tradesmen - bakers, carpenters, blacksmiths or other guildsmen - still wearing their aprons. Jugs of wine were being passed around. Labeo thought that the acetum would put some fire into the bellies of his foot-soldiers. In contrast to the rough-looking workingmen, a smattering of students, wearing tunics as white as sheep, also populated the burgeoning mob.

Agrippa briefed Varro. Confidence and concern laced his tone and stern features. Manius had been taken prisoner. How did he know? The agent, who Agrippa had tasked with shadowing Paulus Labeo, had seen the Briton being carried into the warehouse, before he reported back the consul and mobilised a contingent of soldiers. Agrippa could not be certain that Manius was still being held captive in the building, but it was likely.

"Can we not storm the building now, catch them by surprise?" Varro asked, desperate to liberate his friend - even if he had to climb over a mound of dead bodies to do so.

"No. The bulk of my men are positioned a few streets away from here, close to the Jewish quarter. I want Carbo's mob to march towards their target. At present they are just a group of men. If I attacked now, I could cause that which I am seeking to prevent. Caesar could be labelled a dictator and butcher - and Carbo's ranks could swell, if they are slaughtered. Factions in the Senate House could even legitimise him. When the armed mob close in on the Jewish district however we will have cause to strike. I am confident of their route and approach. I have men ready to close off the street. They will not break through our shield wall. We will also close off the street from behind, trap them in a vice. Archers will line the rooftop. Carbo's would-be army will be forced to surrender - or perish. But that does not mean I will leave Manius to his fate. Firstly, I want you and Vulso to infiltrate the warehouse. Find out if Manius is present. Once the mob have been led off you should have an opportunity to locate him. I should warn you, Rufus, that Manius has probably been tortured. He may even be dead. You need to prepare yourself. You cannot afford to let revenge bubble over. You could compromise yourself and Vulso. I am sure Manius wouldn't want you to forsake your life in a vain attempt to avenge his."

Varro nodded his head, to convey he understood. But should Carbo be responsible for murdering his friend, the agent would not rest until he brought the demagogue to justice. And he would answer for his crimes in Hades, rather than in a courthouse.

*I'll kill him.*

## 23.

The jugs of water and wine were still being passed around, but the ribald jokes and expectant chatter ceased as Publius Carbo made his entrance. He climbed the steps to the raised platform - stage - slowly, carefully. His solemn expression tempered any temptation from the crowd to cheer their political champion. The statesman suppressed the urge to turn his nose up at the unpleasant stench tickling his nostrils, for fear his audience would interpret the gesture of him turning his nose up at them. Carbo held his hand aloft to command further quiet, from those whispering in the congregation. He resembled a priest, about to offer up a prayer - or make a sacrifice. His tunic was brown and cut from the same cloth as others he saw before him. Carbo wanted to impress upon his followers that he was like them, as well as above them.

The demagogue surveyed the crowd below. Sweat dripped upon brows. Some clutched clubs. Some gazed up with admiration and adoration in their eyes - although one might have interpreted a few of the expressions as reflecting gormlessness rather than wonder. Carbo looked forward to a time when women would be attracted to his party too. His pictured them sitting at his feet, hanging on his every word. Giving themselves to him. The younger the better.

That morning he remembered his political antecedents: the Gracchi, Catiline and Clodius. He would honour them and learn the lessons they had to impart. Yet their chief legacy was one of failure. Their revolutions and reforms had not taken root. As much as he would publicly condemn Sulla and Caesar, the republican knew he needed to emulate them. Their ruthlessness. How they won and retained power. Carbo and Labeo had already drafted their proscription lists. Enemies would be exiled or executed. He would appropriate Agrippa's residence. Labeo said he would take great pleasure in requisitioning and redecorating Maecenas' palatial house on the Esquiline Hill. The pair of them would also ensure that any generals were subordinate and loyal to the new regime. He would disband the bulk of the army and mobilise a police force to suppress any dissent directed towards the state. New officials would be recruited, from the ranks of his devout followers. Diplomats would know their place too and not exceed their brief. Carbo smiled to himself, as he recalled a quote by one of Labeo's mentors: "A sincere diplomat is like dry water or wooden iron." Carbo envisioned that he would still plan feast days when in power, but not ones devoted to the gods. Rather they would celebrate the state. He would melt down the army of statues dedicated to Caesar and commission one of himself, if the people so demanded it. He compiled a list of tax rises, which he would implement on the first day of gaining power. The rich would be made poor. He would tax luxury goods and vices, although Labeo advised against upsetting his followers and raising taxes on wine.

"Friends, Romans and comrades," Carbo declaimed, smiling benignly. "Today we sow the seeds of a new Rome. A Rome for all. A Rome for you. Today we come out of the shadows and provide a cure for a pestilence which has plagued this city for far too long. The enemy is inside the gates. They have taken our wealth, women and jobs. They wish to cripple us with debt, subjugate us. Too many of us deal daily with hunger and privation, whilst they swagger around the city, wearing the finest clothes and eating the richest foods. But no more, I say. We will no longer be bled dry by these parasites. The Jews must be driven out, like lepers... We are many, they are few. Today we will turn the tide in this battle, this battle for the very soul of Rome. We must drag them out of their litters, burn them out of their homes, retrieve our money from the war profiteers and vile usurers - and tear down their temples... I want a world of peace, but I will not see Rome further corrupted and ruined on the altar of Judaism... If you are not for Rome, you are against it. You must even denounce your neighbour and consider him an enemy of the state, should he transgress. More than a husband, father or worker you must be a citizen of Rome!"

Publius Carbo drew breath and paused accept the applause and acclaim of the crowd, which numbered over a hundred. Cups and hands were raised, in a salute to their beloved leader. Spittle filled the air as they chanted his name in a low, rhythmic drone. His solemnity had turned into a blazing passion. His voice hammered into every ear.

Rufus Varro blended in, thanks to the worn, besmirched tunic Vulso had given him to change into. A piece of rope replaced his leather belt. His soft sandals had been replaced by hobnailed boots. A layer of dust and dirt was caked upon his fine features. He raised his cup too. The agent hoped however that none of the surrounding mob had noticed him roll his eyes, in response to their leader's vicious, vapid speech. The agent stood next to the equally inconspicuous soldier. No one had given them a second look as they entered the warehouse and mingled among the crowd, hoping to glean whatever intelligence they could.

The cheers and foot stamping grew louder, like the tamp of soldiers marching to battle. Varro was worried at one point that the roof might give way, although he subsequently welcomed the scenario. The mob deserved to be buried under the weight of their own raucous din. The nobleman held up his nose, both at the fetid stench and revolting, plebeian behaviour.

*It never troubles the wolf how many the sheep may be*, Varro thought, remembering the line from Virgil. Carbo would promise them Elysium and deliver Hades. He was using the politics of resentment and division to widen the cracks endemic to society. Varro surveyed the crowd and witnessed a sea of enthralled faces, as if they were listening to music. But Carbo's oratory would prove a Siren's song.

He recalled snippets of conversation, between his father and Tiro, about Lucius Sergius Catiline, who similarly attracted students and young aristocrats to his cause, as well as mobs formed from coarser stock.

"Narcissus was less enamoured with himself. Catiline was an impressive soldier and orator. But he also resembled a spoilt child, whose temper and ambition flailed as wildly as the legs of an octopus. His courage cannot be called into question, as opposed to his judgement. He set himself up as the people's champion. He wanted to cancel their debts - after he had arranged to cancel his own. They swallowed his words like honey. But too much honey will cause a man to vomit... Catiline was as addicted to conspiracy as he was to sex. Women - and men - swooned over his attractive figure. But his reach exceeded his grasp. He was a formidable soldier, who could have served Rome well. Yet he wished to become master over it - and Cicero quite rightly never regretted acting like a dictator, in order to combat the would-be tyrant... Once defeated, Rome largely forgot about Catiline and his cause, until Clodius - that vicious peacock - adopted his mantle. The nobleman became a common street thug, standing on corners like a whore and whipping-up a storm against the establishment. As Diogenes said, "The mob is the mother of all tyrants." Those were dark days. The darkest day was when Clodius forced Cicero out of Rome... Yet it was a happy day when Clodius met his fate. Those that live by the sword invariably end up dying by the sword."

Varro's thought turned towards Manius. The former gladiator lived by his sword, in some respects, His friend just hoped that he would not now die by it.

"Those of you who are poor will soon be rich. Those of you who are powerless will soon be powerful. Together we can take back control of Rome. Together we will drive out the Jews. Let them settle elsewhere. Rome must be a beacon of light, for the rest of the world to follow... Workers of Rome unite! You have nothing to lose but your chains," Publius Carbo proclaimed, to a crescendo of cheers. The sheep wished to unleash themselves, like wolves, Varro wryly thought.

Gnaeus Piso punched his fist into the air and roared louder than most. Although he was grateful for the former senator's contribution to the cause - and he chanted his name - Piso's loyalty was towards the author behind the speech. The enforcer looked forward to a time when the elderly Carbo retired, or was ushered aside, for Paulus Labeo to inherit the crown. He knew how to further their cause. People worship the rising rather than the setting sun and one didn't need an augur to recognise that Labeo was slowly but surely directing their movement. Labeo possessed more ideas, energy and passion. He had the stomach for the fight. Ultimately, the aristocratic senator would always be a part of the establishment, when he needed to be its enemy. Carbo wanted to lead the Senate House, while Labeo wanted to raze it to the ground and build a thousand-year regime. Labeo would be the one to give the order to kill their prisoner.

Lucilla sat in the shade beneath a pear tree, in her garden. Her heart was still beating quickly, irregularly. But all would be well, she told herself. She had done the right thing. Lucilla had settled on declining Pulcher's proposal, even before being presented with his terms. One of which - that she needed to agree never to see her previous husband again, once they were married - she would have refused. Lucilla politely thanked her suitor for his proposal - and mentioned how honoured she felt and how much she enjoyed spending time with him - but asserted that she had no desire to re-marry. She further argued that it was best they no longer saw each other, as they wanted different things from the relationship.

"I do not want you thinking that I am leading you on or lying to you."

Pulcher was perhaps too shocked or crestfallen to notice, but there was an element of irony, as well as sincerity, in the woman's tone. Whereas a few moments before he had been articulate, verbose, the agent was now lost for words. Disbelief (or almost denial) flooded his being. He felt akin a man who had placed a fortune on an overwhelming favourite for a chariot race, only to have his champion finish in second place. Pulcher was not sure he had been refused anything before. The agent had always broken hearts, as opposed to have someone break his. He had failed on a personal and professional level - and further failed to comprehend why.

Anger and ingratitude soon displaced feelings of confusion and sorrow. Yet the spurned suitor did his best to remain civil. An agent should never lose possession of himself. As with most emotions, they bubbled beneath the surface. He was tempted to ask - or demand - whether Varro had whispered poison into her ear and turned her against him. He wanted to know why so much had seemed to change, since only the night before. He wanted to call her a whore, threaten to ruin her reputation and ask for his love tokens back. Yet, Pulcher still owned a number of fine feelings for her. He wanted to give her the benefit of the doubt. He could still win her over too. It would just take time and a fresh strategy. Should he cause such offense now and behave in such a boorish manner she might never forgive him and reconsider his proposal. It wasn't all over, he told himself.

It was all over, she told herself. Even the birdsong seemed plaintive. The sun was shining, but there was little light in her heart. Diana served her a cup of wine, which was barely diluted, hoping that the drink might help her mistress sleep.

Varro had been right, although Lucilla was in no rush to tell him so. Licinius had been introduced to her by Maecenas, in order to spy on her (and read her correspondence with Caesar's wife). Livia always asked her friend to destroy her letters, for fear of them eventually falling into the hands of gossips or her enemies. Lucilla complied with the instruction and always burned the missives immediately, although Maecenas and his agent were unaware of this arrangement.

After Varro departed the other day, she was left with a seed of doubt as to Licinius' intentions. Lucilla needed to know if her suitor - the man who she was considering marrying - was honourable. If it was all an act, it was all worth nothing. Lucilla confided in Manius during the party, asking the bodyguard not to reveal her anxieties to his friend. The Briton furnished her with a plan.

"You should give him enough rope to hang himself."

Lucilla casually mentioned that she would be replying to a piece of correspondence, recently sent by Livia. She composed one letter herself - and asked Diana to write out another letter, pretending to be from Caesar's wife. She put the letters in the drawer of her desk, placing a fleck of ash on them, and left the door of her study open. When she returned, the ash had been disturbed and the letters were positioned differently in the drawer. Licinius had entered the room and reviewed the contents. Lucilla felt violated and wanted to be sick. She was close to crying. Love was nothing without trust and, once lost, it is difficult, if not impossible, to restore.

Lucilla quickly gained possession of herself, however. She decided that she did not wish to cause a scene with Licinius or listen to any more of his lies. She would prove that spies were not the only people capable of putting on an act. Women can deceive too. If the agent acted inappropriately, she would threaten to tell Livia - and Caesar - about Maecenas' attempt to spy on them.

And so, Lucilla listened to his proposal. She took great pleasure in refusing it. She was tempted to try to humiliate and hurt him. She was also tempted to confront him with his crime. The agent was far from retired. But then he might try to tell her the truth. Yet men invariably dissemble the most when endeavouring to tell the truth. Lucilla was just pleased the affair was over. Ultimately, she did not love Licinius. Partly because she knew what genuine love felt like. She was free, again.

Despite the heat her skin prickled, and she placed a brown cloak over her. A wave of loneliness washed over her, as black as the waters of Acheron. Her future seemed dim again. But then Lucilla smiled, wistfully, telling herself that her canvas was blank rather than black. She had a lot to be thankful for. It was a phrase that her mother had often used. Her mother too had endured an unhappy marriage but had argued that she had taken consolation from being wedded to her children. Who she loved dearly - and who loved her back. Her father had been, like Rufus, unfaithful and untrustworthy. Unlike Lucilla's father however, had Rufus changed? Once trust is lost it is difficult, but not impossible, to restore. It struck Lucilla how she had lied to herself the other day, when she couldn't remember the last time she had been happy. She could. It was when she was with Rufus in Arretium, last year, nursing him back to health. Lucilla realised she could spend the rest of her life with him. He just had to ask.

## 24.

Piso ordered his lieutenants to assemble his force outside the warehouse. The heat and wine fuelled their desire to get on with the job. They had an itch they wanted to scratch. Carbo's speech had tapped into a rich seam of envy and resentment. The Jews were the enemy. The cause of all of Rome's ills. Eventually, he would convince his followers that Caesar was responsible for their grievances. Others followed the demagogue out of greed. Varro had overheard more than one man talk about what he was going to spend his loot on, after the raid. It was time to "tax" the Jews. "The broadest shoulders should bear the heaviest burden," Carbo argued. Some seemed veritably jubilant, as they set off towards the Jewish quarter, carrying knives and clubs - like revellers travelling to a party. Many of the pale, rake-thin students appeared skittish, as if a gust of wind could blow them over. A fair few downed an extra measure of wine, to settle their nerves and bolster their confidence. Tarquin Gellius imagined himself encountering the elderly Jew, Benjamin. He would have his revenge on him and the Briton today, he satisfyingly thought. The gods were smiling on him. Gellius also licked his lips, as he pictured cornering a Jewess.

The mob set off, snaking around into the next street, in less disarray than Vulso would have liked. A few of them staggered from too much wine but many marched in good order, their backs as straight as a pilum, betraying some military training. Their leader, Piso, oversaw their departure but then headed into the warehouse again. The throng possessed an air of purpose and animus, the praetorian considered. But a seemingly unstoppable force would soon encounter an immovable object. Vulso believed that Carbo's army of thugs would be no match for professional soldiers. He pictured the shield wall, sharpened spear points poking out, moving inexorably towards the trapped, doomed enemy. A contingent of archers would rain death from above. His fellow soldiers neither loved not loathed the Jews. They would do their duty of keeping the peace and serving Caesar, their paymaster, however.

Varro and Vulso lingered just outside the warehouse. The stench had receded, but an air of danger remained. A contingent of a dozen or so men, who were part of Carbo's retinue, also milled about the building. A few were armed. None gave the two strangers, who kept to themselves, a second look though.

Contrary to Agrippa's orders, Varro was determined to rescue his friend. Despite the heat, a shiver of terror zig-zagged down his spine. But Varro's fear was secondary to his will save Manius. If he was still alive. A greater fear was arriving too late. Anger and helplessness overpowered his normal air of indifference. Varro was willing to lose his life. Fronto would act as executor to his will. He had also entrusted certain letters to his estate manager. One of which would be sent to Lucilla. She should know how I feel, once I get to the next world, he thought.

*Although I should tell her how I feel in this world.*

Varro pictured his friend. When his father had first brought him home, like a stray, he had felt slightly threatened. Manius should not be considered a mere slave, his father had ordered. Varro resentfully thought the Briton would be the son his father never had.

"The barbarian looks like he has come from the underworld, rather than the arena… I am not sure what we should lament the most, his table manners or dress sense," Varro had pointedly remarked to Fronto.

Yet Fronto admonished, rather than agreed with, his young master. The sage estate manager posited that if anyone was displaying bad manners, it was him.

"You need to help educate Manius, as much as he's been charged to tutor you. Nobility has its responsibilities."

It soon turned out that the Briton was the brother Varro never had. There was not a braver, more honourable soul in Rome. Varro never had the heart - or material - to satirise his friend in a poem. The bodyguard had saved the nobleman from injury - and even death - more times than he could recall.

Varro already overheard that a prisoner was being kept in the rear of the warehouse. The scar on his forehead began to itch and he briefly shuddered, recalling the horror of his own torture, before casting it out of his mind - pushing it away with a pole like a barge creeping too close to the riverbank. Varro would not wish such a fate he endured on his enemies, let alone his friend.

"We need to strike now, before it's too late," the agent urgently asserted, whilst keeping his voice low.

"We have our orders. We need to gather intelligence and report back. We can then form a plan as to how best to proceed," Vulso replied, shaking his head whilst repeating Agrippa's words. The soldier was not without courage. Years of marching, digging, fighting and suffering had turned the orphan into a block of iron. But one of the reasons why the praetorian had survived so long was that he cultivated a sense of caution too.

"I have all the intelligence I need. We must get to him, now."

"You shouldn't engage an enemy, when unsure of your opponent's strength," the praetorian, somewhat sententiously, countered. "We do not know the extent of the force behind the door. And even if we could free your bodyguard, we would have to fight our way out. Our orders are our orders. Why would you wish to commit to such a suicidal plan?"

Vulso resisted the temptation to add that his friend may already be dead.

"Because he would do the same for me. If some bastard was torturing your friend, would you leave him to his fate?"

Manius lay on the floor, resembling a corpse. Blood trickled down his chin from where his lip had cracked again. The former gladiator knew a number of his bones had been broken. His body felt like a slab of tenderised meat. He promised that any pain inflicted upon him by his enemies, he would return with interest. Hate was one of the things binding him together. And love for Camilla. The agent pretended to be unconscious. He flinched not on hearing the suggestion that they should discover if the agent had a wife or child - and threaten to torture them in order to extract the information they craved.

*Conserve what little strength you have. Keep your mind alert.*

Manius kept his eyes closed but counted the men in the room. Carbo and Labeo. The latter might have some fight in him, but the former had as much backbone as a jellyfish. The former senator would resile himself from any fight. The man who had tortured him was a former soldier and shouldn't be underestimated. But Manius had just overheard him say he would be leaving soon, to take charge of his men when they reached the Jewish quarter. The two men who had been tasked with hoisting him up and down were an unknown quantity. But it was likely they could handle themselves. They would have to kill or be killed though. Were they ready for that? It could prove that, at some point, he would be left alone with just one guard in the room too. Manius was conscious of not underestimating his opponents. But he hoped that they would underestimate him. The gladiator had one last contest left in his weakened body. He wanted to at least take one of his enemies into the next life with him.

Just as Manius finished counting the people in the room and thinking about how he could even the odds he heard the door open.

Vulso had agreed to accompany Varro inside the warehouse. Their aim was to reconnoitre where the prisoner was being held, judge his physical state and assess the force which was keeping him captive. Should Manius somehow only be guarded by one or two men, then, Vulso conceded, they could look to liberate the Briton. Otherwise they would take their intelligence back to Agrippa and engage the enemy, after they arranged the requisite plan and numbers.

As a ruse to gain access to the backroom Varro would tell the two guards outside that he had intelligence about a wealthy Jew. They knew where his valuables were secreted in the house. Their leader would want to know.

Access proved easy as the two soggy-brained sentries believed Varro's story. Varro and Vulso shut the door behind them as they entered the room.

"Who are you? What are you doing here?" Labeo barked, like a teacher scolding some errant students. The tribune was vexed by the intrusion and interruption.

There was an eerie pause as people turned their attention towards Varro and Vulso, except Manius, who still felt it prudent to pretend to be unconscious.

Varro turned his attention towards the prisoner, prostrate upon the blood-stained floor. His friend was alive, just about, as he observed his chest move up and down. The nobleman's blood was on fire. His heart beat, savagely. The agent had killed, once, before. He hadn't enjoyed the experience, but he hadn't regretted it either.

Even if the room would have been filled with twice the number of opponents, Varro had no intention of leaving without his companion.

"We're here to deliver a message," the agent remarked.

Manius' eyes snapped open on recognising the familiar voice.

Varro had a small dagger tucked inside the back of his belt, but he noticed the hammer and chisel on the chest next to the door and picked the tools up. Just before he did so the propagandist marched towards him, intending to confront and further berate the irksome stranger. Labeo's contempt turned to confusion - and then alarm - as Varro walked purposely forward too. The stone mason's hammer weighed heavy in his hand, but not so heavy that he could not quickly raise the tool and smash it against his enemy's temple. The sound of the low thud and splintering crack, as Labeo's skull was shattered, caused Publius Carbo to wince and flatten himself against the wall. The noise resembled someone breaking open a lobster claw.

The two men who had helped torture the prisoner - Trogus and Papius - sprang into action. Trogus drew his dagger and rushed towards Varro. Papius retrieved his short club from the nearby table and honed-in on Vulso.

Manius pushed through the pain barrier and rose to his feet, turning to confront Piso, picking up the bronze stylus. He was wounded, near defeated, like a lion with a brace of spears protruding from his chest. But he wasn't wholly defeated. He stood, slightly bent over, one arm tucked in, consciously or unconsciously protecting his broken ribs. His left eye was swollen, causing his vision to be blurry. His blood-stained, grimy tunic seemed mottled with scabs.

Vulso saw Papius running towards him, his weapon held aloft, and heard the sound of the guards outside about to open the door. He would not last long trying to fight on two fronts. He would be stabbed in the back quicker than any politician. The praetorian, in an action oft practised on a piece of wood in various camps throughout his time campaigning, threw his knife at the advancing opponent. The blade buried itself into Papius' chest. His legs gave way, as if slipping on a sheet of ice, and he fell at Vulso's feet. The soldier quickly pulled the weapon from the dying man's body and turned to face the door, where he imagined that the two guards were about to enter the fray.

Varro and Trogus faced off against one another. Both men circled each other, neither committing to a rash, compromising attack. Trogus' arm quivered as he held out his weapon, trembling with nerves or exhaustion, from having hauled the prisoner up so many times. Perhaps his tactic was just to keep his opponent occupied and wait for reinforcements. Varro still held the hammer in one hand, the chisel in the other. He was a picture of malice - and concentration. He tried to recall the lessons Manius had imparted to him over the years.

*Be quick in a fight, but not reckless… Counter-attacking can be just as effective as attacking first.*

Trogus' attention was momentarily diverted on witnessing his comrade fall, as the knife entered his chest and he dropped to the ground. Varro remained focussed however and grasped his opportunity, as he moved forward and swung his hammer, knocking the dagger from his hand. Whilst Trogus watched his weapon slide across the floor Varro closed in and plunged the chisel into his sternum.

Piso bared his teeth and growled, more than spoke, as he raised his dagger up to Manius' eye-level. Shafts of light from above glinted off the polished blade.

"I'm going to gut you like a fish."

Manius knew he probably only had one concerted attack in him. Any sudden movement and he was likely to lose his balance afterwards. *You miss, I hit*, Manius thought to himself. He had been drilled as a gladiator, thousands of time, in the ludi – whereby an opponent would look to thrust and connect with his practise gladius. The task was to avoid the padded point or edge of the weapon whilst also, in one fluid movement, counter-attack.

Piso feinted one way but then made thrust his blade from a different angle. Manius read the attack, however. He shifted his body weight, much to the annoyance of his stiff, screaming ribcage, and swung his long arm around. The point of the stylus found its mark. His opponent's jugular vein. Just for good measure Manius ripped the weapon out of his throat, to widen the wound further. Piso, shock replacing rage on his contorted countenance, immediately fell to his knees. Blood gushed out. The former legionary tried to curse his enemy, but he merely emitted a gargling noise, as Piso held his hand up to his gory injury.

"Some chicken, some neck," the Briton remarked. Blood would continue to ooze out of the vein. Soon he would lose consciousness. And then he would lose his life.

*Let the bastard bleed and let the bastard die.*

Vulso shifted the heavy chest in front of the door and positioned himself to act as a brace, in order to further shore up his barricade. Yet, to his surprise, the guards outside failed to try and enter. Something was wrong. Or right.

The two friends approached one another and offered up a subtle nod and fraternal clasp of the shoulder.

"I did suggest that one day I would get to save you," Varro said, his heart still pounding from having fought - and killed - a man.

"I'd be more than happy for you to do so again. Just try not to leave it so late next time," Manius, looking life death warmed up, replied. "No jokes though, for once. It hurts like a bastard when I laugh."

Both men had tears welling in their eyes, but there was no time for the tears to go anywhere else. They turned their attention to Publius Carbo, who was still stuck, limpet-like, to the wall. He had somehow aged since Varro and Vulso had walked through the door.

"Who are you?" the demagogue asked, or rather demanded. But his whimpering voice diminished his authority somewhat.

"I am a Roman citizen," Manius replied, reminding himself and his captor of what he said, while being tortured.

"And I am a patrician, a former senator. Part of Rome's establishment," Publius Carbo haughtily, or shrilly, pronounced, puffing out what little chest he possessed.

"I know," the Briton flatly said, before covering the anti-Semite's mouth with his hand (he had grown more than tired of listening to his voice). Manius then slowly pushed the stylus into the politician's left eye. Carbo struggled for a moment or two, but eventually his body went limp. Death is the solution to all problems. No man - no problem.

Vulso realised that he had no need to fight his way out of the warehouse, as Agrippa had fought his way in. Having observed Varro re-enter the building, Agrippa had second-guessed his intention to ignore his orders and attempt to save Manius. The consul had hoped that Vulso would rein his agent in, or at the very least not join him in any act of recklessness.

Agrippa quickly ordered his men to storm the building and engage the enemy. Most of Carbo's retinue surrendered immediately. The remainder offered little resistance. The guards posted outside the door to the backroom were attracted to the commotion at the front of the warehouse. They thought about trying to escape - but ended up surrendering quicker than a Gaul in winter.

The light blazed through the shutters, illuminating motes of dust and dead, translucent skin. Agrippa pursed his lips and gently shook his head as he entered the room and took in the scene. He fancied that the expression on Labeo's face was one of extreme shock, as though he had just found out he had lost an election. Carbo's mouth was open, as if he were about to sing. Or he had died mid-scream. The room was a picture of vengeance, as opposed to justice. But perhaps, sometimes, vengeance equates to justice. There are worse fates that Carbo and Labeo could have suffered. Agrippa was just at a loss to think of them right now. The main thing was, the Jewish quarter would be safe. Or the main thing was that Caesar would be pleased. Another potential rival or enemy had perished. Or the main thing was, Varro and Manius had survived.

"Firstly, let us deal with the living, rather than the dead," Agrippa remarked, as he instructed one of his men to fetch his personal surgeon, to tend to Manius' injuries. He then turned his attention towards his agent. Varro appeared remarkably calm, given the drama and violence which had just ensued. He wasn't sure whether his sense of duty towards his friend made him a better, or worse, agent. Spies should try to shed their emotions - and any notions of honour or morality, Agrippa judged. It may keep them dead inside. But it would also keep them alive. Yet the soldier wasn't entirely convinced of his own argument.

"Well, this is all a mess," the consul exclaimed, as if rebuking some errant schoolboys. "But messes exist, so we can learn to clean them up. I will be generous and say that you misinterpreted my orders, rather than disobeyed them... I am glad you are both safe. I do not have the time to train up any replacements for you... Few will mourn Carbo. Although I imagine that Nerva will lament that there won't be a trial. The fee he would have earned, either defending or prosecuting him, would have helped pay off his debts... Now, instead of creating a mess, how close are you to cleaning one up? Have you progressed in your investigation?"

"Maybe," Varro vaguely replied, thinking how he was confident he could now re-cover the dagger. The agent was just unsure who he would retrieve it for. Agrippa, or Maecenas.

## 25.

*None of us is without sin.*

Varro walked with a heavy step - and heavier heart - through Rome as he made his way to Tiro's house. He passed through some public gardens and along the river at one point, but still failed to find some fresh air and quietude. The agent felt dizzy, nauseous. Varro thought it might be due to the drama and exertion of the afternoon's events. But, more so, it was due to where he was going. He needed to clear his head, do his job. As much as the agent yearned to be away from Rome, he knew that his work had saved him over the past year - albeit Varro knew it was also now damning him. He felt like he had been tossed into a mortar - and the pestle of life was grinding him down.

*You need to laugh at yourself more, like you used to.*

The investigator did and didn't believe it. *It couldn't be, it couldn't be*, he asserted in his mind, like a choral refrain. But he knew that it could be. That it was true. Tiro had murdered Herennius. Not only would the piece of brown material match Tiro's cloak, but, Ovid was right, the past isn't just the past. It wasn't for Varro (he still loved Lucilla), so why should it be for others? Tiro had killed Herennius out of an act of vengeance, for executing Cicero all those years ago. Hate perhaps lives on in the heart more than love.

It was an effort, strain, to think of his noble friend committing the bloody crime. Tiro was not still Tiro. Rome had lost even more of its lustre, if it had any left in the first place.

Varro reached Tiro's property, Cicero's former residence. The previous owner's shade must have haunted the secretary on a daily basis, just as Varro's father's shade had once haunted him. One might as well try to exhume all the dust from a house, as shoo away all one's memories. Although rich with recollections, the property was now largely devoid of furniture, as Tiro had moved or sold the bulk of it. A few statues and ornaments remained, but the house reminded Tiro of a mausoleum. His footsteps echoed along the marble corridors like he was being followed.

A slave led Varro out into the atrium, where Tiro was spending the afternoon reading. The slave had admitted the aristocrat without forewarning his master, having done so numerous times before. Appius Varro's son was always welcome at the house. The sunlight was weak, jaundiced. The plants were dying. The chipped statues, of Fortuna and Sancus, had their backs turned towards the old man. Tiro was sitting on a large couch, which looked like it might soon swallow him whole, Varro fancied, given his friend's increasingly slight figure. The same wisps of silvery-grey hair covered his liver-spotted scalp. The same bat-like ears protruded from his large head. But something was different. New, subtle shades - of shame and sorrow - were cast over his features, like a grim morning mist. How much had it been life, or Rome, which had ground him down? Varro would have to think more intently on the question, to provide an answer. The brown cloak was spread out on a nearby chair. The agent felt that the world would be able to see where a piece had been torn off.

Tiro squinted a little on first seeing the figure standing before him. It looked like Varro, but his expression was odd. Pained. His tunic was also different. Dirty. Even bloody? If he doesn't know the truth, he probably suspects it, Tiro considered.

*The truth will out. Murder will out. Both expressions are one in the same, in this instance.*

"Rufus, what an unexpected pleasure," Tiro said, his voice cracking. His smile similarly faltered - all but stillborn.

For as many questions as Varro wanted to ask, for as many lines as he prepared on his walk over, a pregnant pause hung in the air. It suddenly felt ludicrous, or incredibly rude, turning up at his old friend's house and accusing him of murder - with little or no evidence to substantiate his claim.

"Or perhaps I should have expected you would call on me at some point, both in your capacity as a friend and an investigator," Tiro added. "You have a new tailor it seems, although I cannot altogether say he's an improvement on the last one. Have you been labouring?"

"My father used to say that just once he would like to see me do an honest day's work. I fear he's still waiting."

"I like to think I have tried to be honest throughout my life, which is no mean achievement when you consider I used to serve a politician. Given my surfeit of perceived honesty, perhaps I thought I had earned a dishonest act. I regret having lied to you Rufus, but I do not regret having murdered the man who killed my master. The only thing I regret, concerning the deed, is waiting too long."

Varro didn't envision his assignment ending this way. There was no sense of satisfaction, or roar of applause. Part of him wished that what Tiro had just said could be unsaid. The agent sat down, lest his legs gave way, on a chair opposite the couch. He breathed deeply, wearily. To grant him more time to compose his thoughts he poured out a cup of water for both himself and his, now, potential prisoner. Varro was tempted to ask for something stronger. Much stronger. It had been the longest of longest days. He still hadn't quite processed the events from earlier on in the day. Both he and Manius had nearly died. Varro felt like a pane of glass, which could shatter at any moment. The gods were testing him - or just being cruel for cruelty's sake. Tiro interpreted his silence as a prompt to talk - or confess - more. Neither party was terribly well-practised in how an interrogation should be conducted.

"I owed my master one last service, before I left Rome. I know that probably sounds foolish. But you're wise enough to know that's why it's true. People will argue that foolishness is the province of the young - just look at those self-righteous students who blindly follow the likes of Publius Carbo and his ilk. But everyone can contract foolishness. It's like the common cold. Foolishness may well be our most defining quality. It can cause us to commit acts of wickedness, or be a spur to be brave and virtuous… I could never quite free myself of knowing what my duty was. I suppose my decision to leave Rome brought the issue to a head. Vengeance never wholly subsides. It's like a scorpion, ready to strike after seemingly remaining dormant… I know I have lived my life in another man's shadow. I served him, even after he died. But Cicero's life, cause, was fundamentally a noble one. Perhaps all the more noble for being tragic. I, more than anyone, knew his flaws. I lived with him daily. When one gets close to a portrait one can see the cracks in the paint and misplaced brush strokes. But it's important to step back sometimes and take in the picture as a whole. Despite his vanity, despite his political chicanery, Cicero was a force for good in Rome. He sacrificed his life for Rome, long before he died for it. Herennius deserved his fate. He deserved to die many deaths, for the crimes committed after executing my master. I kept track of his life, hoping that he would one day do something so atrocious that it would heat my blood to such an extent, that I would be compelled to slay the monster. But I remained a coward, to my shame, for far too long. Ironically, I now finally feel free, even if it means I will soon be incarcerated."

Tiro spoke as much to himself, as he did Varro. His rheumy eyes grew teary as he remembered his master. His lip curled, as he pronounced the name of his victim. Varro didn't quite know how to react. He was a cracked mosaic, made-up of countless tiles: shock, abhorrence, compassion and confoundment. Tiro paused in his confession, to quench his thirst. Another awkward silence hung in the air, like a vulture circling a carcass. This time Varro felt obliged to speak.

"Can you tell me more about the night in question?"

"I was willing to wait that evening, all evening if required. The gods knew I had waited for years. It was Lucilla who informed me about the gathering, in an offhand comment about the party she was due to attend. I imagined it would run on late. Herennius would be drunk by the end of proceedings. I stood across the street from the house, shrouded in darkness. I counted the guests in and I counted them out. I was surprised to see Lentulus Nerva in attendance, until I discovered that the advocate had sold his daughter to the fiend. Nerva once came to visit me, shortly after Cicero died. He made a prepared, spontaneous speech about how much he admired my master. But in truth he was angling to gain access to Cicero's client list… Once the guests departed, I approached the house, offering up a prayer to the gods that Herennius would be still awake - and alone. My prayers were answered. The gods were on my side. Herennius answered the door himself, imagining that I was one of his guests, returning to retrieve something they had forgotten. He was confused by my appearance. I explained that I was leaving Rome and in the process of selling some of Cicero's valuables. I thought he might be interested. On remarking that I was desperate, and therefore he thought he could take advantage of me, he let me in. My host was still drinking heavily at this point. He didn't suspect for one moment that my motives were anything but pure, or pecuniary.

"I am glad you do not have any hard feelings relating to what happened all those years ago, he explained. I have all but forgotten about it. Business is business. He picked up the golden dagger, which had been a present from Antony and Fulvia, and gazed at it fondly as he spoke. It was at that point when I struck. Vengeance gave me the strength of a man half my age. I was confident that I could do it. I had pictured murdering him for so long that I considered myself well trained, in some respects. The knife belonged there. The thin blade went through his chest and punctured his lung. He barely made a sound as he fell. He turned and landed on a couch, softening the noise of his fall. There was not a spot of blood on me. I planned beforehand to make the crime look like a robbery, so I took what valuables were to hand, including the gold dagger. I have kept everything, not that I consider them trophies of any sort... I never imagined that you would be placed in charge of the investigation, although I didn't discount that I might somehow be on someone's long list of suspects. I do not suppose you could disclose what led you to suspect me?"

"You snagged your cloak on the gate, as you entered or exited the scene."

"The apparel oft proclaims the man," Tiro muttered, wistfully - permitting himself the faintest of smiles. He felt more resignation, than rage, at being caught. "It seems your application now exceeds your laziness. You will be considered an effective agent. Be wary of where the path of your new vocation may lead you though, Rufus. A life dedicated to deception will invariably cause you to deceive yourself. You will have to lie for a living, even more than a politician or lawyer. You will often be asked to distort the truth, to such an extent that your soul may be distorted too. The darkness always returns and dominates, Cicero once told me. As ever, he was right. Even though I have finally paid my due to my master, I cannot envision seeing much light for the remainder of my days. I worry that, as an agent for Caesar, you may be travelling down a path from which you will be unable to return."

Varro let his friend's words linger. Perhaps Tiro might muse upon how much his own soul had been besmirched and distorted, from killing a man in cold blood. The unassuming kindness and cheerful humour, which he had always esteemed Tiro for, had disappeared from his aspect. He seemed hollowed out. Only sorrow remained. If that. Varro wondered how, haunted by his duty and grief, had Tiro been able to remain so kind and cheerful in the face of such an unjust world? The agent didn't quite know whether to admire his friend for his (tragic) heroism - or condemn him for his fraudulence. Surely his goodness was just an act? Varro desperately wanted to believe in Tiro's decency, rather than deception. The gods only knew how Rome needed every decent man it could find. There were precious few in the Senate House.

"You say you owe a duty to Cicero, to avenge his death. Popilius, Mark Antony and Fulvia have already met their fate. Lepidus, should you consider him responsible, is famous for his obscurity, and living in exile. Herennius was only following the orders of Caesar. Should I be worried that you will one day pay him a visit in the middle of the night?"

"I made my peace with Octavius a long time ago. In some ways he avenged Cicero too, defeating Antony and his she-wolf of a wife. Shortly after my master's death Octavius visited me. He sought my forgiveness. I said it was not my place to forgive him, but in some ways it was. Caesar confessed how he would carry the burden of Cicero's death throughout his life, but he hoped it would make him stronger rather than weaker. When he signed other death warrants, it would give him pause. When he enacted legislation, he would ask if Cicero would approve. His library would always have a place for his books... The split between my master and Octavius was perhaps as fateful as the split between Caesar and Pompey, when Julia died. Such personal relationships can and do shape the entire world, for good or ill. Mainly ill, it seems. For once, I thought Octavius was exercising his conscience, rather than his charm, when he spoke with me in private. He seemed genuinely contrite and I was willing to give him the benefit of the doubt. Octavius didn't have to visit me and offer his condolences. But he did... My master was genuinely fond of the boy, as he was when he first met him. He often imagined he could serve as a mentor to Octavius, as Aristotle had tutored Alexander the Great. Cicero was not one for taking back his words, but he always regretted saying that Octavius should be praised, honoured and disposed of, once he defeated Antony... Your father told me a story of how he visited Octavius one day, and he overheard him talking to a boy in his garden. The youth was reading a book, written by my master. He went to conceal it on seeing Caesar approach, no doubt fearing the great man would disapprove of his choice of text. Caesar saw the book however and perused several pages, before remarking: "An eloquent man, my child, an eloquent man, and a patriot." I can think of fewer finer epitaphs for my master. Your father also mentioned that there were tears in Octavius' eyes, when he spoke. So, in answer to your question, I will not be paying Caesar a visit in the middle of the night. I imagine there may well be a queue outside his house, of those with a grievance against him, already."

There were tears welling in Tiro's eyes too, when he made his confession - albeit Varro couldn't quite decide on the cause of his tears. Was he reliving the grief of his master's passing? Was he crying from shame and the failure of getting caught? A fear of punishment and death? Guilt?

"Does anyone else know of your crime?"

"No. You are the first person I have told. I thought I owed you the truth, Rufus. I came close to telling your father once, about my duty and desire to murder my master's executioner. It was when I eventually told him about that final, fateful day. I've never spoken to you about Cicero's death. I have sufficiently replayed the scene in private, not to want to air it in public. But you should know. Through the biography I have completed, history will know too... Octavius, Antony and Lepidus formed their triumvirate, carving up the world and signing the death warrant of the Republic. The proscription lists were the first order of business. Apparently, Antony added a name to the list just because he wanted to get his hands on the man's collection of Corinthian bronze statues. Octavius fought hard for two days to remove Cicero's name from the list. But not hard enough. Upon hearing the news my master planned to join Brutus in Macedonia. We disembarked but then Cicero made the decision to turn back. He said he experienced a presentiment, that there would be a storm - although I had never known him to be a slave to superstition before. He also argued that if he returned to Rome, he could change Octavius' mind. "If I could just talk to him. I need only tell him that Julius would have never given a similar order," he explained. In truth, I believe Cicero was just reluctant to leave centre stage. "I will die in the country I have so often saved," he pronounced. Yet he resolved to travel down the coast and leave for Macedonia once again. The night before we intended to disembark, Cicero and I enjoyed a meal together. We talked long into the night. He asserted that Rome had been cleaved in two. Its citizens were either sons of Caesar, or sons of Cicero. Or, its citizens were sons of whores or soldiers. His spirit had also been cleaved in two. "The only thing that the two opposing sides can agree on, Tiro, is that they could not cope without you," he remarked. "My only regret is that I did not set down in writing how much I have to thank you for. You define the meaning of loyalty and friendship" The following day we were apprehended, within touching distance of our vessel. We were tantalisingly close to our freedom. Popilius Laenas led the wolf pack, sent to hunt Cicero down. He was far from the bravest military tribune to ever serve Rome, but he may have been the most sycophantic. His soldiers ambushed us along the shore, as we appeared out of the treeline. Cicero was being carried in his litter. He was reading Medea, by Euripides, at the time. I read the play every year, on the anniversary of his death. I dare say I know the entire text by heart. "Hate is a bottomless cup; I will pour and pour... I understand too much the dreadful act I'm going to commit, but my judgement can't check my anger... Who can stop grief's avalanche once it begins to roll?... Death is the only water to wash away this dirt." Myself and others in our retinue were willing to take up arms against Popilius' men but Cicero was resigned to his fate. "It's fine, Tiro," he calmly stated. "This is one situation where I cannot call upon your service. No one pays his secretary that much. I have witnessed enough bloodshed to last me four lifetimes. Keep your weapons sheathed. At the end, at least, I would like to find some peace." I will never forget how, after he here spoke, Cicero nodded at me - as if to say that he was ready for death. Or the nod could have been a prompt to remind me to record his last words, for posterity. Perhaps, in the next life, I will be able to ask him and find out. Herennius did not hesitate in carrying out Popilius' command to execute my master. Indeed, he grinned, almost lasciviously, in response to the task. Cicero extended his head, out of the litter. His face was wrinkled and strewn with sweat and dust. Wisps of grey hair blew in the wind. The sea hissed in the background. Tiredness hung over his expression, like a veil. Yet there was still nobility in his countenance - and soul. "Come here, soldier. There is nothing proper about what you are doing, but at least make sure you cut off my head properly," he remarked to Herennius, checking and chiding the brute. I imagine Herennius had never encountered someone who met his end with such dignity and humour. He slit his throat. Blood soaked the sand. The image is still branded in my mind's eye. As per Antony and Fulvia's instruction, the soldier commenced to hack off my master's head, so it could be presented to the triumvir as a trophy. I am not quite sure what else to say. I hope you can understand why I thought Herennius deserved to die. Should someone kill

Manius, would you not want to avenge his death? I will equally accept any punishment. I fear my walking stick may snap, should I attempt to flee."

Tiro raised the corner of his mouth in a wan smile. He seemed uncommonly brittle. His skin was like parchment or Varro imagined that, if he touched his old friend, he might turn to ash.

## Epilogue.

"Sometimes justice equates to mercy," Varro argued, as he explained to Tiro how he would not be apprehending his friend. The authorities would remain none the wiser about his crime.

"Your father would have obeyed the law and reported me to the authorities."

"I am not my father, for good or ill. Rome's loss can remain Puteoli's gain," Varro remarked, thinking how Tiro's conscience may haunt him now in a different way. Any time spent incarcerated would be tantamount to a death sentence for the old man. He may well be executed, as a punishment to fit the crime. But Varro did not want his friend's death on his hands.

"How will you explain that you have retrieved the dagger, but not apprehended the murderer?"

"As with one of my poems, I will make it up as I go along."

Varro held the golden, bejewelled knife in his hands. It was heavier than he expected. He found himself agreeing with Ovid. It was a shiny yet vulgar object. As spotless as the glowing blade was, the agent looked at the dagger with an expression of distaste or disdain, as though blood was dripping from its tip.

Varro walked the streets of Rome again, trying to provide a semblance of order to his chaotic thoughts. His mind flailed, like a half-severed limb. The idea of virtue seemed even more of a confidence trick than normal. Part of him wanted to descend into the Subura, have the earth swallow him up. Each laboured breath he took resembled a world-weary sigh. Muscles ached in his body, which he didn't know he had. He craved a cup, or jug, of wine - even if it made his headache worse.

One issue which buzzed around in his headache, like a gadfly, was the mystery concerning the murder of Sestius. There was still a missing piece of the puzzle out there. Tiro had professed to having nothing to do with it. "Ironically, Sestius may have been the victim of a common robbery, the kind that I had intended Herennius' murder to look like." Varro was confident there was more to it than that, however. Nerva could well have been behind the killing. Or even Cornelia. Sestius was as much assassinated as murdered too, which meant that Pulcher would remain a key suspect. But Varro judged that Caesar would allow the mystery to remain unsolved, as he would soon possess his coveted trophy.

The temptation was but fleeting, to deliver the knife up to Maecenas. But he could not commit such a dishonourable act. Even if it was a conceit, it was a good conceit. A good lie.

*I owe a duty to Agrippa.*

Varro was wary of selling what little he had left of his soul to Maecenas. He heeded Tiro's words, that once one starts down a certain path it is difficult, if not impossible, to find your way back. Varro had scant desire to be in

Maecenas' debt, or have Maecenas be in his. Manius' advice chimed in his ears too. He needed to trust Lucilla, that she would see through Licinius' act.

*She's a keen theatre attendee. She can recognise a second-rate performer when she sees one.*

He did not want anyone's help, least of all Maecenas', in winning Lucilla back. Varro resolved to tell his former wife how he felt. If he lost her, so be it. But the past wasn't dead. It wasn't even past.


Agrippa flexed his hand from the strain of replying to various correspondence and looked up to greet his agent. The consul appeared to be his usual sedate, equitable self, as though he hadn't drawn sweat all afternoon. As though he hadn't mobilised the Praetorian Guard and ordered an assault on a warehouse or prevented a riot from destroying part of the city. As though his agents hadn't murdered a tribune and former senator. It was business as usual.

Varro first asked after Manius. Agrippa's surgeon had tended to his injuries. Manius was back home in bed. The consul had visited him and explained to Camilla that her husband was a hero, having assisted his force of praetorians in quelling an attack on the Jewish quarter.

Agrippa permitted himself a smile when Varro revealed that he had the dagger in his possession. The consul pursed his lips and ruefully shook his head when holding the item in his hand, however.

"All this, for this?"

The agent recounted how, as much as he could have reason to suspect a veritable legion of people, his investigation was leading nowhere. Varro judged that Herennius was the kind of man who would want to keep his riches close. And he was surprised by the lack of valuables he had found during his principle search of the house. His conclusion was that the dagger could still be at the property, hidden away with other valuables.

"When I ventured down to the cellar again, I noticed something strange yet familiar about one of the wine racks. The piece of furniture, similar to something in my own cellar, had a false back. The wine rack was on a hinge. When I pulled it open, I saw an alcove containing the knife. Herennius must have put it back there at some point in the night, before he was murdered. I couldn't quite believe it."

"I cannot quite believe it too," Agrippa replied, arching an eyebrow in scepticism. "If I ask you no questions, you can tell me no lies. You are a spy, after all, Rufus. I must allow you to keep some secrets. The main thing is that Caesar will be pleased. You have completed your assignment. You are beginning to make a name for yourself."

"I know."

*That's what I am afraid of.*


Varro headed home, ignoring the drizzle peppering his face. The rain freshened and fuelled the acrid stench, which covered the city like a second skin. Despite various issues resting on his mind Varro's body needed to rest even more, and he quickly fell asleep.

He woke, washed and dressed, whilst fending off some subtle, and not so subtle, advances from Aspasia. Varro then accompanied Fronto in paying a visit to their friend.

Camilla was understandably mired in a state of worry, although she was also visibly proud when recounting how the consul had called at the house and praised Manius as a hero of Rome. "I was tempted to say that next time Rome should find someone else to play the hero," Camilla remarked. She also expressed relief when the surgeon reported that Manius would not suffer any long-term injuries.

Varro entered the room alone. Viola lay on the bed, her head resting on her master's shin (which was one of the only parts of his body which wasn't in pain). The dog hadn't left his side since he came home, even when Camilla had called out that her dinner was ready.

"I've looked better, I imagine," Manius said, good-humouredly, to his friend. His face was bloody, bruised and swollen. Lumpy. Ironically, he looked like a gladiator after a hard-fought contest.

"I've seen you after a hangover. You've looked worse," Varro replied, offering up a smile whilst writhing with sadness and anger on the inside, at witnessing his tortured friend.

"Unfortunately, I may have found a job that's even more perilous than being your bodyguard," the agent said, whilst wincing slightly in pain as he shifted his body position on the bed. The hurt he was suffering meant little to the Briton, compared to the hurt he felt at having to deceive his wife. He realised now how much of a double-life he would have to lead. Manius told himself that what Camilla didn't know couldn't hurt her. He felt his reasoning was logical, yet somehow rang false. The Briton desisted from cursing his fate - and new profession - entirely though. The lives of Benjamin and countless others had been saved due to his actions. He had paid in blood - and no one could know about his sacrifice - but the price had been worth paying, Manius judged. Publius Carbo's new kind of politics would not take root, at least until some other vile demagogue picked up his baton.

Varro told his friend about Tiro.

"I have known the man almost all my life. But it seems I may not have known him at all. Some of the things he said, or rather the way he said them, chilled me to the bone. Vengeance, rather than virtue, sustained him. I thought him the best of men. He still could be the best of men... We must keep the truth from Fronto. I do not want him thinking less of his friend... Am I doing the right thing, in letting his crime remain unpunished? I still believe him to be a good man. Perhaps, in a life filled with so many acts of kindness, Tiro is owed some kindness back. Who knows? Duty and truth. I fear I still own more questions than answers. Nothing exists except atoms and empty space; everything else is opinion."

Manius puffed out his cheeks in astonishment, whilst Varro gave his report of the afternoon's events. The world was as broken as his ribs. If any other man would have accused Tiro of murder, he may not have believed them. At times the Briton looked pained - but it had nothing to do with his physical injuries.

"I'm not sure I have any answers for you either. All I know is that the more I get to know people, the more I love my dog," Manius half-joked, as he lovingly stroked Viola behind the ear and fed her a treat.

The lamp flickered. The consul yawned. He felt like he could fall asleep on a stone slab, or bed of nails. But he would wait up some more until he retired. Not only did Agrippa want to reply to one last letter, but he wanted his wife to fall asleep before he entered the bedchamber. Her augur had decreed it to be one of their nights when they should couple. She liked to keep to his schedule. Even more than for herself, she wanted a child in order to please her uncle. But tonight, as with other nights, Agrippa was not in the mood. If need be, he would explain to his wife that he was suffering from a headache.

Yet the consul was in a good mood. It was far from the noblest sentiment he had ever experienced but Agrippa revelled in Maecenas' failure, more than even his own success. He grinned, mischievously, as he recalled the message he had sent to his ally earlier in the evening. He pictured Maecenas' crestfallen expression, indeed he raised the corners of his mouth in correlation to the lowering of his rival's. He had bested Maecenas, on various fronts. Varro had told Agrippa of Maecenas' attempt to recruit him as an agent, as well as a poet. *All is fair in love and espionage.* Varro declared that he wanted to be "honest" with his employer. Honesty was not the most valued trait in his profession. Agrippa had a niggling suspicion that Varro was being honest about his dealings with Maecenas in order to make him more inclined, susceptible, into believing his story about recovering the dagger.

The object lay on his desk. It had seemingly been Herennius' most prized possession, even over his wife. His greatest trophy. Agrippa remembered how Popilius Laenas commissioned a statue of himself, wearing a wreath, seated beside Cicero's severed head, after Antony had lauded him and paid a bonus. The act - and work of art - were both monstrosities. Agrippa could no longer smile, thinking about the shameful death of one of Rome's greatest citizens. Although the politic statesman had been an opponent, Agrippa had always been fond of Cicero. His wit was as sharp as any soldier's blade. Caecilia had been fond of him too. She was the daughter of Atticus, Cicero's confidante and friend. "When he dies, a light will go out across the entire empire," she once remarked. Octavius remembered Cicero with affection as well. Agrippa often noticed his companion reading Cicero's works. He regularly endowed libraries with his books - or sent copies out to friends as gifts. Agrippa considered it more likely that the garish dagger in front of him would remind Caesar of the guilt he felt at his death, rather than the affection he felt for his old mentor. But perhaps that was the point.

Agrippa read over the letter in front of him once again. The governor of a province in the East had caught one of his agents embezzling funds. The veteran spy, Lutatius Calenus, had been claiming money in order to pay non-existent sources of intelligence. The assets were not real. But the fraud was. The governor was calling for Agrippa to recall and punish the agent. Yet Calenus also oversaw a couple of genuine assets, ones which provided regular, valuable intelligence. Agrippa would instruct the governor to keep the spy in his post. He may not be a good man, but he is a good agent, the consul would argue, lamentably. It was a far from perfect world.

*May the gods save us, for we seem unable to save ourselves.*

The light was incandescent. He would castigate his slaves for burning too many candles. Gaius Maecenas paced around his study. Incandescent with rage. He scrunched up the message from Agrippa in his left hand. The soul of civility became the soul of resentment. He wanted to stamp his foot, smash the mosaic depicting a scene from Virgil's *Georgics* which lay beneath his feet. In his right hand he carried a stylus, which he was tempted to use to score across the faces of the portraits on the wall. He resented their judgmental, superior expressions. A fine alabaster bust of Augustus sat on his desk. He was a heartbeat away from storming across the room and throwing the ornament against the wall. The bust had been a gift from Caesar, which was why he did and didn't want to destroy it.

The political fixer called for more wine, bellowing out the order. The shrill noise echoed throughout the marble-clad home. He should not have to wait for whatever he desired. He was descended from Etruscan royalty (or so he commissioned Horace to posit in one of his poems).

Maecenas breathed, seethed. His usually smooth brow grew corrugated with severity. No amount of sonorous poetry, or sweet nothings from mistresses or an Adonis, could quieten his animus now. He could consider himself the third most powerful man in the world. But it wasn't enough. Maecenas sat down, still holding the message in his recently scrubbed and manicured hands. Despite the gnawing pain it caused, throbbing like a bee sting, he read over Agrippa's short letter again.

*"Dear Gaius,*

*It gives me great pleasure to tell you that one of my agents has retrieved the knife. Our treasure hunt is over. I am letting you know, as it still may be the case you are attempting to procure the item for Caesar. I wouldn't want you to go to any further trouble for nothing... I understand that you have made an approach to Rufus Varro, to recruit him to your stable. I am sure he is flattered by your offer but, unfortunately, he is content to remain with his current patron... You should come over for dinner soon. I have recently employed a new cook, Tillius Silanus. I understand your new cook studied under him..."*

Perhaps the dour, prudish widower was not devoid of a sense of humour after all, Maecenas considered. As goading - galling - as the letter was, Maecenas was further put out by reports coming in that Agrippa was responsible for saving Rome, or at least the Jewish quarter, from an attack by Publius Carbo's followers. It was just a shame that the consul didn't tragically die during his bout of heroism, Maecenas posed. He felt deficient, diminished. The spymaster had been unaware of Carbo's activities. Before, he would have known what Carbo was going to do, before he knew it himself. Maecenas could blame his agents for his lack of intelligence, but he knew he was to blame too. He castigated himself. Maecenas knew that Caesar always asked the same question he asked of anyone. How useful a man is he to me? If he lost the support and confidence of Caesar, Maecenas knew that his enemies would move against him.

*You've been enjoying the good life for too long. You have grown weak, culpable. Your days have been filled with poetry, rather than politics... At least I will no longer have Licinius as a distraction... Never reward failure. He says he can win the woman back, but his heart, or head, have not been in the assignment. Both Lucilla and the dagger slipped through his fingers. I will send him on a mission now, situated at the arsehole end of the empire... Varro will rue the day he disappointed me too. No one says "no" to me, without suffering the consequences... I will bide my time, but eventually an opportunity will arise to right the wrongdoing. Vengeance is a dish best served cold. I almost feel sorry for him. Almost... I may have lost a battle, but I will win the war...*

"More wine!"

"More wine," was usually his first thought on such occasions but Varro wished to be sober when he met with Lucilla. He could always have a drink, to celebrate or commiserate, after his conversation with her. He had been less nervous when he first proposed, all those years ago. The poet had also been less in love, as much as he had been in love with Lucilla back then.

"Are you surprised?" Varro said to Manius, after citing his intention to ask Lucilla to marry him the night before, as his companion convalesced.

"I am just surprised that it has taken you this long to realise how much you still love her."

A storm in the night, which Varro had slept through from exhaustion, had cleared the muggy air. Virgin white clouds scudded across a startling blue sky. Varro walked with purpose towards Lucilla's house. He barely spared a thought for the likes of Maecenas, Nerva, Publius Carbo or even Tiro. They were ghosts from his past, more than shades at his shoulder. Rather he thought of Lucilla and his villa at Arretium, and the prospect that the former would come away with him to the latter. He started to pick out which books he would take away with him, prioritising those which she would enjoy too. He looked forward breathing in lungfuls of fresh air, gulping it down like wine. He promised himself that he would write again. But not poetry. Instead he would try to write a biography of Cincinnatus.

"I do not believe that my mistress is admitting visitors today," Diana pronounced, with even more piquancy than normal - eyeing Varro with suspicion at best or, at worse, unfiltered antagonism.

"I am sure if you put in a good word for me, you will get her to change her mind," Varro replied. The slave noticed a hint of desperation, as well as playfulness, in his tone, however. He wiped his sweaty palms on his tunic more than once and there was a rare vulnerability, or diffidence, in the nobleman's expression. The scar on his forehead itched, again.

Diana disappeared but shortly afterwards another slave opened the door and led Varro out into the garden. A smudge of dirt marked her left cheek. Lucilla wore an apron and ill-fitting dress which did little to flatter her figure. That she wasn't always obsessed by her appearance made Lucilla all the more attractive.

A mellow, sumptuous smell of freshly picked apples scented the air. He could smell honeysuckle and love-lies-bleeding too.

"I am just gardening," she said, curious and a little worried by his strange expression. Although she still smiled upon seeing him, beaming like the serene sunshine proliferating the scene.

"I am a professional investigator. I can deduce such things now, would you believe?"

"And there I was thinking that the only thing you took professional pride in, was a life dedicated to indolence," Lucilla replied, with equal good, sarcastic, humour.

The smile fell from his face, however, when Varro asked Lucilla to sit down on a nearby bench. He licked his lips and yearned for a cup of water to moisten his parched throat. But the words couldn't wait. They had waited long enough. He gulped and tried to catch his breath. The agent had perhaps been less anxious during the attack on the warehouse, the day before.

"You sound serious, which is rare for you. Usually you are only serious about treating life as a joke," Lucilla remarked, growing a little anxious herself. Although, she was still pleased to see him. She wanted Varro to be one of the first to know she had ended her affair with Licinius.

"I am going to be serious - and sincere - for a moment or two," Varro declared, as he sat down on the bench next to her. His hands were trembling. "If I do not say something now, I fear I never will. I have recently told Fronto and Manius how much you mean to me. It's somewhat more important though that I tell you... Please do not think I am here just because I want to spoil your relationship with Licinius. I will respect any choice you make... I have loved you for some time. Indeed, I probably never stopped loving you. I have never quite deserved you, but I would be a wretch should I be with someone who I do deserve... When I am with you, I don't want to be with anyone else. And I am half the man I could be, when I am not with you. "We are each of us angels with only one wing, and we can only fly when embracing one another," Lucretius wrote... Growing old with you will help me stay young. Give me something to live for. I have no desire to be married to my work anymore. I can survive without Caesar - and Caesar can survive without me... I have taken things, all my life. But the only way to become more than oneself is to give something of oneself. I hope it doesn't sound too much of a joke to your ears, but I am ready to be faithful and honourable. If you believe in me, then I will believe in myself."

Varro here took a breath and caught Lucilla's eye, to try and gauge her reaction to his confession. He felt he might be coming across too desperate, feverish. "Love is a disease though," he had once written. In contrast to his febrile manner Lucilla appeared calm, but not cold. Receptive, but unresolved to any decision.

Varro pictured her earlier, whilst walking to the house, wearing her favourite silk dress and finest jewels (ones bought before her affair with Pulcher). But this was more beautiful for being real. Lucilla removed her headscarf. Her glossy hair tumbled down her kind, elegant features. She tucked a few strands behind her ears, but some remained hanging in front of her face. She had loved him for the man he used to be - or could be again. But she realised, over the past year or so, how she loved her former husband for who he was now.

"I remember this time last year. I said how sorry I was, for everything - and you believed me. I need you to believe me now, when I say that I love you. I may even love you more than Manius loves Viola," Varro said, hoping that his joke might ease the perceived tension in the air.

He just wished her to say something back now. Anything. But Varro's wish wasn't granted.

Instead, Lucilla rose to her feet. He tried to breath in her perfume, but she wasn't wearing any. She took a step and he considered she was just going to walk back into the house, without saying uttering a sound. Actions can speak louder than words. Varro thought he was about to lose her forever and he hung his head in grief accordingly.

But Lucilla lifted-up his face in her soft hands and gazed, tenderly, into his teary eyes. She first bent over and kissed him on his brow. His scar stopped itching. Lucilla then kissed Varro full on the lips, before smiling that smile which made him smile. Finally, the graceful woman kneeled in front of the elated nobleman and took his hands, which had stopped trembling, in hers. She was grinning ear to ear - and tearing up too.

"Rufus Varro, will you marry me?"

**End Note.**

*Spies of Rome: Blood & Vengeance* is a mixture of fact and fiction. Should you be interested in reading more about the real life characters featured in the book then you may find the following titles of interest: *The First Emperor*, by Anthony Everitt; *The Roman Revolution*, by Ronald Syme; *Marcus Agrippa*, by Lindsay Powell.

Should you be interested in reading more fiction about the era then I can heartily recommend the relevant works of Steven Saylor, Peter Tonkin and Robert Harris.

Please do get in touch should you have enjoyed reading the Spies of Rome series. I am grateful to all those readers who still write to me about the *Augustus* and *Sword of Rome* series too. You can contact me at richard@sharpebooks.com

Rufus Varro and Manius will return in *Spies of Rome: Blood & Secrets*.

Richard Foreman.

**Blood & Secrets**

**Richard Foreman**

# SPIES OF ROME

First published in 2019 by Sharpe Books.

*"The difficulty is not so great to die for a friend, as to find a friend worth dying for."*
Homer.

*"We men are wretched things."*
Homer.

## 1.

Night, as black as the Acheron. Thunder rumbled in the background like a presumed dormant volcano, stirring. The distant storm growled but had yet to bare its teeth. But it would.

"It's good to see you again," Rufus Varro remarked to his late-night, unexpected guest - Aelius Vulso. The nobleman welcomed the praetorian, who was saddle sore but undaunted, to his country villa. Vulso walked across the threshold and noticed marble tiles - and some wording - on the floor. A quote from Aristotle:

*"It is during our darkest moments that we must focus to see the light."*

Varro warmly shook his hand and poured the soldier, who had travelled from Rome, a large cup of wine. "Of course, given that you are likely to be a harbinger of bad news, you are the last person I would wish to see again."

The former spy first encountered the praetorian during a mission to liberate Varro's bodyguard, Manius, from being tortured and held prisoner by the demagogue, Publius Carbo. The three men had shared more than one joke and jug of Massic since that day. Vulso could be as stern-faced as a lictor at times, but there was no doubting his courage and sense of honour, Varro considered. His men would follow him into the fires of Hades - and the officer would lead them out again too. Vulso was as tough as the old leather boots he wore. The soldier appeared slightly ill at ease however, having to visit his friend in an official capacity. His firm features were shiny with sweat. He gleamed like a freshly painted statue, the poet fancied.

An oil lamp glowed between them above a rosewood table, as the two men sat facing one another on soft-cushioned sofas. Varro encouraged his friend to help himself to the various dishes to hand which were left over from supper: honey-glazed ham, spiced mussels and asparagus tips.

Vulso downed his wine and thanked his host as he refilled his cup. As he caught his breath and quenched his thirst the praetorian took in his friend. He hadn't seen Varro for several months, after taking the decision to spend over half the year at his house in Arretium. "I'm tired of Rome. It may well be tired of me in return. Familiarity breeds contempt. Maybe absence will make the heart grow fonder, due to spending the summer in the country," Varro explained, before departing. Some things had changed. Some things hadn't. The same black curls hung over his brow, concealing the same horizontal scar. His eyes were less bloodshot. Varro drank less and slept more nowadays. He was glowing, with health and happiness. The smile was fulsome, rather than mocking or wry. Varro remarried his first wife, Lucilla, a year ago. Lucilla had given him a second chance, after the wastrel had given himself a second chance. Their mornings were spent walking and swimming in the sea. During the afternoon Varro would write, whilst his wife painted or tended to her garden. During the evenings they would have dinner with Manius and his wife, Camilla. The couple arrived last month. Camilla was expecting their first child.

"You are looking well, Rufus."

"Not working for the glory of Rome can do wonders for one's constitution - and soul. The only thing I need to get up for in the morning is my afternoon nap. I trust you are well too, Aelius."

"My sword has spent more time in, rather than out of, its scabbard of late. I'll leave you to decide whether that's a good thing or not," the broad-shouldered, barrel-chested soldier replied, shrugging.

"As much as I would wish it to be so, it's unlikely that this is a social visit. I take it that you have a message for me?" Varro asked, the smile falling from his face. His smooth, aristocratic features became pinched. He thought that Arretium might be faraway enough for him to remain untouched by the tentacles of Rome. He was wrong.

"I do not have any detailed message to pass on, Rufus. Agrippa has just asked me to accompany you back to Rome. I am as much in the dark as you. I thought you were retired."

"I thought so too. Perhaps I can't quite call myself a former spy yet. Perhaps no one can," Varro replied. His haunted expression was allied to a world-weary sigh, before he forced a half-smile. He thought of Lucilla. The nobleman promised his wife that he would no longer work as an agent for Agrippa. He had been tortured and nearly killed during his first assignment (Varro had a scar on his forehead, which served as a daily reminder of the ordeal). Manius had been tortured and nearly killed during their last mission. Even when he was a poet, the critics weren't quite as cruel as the likes of Lucius Scaurus and Publius Carbo, he judged. As an agent, working for Agrippa, he had often been charged with uncovering the truth. But perhaps it was the job of a spy to keep secrets hidden, rather than reveal them. Varro winced slightly as he remembered Tiro. Cicero's former secretary had been one of the noblest men he had ever known. A friend and mentor. Yet Tiro had proved himself to be a killer. A victim of his baser instincts. Or could he not argue that Tiro had murdered the brutish slave trader, Herennius, out of a noble duty to avenge the murder of his old master?

Varro gazed outside. Vulso was reminded of the vacant, long-distance stare of veteran soldiers he had witnessed over the years. Usually the nobleman could see a vista of pearlescent stars, or the outlines and faded colours of the flowers Lucilla planted in her garden. But the swollen darkness swallowed everything up, like a leviathan gulping down a fleet of fishing boats. The lamps on their bows extinguished. The night was blacker than the most violent bruise. Blacker than a widow's garb. Blacker than a god's humour. Unlike previously, when Agrippa summoned him, his heart failed to beat with any atom of intrigue. Duty no longer stiffened his sinews. He didn't feel that the shade of his father would be proud of him. Varro felt as if he were Odysseus, being ordered again to Troy, after finding his way back to his wife and home. He was Sisyphus. Having struggled to roll his boulder up a hill, it had just rolled back down again. The past year had been akin to a pleasant dream. But he was about to be dragged back to reality. Varro grimaced, recalling some of his previous assignments and experiences. Priests had defiled virgins, vestal or otherwise. Guilds formed themselves into riotous, rapacious gangs. Tax officials bled provinces dry, filling their coffers to fund political campaigns. Siblings poisoned one another – bitter rivals, competing over a mistress or, more often than not, over an inheritance. Slaves were beaten to death, their bodies burned. Sometimes they were burned alive. Gladiators were forced to fight when wounded. The practise was tantamount to a death sentence. Advocates colluded with criminals to bribe or assassinate witnesses. The city was infested with rats, cockroaches and, worse, politicians. The air was rib-thick with cheap perfume and vanity. Nausea was normal. Varro was sick of Rome already, and he hadn't even stepped inside its walls again. Whether they knew it or not, every soul there was guilty of something: folly; theft; dishonour. Innocence was an even rarer commodity than honesty. Some forms of innocence could be bought, via expensive advocates or rigged juries. But, all too more frequently, innocence was sold - and not even to the highest bidder. It was often given away, as freely as an exhalation of breath. A sigh. Varro wasn't quite sure if he thought less of Rome or Man. The race to the bottom between them was close to a tie. The gods only knew how he would have scorned Rome and Man even more, if not for Manius and Lucilla.

The spy hadn't seen it all, but he had seen enough. Agrippa had pimped him out enough to vulnerable wives. He had seduced them in order to gain incriminating intelligence, against their husbands. But he would not now be unfaithful to his wife. Even if the fate of Rome - sordid, pernicious Rome - depended on it. Varro had given a solemn vow that he would remain true to Lucilla. His past behaviour would remain in the past. The spy wanted to be at least half as honourable as Manius and Vulso. Agrippa, Rome, owed him more than he owed them. If Caesar was all powerful, a demi-god, then why did he need the help of a crapulent, failed poet?

Manius entered the triclinium. Like Varro, he greeted the praetorian warmly. And like Varro, he knew Vulso's presence presaged the news that they would need to return to Rome. Manius suspected Agrippa would call upon them again. He just hoped it wouldn't be so soon. Despite having retired too from Agrippa's employ, despite his wife being due to give birth, the bodyguard would loyally accompany Varro back to the capital. It had been some time since Manius had needed to protect his friend. The spy had ceased to put himself in harm's way or conduct adulterous affairs. Nights spent drinking and gambling in the Subura were few and far between, since he had remarried.

"You may no longer need my services anymore," the bodyguard posed, a few days ago.

"I am sure I'm still capable of offending people and getting myself into trouble. I don't altogether like me, Manius. I don't see why others should either," Varro drolly replied, a smile flickering on his lips. "Given that I will be spending half my time in the country now, you may wish to consider yourself semi-retired. The greatest threat to my life under this roof is Diana's cooking."

Accompanying Manius inside, after the two men had attended to the horses, was a young, fresh-faced soldier. Titus Macer. Bright green eyes glinted beneath his smooth brow. As boyish as his countenance was his chest was as broad as a scutum, his arms knotted with muscle. Varro, who had encountered Macer a few times back in Rome, thought how life had yet to sow worry lines into his features. Wine had yet to redden his nose. A woman had yet to sour his heart. He still might have faith in the gods or ruling class. He still believed war was a source of honour and glory. Varro wasn't sure if he envied how the adolescent had most of his life ahead of him - or pitied him for it. Life was largely unpleasant.

Agrippa spotted the youth on a training ground, practising his archery, last year. Much to the consternation of the aristocracy in Rome the consul believed in promoting talent over lineage. Remembering how Lucius Oppius had taken him under his wing, back in Apollonia when he was nineteen, Agrippa instructed Vulso to mentor the archer. Hopefully some of the veteran's virtues would rub off on the young soldier.

"What's the news?" Manius asked. The bodyguard cut an imposing figure. But despite suffering all manner of privation and anguish, he was still able to smile in the face of an iniquitous world. The Briton had seen his village burn and had been sold into slavery as a child. He had then been forced to fight in the arena, as a gladiator. Yet he had endured, retaining a sense of decency in an indecent world. Appius Varro had bought his freedom one day, after watching him fight. He brought Manius into his household. The gladiator was charged with tutoring the nobleman's son in swordsmanship, before serving as his bodyguard.

The thunder grew louder, as ominous as an augur in a grouchy mood. Lightning would soon slap against the earth, like a master whipping a slave.

"We're being summoned to Rome," Varro replied, devoid of enthusiasm.

"Do we know why?"

"I'm not sure yet. But it's unlikely Agrippa wants to call us back just to tell us that all is well."

Varro went to bed, but the storm woke him and his wife up. A couple of candles illuminated the chamber. Landscape paintings, by Lucilla, awash with light and colour, decorated the walls. Marble busts, of Sophocles and Plautus, sat on a table opposite the bed. The busts were a present from Lucilla to her husband, to help serve as an inspiration as he wrote his plays. The poet had become a playwright, after encouragement from his wife. Varro had composed both a comedy and tragedy in the past year. *The Honest Aedile* and *The Tragedy of Hector* had been staged, in and outside Rome, and theatre managers constantly badgered him, asking when he would be able to finish his next work.

As much as Varro tried to act as if all was well, as he reported on Vulso's arrival and his message, Lucilla remained unconvinced. She didn't know her husband completely. But she knew him enough. His body was taut, like a bow string. His features pained. Lucilla wrapped her slender leg around his and she rested her head on his chest, as if it were a pillow. She laced her fingers in his. Varro couldn't quite tell if she squeezed his hand from consolation, anger or frustration. Lucilla desperately didn't want him to leave. But she knew he needed to. She respected Agrippa but wasn't particularly fond of him right now.

Above the clamour and clap of thunder – and the thrum of rain against the tiled roof – Lucilla spoke to her husband:

"Would you like me to come back to Rome with you?"

"I would prefer to have you with me in Rome – and of course in my bed. But Camilla needs you here even more. The baby may arrive early. I will write to you every day, if I can. You know that, if I have a choice, I will refuse any assignment."

A fork of lighting plunged down upon the earth, like Neptune's trident, and for a moment the darkness rescinded. Varro could see the contoured landscape again, its farmsteads, streams and trees. But the moment, an aberration, ended.

"You will be my hero if you behave like a coward and run away from any danger."

"What do you think I've been conditioning myself for? I can run – and swim – faster than ever. Manius will also be with me. I am too cowardly to stop him. I may be back before you know it, however. This could all prove to be an anti-climax," Varro remarked, reassuringly. "Most things are in life."

"You know that won't prove to be true."

"I know. But I thought I might start lying to myself and others again. I need to rehearse, before I return to the stage. Spies are not renowned for their honesty."

"I appreciate how Agrippa may ask you to deceive someone. But remain true to yourself. You have changed a lot over the past two years," Lucilla remarked, raising her head to look her husband in the eye.

"For the better I hope."

"Well you were in the enviable position where you couldn't much change for the worse."

Varro laughed. He matched, or eclipsed, the amount of devotion in his wife's expression. Her skin glowed in the candlelight. He wanted to kiss her brow, neck, breasts and smiling lips. During the years when Varro gambled heavily, he often would pray to the goddess Fortuna for good luck. But his greatest piece of good fortune, he realised, was finding and marrying Lucilla. And then remarrying her.

"I should write this down. This is all good material for a future play."

"A husband and a wife trading insults? People can stay at home, rather than venture out to the theatre, to play out that scene. Should you ever turn our story into a drama, will you write in a happy ending?"

"I'm far too terrified of you to write anything else. Despite the storm, despite my having to leave, let's give this evening a happy ending," Varro asserted, with a piratical grin, running his fingertips down her spine.

313

After they made love Varro pretended to be asleep. He did not want his wife worrying about him. Already he was playing the spy again. Deceiving people. He lay awake, feeling as exhausted as a pack mule. Rather than returning to Rome as a conquering hero, he felt more like a condemned man, awaiting his sentence.

*Happy endings may exist in myth and literature. But not in the real world.*

## 2.

Morning.

The skies were clear but the rain, from the storm, still soaked the ground.

"I wish the storm had never ended, so you wouldn't be able to leave," Lucilla said to Varro, just after she woke.

"I have often wanted for the earth to swallow me up. Today could be my chance, given the sodden earth."

The carriage waited outside the villa. One of Varro's attendants, Milo, sat on top, with the reins in his hands. Macer sat next to him, with his weapon and a bag of arrows stashed behind. He repositioned his sunhat, gulped down some water and wiped his mouth with the back of his hand. He wore a bow-shaped grin on his face as the water sloshed down his throat and the image of Sabina swished around in his mind. He pictured the slave girl's coquettish features and satin flesh. He looked forward to returning to Rome and seeing the slave, who was attached to Varro's household. The soldier would continue his campaign to win the girl's heart.

Aelius Vulso sat on his horse. The chestnut mount, which he named Mars, was as sturdy and muscular as its owner. Its hooves scraped along the ground. Mars seemed keen to setoff, like Vulso. The praetorian pursed his lips, thinking how they were wasting daylight by tarrying too long – as he waited for Varro and Manius to say goodbye to their wives. If they had been soldiers, under his command, he would have given them short shrift.

Vulso was already thinking about being back in Rome. The officer had a batch of new recruits to break in. They needed to be work-hardened like a piece of iron, and then polished. They should take pride in their duties and uniform. They shouldn't pick-up bad habits, or a pox. Vulso started to turn over, in his head, the speech he would deliver to the green recruits:

*If, or when, you lie with a whore then make sure she's as clean as your blade. Maintain your discipline, as well as you maintain your uniform and kit... Your first duty is to serve Caesar. But Caesar is Rome, so you need to serve this city – and its people – with a similar sense of duty. You cannot just cut down a Roman citizen, as if he were some whining Gaul or hairy-arsed German... No doubt some of you have joined the Praetorian Guard because the pay and conditions are better, and the length of service shorter. If you think that you have landed on your feet, I'm here to knock you to the ground. You will learn the virtues of duty and loyalty, even if I have to pummel them into you. Some of you may well wish yourself back in the legions, in some shit-filled ditch at the arse end of the empire, compared to the Hades I'll create for you. The Praetorian Guard is the home of Rome's elite. I don't care whether you're the son of a patrician or pleb, you will follow orders. You will learn how to stand in a line and fight for the glory of Rome, as well as fight for the man standing next to you. I will teach you the meaning of suffering, and the meaning of honour.*

Vulso wryly smiled to himself as he noticed the small scar on his knuckle, from where he had punched the front teeth out of a recruit, a couple of years ago, for making a joke during his speech. He didn't make any jokes afterwards. Vulso mused that it was almost worth paying a new recruit to open his mouth inappropriately, in order to make an example of him and cement his authority.

Varro embraced his wife one last time and breathed in her jasmine perfume, hoping that the smell might linger in his nostrils or rub off on his clothes.

"There are worse fates than having you leave. I just cannot think of them right now," Lucilla said, wistfully. She wanted to put on a brave face, so her husband wouldn't worry too much.

"There is one consolation. I won't have to suffer Diana's meals while I'm away," Varro replied, making reference to his wife's attendant. Diana had served Lucilla for several years – and had never forgiven Varro for his mistreatment of her mistress during their first marriage. The crinkle-faced servant still offered up the odd expression of distrust and animus, whether she was positioned behind Varro's back or not.

"You should be careful of your words. Diana might be tempted to poison your food, the next time she cooks for us."

"I'd welcome her doing so. The poison may add some much-needed flavour," he drily countered.

Lucilla laughed, although her fine eyes were moistening a little with tears. Varro forced an unconvincing smile in reply. He thought about the words he had written yesterday morning, for his latest play. The scene concerned the departure of Tiberius and Gaius Gracchus one morning, on the day of the former's murder.

*"We two must set out on our goodly path,*
*Even if only one of us returns.*
*For the prize will be worth the sacrifice.*
*Should one of us die, then let it be me*
*My brother."*

Varro thought how he and Manius had cheated death before. But the odds were against cheating death forever - even if you were as immortal as Achilles. Although Varro was not one to fall prey to superstition, he still experienced a chilling presentiment and hoped that his words were just words - and wouldn't prove prophetic.

Manius had suffered blows in the arena which had wounded him less, compared to the sight of his pregnant wife sobbing as he climbed into the carriage to disembark for Rome. Camilla's eyes were already puffy, from having cried the previous night. She said that she understood why Manius had to accompany his friend, but her words lacked conviction. Camilla felt her baby kick in her stomach. She was close to pleading with him to stay – and argue that she was scared and needed him to be with her at the birth. But Camilla bit her tongue. Neither of them could forgive themselves should something happen to Varro, through Manius' absence, whilst he was in Rome.

Lucilla took the hand of her friend and hugged her, whispering words of support as Milo flicked the reins and the carriage moved off. The wheels crunched upon the gravel, like a soldier's hob-nailed boot crushing a cockroach. Comforting Camilla would help distract Lucilla from her own frustrations and sorrow. At the same time, she cursed Agrippa's name. But as Varro reminded her the night before:

"It wouldn't be wise to say "no" to the second most powerful man in the world."

The blazing sun began to dry-out the ground. Gulls carped overheard, either celebrating having found some food, or bemoaning the lack of it. The long grass bent over, like a throng of hump-backed old men, as the breeze passed through the fields.

When the carriage reached the crest of a hill Varro stared out the window. The expansive, serene sea bordered the horizon, framing the beautiful, bucolic landscape. The agent wished he could have spent just one last morning with Lucilla, on their secluded stretch of beach, within walking distance of the villa. He pictured droplets of water on her shoulders and back, as she came out of the sea, as elegant and captivating as any nereid. He wanted to kiss her salt-tinged skin and lips one more time. Varro told himself that he would be able to do so, once he returned. But their idyllic existence would never quite be the same, he lamented.

*All things must pass.*

And not all the scenes between them were perfect on the beach. Varro remembered how they rested next to one another, on the fine golden sand, just the other day. The comfortable silence between them ended when Lucilla mentioned how she had received a letter from their mutual friend Tiro.

"He writes that he has finally finished editing Cicero's correspondence. We should invite him to stay for the weekend soon."

Varro was non-committal in his response. The agent had yet to share with his wife the conclusion to one of his investigations last year. Tiro had murdered a man. He didn't have the heart to spoil Lucilla's admiration and affection for the sage secretary. But nor did he want to countenance having Tiro cross his threshold. His skin still prickled as he recalled the gruesome crime.

*Not all things pass. Sometimes I wish I could be a lotus-eater. Sometimes the truth is not worth knowing.*

Lies can leave their own form of scars. They just remain unseen, beneath the skin, Varro considered. Secrets can fester or become gangrenous. Philosophers proclaimed that life should involve the pursuit of truth. But falsehoods bind the world together, as much as truth. Lies can be virtuous. Deception can save a marriage, for the good of the children. A lie by a diplomat, regarding a minor clause in a treaty, can cement a peace or trade agreement. A lie, during a political campaign, can secure the election of the worthiest candidate. The truth is far too self-righteous and overrated, Varro half-joked to himself. Yet lies leave scars.

Occasionally, Varro could hear Milo shout out some instructions to his team of horses, and the creatures would whinny in reply, although nothing changed in relation to the uneven ride. Usually the attendant would take it slow along the stone and rut-filled track, but Varro suspected Vulso was setting a brisk pace. Often Varro would drink plenty of barely diluted wine to send him to sleep, or he would stop-off at a tavern or two. He was friendly with many of the landlords between Arretium and Rome - and had been even friendlier towards some of the serving girls before remarrying.

The soft-cushioned seats alleviated some of the jolting movements of the carriage, but they couldn't alleviate them all. In order to distract himself, from both the uneven ride and his brooding thoughts, Varro re-read a letter, sent to him recently by Gaius Macro. Macro was a former poet and drinking companion. On more than one occasion the rumourmonger had served as an unwitting informer during an assignment. Every month or so he would write to Varro to recount the latest gossip from the capital.

*"The trickle is now turning into a foaming torrent, in relation to the rumour that Caesar lies on his death bed in Tarraco. Augustus may not prove to be so divine after all. Livia is by his side as is, tellingly, Marcellus. Caesar may well choose his nephew as his heir. Tiberius is sometimes mentioned in the same breath, but he is in Rome and has not been summoned to be by Caesar's side. A storm cloud hangs over the future. But surely Augustus will nominate Agrippa as his successor, else he may create a power vacuum. Agrippa has never seemed one to grab power, but nor will he relinquish it to an unproven boy, in the shape of Marcellus... But not even the gods know what will happen, if Caesar passes. Rome has tasted peace and prosperity. There will be no appetite for factionalism and civil war among the people. The Senate House may try to assert itself, to restore the old order, but its bark, or annoying yapping, will be worse than its bite I imagine. The Praetorian Guard – and the majority of the legions – will be loyal to Agrippa. Yet Caesar will eventually want power to pass onto his bloodline. Agrippa may be instructed to transfer his office onto Marcellus, once the time is right. Rumour has it that Caesar is arranging for his nephew to marry his daughter, to secure his dynasty and legacy. If true, Marcellus may well have more difficulty controlling his wife than keeping order across the empire. Julia is gaining quite a reputation, which she seems to be revelling in. She enjoys her wine, as much as Bacchus - and she could tire Priapus out in bed. Yet, despite or because of her love of hedonism, the people have taken to her. She is generous and witty. Crowds cheer her name, when her litter passes through the streets. She smiles and waves back with genuine delight and affection. Julia and her fellow bacchantes are often seen carousing deep into the night - or stumbling home early in the morning. Julia also throws regular parties at her own house (the vestibule hosts a mosaic, which quotes Epicurus: "Pleasure is the beginning and end of living happily"). She even invites commoners. It amuses her to watch members of the aristocracy interact with them. The girl also invites actors, artisans, courtesans and charioteers. People camp outside the house, during the gatherings. Julia sends out food and wine to them. I attended*

*one of the parties last month. There was plenty of flesh on show. Unfortunately, my wife accompanied me. She was dressed up in her finery, but her stony, priggish expression made her resemble the Medusa. I imagine how Caesar cannot be best pleased with his daughter's indecent, un-Roman behaviour. Perhaps that's why she does it, to gain his attention. But who would dare censure her, aside from him? Who else can claim to be the daughter of a demi-god? Julia is still to turn sixteen years old I believe, yet she has the love of Rome. The daughter of the First Man of Rome understandably has a bumper crop of friends and suitors. She seems particularly fond of that young poet you took under your wing, Publius Ovidius. Gaius Maecenas recently tried to recruit him to his stable of writers again. Ovidius said no. Maecenas is peeved, believing that you influenced the youth's decision.*

*He may also be ruing you declining his offer of patronage – and be envious of your recent success. Audiences are still flocking to your plays and there are a few lines which are even coming into common parlance:*

*"When you're going through Hades, keep going... Woman, that was the gods' second mistake..."*

*...I desperately need you back in Rome, my friend. My wife is urging us to spend more time together. I can stomach her cooking, but not her conversation. She has also recently nagged me into joining her on shopping trips. She thinks she can compensate for losing her looks through buying a wealth of cosmetics and new clothes. The more money and time I spend on my wife, the less I am able to devote to my mistress. I dearly wish she would take a lover for herself, be someone's mistress. I would be more than happy for another man to lavish gifts upon her, to save me from doing so. But who would want her as a lover, after they have met her?*

*...I should warn you that your past transgressions may come back to haunt you when you return. I attended a party the other evening and overheard someone mention your name. It was Livius Galba. He's baying for your blood, for trying to seduce his wife. I was going to point out to him that you succeeded in seducing Hypatia. He was spitting out more curses than a drab, when damning a customer for leaving without paying. He promised that he would thrash you like a disobedient dog if he saw you though, so perhaps it's best you remain out of his sight. His bark may well be worse than his bite, however. He is due to leave for the front again soon as well.*

*Galba is not the only person of note you have upset it seems. Lentulus Nerva has been cursing your name too. He is claiming he has suffered a loss of business, as an advocate, after you dragged him into the investigation, when Herennius was murdered. He also argues that, due to the suspicion surrounding his daughter in her husband's death, she is now finding it difficult to marry again. I fear you are collecting more enemies than my wife collects shoes, or tedious after-dinner anecdotes.*

*I should here assert that not everyone in Rome bears a grievance against you. I encountered the actress, Sulpicia, the other evening. I bathed in some reflected glory by knowing you (I'll accept any kind of glory nowadays). She is keen, to say the least, to perform in your next play. She is willing to audition for you. She can sing, dance and pointed out that she would be happy to show off her other talents, in private. Such was the heat in her eye that I am tempted to become a playwright myself. Although I much prefer riches to fame, so it's best I remain a property developer.*

*Decimus Bibulus has released his new collection of verse. He still has the uncommon ability to use ten words, when one, or none, will suffice. His similes are as stale as the bread served in the Subura. Even the lines he plagiarises are forgettable. Women will use the book as a sleeping draught. But perhaps I am being too harsh. Or not harsh enough. His father has of course arranged to purchase a legion of copies. Every household will have a copy by their fire. Once they read the book however, every household will toss their copy into the flames."*

Varro took a break from reading Macro's letter and glanced across at Manius, sitting opposite. As much as the former gladiator could appear brutal and fearsome when engaged in combat, his usual expression was open and good-natured. It was far more good-natured than his own, the nobleman fancied. An amused, or mocking, look was often plastered on his own countenance. Or, before he had remarried, Varro could appear a picture of melancholy. He had been a poet, after all.

Yet the Briton's brow was now knitted in pensiveness, or fretfulness, as he ran a sharpening stone along his blade. Varro thought how, for once, his friend looked old. He wondered how much his own experiences as an agent had aged him over the past couple of years. Thankfully Lucilla made him feel young, alive, again. Varro shared his companion's anxiety, however. He mentioned, when they set off, how they were journeying into the unknown:

"Perhaps we should have paid a haruspex to sacrifice a bird for us and read its entrails, to divine our fate."

"Or we should have paid a haruspex to roast us a bird, so as to have something to eat," Manius replied, regretting the scant amount of food they had brought for the trip.

The bodyguard stopped sharpening his sword. Both men forced a smile.

"There are worse fates than travelling back to Rome. At least you will get to see Viola again," Varro remarked, whilst failing to mention how much he had missed her too. Even the melancholiest of poets couldn't be unhappy in the ebullient dog's company.

"Aye, they'll be some sunshine pouring through the clouds," Manius said, his smile becoming genuine as he thought of the black and white mongrel, who was being looked after by his friend's estate manager, Fronto. The dog had been a stray, rescued from the streets. But somehow, equally, the dog had saved the Briton, who sometimes felt like a stray in the capital. "I also need to re-engage with my business and pupils."

"Without you, I fear that some of your students may accidentally slice their feet off or poke their eyes out. Of course, what you should be teaching the scions of our senatorial class, should they wish to become statesmen too, is how to stab a rival in the back."

"You could be in Rome again already, given your cynicism. Politicians can't be all bad."

"I am sure that there are some good eggs, amongst the rotten ones. I have just never encountered any. Self-interest and dishonour seem to be as much a part of them as skin and bone. But perhaps I am being too unfair. One should never discuss politics when sober. Agrippa has the safety of Rome and its best interests at heart. Or the safety of Caesar and his best interests at heart. Doubtless, Agrippa would dutifully argue that they were one in the same thing. Thankfully, we're used to riding towards the unknown. It wouldn't quite be the same, if we knew what was going on," Varro said, philosophically.

Manius raised a corner of his mouth and nodded, whilst sheathing his sharpened sword.

He would have cause to draw it again soon, however.

### 3.

Vulso suspected something was amiss, as soon as he spotted the sideways pointing wagon, blocking the road. The wagoner waved to the soldier, beckoning him to approach and assist him. He pointed to the far side of the vehicle and exclaimed that his wheel was broken.

Milo slowed the carriage to a halt.

The praetorian gripped his sword. He was about to instruct Milo to ride on, around the obstruction – but it was too late. Over a dozen men swarmed out from the treeline, which flanked the right side of the track. They carried an array of weaponry (spears, knives and cudgels) and let out a garbled war-cry. At the same time a brace of archers appeared from behind the wagon and immediately aimed their bows at the mounted soldier. Vulso turned to the skittish Macer and, holding up the palm of his hand, ordered him to stand down.

The soldier took in the group of bandits, as they formed a horseshoe around him and the carriage. Tough, leathery visages were fixed upon him. Some offered up toothless smirks, and some snarled. They wore faded tunics, marked with all manner of stains (wine, oil, blood) and their weapons were mottled with rust. They were a vicious, but ill-disciplined, rabble, Vulso surmised. Violence was a way of life, as valid (or more valid) as any other. A number of them darted glances towards the figure, sitting on the wagon, who propagated the ruse. Vulso surmised that he was the leader of the brigands.

Syrus Bursa stepped down from the wagon. His nose was flat, broken and red, from a lifetime spent drinking and brawling in taverns. His hair and beard were slick and shiny with grease. His build was stocky and muscular, like a fighting dog's. Unlike the others, his shoes and tunic were of a good quality – and he also carried a sword. Bursa had worn a friendly expression on his face when calling for the soldier's assistance a moment ago, but he now scowled like a jilted lover. When he saw the nobleman, along with his bodyguard, step down from the carriage he pointed his sword at his target.

"Are you Rufus Varro?" he exclaimed; his voice as rough as cheap parchment. The sentence was as much a statement as a question. Bursa served as an enforcer for a stonemason's guild in Rome. His instructions, given to him by Cervidius Stolo, the leader of the guild, had been to recruit a group of trusted men – and rob and murder the nobleman, at his villa in Arretium. The money he was being paid was good. Bursa had additional motivation. The client, who had approached Stolo, mentioned that Varro had been involved in the murder of Publius Carbo. The enforcer had been an ardent follower of the demagogue, sharing his hatred towards Jews. Upon witnessing the expensive carriage from a distance, which he had been told about during a briefing for the assignment, Bursa decided to arrange an ambush. The surprise attack had worked perfectly. The mounted praetorian was at the mercy of his archers. The old man and boyish soldier, sitting on the carriage, posed little or no threat. The same could not be said for the nobleman's bodyguard. He had been briefed about the former gladiator beforehand. "He is not to be underestimated. Others have underestimated him in the past, and have the scars to prove it," Stolo had warned, passing on the client's advice.

Vulso realised the group surrounding them were assassins, as opposed to brigands. They were surrounded, like his father had been, serving under Julius Caesar at Alesia. It was either fight - or die. While their leader directed his attention towards Varro, Vulso caught Macer's eye. With the subtlest shift of his head and eyes he indicated to the archer that he should take out the enemy bowmen first. But not yet. Now was not the time to strike. Macer nodded in reply, acknowledging the order, as he wiped his perspiring palms against his tunic.

"Speaking," Varro replied, equitably, his tone unashamedly aristocratic. "Who am I addressing?"

"That doesn't matter. You're a dead man walking," Bursa said, smirking. The enforcer was already envisioning getting paid - and spending the money on women and settling his gambling debts.

"Aren't we all? Can I ask who paid you to come here?" Varro asked, trying to solve the mystery of the confrontation, whilst surveying the men and weaponry around him. Vulso and Manius wouldn't surrender without a fight.

"You can ask, but I don't have an answer for you. I never met the man who ordered your death. He did say that he was happy for you to suffer, before we killed you, though."

A few of the men, who heard Bursa's comment, sniggered. One of which was a hulking thug, with a lazy eye and pock-marked skin, who glowered at Manius. Challenging him. Goading him. Aulus Strabo had a face that you wouldn't want to encounter on a dark night, or during the day either. Even if you punched him several times, he couldn't get any uglier. He was a big bastard. But he would soon be a dead bastard, the Briton thought. The key to victory would be Macer, Manius calculated. If the young bowmen could take out the opposing archers, before they could cut down Vulso, then they had a chance. He hoped the youth had been bloodied, and he had shot more than just training targets before.

"I am not sure how much you're getting paid, but I would be willing to pay double your fee, if you would do me the courtesy of not brutally murdering us," the aristocratic posed, the soul of civility - albeit Varro kept a hand clasped around his sword as he spoke. He wondered, could the attack be linked to his impending assignment in Rome? Thoughts swirled around in his mind, like fireflies slipping through his fingers. But he couldn't be distracted too much by the issue of who was pulling the strings behind the scenes. He could figure that out afterwards. If there was an afterwards.

"I would kill you for nothing, to avenge the death of Publius Carbo. He would have created a new, better Rome for the people. Jews would have been banished and the workers would have united under one banner. A new order would have been established, built on the ashes of the old. But rumour has it you took that future away, by executing Carbo. Did you kill him?" Bursa asked, his face balled up like a fist, his heart thumping with malice.

"Yes. And my only regret is that I only got to kill him once," Varro replied, calmly and drily, his eyes flitting to the side, in order to measure who might attack him first from the group.

"You think you're funny. But I intend to cut the smile from your face. If you submit to your fate without a fight, however, I will allow your companions to go free."

"Let's hope that you are an even worse assassin, that you are a liar."

The tension in the air congealed. Both sides awaited an order, like a crowd waiting for a chariot race or boxing bout to start.

A couple of the thugs near Vulso closed in. But the soldier welcomed the encroachment. They were now in range. He also noted how the two archers, who had had been assigned to train their weapons on him, had lowered their bows. One had even un-nocked his arrow. Now was the time to strike.

"Macer. Engage!" Vulso bellowed, his stentorian voice carrying through the valley.

The archer reacted immediately. He grabbed his bow - whilst springing to his feet – and nocked an arrow in one fluid movement. His arm bulged. His chest expanded. The string bit into his fingers for a second, before Macer unleashed the arrow and it thudded into his enemy's sternum. If he hadn't been bloodied before, he was now. The second archer in Bursa's gang hesitated and fumbled, trying to re-position the shaft on his weapon. There's the quick and the dead. The stonemason was the latter. Macer aimed for the brigand's heart, but the arrow buried itself in his bearded throat. Blood spat out and splattered upon the ground.

Vulso was quick to attack too. He shouted out a command to his horse and Mars reared up, letting out his own species of a war cry. The mount's front legs flailed out at the enemies closest to him, knocking them to the ground. The praetorian then kicked his heels into the horse's flanks. Whilst mowing down one enemy Vulso also whipped his sword upwards, slashing an opponent's face from chin to forehead. The sound of a blood-curdling scream sliced through the valley.

Bursa's men initially froze, but they didn't remain slack-jawed for long. Two spearmen rushed Manius. Thankfully they were untrained in throwing the weapon. The Briton took out the closest by throwing a dagger, which hung down from his belt, into the bandit's breast. The blade scythed through his top ribs. The second assailant was Aulus Strabo. The brawny enforcer jabbed his spear forward. The triangular blade drew blood from the bodyguard's upper arm, but he dodged inside and buried half his gladius into Strabo's stomach. The big bastard was dead. But there were still plenty of other bastards to kill.

As much as he had focussed his attention towards his conversation with Bursa, Varro was quick to draw his sword and become a man of action, rather than just words. He deflected a spear thrust from an assailant and then wounded his opponent in the arm, causing him to drop his weapon and retreat, like a scolded dog. Varro picked up the spear and used it to fend off the next attacker, whilst moving closer to the carriage. He realised that Vulso and Macer would win them the fight, if winning the fight was possible. He tasked himself with standing by Macer's side of the carriage and protecting the archer, as he continued to rain arrows down upon the enemy. He also tasked himself with staying alive.

Bursa's blood was up. He could no longer consider that his plan was working perfectly. All that mattered now was killing nobleman and getting paid. He had no desire to challenge the praetorian or bodyguard. Whilst Varro was occupied with keeping two men at bay in front of him, Bursa would take the opportunity to outflank the aristocrat. Varro was blindsided. Manius saw the danger but he had his own combatants to deal with. All he could do was call out to his friend. But it would be too late.

Bursa held his sword aloft, ready to bring it down upon Varro, like an executioner's axe. But it was the stonemason who was cut down. Macer's arrow entered the top of his brow - and the tip protruded out the back of his neck. Once you cut off the head, the body will fall. Their paymaster was dead. A retreat turned into a rout and a few of the gang were able to disappear back into the woods. Vulso continued to butcher anyone within range. His blade was streaked with blood and gore - and flecked with tiny pieces of bone.

The fight was over. Manius plunged the tip of his spear into the throats of those who were on the ground wounded, as if he were plunging a spade into virgin soil. Either he was being merciful, by putting the injured out of their misery, or vengeful. He noticed a hammer-shaped tattoo on a number of the fallen, suggesting membership of a gang of guild. He flagged the mark up to Vulso, who dismounted from his snorting horse.

"It shouldn't be too difficult to track down the gang and its leader," the praetorian argued.

"Will he talk?" Manius asked, his face freckled with spots of blood.

"I'll cut off his cock before his tongue. He'll talk."

Varro, whilst trying to catch his breath, turned to Macer, who had climbed down from the carriage, with the intention of retrieving his arrows.

"You fought well, Titus. I owe you my life. Thank you. How about I start paying you back with a jug of Massic, when we return to Rome?"

The young bowman nodded, enthusiastically, with a wide grin on his perspiring face. Varro couldn't be sure if the smile was due to the pride he felt at shooting well, or the relief at surviving the bloody encounter.

"You're as popular as ever it seems," Manius remarked to his friend. "Who do you suspect wants to kill you?"

"Your guess is as good as mine. It could be anyone who has ever met me - or has had the misfortune to read one of my poems," Varro replied, trying to make light of the situation. The graver the situation, the glibber he sometimes became. But his hands still trembled, and his breathing was still laboured. The lines from his play poured into his thoughts again, like a poison. He was worried for Manius, as much as himself.

*We two must set out on our goodly path,*
*Even if only one of us returns.*

*For the prize will be worth the sacrifice.*
*Should one of us die, then let it be me*
*My brother.*

His natural glibness couldn't entirely mask his unease. Varro envisioned the scenario of the gang entering his home. He could have been murdered in his sleep, along with Lucilla. Perhaps he could argue that Agrippa's summons was fortuitous.

*Are the gods on my side after all? If they are, then why didn't they strike down my enemies before they even reached me?*

Whether sent by the gods or not, a sheep farmer, who Varro knew, approached the carriage. Acilius Pollio, riding his cart, puffed out his cheeks on witnessing the bloody scene before him. Many a rictus and grimace were fixed on the faces of the contorted corpses. Flies already started to buzz around and land on lips and glistening wounds. Pollio had little time for bandits though. They plagued the lands, like vermin. At least in death they might do some good, by acting as fertilizer, the sanguine farmer considered.

Vulso gave instructions to Pollio to visit the nearby barracks and pass on a wax tablet to its senior officer. The message contained information about their encounter. The corpses needed to be collected and disposed of. Vulso also issued orders, under the authority of Agrippa, to seek out any fugitives, who had escaped through the woods. They would be wearing besmirched tunics, probably carrying weapons and some would have hammer-shaped tattoos on their necks.

Varro asked Pollio to pass on an additional message to the commanding officer at the barracks. He wanted the centurion to provide him with a handful of men, to help guard his house while he was in Rome. In order not to alarm his wife, the soldiers should explain that Varro was paying them to help with building works. During the evenings they should stand sentry, at the front of the house. The nobleman would pay the officer and his men handsomely for their assistance.

"Are you going to Rome then?" Pollio asked, masticating like a cow, with wiry grey hairs sticking out of his ears, nose and chin.

"Yes. Have you ever been yourself, Acilius?" Varro asked.

"No. I'd rather pull out what few teeth I've got left in my head than go there. I wouldn't want to be around all those priests and politicians in the capital. I already have enough manure to deal with as a farmer."

Varro let out a burst of much-welcomed laughter, before setting-off again on his journey.

## 4.

Night was drawing in, like a grey-faced widow wrapping a black shawl around her. But the lights of Rome glimmered in the distance, and Milo lit the oil lamp next to him. The faint odours of ordure and sulphur increased as they closed in on the capital.

Varro shifted in his seat uncomfortably and downed another cup of wine. Part of him was still tempted to turn back. He wouldn't sleep easily until he was with Lucilla again. But he needed to move forward. The real enemy was in Rome, not decomposing just outside Arretium. To protect Lucilla, he had to uncover who hired the gang and, most likely, end them. Vulso had once told him that the rule of the battlefield was kill or be killed. Perhaps the same rule applied to the world of espionage. Although he would have to wait for the answer, the agent kept asking himself whether the assassination attempt on his life was linked to Agrippa's summons.

In order to distract himself from his needling thoughts, Varro stared out the window - as the carriage creeped slowly forward in the traffic. Despite the fading light he could still make out some of the words engraved on the tombs, which lined the road into the capital.

Ornate scrollwork and quotations from Hesiod and Ennius decorated the marble edifice of one Fulvius Sertorius. The small monument also boldly declared, in raised golden lettering,

*To a devoted husband and loving father. A good Roman.*

Some may have been moved to tears by the simple, touching dedication but Varro was nearly moved to laughter. Sertorius had been a colleague of his father's, having served as a Roman diplomat. The haughty patrician was certainly devoted to his various mistresses, Varro recalled. His love didn't extend to all his children too. He expelled one of his sons from his household for wanting to marry a low-born Greek woman. The diplomat also arranged for his youngest daughter to marry a known pederast, in exchange for the husband- to-be granting Sertorius the use of his villa in Pompeii. If being "a good Roman" meant being unfaithful, corrupt and vain then Sertorius could have been called an exemplary Roman, Varro judged.

A more modest tomb, housing both a husband and wife, attracted Varro's attention, mainly because of the verse inscribed upon it.

*One kiss can lead to many more*
*One day can lead to forever*
*Two ships can seek out the same shore*
*In death, as in life, together.*

The poetry was not the most accomplished he had ever encountered, although it was far from the worst, given that he owned books by Decimus Bibulus. But the sentiment was sweet and sincere. Varro couldn't read the names on the tombstone, due to the inky darkness, but he pictured a doting, devoted couple. Their hair was grey, but there was still a glint in their eyes.

The husband was politely filling his wife's winecup before his own. They laughed at their own, private jokes. They could barely remember last week, but scenes from their courtship were vivid. Varro thought that should he die a day after Lucilla, he would die a happy man.

Once inside the walls of the city Vulso veered off towards Agrippa's residence. Varro promised that he would visit Caesar's lieutenant in the morning. He was tired and of little use to anyone right now, the spy argued. If Agrippa could not wait to see his agent then he should send a messenger, though he warned Vulso that it might be easier to wake the dead this evening.

Varro and Manius made their way through the half-lit city streets. The smell of garum and wine wafted through windows. Some citizens were making their way home, after making an offering in a temple, before they closed their doors for the night. Some made their way to the taverns, carrying their lucky dice or hoping that their favourite whore would be available. A fair few litters crossed their path as they grew closer to the Palatine Hill. In days gone by the smell of perfume emanating from the litters might intrigue Varro, as to who was inside. As they ascended the Palatine Hill the smell of garum turned to that of red mullet. Besmirched concrete turned to polished marble. Tunics turned into togas, some patterned or embroidered. People didn't have to watch their step so carefully, for fear of stepping into dung. Instead of the sound of commoners throwing piss out of their windows, one could hear the far more welcome noise of trickling fountains.

Varro surprised himself by how much relief and comfort he felt at being back home, when he walked through the door and entered the triclinium. When Fronto rose to his feet, Varro could hear the old man's bones click. Perhaps because he had not seen him for six months, where previously he had seen his estate manager every day, Fronto appeared significantly older. His stoop was more pronounced, his skin seemed increasingly liver-spotted. Fronto's wrinkled, hoary countenance lit-up at seeing his master, however. The estate manager had been a surrogate father to Varro over the years. He had overseen the boy's education, when Appius Varro had been a distant or largely absent figure in his life. Perhaps Varro would not have been a poet, or now playwright, if not for Fronto helping to instil a love of literature in the youth. The nobleman had also inherited his estate manager's dry sense of humour. Fronto had missed his master over the past six months. It had proved the longest period of time the two men had spent away from each other. But Fronto had been overjoyed when Varro remarried the love of his life. Living in the countryside had been good for Varro's soul, and he had found some purpose and success as a writer.

"I see that you are still waiting up for me," Varro remarked, beaming fondly at his friend, before embracing him.

"Agrippa sent a message to say you were due. Is Lucilla well?"

"She's fine - and sends her best wishes. I did of course say to her to save her best wishes for someone far more highborn, but she insisted, Varro joked."

Manius beamed too, observing the food on the table, before embracing the estate manager, who had warmly welcomed the young, foreign gladiator into the household many years ago and made him feel at home. Fronto noticed the bandage on the bodyguard's arm, covering the wound from earlier, and raised a quizzical, bushy eyebrow.

"It's nothing. I'm certainly in far better condition than the man who caused the injury. I'll explain later. I'll go through what happened, as I go through the feast on the table over there," the Briton said, licking his lips, as his stomach yearned to be introduced to the plates of squid and lamprey on display.

They heard her first, her claws sounding on the tiled floor as she scampered through the house after hearing the longed-for voices. Viola appeared. Her tail wagged so furiously, it seemed to shift her entire body back and forth. The sweet-natured, adorable mongrel barked and howled in elation (although some of the barks and howls may have been emitted out of a sense of castigation, for Manius having been absent for so long). She leapt up and licked the tip of his stubbled chin. Manius soon got to his knees and then just lay on the floor, whilst she trod over him and licked his hands, arms and face, as if he were made from sausage meat.

"I think she may have missed you," Varro said, thinking that, even if they had drunk several cups of wine, there was not a soul in Rome happier than Viola this evening.

The three men sat down to eat and caught-up with various pieces of news. What with Varro saving money by not drinking and gambling so much – and not having to pay his divorce settlement anymore – the estate manager reported a sea change in his master's finances.

"You can afford to be a wastrel again, or invest in modern art," Fronto drily remarked. "I have placed a set of accounts in your room, should you be interested in perusing them. I have also left a mound of correspondence in your study. As well as receiving written plaudits from your devoted public, I've received an ongoing string of visitors daring to knock on our door, intent on seeing you. Mainly actresses. You would think that I wouldn't grow tired of meeting a host of doe-eyed young women, wearing sheer dresses and offering to sit on a casting couch. But you would be wrong. I'm an old goat rather than a young ram. Would-be poets are also making a pilgrimage to our door. I think I preferred it when people ignored or criticised your writing. Anonymity is like making a tax payment. Once it's gone you can't get it back."

"There's no need to worry too much. I've every confidence that I'll write a spate of second-rate plays soon and my fame will dissipate, far swifter than it came to fruition." Varro replied, before popping another stuffed olive in his mouth. "But you must excuse me. I fear I might dissipate, if I do not get some rest. To quote Homer, rather than a second-rate playwright, "There is a time for many words, and there is also a time for sleep." I will leave Manius to fill you in on events."

Diana prepared some warm milk for her mistress, but Lucilla's stomach remained unsettled. The late-night arrival of several soldiers confused her. She sensed something was amiss, that she wasn't being told everything. The officer in charge just reiterated that his men had been ordered to assist with some building work at the house, and that they should billet at the villa too and guard the property, as there were reports of bandits operating in the area.

Despite the balmy evening air, a shiver still ran down Lucilla's spine. She couldn't sleep. Instead of goose feathers, she felt as if she was resting on a bed of hot coals. She already desperately missed Varro. The house seemed empty. Lucilla had spent the evening comforting Camilla, as much as she needed comforting herself.

"I always pictured Manius being with me, when the baby was born. He can be surprisingly tender and gentle," Camilla remarked, her eyes red-rimmed from tears.

Lucilla didn't doubt it. She offered up a prayer for the Briton to be safe, as well as her husband. Without Manius, she probably would have been a widow rather than wife, from during the time when they were first married. She couldn't ask for a better bodyguard or friend for Varro.

"Manius will return in time for the baby being born, I am sure of it," Lucilla asserted. For the first time since knowing her, she felt that she was knowingly deceiving her friend. Giving her false hope.

Lucilla buried her head in her pillow and prayed to Hypnos, to deliver her. But her skin prickled, and her imagination continued to torment her as she dwelled upon the demands Agrippa could make of Varro. Caesar's lieutenant could order her husband to travel to some far-flung land, rife with enemies or disease, in order to assassinate a head of state. He could be told to seduce the wife of a diplomat or senator and to extract intelligence. Both propositions caused Lucilla to shudder, as if she were experiencing physical pain. She couldn't quite decide which scenario was worse.

Lucilla lit the bronze oil lamp next to her bed. Wishing to spend the dead time of the night more productively, she decided to read. She walked across to the bookcase, on Varro's side of the room, containing a host of scrolls. She scrunched her toes on the Persian rug that Livia had bought her, as a wedding present. Caesar's wife still occasionally wrote to her friend. Lucilla had often provided Livia with advice, on financial matters or buying paintings, when the pair of them lived in Rome.

Lucilla perused the tags on the scrolls, which identified the wide selection of books. Literature had been her guide and comfort when she was growing up. Books, rather than sophists or her parents, had educated her – which was probably the cause of why the independent-minded woman was wiser than most. Lucilla wondered whether she should read something engaging, which might help her take her mind off her troubles - or read something dull which might usher her off to sleep. A flicker of a smile briefly animated her elegant features as she took in the row of scrolls containing the works of Homer. Lucilla remembered when Varro first courted her. He introduced the poetry lover to a game he played. *Homeric Lots.* Varro would roll the dice he carried with him three times, to select the book, passage and line from *The Iliad* or *The Odyssey*. The line was then supposed to indicate or predict the roller's fate. A further flicker of a smile animated her tired features as Lucilla recalled the first time she played the game with Varro, over a jug of wine. She couldn't help but laugh, along with Varro, as he rolled the dice and read out the all too true line from Homer:

*"We men are wretched things."*

She was not one to normally fall prey to superstition, but Lucilla felt compelled to play the game once more to divine her fate. She checked for Varro's dice in the drawer. Whereas before they had remarried, he would carry his lucky dice with him at all times, Varro no longer gambled. Gambling had helped ruin his first marriage. He did not want to bet that he could do so again. Lucilla clutched the ivory dice, spotted with gold, and threw them – trying to remember the system Varro had devised (as if there was some kind of science to the game). She retrieved the correct scroll and ran her finger down the parchment to locate the right passage and words. The tired, distraught woman recoiled, like a hand quickly drawing away from a flame, when she read the requisite line.

*"The difficulty is not so great to die for a friend, as to find a friend worth dying for."*

Lucilla thought of her husband - and Manius - and experienced a bleak premonition that, somehow, one of them would not come back from Rome alive. Her legs nearly buckled, as if she were a new-born lamb. The curtain suddenly billowed out from a gust of wind. Some storms don't involve thunder or lightning. The thrum of crickets in the garden sounded more like locusts. The moon slipped behind a cloud and the sound of laughter, from when Lucilla had first played the game, seemed a world away.

## 5.

Varro woke, in a sweat. The blast of heat pouring through the window resembled the tongues of flames which had licked his visage in the dream, or nightmare, he had just endured. During the dream he had ridden back home, with Manius and Vulso, to his country villa, his horse snorting and streaked with perspiration. The house was wreathed in fire and belching out smoke. The marble columns and flowerbeds were charred. He heard Lucilla scream from inside and pictured her contorted semblance, melting like wax. He tried to enter the burning building, but the earth was as soft as a bog – and Vulso held him back. When Varro looked to Manius to help him he saw the once towering figure brought to his knees, sobbing like a child as he mourned the death of his wife and baby. Above the sounds of the nightmare Varro heard the shrill laughter of Gaius Maecenas, who sat upon a black mount, with white fetlocks, holding a torch aloft. Varro reached for his sword. But as he went to draw his blade, he found that it was absent and he stood impotent, with just the hilt in his palm.

It was at that point that Varro woke-up, the nightmare visions still branded upon his waking mind. The images were fantastical, but the feelings of grief, desperation and rage were real. Should Maecenas have been in the room, he would have killed him. He was more than just a suspect, he was guilty, in Varro's mind, of ordering his assassination. The two men had crossed paths a year ago. The spymaster owned enough animus and motive to murder Varro. Crucially, unlike other figures he could suspect of wanting to kill him, Maecenas possessed the resources and intelligence network to know his location and recruit the criminal gang. The lauded patron of the arts, who had championed both Horace and Virgil, had also served as governor of Rome, whilst Octavius was absent from the city during the civil war. Maecenas was a political enforcer for Caesar, who promoted his master's interest (through bribery or blackmail) whilst weeding out his enemies. He was charming and ruthless in equal measure. He oversaw agents and assassins across the empire, employing them to serve his own interests as much as Rome's. Rumour had it that he even encouraged his wife to become Caesar's mistress, in order to gather intelligence on him. As much as Rome's establishment and elite may have hated Maecenas, they also rightly feared him.

Varro had earned the equestrian's enmity by embarrassing him last year, through completing an assignment for Caesar, which Maecenas had originally been charged with carrying out. The incident had caused the lieutenant to further fall out of favour with the princeps - while his rival, Agrippa, was granted further honours. The poet had also refused Maecenas' generous offer of patronage. The former governor of Rome was not accustomed to hearing the word "no". Despite his cultured manner and veneer of civility, Varro had been a witness to - or a rather victim of - Maecenas' animus. He possessed the vanity of a peacock, yet the venom of an asp.

*We men are wretched things.*

Such was the vividness and potency of his nightmare that it somehow served as proof of guilt for Varro. Were the gods presenting him with a prophesy, that Lucilla was going to die? Or were they warning him of danger, so he could prevent a catastrophe? Between saving Lucilla, or damning Maecenas, there was no choice to make, Varro judged.

*Kill or be killed.*

He plunged his head into a basin of cold water, that a slave had stealthily left in his room earlier. The nobleman dressed himself in a plain, white tunic and put on a pair of comfortable sandals, crafted from softened ox-hide. Varro turned his thoughts towards his imminent meeting with Agrippa. It cast a shadow over his day. He wanted to get the appointment over and done with, like a session with a surgeon to get a tooth pulled. Agrippa had placed Varro in more danger than anyone else he knew, yet there were few men that the agent trusted more. It was difficult for even the consul's enemies to dismiss his ascent and achievements, as much as the patrician class might look down their aquiline noses at the commoner (although they were doubtless too cowardly to insult him to his face). Caesar may well wear the crown, but Agrippa helped place him on his throne. He recruited his armies, built his navy, constructed his aqueducts, rennervated his temples and defeated his enemies, on land and sea. He fed his people, through managing the grain supply, commissioned his statues and recruited his spies. Unfortunately, Varro was one of the latter.

He yawned and attempted to flatten his unkempt hair as he walked into the triclinium. Varro's weary eyes widened in surprise slightly as he was met by two lantern-jawed lictors, looking as lugubrious as Germans. Manius, Fronto, Vulso and Agrippa were also sitting on his couches. The mood was sombre, as if somebody had just died. Agrippa rose to his feet. He was wearing a toga, which was rare for the former soldier. Although his stocky figure filled out the mass of finely woven material the garment didn't quite hang right. He constantly adjusted its folds. Varro also observed that Vulso was out of uniform.

"Either you woke early, or I woke-up late," Varro remarked.

"Or both happened," Agrippa replied, his voice somewhat stiffer than his host's. He then smiled, however, conveying how pleased and relieved he was to see his friend. The smile was wide enough not to appear perfunctory, but not so wide as to seem false or misplaced, given the circumstances of his visit. Varro half-smiled in return. He was happy to see his friend, but less happy to see his employer.

"I hope I am not going to be required to change and don a toga as well. The moths may have feasted on it in my absence," the nobleman said, as he took in his august guest. Agrippa appeared noticeably older, worn down like a blacksmith's hammer that had been used too many times. Crow's-feet perched around his eyes. His hairline had receded and was marbled with grey. Whereas his palms would have once been worn from holding a sword, Varro noticed blisters on his thumb and finger from where the administrator had been gripping his stylus. Yet still his jawline was firm, like the prow of a ship defiant in a storm, and one could discern his soldier's build beneath the formal attire.

"I have no intention of depriving your moths of their breakfast. I am due to visit the Senate House later, in order to present some legislation and give a speech. I will keep the speech short. With every fourth line a Roman politician utters, he is almost obliged to insert a lie. Therefore, the briefer the oratory, the more honest it will be. If my audience falls asleep, at least I can blame things on the heat. People have labelled this heat "insufferable". My definition of insufferable involves senators and mimes," Agrippa drily explained, resisting the temptation to add his wife to the list. "I would ask if you had a good journey, but Vulso briefed me last night. What with you travelling all the way from Arretium, I thought I should at least do you the courtesy of travelling across Rome to see you. We will discuss the events and implications of your unexpected encounter soon. But I must first talk about why I have summoned you to Rome. Or rather why Caesar has summoned you to Rome. I did explain to him that you were no longer an active agent, but he insisted that you would come out of retirement. It's not wise to say "no" to the most powerful man in the world."

The grass felt soft and cool against his feet as Varro strolled out into the garden, along with Agrippa. Although he had not missed the array of odours that Rome had to offer, Varro found that he had missed the view from his garden. Smoke whorled up from bakeries and tanneries across the seven-hilled city, melting into the ether. The capital was a glorious mix of industry and indolence, virtue and vice. Rome wasn't all bad. Not all of its one million souls were iniquitous. The air rippled and shimmered from the sultry heat. Rome was man's greatest feat, which was why it deserved the world's admiration – and opprobrium.

The irony wasn't lost on the two men as they sat upon a bench next to a statue of Harpocrates, the Greek god of secrets, silence and confidentiality. Varro fancied that he saw a look of disapproval on the god's usually impish face – in response to the fact that Agrippa was about to dishonour the concepts of silence, secrets and confidentiality.

"How's Lucilla keeping? I was glad she was foolish enough to take you back."

"So was I. She is fine, thank you. She sends her regards," Varro replied, practising his ability to deceive again. "And how is Marcella?"

"You would do better to ask her soothsayer. She spends more time with him, than me, nowadays. He tends to instruct her on how she should be feeling. Not that I am complaining. It could be worse. She could share her time and feelings with me. I think I used up all my good fortune, in terms of married life, when I wed my first wife," Agrippa said. At first a wistfulness shaped his features, but then he appeared pained, as he remembered Caecilia. He would have sacrificed, in a heartbeat, all his wealth and power to spend just one more day in her company. The widower told himself he would see her in the next life. Unfortunately, in this life, he had been forced into a pantomime union, by Caesar, for the good of the empire and his bloodline. Although Agrippa remained faithful to his young wife, he probably possessed more affection for his sword or horse than he did Marcella, Varro fancied.

"The gods are not known for being generous with their store of good fortune, which is why we're encouraged to make our own luck. I fear I may be experiencing a bout of bad luck myself, however. Otherwise we wouldn't be sitting here."

"I wish we could be sitting here just as friends, Rufus. I feel partly to blame for your misfortune. Believe it or not but I have frequently sung your praises to Caesar. You may have sometimes been a reluctant agent, but you were a proficient one. You were an honest spy, if there is such a thing. You never tried to enrich yourself during your assignments - or tell me just what I wanted to hear. Although I must confess, I had my doubts about you initially. It seems a lifetime ago when I first turned-up at your house. You were hungover. The bags under your eyes were so large, they could have carried the dregs of wine you left in your cup from the night before."

"I'm offended. I would have downed those dregs," Varro replied, recalling the scene of his first meeting with Agrippa. He initially thought that it was a joke, or dream, when the consul entered his bedroom and ordered him to wake and get dressed. Fear sobered him up, like a bucket of icy water.

"You were over-privileged, over-indulged, over-fed and over-sexed back then."

"That's unfair. I wasn't over-fed."

"You said that you had risen late due to staying up, to finish composing a poem. Thankfully you became a more accomplished liar, as an agent. Your profession demanded it. You didn't care about much during those days, including your own welfare."

"I cared about my apathy. I was passionate about my indifference."

"Indeed. I had every confidence that you would be able to seduce Cassandra. I had less confidence in your ability to do your duty and succeed on other fronts. But you proved me wrong, Rufus, and maybe you even surprised yourself. Caesar was grateful and impressed. As was I."

"I am starting to wish that you would revile me and denigrate my talents and achievements," Varro commented, with little or no irony. His eyes had briefly narrowed – and his features became taut, in a twinge of discomfort – as he heard her name again. He felt guilty that he had seldom thought about Cassandra, since remarrying Lucilla. But the image of her gory corpse haunted his inner eye once more.

"You were warned that you could become a victim of your own success. Caesar has cause to call on you. Last month a young nobleman, Marcus Corvinus, was found murdered in his swimming pool. He had just finished hosting a small party for a circle of friends. The body was found, floating in the bloodstained water, in the morning, by slaves, with a knife wound in the top of the skull. Corvinus had recently returned from studying philosophy at the academy, in Athens. He was a promising poet, apparently. I will let you be the judge of that. Corvinus wasn't just academically gifted though. He was famously handsome, an accomplished horseman and was planning to serve as an officer in the army. Greatness beckoned, by all accounts. Corvinus was popular, perhaps too popular. He was a victim of his own success too. The would-be Mark Antony was, to put it mildly, amorous. If we start from the supposition that he was murdered by an ex-lover, then we could list half the inhabitants of the Palatine Hill as potential suspects. He could have also been murdered by a cuckolded husband. Such crimes have happened before and will happen again. Corvinus was a nobleman, poet and seducer. Sound familiar? Perhaps he thought he was the heir to your throne, after your abdication."

Varro raised the corner of his mouth, but barely smiled, and rolled his eyes in response to Agrippa's joke. He had never been proud of his reputation, which preceded him – or followed him around like a shadow.

"I'm intending to die in my bed, rather than in a pool of blood. My days as a priapic poet are behind me. My future is as a prosaic husband," Varro replied, thinking how those words would have never passed his lips when he had first met Agrippa.

"The daughters – and mothers – of our patricians were not the only ones to adore Corvinus. His father, Porcius, also doted on him. Porcius was an ally of Julius Caesar and, even before the Battle of Mutina, supported Octavius. He pledged financial and political capital to our side, in periods of both war and peace. Critics of Caesar are quick to highlight instances of him punishing treachery, but they conveniently forget his virtue of rewarding loyalty. Porcius recently wrote to Caesar, imploring him to track down his son's murderer and bring him to justice. Porcius is a good man. Rome owes him a debt of gratitude, regardless of his relationship with the Octavius. I visited the old man a few days ago. He used to be politically active, host dinner parties for writers and give lectures on philosophy. Now he barely leaves the house. He sits in his wine cellar, tearing out what little hair he has left and mourns his son. He's the sum of his rage and grief. Even if you are able to identify his son's killer, I fear Porcius will still be a slither of the man he was."

"I'm pleased you said if, rather than when, I identify the murderer. I could have more chance of finding an honest Egyptian than apprehending the culprit. Do we have any lines of inquiry? Are there any witnesses or suspects?"

"The good news is that we have a prime suspect. The bad news is that we do not know his whereabouts. A young poet, Felix Plancus, attended the party, but he vanished the next day, after stealing his father's purse and a few, portable valuables from his home. Innocent people do not usually flee the scene of a crime and then go into hiding."

"How do we know if he is still in the city?"

"Because he made another appearance at his family home on the Capitoline Hill a few days ago. His mother caught him in her bedroom, liberating the contents of her jewellery box. She reported that he didn't say a word to her, and quickly retreated out of the window. But she believes her son is innocent and wants us to find him."

"Are you absolutely sure of his guilt?"

"Nothing is certain, aside from death and Roman taxes. And you may uncover other suspects. But the sooner you locate Plancus the sooner you will be able to return to Arretium, I warrant. I have posted watchers across the gates of the city, but that doesn't mean he won't try to escape. If he is able to leave Rome, however, the chances of us apprehending him will be significantly reduced. He will be desperate for money, I imagine. I have a list of a few of his friends, who he may reach out to. Shake the tree. See if any fruit falls. The fate of Rome doesn't depend on your assignment. But Caesar does want to honour his promise to Porcius. He believes that, having tracked down Herennius' dagger a year ago, you will be able find Corvinus' murderer. He also believes you will be duly discreet, during your investigation."

"Why do I need to be so discreet?"

"Because Caesar's daughter and stepson were also present on the night of the murder."

## 6.

Manius picked at some finger food, although he had little appetite for once. He stared out the window, pre-occupied. Fronto noticed him tap his foot and chew his nails. The estate manager imagined that the bodyguard could be troubled by any number of worries, jabbing at his side like a gladiator's spear. Manius was embarking on a fresh assignment. His closest friend had been targeted by an assassin – and probably would be again. Yet Fronto fancied that, more than anything, Manius was thinking about his wife and unborn child. The hulking, fearless Briton felt powerless and scared.

Macer entered the room, adjusting his tunic, his hair dishevelled. If he looked anymore sheepish, he would have wool sprouting out from his ears, Vulso thought to himself. The praetorian had given the archer leave to disappear earlier – and spend some quality time with Sabina. The girl led the soldier back into the staff quarters of the house, where the two of them could be alone. Macer brimmed with pride as he told the story of how he had saved Varro's life, during their perilous journey from Arretium. He was occasionally distracted in the telling of his tale, when he caught glimpses of Sabina's upper thighs and bosom, beneath her skimpy dress. The Greek slave, with almond eyes and ambitions of becoming a freedwoman, liked the young soldier. When he was not being lusty, he was courteous. His prospects were good. Despite his age he was already a member of the Praetorian Guard. He had the body of a gladiator, but boyish features of a eunuch. She could attest, from first-hand knowledge, that he was no eunuch, however.

Macer blushed and grinned at his commanding officer.

"I hope you put a similar smile on the girl's face," Vulso remarked. He could still just about remember being a young soldier - and being directed more by what was between his legs than between his ears. As much as Vulso might have been tempted to rib the bowman some more - and see his visage grow redder than carnelian - he wanted to turn to the issues at hand. Agrippa had briefed Vulso, Manius and Fronto about the assignment to investigate the murder of Marcus Corvinus and find Felix Plancus.

"I remember hearing some gossip about the crime when it happened, last month," the praetorian remarked. "Opinion was split. Some called it a tragedy, believing that Corvinus was bound for high office, or military glory. Others explained that the philanderer received his just desserts – and he was stabbed with the horns of a cuckold. Sooner or later his transgressions would catch up with him. And they did. Agrippa mentioned that you once gave Corvinus some lessons in swordsmanship. What was your impression of him?"

Manius shrugged his shoulders, to indicate he had no great insight to offer, and replied:

"He was an accomplished student, physically strong and intelligent. He had a confidence that often spilled over into arrogance. Corvinus knew he was gifted, and he wanted everyone else to know it too. Either he didn't see his attacker coming, or he knew and trusted him. Otherwise he would have put up a decent fight."

"I caught wind of a couple of interesting rumours, after news of the murder spread," Fronto said, in his slow, considered voice. "Firstly, the gossip was that Julia became one of Corvinus' conquests. Apparently, he composed some lewd, compromising verses about her, which found their way to Caesar. The murder may have been the result of a father protecting the reputation of his daughter. Although, that being the case, it would mean that Caesar has initiated an investigation against himself. But stranger things have happened in Rome. The other main suspect at the time, who people twittered on about for a few days, was Senator Gnaeus Silo. Shortly before his murder, Silo attacked Corvinus at a party. The rumour, which was just a rumour, was that Corvinus had not just seduced the senator's wife - but had raped her. When questioned after the murder, Silo provided a cast iron alibi. But, as we know, alibis are as easily purchased as whores in Rome. Silo has a known violent temper. He has flogged at least two of his slaves to death, over the years. His first wife also died in suspicious circumstances, a month after he discovered evidence that she was having an affair. You will need to pay a visit to Silo, during the course of your investigation."

Manius nodded, but then gently shook his head in ruefulness. The investigation would take longer than expected. There would be more questions than answers, as weeds outnumber flowers. The Briton felt a twinge of anguish, believing he wouldn't be present for the birth of his first child. The world was unfair. But, thankfully, he knew that already.

"You are to question, but not interrogate, Julia and Tiberius. They may be able to shed some light on Plancus' character and location - or identify other possible suspects. Tread carefully. Caesar's daughter and stepson must be beyond suspicion. Caesar is all too aware of his daughter's behaviour and indiscretions, but that doesn't mean that he will want you to point them out to him. I have already sent messages to Julia and Tiberius, informing them that you will be calling over the next day or so. Julia sent a message back, saying that she is looking forward to meeting you - having read your poetry and seen your plays. She is curious to see whether you live up to your reputation. Do not let her youth fool you. I have known Julia since her birth. She is as intelligent as any woman, or man, twice her age. I am fond of her. She enjoys a good joke, but her licentious conduct is proving to be no laughing matter. Although she can quote Aristotle better than any philosophy student, Julia does not embody his virtues and lessons of restraint. As well as her images appearing on coins, you may have observed a few bawdy images and graffiti comments about her, scattered throughout the city. I would argue though that, however salacious the gossip is about Julia, the reality may be even more colourful. You are already in the young woman's good graces. I just don't want you to find yourself in her bedchamber," Agrippa warned, his features becoming rigid, like quick-drying cement.

Varro offered up a chuckle, whilst shaking his head.

"You have no need to worry on that front. I will make it clear to Julia that I am happily married."

"That will only increase her attraction to you, I imagine. You could prove an irresistible challenge. Others have believed themselves immune to Julia's charms before, yet they fell for them."

"You should be mindful of your conduct in Julia's company, for fear of earning Caesar's displeasure" Agrippa reiterated, appreciating how Varro could be tempted to behave more like a satirist than diplomat at times. "But you should be even warier of your behaviour towards Tiberius, for fear of earning his mother's wrath. Livia is not a woman to be trifled with. Even your marriage to one of her closest companions will count for nothing, should you upset her precious son. Livia dotes on him. She is ambitious for him, perhaps far more than he is ambitious for himself. Despite or because of Livia's influence over him, Tiberius is turning into a fine Roman. I have heard favourable reports concerning his bravery and professionalism whilst fighting under Caesar in Spain. Although Augustus has been championing Marcellus in official dispatches, Tiberius has earned the respect of the ordinary soldiers. He has already been helpful in providing information about Corvinus and Plancus. I am sure he will similarly assist you in any way he can."

"It will make a welcome change, someone volunteering information during an investigation. Usually people are about as helpful as a hole in a bucket, or a one-legged cavalry horse," Varro said, resisting the urge to both yawn and call for a jug of Massic.

"But it's important I now assist you, Rufus. The events in Arretium are as alarming as they are baffling. We need to identify who was behind the attack, before they have an opportunity to strike again. It may take at least a day or two for your unknown adversary to receive word that his assassination attempt has failed. If he dares to plan another attack, as opposed to abscond, that cannot be arranged overnight, either. We have a window of opportunity, for the hunted to become the hunter. I have sent a message to the garrison commander in the region to double the guard posted at your house. I have assigned Vulso and Macer to accompany you during your task to locate Plancus, as well as serve as additional protection for you. But who do we need to protect you from? Have you slandered anyone in your plays, who may have the cause and means to exact their revenge?" Agrippa remarked, with a raised, almost reproachful, eyebrow.

"No. As much as the plays may offend some sensibilities, they do not insult any specific individuals," Varro said. "I have heard a recent report that Livius Galba is baying for my blood."

"Do you blame him? You did cuckold him. Under the law, should you be of an unenviable social rank, Galba would have had the right to execute you, without fear of prosecution. But Galba can be full of bluster, as well as brutality. He also has some semblance of honour. He would want to be present or involved in your punishment. I will send him a carefully worded letter, to warn him off, should he still harbour any ideas of violence towards you. An attack on one of Caesar's agents is an attack on Caesar himself, I'll subtly convey. We shall identify your adversary soon enough. I have instructed a number of men to visit the relevant docks and taverns, to locate other tattooed members of the gang – and their leader. Once I've gathered the requisite intelligence, I'll send word. I can arrange more men, should you need them to apprehend the gang leader. Vulso will interrogate, rather than question, him."

Galba wasn't the only one baying for blood. Attempting to assassinate his agent and friend was an act of war. When Agrippa heard about the attack, he was willing to fix his sword around his waist again and dirty his blade. The culprit would not have his day in court. His body would be buried or burned. Un-mourned.

"There is one other person I have thought of, who may be pulling the strings behind the scenes. Maecenas is not one to forgive and forget. He has the motive and means," Varro said, his face twitching as the image of the spymaster, from his nightmare, flashed through his mind.

"It's unlikely. I have never known Gaius to employ the services of a criminal gang before, to carry out an assassination. Indeed, he has nothing but contempt for the guilds. They are on a long list of things which he sneers at. There is also the argument that if Maecenas wanted you dead, you would be dead. If, however, there is firm evidence that he is involved in any plot, he will be brought to justice. Caesar will not protect him. But, trust me Rufus, Maecenas wasn't behind the attack."

Gaius Maecenas marched into his opulent study, adjusting the pleats in his toga. He was freshly shaved. His skin had been perfumed with crocus oil and cosmetics disguised the burgeoning liver spots on his temples. His hands were manicured, his nasal and ear hair plucked (along with any grey hairs sprouting from his chest). Although he had instructed one of his young, handsome slaves to give him a massage and relieve him of his anxiety during the morning, Maecenas could still feel tension in his shoulders.

His wife, Terentia, had already left the house. She said she was out shopping for the day and seeing friends, but Maecenas didn't need to have her followed to know that she would be visiting her new lover. After being Caesar's mistress, he would prove second best. Terentia had been one of his greatest assets, when she shared Caesar's bed. But now that wellspring of intelligence had run dry.

It could soon be the case, however, that the spymaster needed to find someone to share Caesar's nephew's bed. He had already befriended Marcellus and opened-up a line of communication. Over the past few months he had often written to the youth and sent him gifts, such as books or pieces of jewellery. He had already sowed the seed in the adolescent's mind that Maecenas could help guide him through the labyrinth of Roman politics. Should Caesar die from his latest bout of serious illness – and Agrippa be named as his successor – then Marcellus needed to see Agrippa as a rival. Marcellus should be encouraged to feel he is the rightful heir - the blood heir.

But should Caesar pass his ring to his nephew, he should be made to view Agrippa as a potential threat. One that should be addressed and nullified.

Maecenas reached his desk. He smirked upon seeing a pile of love letters, which one of his agents had secured. They proved that an influential senator, Publius Strabo, was conducting an affair with his daughter-in-law. Doubtless there were some others in the Senate House who would privately admire their colleague's behaviour, but most would admonish him if the scandal were made public. Strabo's influence could now be added to the store of Maecenas' influence. Sitting on the other side of his desk, like a squat, ugly toad, was the latest book of verse by Crispus Rullus. The young poet wasn't fit to polish the stylus of Horace or Virgil, but he had invited the aristocrat into his inner circle and taken him as a lover. Rullus had dedicated the book to his patron and mentor - but it was far from the greatest poetry ever to honour him. Rullus had tried too hard, or not tried hard enough. The lady - another ubiquitous Lesbia figure - had inspired him too much, or not enough.

Maecenas smoothed down his already oiled hair and made a mental note of who to invite - and more importantly who to snub - in relation to his forthcoming dinner party. He was distracted however by one of his agents, Vedius Sallust, entering.

Sallust had a furtive expression and upturned nose, like a rat sniffing the air. Despite his untrustworthy countenance Maecenas trusted the veteran spy. He had proved his loyalty on countless occasions. Sallust took particular pleasure in delivering bad news to an adversary, in the form of blackmail or extortion, on Maecenas' behalf. Secrets were treasure, to be snuffled out like pigs uncovering truffles.

"What's the latest news?" Maecenas asked, demanded. The smirk had fallen from his face, like a scab. His lips were pursed, in worry or determination - clamped shut like the jaws of a shark.

"Rufus Varro returned to Rome last night. The attack must have failed, or Bursa didn't intercept him. He's had a lucky escape it seems," Sallust reported, snorting in derision or respect. When the agent spoke, it sounded like a piece of phlegm was permanently attached to the back of his throat.

"We must find and kill him immediately," Maecenas replied, seething, baring his teeth - like a shark.

## 7.

Agrippa departed. Varro joined his companions and discussed a plan of action. He lifted his weary heart and rose to his feet, soughing like the wind. More than the will of the gods, Caesar's will must be honoured and obeyed. Another day, another assignment. Arretium seemed far more than just a day's journey away. Varro could no longer smell his wife's perfume on his clothes. But he wished he could.

The agent resolved to first visit Caesar's stepson. He hoped Tiberius could provide him with the name of a close confidante of Plancus. They would then discover their suspect, hiding at his home. Plancus would confess to the murder and they could return to Arretium, before the baby was born. That's what Varro hoped. But the agent was experienced enough to not put too much faith in his hopes.

Varro, Manius, Vulso and Macer made their way across the Palatine, weaving their way through the busy streets like fishing boats negotiating clusters of sharp coral in the shallows. Breathless slaves, their faces slick with sweat, were running an array of errands. Petty officials were burdened, like pack animals, with scrolls and wax tablets. Queues had already formed at wine stalls, with customers looking to quench their thirst in the unrelenting heat. Bedraggled tunics brushed against rustling silks. Friends traded morsels of gossip - or bewailed the state of their finances or marriages (with the latter often causing a strain on the former, or vice-versa). Scrub-faced boys were being taken off to the gymnasium (some skipped, some dragged their feet, lumbering like aged oxen). Mothers and daughters, dressed in their finery, were making their way to the temple, to make an offering. The daughters would be praying for a wealthy, handsome suitor to make a marriage proposal. The mothers would just be praying that he would be wealthy.

Varro couldn't help but catch snippets of conversation, as the flow of pedestrians grew congested through the presence of litters clogging up the streets. A couple of food vendors swapped news on past and forthcoming chariot races. A trio of women complained about the rising price of squid at the fish market, situated just outside of Rome. Varro sensed that it was more than just the merchants he overheard, who were concerned about the issue of Caesar's health.

"May the gods preserve him."

"The people may raise a riot, after their grief subsides, should he perish. Law and order, peace and prosperity, may be thrown out the window, like a bucket of shit."

"Those parasites in the Senate House may look to raise taxes too, given half the chance, and make a power grab if Augustus passes."

Despite the muggy heat Varro's party all donned cloaks, beneath which hung swords and daggers. Macer also carried a cloth bag, containing his bow and a clutch of arrows.

An assassin, or death itself, could be stalking him, Varro told himself, as he licked the sweat off his upper lip. His eyes flitted from side to side occasionally, surveying possible adversaries. Ironically, the more unassuming and anonymous people looked, the more they were likely to be a professional killer. Fatalism hung in the air, like the thick stench of ordure. Thoughts flailed around his mind, like an untethered sail in a storm. He was tempted to march across the city and confront Maecenas. But the only evidence he had, to accuse him of a crime, was that he had featured in a bad dream. Could he not just defy Caesar and Agrippa - and return to Arretium? One death sentence is the same as another. Perhaps he should at least order Manius to be by his wife's side. But he knew his friend would defy him.

A motley-dressed juggler appeared from out of nowhere in the crowd. Sweat cut scars through his make-up. He grinned, toothily, whilst juggling a set of polished knives. For a moment Varro imagined that the street entertainer might be an assassin. Out of the corner of his eye he saw Manius reach beneath his cloak and clasp his dagger. But the juggler passed harmlessly by. Varro exhaled, and was close to laughing at his paranoia. He mused how it was more likely that he would be bored to death by a juggler than stabbed by one.

Varro told himself that an assassin, or death, wasn't stalking him. He needed to concentrate on what was before him, rather than anything hidden, or non-existent, in the shadows. The agent turned his attention to the assignment at hand. Although Varro had remained largely impassive during Agrippa's briefing, the names of Felix Plancus and Marcus Corvinus were familiar to him.

He had encountered Corvinus a couple of years ago, at a party. He was in his late adolescence then, wearing a Pompey-quiff hairstyle, which had somehow become fashionable for the summer. Corvinus had sought Varro out from across the room, impressing upon him how much he enjoyed his poetry – and boasting how he had recently seduced the daughter of their host. His poetry was the soul of mediocrity, but the youth was uncommonly handsome. His features were chiselled, his hair as golden as the gaudy pieces of jewellery he wore. Varro recalled how Corvinus plucked his eyebrows and wore more perfume than all of his mistresses combined. Rumour had it that, in order to insert himself into certain social circles and further his aspirations, Corvinus had prostituted himself out to influential senators and patrons of the arts. Varro recalled a piece of gossip that Maecenas had taken an interest in the young poet. He had even given him the nickname of "Ganymede," as a result of Corvinus' habit of handing Maecenas his wine-cup. Could Maecenas be involved in his ex-lover's death?

Corvinus had a pronounced air of conceit about him. But he was a young man. That's as it should be. The aristocrat looked down his Roman nose at most things. But that was all too depressingly normal too. Arrogance is almost the birth right of the patrician class. Women were conquests, instead of companions. The more, the merrier. Every woman was fair game, whether a wife or virgin. The philosophy student had read Plato's *The Republic* and concluded that he had gold in his soul. He was destined for great things, whether he donned a toga or military breastplate. It was in his blood. Corvinus was entitled to run-up debts which he couldn't repay, but he knew his father would. He was accustomed to staying out until the early hours of the morning and then summoning his litter bearers to rush across the city and carry him home, while he slept in a pool of vomit. He felt entitled to demand that high-priced prostitutes offer him a discount. And they would grant him one, not because of his prowess as a lover but it would encourage loyalty and repeat business. Agrippa had been right. Corvinus' behaviour was all too familiar to Varro. It was unsurprising how Corvinus had gravitated towards Caesar's daughter, or perhaps Julia had been attracted to Corvinus. Life was one long party for the gilded elite. Varro knew, because he had once been one of the partygoers too.

Varro was a little surprised that Plancus was part of their set though. Again, he had encountered the youth a few times over the past couple of years. Plancus was slight, studious. Although his poetry may have aimed to be confident and flamboyant, the poet was diffident and dull. His expression often appeared anguished, or apprehensive - like he was a maltreated dog, expecting to be beaten. Varro remembered another aspect of his personality. Plancus was often desperate to please. Too desperate. During their first conversation the would-be writer offered to work as a copyist for Varro - and attempted to flatter him.

"Your poetry has changed my life," Plancus enthused, batting his eyelashes.

"Really? I wish it would help change mine," Varro drolly replied, catching the eye of a serving girl to refill his cup. He also did his best to suppress a yawn of boredom, despite or because of Varro being the topic of conversation.

He recalled attending a dinner party a week later. Plancus was in attendance too. The youth had been asked to give a reading of a few of his poems. It was painful to watch. His hands trembled as he held up the scroll. His voice was reedy, as feeble as his scrawny body. It barely carried to the front of the room, let alone the back of it. Giggles and heckles served as a chorus to the performance. Plancus blushed so much, Varro feared he might catch fire. For once, the satirical nobleman didn't laugh or mock his fellow poet. Rather he felt sorry for him. Plancus was trying to bare his soul to the world, through his work, and the world was laughing at him. He had some talent as a poet. But not enough. Already Felix may have seen himself as the runt of the litter in his family. He lived in the shadow of his two brothers, who were making names for themselves in the army and Senate House. Unlike the other guests around the table on the night when Corvinus died, Plancus was an awkward, sensitive soul. Who had invited him? And why?

Varro would have once thought that the diffident adolescent was incapable of such a brutal act. But working as a spy had provided him with added insight. Light had been shed on the darker aspects of Man's make-up. Varro would have once considered that he was incapable of murder himself. Yet he had killed – and on more than one occasion. Anyone with a heartbeat can be prone to a crime of passion.

And what of the crime? Varro re-apprised himself of the events of the fateful night, as reported by Agrippa, before questioning Tiberius. He had no desire to unwittingly offend Caesar's stepson. Or come across as being ill-informed or unprofessional.

The guests - Julia, Tiberius and Plancus - arrived separately, just after sundown. Julia and Tiberius were accompanied by their bodyguards (former lictors, who had served under Caesar). The bodyguards were instructed to remain in the house whilst the party took place in Corvinus' garden, which contained a small swimming pool. The group worked its way through several plates of food and more than one jug of wine. The atmosphere was cordial. Laughter, rather than raised or discordant words, could be heard from inside. It was noted that that Corvinus often teased Plancus (by ridiculing his poetry), but apparently the victim of his jokes took things in good humour. Tiberius left first, shortly followed by Plancus. In order to cool off, during the balmy evening, Julia joined Corvinus for a dip in the swimming pool at the end of the night. Julia eventually departed too and Corvinus dismissed his slaves. At some point after that the murderer entered the garden, through the back entrance (which had been left unlocked). Varro asked Agrippa if someone could have slipped through the entrance noiselessly. Agrippa replied that they could. There was no sound or evidence of a struggle between Corvinus and his killer. The body was found face down in the swimming pool at sun-up, by a slave. The water was cloudy red. Corvinus had been murdered by a single blow, from a wide-bladed weapon, in the back of his head. Nothing had been stolen. Was the murder a crime of passion? Or had Corvinus been the victim of a professional assassin?

Varro was now only a couple of streets away from the address Agrippa had given him, for Tiberius. He was conscious of recalling what he knew about Caesar's stepson, before crossing his threshold. His first memory of Tiberius had to be mined from several years ago. Varro had been part of the crowd, which had witnessed Caesar's triumph, celebrating his victory at Actium. Rome was, finally, at peace. Sunlight poured through the jubilant streets. Caesar and his entourage showered the adoring mob with coins and foodstuffs. Caesar rode in his chariot, albeit Varro couldn't remember if there was a figure whispering in his ear, "Remember you are mortal," like participants in previous triumphs. A serious looking boy was positioned to the left of Caesar, clad in a gold-hemmed tunic. He wore his hair long at the back. The style was synonymous with his Claudian ancestry. Voices from the crowd chanted the boy's name and encouraged him to wave back but his expression remained imperious. Impervious. Either he was too shy or overwhelmed. Or more likely the haughty boy had no intention of debasing himself and pandering to the mob. In contrast, posted to the right of Caesar (a position considered more prestigious), was Marcellus. Caesar's nephew didn't harbour any reservations in relation to responding to the crowd and duly waved his sword in the air. Octavius beamed with paternal pride and affectionately rubbed the boy's head.

Although Varro had never met Tiberius, Lucilla had. He tried to remember some of her comments:

"Despite meeting him several times I can't say I know him that well. Like a book of verse by Decimus Bibulus, I thought he was unreadable. Like most aristocrats, he keeps his emotions under lock and key. He was always polite, but seldom warm... Although Caesar took him in, I imagine that Tiberius still considers himself to be more Claudian than Julian, which of course doesn't diminish his pride and sense of superiority... Caesar brought Tiberius into his household, after his father died when he was aged nine. I believe Octavius is fond of his stepson, without ever wholly wanting to favour him. Tiberius has always been keen to honour Caesar. But as much as he wants to impress his stepfather, he may be fighting a losing battle... Livia dotes upon him, although Tiberius doesn't always reciprocate his mother's adoration. She is always eager to promote his interests, regardless of whether Tiberius sees them as his interests too... He is well-versed in Greek and Roman literature. I know he is a keen patron of public libraries too, donating books and capital... You will not be surprised to hear that Tiberius has tried his hand at writing poetry. He once showed me a couple of his verses. They were traditional, formal in tone, but he is not without some talent... Dare I say it, but I think he was sweet on me at one point. Livia has been conscious of protecting her son from the fairer sex over the years. Perhaps she does not want a rival for his affections, frustrating her ambitions for him."

Aelius Vulso, who had hung back from the rest of the group to spot any potential assailants or agents following them, quickened his pace and caught up with Varro.

"We're nearly at the address, are we not?" the soldier asked. "Have you ever met Tiberius before?"

"No. I'm afraid not. Have you?"

"No. I have heard a few reports about him though. He has gained some deserved plaudits as a military tribune. Some noblemen and tribunes hide themselves away, closer to Rome than to the frontline, when they secure their commissions. But Tiberius had been a man of action, apparently, rather than just an administrator, in Spain. He led by example and bloodied his sword. Caesar's stepson has also gained a reputation for being a hard drinker. Tiberius Claudius Nero earned the title of "Biberius Caldius Mero". Drinker of hot wine with no water added."

"There are worse - and catchier - nicknames," Varro replied, thinking how the gods of irony might strike him down should he start criticising another nobleman for drinking too much.

347

## 8.

Varro stood in the tastefully decorated triclinium. The floor was an expansive mosaic – of a Greek, geometric design flecked with gold. Expensively crafted rugs from Persia also covered the floor. A copy, or the original of a painting by Iaia of Cyzicus, dominated one of the walls. The image depicted Achilles mutilating the body of Hector. Varro had always admired the latter over the former, for his heroism in the face of defeat. Hector soldiered on, even though the gods conspired against him. Bookshelves lined all other walls. A bronze bust, of Gaius Claudius (the consul turned dictator), sat proudly on a plinth of Numidian marble in the centre of the room. Gleaming silver plates - filled with oysters and thinly sliced radishes and pears - sat on a glass-topped table. Varro noticed both military maps and astrological charts on the table too, which Tiberius had been studying when he entered. It seems he took an interest in both the heavens and earth. Varro also observed a letter on the table. He recognised the handwriting as Livia's, from the correspondence Lucilla had received over the years. The agent was unable to read the letter, however, as Livia and her son shared a special cypher.

The two aristocrats sat down on plump-cushioned couches, across from one another. Varro was furnished with a gem-encrusted goblet of wine, by a slave boy. He noticed that the slave did not bother to ask his master if he wanted his wine diluted with water.

"Agrippa trusts you. And I trust Agrippa," Tiberius said, without ceremony. "Far more than I trust others, who surround my stepfather like piglets suckling upon a teat."

"Thank you," Varro replied, uncertain of what he should be grateful for. Despite his tender years, there was a forcefulness to the youth's tone. He was eager to project his authority and dignity.

"I already know something of you, Rufus Varro. You are a nobleman and poet. You are married to one of the most esteemed women I know. Caesar speaks highly of you too. In a way, such has been the advanced praise of your character, I can only now be disappointed by you," Tiberius stated, hiding his expression through burying it in his wine cup.

Varro was unsure whether his young host was joking. Military life had bulked-up his figure. His features were lean, hard (in contrast to the rounded cheeks he displayed in the portraits Varro had seen of him; Livia had also commissioned paintings and statues which made her son resemble Caesar). A set of straight, clean teeth were housed in rosebud lips. Tiberius still wore his hair long, in a Claudian style. His toga was as pristine as his teeth, like a freshly wiped wax tablet. His eyes were large, seemingly sucking everything in and dismissing everything simultaneously. There were few things which Tiberius didn't seem contemptuous of, given the haughty superciliousness in his expression and tone. But Varro considered how the gods of irony might have a fresh excuse to condemn him, should he criticise his fellow aristocrat too much for such an outlook on life. His nose was as long and straight as the Appian Way, the poet mused, the famed road that his Claudian antecedents had built for the glory of Rome (and to provide a major artery for troops to move across the country and quell any uprisings). The pimples on his face gave the impression that Tiberius was a boy trapped in a man's body. Whether due to his military training or not, Tiberius moved with a stiff gait, as if the toga he wore was wrapped too tight. Tiberius desired to project manliness and authority, but his voice was still somewhat comically that of an adolescent. His chest was as broad as an axe, but his lungs were as narrow as a dagger.

Varro and Tiberius were alone in the triclinium. Agrippa warned his agent beforehand how Tiberius might not want to share the room with commoners, when being interviewed. Manius, Vulso and Macer were asked to wait in a small reception area at the front of the house.

"I dare say I disappoint everyone, sooner or later. I understand that you have been briefed in relation to my visit. Thank you for sparing some time to answer my questions."

"I am just doing my duty, as any Roman should. Marcus was a dear friend. He had even requested to serve alongside me in Spain. Rome is poorer for his light being prematurely extinguished. Marcus would have added to the glory of the empire, whether serving in the army or Senate House," Tiberius posited. For once his voice broke a little with grief. Or maybe his throat became dry. Which he remedied with a large mouthful of wine.

"Can you tell me a little bit about the night of the murder?"

"There is not much to tell. Marcus was his charming self, as he hosted a drinks party for a few friends. He certainly didn't exhibit any signs that someone was intending to kill him."

"I was told Corvinus exercised his wit and ridiculed Plancus throughout the evening."

"No more than usual," Tiberius replied, shrugging.

"And who invited Felix Plancus?"

"Marcus did. I think he liked to keep Felix at hand, like a pet. Or acolyte. Marcus would often mock him and his poetry, but he did so out of affection, not malice. If Felix did murder Marcus – and I have my doubts that he did – I do not believe that the motive was borne from any resentment over a harmless slight or joke."

"If you do not believe that Plancus is responsible for the crime, why do you think he has gone into hiding?"

"You would have to ask him to find the right answer. But maybe he witnessed the murder and is in fear for his life. Felix possesses a weak, meek character. For him to assault Marcus would be akin to a dove growing talons and attacking a hawk. He is frightened of his own shadow. Felix also adored Marcus, like a dog adores its master. Yet if the trail of evidence points towards him, I appreciate that you must apprehend him. If Felix did kill Marcus, he must be brought to justice. No one should be above the law."

"Could Plancus and Corvinus have been lovers, rather than just friends?"

"It's possible. Anything is possible, where Marcus is concerned. In more than one poem Felix declared his love for Marcus."

"Sometimes we hurt the ones we love," Varro argued. "Do you know of anyone else who might have exercised a grudge against Marcus - and have wanted to kill him?"

"Should you have to interview everyone in Rome who would wish injury on Marcus then you will be interviewing suspects till you are in your dotage. Unfortunately, for every lover Marcus collected, he would have collected an enemy too. Or more than one enemy, in the form of a cuckolded husband and spurned mistress. Marcus had more lovers than Zeus. To add insult to injury he would compose satirical verses about his conquests. I understand you were not dissimilar to him, not too long ago," Tiberius remarked, arching an eyebrow. Although under half his age, the youth acted like he was a father, chastising a son. Varro was tempted to laugh at the boy's attempt to censure him, but he thought better of it. He suspected Caesar's stepson was not used to people laughing at him.

An awkward silence hung in the air, like harpist waiting for a fellow musician to play a refrain. Eventually Varro replied:

"Long enough ago, I hope. Any enemies I have nowadays are probably more worried about their hair and teeth falling out, from old age. Or they have lost their wits and forgotten about any offence I caused."

"Unfortunately, Marcus did have several enemies. Some had a genuine grievance. Some were just envious of him. Should you ask me who you should be investigating, you should not discount Gnaeus Silo as a suspect. They had a public disagreement recently, and Silo vowed to kill Marcus. Apparently, Silo has an alibi, but I will leave it to you to investigate the veracity of that claim. In terms of another suspect, I believe that Quintus Trebonius swore he would take his revenge against Marcus, in recompense for him stealing his army commission. Marcus could win and lose friends on a daily basis. He could charm or condemn in equal measure. He frequently borrowed money, with no intention of paying it back. He could be callous towards his mistresses. He would grow bored - and discard them like a child will throwaway a toy, that no longer amuses him. Marcus was seductive, as well as selfish. But great men should be forgiven for their minor indiscretions. He could captivate an entire room, when he spoke about philosophy or recited a poem. He borrowed so much money, because he was generous towards his friends. Despite his own faithlessness, Marcus engendered loyalty in his close companions. He was brave. Talented. His divine spark burned brightly. He was devoted to his father and wished to honour his family name. Marcus should be mourned, for the hero of Rome he would have been. We should honour him. I am still in a state of solemn grief. But I am angry too. Should his murderer walk into this chamber right now, I would grab my sword and run him through," Tiberius stated, losing a little of his self-possession. His hand trembled as he reached for his cup again. His eyes moistened with tears as he remembered his friend.

Varro attempted a consoling expression, although he wasn't sure how much of a balm he was providing. He felt sorry for the adolescent, imagining how bereft and angry would be, should someone murder Manius. Varro turned his head and stared at a bust of Plato carved out of Porphyry marble, on a stylish bronze table, by the sofa.

"It was a gift from my stepfather. The piece once belonged to Sulla," Tiberius said, remembering with pride the moment Caesar presented his him with the bust. It had been after Tiberius had given the eulogy at his father's funeral. He had only been nine, but he had composed the eulogy himself and compelled the mourners to weep with his performance.

"It's funny that a dictator would prize a statue of the author of The Republic," Varro posed.

"It's not that funny," Tiberius said, humourlessly. "Even Pericles displayed shades of being a dictator. We are all a patchwork of contradictions. And thankfully so, otherwise people would be even duller than they are. You have recently become a playwright. Drama is essentially conflict. Your characters must be full of conflict and contradictions, if you are aiming for art to imitate life. In life, unlike art however, few things are resolved. Although I understand that you have found a happy ending yourself. You were a lucky man to marry Lucilla once, let alone twice. I was often in the same room when she called upon our home. Even when my mother poured scorn on you – and highlighted your infidelities – Lucilla did not speak ill of you. Perhaps she thought it was a bit rich, having my mother lecture someone on how one shouldn't tolerate a husband's unfaithfulness. My stepfather makes even Marcus seem chaste. The apple has not fallen far from the tree in relation to his daughter," the Claudian nobleman remarked, pursing his lips in disapproval. "I understand you will be interviewing Julia too."

"Yes, I will be paying her a visit later on today."

"I hope she can be of some assistance as well. Julia has dedicated her life to the pursuit of pleasure, rather than duty, though. Whatever she wants, she takes. She does not honour the gods, or her father. The Forum is just another place to fuck, for her. You should be careful my stepsister doesn't take too great a liking to you, Rufus Varro, lest your happy ending comes to an end. Julia has a taste for both poets and husbands. You will be two feast days in one for her. I do not believe that Caesar will tolerate her unseemly behaviour for too long. The closer Marcellus gets to becoming a son and heir, the less need he will have for a daughter. I pity her husband, whoever she marries. She will cuckold him before the wedding night is over."

Tiberius took a large swig from his winecup after he spoke, as if he wanted to wash away the names of Julia and Marcellus from his throat. As intelligent and mature as the youth appeared, a childish petulance still understandable eclipsed a sense of wisdom and restraint.

"You still see your stepsister. She was present on the evening of the party - and may have been the last person to see Corvinus alive. Not counting his killer. Can you tell me if they were more than friends?"

"Neither are famed for their celibacy. In their ability to seduce and sacrifice their lovers, in the blink of an eye, they may have been a perfect match for one another. But it's best that you ask Julia that question, when you meet her.

And yes, I still see her occasionally. Thankfully our paths do not intersect too much," he said. Again, a forced, formal smile was followed by a pinched expression - and Varro pictured again the image of a disdainful child, riding next to Caesar during the Triumph.

The two men spoke for a while longer. Tiberius mentioned that his father was friends with Appius Varro.

"Your father honoured Rome. He was an asset to the ruling class. Governance was in his blood. I am surprised that you have not chosen to follow in his footsteps and pursue the course of honours," Tiberius said, as he glanced, not without some pride, at the image of Gaius Claudius.

"I fear that the course of honours will ultimately lead me down to Hades, rather than to the heights of the Senate House. Becoming a politician really would ruin my happy ending – although as a playwright I am used to making things up, which could aid me in any candidacy to become a statesman."

Again, Varro couldn't discern whether his host grimaced or smiled in reply, as his features were hidden behind his winecup.

The agent asked a few more follow-up questions. Although Tiberius was unable to suggest a chief suspect, who could be providing refuge for Felix Plancus, he did provide Varro with a comprehensive list of the fugitive's closest friends. Tiberius also asked the agent to keep him abreast of any developments in the investigation.

"You have an impressive library," Varro remarked, as he rose to his feet and surveyed the row of scrolls along the wall.

"Thank you. But what you see before you is merely a branch, rather than the whole tree, in relation to my collection. A room without books is like a body without a soul," Tiberius exclaimed, quoting Cicero, soullessly.

Varro reconvened with his companions out in the street. They looked at the agent with an air of expectancy. Unfortunately, he couldn't provide either answers or certainty.

"How did it all go?" Vulso asked. He refrained from complaining that all they had been offered while waiting for Varro was bread and water. Thankfully or not, as a soldier, he had suffered worse meals.

"It went well, I'm sorry to say. Too well. Tiberius cooperated. He furnished me with a list of Plancus' friends. Although he does not think Plancus is guilty. He has provided us with a couple of other suspects to investigate. He believes we should scrutinise Silo's alibi. He also believes that we should consider one Quintus Trebonius as a suspect. We will be obliged to investigate both, which could take some time," Varro said, sighing and rolling his eyes. Out of the corner of his eye he saw Manius' shoulders slump. The Briton didn't say anything about the delay to returning to Arretium. But he didn't have to.

"So, what was Caesar's stepson like?" Macer said, eagerly. The bowman was keen to take some gossip back to Sabina.

"Even for a Claudian, he was a snob. Cato wasn't as self-important, nor Brutus as self-righteous, at the same age I imagine. I didn't know whether to be worried, or amused, by some of the things he opined. Tiberius has been expensively educated, but he has a lot to learn. One may argue that there is much to admire about the military tribune. But there is something out of kilter about his character. I am just glad Tiberius is some way down the list, in regards to Caesar choosing his successor. So, there you have the stepson. It's time to now meet the daughter."

## 9.

A slender, dusky, barefooted slave led Varro and his party through the house, towards where her mistress was relaxing, in the garden. Her perfume, infused with rosewater, trailed in her wake like the train of a gown. Varro mused how he had rarely seen such a provocatively or richly dressed slave. Her figure-hugging dress - dyed in sea-green, purple and saffron-yellow – must have belonged to her mistress. Similarly, Julia must have given her permission to wear her jewellery. The young woman sounded like a tambourine, as numerous bracelets and anklets jangled together with every stride and rhythmic movement of her hips.

Vulso glared at the slave and licked his lips, as if imagining himself biting into the pert posterior, like it was a pomegranate. Macer was similarly entranced, his eyes as wide and round as a hoplite's shield, and conveniently forgot about Sabina. The bowman remained slack-jawed as he took in the magnificent house. The property appeared lavish and opulent from the outside – with its marble colonnades, decorative coloured glass and bronze statuary. The interior matched, or surpassed, the exterior. The inside was awash with marble flooring, intricate mosaics, silver mirrors and pieces of furniture inlaid with ivory and gold. The atrium was home to a pond, filled with koi carp. Varro noticed a couple of large paintings by Arellius, with more flesh than clothes on show. As he viewed an awe-struck Macer out the corner of his eye he thought how the praetorian would need to grow accustomed to such households. Should Rome experience an uprising or riot the archer would be ordered to guard such homes and their owners.

It was said that Caesar lived modestly, in his small property on the Palatine. But the apple had fallen far from the tree, in another orchard, it seemed. No expense had been spared throughout the ostentatious residence. The house gleamed, dazzled. Everything was impressive – but somehow vulgar too, Varro ruminated.

The agent and his companions were shown into a small, octagonal-shaped grove, through a narrow entrance, situated within a larger garden. Ornate trellis work served as walls to the grove, intertwined with myrtle, vines, budding flowers and suggestive paintings. Varro reasoned that, as well as serving as decoration, the plants and paintings prevented prying eyes from spying into the intimate alcove. Despite the smell of the various blooms, Julia's aromatic perfume, laced with myrrh and spikenard, cut through the air like a knife.

Caesar's nubile daughter was reclining on a purple sofa, dressed in a scarlet dress made from luxuriant Coan silk. One of her smooth, tanned legs accidentally (or artfully) hung out of the slit in her dress. Julia rose to greet her guests. A playful smile danced on her glistening lips. She took in the four men, sucking on the tip of her finger, apprising them like a widow might assess the stock during a slave auction.

"Rufus Varro. I hope you will be worth the wait. I received a letter from Marcus Agrippa. I am surprised that he didn't call upon me himself. I imagine that he would have been pleased to get out the house, especially if his wonderfully dull wife was at home. Your attendants look good enough to eat. I could feast upon the sight of you and your companions all day. But I must speak with you privately. You will be welcome to feast upon my hospitality while I steal Rufus away from you. I have provided some refreshments in one of the reception rooms in the house. Herminia, please see to their every need and whim," their hostess instructed, her tone as sweet as honey. The mistress of the house addressed Varro with a disarming amount of confidence – and even familiarity. It was as though he was an ex-lover. Or soon to be lover.

The comely slave girl beamed, bowed and led Manius, Vulso and Macer back into the house, where a veritable banquet of food was waiting for them, to be washed down with a selection of ruby-red wines.

"Alone at last," Caesar's daughter remarked, tucking her hair behind her ears, revealing a pair of diamond earrings. Her smile added a layer of luridness to its playfulness. "But tell me, who was that large attendant in your party? He seems like the strong and silent type, which I've found to be one of the better types. I noticed that he refrained from ogling me, which was both courteous and rude at the same time. He didn't seem interested me, which of course interests me."

"Manius is my bodyguard."

"Is he a eunuch?"

"No, he's happily married."

"Ha! There's no such thing, in my experience. You may as well say that there's such a thing as an honest politician. Or an honest woman, come to that. And what of your other companions? Although I have scant interest in the boy. Boys only know how to satisfy themselves. The pups know not how to satisfy women."

"They're soldiers."

"Yawn. I have had my fill of soldiers too. They can't help but be rough and uncouth. They feel they need to dominate and conquer, and frantically move about your body as if they are on manoeuvres."

Varro smiled in reply. He couldn't quite be sure if he was doing so out of politeness, humour or awkwardness. He took in the woman, or rather girl, in front of him. The make-up she wore gave the impression that she was older than she was. Her body wasn't quite fully developed, but Varro could easily imagine how many men would admire and women envy her figure eventually. Her features were fine, attractive – similar to the statues and portraits Varro had seen of her father. Her blue-green eyes (framed within curled, coquettish eyelashes) were bright – teeming with life, like her fishpond. Occasionally, however, her expression could be, like her father's, scrutinising or inscrutable. Her fair hair was styled in a bun, and held in place by a large shiny, sharp, silver hairpin. Varro fancied that Julia was wittier – and wiser – than her stepbrother, although that wasn't such an insurmountable task. Caesar's daughter had plenty to learn too though. She wanted to gleam, dazzle and shock. She was impressive, but vulgar. She seemed to be wearing more perfume than a courtesan, as if her small hands had accidentally dropped the bottle over her. Her shimmering silk dress possessed a plunging V-shaped neckline, although there was little to see. An inverted V-shape dominated the bottom half of the garment. The material was so sheer that one could see the odd mole and blemish beneath the dress. At least the material was slightly thicker around the girl's waist. Julia, or her dressmaker, still had a kernel of modesty left, Varro thought.

"Thank you for sparing me your time."

"It's my pleasure. Or, hopefully, it will be your pleasure," Julia said, arching her eyebrow, suggestively. But then she smiled, amused at her own joke, flashing her white teeth like a blade. She kept her gaze fixed on Varro, eyeing up his chiselled features and well-conditioned figure, as she took a couple of steps backwards and reclined upon her sofa again. The agent took in her black, soft leather slippers which, open-toed, revealed red-painted nails. A bracelet, coiled around her tawny forearm, resembled an asp. The head of the snake was open-mouthed and contained a sapphire.

Varro also couldn't help but observe two finely crafted statues, carved from Luna marble, flanking Caesar's daughter.

"I take it you recognise Bacchus. From what I have heard, you were a devotee of the god, when you were younger."

"I'm not sure any god would be entirely pleased to have me as a devotee – and I wouldn't wish to be a worshipper of any god who had the poor taste to welcome me into its cult."

Julia laughed. The unaffected, sparkling sound filled the grove, jangling like Herminia's jewellery.

"I remember overhearing your wife, or she was your former wife then, calling you witty, several years ago. She was telling the truth. Perhaps there is at least one honest woman in the world. The other statue is, of course, Aphrodite. You may have seen coins attesting to my affinity with the deity. Although you may not zealously follow any god, I am hoping that goddesses still possess the ability to captivate you," Julia remarked. Again, she smiled – either playfully or amorously.

"Any goddess would hopefully divine I am happily married too."

"I think I might have to start praying to the gods, that you have not grown old before your time, Rufus. I have read some of your poetry. You used to be bored. But now you may be boring. You were once hailed as a new Catullus. But you are doing a better impression of Horace, hiding yourself away and living an inextricably tedious existence in the countryside. The countryside is overrated. I couldn't bear living a life of so-called domestic bliss. The birdsong will be drowned out by the sound of a bleating spouse. The smell of dung will overpower the scent of wildflowers. The only man I'd be able to fuck is a slave or, worse, my husband – as there wouldn't be anyone else's husband around to have fun with," Julia argued, before sipping some wine and running her tongue over her top lip. "But, alas, you have not come here to have fun, Rufus Varro. You wish to interview me about the evening of Marcus

Corvinus' murder. I should of course be offended that I am not being considered a suspect. Do I not possess the necessary strength and courage to kill a man, if my life depended on it? Or if my honour, or dishonour, depended on it? My father has been responsible for tens of thousands of deaths, can his daughter not be responsible for just one? But I should be answering your questions, rather than asking you to answer mine," Julia added, adjusting her dress slightly, so that Varro could see more of her bosom and thighs. Was she hoping to shock, embarrass or distract the agent?

"Could you tell me about the night of the murder?"

"We had an enjoyable party – and then Marcus was killed." Caesar's daughter stated. For once the smile fell from her face. The make-up around her eyes cracked a little. But her mask, or true semblance, soon returned. "Most of my memories were washed away by the wine I drank, but I do not recall any air of tension during the night. Marcus may have teased Felix, but we all like teasing and being teased, do we not?"

Mischief sparkled in her eyes, like petals of light strewn across water. Julia looked like she as on the cusp of laughing, or pouncing.

"You were the last to leave, were you not?"

"Yes. Marcus was still relaxing in his pool. I left, accompanied my bodyguards, through the front door. Perhaps if I had left through the door in the garden, I might have spotted the assassin, or scared them off. To save you the embarrassment of asking whether Marcus and I were more than friends, I will tell you. We were lovers. But by being lovers, we were *less* than friends. Our relationship was casual, at best. I cannot rightly remember who seduced who. He was a dish I had to sample. I wanted to satisfy my curiosity with Marcus. His reputation, like yours, preceded him. I saw women fall into his lap, or he fell into theirs. He was as handsome as Paris, and as cunning as Odysseus. You would have admired his seduction techniques, far more than you would have admired his verses. He could leer at a young girl, or her mother, and it almost seemed like the straps of the dress they were wearing would unfasten themselves. My curiosity was satisfied, but little else. The most important love affair in Marcus' life was the one he conducted with himself. The most alluring gown could never compete with the sight of himself in a mirror. He duly craved to be the centre of attention during the party - and succeeded. Even though I was present and competed for the honour."

"And what of Felix Plancus? Was he a friend or lover of the victim?"

"He was both. Or perhaps their relationship was more like deity and supplicant. Sometimes Felix would just stare at his idol, doe eyed. He would always be ready to fill his winecup or lend him money. He would be the first and last person to applaud Marcus when he recited one of his second or third-rate poems. I think Felix even enjoyed it somewhat when his master ridiculed him. At least it meant that his hero was then paying attention to him. Felix was unhealthily obsessed with Marcus. Obsession can be wonderfully comic to an outside observer. Yet zealots can be dangerous too. Marcus may have created a monster – and then the monster turned on its creator and slew him.

I find it difficult to believe that Felix is guilty, however. He is guilty of writing some turgid verse, certainly. Felix always stressed how much pain he went through, baring his soul, when composing his poetry. If only he knew how painful it was to listen to his verse."

The cat has claws, Varro thought to himself. He didn't have the time to interrogate the merits of Plancus' poetry, however.

"It seems that Corvinus had plenty of other enemies, who could serve as suspects. Are you familiar with Gnaeus Silo?"

"Yes, but thankfully not too familiar. I understand Marcus slept with his wife, Marilla, recently and Silo didn't take kindly to his behaviour. The two rams butted heads. I'm bemused as to why people think monogamy can work - or be fun. Even the gods are unfaithful. Should we not look to imitate the gods? You will not find any fidelity in nature, either. Silo may not display the greatest endurance as a lover, but he does possess the stamina to hold a grudge. Gnaeus has an alibi for the night of the murder. He could probably purchase half a dozen more, if called upon to do so. Rumour has it that he has also employed the advocate, Lentulus Nerva, to assist him should he have to answer further questions in relation to the crime. As much as Nerva is known for taking on the guilty, his clients tend to walk free."

"I spoke to your stepbrother and he mentioned that a Quintus Trebonius nursed a grievance against Corvinus too. Is that right?" Varro asked, noting her comments about Silo. It would be difficult to prise a confession out of the statesman, given Nerva's potential involvement, but he would cross or fall off that bridge when he came to it.

"Marcus generated grievances, as goats churn out milk. His sins were as countless as the stars. One of Rome's favourite sons was far from universally loved. But what did you think of one of Rome's other favourite sons, my ebullient stepbrother? I've seen marble busts of Cato smile more, and one is more likely to hear the sound of a unicorn farting, as opposed to laughter, in his household. I feel sorry for Tiberius though. He can do no wrong in the eyes of a mother, who he cares little for. And yet he can never entirely satisfy my father, who he desperately desires the approval and admiration of. I must confess, I haven't seen Tiberius since the night of the murder. From reading Plato's Republic, he concluded that he had gold in his soul – and therefore shouldn't react to anything. He was taciturn on the night of the party, and I can't imagine he is garrulous now. I still can't quite decide whether he revered or reviled Marcus," Julia said, before yawning. "Excuse me. I had a late night. I was courted by a trio of suitors. I think I can still remember the names of two of them. They tripped over themselves to fall at my feet. They puffed themselves up and tried to deflate one another. I was their moon or muse. They flattered me but, more enjoyably, they amused me – and not in the way they intended. They showered me with gifts, which I will pass on to my slaves. Or I will shower the people with them, when I am next passing through the city in my litter. I'm all too happy to keep the dressmakers and jewellers of Rome in business, although I fear I am responsible for inspiring too much uninspiring poetry. Their words failed to warm my heart, but the parchment will help fuel the fire this winter. I'm just joking. Or am I?"

Her voice was sometimes sultry, sometimes sarcastic. Varro thought the girl was akin to a restless frog, jumping from one subject and mood to another, in the blink of an eye.

"You are developing a reputation yourself it seems, Julia. Take it from someone who knows though, it's a lot easier to gain a reputation than to lose one," Varro warned, hoping that he was coming across as sincere rather than sanctimonious. The girl's soul was burning brightly, but she could also burn out.

"I like you Rufus Varro. You are one of the few men I know who I would prefer to laugh with, rather than at. I would love to get you into bed for the quality of the pillow talk, as well as to assess your prowess as a lover. I have a confession to make. I became a little fascinated with you, around a year ago, when I first started to read your poetry. I saw you as a kindred spirit. We are all alone in the world. But I felt less alone in the world when I read your satires. You know that a desire fulfilled is a desire negated. But that shouldn't dissuade us from pursuing further desires. As dull as Horace has become, I agree with him when he says that we should seize the day and suck the marrow out of life. I adored that you never cared about what anyone thought of you. You rebelled against your father and your class, like Prometheus against the gods," Julia said, impassioned. She had now swivelled her legs around, off the sofa, and was leaning forward intently.

"You shouldn't believe everything a poet writes. Myself, or Horace too. I think I even once wrote that I was "a truth-teller". I am surprised that an advocate didn't sue me for fraud. As much as you may have been fascinated with Rufus Varro the poet, I am just Rufus Varro the man now. Or Rufus Varro the husband," he replied, thinking how much he would soon like to become Rufus Varro the father. For Lucilla's sake, as much as his.

"I always thought Lucilla to be a lucky woman, although she was clever enough to make her own luck. When she used to visit my stepmother, I thought her beautiful, so much so that I should have envied and despised her. But she made me laugh, and sometimes brought me books to read. I also remember a piece of advice she gave me. When people tell you to be cautious, be bold. And when people tell you to be bold, be cautious."

Varro smiled, appreciatively. The agent pictured his wife. The image was bittersweet.

"That sounds like Lucilla."

"Please pass on my regards to her, when you next see her."

"I will."

"If you also pass on my regards to Marcus. My father's closest friend is one of the only men who I could ever marry, because I know that he would never wholly love me back. His heart belongs to another – and not his wife. Well, not his current wife. I might have praised infidelity earlier, but I admire Marcus for staying faithful to Caecilia. He stands in stark contrast to my father, who may well preach the virtues of being a good husband and father.

But he does not practise what he preaches. The only thing he remains faithful to is inconstancy. Yet given who he is married to, I cannot altogether condemn him. If you were married to Livia, would you not seek solace in the arms of another woman? Livia is more likely to whisper poison, than sweet nothings, into a man's ear. Or whisper incessant words of praise for her precious son, Tiberius. She is more likely to bore you to sleep, faster than any sleeping drug can work its magic."

In the same way that Tiberius had looked like he was chewing a wasp, when he mentioned his stepsister or Marcellus, Varro noticed how a sour expression came over Julia when she mentioned her stepmother.

"I will pass on your regards to Marcus too."

"Thank you," the girl replied, warmly rather than flirtatiously, and then yawned. "I won't have any need of a sleeping draught myself, it seems. I need to get some beauty sleep, not least because I am hosting a party this evening. I must insist that you attend. You will be welcome to bring your companions. Particularly Manius, of course. I may try and seduce you too. I will instruct Herminia to keep filling your winecup, so I can take advantage of you. Unless you would like to take advantage of me. Some of Rome's finest families will be attending, but do not let that put you off. I will even send out invites to Gnaeus Silo and Quintus Trebonius, to further tempt you. What do you say?" the girl asked, her eyes bulging and gleaming. Ripe or overripe. Amused and dictatorial at the same time. There were queens who were less used to getting their own way, Varro fancied.

"Be bold, Julia. Be bold."

### 10.

Varro asked Caesar's daughter a few more questions, before he took his leave. Her perfume was making him a little nauseous and he craved the "fresh" air of Rome. Julia mentioned she had no idea where Felix could be hiding, although even if she did, she might be hesitant in revealing his location.

"I could be condemning an innocent man to death, and my family already has enough blood on its hands... You said that my father asked you to investigate who murdered Marcus, in order to honour his friendship with Porcius Corvinus? You should know that my father does little out of the goodness of his heart. He's a political animal. He possesses ulterior motives, as you and I possess vintage wines in our cellars. I have been told that Porcius promised my father a significant donation and use of his gladiators, to help Marcellus stage some games to boost his popularity with the people. But now Porcius will only agree do so if his son's murderer is brought to justice."

A blast of dirty, vermilion heat hit Varro as he entered the street. The heavy, bracketed door slammed loudly behind him. He wasn't sure if the imposing entrance was meant to keep people out or trap them inside. The paving stones were worn smooth, perhaps from the constant traffic of party guests and would-be suitors calling at the house.

"So, what did she reveal? That wasn't already on show," Manius half-joked to his friend, before letting out a burp. His belt, fastened around his tunic, began to cut into hips a little from the food and wine he had consumed, along with his other companions.

"Not much, at most."

Varro sighed, like a man who had lost his sword but found a rusty dagger. He still didn't know if Corvinus was murdered by Felix, a professional assassin or another one of the victim's numerous enemies. He still couldn't confirm Silo's alibi. He was no closer to finding Plancus. No closer to going home.

Motes of dust hung in the air, like insects, as Varro sat in his study. Slashes of light cut through the slats in the shutters on the windows. He gulped down another cup of water. The cool liquid ran down his parched throat, like a stream running through a desert. Although Fronto had placed freshly cut flowers in the room the musty smell of parchment still pervaded the air. Varro flexed his hand and read over the contents of his letter to Lucilla.

*"Rome is much as I remember it, I'm sorry to say. I'm missing you and the quiet life even more than I expected. I doubt if even Odysseus missed Penelope this much. The definition of Hades is other people. And Rome is full of people. A small consolation has been seeing Fronto again. He is much as I remember him, I'm pleased to say. His body may be drying out, like a date in the sun, but he still has a knowing glint in his eye. The house is in good order, as is the garden. The roses you planted are in bloom.*

*So, why was I summoned to the capital? I have been asked (if asked means ordered), by Caesar no less, to investigate the murder of one Marcus Corvinus. Unfortunately, Corvinus had more enemies than Decimus Bibulus has lines of poetry which don't rhyme properly. The one bright spot is that there is a chief suspect, Felix Plancus, whose fleeing of the scene would suggest he is guilty. I am hoping that the gods will smile on me and we will find Plancus quickly - and he will confess to the crime. I do not wish to bore you with the details of the murder here (you can look forward to me doing so when I get back) but should you somehow know of Corvinus or Plancus then I would welcome your thoughts, concerning their characters.*

*Our journey to Rome was eventful, but again I will tell you more about it when I return.*

*Being an agent has reminded me why I no longer wish to be an agent. My heart isn't in it. But a heart is one of the last things an agent should possess in this game. Aye, it often feels like a game – a game that you can only lose, in one way or another. I feel like I'm scrabbling around in a mudheap, searching for a piece of shit. My investigation so far has only taken me to the heights of the Palatine, as opposed to the bowels of the Subura. Today I encountered both Caesar's stepson and daughter. I'm moving up in the world, unfortunately.*

*I first met Tiberius. He's half boy, half military tribune – and all Claudian. I can't quite decide whether to consider him more or less than the sum of his parts. He seems keen to follow Caesar's orders, but he's only human – and far keener to give out orders. Tiberius mentioned how he was fond of you, but take it from someone who knows, it's not always a blessing to have a Caesar hold you in high esteem.*

*I next met Julia. I remember you saying how she was a shy, intelligent girl, that her friends and tutors were vetted by her father. Livia also ensured that certain Roman virtues (whatever they are) were instilled in her. But you argued that sooner or later Julia would realise she was a Caesar. A law unto herself. Suffice to say, shy would be one of the last words to describe the girl now. She is mercurially intelligent, however. I couldn't quite decide whether she was being genuine or glib at times. Perhaps I deserve to get a taste of my own medicine. But Julia has broken free of her cage – and she is now a man-eater. I worry that her licentious behaviour is a way for her to attract her father's attention. She may regret it when she finally does.*

*But I have devoted enough of my attention to the Caesars for one day. How are you? And how is Camilla? I hope that the baby will wait for his father to return before he, or she, makes their entrance. Given the drear state of the world, I'm not sure how eager I would be to come into it."*

Varro suffered a rare bout of writer's block, as he deliberated what to write, or what not to write, in relation to the issue of when he would be travelling back to Arretium. He pictured Camilla asking Lucilla about their due date, as soon as the letter arrived. Varro shifted in his chair, uncomfortably, as he re-read the line about telling his wife that his journey to Rome had been eventful. He told himself that he wasn't lying. But he felt as dishonest as a priest.

Each breath was akin to a sigh. The agent craved something stronger than water as he started to tally-up how much additional time he would require, to complete the investigation. He would arrange to pay a visit to Silo and Trebonius. He wanted to visit the scene of the crime too, in order to paint a clearer picture of events. As awkward as it would doubtless be, he would interview the parents of the victim and possible culprit.

Varro was about to bury his head in his hands, when he was distracted by an attendant entering. Agrippa and his agent had been trading messages throughout the afternoon. There was a chink of light and some potential good news. Agrippa had obtained some intelligence on the location of Cervidius Stolo, the guild leader of the men, branded with hammer-shaped tattoos, who had attempted to murder Varro. They also revealed the name of his lieutenant, Bursa, who had led the band of brigands. Frustratingly, Agrippa ordered that Manius and Vulso should take charge of apprehending Stolo. While they were doing so his agent would accept the invitation to attend Julia's party this evening. Hopefully Silo and Trebonius would be present too. Wine might lubricate one of their tongues, Agrippa argued, although Varro was more interested in wine lubricating his own tongue first.

Varro initially heard the sound of the blade scraping across the sharpening stone, before he saw the silhouette of Manius, sitting on a chair in the garden. The Briton had a habit of ritually sharpening his sword whenever he was anxious. He had always done so before a gladiatorial bout. Varro recalled how he often did so too when he first courted Camilla, fearful as he was that her father would find out about their relationship and forbid his daughter from seeing the lowly, foreign bodyguard.

Manius stared out across the city. Smoke melted into the Stygian night. A breeze hissed through the nearby cypress tree. People looked like shades, lemures - as though the tombs of the necropolis, the city of the dead outside Rome's walls, had opened its gates.

Varro sat down in silence next to his friend. The only sounds that could be heard were that of wine sloshing into a cup, and a blade being sharpened. The two men had spent many an afternoon and evening in the garden, sharing a joke and a jug of Massic. Varro took a sidelong glance at his companion. The Briton's expression reminded Varro of when Manius had first entered the household, after his father had bought the gladiator's freedom. The youth was suspicious of the aristocrat's generosity and kindness. His freedom and new life were surely too good to be true. Apprehension was etched into his features, like tiny scars. His eyes regularly darted around the rooms he entered, perhaps searching for potential weapons or exits. The habit would prove useful, for being a bodyguard and spy.

Manius had initially been wary of the young nobleman in the house, and rightly so. Varro treated the foreigner with thinly veiled disdain or pronounced indifference. He didn't want to give the impression that the feral Briton was his equal, or a rival. The aristocrat would speak to his father's pet as if he were a slave. Yet, with time and Fronto's encouragement, Varro got to know and like the ex-gladiator. His affection understandably increased for the Briton after Manius prevented all manner of drunks and aggrieved gamblers from beating him to a pulp. If not for his friend, he may well have shared the same fate as Marcus Corvinus – and been murdered by a cuckold or spurned lover. Varro now considered his bodyguard the bravest and most honourable man he knew.

Varro also admired Manius for his good humour, although at present he appeared as overjoyed as someone who had found a piece of mud in a mound of shit. His stubbled jaw was as square as his shoulders, as he gritted his teeth. The agent wished he could offer up some hope to his friend, that he would return in time to be there for the birth of his child. But he felt he would just be offering up lies.

"How's the Alban?" Varro asked, as Manius glugged down half a cup of wine.

"It's as dry as an old drab's –", Manius remarked, yawning before he could finish his analogy. "Or as dry as your sense of humour."

"Perhaps we should take some back to Arretium with us. Let's hope it doesn't become a vintage before that happens. Am happy to use it as an excuse to send you back too. You don't have to stay," Varro remarked, offering his friend a lifeline to see his wife and be there for the birth of his child.

"I know I don't have to stay. But I will. I wouldn't want you to get into even more trouble than you're likely to get involved in already. Camilla understands," Manius answered, hoping rather than expecting that his wife would forgive him. "She has Lucilla with her there too. She may get even more broody once Camilla has the baby."

"Aye, I've thought about that. We're still trying to have a child. One doctor said that it may be my fault. Another doctor argued that Lucilla may not be able to become pregnant, given the complications she suffered before," Varro replied, thinking how the doctors employed as much science in their opinions as a soothsayer when coming to their conclusions. One of the doctors had a runnier nose than Viola, fewer teeth than a jellyfish and a more pronounced stoop than Fronto, Varro recalled. *Physician, heal thyself.* The doctor charged more for his time than the most expensive courtesan. He recommended all manner of absurd treatments (such as drinking bat's urine and rubbing snail slime on her stomach) to help his wife conceive. "Lucilla says that she is happy and doesn't mind not having children. But I know she does mind. As a husband, who lied to his wife throughout his first marriage, I can tell when she is lying to me. Or perhaps my time as an agent has helped me divine the truth. Although, as a spy, we're encouraged to think that everyone is lying to us, all the time."

"The gods may provide an answer. Or you can adopt," Manius suggested, wanting to offer some hope to his friend.

"Perhaps the gods do not want another Rufus Varro out in the world."

"But they would want another Lucilla."

"They would indeed, if they've got any sense. Which is yet to be proved. But Lucilla will make a good mother. Good enough to hopefully compensate for my copious deficiencies as a father."

Manius grinned in reply, although rather than his comment Varro thought that his friend was likely smiling at the appearance of his dog. Viola jauntily padded across the lawn. The mongrel leapt up and put her front paws on the nearby table, to check for any possible scraps of food. She then sided up to Manius and leant against his leg.

Varro filled both their cups and downed his own measure immediately.

"How are you bearing up? I imagine you want to get back to Lucilla, as much as I want to see Camilla."

"Well nobody's tried to assassinate me today so I suppose I should be grateful for small mercies. Although I'm acutely aware that the day isn't over yet. Agrippa is furnishing me with some of his bodyguards to escort me to the party this evening. Once you've finish questioning this Stolo we may have something to celebrate, in the form of knowing the name of the man - or woman - who is trying to kill me. Or if we fail to have something to celebrate, we'll have accumulated enough sorrows to drown. Either way, we should meet later. I was thinking we could all pay a visit to Bassos at *The Golden Lion*. He'll welcome our company and coin. The latter more than the former. But who could blame him for that?"

Manius nodded, and stroked Viola behind the ear. He looked forward to enjoying a drink with his friends later that evening. It would help take his mind of various things. But right now, he wanted to focus on his current assignment. The plan was to abduct and interrogate the guild leader, in order to extract the requisite information. Manius was willing to torture - and kill - Cervidius Stolo tonight, if necessary.

*There will be blood.*

## 11.

A wave of noise - the drone of conversation and tintinnabulation of laughter - hit Varro, like a blast of heat from the mouth of a volcano, when he entered the room. His eyes narrowed, wincing, from the cacophony of colour. The dressmakers and dyers of Rome were having a profitable year. There was not a plain, matronly stola in sight. Teeth and gems gleamed. Smooth, burnished flesh glowed in the candlelight. There was almost an unofficial competition taking place as to who could wear the most revealing item of clothing.

Varro surveyed the scene, his nostrils prickling with perfume and incense. The large, square reception room was brimming with people. Sofas lined the walls, where women sat on the laps of groping men. A couple of jugglers weaved their way through the chamber, but the glassy-eyed revellers barely noticed them. Julia's bodyguards, who Varro had encountered earlier in the day, were now dressed in short skirts, their muscular torsos glistening with oil. They wore black eyeliner and flowers in their hair. Their jaws still jutted out and their expressions remained stony, but they looked ridiculous, emasculated. Dozens of lithe serving girls kept topping up winecups to quench the party's thirst, like a bucket chain of people trying to extinguish a fire. Erotic paintings and statuary adorned the chamber. A bronze Priapus bared all. By the end of the evening a few guests would hang their cloaks on part of the statue. A painting of Bacchus, with supplicants laying at his feet like a mound of corpses defeated in battle, dominated the wall to Varro's left. To the right of him the nobleman observed a procession of couples, in various states of inebriation, ascend the stairs, which led to several bedrooms. The scene reminded him of a high-class brothel. Sometimes the women led the men, sometimes the men led the women. Varro grinned when he watched a plump, flushed guest stumble down the staircase, his wig comically askew on his bald head and his breasts jiggling.

Varro didn't quite know whether to feel amused, or ashamed, as he realised that there were several women in the room who were daughters of mistresses he had slept with over the past ten years. He recalled a few of them. *Albina.* She proclaimed she loved the poet, with all her heart, after just a week from beginning their affair. Varro responded by saying that he loved the way her braided hair cascaded down her back. *Domitia.* The wife of the wealthy shipbuilder used to lavish her lover with expensive gifts, which Varro then passed onto his other mistresses to win their favour. The daughter of Balbina was almost the mirror image of her mother. Varro cringed as he remembered their dalliance. Dread, rather than devotion, flooded his being when, lying in bed one night, Balbina announced that she wanted to have a child with Varro. He (just about) feigned enthusiasm for the idea - but spent the next couple of months carefully keeping note of the woman's cycle, to avoid any accidents.

Varro experienced a sudden presentiment, which tore him away from his reverie - like a slave being dragged through the market with a chain around his neck. His heart stopped and he felt a catch in his throat. The hairs on the back of his neck tingled and, despite the balmy air, a chill ran down his spine. The agent sensed someone linger just beside him. Whereas his unknown adversary had at first used the hammer of Bursa and his brigands to bludgeon him to death, he imagined that the second attempt would involve a lone, professional assassin and a thin blade between his ribs. There was indeed someone next to him. But Varro breathed out, with relief, like steam escaping from a pot, when he heard the familiar and friendly voice.

"I thought you might consider yourself too married to attend this party," a young man remarked. "Although there are plenty of other married men here. Indeed, they're attracted to such gatherings - and its hostess - like moths to a flame. Julia mentioned you would be here. What a Caesar wants, a Caesar gets."

Publius Ovidius Naso. *Ovid.* The wine and late nights meant that the poet no longer appeared as fresh-faced as he used to. Varro wasn't going to criticise him for that. His frame was slender, rather than scrawny. Should wild beasts devour the youth in the arena, they would still feel peckish, Varro fancied. His voice was clear, playful - and his mind was as nimble as a Greek acrobat. His eyes twinkled with mischief - and a mercurial intelligence which could both enlighten and eviscerate. He seemed to have been born with a wry smile on his face, and he often appeared as if he were on the cusp of laughing. Ovid wore a white, laundered tunic, bordered in green, with an ostentatious belt-buckle, in the shape of a harp.

The two men had first encountered one another during Varro's investigation into the murder of Herennius. The agent was immediately impressed by the adolescent's coruscating talent. His poetry was witty, lyrical and insightful. Lucilla had mentioned how Ovid reminded her of Varro, when he was younger. Ovid could be scabrous and satirical at one moment, touching and tender the next. Varro championed the budding writer by introducing him to relevant patrons who arranged events, where Ovid could recite his verse. Varro also provided the poet with an open invitation to make use of his extensive library, although the pair made more frequent trips of the nobleman's wine cellar.

"Evening Ovid. You're a welcome sight. I was worried I might have to talk to one of my aristocratic tribe or, worse, a beautiful young woman tonight," Varro replied, whilst deftly stealing a cup of wine off a silver tray, from a passing serving girl. "I am here for business rather than pleasure. I will need you to be discreet, far more discreet than that women over there who seems to be, by accident or design, wearing more of her bosom outside rather than inside her dress."

Varro proceeded to find a quiet corner and briefed Ovid about his assignment. As the agent suspected, the poet was familiar with all the guests at Corvinus' party. Varro welcomed any intelligence he could provide him with. Ovid would be honest in his comments. Brutally honest, should the satirist have consumed more than a couple of cups of Massic.

"Rome's loss is poetry's gain, given the quality, or lack of quality, of Marcus' verse. He used to hound me to read and critique his poems. I think we remained friends because I declined to do so. But be aware that it may be envy talking, when I speak about Marcus. He was as handsome as Adonis and had the ability to borrow more money than me as well. We shared a couple of mistresses - and I know they prized the more attractive and affluent suitor over me. Women are only human too, I think. But as wicked as Marcus could sometimes be, he didn't deserve to die. If you ask me who murdered him, I would have to bet on the favourite. Felix was in love with Marcus, of course. Which is why I can believe he killed him. He felt betrayed, spurned or possessive. Felix might have thought to himself, if I can't have him then no one can. Love can be poisonous, as well as ambrosial."

"Has Felix contacted you, to ask for money? You are friends, no?" Varro asked, fishing without expecting to catch anything.

"I would indeed call Felix a friend. He would often write letters to me, but as such he knows better than to ask me for money. The only thing I own are my debts. Anyone who thinks they can make a profit out of poetry should be crucified, upside down – in order to get some blood rushing to their head. Do I know where your chief suspect is? Most poets live in their own little world, but I imagine that Felix has secreted himself in some dank, dark corner of the city until he can raise enough funds to escape."

Another burst of braying laughter drowned out the noise of intricate flute-playing. Although there was plenty of room between Varro and the marble pillar he stood close to, a fellow guest brushed-up against him when she moved past. The lissom woman smiled, enticingly. Varro smiled in reply, amused. Or bemused. There was a time, even during his first marriage, when Varro would have seduced the woman, whose dimples seemed embedded in her cheeks like gems studding a sculpture. Or he would have let the temptress believe that she was seducing him. But Varro was too faithful, tired or content to conduct any more illicit affairs. Ovid had once asked him why he no longer partook of forbidden fruit, as it was the sweetest fruit after all.

"If you are careful, Lucilla need not know."

"But I'd know," Varro replied, knowingly.

Once the woman was out of earshot, although the scent of her moreish perfume lingered, they continued their conversation:

"It seems that Julia, as well as Felix, consider you a friend. Or at the very least she is a keen admirer of your poetry," Varro asserted, recalling how a couple of mosaics he had seen at the house had quoted lines from the young poet.

*"We are ever striving after what is forbidden, and coveting what is denied to us… Love is a kind of warfare."*

"Annoyingly, Julia views me as just a friend. It's almost a cruel a fate as being an enemy. I would rather she seduce or dominate me – as she does with others. I must be among a select few in this room, of men she hasn't bedded. Suffice to say I do not feel that special as a result. If you haven't already noticed, Julia is more like her father than she might prefer to admit. She is a political animal, far more than she is Aphrodite. Many of the guests are scions of Rome's leading families, optimates and populares. Julia is courting favour, or she is allowing them to court her. I feel like I am but a foot-soldier in love, whilst she is a general. To be chewed up and spat out by her is even an honour. Her youth is part of the prize, but it is also a mask to her wisdom and cunning. Julia is as alluring - and devious - as Cleopatra on her best, or worse, day. She is a rare creature, or some might argue beast, who can call upon the support of the common people in the Subura and the elite in the Forum."

Varro found himself staring - intrigued rather than bewitched - at the young woman through the shimmering throng. She tossed her head back and emitted a throaty laugh, whilst her fingertips grazed against the bare forearm of the young man she was conversing with. Desire and deference oozed from the youth, like a tongue lolling out the mouth of a dog. She smiled, like Circe enslaving yet another devotee.

"Rome has worshipped far worse deities and mortals," Varro argued, albeit he had no wish to dwell upon the likes of Sulla, Clodius and Pompey to further his point.

"You should be aware that it might not be Rome's love Julia yearns for tonight. Rather she may have set her sights on you, as if she were Cupid wielding a bow. I witnessed a telling look in her eye when she mentioned your name earlier," Ovid remarked, with traces of caution, playfulness and even jealousy in his tone.

"She will be wasting an arrow."

"By refusing her you may increase her desire even more. We always want what we're not allowed. Set constraints on a person all you like, but the mind remains adulterous. You cannot regulate desire," Ovid argued, quoting lines from his own poetry. "Julia will view you as a challenge, or trophy. Did you not lick your lips and gird your lions even more for those women who were difficult to ensnare? Julia may see you as a fortress, that she must besiege. She could starve you out, over time, or capture you by force. You probably do not know about Lucius Melito. Rumour has it - and I have found that there is often a grain a truth in salacious gossip - that Lucius, a happily married man, spurned Julia's advances. In reply she blackmailed him, threatening to tell her father that he had raped her, if he refused to submit to her. Suffice to say, Lucius is now less happily married."

Varro heeded Ovid's warning, but explained how he was not attending the party to further his relationship with Caesar's daughter. Instead, he wanted to get to know his two possible suspects, Gnaeus Silo and Quintus Trebonius. Ovid picked out Silo. The blustering statesman was standing close to a Nubian sword swallower, who was wearing a couple of phallus-shaped daggers in his belt.

"That's him. Balding. Beak-nosed. An expression of distaste set, like cement, on his face," Ovid said, turning his attention away from Silo and towards the delectable morsel to his left. The girl's dress was so sheer and tight against her figure, the garment seemed like it was painted on. Although his hostess may have only be interested in him for his poetry, that did not mean that Ovid wouldn't lower his sights and seduce one of Julia's guests.

Varro took in his suspect. He reminded the agent of a statue on the Capitoline Hill of the general, Gaius Marius, Caesar's uncle, a bull of a man with a large forehead and short temper. Silo's ears were uncommonly large - and would crimson when enraged. Certainly, the powerful ex-soldier possessed the strength (as well as the motive and temper) to plunge a knife into the top of Corvinus' skull. Even if feeling inebriated, or lusty, Varro would have thought twice about seducing Silo's wife. He was not a man to rile or ridicule. His nostrils seemed perpetually flared in ire, his lips pursed in displeasure. Varro recalled Ovid's words: "He once flogged a slave half to death for serving him green, instead of black, olives. His hands are reportedly calloused, from overusing his vine stick... Silo can fall into a rage quicker than I can fall into a drunken stupor. I was there at the party when he attacked Marcus. He gnashed his teeth so fiercely that I thought they might drop out. His eyes bulged, like the swell of a pregnant woman's stomach. Silo wanted to kill Marcus that night, as much as too plus too equals four. The question is, does it all add up that he murdered Marcus on the night of his party?" As tempted as Varro was to introduce himself to Silo, he reined himself in. It would be wiser to question his suspect in a more sedate setting. Given his erratic temperament, he would prefer it if Manius or Vulso were present too. Varro also needed to investigate his alibi first, before he could challenge the senior statesman about it.

Julia made good on her promise, luring Trebonius to the gathering. It was likely Varro could have picked out the self-aggrandising soldier even without Ovid's assistance. Trebonius had a stiff military bearing, allied to haughty, aristocratic expression. A sharp, hard jaw tapered into a non-existent chin. An upturned nose hung above a thin, humourless mouth. At one point he dipped his finger into a bowl of water and smoothed down his arched, sculptured eyebrows. Trebonius wore a large, silver brooch in the shape of a hawk, or eagle, on his breast. An ornate dagger hung off his hip and the agent couldn't help but wonder if it was the right size to serve as a candidate for the murder weapon. The nobleman could trace his ancestry back to Tarquin the Proud. But his family had fallen from grace in recent times. A large portion of its wealth had been appropriated. The clan had been on the losing side, during two civil wars, having supported Pompey and Mark Antony. Varro thought the young man had reason to look gaunt and glum. He probably would have expected that, having been invited to the party by Caesar's daughter, she would have attended to him more. He may have believed that her father had asked Julia to invite him, or he may have hoped to convince her to put in a good word for him to Caesar.

Thankfully Ovid knew the young officer - and was not devoid of gossip about him.

"He calls himself the "new Scipio," although it's telling that no one else grants him that title. He was keen to secure a commission in Spain in order to catch Caesar's eye to advance his career in the army. He was understandably put out when, at the last moment, his promotion was rescinded, and Marcus was offered his prized commission. Trebonius has now been ordered to serve in some distant backwater called Tomis. He was close to putting himself on the map. Most maps don't even include Tomis. I would prefer to be banished to Hades. It's more populated, closer to Rome and its habitants know how to have a good time. Julia offered up a juicy titbit of gossip, which she said came from Marcus' lips himself, during some pillow talk," Ovid remarked. The two men leaned in towards each other, as the poet lowered his voice. "Apparently, it was Gaius Maecenas who fixed things so that Marcus secured the commission in Spain, in order to spy on Tiberius. By getting close to Tiberius, perhaps he hopes to get closer to Caesar again too. Maecenas is the kind of man to hedge his bets and ingratiate himself with both Marcellus and Tiberius - and ride two horses, in preparation for when Caesar proves himself more man than god."

*Maecenas.*

## 12.

Aelius Vulso had spent time in less salubrious establishments, compared to *The Silver Anchor*, over the years. He just couldn't remember them right now. The tavern was located close to the river, a stone's throw away from the docks, within a warren of backstreets. The praetorian sat with Manius on a table in the corner, with some food and a jug of acetum in front of them. The bread was hard enough to hammer a nail into the wall with and the unspecified meat in the stew was tougher - and less tasty - than his leather boots. The wine was acidic enough to strip the enamel from one's teeth. But no one complained. You get what you pay for.

A fair few of the customers had turned to scrutinise Vulso and Manius when they entered, but no more or less so than they would have done for any strangers. Fronto had provided them with a couple of old tunics, belonging to slaves at the house, so they blended in. The two men had also rehearsed a back story, of being dockers from Brundisium searching for work in the capital, should they have to engage with anyone. Unsurprisingly, no one was eager to accost the inhospitable looking soldier and ex-gladiator, however.

Manius couldn't quite decide which was more overpowering, the smell of rancid garum or fresh shit. His eyes briefly flitted around the tavern. The beams above were cracked and the floorboards were warped. A few rusty anchors and yellowing shark jaws decorated the walls, along with an array of damp patches. The wealth of cobwebs strewn across the room seemed to be the only thing still holding the place together. Every now and then Manius heard the unedifying noise of someone sniff and/or spit. *The Silver Anchor* was old, weathered and piss-soaked – much like most of its custom. The patrons were mainly dockers and sailors, although the Briton also noticed a few figures with hammer-shaped tattoos on their necks, which suggested that it was a regular drinking haunt for Stolo's stonemason's guild too. The Briton was briefly attracted by the sight of two bleary-eyed sots playing dice in the corner. The first man was so scarred it appeared as if his face had been carved up and sewn back together again. The second had a facial tic, which increased in virulence as the stakes grew higher during their game. The dice resembled spheres more than cubes from overuse. Occasionally Manius heard snippets of ribald conversation and cackling laughter from the two men (what conversation he could hear, through their guttural accents and slurred speech).

A couple of serving women, twenty years past their prime, worked the tables in the tavern. Their feet were as worn as their expressions. When they were finished for the night, they would offer themselves, at a competitive price, to any willing patron. The owner had converted a cupboard upstairs into a small bedchamber. One of the women had been cruelly nicknamed Polyphemus, due to only having one working eye, and the other was called Venus – in a spirit of sarcasm rather than flattery. The former walked with a slight limp and the latter spoke with a slight sibilance, from missing a few front teeth. You get what you pay for. Manius fancied that they had glowered into the jug earlier, as an explanation to why the milk had curdled.

The Briton hadn't turned up in order to sample the food or company at the tavern, however. He ground his teeth in determination and gripped his winecup firmly, in preparation for clasping his cudgel later. Although he wouldn't enjoy torturing Stolo, he had no qualms about doing so. Manius needed the name of the man who had tried to kill his friend - and he would be willing to prise it out of him, as if he were cutting out an arrowhead lodged in a wounded soldier's chest.

Caesar may have been the First Man of Rome but Cervidius Stolo considered himself the First Man of *The Silver Anchor*. The stonemason sat at a table on the mezzanine floor of the establishment, looking down upon the rest of the tavern. It appeared that he didn't have to suffer the same menu as other patrons. Despite his advancing years, Stolo had retained a brawny figure, through the physical exertion of his profession. His leathery countenance was shiny with grease from where he had recently devoured a plate of sausages. His large, shovel-like hands dripped with gold rings, studded with tiny rubies and amethysts. They were worn as weapons, as well as for decoration and status, having shredded the faces of his adversaries over the years. A few friends, or attendants, sat next to him on the sole table on the floor. Stolo dominated the conversation and often barked out orders. His rasping voice was as rough as the bare brick wall behind the table. A puffy-eyed young prostitute leaned into him and occasionally nibbled on his ear or placed a hand between his legs. In reply Stolo would squeeze the girl's breasts and enthusiastically slap her rump. When he offered an opinion on any and everything his companions would nod sagely in agreement – and when he cracked a joke it was to a regimental refrain of laughter. Clearly, he was in good spirits. Clearly, he hadn't heard word back that the assassination attempt on their latest target had failed - and that Bursa would no longer be able to pay his guild membership fees.

Before setting out for the evening one of Agrippa's agents had briefed Manius and Vulso on Stolo's life - and crimes. It was during the turbulent time of Clodius and his period of mob rule when the apprentice stonemason first got a taste for violence and power. Rumour has it that he liked to torture and kill people using his stonemason's hammer and chisel, Agrippa's agent reported. Stolo worked his way up through the guild, through force and bribery, to lead the organisation. The guild recruited from other professions. There was strength in numbers, he believed. "The workers of the world should unite," was one of his recruitment slogans. As well as looking after the interest of his guild members, Stolo was diligent in looking after his own interests. A taste for violence and power was accompanied by a taste for some of the finer things in life. But they needed paying for. And crime paid. Stonemasonry was just one of the concerns of Stolo's guild. Politicians would employ the gang to support them at rallies or have them break-up the rallies of their opponents (the guild had strong ties to the demagogue Publius Carbo, and its members were part of the force which planned to raid and destroy the Jewish quarter in the city). The gang was responsible for an ongoing scheme of larceny – as they pilfered from docks, ships and warehouses and then sold on the stolen goods. Stolo was also brazen in using his army of enforcers to intimidate and extort protection money from small businesses in the territory he operated in. If shop owners or tradesmen failed to pay, they would suffer a beating - or their place of work would be burned down. The guild leader had also been known to fulfil unwritten contracts to rough-up, or kill, designated persons. "Business is business," he would argue, matter-of-factly. "If I don't do the things I do, somebody else will. And they're unlikely to give me a share of their profits."

Manius and Vulso had met with another of Agrippa's agents, Vindex, a couple of streets away from the *The Silver Anchor*. Vindex described what Stolo looked like. Nobody wanted to abduct and torture the wrong man. Vindex grinned wolfishly whilst saying, "Not again." They went through the plan once more. It wasn't fool proof. But it would suffice, hopefully.

Stolo stretched, belched and, half-drunk, made his way downstairs, slapping the arse of the young whore once more. The gang leader yawned cum roared as he headed out to the courtyard to relieve himself in the iron trough outside. There was no reason to think there was anything suspicious or untoward when the two strangers made their way outside too, if indeed any of Stolo's companions noticed. Their weapons were concealed beneath their cloaks.

The courtyard was ill-lit, due to the parsimonious owner of the tavern wanting to save on lamp oil. More than half the establishment's patrons missed the trough at some point when relieving themselves. The thick, pungent odour of urine filled the air, like a morning mist. The smell would have made customers retch, if they were not so inured to it.

Vulso wiped the perspiration from his palms and glanced upwards, to witness the silhouette of Macer on the adjacent rooftop, ready to nock an arrow should any of Stolo's confederates enter the fray. The praetorian proceeded to walk towards the latrine at the rear of the courtyard, where his target was standing.

Stolo turned to the stranger, who approached him on his right.

"Wine goes through you quicker than you think, eh?" the stonemason posited.

"Aye, but it's a blessing. Better out than in, given the swill I've drunk tonight," Vulso replied.

Stolo's grin quickly turned into a stricken grimace, as Manius came up behind the guild leader in his blind spot and punched him in the right kidney, knocking the wind out of him. Confusion flooded Stolo's being, before terror overwhelmed him. The Briton wrapped a powerful arm around Stolo's neck and placed a hand over his greasy mouth. During his training as a gladiator, a Greek wrestler had taught Manius a special way with which to choke and immobilise an opponent. Stolo initially struggled and flailed, attempting to kick the trough over, but soon lost consciousness and his body grew limp as a rain-drenched leaf.

Manius grabbed Stolo and dragged him along the courtyard towards the exit in the corner. Vulso drew his sword and walked backwards, keeping an eye out for anyone who might come through the door of the tavern. Thankfully the alleyway at the back of *The Silver Anchor* was dark and deserted. Vindex was waiting for them on at the end of the alleyway, along with a litter and several praetorians, dressed as litter bearers. Stolo was bundled inside. His hands and feet were tied up and mouth gagged, as if he were a bound suckling pig, ready to be feasted upon.

Once Stolo was secure inside the litter Vulso and Manius shared a look and puffed out their cheeks in relief. There was no sign of a struggle back at the courtyard. Even if they suspected that their leader had been abducted there was nothing they could do about it. Back at *The Silver Anchor* his companions were surprised by his absence, but not alarmed. They were more concerned with instructing the owner that Stolo would be paying for their drinks for the night. The buxom prostitute was content too, as Stolo had paid for her time up front.

## 13.

Varro welcomed the cool breeze brush against his flushed skin. Crickets chirruped in the bushes below, seemingly enjoying their own party or complaining about the raucous noise from the revellers inside. The moon slipped in and out of view, behind dappled clouds, like a trickster palming a glinting coin.

The nobleman decided to take some air and stood on the balcony. Ovid had slinked away, like the rear of a Gaulish army. Varro suspected that the priapic poet had spotted an ex-lover and wanted to avoid them. Or he had observed a prospective new mistress and was preparing to launch a fresh campaign. Varro wryly smiled as he remembered something the poet said, when pointing out one of the female guests:

"That's Galla over there. She's renowned for experimenting with various cosmetics to help her keep looking young. She led the craze for the noblewomen of Rome to smother their brows in axle grease, to help prevent wrinkles. Her latest treatment involves smearing her cheeks with crocodile excrement to lighten her complexion. She gets, quite literally, shit-faced every night."

Silo and Trebonius had both absconded too, but Varro was determined to catch-up with them over the next couple of days. As much as they would want to bar their doors to the agent, they would not want to refuse to cooperate with someone acting for Caesar. Questions needed to be answered.

Varro barely gave Silo and Trebonius a second thought, however, since Ovid had mentioned Maecenas' name. The searing image of the political agent, from his nightmare, plagued his inner eye again. A theory began to take shape in the agent's mind, like a potter moulding clay. It was not beyond the realms of possibility that Maecenas was behind Corvinus' death. Corvinus could have become a liability, as opposed to an asset. If Corvinus had been indiscreet with Julia, it was likely that he had been indiscreet with others. The spymaster could not afford for Caesar to find out that Corvinus was intending to spy on him, through his stepson or otherwise. Corvinus' secrets, and ability to compromise Maecenas, would have perished with him. Dead men can't testify. It wouldn't have been the first time Maecenas had employed a professional assassin to carry out a murder too, Varro considered.

A further thought started to form in the playwright's mind, as if the two strands of a plot were joining together. If Maecenas had gained advanced knowledge that Caesar was commissioning him to investigate the murder, it was feasible the spymaster could have had the opportunity to employ Stolo to eliminate the agent, before he could uncover the truth.

Varro heard footsteps behind him on the balcony. As softly as they sounded, he didn't experience any premonition that an assassin was about to strike. Rather he smelled Julia's musky perfume. Caesar's daughter had watched Varro stroll out onto the balcony, unaccompanied. She asked an attendant to fetch her favourite silk gown. Before she walked outside Julia also instructed her bodyguards to stand sentry at the door and prevent any other guests from disturbing her.

"Great minds think alike. I often come to this spot to think, or empty my mind," Julia breezily remarked, unable and unwilling to suppress her delight at seeing the nobleman. It wasn't just the wine in her stomach which stirred her desire. She wanted him - and wanted him to want her. She wanted him to see her as a woman, an experienced lover, rather than a capricious girl. Julia had checked her appearance in a mirror, before venturing outside. She moistened her ruby lips, adjusted her fringe and untwisted the necklace, made of gold and pearls, which hung down, just above the swell of her breasts. "Did you have an opportunity to meet Gnaeus and Quintus?"

Varro turned, making sure he only half-smiled. He didn't want to over encourage the girl, to lead her on – or have her think that she could lead him on.

"Unfortunately not. Or fortunately not."

"I saw them arrive. Thankfully I saw them leave, before I could play the hostess and engage with them. I am sure that if either of them are guilty, you will get your man. My father speaks highly of you, which is rare. My father also says that you are in credit with him in terms of favours, which is even rarer. Usually it's the case that people are indebted to him. He once asked my advice in relation to sending you - and Lucilla - a gift. You could of course consider me a gift and unwrap me right now. You would just need to tug on this, and all will be revealed," Julia suggested, as she clasped one end of the belt fastened around her gown, dyed imperial purple.

It wasn't the first time that a wine-fuelled young woman had stood before Varro and offered to disrobe. Irritation, rather than temptation, shaped his mood though. Whether Caesar's daughter was game-playing or offering herself in earnest, he didn't want to pull upon any cord and see things unravel. Nor did he wish to offend Julia by beating a hasty retreat. He just needed to change the course of the conversation.

"Can I ask you a question?"

"If the question is the one I'm hoping for, the answer is yes."

Again, Varro thought it best to gently ignore Julia's coquetry and advances. He pictured Lucilla, like reciting a prayer to ward off an evil spirit.

"Did Marcus Corvinus reveal that he was working for Gaius Maecenas? And that Maecenas organised his commission in Spain, on condition that he spy on Tiberius and your father?"

Julia removed her hand from her belt and let out a short sigh of frustration, or tedium, before replying:

"He did. Marcus mentioned it as a boast, but I think it was to his shame that he was willing to act like a lapdog for Maecenas and exploit his friendship with Tiberius. He made me promise that I wouldn't inform my father or Tiberius – and, as much as some people may sneer behind my back that I am without honour, I like to keep my promises. But I didn't promise Marcus that I wouldn't tell Ovid, or you. Ovid is a very fond of you, as you may already be aware. He made me even curiouser about meeting you. He once said that you were one of only a few people in Rome he wouldn't satirise, because you were too self-deprecating already. I think he wants to be you - but with the readership of Horace and Virgil," Julia half-joked, as she sat down on a bench facing Varro and crossed her legs, revealing her bare thigh. "Please, come sit down next to me Rufus. I promise not to bite, unless you want me to."

"I am fond of Ovid too, although I worry that as much as his tongue may talk him into trouble, it may not always possess the charm and power to talk him out of it," Varro replied, planting himself on the other side of the bench to Caesar's daughter. Not too close or not too far away from her.

"Marcus was envious of Ovid and his talent, not that he would ever have admitted it. Can I ask if you envy anyone?"

"I can say with some confidence that I possess plenty of reprehensible character traits, but envy isn't one of them."

"If anyone else would have said that, I wouldn't have believed them. But I believe you, Rufus."

Julia here gazed upon Varro with admiration rather than lasciviousness. He was handsome, but that wasn't (just) the attraction. His considerable wealth meant nothing to her. She probed his expression - or got lost in it. His eyes could be bright, doleful or playful. Like hers. He could tragically make a joke out of anything. Like her. She wanted to tell him how serious she could be too, however. She wanted to tell him how much philosophy she had studied - and how much of his poetry she had read. She had a thirst which, no matter how much wine she drank, she could never quench. "No amount of tears can wash the loneliness away," she wanted to express, quoting a line from his latest play. Her lust could never fill the hole, left by an absence of love. A devotion to pleasure wasn't the beginning and end of living happily. It just seemed that way sometimes.

"It's the only thing in my life that people should envy me for. But tell me, do you know if Maecenas discovered that Marcus divulged his secret to you, or anyone else?"

"You wish to use me, it appears. If only you would use me like other men wish to use me. I certainly didn't divulge anything to Maecenas. We may have recently shared some lovers, but we are not in the habit of sharing information. He does have excellent taste in art and literature. He is one of the only people in Rome to possess a better stocked wine cellar than myself. But it wouldn't surprise me if Marcus boasted of his exploits to others. He was well practised, to the point of being pitch perfect, in singing his own praises. Are you imagining that Maecenas could be responsible for Marcus' death? He could have felt desperate enough to silence him. He is losing influence with my father, faster than his hairline is receding. The great Caesar no longer trusts him, which is ironic seeing that my father was the one to take his friend's wife for his mistress. Livia may be faithful, out of fear rather than devotion, but my father is unfaithful enough for the both of them. At least I am honest about my lack of virtue. My father still tries to be one thing to the world, and another to his wife and family. He should identify himself with Janus, rather than Apollo.

But Maecenas shouldn't feel overly aggrieved. I am not sure if my father wholly trusts anyone."

Varro mused how there were some who argued that Julia was shaming her father as a consequence of her debauched behaviour. But could it not equally be the case that Caesar's daughter had a will to punish her father, and her behaviour was a consequence of that?

Although she wasn't proud of the fact, Julia wasn't much interested in Gaius Maecenas, or the death of her friend, right now. She just wanted Varro to lean over and take her. He could bite her lip and draw blood. He could either tenderly clasp her hand or hungrily devour her. That part didn't much matter. That he could resist her, that he loved his wife, only increased her desire. Other rooms might be occupied, but her private chambers would be free. She could instruct one of her attendants to bring wine and food up to them. And then bid them not to disturb her until morning.

"I am grateful for your help, Julia. The information will hopefully prove useful," Varro said, thinking how he now had intelligence which he could exploit to blackmail Maecenas - as the spymaster had blackmailed countless others over the years.

"Is it not customary for agents to offer a reward for people who provide them with valuable information?" Caesar's daughter asked, her eyes twinkling with coquettishness once more. Julia had been playing a part for so long now she couldn't really tell when she was putting on a performance or not.

Varro's heart began to beat a little faster, from anxiety rather than ardour. He realised how dry his mouth was. The image of Lucilla loomed larger. The warm breeze wafted the smell of her perfume into his face, as if it were conspiring with the girl to seduce him. He felt like he was engaged in a sword fight, but all he could do was parry, rather than attack.

"It is," Varro replied, his tone less sure of itself than usual. He gulped before speaking.

"Then I would like just one kiss, as payment."

For once the confident, insouciant, nobleman appeared fretful - almost comically so. How wise would it be to say no to the daughter of the most powerful man in the world? Could this not somehow be his crowning conquest? In some ways Julia was the most powerful woman in the world, or certainly second - after Livia. It would just be one kiss. It wouldn't mean anything - aside from it meaning everything. Varro had been able to remain faithful since remarrying Lucilla. When she had proposed to him, it was the first day of the rest of his life. He loved her, more than life itself (albeit this was partly due to Varro not being entirely enamoured with the world). One kiss would be nothing, especially considering past transgressions when he was first married to Lucilla. A woman scorned he could deal with. Practise makes perfect. But a Caesar scorned?

"I am afraid my heart wouldn't be in it."

"It's not your heart, but another part of your person, that I'm interested in," she whispered, luridly, leaning into him. Her chin nearly rested on his shoulder. She was fifteen, going on fifty, Varro fleetingly thought. Yet he also thought how, if fifty, he would have considered how she was behaving childishly. Rome seemed so utterly tawdry and tiresome.

As much as Julia always got her man she drew back when witnessing the discomfort on Varro's face. He shifted uneasily on the bench, as if he were sitting on hot stones from a bathhouse. Should she pounce, she sensed he would recoil. The cost of the kiss would be too high if she lost Lucilla as a friend. And what if she forced Rufus to sleep with her? He would spend the night with her but then creep out of her room - and life - for forever come the morning.

"I am sorry if you thought you were inviting Rufus Varro the errant poet this evening. Unfortunately, Rufus Varro, the faithful husband, has turned up."

There was a moment when he thought the young girl might flare her nostrils and snort fire, in response to being rejected. Her hands bunched themselves into small fists. But she merely breathed out and smiled.

"It's still not been a wasted invite. Instead of stealing a kiss, perhaps I might take up some of your time and write to you and Lucilla at some point?"

The masked slipped. The twinkle in her eye dimmed. Caesar's daughter now appeared diffident, as opposed to demanding and dominant. The agent gave her the benefit of the doubt that it wasn't an act. If it was an act it was unerringly convincing. He was tempted to suggest to Julia that she could become a spy too, but he didn't want to put any such ideas in her head.

"We would both like that," Varro replied, warmly and evenly. He felt a surge of pity for the vulnerable girl. Despite making a show of having a string of lovers Julia seemed intensely isolated and lonely.

"I suppose I should get back to my party. Duty calls. If my face isn't aching from smiling too much, I may think that something is wrong. A mob of patricians need entertaining. Even aristocrats need their own form of bread and circuses. I promise to write to you. And as you know, I always try to keep my word, which is why I seldom give it. Will you be coming inside and re-joining the party too?" Julia remarked, getting to her feet, smoothing any creases from her gown, moistening her lips with her tongue and fixing her smile again.

"Not quite yet. You can have too much of a good thing. I'm going to suffer my own company for a little longer," Varro replied, missing Lucilla more than ever.

## 14.

Aelius Vulso had arranged for someone to spill pig's blood on the floor, close to the chair which Stolo was bound to. The sight was unavoidable and disconcerting. Manius stood by the glistening stain, sword in hand. Glowering. The equally intimidating praetorian stood a few paces away.

The warehouse they were in was relatively secluded, although Vulso posted a few men to patrol the building. A couple of oil lamps and a brazier, with a branding iron nestled in its orange coals, provided some light. Hooks hung down from beams which criss-crossed the ceiling. The pungent smell of rotten meat - death and decay - hung in the air too. A long-tailed, black rat scurried along the floor and darted into an egg-shaped hole in the wall. It was unlikely that the gang leader could make a similar escape.

Stolo stirred, dehydrated and disorientated. He didn't know where he was, when it was or who the men were who had abducted him. The last thing he remembered was being assaulted in the courtyard of the tavern. His chin was wine-stained. He could feel his bare feet on the stone floor, from where his captors had removed his shoes. The ropes bit into his wrists. Stolo squinted, taking in his surroundings, and shook his head, as if he were trying to shake off a hangover.

The gang leader noted the patch of blood on the floor, which he reasoned had come from a previous prisoner. He took in the iron-wrought countenances of his captors. He considered them foot-soldiers. He ultimately needed to speak to their superior to negotiate a deal and extract himself. Stolo's attention was naturally drawn to the nearby wooden table as well. Resting on which was a mallet, a meat cleaver, pliers, several slightly bent long nails and a stonemason's hammer and chisel.

"Who are you? Where am I? Do you know who I am?" Stolo said, or rather croaked. His throat was sore, his voice raspy – as if he had just inhaled clouds of black smoke from a fire. He posed the first two of his questions in a state of bewilderment. The last contained a hint of menace.

"This is an interrogation. You're required to answer questions, not ask them," Vulso stated, his voice as flat as the head of the mallet beside him.

The gang leader was all too familiar with interrogations and torture sessions. Stolo had taken part in several over the years, albeit his role in them was somewhat different to his current one.

"What do you want to know? I want to help. But I am just the head of a stonemason's guild. You are talking to the wrong man."

"I just want a name. Who hired you to murder Rufus Varro?"

"Who? I don't know what you're talking about."

As convincing as Stolo's performance was it wasn't convincing enough. There was a flicker of recognition in his eyes when he heard the name.

"You're about to find out that ignorance isn't bliss," Vulso said, turning to Manius and nodding.

The Briton didn't hesitate. He picked up the mallet from the table and smashed it against the prisoner's toes. Stolo's head snapped back and he howled in agony, like a wolf baying at the moon. A tooth-sized piece of bone flew off in one direction and a scrap of flesh squirted in another.

Outside, a couple of soldiers standing sentry heard a faint scream from inside and shared an amused look, as they watched a group of birds scatter from the roof of the warehouse. They had every confidence that Vulso would extract the information he was after. The praetorian would be thorough. They nearly, but not quite, felt sorry for the doomed prisoner.

Vulso didn't take any overt pleasure in torturing a suspect, but neither would he shirk from the task. Violence worked. It was a valuable and necessary tool. A stock part of his trade.

His battered, bloody foot throbbed and felt like it was on fire. Stolo gnashed his teeth and cursed the men in front of him, under his breath. He vowed he would find, torture and execute them, once he was free. He would slaughter their families too, if they had them. But he needed to deal with what was happening now. He still didn't know if Bursa had found and killed Varro. He could collect the remaining fee owed if so. And what had happened to Bursa and his men?

"Bursa already gave us your name," Vulso said, lying.

"What happened to Bursa?" Stolo remarked, the resistance draining out of his voice, as blood seeped out of his foot.

"You will see him soon enough. You can ask him yourself," Manius said, stolidly. Blood freckled his cheeks, from where he had smashed open the prisoner's foot, squishing it like a piece of fruit.

"You're going to give me the name I'm after, even if I have to work through the night. I have all sorts of incentives on this table to compel you to talk. Firstly, I'll employ the hammer and chisel to cut off your fingers and toes. I will then use the pliers to pull out what few teeth you've left in your head. This will just be the appetiser course, before we get to the main meal. The branding iron is heating up nicely. It'll soon melt through your flesh as easy as a tax collector will go through your accounts. Your skin will melt like wax and the putrid smell will make you retch. But vomiting will be the least of your concerns at that point. I will brand your bollocks and cook your eyes. I'm practised in inflicting a horrific amount of pain, whilst preventing a prisoner from dying. Trust me, you will be confessing your deepest, darkest secrets by then. I am giving you the opportunity to talk now, however."

Stolo's eyes briefly flitted from side to side, weighing up each option. The issue was whether to betray his client or not. There was little or no real choice to make. The gang leader would save his own skin, even if another's skin was flayed as a consequence. He remembered some of the incidents of torture he had presided over. He had no desire to be disfigured, broken or die from his wounds.

"I will cooperate. I didn't like the haughty bastard anyway. But business is business," Stolo stated, sneering in reaction to thinking about the figure, or from the pain in his foot. He just wanted to put the whole unpleasant business behind him. He just hoped that he wouldn't have to spend too much time and money having to recruit more men, to replace any he lost. He would have to now write-off the second tranche of his fee, but so be it. Stolo revealed the name.

Manius offered up a grim but confirmatory nod to Vulso, to convey that he believed Stolo was telling the truth. The name was familiar and unsurprising. Vulso nodded in reply and moved aside, so the Briton could stand directly in front of the prisoner, his sword still in his hand.

"Is that it? What else do you want to know? What happened to Bursa? Where is he now?" Stolo asked, spewing out questions like a camel, spitting.

"He's dead," Manius declared, as short and sharp as a drumbeat.

Stolo screwed up his already bitter countenance, in confusion and antagonism.

"But you said I would see him again soon."

The bodyguard thought about how, if the man in front of him lived, he would still pose a threat to Varro. The gang leader might also look to hunt himself down, as well as harm Camilla and his new-born child. Vulso's men were already prepared to dispose of the body in the river. Stolo was a dead man, as soon as he was abducted. He just didn't know it.

The stonemason's features began to crumble, his complexion began to grow pale, as he realised the import of his captor's words. There was a hoarse intake of breath. He wondered if the blood on the floor belonged to Bursa.

"You will," Manius replied, free from pity or perniciousness, before punching the tip of his sword through Stolo's chest. The blade scraped against bone. Death is death.

## 15.

The tavern was busy, raucous – but the atmosphere congenial. The sawdust on the floor was used to soaking up wine rather than blood nowadays. Food was being wolfed down, and no one was wincing on tasting their first mouthful of wine. Manius noticed a new menu, new furniture and new whores. Bassos had changed over the past year too. He had lost weight, his clothes were smarter and his manner seemed less fraught. His posture had even improved. The weight of the world no longer seemed to be on his rounded shoulders. His teeth were clean-*ish* and what little hair he possessed had been combed.

Varro and his bodyguard had been loyal, regular customers years ago. Bassos caught sight of the Briton and wended his way through the crowd. The landlord instructed one of his slaves to provide a table and chairs for his old friend and his guests. When Manius introduced his companions and discovered they were soldiers - praetorians no less - he provided the first jug of wine on the house, knowing that others would follow. He hoped the wine would whet the soldier's appetite to try out other wares in the tavern.

"My girls are the best in the Subura," Bassos boasted. As much as the landlord's appearance had changed, he still saw himself as a salesman. "We have a special deal on for two of our most popular fillies. There's Nefertari, an Alexandrian. It'll be all too easy to imagine you're bedding Cleopatra herself. She'll coil around you like a snake and swallow you whole. And then there's Nessa, a Briton like our friend Manius here. She's clean, yet dirty. The exotic redhead is wild like a barbarian, but in a good way. Men, not just women, need to be ravaged sometime, eh? You can book to see them both in the same session. You will have the world in the palm of your hand - east meets west. Two women. One price. You don't need to speak their languages, as they speak the language of love. You may initially think the cost is on the high side, but quality is quality. Or, due to the fact that you will have two lovely ladies serving your will and whim, quality is quantity."

Whilst Macer remained rapt by the landlord's lurid sales patter, and Vulso attempted to negotiate down the price, Manius was understandably pre-occupied. The mystery had been solved as to who was behind the assassination attempt, but the threat still existed. He barely registered the shapely serving girl putting a cup of wine in front of him - or heard the laughter of nearby patrons telling a joke about a three-legged goat, a fascinum and a one-eyed Vestal Virgin. Varro's past was coming back to haunt him, again. Manius knew that the man who had wanted to murder him once would be doubly determined to murder him a second time. To finish the job. By killing Stolo, Manius had hopefully been able to buy some more time. Should any of the brigands make their way back to Rome, they would not be able to report back to their gang leader – who could subsequently inform his paymaster. Yet their adversary had the experience and means to arrange surveillance on Varro's home. It would now be a race. Could Licinius Pulcher get to Varro first, or could they get to him first?

Agrippa heard his wife outside his study, admonishing a slave for not bowing to a statue of Fortuna in the hallway. The unctuous astrologist, Toranius, had advised Marcella to encourage her staff to worship the god in order to win favour with the deity. Agrippa rolled his eyes so much it appeared at one point as if he might be staring at the back of his head. He was worried that his wife might be about to check on him, to ask him to come to bed and sleep with her - out of a duty to provide a child for the glory of her family and Rome. Agrippa was just about to rest his head on his arms, on his desk, to pretend to be asleep, when he realised that her querulous voice was receding. He felt like offering up a prayer to Fortuna as a thank you.

A strong gust of wind squeezed through the shutters and extinguished one of the candles on his desk. He didn't interpret the incident as a sign that he should retire for the night. Instead he used another candle to reignite the dormant one – and worked on. Before composing a reply, he read over the letter from Caesar again. The good news was that Caesar was recovering. Some were probably already writing their eulogies, but they were wasting their time. The vultures had no need to circle. Over the years Caesar had been accused of possessing a weak constitution (or he was adept at pretending to be ill, especially on the eve of battle), but he was hardier than they thought. Agrippa was relieved, for more than one reason. A body needs a head, a ship needs a captain and Rome needs a Caesar, even if his name was Agrippa. Out of a sense of duty, rather than ambition, Agrippa would have become the First Man of Rome if his friend passed. But he would have done so reluctantly. His gentle, internal sigh of relief could be heard from Hades and Elysium. The letter did not just concern itself with the subject of his friend's health, however.

*"...Please keep me abreast of how Rufus Varro is progressing with his investigation. By finding Plancus, he will be also be solving the crime and we can communicate the good news to Porcius Corvinus. The son of Appius Varro is more like his father than he might think. He is shrewd and tenacious. He is a keen judge of people, in that he thinks little of them. Ironically, people trust him and still unburden themselves. Our spy has an honest face it seems. Perhaps he will discover things about Julia and Tiberius that I'm unaware of, albeit I might prefer not to know. There are some secrets that I'm happy to remain so.*

*Julia has refused to reply to my previous two letters. By all accounts she is behaving like a dog in heat - and needs a leash. My warning shots across her bow are failing as deterrents. If she was anyone else, she would have received one warning shot, at most. I will not be ignored or defied. People may applaud her for her generosity and gregariousness, but Julia cannot continue to bring our name into disrepute. Caesar's daughter must be beyond suspicion, or reproach. I am the First Man of Rome. She must appreciate she is part of the first family of Rome – and act as an example to Roman citizens across the empire. She must uphold the traditional Roman values of the Senate House, not the standards of a whore in the Subura.*

*Once I have regained my strength and returned to Rome, I will arrange for Julia to marry Marcellus. Rome will celebrate the union. We will increase the grain dole for the month and put on various spectacles in the arenas. Marcellus can be the one to put her on a leash. Pregnancy will slow her down and motherhood will temper her excesses.*

*You would think I would be tired of fighting a losing battle, in relation to our seemingly endless campaign in Spain. But I will subjugate my enemies in Spain, as well as my daughter. Caesar must be Caesar. Our enemy in Spain used to be Hydra-headed. You killed one man to have him replaced by two. Each hiding behind the next tree, carrying a blade. But we will burn down the forests if required, to flush them out and secure victory. Dare I say it, but the tide has already turned. Our enemies are the ones realising that they are fighting a losing battle. Thanks must go to Marcellus. He is learning his trade – and a Caesar's trade is war. Tiberius has performed admirably too. Although I am wary of mentioning him more in dispatches, lest the praise goes to his head and he overshadows Marcellus.*

*How is Marcella? As much as I must reprimand my daughter for her flightiness, you have earned your infidelities. A mistress would do you the world of good. Adulterous affairs have certainly saved my marriage. Do as I do, not as I say in official proclamations. I can of course recommend a number of women who know how to be discreet and indiscreet in the right measure. Some of their husbands might even be honoured that you would choose to take their wife as a mistress. By keeping their spouses occupied, they will also have greater freedom to conduct their own affairs. Surely the most tempting dish to sample will be Terentia? You can screw both her and Maecenas at the same time. I dare say he might be willing to pimp out his wife to you though, as he did for me. You can, like me, feed Terentia false information to take back to Maecenas and let him sweat and squirm over nothing.*

*...I almost long for a time when all we needed to worry about was civil war, famine and insolvency..."*

Agrippa was just about to compose his response to the letter when one of his attendants entered, announcing that he had a visitor.

"Who is it?" Agrippa asked, vexed a little that someone was calling at such a late hour.

"Gaius Maecenas."

Manius had sent word to Varro that they were drinking in *The Golden Lion*. The message provided the agent with the perfect excuse to extricate himself from the party. Half a dozen praetorians accompanied Varro as he descended into the Subura to rub shoulders with a different class of thieves and debauchees.

Bassos greeted Varro warmly when he entered, his chuckles chiming like a purse clinking together, and showed the nobleman to his party. Varro was pleasantly surprised by how busy the tavern was – and that the landlord was so hale and hearty.

"You are looking well and are in good spirits, Bassos."

"I had a stroke of good fortune, since we last met. My wife died. She clutched her chest one evening and her heart stopped beating. I always thought that she would die through choking on her own bile. At least it proved that she had a heart, which some people doubted. She was queen of the harpies, sourer than the cheap acetum she forced me to sell. Every morning I woke up next to a nightmare. As you know, she disapproved of me drinking. She also banned me from sampling my girls. But I am my own man again. I've made changes to the business, which have worked. I may even open another tavern. Or a brothel. I now wake up to a dream. I can vouch for the charms of my girls. My patrons have even nicknamed me the "Merry Widower". I told myself when I got married, that it was the happiest day of my life. But I know better now, that the happiest day of my life was when the harridan died," the roseate landlord exclaimed, like a man whose prayers had been answered. He noted a couple of well-dressed, middle-aged customers enter – and ogle his girls. Bassos politely excused himself and greeted his new patrons. He would be able to negotiate up his prices, he thought, licking his lips as much as his guests. Fools and their money are easily parted.

"We found Stolo," Vulso remarked to Varro, as the latter took a seat around the table and poured himself a large measure of wine. "If someone wants to find him now, they'll have to take a deep breath and search at the bottom of the Tiber."

"Stolo gave us a name," Manius said, his features puckered, as if the Briton wished he hadn't uncovered the truth. "Licinius Pulcher."

Varro reacted to the name like it was a bad smell. *Pulcher.* The rival agent had worked under the aegis of Gaius Maecenas. The handsome aristocrat had served as his lover, as well as his spy and assassin. Like Varro, Pulcher was often employed to seduce women and gather intelligence on Rome's enemies. It was a coin toss as to whether the initial rivalry between the agents was borne from them being too similar or too different to one another. Pulcher first made a name for himself through seducing a Vestal Virgin, and gaining access to Mark Antony's will, which was used against him by Caesar in the propaganda war. A veneer of civility and charm masked a vicious heart. Pulcher was one of Maecenas' most effective assassins, Agrippa reported. "He's adept at using poison or a blade. Maecenas directs his man like a ballista bolt, and then unleashes him." But Maecenas had cut ties with Pulcher last year. The agent failed in his assignment to locate Herennius' dagger, after his murder. Pulcher had also failed to seduce and marry Lucilla, in order to intercept her correspondence with Livia. Spurned and resentful, Pulcher abandoned Rome, to lick his wounds. He had cause to blame Varro for ruining both his professional and personal life. Varro had embarrassed Pulcher by locating Herennius' dagger. Maecenas' agent had also developed genuine feelings for Lucilla, during his assignment to seduce her. Yet she had returned to her first husband, who had wronged her during their first marriage. Did Pulcher still carry a torch for Lucilla? Had Bursa been given orders to spare her, as well as kill him? Varro used to joke that he had a lot to thank his rival for. If it wasn't for Pulcher then Varro might not have been prompted to re-declare his love for Lucilla. "The man who nearly married my wife unwittingly played Cupid."

Varro recalled a throwaway piece of gossip in a letter from Gaius Macro, a couple of months ago. His friend reported that Pulcher had returned to Rome, after inheriting his wealthy uncle's estate. The aristocrat was now a plutocrat as well - and was on the hunt for a wife and an entrance into politics. He clearly possessed the means and motive to hunt down Varro.

Manius couldn't help but observe the anxiety etched in his companion's expression. Varro briefly raised his head to the heavens, as if offering up a prayer – or checking to see if the Sword of Damocles was hanging over him. He tried to put on a brave face, but the mask slipped. Both men knew Pulcher would strike again, if unchecked. The bodyguard wanted to reassure his friend that all would be well. That they now knew their adversary was to their advantage.

"Don't worry Rufus, we'll find him. Pulcher doesn't know it yet, but he's a dead man."

Agrippa placed a blank piece of parchment over Caesar's letter to him before Maecenas entered. His guest had the morals of a snake and eyes of a hawk. In an instant he seemed to take in the positions of Rome and its enemies, displayed on the map across the wall to his left. Maecenas also took in his rival, wearing a plain tunic. *For a plain man.* The two men had known each other for so long, Maecenas could never quite remember the initial grievance he had against him. Yet certain differences seemed irreconcilable. They would always be chalk and cheese. Maecenas was urbane, cultured. The equestrian preferred the company of poets. Power was an end in itself. Agrippa had been brought up in the countryside, a rural backwater. He had just been lucky enough that the young Octavius had lived in the backwater too, as a child. His life would have come to nothing, if not for his friendship with Caesar. Although Maecenas could have made the argument, that Caesar would not be Caesar if not for his friendship with Agrippa. But Maecenas was reluctant to grant him any such praise in public. Agrippa preferred the company of soldiers, to poets and politicians. Power was a consequence of doing his duty. Although the two men were aware that Caesar played them off each other - employing the stratagem of divide and conquer - they still willingly played along. When the three men were together Maecenas would deliberately engage Caesar in conversations about poetry and philosophy, in an attempt to belittle Agrippa and exclude him. Yet often, out of sympathy for his friend or to amuse himself, Caesar would reminisce with Agrippa about past military campaigns, ousting Maecenas from the discussion.

The silver thread lining Maecenas' tunic - which was bordered in a colour close to but distinct from imperial purple - glinted in the candlelight. A few hairs were out of place on his oiled scalp, which could well presage that the world was about to end, Agrippa thought to himself. Maecenas strode into the room with purpose, a little breathless for once. Perspiring, for once. Fraught, for once.

"Thank you for seeing me, Marcus. Although after I have spoken you may wish that your attendant would have barred my entry," he half-joked, unconvincingly. Sheepish rather than waspish.

Maecenas proceeded to explain how his former agent, Licinius Pulcher, had returned to Rome, with the intention of murdering Rufus Varro.

"Licinius is no longer himself. His wits have been addled, like some tragic hero being punished by the gods. We had dinner a month ago. I initially thought he might want to meet, in order to ask that I recruit him again. But he spent most of the evening railing against Varro. Licinius declared his love for Varro's wife, Lucilla - arguing that Varro had poisoned her mind against him... Licinius asked me if I wanted to see Varro dead. I was firm in expressing my opposition to the idea. Unfortunately, I underestimated his passion and determination to punish Varro. After I had any opportunity to stop Licinius, he arranged to have Varro assassinated, hiring a criminal gang to travel to his villa in Arretium. I have a letter in my possession, which will provide evidence to both condemn Licinius and exonerate me from any wrongdoing. Thankfully the assassination attempt failed. But I imagine Licinius' blood is still as hot as the pyre which consumed Dido. He still poses a threat to Varro's life," Maecenas remarked, feigning concern for the welfare of Agrippa's agent.

Agrippa wanted to roll his eyes at his guest's use of another literary allusion. He could be as garrulous as Nestor at times. As much as Maecenas pretended to worry about Varro's fate, Agrippa suspected that his rival had come to him because he was worried about his own safety. After Pulcher had finished with Varro, he might come for the man who had ended his career and forced him out of Rome. Maecenas could also implicate him in the plot to murder Varro. And the spy had become a potential liability to the spymaster. He was a keeper of secrets, which could compromise Maecenas. Pulcher knew, quite literally, where the bodies were buried. There were times when Maecenas had operated outside of Caesar's interests. Family and friends could also avenge his victims, should Pulcher expose Maecenas' involvement in their demise.

"We need to find and kill him immediately," Maecenas argued, hoping that he could convince Agrippa to deploy the Praetorian Guard. "If we merely apprehend him, he could still arrange to murder Varro. We both know that the law does not always deliver justice. Given his new-found wealth, Pulcher will be able to hire the best advocates, or bribe a jury, to evade punishment. We should forego any trial – and execute Pulcher before he can do any more damage. I know I should have come to you earlier, Marcus, but hopefully I have not come to you before it's too late."

Agrippa remained impassive whilst listening to Maecenas explaining himself. Occasionally he acted surprised or disappointed. At one point, Maecenas even wrung his hands in apology. He told himself he would gift Agrippa a temporary sense of superiority, in order to secure his assistance in neutralising Pulcher. Maecenas was accustomed to manipulating people because they were indebted to him, but he would now act as if he would be in Agrippa's debt.

"I am grateful for you coming to me, Gaius. As you know, honesty is the best policy. I agree that we need to find and eliminate Pulcher," Agrippa said, magnanimously, after sitting in silence for an extended amount of time. Waiting to pass judgement. Agrippa wasn't surprised that Maecenas was willing to sacrifice his former agent, as if Pulcher were making an offering to the gods - a bull about to have its throat slit. His guest, sitting on a low chair on the opposite side of the desk, forced an amiable expression and shifted uncomfortably in his seat. Maecenas had a history of switching some allegiances, as if he were merely changing a tunic. Pulcher had become dead to him.

"I have just received some intelligence, in relation to Licinius' location. He is currently residing in a villa just outside of Rome. The property is far from impregnable, but you will need to mobilise a significant force of praetorians to crack the egg. Licinius has recently employed over twenty bodyguards. A cornered animal is a dangerous animal."

Agrippa promised that he would muster the Praetorian Guard. But that he, rather than Maecenas, would oversee any operation. The former general feared he would lose a few men during the mission. He scrutinised his colleague/rival, briefly flaring his nostrils and wearing thunder on his brow. Agrippa wanted to tell him that, should Maecenas be deceiving him, he would personally thrash him half death. If not kill him entirely and rid Rome of its serpent. He wanted to disclose how Caesar often ridiculed Maecenas behind his back – and how much Terentia had mocked him too. And he wanted to reveal how the equestrian wasn't the only Roman who could play a part. Shortly before Maecenas arrived, Agrippa had received a message from Vulso, making him aware that Licinius Pulcher was behind the assassination attempt on Varro.

As tempted as Agrippa was to lambast and chastise his rival, he did something far more galling. He patronised him.

"You are right that you should have come to me earlier, Gaius. I have the authority and experience to resolve such issues… You shouldn't ever allow your pride or fear to prevent you from approaching myself or Caesar…"

Maecenas nodded as Agrippa spoke - lectured him. His bloodless lips remained pursed, although occasionally the corner of his mouth twitched in frustration or malice. When he thanked Agrippa - and apologised to him once - the words felt like hot coals on his tongue. But the cultured Roman would not give his rival the satisfaction of displaying too much emotion. Emotion was a form of puss, Maecenas considered. He would play the chastened inferior - and take his medicine. As much as it tasted like poison.

Agrippa thanked his rival and then dismissed him, like a mid-ranking member of his staff. He was disrespectful. But not too disrespectful. He would temporarily ally himself with Maecenas, for the sake of Varro, but that did not mean he would wholly trust him.

Much to Agrippa's relief his wife was asleep when he entered his bedchamber. He thought of Pulcher and pictured the villa his men would attack the next day. It was time to make war, not love, the soldier determined.

## 16.

Varro slept fitfully throughout the night. His linen sheets were damp with sweat. His head hurt, like it was trapped in a vice, from the copious amount of wine he had drunk. He repeatedly downed cups of water, to quench his thirst and avoid dehydration, and filled up more than one piss pot during the night. It was not the first time he had spent an evening intermittently sleeping, drinking and relieving himself. Fronto had argued that Varro was lucky, he only did so after a session in the tavern. When he reached old age, he would do so on a nightly basis, regardless of how much wine he consumed.

The stinging heat filled the room, like invisible smoke. Varro had locked his shutters, out of an irrational or not fear that an assassin could climb through his window and slit his throat. For so many years he had, from an instinctive or philosophical viewpoint, devalued life. He had been indifferent to life and death – attesting to the fact through his writing:

*Life is a necessary evil, a disease. Sleep provides a balm and death gifts us the cure… Would that the gods lift-up the clouds and stamp on us, like insects. Put us out of our misery.*

But how cruel were the gods, or how cruel was life? Varro had found Lucilla - something to live for. And now death was stalking him like a jilted lover.

The agent was also unable to sleep from the thoughts and questions pricking his mind, like fat sizzling in a pan. Where was Plancus? Was he hiding out in a neighbouring house or halfway to Alesia or Jerusalem by now? What was Silo's alibi, and how could he unpick it? How could he trap Trebonius into revealing his involvement? If he was involved. And then there was Maecenas…

In order to take his mind off the deluge of questions sluicing through his thoughts Varro tried to think about his latest play. The tragedy wasn't even finished but already he was being approached by actors and actresses, wanting to win a part in the production. A smile finally formed on Varro's pensive features as he remembered his encounter with an actress the previous night, as he was leaving the party. He was nearly at the door, having worked his way through a crowd of sycophants and sirens, like a forester hacking a path through a dense wood.

"Are you Rufus Varro, the playwright?" the young woman asked, after shuffling quickly, in a tight-fitting dress, to intercept the famed writer. Her voice was as soft and pliable as the silk belt coiled around her lissom waist. Helvia was a dancer turned actress. Tendrils of auburn hair hung down, framing a comely, oval face. A face which was home to a porcelain brow, pronounced cheekbones and four distinct smiles (seductive, amused, polite and friendly). A beauty spot had also been painted above her upper lip, according to the latest fashion. Helvia was accustomed to being adored. Poets had dedicated verses to her – drooled over her. Helvia considered that love should be bought, as opposed to earned. Although it was unlikely that the actress believed love existed. Desire, yes. But love, no. She had recently become the mistress of Senator Julius Crispus, after the senator's son had bedded her. Some gossiped that Helvia used the younger man to get to the older, wealthier, one. Crispus had promised that he would divorce his wife and marry Helvia, but the senator wasn't renowned for keeping his promises.

"Yes, unfortunately," Varro replied, drily.

Helvia seemed slightly befuddled by his answer, as though Varro was working from a different script to the actress. His eyes didn't widen on seeing her. But she soldiered on, keen to deliver her lines.

"My name is Helvia. I just wanted to tell you how much your last play inspired me. Your words touched my soul," the practised performer remarked, fingering a pendant around her neck, drawing attention to her perfumed breasts. Her dyed, diaphanous dress left little, or a lot, to the imagination.

"That's very kind, thank you," Varro said. He was going to ask how his words had inspired her, believing that he might be amused by her answer, but he had no desire to prolong their conversation. He was keen to join his friends in the tavern.

"I do so hope, as do others, that you are working on another play. And I do so hope that you would consider me for a part in your next work. Julia may have mentioned that I am an actress. I am not just a pretty face. I would do anything to learn from you and perform for you on the stage. Anything. My friend and patron, the statesman Julius Crispus, would even be willing to help fund the production should you offer me a part. I am sure that other actresses have offered to sit on your couch and rehearse for you. But when it comes to casting for roles, please think of me too. You write so well for women. You know how a woman thinks," Helvia said, mixing and matching her four smiles as she spoke.

Varro thought of about half a dozen satirical comments to reply to the actresses' final assertion, but he kept his words sheathed.

"Rumour has it that you know your way around a woman's body too," Helvia added, leaning into the attractive playwright. Smiling, seductively. Whispering. Varro smelled the Massic on her breath, observed the ribbon-like wine stain encircling the inside of her mouth.

"You shouldn't put too much stock in rumour. Like my plays, my prowess as a lover had been overpraised. I fear it would take me an age just to undress you. You might interpret my slowness as being a tactic to prolong the anticipation - but really, I am just uncommonly clumsy. If I somehow got you on my couch, I'd probably bore you to sleep," Varro argued, the soul of earnestness.

Helvia, again, appeared somewhat perplexed. An expression of confoundment vied for sovereignty with a polite smile to win the battle to shape her youthful features. In the end she made a leap of faith and offered up a laugh, Men liked it when she laughed at their jokes.

"You are trying to tease me. But that's fine, as I would love to get to tease you in return and show you how talented I am," she posed, her features dripping with luridness. The actress would be happy to surrender her body to the aristocrat for the night, in order to be master over his heart later and secure the role. They were just trading assets. Helvia wanted audiences to adore her, as well as a string of suitors. The playwright was married, but that would most likely increase her chances of seducing him, she believed. Helvia preferred married men. They were not such a drain on her time. She resolved to send a messenger to his house in the morning and invite him to the love nest that Crispus rented for her.

Varro mused how, years ago, he couldn't think of anything more enjoyable than auditioning a harem of aspiring actresses, with a willingness to impress and please. "You can have the pick of the crop - pluck the ripest fruit from the bough," Macro had recently enthused in a letter. But Varro was too tired, old or, preferably, too much in love to relive past triumphs or transgressions.

*Perhaps Julia is right. I am now boring, as opposed to being bored.*

Varro offered up his own form of a polite smile and excused himself from the beguiling, or bewildered, actress. When she asked for his address and proposed they have dinner the following evening Varro explained that it was likely he had to leave Rome in the morning. Helvia concluded that the aristocrat preferred bedding men to women, such had been her abject failure to captivate the playwright.

The nobleman did attempt to relive past glories in relation to the levels of wine he consumed through the night, once he reached the tavern. Oblivion is a warm and welcome destination, especially when accompanied by friends. His memory was hazy, but he did recall Vulso coming back, his legs wobbling a little, from visiting Nefertari and Nessa. "Money well spent," he exclaimed, breathlessly. Macer was tempted to venture upstairs too but thoughts of the expense, or Sabina, made him think twice. The young archer did his best to keep pace with the rest of the seasoned drinkers around the table, not wishing to lose face with them. He wanted to prove his manhood, earn their respect. As a result, Macer spent the dregs of the evening in a cycle of drinking, vomiting and sleeping. He declared his love for Sabina, on more than one occasion, although no one listened, not least because his companions couldn't understand his garbled speech. Varro also remembered how they spent a portion of the evening making various toasts: to friendship, the demise of Publius Carbo, competitively priced whores and the death of the landlord's wife. The most enthusiastic clinking of cups came after Vulso proposed a toast to finding Licinius Pulcher.

"Let's kill the bastard and go home," Manius announced.

"I'll drink to that," Varro enjoined.

The morning light scorched the back of his eyes. His skull felt bruised. His mouth was dry, like he'd been chewing sand. Varro stretched out in bed and felt bones click which he never knew he had. He washed, dressed and entered the triclinium. Manius was up, hunched over a wax tablet, composing a letter to his wife, as he gulped down another cup of water. The Briton was nursing the kind of hangover he used to experience when Varro was on a roll and wouldn't leave the dicing tables. It was like old times. Too much like old times.

The friends nodded to one another and lazily raised their hands, to serve as a greeting. Varro realised that he couldn't remember how he got home. He had a vague memory of someone pouring some effluence out a window, above his head. The agent argued that he was used to life shitting on him, so it wasn't worth complaining if a Roman citizen imitated life. No doubt Manius took care of him as he stumbled homeward and, after reaching the house, Fronto made sure he got into bed. The estate manager would have provided him with his ewer of water as well.

"The events of last night are flitting in and out of shadow. I hope I didn't make a fool of myself," Varro said, after yawning.

"Ask me no questions and I'll tell you no lies," Manius replied, raising a corner of his mouth, as if amused by one of the events from the previous evening.

"That bad?"

"It was fine, partly because I've seen worse," Manius remarked, stroking Viola, who was curled up at his feet. Or rather she was on his feet, hoping to trap him, so they spent the day together.

Varro clasped a fraternal hand on his friend's shoulder, leaving all manner of things left unspoken. What also remained unspoken was the news that Varro wanted to give Manius. His new family could make use of his house in Rome, while he based himself in Arretium. Manius would provide some company for Fronto. He could also sell his own house, and save money on rent, by living on his estate. Viola would enjoy the large garden too. Varro had discussed things with Lucilla, as it was her home as much as his.

"It's one of your better ideas."

Varro and Lucilla intended to tell Manius and Camilla after the baby was born.

Vulso entered. He was back in uniform. His features were set firm, like a keystone set above an arch. His hand was clasped around his sword, as he marched purposefully into the triclinium. He had woken early. His hangover was already a memory. The soldier's brow was corrugated in determination, or bellicosity. Varro thought that the praetorian might deliver more bad news. But he was wrong.

The veteran's face broke out into a grin when he saw his friends.

"Good news. We've found Plancus," Vulso announced.

Varro's mind suddenly became alert, like a hound taut with anticipation.

"What has he said?" the agent asked, eagerly.

"Nothing. He's dead."

It was a beautiful day, one that could almost prove the existence of the gods. The cool, blue sky was fretted with wisps of cloud, and awash with clement sunshine. The storm, the previous evening, had cleared the air. Lucilla wondered if the tempest, which had come in from the sea, had reached Rome and Varro. Some storms die out, some thrive. The dewy fields basked in the light, seemingly turning greener as the day progressed. Flowers turned their heads towards the sun, like a group of senators craning their necks when a pretty woman walks past.

As pleasant as the view was out the window Lucilla averted her gaze back towards Camilla. The expectant mother was in bed, with extra pillows propping up her head. The room had been aired and cleaned. The bedsheets had been laundered that morning. The silver ewer and cup, filled with water, had been polished to a standard that Vulso would have approved of. Lucilla had also removed various extraneous pieces of furniture from the chamber, so the surgeon and his attendant had more space to move around in. Camilla had just endured her first contractions. The privileged daughter of a wealthy merchant had never experienced pain like it before, and she began to rue her words to her husband, that she wanted as many children as possible. Her features were contorted, at differing times, with anxiety and elation. Her face was glazed in sweat. Tendrils of hair were stuck to her cheeks, like wet long grass sticking to smooth stone.

Camilla called for Manius to be with her, more than once. She often felt like she was the safest – and luckiest – woman in the world when she was with him. But she felt less safe and lucky right now. Lucilla observed her friend's distress and held her hand, offering soothing words of support.

"I have sent for Septimus. He will be here with his attendant soon."

"Thank you, for everything, Lucilla. I promise to be here for you, when you have your first child," Camilla replied. Manius had never told his wife about how Lucilla had lost two unborn babies when she was first married to Varro.

Lucilla forced a grateful smile, but twinges of regret and dejection soon shaped her expression as she averted her gaze and stared back out the window. She had imagined holding Camilla's baby, wondering whether she would feel a sense of boundless joy or boundless envy. She masked it well, but her mood could be as changeable as the weather. As serene as Lucilla seemed on the surface, who knew the strengths of the currents pulling beneath? There were moments when she intensely envied her friend – and thought that she deserved to have a child before the younger woman. As content as she felt since remarrying, she still didn't feel complete. Only a child could fill the hole inside her. Lucilla had yet to tell Rufus how she felt. "Everyone must keep some secrets. Anyone who isn't hiding something isn't worth knowing," he had written, in his first play. Even if they adopted a baby, that would be enough. Be more than enough. She raised the subject a couple of times, but his enthusiasm was conspicuous by its absence. "Whatever makes you happy," he had said. But she needed him to be happy with any decision too. Lucilla remembered how Rufus used to argue that he didn't want to bring a child into the world – and that it had more to do with the world than with the child. The world was cruel, vain and, more often than not, dull, he argued. Lucilla sometimes thought that Rufus wasn't keen on having children as an act of rebellion against his dead father, or class. His name, history, would die with him. The chief reason why Varro wasn't keen on having children however was that the surgeon who had attended to Lucilla, when she lost her second child, warned him that his wife could die if she fell pregnant again.

Both Lucilla and Camilla grew distracted from their thoughts when they heard voices from outside. Burrus, a grizzled veteran, was talking to Piso, a new recruit. Burrus decided to tell a few jokes, to help kill the time as the soldiers made a routine patrol of the property.

"So, I went to get my hair trimmed the other day," Burrus said, his gravelly voice as rough as his manners. "The hairdresser asked how would I like in cut? In silence, I replied. Ha! That's not olden, that's golden lad. Now, listen, what I'm about to tell you isn't a joke. It's a true story, that actually happened. It was the night before the Battle of Pharsalus, and a group of Caesar's soldiers captured a decurion from Pompey's camp. At first, they beat him and interrogated the peacock. The wine flowed as much as the blood. The officer in charge of Caesar's men then tossed a noose around the strongest branch of the nearest tree - and pulled out some dice. He said to the poor bastard decurion that if he threw a one to a five then he would hang him. "What happens if I throw a six?" Pompey's man asked, through a mouth of broken teeth. "Then you get to throw again." Ha! How do you like that one?"

Burrus slapped his thigh as he let out a throaty cackle, before he snorted and spat out a gob of phlegm.

Lucilla smirked, easing the tension in her expression. She made a mental note of the joke, so she could tell it to Rufus when he returned. Although her husband often appeared amused - and it was not always clear what he was amused by - he seldom laughed out loud when sober.

## 17.

"The old Jewess, who rented the room out to Plancus in the Subura, found him first thing this morning," Vulso explained. "He was laid out on his bed, having plunged a knife in his throat. I'm not sure if we should consider the stupid bastard courageous, or cowardly, for taking his own life in such a way. He was a poet though. The fool probably thought he was Cato re-born. Agrippa has asked that you visit the scene. The corpse and the note Plancus left are still in place. The letter confesses how he murdered Corvinus. He waited until Julia left. He says that he loved Corvinus, that it was a crime of passion and all that rot. He killed himself because he felt guilty. He didn't want to bring any further shame to his family. Anyway, it's all now a dead issue it seems. It looks like you can both go home."

The praetorian was pleased to be the harbinger of such good news, having previously felt ill at ease, having acted as the messenger to summon Varro and Manius to Rome in the first place. He felt a small pang of regret, that he was unlikely to experience the hospitality of Caesar's daughter again or learn how an investigation could unfold. But he welcomed the fact that his assignment was over. He was a soldier rather than spy. He was used to marching, as opposed to sneaking about. Vulso looked forward to returning to his duties, chipping away at the blocks of stone of his new recruits and shaping them into praetorians worthy enough to wear the uniform. He hadn't drilled his men for several days.

*Their holiday will soon be over.*

Vulso also looked forward to hunting down Licinius Pulcher and running his sword through his gullet.

Manius immediately appeared buoyed by the news of the suicide. He breathed out, but the last thing he felt was deflated. The word "home" seemed as sweet as wine, sex and victory. He would offer to start making the arrangements, for the journey back to Arretium. There was still a fair chance he could be present for the birth of his child.

Questions – and prayers – had been answered, Varro mused. The investigation was over. There was no need to interview Silo or Trebonius. He could avoid an awkward encounter with the father of the victim. He would be spared the onerous task of interrogating Plancus' friends. Varro was free to travel back home. To Lucilla. The agent felt akin to Tantalus, finally being able to pluck the fruit from the bough and drink water from the pool. The gods were no longer punishing him. But his mood failed to soar. His wings still felt clipped. Perhaps the writer in him wanted Plancus to be innocent – and for there to be a greater store of intrigue and treachery involved in the crime. He thought there might be a twist in the tale, that comedy would turn into tragedy, or tragedy into comedy. But the simplest solution is often the right one. Plancus murdered Corvinus. And now Plancus was dead. Justice had been done. The investigation had been neatly tied-up. But were things too neat?

Caesar would be satisfied, which of course was the most important consideration.

On hearing the news that his assignment had run its course Varro's hangover subsided. The agent suddenly craved a drink again. To celebrate. He could soon kick the dust of Rome from his feet. The city had fed on the morsel of his soul for long enough. A burden, or curse, had been lifted. But not entirely...

Varro felt like he was a man trying to swim in two opposing directions. He had made a promise to his wife to return as soon as possible. He had made a similar promise to Manius. But he had also given his word to Agrippa to do his duty. He had made a promise to the ghost of Corvinus, that he would find his murderer. He could make a further promise to Plancus, to clear his name should he be innocent. Varro told himself that he owed more to the living than he did to the dead, but still he would visit Plancus' hovel in the Subura.

*What will be will be.*


Varro and Vulso, accompanied by a couple of praetorians, made their way across the Palatine and down into the Subura. Manius remained behind, to make the provisional arrangements to journey back to Arretium. He also wanted to write a letter to his wife, to send word ahead of his imminent arrival. He was unsure whether to include in the letter the news that he was bringing Viola back with him. Camilla didn't quite love the mongrel as much as the Briton. But no one did.

Death no longer seemed to be stalking him, Varro half-joked to himself as a noisy funeral procession which was heading towards him veered off down a side street and the caterwauling receded. He was perhaps more concerned that the mimes leading the procession might have been stalking him, when they made eye contact with Varro and gesticulated with pronounced vigour.

The heat was clammy, dirty. It felt like Varro was wearing a dusty, scratchy woollen hood over his head. Clusters of insects congregated in the air over mounds of dung and refuse. They giddily flew about, reminding him of Julia's party guests.

Toga-wearing senators, walking towards the Forum, were a self-conscious picture of stoicism in the face of evident discomfort, as they sweated in their heavy garments. One sour-faced official lost his temper however as he lashed out at his slave, who accidentally dropped a couple of scrolls he was carrying. The grey-beard's walking stick suddenly resembled a centurion's vine staff, as he thrashed the Nubian several times. Varro was tempted to grab the stick from the official and use it on him, to teach the vicious bureaucrat a lesson, but it was far too humid to play the hero. The oppressive heat sapped his courage – physical and moral.

During their walk across the Palatine, Vulso further briefed Varro about Agrippa's meeting with Maecenas the previous evening. The plan was to apprehend, or execute, Licinius Pulcher.

"Agrippa has dispatched a couple of agents to scout ahead. As well as assessing the strengths and weaknesses of the enemy's defences, they will be able to track Pulcher should he leave his location."

Varro was understandably relieved that Agrippa had found Pulcher so quickly. He was just wary that the intelligence had come from Maecenas. As Agrippa had once said himself, "The day you trust Gaius Maecenas is the day he puts a knife in your back." Varro couldn't shake the suspicion, buried deep inside of him like a gallstone, that they were all puppets in a play, directed by the spymaster. Maecenas was well-practised in the arts of ulterior motives and misdirection. He recalled a recent election, which he rigged like a chariot race in the Circus Maximus. Maecenas had declared his support for Lucius Bulla. He offered to manage Bulla's campaign and fundraise for the merchant. By doing so Maecenas grew close to the candidate - and uncovered compromising information about the man he purported to support. Bulla withdrew from the race, a few days before the vote, and his rival won the election at a canter.

"Was Agrippa not sceptical of Maecenas' change of heart about his former agent?"

"Agrippa argued that he would have been more suspicious of Maecenas if he didn't betray his former agent. Maecenas wants Pulcher dead for the selfish reasons that his ex-lover may well come for him next, after he gets his revenge on you. Pulcher is also a keeper of Maecenas' secrets – and crimes. If Pulcher dies, the information dies with him. The wily, old fox, or snake, knows what's best for him. Deceiving Agrippa is tantamount to deceiving Caesar, which wouldn't be the wisest career move… It's better to be safe than sorry, though. Agrippa has forbidden Maecenas, or any of his men, to be present when we capture Pulcher… I know the property. It'll be a tough nut to crack. But I'll make sure we bring a big enough hammer. The walled villa is close to a back road. A river could also provide Pulcher with a means of escape. But we'll besiege and encircle the bastard if we need to. The noose will tighten, with his neck in it. I'll get him, I promise Rufus," the soldier remarked, honourably and earnestly, clasping his sword.

"Not if I get to him first. I have every faith in yourself and your men that you will get the job done, Aelius. But I hope you understand that I'd like to be present too. I want to see Pulcher dead. Manius wouldn't want to miss out on all the fun too."

Vulso nodded. He had already arranged additional horses, having second-guessed Varro's decision.

Clumps of people parted and allowed the formidable looking praetorians through, like a plough cutting through virgin soil, as they descended into the crowded Subura. The soldiers were viewed with suspicion, or outright antagonism, once the labyrinthine streets of the district swallowed them up. The locals judged that the authorities were coming for one of their own. It would be a brave man to challenge Vulso and ask him to turnaround, however. Bleary-eyed whores stared out of windows, either having just woken up or just returned home. Cadaverous faces, studded with eyes which glinted like blades, could be glimpsed in dark alleyways. Before they vanished. Barefooted, malnourished children, with swollen bellies and hollowed out expressions, didn't know whether to admire or fear the hulking soldiers. Praetorians could be both heroes and villains.

Varro was pleased he wore boots rather than sandals, as he traversed through streets covered with a layer of slick grime. Occasionally the pungent aromas of stale acetum, and staler garum, could be smelled over the stench of fresh ordure. Rats, more populous than drunks and beggars, darted in and out of sight.

More than one quarrel could be heard emanating from the apartment buildings lurching over them. Wives scolded husbands, and husbands berated wives – the noise carrying further than a siren song.

"You pissed your money up the wall, drinking again," one woman screeched, either dropping, or more likely throwing, a clay cup as she made her salient point.

"Well, I wouldn't piss on you, even if you were on fire," the husband countered, slurring his words.

"I'd piss on you though, if I thought you'd drown."

The streets were saturated with privation. Varro wondered if anyone was running a wager on which building would collapse next. The sound of rustling silk was alien to the neighbourhood. A family huddled together at the entrance to a recently burned-out apartment block – their worldly possessions contained on their laps. Other besmirched, browbeaten countenances went about their business. Teeth like cinders. Clothes patched-up or threadbare. People shuffled rather than strode. Hunched over, from life dragging them down day after day, year after year.

Little sunlight, hope or prosperity shone through. The nobleman seldom frequented the Subura during the day. He had always visited its taverns and brothels at night. He had always been accompanied by Manius too. Varro would have probably been robbed and died a thousand deaths, without his protection. Plancus was right come to the Subura to disappear. No one would want to linger and search here. People kept themselves to themselves. Even tax officials gave the district a wide berth. It was difficult to tax the destitute, as a percentage of nothing is nothing.

Yet Varro was wary of tarring everyone with the same brush. There were plenty of inhabitants of the Subura who tried their best to live as honestly and honourably as possible, in a city not renowned for its honesty or honour. They just wanted some food – and wine – in their bellies. To celebrate a win at a chariot race and to see their children healthy and happy. The aristocrat had drunk with plenty of rogues and characters in the local taverns. Their sense of humour was as developed and robust as any Roman satirist. It was important, if not essential, to laugh in the face of a rancorous world.

As they came to the dilapidated apartment block they were greeted by the equally dilapidated landlady, Marta. She had managed the lodgings, for decades, with her husband, who had recently passed. The widow had a squashed, shrewd, distrustful expression. Grey, wiry hairs, like baby snakes, sprouted out of the black shawl which covered her head. Her face resembled a scrotum. Beneath her widow's weeds Marta must have been the size of a child, Vulso thought. Her chin was covered with more hair than Macer's. Despite her frail frame her voice was strong and forthright.

"You're late. You should have been here earlier. I don't see why my day should revolve around you, or a corpse."

"I am sorry for our tardiness and any inconvenience caused. We will duly compensate you for your time," Varro cordially remarked, offering up his best, conciliatory smile.

Marta grunted in assent.

"Come with me. He's up on the second floor," the landlady exclaimed, before masticating like a cow.

The stairs groaned, perhaps in sympathy with their owner. Vulso dared not grasp the bannister, lest it came off in his hand. The smell of bread and fish stew emanated from the kitchen at the rear of the property. There was an extra charge for food at the dwelling.

Due to Marta travelling at a snail's pace, if the snail was lame and blind, Varro had a chance to glance inside some of the rooms in the house. They were small, spartan, dingy. Most were festooned with dust and cobwebs. The landlady provided a cleaning service, for an additional charge. Candles and a washbasin were extra too. The floorboards were warped, the curtains threadbare. The only attractive thing about the room was the price.

It had been some time since Varro had encountered a dead body. He didn't want to embarrass himself or Vulso and retch. The scowl he would receive from the old crone might also burn a hole in him too. The aristocrat could stomach a lot more since becoming an agent, for good or ill. Varro recalled other corpses he had witnessed over the years. Some people died with a shocked expression on their face, as though the inevitable still took them by surprise. Skin could be like cheap leather, or ashen or translucent. A mouth could be comically contorted, in agony or in a silent, primal scream. Raging against death, or life. Some corpses appeared at peace, however, as if they were sleeping rather than deceased. People died in different ways. But people died.

*How will I die?*

Before Varro had a chance to answer the question, Marta turned around and addressed him.

"He was a good boy. He paid his rent promptly and was always polite. I thought he was just hiding from his creditors. I didn't know he was a fugitive. If I did, I would have called you here earlier. The law is the law. It's such a shame though. He kept himself to himself. He often just stayed in his room and read. I should have guessed something was awry. The boy was always fidgeting. He chewed his nails so much I thought he might gnaw off his arm. He lost weight. It fell off him. You need fattening up, I said. You should get a woman to cook for you. He had everything to live for. I told him, you need God in your life. I wept and prayed for the poor child when I found him this morning. Is there some sort of reward? A good deed is its own reward of course. But coin is coin. I can't eat virtue or spend kind words."

They finally reached the second floor. Plancus' room was at the top of the house. The slanting roof almost cut the space in half, although Varro doubted the lodger received a discount on his rent. He felt a wave of pity, rather than nausea, as he saw the dead youth splayed out on the bed. The knife still protruded from his bloody throat.

"Thank you for your assistance. We can take things from here. If you would like to wait downstairs. I promise that you will be amply compensated for your troubles," Varro remarked. He no longer wanted her voice needling his ear. The agent needed some quiet and scope to think.

*She's as irritating as leprosy.*

Vulso pointed out Plancus' note on the desk but then decided to wait outside. Varro sensed some foul play at work immediately, without even scrutinising the scene. Something didn't smell right – and it wasn't just the landlady's fish stew. The agent approached the narrow, coffin-like bed as dispassionately as possible. Plancus had been wearing a bark-brown short-sleeved tunic when he died. He had certainly not been at peace when he perished. A rictus of terror was still plastered on his bloodless countenance. Varro noticed how his scrawny arms lay by his side. They were also bloodless. Surely the hand that he used, to hold the knife, should have been covered in blood. Vulso had assured him that the body remained untouched. He would check with the landlady to see if she or anyone else had placed Plancus' arms by his side, or had washed his hands, but he was confident of the answer. The faint but discernible fingertip-sized marks on the youth's biceps, from where someone had grabbed him and potentially pinned him down, added further credence to Varro's suspicions. That Plancus had been killed by someone else's hand.

The corpse's face was dusted with salt. Plancus had been heavily perspiring before he expired, Varro judged. He also glanced down at the dusty floorboards. There was an array of large boot prints, especially around the bed.

The agent peered over the small balcony at the far side of the room and surmised that it would have been possible for a couple of assailants to scale the walls of the apartment building, although there was no evidence anyone had done so.

Finally, Varro went over to the desk and examined the note Plancus left. He recognised that it was the same handwriting to that of the poems he had been sent by the youth previously. Yet the script was more spidery, jittery, than usual. The agent pictured Plancus composing the letter, his hand trembling as someone held a knife to his throat.

*"I killed Marcus Corvinus. He died by my hand alone. I entered the garden, late at night, and murdered my friend while he was in his pool. He was my lover. Jealousy compelled me to kill Marcus. It overtook me, like a poison. Guilt and shame have compelled me to end my life. It is only just that the same hand which murdered Marcus will murder me, using the same knife. A light*

*has gone out in the world, since his passing. I despise myself and my wicked crime. I have brought shame to my family. They should no longer have a murderer and fugitive as a son. I am sorry."*

Varro arched an eyebrow. He leaned over the bed and scrutinised the knife again, half lodged in Plancus' throat. Although the agent hadn't seen the weapon or wound, in relation to the murder of Corvinus, he had been told that the knife was large. The dagger used to kill Plancus was not.

The discrepancy between the weapons was one of many pieces of evidence which suggested he was standing at the scene of a murder rather than suicide. But even if he could prove, beyond a reasonable doubt, that Plancus had been killed, what then? Who could he accuse of the crime? There were no witnesses. Advocates were not necessarily known for their dedication to justice and truth. Lies came as easily to lawyers as swimming did to sharks.

*Maecenas.* Again, the agent's thoughts turned to his old adversary. Did Corvinus confess a telling secret to Plancus, which could compromise the political fixer? Although it seemed - *seemed* - that Maecenas was guiltless of being behind the assassination attempt on his life, that did not mean that the spymaster was guiltless of being behind the murders of Corvinus and Plancus.

But he had no proof at present of Maecenas' involvement. The death of Plancus was still as much of a mystery as the death of Corvinus.

*Viola chases her tail less.*

Varro's heart went out to Plancus, as he gazed at his bloody corpse. He spared a thought for his parent's too, who would soon be bewailing their son for different reasons. Yet, as an act of will, the agent hardened his heart. It was perfectly possible that he was staring at Corvinus' killer. Should he not just take the win? He need only report to Agrippa that the suicide appeared genuine – and he could go home. It would be a lie, of sorts. But he was a spy. His job, or vocation, was to deceive. As a former philosophy student Varro was well-rehearsed in being able to argue for two, opposing points of view. He could make a convincing argument for Plancus murdering Corvinus - and then committing suicide. Even if Varro voiced his doubts, he imagined that Caesar would be willing to let sleeping dogs lie.

The agent let out a curse of frustration beneath his breath. He was tempted to pick up the clay cup on the nearby table and smash it on the ground. Instead, he sighed wistfully. Death and corruption were still no excuse to act in an uncivilised manner, the aristocrat considered.

## 18.

Despite the tantalising promise of returning to Arretium and Lucilla, Varro found himself trudging home, after he finished making a payment to Marta.

"Will you be open to negotiating?" the landlady asked, either probing him with her good eye or just squinting in the sunlight.

"Yes, but I will only be able to negotiate down."

Marta took the money, tightly clutching the coins in her hand, wishing that she could receive a similar sum for all the lodgers who died in her beds, from suicide or other causes.

Varro ascended the slope leading up to the Palatine, fresh air and pristine sunlight. He half-joked to himself that he was feeling so weary, burdened, he might even be developing a stoop. His footsteps were as leaden as a child's however, travelling to school or heading home, knowing that his father would punish him for another instance of bad behaviour. Or, as the agent thought of where he was in relation to the dead ends of his investigation, he imagined himself akin to Sisyphus again.

*The boulder rolls up the hill. The boulder rolls down the hill. And so on.*

In contrast, Varro observed a notable spring in Manius' step, when he returned home. He seemed almost as happy as Viola, if that were at all possible.

Varro resigned himself to lying to Agrippa. He reported that it was a suicide. Or he said that it "appeared" to be a suicide. The writer was, as ever, careful with his words.

*Euclid may disagree, but some circles can be squared.*

He heard the shade of his father whisper in his ear, criticising him for not finishing the job. But Varro had ignored his father enough when he was alive. It was easy to dismiss him in death as well. There had been plenty of crimes in the past which went unpunished. There would be plenty of crimes which would go unpunished in the future too. One more wouldn't make a difference.

As well as ending the assignment in order to travel back to Arretium for his friend's sake, he was doing so for selfish reasons, Varro concluded, as he sat in his garden. Alone. He closed his eyes, attempting to block out most of the world. The grass cooled his warm, aching feet. A merciful breeze lapped against his face, like waves lapping against the shore. Occasionally there would be a lull in the wind blowing against his skin and he would be tempted to call for one of his slaves to stand by his chair and fan him.

When he finally opened his tired eyes, he noticed a row of pert flowers bordering part of the lawn. They were the same purple and white blooms which brightened up part of his garden in Arretium. He remembered the scene, when he sat and watched Lucilla plant the flowers. She wore an old dress, which wouldn't have appeared out of place on a slave. Yet the dull, grey garment still couldn't diminish her beauty or spoil her elegant figure. A smudge of dirt marked her chin. She gardened, similar to other things, with efficiency and care, patting down each plant and brushing off any soil from the leaves or petals.

"You're more than welcome to help," Lucilla suggested, turning to her husband. Varro was soaking up the sun, reading, reclined in his favourite cushioned chair. A slave had just refilled his winecup and delivered another plate of dates and thinly sliced pieces of pear. The nobleman was a picture of indulgence and indolence.

"I'd prefer not to get my hands dirty. You're doing a splendid job by yourself too," Varro replied. A smile peeked out from beneath the brim of his sunhat.

"If you look after your garden, then your garden will look after you," Lucilla remarked.

"If you're offering up that maxim to be included in the next play, then I'm afraid that I can't help you out on that front either."

His smile was as crisp and bright as the midday sun. Lucilla raised a corner of her mouth, in a nod towards a smirk, but she wasn't quite as amused as her husband by his words.

"I take it that you're going just going to sit there, read and drink wine for the rest of the afternoon?"

"I doubt if I'll sit here all afternoon. I need to go inside at some point. I wouldn't want my reading to eat into my nap time," Varro drily replied, before yawning. Somehow, even when yawning, he remained smiling.

"Talking of eating," Lucilla replied, turning to her attendant, who had just come out into the garden. "Diana, will you be fine to cook dinner this evening?"

"Yes, I can cook you your favourite. Trout, in a cheese sauce," the gnarled woman answered, full knowing how much her mistress' husband disliked the dish. But Varro merely rolled his eyes and shared a conspiratorial look with his wife. Amused. Enamoured.

Every day was less of a day without her, Varro fancied. The curse of Sisyphus didn't feel so terrible, with Lucilla helping to roll the boulder up the hill. It was less than half the weight. He wanted to end the investigation in order to go home and view the light in her eyes when he revealed he wanted to adopt a child. Not just because it would make her happy. But that it would make him happy. It was the right thing to do. Varro was determined not to repeat the mistakes his father made with him, albeit he was confident of making his own ones. The world needed condemning.

*But it isn't - quite - all bad.*

Just as Varro was about to hammer the final nail in the coffin of his investigation, to find Corvinus' killer, there was a knock at the door. The unexpected guest was shown out into the garden. Questions would now be answered.

Clouds blocked out the sun. The temperature dropped. The sweat on Varro's back chilled a little as he stared, his mouth agape, at the familiar face of his visitor. But as much as the face was familiar, his demeanour was strange. Ovid's usually carefree expression was careworn. Varro had seen the poet hungover, plenty of times, but his pallor and unease were not due to a surfeit of wine, he judged. Ovid's hair was unkempt, and his tunic marked with food and drink stains. The poet was normally well attired, presentable.

"Fail to prepare, prepare to fail," Ovid had once told his friend. "You never know when you might encounter the love of your life. Or, even better, your love for the coming night ahead."

His friend was clearly in some distress. Ovid's head darted about, bird-like, checking to see if anyone might be spying at him from over the garden wall. Sweat was pouring off him, like someone had just thrown a jug of water in his face. The jittery youth was carrying a bag over his shoulder, clutching it tightly, guardedly, as if it contained the only copies of his latest poems. Ovid met Varro's gaze. His bottom lip quivered, as if he were about to cry.

"Ovid. It's good to see you," the nobleman said equitably, reassuringly. "Please, come, take a seat. Would you like anything to eat?"

Ovid shook his head, fearing that he wouldn't be able to keep any food down. Varro led his friend over to where he had been sitting, drawing up another chair. Ovid sat down, just before it looked like he might collapse. Varro poured a cup of wine for his guest. The youth's hand trembled as he moved it towards his lips – spilling a few drops as he did so. A couple of fresh stains joined the old ones on his tunic.

"You seem troubled, my friend," Varro remarked. "How are things?"

"Things have gone to shit. Things may well never be the same again."

"What's wrong?"

"What's right? Nothing's right. But then we've always known that. I've just obtained another piece of evidence which proves our theory."

Ovid wiped his brow again, licked the sweat off his upper lip and retrieved a tightly bound scroll from his bag.

"I received a letter. It's from Felix. It was delivered last night, while I was attending the party. My slave put it with a pile of other correspondence. I didn't read the note until this morning. I can't guarantee I'm not being watched. I'm more scared of her than him. She has spies everywhere, more than Agrippa or Maecenas."

The agent took the scroll out of Ovid's shaking hand. As much as he was tempted to do so, he didn't snatch the parchment and open it up immediately.

"You will be safe here. Manius is inside, along with a contingent of praetorians," Varro remarked. He chose not to reveal that the soldiers were present due to the threat on his own life.

"Thank you, Rufus. I didn't know who else to turn to."

Ovid exhaled and appeared visibly relieved, having handed Varro the scroll. A problem shared is a problem halved, supposedly. The nervous poet still fidgeted however and glued his gaze to Varro's reaction to Plancus' letter.

*"My dear friend. Perhaps, because I am entrusting you with this, you are my dearest friend. I have not named you, just in case this letter falls into the wrong hands.*

*I have written to you because I must tell someone the truth, even if you will be unable to share the contents of my message for some time. But I need to confess the truth, before it's too late. I will either flee from Rome soon – and disappear into the aether - or I will be murdered, like Marcus was murdered. By Tiberius.*

*I should have travelled home after the party. But there was a knot in my stomach which I couldn't untie – a Gordian knot which I should have just cut – when I dwelled upon the misery that Marcus had chosen Julia over me. Marcus whispered that he would see me the following evening, that he would think of me when he was with her. Even at the end I still swallowed his lies and love. When I waited behind the garden wall and overheard them together, every groan was like a spear thrust into my chest. I felt like opening-up a vein and composing a poem in my blood. My Lesbia was betraying me. Yet still I loved Marcus. I must have loved him, otherwise it wouldn't have hurt so much. He told me before too that, if I wanted him, I would have to share him. I would have forgiven him anything. He was Catiline and Brutus reborn. I could even forgive him ridiculing and plagiarising my poetry. No one knew him like I knew him. No one loved him like I loved him. He told me I was his true love. As much as he could be mocking and arrogant in public, he could be tender, sweet and generous in private. When he spoke about philosophy, you felt like you were in the presence of a character from Plato's dialogues. I know you never quite felt for his charms, which I envy you for in a way. Love is a fever and the cure. But I fell for him completely. In some ways, I feel like I am still falling.*

*I was gripped by jealousy, as surely as a hand can grip the wrong end of a poker. And I wasn't the only one gripped by jealousy. Tiberius was drawn back to the house. Unbeknownst to me, he was standing around the corner. Waiting – and listening – like me. We overheard part of their conversation.*

*"You will be welcome to stay the whole night," Marcus said to Julia.*

*"You couldn't afford me for the whole night," she replied, laughing and mocking him. As you know, Julia often likes to play the courtesan. However, it's her lovers who feel used, that they've prostituted themselves.*

*When he heard Julia leave, Tiberius entered the garden through the back door.*

*"I'm glad she's finally gone," Marcus exclaimed, at seeing Tiberius. "I know it may come as scant consolation, but when I was with her, I was thinking of you. I feel like I am living a lie when I am with her. But you know how demanding your sister can be. If I refused her, she would not be forgiving. We will soon be together though, away from Julia and Rome. Fighting side by side. Sleeping side by side. In Spain."*

*I couldn't hear Tiberius' reply. What I did hear was the rasping sound of a blade being removed from its scabbard. And then I heard splashing and a slight sluicing sound – of, what it turned out, was noise of the blade penetrating Marcus' skull. Something was wrong and, without thinking, I rushed into the garden. If there was a struggle ensuing, my intention was to save Marcus.*

*Yet I was too late. I stood in the doorway, as if I were Patroclus having witnessed the death of my Achilles. The knife had already been plunged into his skull. Tiberius was standing over him. He shifted his focus from the wound he had inflicted and met my gaze. Blood trickled down Marcus' forehead and his killer let the body slide into the pool. Foolishly, for a moment, I was worried he might drown – before I remembered he was already dead. You would have thought that Tiberius' expression would have been imbued with remorse or rage. But no. It was a look of triumph, satisfaction and "you're next". I have witnessed gladiators enjoy killing less. You might think that the crime was committed in the heat of passion. Yet his countenance was cold, chilling.*

*I remember observing a pitcher of water on a nearby table. I was nearly compelled to use it as a missile - or clasp its handle and wrap it around the monster's head. To my shame, I was a coward. I regret my actions, or inaction. I wish I could have done something, though more so I wish I had just travelled home after the party.*

*Marcus perished immediately. He would have wanted a soldier's death, or a philosopher's death. Instead he was butchered, sacrificed on the altar of Tiberius' jealousy and cruelty. Should we thank the gods for small mercies, that he died so quickly? If the gods have any devotion to justice, then Tiberius will not experience such a merciful demise.*

*I ran, as if Cerberus were at my heels. I needed time to think. I couldn't spend the night at my family's home, for fear of Tiberius and his bodyguards breaking in and slaughtering us all in our beds, to silence us. I realised I needed funds, immediately – and that I should go into hiding. The more squalid the hole I found, the better. My plan was to contact my friends and raise money, to flee Rome. But friends turned their backs on me. I feel hollowed out. My faith in my friends – and the world – has diminished to near extinction. My fugitive status has condemned me, in more ways than one. You might argue that I should have immediately reported the crime to the authorities. But who would have believed me or have dared to apprehend Tiberius? Caesar would have ended the investigation before it began.*

*I feel trapped, enfeebled. I feel like I have been murdered. My life is now over. The truth is a death sentence – and I am sorry for burdening you. But one day you may have the audience of Horace and Virgil and be able to share the truth, without fear of punishment from Caesar or Tiberius.*

*I intend to leave Rome, the day after tomorrow. I have caught word of a large funeral procession leaving the gates of Rome for the necropolis. The authorities will have probably posted watchers on the walls, but there is safety in numbers. Ironically, or poetically, a funeral will provide salvation.*

*If I do not escape the city soon, I will be found and killed. I was nearly apprehended yesterday. I was chased through the Subura by two men. Thankfully I evaded capture. My rag-like clothes befit my state, yet they proved an asset through allowing me to blend into the crowd. I am unsure whether Tiberius or Caesar himself dispatched people to find me. Marcus once told me too how Livia has a far more extensive and ruthless network of agents than Agrippa or Maecenas. She will do anything to protect her son.*

*I am running out of parchment and time. Perhaps one day we will meet again and share our verses, on Mount Parnassus. I do so esteem and envy your gifts. The greatest gift you gave me was that of your friendship, however."*

The parchment weighed like a slab of lead in Varro's hand. His mind was ablaze, as it struggled to fully comprehend what he had just read. He tried to imagine Tiberius murdering Corvinus, with Plancus looking on, but the poet's imagination was somehow deficient. Incredulous. A torrent of sympathy flooded his being, as he put himself in Plancus' shoes. The adolescent had seen his friend and lover murdered. His existence had been turned upside down. Terror must have coursed, like blood, through his body. Had he been brave or cowardly to hide himself away? Varro admired his will to keep his parents safe, however. Any admiration the agent cultivated for Corvinus further dissipated. Corvinus reminded him of his past self. Manipulative. Self-interested.

Ovid's febrile manner diminished - but didn't vanish completely.

"I pity anyone who considers me their dearest friend. He must be desperate. I have spent half this morning cursing Plancus' name, for involving me in his plans. Why did he choose me to confess to? I am as loyal and reliable as a whore. Yet I feel sorry for the fool too. Can we help him, without compromising ourselves? Can we get some money to Felix? I will repay you, albeit my list of creditors is as long as my list of ex-lovers. There are some names which occupy both lists, of course. But we must assist Felix if we can. He is innocent. If we cannot save the innocent, then what hope is there for the guilty, like us?" Ovid argued. His strained voice was scarce above a whisper, as he leaned towards his host. His knuckles were as white as snow covered mountaintops, as he gripped the arm of the chair he was sitting on.

"Felix is now beyond saving I'm afraid. Or he has been saved, delivered. He was found dead this morning," Varro said, sorrowfully. "He was discovered in a lodging house in the Subura."

"How did he die?"

"He was stabbed, in the throat. I examined the scene myself. It was made to appear as if Felix committed suicide. The bastards even forced him to compose a final letter, confessing to the murder."

Both men paused, imagining the grim scenario. Ovid shook his head, mournfully. Although twinges of grief were ultimately eclipsed by pangs of fear.

"It pains me that Felix has died. He may have been a second-rate poet, but he was harmless. He retained a sweetness that not even this city could blight. I imagine that few will attend his funeral. I should compose an elegy, one that will wring tears from the heart. But the poem would need to remain unread. I must keep my distance, like a lover I've recently spurned and do not want to cause a scene in public with. I know my behaviour may be deemed ignoble. But better to be ignoble than dead. For once poetry seems unimportant. Poetry is, at heart, frippery. Verbal perfume. Poetry can linger for a while, but it will fade. I have no desire to fade or die right now, however. This letter is a death sentence. It's poisonous. I cannot use it as evidence to expose Tiberius, as it will expose myself. I feel like a dead man walking. At best I would be banished, exiled, if Caesar found out that I knew the truth. I do not want to keep this letter in my possession any longer. You can keep it. I would burn it, if I were you. We can just pretend it never existed. Or you can be the friend he refers to in the note. But even if the authorities believed Plancus' version of events in his letter, they would still dismiss the contents. This letter, like justice, can never see the light of the day. Caesar's authority and dignity will be tarnished if he allows Tiberius to be put on trial. Yet, if his stepson escaped punishment, Caesar would be accused of corruption. The walls of Rome would be strewn with caustic graffiti. I am intending to leave Rome for a few months. Against the bold, daring is unsafe. Out of sight, out of mind. The dust needs to settle. Time is the best doctor. I have a mistress, currently residing in Ravenna. Her husband, who was as old as the hills surrounding the town, has recently passed. I am developing an urge to accept her hospitality and comfort the widow. I shouldn't laugh though. We should be weeping."

Varro didn't wholly admire Ovid's response to Plancus' letter, yet he understood it. The revelations in the correspondence - and his friend's gruesome death – were a lot to bear. Varro decided he would give Ovid some money to clear his debts and finance his trip to Ravenna. Hopefully his new mistress would take his mind off things.

The agent also spared a thought for Tiberius. Caesar's stepson had asked Varro to inform him of any developments in the investigation.

He was about to do so.

**19.**

The room was windowless. Tiberius often locked himself - and his lovers - in. Away from prying eyes. The chamber was decorated with fine works of art - paintings and sculptures. Eroticism blended with militaria. A couple of couches sat opposite each other. A glass-topped table, standing on iron, lion-footed legs, stood in the middle of the room. Incense burned in one corner. A shield, once belonging to the dictator Lucius Cornelius Sulla, was mounted in another, close to a murmuring brazier. Candles lined the walls, like a shrine in a temple.

The private chamber was adjoined to a bedroom and a small bathhouse. Tiberius had recently bathed himself. First, he had sweated in a hot bath, using a strigil to vigorously scrape away any dirt and dust from his skin. He then plunged himself into a cold pool, refreshing and numbing himself. Tiberius recalled, during his ablutions, how he had scrubbed and scraped Marcus' blood off his person, after he murdered his lover. He believed his body to be clean and his conscience clear.

Tiberius stood over a large wooden bowl, which sat on the glass-topped table. He clasped a vine cane and used it to prod the two scorpions in the bowl – or arena – together. Caesar's stepson had imported a new batch of the creatures, which marked his star sign. He wanted the scorpions to do battle for, like gladiators. Tiberius had long been fascinated and enamoured with the species. As a child he would carefully hold his pets by the sting and let their claws pinch his fingers. Sometimes they would draw blood – and he would lick it like honey. As a student he also composed verses, in Latin and Greek, in praise of the creatures. The nobleman would force slaves to be stung, to scientifically assess the potency of different types – and because the acts of cruelty amused him. He even experimented with slaves being stung in their eyes, to see them comically balloon up. Tiberius also arranged races, using a specially constructed model, based upon the Circus Maximus. The victor would be allowed to eat the losers.

A wax tablet lay on the table as well. Before Tiberius wiped it clean, the tablet contained the news of Plancus' death. The youth would have mourned one of his scorpions more. Plancus was weak, over sensitive. Corvinus had kept him around for his amusement. He nicknamed him his "Patroclus." Tiberius felt offended that he had shared the same lover. He knew women who acted less effeminately than the dead poet. Yet Plancus was now gone. The sole witness to his crime would never be able to testify against him. Caesar's stepson had got away with murder. He smiled to himself as he planned to write a letter to Plancus' parents, to attempt to console them during their loss. He would even say that he didn't believed that his friend Felix was capable of such an act of violence, and that he was innocent.

Tiberius would also write a letter to his mother, employing the coded cypher they shared, informing her of Plancus' death – albeit her agents, who had arranged the "suicide," had probably sent word already. Tiberius had advised that Plancus could be spared, due to being too fearful of accusing Caesar's stepson of the killing. But he knew that as soon as he informed his mother of the situation, she would dispatch her agents to silence the unfortunate witness. "Death cures all ills," she had once told him, after hearing the news that a senator, championing the cause of the old republic, had died in mysterious circumstances. The self-satisfied smile on her lips suggested that the circumstances of his death were not such a mystery to her.

A second wax tablet rested on the table, containing the news that his stepfather was recovering from his recent illness. His surgeon, Antonius Musa, had worked another miracle in Tarraco. The physician was worth a thousand priests, praying for the Princeps. Tiberius was slightly conflicted on hearing the good news. He knew that Rome needed a Caesar. Should his stepfather perish then Rome could be plunged into chaos. An uncivil war. There would be a grab for power. Factions would be unleashed, fighting over Rome like a pack of dogs fighting over a bone. A Caesar was needed to maintain order and lead. The empire was a wolf, which one needed to constantly hold by the ears. The earthly problem of Caesar's successor had to be resolved, before Augustus could finally ascend to the heavens. Yet Tiberius would be willing to help solve the issue. His education, experience as a commander, name and bloodline meant that he was fit to lead. Inspire. Perhaps his stepfather dying now would be the right time to stake his claim, before he officially passed his seal onto Agrippa or Marcellus. Before he had other children or grandchildren, to weaken his own legitimacy. Tiberius dreamed of seizing power, for the good of Rome. He would be a just leader, and return (some) authority to the Senate House and great families of Rome. Nobility has its responsibilities. As a member of the Claudii, Tiberius often exclaimed how he was duty-bound to serve Rome – although, after a few wines, he would state how Rome existed to serve him. Tiberius often thought about optimum tax levels. *It is the duty of a good shepherd to shear his sheep, not to flay them.* He planned, in his mind, the games he would hold to celebrate his ascension. Which exotic beasts he would import to perform in the arena. Which plays he would commission and which poets he would patronise, to mark the epoch. He would arrange for the Praetorian Guard to wear an emblem of a scorpion on their shields and breastplates. Power was so near, yet so far away. He calculated he could bide his time, however. A scorpion should strike, only if it knows it will defeat its prey. His mother would continue to champion his cause, though he would curtail her influence should he gain power. He would court Maecenas' favour – and allow the political agent to court him in return. Should Tiberius be unable to succeed Caesar, he vowed to banish himself from the city. He would be content to live on an island somewhere, couched in luxury and small pleasures. Master of all he surveyed. Recalling the words of Julius Caesar, Tiberius would rather be the first man in a village than the second in Rome. He could not serve under Agrippa, a mere commoner, or Marcellus – a peacock. His pride wouldn't allow it, in the same way that his pride wouldn't permit Marcus Corvinus to turn him into a fool and victim.

The scorpions grappled, each vying to bring their stingers into play, after circling one another like boxers. Tiberius enjoyed it when one competitor stung the other and then, with the opponent paralysed, the victor eviscerated its foe.

Tiberius took another large swig of wine and folded a piece of cured meat into his mouth. He glanced into the bedchamber. Despite the thought he expended on politics and his future, Tiberius desired a distraction. He would soon be joined by the courtesan, Fausta. One of her many attractions was that she liked to be dominated in bed. Which was fortunate, as Tiberius liked to dominate as a lover. Fausta had already agreed to dress up as a boy, during their time together. She would be discreet. Whatever happened in his private quarters, remained in his private quarters.

Yet, before Fausta arrived, Tiberius would quickly deal with his other visitor. He had instructed his attendant to make Rufus Varro wait for a prolonged period of time, before showing him through. The nobleman needed to know his place. The investigator would arrive at any moment now though. No doubt Varro was here to relay the news of Plancus' suicide - and his letter, confessing to the crime. He was tempted to present a show of being shocked and saddened, but he decided to be honest and stoical and reveal that he had already been informed of events. The sooner the agent departed the better.

Although Varro was sufficiently emboldened to confront Tiberius, he was still fearful enough to invite Manius to accompany him. The bodyguard waited in the corridor as Varro entered the room and closed the door behind him. The agent's manner was cordial, relaxed. Though he had a look of thunder on his brow as Varro travelled across the Palatine. Injustice burned, as much as the searing sun. The agent's pride rankled too, from the youth having misled him so comprehensively. He had been his dupe. During their first interview Tiberius must have been laughing at him on the inside, from knowing the gruesome truth.

But now it was Varro's time to pretend not to know the truth. The agent had underestimated his interviewee last time. But Tiberius would here underestimate him. Even before becoming a spy, Varro was well practised at deception and playing a role. Feelings, passions, must be suppressed. Suffocated. As much as Varro was determined to initially play a part, he ultimately wanted to rip the mask off the pernicious adolescent. Even if he was the only witness to his true face. Or maybe the gods would be watching – and they would punish the guilty. But divine justice was far from prevalent in the world, even when taking into account that the gods could work in mysterious ways.

Varro willed himself not to be taken back by how young the killer was, when he saw Tiberius. He noticed a few pinpricks of blood on his cheeks, from having scratched the heads off a few pimples. Youth was sometimes not credited with how innocent it could be, but even more so Varro considered how youth wasn't credited with the amount of wickedness it could inhabit. He sometimes thought how it would be easier to flatten the seven hills of Rome than reduce the cruelty in the world by just a fraction. Yet it seemed to him it would be equally difficult to increase the goodness in the world. If goodness existed. Goodness was a flitting shadow at twilight, a conceit. Yet wickedness was all too real. Solid.

"Rufus Varro. Welcome. I take it that you have come here to deliver news pertaining to your investigation. If you have come to report the sad event of Felix's suicide then I am afraid you have had a wasted journey, I'm sorry to say. News travels fast in Rome, like so many smells from some of the more plebeian districts in our city. It is a shame that Felix took his own life. He always admired Cato and Brutus and spoke of their noble, Roman deaths. It is a tragedy. Suicide is no laughing matter. His family will be devastated. Not to sound insensitive, but you must be relieved that your investigation is over, however. I am still trying to comprehend the situation. It was surely a moment of weakness rather than wickedness, which caused him to commit the awful crime. You must take no pleasure from being right, but you did say that we hurt the ones we love. We may be able to argue that Felix deserved his fate, given the viciousness of his actions. But all life is valuable," Tiberius said, plaintively.

"Some life is valuable," Varro drily countered, as he noticed the large mosaic, of a black scorpion, he was standing on. The central image was bordered by a circle of smaller, red, scorpions, either forming a ring to protect their queen or marching aimlessly around, just following the tail of the one in front.

Varro allowed Tiberius to speak, like an angler letting a fish run with the bait.

*Let him keep digging a hole for himself. One deep enough to bury himself in.*

"I understand that Felix wrote a note, explaining things," the aristocrat remarked, unable to suppress a yawn. He idly thought if there would be ample time to nap, before Fausta arrived.

"He did. Before he was murdered, Felix wrote me a letter. Explaining everything, as you say," Varro replied, knowingly. His gaze hardened, like water turning to ice. "You were right. My investigation is over."

Caesar's stepson's suddenly felt less than imperious. The winecup felt heavy in his hand and he placed it back on the table, without drinking from it. For a brief moment the ground seemed to give way and the murderer imagined that a detachment of praetorians might come marching through the door, to apprehend him. His stomach churned and his mouth twitched, in thinly veiled distress or anger. Yet the moment lasted but for a moment and the soldier reined himself in. He forced a smile, trying (but failing) to mirror the confidence and calm of the agent in front of him. The smile soon turned into a snarl. The aristocrat was like a dog, about to bark. He strode towards Varro - and made himself bigger, in an attempt to intimidate his accuser. He puffed out his chest and even lifted his heels of the ground.

Yet Varro remained undaunted. He seemed nerveless. Agrippa had once advised his agent. "There's nothing wrong with being nervous. You just shouldn't seem nervous. Spying is all about seeming."

"You are either brave or foolhardy," Tiberius stated, his nostrils flared. "I can't quite decide which. You are not here to apprehend me, however, and you're wealthy enough not to ask for a bribe to keep silent. Not that you have much to blackmail me with. A dead man's testimony? Which can be claimed is a forgery. You will make more enemies than allies should your spurious evidence ever see the light of day."

Varro's gaze didn't flinch. He almost wanted the arrogant aristocrat to attack him, so he could fight back. Deliver some real justice, for Corvinus and Plancus.

"I can't quite decide whether I'm being brave or foolhardy either. I remember the first time I ever saw you. You were even more of a child than you are now, if that's possible. It was the day of Caesar's triumph – and you were riding, along with Marcellus, on the lead chariot. There was someone whispering in your stepfather's ear, "Remember that you are mortal." I have not come here to apprehend or blackmail you. I just wanted to look you in the eye and remind you that you are mortal. That you're human, or rather inhuman."

Tiberius let out a growl cum laugh. He reached for his cup of wine again and gulped down the contents, smacking his lips afterwards.

"You should mind your tone, lest I choose to remind you how mortal you are. I've killed once. I can kill again. I wonder, how surprised were you when you read Felix's letter and found out about my moment of weakness? Or, one may postulate, my moment of strength," Tiberius asserted. The confident, cold gleam was returning to his aspect. The sparkle in his eye was akin to when he watched his scorpions torture and kill the spiders and rodents he placed in the arena with them. "Were you not listening to me when I said that I had my doubts that Felix murdered Marcus? I was being honest with you. But, I must confess, I was lying to you at another juncture during our previous meeting. I said that no one should be above the law. You have doubtless asked yourself the question, why did I kill Marcus? The answer is, because I could. Some people can and should be a law unto themselves. A Caesar and a Claudian should. You can take your pick as to which to call me. Not all men are created equal. Some men, who seem superior, like Alexander, Sulla and Julius Caesar, are superior. They take, but they also give back – and forge a better world for others. If they have some blood on their hands, so be it. The eagle has no need to concern itself for the earthworm. You might argue Felix was innocent. But the innocent are punished every day. It's what makes them innocent, one could argue. His greatest ambition in life was to be a catamite. And I killed Marcus because it was his greatest ambition to turn me into his catamite. On the night of the party he promised he would do his best to get rid of my sister – and spend the evening with me. He lied to me and dishonoured himself. I knew they were lovers. My sister is accustomed to getting whatever, or whomever, she wants. She can prey on a man, like a leech. A succubus. She is a law unto herself too. But Marcus always promised me he didn't possess any true feelings for Julia. And I believed him. But then I heard the two of them rutting, from behind the garden wall. I heard Marcus employ the same terms of endearment for her, as he uttered for me. I felt like a cuckold. Betrayed. He made a fool of me. Marcus became a cause of pain, which needed to be removed from the world. His murder was an act of surgery. I suppose that Felix's murder was another small act of surgery. When he walked into the garden he was accidentally walking onto a battlefield, one which he was ill-equipped for. His face was as pale as the moon above us. Part of me wanted him to escape Rome and live happily ever after. But he was already dead, a ghost. Yet he was resourceful enough to send you a letter, make his final confession, before he perished. Believe it or not but it was not my decision to murder Felix, and make it appear like suicide. That honour belongs to my mother. Caesar is more merciful. You may not fear me Rufus Varro, but you should fear her. You do not want to make an enemy of her."

"And she does not want to make an enemy of me," Varro replied, firmly. Menacingly. "Should she even raise a little finger against myself or my friends then any ambitions she nurses for you will turn to dust. I could live with your demise, but I suspect she couldn't. I have arranged for the evidence against you to be placed in safekeeping, should I share the same fate as Felix. Silencing me will not suppress the truth, but rather give voice to it," Varro said, lying. He hadn't placed the letter into safekeeping, but he soon would. "My days contemplating suicide ended when I discovered sex and Falernian, so my death will be considered suspicious if it seems I have died by my hand, or any other's. I have every confidence that you will never be prosecuted for your crimes, but that doesn't mean you won't suffer some form of punishment should you or your mother roll the dice against me and the truth is exposed. As you said, news travels fast across Rome. Given the choice between preserving his own honour, or yours, I know who Caesar will sacrifice. Even your mother will not be able to save you. When eagles fall, they fall from great heights – and end up lying next to earthworms. To be out of favour with Caesar must be similar to dying a death of a thousand cuts."

Tiberius tried to smile, through gritted teeth. He shook his head, refuting the words he was hearing, But he knew what the agent was saying was true. Varro had engineered things so, if Tiberius brought about his downfall, he would bring about his own too. It was a stalemate. Yet it felt like a defeat, given his sense of triumph earlier.

"I underestimated you. But I would not overestimate Caesar's support, should you choose to reveal the truth and expose the imperial family to such scandal."

"I have no intention of overestimating or underestimating Caesar. The truth will soon be leaving Rome with me. I will be back in Arretium before the end of the month. Think of me as a modern Cincinnatus. I will be ploughing my fields, so to speak, keeping myself to myself. But if called upon, should you continue to act as law unto yourself, then I will return to Rome to bring you down, even if I bring myself down at the same time," Varro asserted, meaningfully. Icily.

Tiberius believed that the agent would honour his promise to keep silent. The agent would also honour his vow to expose him, should he transgress again. In turn, Tiberius wouldn't inform his mother about the agent's knowledge of his crime. She could cause more harm than good, by moving against Varro. The disgruntled aristocrat emitted a sound. Part snort of derision. Part sigh of resignation.

"It seems we can have an accord, Rufus Varro. I am grateful for your discretion. You know how to work in the shadows and act in the best interests of Rome. I could use a man with your virtues and talents in the future, should you be open to a position of service," Tiberius said, hoping, like his stepfather had done in the past, to turn an enemy into an ally.

Varro did his best to suppress his laughter - but he couldn't fail to appear amused by the conceited aristocrat's advances. He was drinking wine while Tiberius spoke. It was small miracle that he didn't choke on the vintage or spit it out. After recovering, the agent wanted to leave the would-be Caesar in no doubt as to his future as a spy.

"I'm retired."

## 20.

Something was wrong, Licinius Pulcher thought to himself, as he paced around his bedchamber. His expression turned into a brief rictus, or wince, as if he had just peeled off a scab. Stolo should have sent word by now. During his time as an agent Pulcher had learned to be patient. But this was different. He needed to know, either way. Was Rufus Varro dead? He resolved to send one of his attendants to Rome, to call upon Varro's house and ask after him. He would also order his man to meet with Stolo and demand an update. Stolo had given his word that his lieutenant could be trusted to complete his task, but his word was worth about as much as the shit clinging to the cracks in his sandals. Guild leaders were as practised as politicians at dissembling.

From a distance the aristocrat appeared as attractive as ever. His figure was trim and muscular. His freshly pressed tunic was bordered with silk and embroidered with gold thread. His sharp eyes darted about and took everything in, whilst giving nothing away. But Pulcher's usually smooth features had sprouted wrinkles. His usually oiled, sculptured hair was unkempt. He was a satin cushion, suddenly looking worse for wear. The stuffing was coming out of him. A cool breeze fluttered through the shutters. But it did nothing to temper his prickling skin and heart. The scene outside, of a gently sloping lawn leading down towards a dimpled, tranquil river, stirred not an atom of calm. Pulcher needed to know Varro was dead. Nothing else mattered. He pictured the poet's smug face, heard his glib speech. That he had found fame as a playwright rubbed salt in the wound.

The former spy took little pleasure in the cup of Falernian he downed. Similar to his rival's bedchamber, Pulcher's walls were made-up of shelves filled with books. Works of poetry and history populated the room, as if the scrolls had been breeding behind his back. Both agents were well-read, as well as being well-versed in the art of seduction.

Both agents had fallen in love with the same woman too. If not for Varro, Pulcher believed that he would have been married to Lucilla right now. Maecenas had ordered his trusted agent to seduce Lucilla, so he could get close to Livia's confidante and read their correspondence. But Pulcher developed genuine feelings for the cultured, beautiful woman. She unwittingly seduced him and gave the weary agent a glimpse at a different world. He was ready to marry her and retire from working as an agent for Maecenas. Varro, however, had sowed seeds of doubt about Pulcher in her mind. Varro encouraged her to test and trap Pulcher, he believed. At the same time his rival had embarrassed him professionally, undermining him in the eyes of Caesar. So, at the same time as being rejected by Lucilla, he was spurned by Maecenas, like an old lover who could no longer please him. The past year would have been different, if not for Varro. He would have been married to Lucilla. With his new-found wealth they would have been a formidable, feted power couple in Rome. He could have befriended Caesar and replaced Maecenas as his one of his key political agents. Aye, once Varro had been disposed of, he would turn his attention to his former mentor. Pulcher had spied for Maecenas, prostituted himself, killed for him. Yet he had cast him out, like a leper – or a vintage wine which had suddenly turned sour.

Pulcher had been left out in the cold over the past year. He abandoned Rome, travelling south. He devoted himself to a life of pleasure, but no wine could wash away the bitter taste of resentment in his mouth. No dish could satisfy him as much as the desire for revenge (or, as he viewed it, for justice). No mistress or whore could make him forget about Lucilla. Regrets – and a malignancy towards Varro – gnawed at his heart, as the eagle suppered on the liver of Prometheus.

When Pulcher's inheritance came through he was determined to return to Rome and solidify his vengeance. He first thought about ruining his opponent's marriage by paying a skilful courtesan to seduce him. Pulcher was also tempted to besmirch the nobleman's reputation by spreading scandalous rumours about him. He often imagined attending the same party as Varro and poisoning his winecup. Or sneaking up behind Varro at night and sliding a knife in between his ribs.

Pulcher was content to pay somebody else to bloody their hands, however. He had everything to lose if he was caught in the act. So, he had employed Stolo's band of brigands. The main thing was that he was still the author behind his enemy's demise. Pulcher realised that he couldn't start a new chapter in his life without bringing the last one to a close – and creating an unhappy ending for Varro.

The former agent decided to travel to Rome himself. Confront Stolo. Demand answers. He would also, during his trip, look to buy a property in the capital for when he would need to stay overnight. Pulcher would call upon Caesar's daughter as well. Getting close to Julia could improve his chances of getting closer to Caesar. She could prove to be a font of intelligence, through careless pillow talk. Pulcher would attend her next party and seduce the girl, or duly give the impression that she had seduced him.

Dusk was beginning to bleed into the pale blue sky, like wine darkening water. Clouds were gathering across the firmament – as, unseen, soldiers were gathering outside the front of Pulcher's estate. Preparing to attack.

It had been a long day, Varro wearily considered. His arse ached from the ride. His head ached from the sun - and life - pounding upon him. But it still could be a long, bloody night ahead. The agent was crouched down, grass tickling his chin, as he hid within a line of dense woodland which ran along the road, opposite Pulcher's villa. The pungent smell of body odour and garum, from various praetorians laying alongside him, coloured the air. The soldiers filled their lungs and flexed their hands, ready to grab their swords and leap up, like dead men springing from their graves, once the time was right. The soon to be besieging force barely blinked, as they took in their target.

A patina of moss and bird shit decorated the walls. The large, black, thick oak door was barred – and further strengthened with iron brackets. A couple of guards manned the walls above the entrance.

"It might be a tough egg to crack," Vulso had remarked. "But crack it we will."

Varro watched the wagon, laden with wine, trundle along the road, towards the villa. Yet his inner eye pictured the corpse of Plancus on his gore-strewn bedroll. Few would mourn his death – and no one would be punished for it. As the agent took his leave from Caesar's loathsome stepson earlier, he rightly, painfully, concluded that justice hadn't been done. But he was a spy. Justice wasn't part of his brief, Varro argued with himself. An agent's mission was to deliver up intelligence, that his paymaster wanted to hear. Agents often avoided telling the truth. Should Varro reveal the truth to Agrippa or Caesar, he would cause more problems than he would solve. Just tell the powers that be what they wanted to hear. The truth needed to remain secret. For once, he wouldn't even share his findings with Manius, Lucilla or Fronto – lest he placed them in danger.

Manius was dutifully placing himself in danger already, however, as he accompanied Vulso and a couple of other praetorians on the wagon. Agrippa had suggested the ruse of pretending to deliver wine to the residence, in order to have the enemy open its doors to the contingent of soldiers.

The Briton sat next to Vulso at the front of the wagon. The latter believed that it was no time to blood a batch of new recruits. He had selected a group of battle-hardened veterans for the assignment. Loyal. Lethal. Pugnacious. Professional. Some had fought under Agrippa at Philippi and Actium. One of the praetorians, Ulpius, spoke to Manius as they approached the house. Ulpius chewed a piece of dried goat's meat ‑ and often spat out gobbets of phlegm ‑ as he talked. He had a guttural accent, as thick as pottage, and the Briton barely understood one out of three words he said.

"I remember seeing you compete in the arena, many years ago. Some retiarius bastard trapped you in his net and buried his trident in your thigh. They then started to play to the crowd. He was from Gaul if I remember rightly. Usually they turn their back on an opponent with the intention of running away. We all thought you were finished. That trident in your leg must have smarted a bit, eh? Must have hurt even more when you pulled the weapon out and launched it into your opponent, as the silly fucker tried to get the arena to chant his name. I remember the day because I placed a bet on you. And I remember paying for a whore with my winnings. And I remember the whore because she gave me a pox. I must have scratched my dick so much afterwards, I'm surprised it didn't wear down to nothing. By Venus, she was a lively filly though. What a ride! The pox was almost worth it. Almost. But it's good to have you with us, Manius. Save some of the bastards for the rest of us. I don't want you and Vulso killing everyone."

Manius merely half-smiled and nodded. Rather than past glories, he was focussed on the imminent fight. Only one kill mattered to him. He needed to kill Pulcher. Then he need never kill again (although he had made – and broken – such a promise before). Once they had secured the entrance, Manius would scour the house for his quarry. Agrippa's agents, who had kept the house under surveillance, reported that Pulcher was still inside the property. The former gladiator had oiled and sharpened his sword, which lay under a blanket by his feet, before setting off from Rome. He had also spent part of the morning practising throwing his dagger, at a wooden target, in preparation for the assault.

The brace of guards, standing on the parapet above the entrance, remained relaxed as the wagon approached. They had no reason to be suspicious, or on alert. They received deliveries every day. Vulso noted how each guard carried a bow. But Agrippa's agent had forewarned him about the archers. The agent had also reported that the household contained around twenty slaves (but many were women, young boys and old men) and around two dozen bodyguards. They were well-armed and seasoned professionals, no doubt former soldiers or ex-gladiators. The agent also briefed Vulso that, once inside, he would encounter a courtyard filled with approximately ten guards sitting around, carousing. "Half the battle will be about securing the entrance, preventing the enemy from defending the villa from a position of strength. Once your men are inside, in numbers, then you'll soon be tasting victory – and drinking the wine you're carrying," the agent remarked.

Manius glanced up at the bowmen on the walls. Their powerful arms and chests signified that they were professionals. Well-practised. The Briton recalled the way Macer had turned the tide, during their skirmish on the way to Rome. From their elevated position the two archers above him could wreak similar damage and decimate the ranks of the attacking force. The bowmen probably had an arsenal of spears to hand too – and if supported by more men could turn defeat into victory, when the praetorians broke cover from the treeline and stormed the villa. Vulso had a plan to nullify the archers, but few plans ever remain intact once one engages the enemy.

The sun-baked ground beneath him was bone hard, but he was ready to spring up from it as if it were made of sponge. Varro's body tensed and he felt his heart pound in his chest, like a prisoner banging a fist against his cell door, as he watched the wagon come to halt. They would soon know if their ruse would succeed or fail. He pulled the strap again on his small, round shield, so it bit further into his forearm. He licked the sweat off his top lip, as brackish as tears. Agrippa had sent over a message back in Rome, saying that he did not expect Varro to take part in the assault. But he was not about to let his friends fight his battles for him. He wanted to see Pulcher's corpse. Unlike the memory of Plancus' bloody body, Varro would welcome the image.

A shutter abruptly slid open, at the heart of the oak door. Vulso took in the dark, close-set eyes and broken nose. The thuggish face scrutinised the unexpected visitors. Manius faked a yawn and appeared bored, as if desiring just to get the delivery over and done with. Ulpius, and the soldier sitting next to him, Ravilla, both wore sunhats to conceal their military haircuts.

"State your business," the less than hospitable figure demanded. His voice was raspy, like the sound of an unoiled blade being drawn from a rusty scabbard.

"We're here to deliver a consignment of wine. It's a gift for your master, from Lucius Curio," Vulso exclaimed. Agrippa had given the praetorian a name to use. Curio was a known acquaintance of Pulcher's.

There was a short pause – and then a grunt of assent or gratitude. The man greeting them, if greeting was the right term, was Flavius Piso. Piso was a former lanista, who now commanded a group of mercenaries. Swords for hire. Piso's men didn't come cheap, but he argued that "you get what you pay for." The Etruscan wasn't one to take prisoners, unless they could command a valuable ransom.

Piso snapped out an order for a couple of his men to unbar the door. Vulso wiped his sweaty palms on his grubby tunic and shared a brief look with Manius, to let the Briton know that he was ready – and to assure himself that his friend was ready too. The large door, wide enough to swallow the wagon up, creaked opened.

Vulso flicked the reins and entered the lion's den.

## 21.

Vulso pulled on the reins and slowed the wagon, ensuring that the back of the vehicle was still located in the doorway, to help prevent the enemy from quickly barring the entrance.

Manius surveyed his opponents. Their leader seemed to be the man who had spoken to them through the shutter. He was lean, grey-haired and his chin jutted out like a cliff. He had a severe centre-parting, and a severer expression. He possessed a face that one wouldn't altogether trust – and one that you wouldn't want to betray either, Manius judged. The men he led were not to be underestimated. They numbered over a dozen, but more could be called upon if the alarm was sounded. They were well-conditioned and well-armed. Well-maintained swords and daggers hung down from belts. Many were lank-haired, bearded and brutish. Their eyes were slightly glazed, from an afternoon spent drinking. But wine often fuelled violence, instead of quelling it. Not even Pythagoras could come up with a theorem to calculate how many men the mercenaries had killed over the years. The Briton suspected that more than a few were foreign born – Germans, Spanish and Gauls. Manius couldn't help but note one barbarian, wearing leather trousers, sitting in the corner. Mago. He was equal, if not superior, in size to the bodyguard. A double-bladed axe lay within his muscular arm's reach, although he appeared more interested in the plate of salted ham on his lap, than in the strangers who had newly arrived. He didn't appear ready for a fight. But Manius was.

Piso wondered if the wine delivery consisted of various vintages, for his employer's cellar, of if the consignment was of a sufficient quality (or lack of quality) so that Pulcher would share it with his men. He would refrain from disturbing his employer at present, with news about the wine. The irritable – and irritating – nobleman had been in a foul mood for a couple of days now. Not even Mago was strong enough to remove the stick from his arse, Piso joked to himself.

The wagon was in position. It was time. Macer and a handful of archers dashed forward. He had his orders. The praetorian was keen to prove himself. Vulso had promised him a month's leave if he made his arrow count. Varro had added that he would grant Sabina a month's leave too – and provide enough coin for them to visit a coastal resort. The guards on the wall had their backs turned, as they took an interest in what was happening inside the courtyard. Macer lined up with five other archers. Three were tasked with targeting the guard on the left, three targeted the guard on the right.

Macer nocked an arrow. The shot would be difficult, but as Vulso told him, "Difficult is not the same as impossible." He pulled the string back, his chest expanding, and judged the required arc of flight. The young bowman took a breath and then took the shot. The guard's focus was averted when he heard an arrow, unleashed by one of Macer's fellow archers, clatter against the stone wall beneath him. But the guard was still not alert enough to see or avoid

Macer's missile. The arrow punched into the guard's shoulder with such power that it forced the mercenary backwards, causing him to fall off the parapet, into the courtyard below. As Macer's countenance broke out into a picture of satisfaction, having witnessed his arrow hit its mark, he felt the ground quake beneath him as the squad of praetorians ran by him.

There was a moment of stunned silence as the mercenaries in the courtyard took in their groaning companion, the arrow still lodged in his shoulder. But then it was as though the gates of Hades opened. Vulso was the first to react. The praetorian threw the blanket off his feet, beneath which lay a cache of spears and a couple of swords. First, he grabbed a pilum. The sinewy, scar-faced mercenary standing closest to the wagon took a step backwards, but not quickly enough to avoid Vulso jabbing the point of his weapon through the jelly of his eye and into his brain. Without hesitating, or seeing his victim fall, the soldier launched his spear to cut down the leader of the mercenaries. Piso had just bellowed out an order for one of his men to sound the alarm. As a bell was rung, to call for the rest of his comrades to muster in the courtyard, the pilum skewered the Etruscan. His rasping voice turned into a croak – and then a death rattle. Vulso reached for another pilum and set out his stall to fend off other opponents.

Manius was swift to react too, realising that he needed to remove the threat of the brutal axe-wielding barbarian, whose plate of food had dropped to the floor in his rush to clasp his weapon. Twig-like strands of hair hung down over his bony forehead and black, glowering aspect. He barged one of his fellow mercenaries out of the way, to make a beeline for the wagon. Manius launched his javelin but, through either luck or skill, the barbarian swatted the pilum away with his axe. He then beat his chest and let out a roar cum growl cum howl in triumph – but as he stretched out his arms and raised his head to the skies Manius took the opportunity to unsheathe his dagger and throw it into the soft, sweet spot at the base of his neck. The mercenary staggered around for a few steps, like a drunk, and crashed to the ground, like a giant oak being chopped down.

"Run hard, but not too hard," Vulso had advised his men earlier. "When you come to swinging your swords, when you get to the courtyard, I don't want you falling over from exhaustion... Keep a good pace and keep your shape."

Varro kept pace and remained in the frontline of the praetorians rushing towards the villa. The force was small enough to approach the house, undetected, but large enough to overwhelm the enemy. Varro tried to keep a clear mind and hoped that the beads of sweat running down his brow wouldn't drop into his eyes. His first objective was to reach Manius. The pair would then commence to search for Pulcher. They could get lucky and Pulcher could come out into the courtyard to join the fight. More likely though, the former agent might try to conceal himself, somewhere in the house. Or he could attempt to escape through the back of the property. But Vulso had posted men there to prevent any retreat - and holed the boat which could be used to cross the river at the rear of the estate.

As much as Varro was dressed differently from the advancing praetorians, the grim determination on his face matched the soldiers' focus. If anything, his expression was even more determined. Fiercer. He briefly saw his reflection in his polished blade and didn't recognise himself. Varro would spend his last day, being a spy, as a soldier. Instead of a spy or soldier, however, he yearned to be husband – and father.

Curses rang out on both sides. Vulso, Manius, Ulpius and Ravilla were now surrounded. Vulso noticed one of the mercenaries grab the bridle of one of the lead horses on the wagon. His intention was to pull the vehicle into the courtyard, to allow his confederates to bar the entrance to the oncoming praetorians. The creatures had remained remarkably calm during the storm around them. They were superior specimens, muscular and groomed. If Piso had been paying full attention, he would have realised that the mounts were far too fine to be mere cart horses. Vulso called out a command and Mars duly reared up and felled the mercenary. The sickening crack of the hooves stoving in the Spaniard's chest could even be heard above the wild cacophony of other the battle. Whilst Vulso was momentarily distracted however, a mercenary thrust his spear forward and the leaf-shaped blade sliced open his calf.

"Bastard," he exclaimed, as he parried a second attack, aimed at his thigh. As much as the soldier was willing to slay anyone in front of him, Vulso knew that the tactic should be to just hold the enemy off and ensure that the door remained open. There was still a chance that the attack could fail, if the entrance was barred. His men would be caught in a killing zone, if they were locked out. Spears and arrows could rain down upon them from the parapet if the mercenaries organised themselves. The enemy could also retreat in numbers through the back of the villa – and Pulcher could slip through their fingers. Ulpius let out a howl of pain as a mercenary plunged a sword point into his midriff, albeit it was swiftly succeeded by the crunching sound of Manius punching his sword through the attacker's collar bone.

Vulso realised that that they wouldn't be able to hold out for much longer. But they wouldn't need to. The cherished, familiar sound of armour rhythmically clinking together grew louder. A wave of iron was about to crash into the villa. Vulso reached down and flicked the reins once more. The wagon fully entered the courtyard, so his men could freely pour through the entrance. The praetorians swarmed through. A number of mercenaries formed themselves into a line – but that just gave the frontline soldiers a greater target to launch their volley of javelins at. A few of the enemy decided it would be wise to surrender at this point. But their blood was up - and the praetorians executed the unarmed men. The dead and dying were trampled on as the soldiers rushed to get to those mercenaries who were attempting to retreat, realising that to battle on was hopeless. They were not interested in prisoners. Vulso, funded by Varro, had offered a significant reward for anyone who cut down the owner of the house. As they didn't know what Pulcher looked like, everyone was fair game. If the former gladiators could contest the soldiers individually then they would have backed themselves, but the trained soldiers were greater than the sum of their parts. They advanced together, killed together – stabbed necks, faces and groins together. Some of the enemy might have been classed as barbarians, but it was the civilised Romans who fought with greater savagery.

A breathless Varro joined Vulso and Manius, as they clambered down from the wagon. Blood spotted their battle-weary countenances, but thankfully it wasn't theirs. The agent noticed the unpleasant gash on the praetorian's calf, however.

"You okay?"

"Call this a wound?" the veteran scoffed. "I've had whores put scratches in my back which have hurt more. We'll finish things off here. Go inside and get the bastard. Ravilla, follow our friends here and watch their backs. Ulpius, stop mewling. It'll have to be a more accurate spear thrust than that to find and cut of your small cock."

The praetorian's voice was dust-dry but he still barked out a couple more orders as Varro and Manius made their way towards the house. He glanced at the wagon and felt like smashing open one of the large amphora of wine and dunking his head into it. He surveyed the courtyard and allowed himself a moment of respite - and thanked the gods. It appeared that he would be carrying a few injured men back to the barracks, but no corpses.

Night was descending, like a veil being pulled over a widow's pale face. The blood, slickening the flagstones, appeared more brownish than red. Varro experienced a few twinges of compassion, and horror, as he witnessed a sobbing mercenary writhing on the ground, attempting to put his intestines back into his stomach. Every time he thought he was close to completing the task they would wriggle free, like eels.

They walked up the flight of steps outside the house, but Varro felt like he was descending into the underworld. Death or deliverance awaited him. Few lamps were lit in the interior. Vulso squinted in the gloom and watched his friends enter the villa, the darkness swallowing them up.

The screams from the courtyard pierced his ears, but not his heart. Pulcher judged that he had paid Piso and his mercenaries well. It was their job to spill their blood for him. When he heard the alarm Pulcher had sped to the nearest first floor window, which overlooked the front of the house. His stomach churned, with fear or bile, as he witnessed the horde of praetorians advancing. He also spotted Manius in the courtyard – and judged that Varro couldn't be far away. A shocked Pulcher spat out a curse, like a cobra spitting venom, but the mystery of how his enemy had found him could wait. Questions could be answered later – although his immediate thought was that Maecenas had betrayed him. Killing was second nature to soldiers, but treachery was second nature to the spymaster.

The task now was to escape, survive, Pulcher determined. He duly commanded a number of passing mercenaries to follow him, rather than run out into the courtyard to be slaughtered. Their comrades were all but dead. But that didn't mean they had to share their fate. The battle was lost, but

Pulcher could still win the war. *Live to fight another day.* If he escaped, he would be willing to pay for an army of assassins to hunt down and kill Varro.

Pulcher ordered his band of mercenaries towards the back of the house. One of the first-floor bedrooms led out to a terrace, which contained steps leading down to grounds which contained a fast-flowing river. The plan was now to reach the sole boat, moored on the small pier, and cross the water. *Go where the enemy can't follow.* Pulcher let out another curse however, as a small force of praetorians scrambled out of the woods, which bordered the neighbouring estate, and decamped themselves on his back lawn. They were waiting for him to be flushed out. Pulcher calculated that, although his mercenaries may not be able to defeat the soldiers, they may be able to distract them long enough for him to reach the boat and flee. He cursed his slaves for running away, as they could have been used as a diversion and sacrifice too.

Pulcher briefed him men, spoon feeding them false hope.

"The bulk of the enemy – and their best troops – are at the front of the house. Those men outside are doubtless new recruits, a reserve force. I have every confidence that we can swat them away, like insects. For any man who joins me, crossing the river to make our escape, I will double his pay," the nobleman exclaimed, drawing his sword in readiness.

Varro and Manius were now halfway up the main, marble staircase. Even in the half-light Varro could see that the house was expensively furnished. Pulcher may have been morally bankrupt, but he could still afford the finer things in life. Agrippa mentioned that the villa had once belonged to Marcus Crassus. He would bring his curvaceous mistresses here, although the only figures he truly appreciated were those which his accountant gave him.

The two men nodded to one another once more, giving the signal to proceed. Even in the gloom Varro could see how his friend's muscular body was taut, alert – his ears pricked to attention, like Viola's when she she heard that call that her dinner was ready. They could be ambushed at any moment. An enemy could appear out the darkness in an instant. The murky light only fuelled his fear. But fear needed to be defeated, along with Pulcher. Varro was ready to raise his weapon at any moment, should he witness the glint of polished metal or hear a battle-cry. He observed how Manius' sword no longer glinted, as blood smothered the blade. Ravilla followed behind, lest they were attacked from the rear.

Ravilla would soon hear the cacophonous noise of his fellow praetorians, entering the lavish property like a plague of locusts. Intent on looting. "When the bastard owner's gone, he won't have need have any of his possessions," Vulso had told him men, during their briefing before the attack. "He'll just need a couple of coins for the ferryman. Feel free to plunder everything else. But get the job done first."

Pulcher was just about to lead, or rather follow, his men outside, when he heard a voice coming from inside the house.

"This way."

The voice was familiar – yet hated. Pulcher involuntarily gripped his sword tighter, to the point where his white knuckles almost shone in the darkness. As the mercenaries made their way down the steps Pulcher turned back. He might never secure such an opportunity again. To have Varro die by an assassin's hand was fine, but for him to die by his own hand was infinitely finer. More honourable. More visceral. More satisfying. If he killed Varro and was cornered by the enemy, he could still surrender. There was a chance that he could purchase his freedom. The commanding officer could be susceptible to a bribe. Even if he was apprehended and taken back to Rome, all would not be lost. He could afford to hire the best advocates. Testimonies could be refuted, evidence contested. Did he not have a right to murder Varro too, having trespassed in his house? Juries could be bought, or intimidated. The worse that could happen would be banishment. But he could live with not returning to Rome, knowing that Varro would never be returning too.

*It's fate that he's here. Kill him.*

Varro moved forward, his boots sounding on the polished, tiled floor. He could feel the breeze grow stronger from the room at the end of the corridor, to the point where it began to chill his sweat-glazed cheeks. He heard a drumbeat of footsteps, retreating downstairs, into the garden. He thought how it was all nearly over. This would be his final day, as a spy. Agrippa had once told him that he accepted his offer of becoming an agent because he was partly damaged.

"You're not the first spy I have ever recruited to be damaged in some way. Working for the glory of Rome, redeeming yourself, will somehow fix the damaged part of you."

Perhaps there had been a modicum truth to what Agrippa had said, back then. But his work as an agent hadn't fixed him. Lucilla had. Should he go back to a life of service to the state, for the glory of Rome, it would be the cause of him being damaged again, not the cure. That much was clear, in the darkness.

Pulcher waited, his razor-sharp gladius at the ready. He willed himself to control his breathing and, at the last moment, he would even hold his breath. His black heart seemed to be pumping black blood. He briefly pictured Lucilla. As much as she was a vision of beauty, the image solidified his animus. Varro had been the author of his rejection. Dejection. But now Pulcher would be the author of his enemy's end. Another footstep sounded outside the room. One step closer to death. But wait. *Let him come to you.* The raucous din of the clash of arms beginning to take place outside in the grounds faded into the background.

One more step. Could he hear his enemy breathing?

It was time to strike.

The former assassin smoothly and swiftly appeared at the doorway and turned, to thrust his blade into his enemy's stomach. The point of the gladius hit its mark - and glided through flesh like a hot knife through butter. Pulcher's eyes shone with spite and triumph. His lips receded over his gums and his teeth gleamed in the darkness, as did the whites of his enemy's eyes, as they widened in shock and agony. Pulcher wanted to stare the man in the face, let him know who had bested him. But it wasn't the face Pulcher expected. Manius' sword clanged upon the tiled floor. His innards burned, as if he had swallowed hot shards of glass. The house grew even darker.

Varro froze for a moment. Or more than a moment. He noticed the tip of Pulcher's blade protrude out of his friend's back. Manius was surely as good as dead. Pulcher hesitated not however, having observed Varro standing just behind his wretched bodyguard. He would unsheathe his gladius from out of the Briton's body and slay his rival too. But for some reason, which at first confounded him, Pulcher couldn't dislodge his weapon. Mustering his remaining wherewithal and strength Manius gripped his own hands around his enemies, to prevent him from drawing his sword. It hurt like the fire of Hades to do so, but it was worth it. Varro's moment of hesitation passed – and with his face contorted in more malice and violence than he thought possible, he stabbed the defenceless Pulcher through the throat. Blood briefly gurgled from the mortal wound, like a pot boiling over.

Pulcher dropped to the ground and Manius slumped to his knees. The bodyguard's tunic crimsoned. Varro could see his expression clearer, as it grew paler. Ashen. The agent frantically called out to Ravilla to fetch a surgeon. The praetorian raced downstairs but, having observed the wound, knew that it would be futile. The brave Britain was a dead man, he just didn't know it yet. Or perhaps he did.

Varro slumped to his knees too and held his friend's hand. For a moment Manius summoned the strength to squeeze it back. The nobleman felt like the lifeblood was draining out of him, as well as his bodyguard. His brother. Varro wished he could be dying in his place. He deserved to die in his place, he believed. Tears moistened his eyes and then flowed freely. The last time he had cried had been the night after Lucilla had proposed to him. But those had been tears of happiness.

"Well, at least we killed the bastard. You can retire. Although it looks like we're both be retiring now," Manius emitted, his voice as weak as his enfeebled body. He raised a corner of his mouth in an attempt at a grin. It was almost his final feat of strength.

"That's nonsense. We both know that you'll outlive me. Just stay awake. Stay with me. Please," Varro replied, sobbing, feeling his friend's hand grow limp and colder. The agent was broken. Far worse than just damaged.

"Tell Camilla that I love her. You've been a good friend, Rufus. You're a good man," Manius said, eking out what words and energy he had remaining, despite the excruciating pain he experienced when he spoke. The blade seemed to be biting into his innards.

"You'll be able to tell her yourself. Just stay awake. Keep talking. Say something," Varro pleaded, feeling helpless. Hopeless. He witnessed his friend close his eyes and his head loll to one side.

"There is a time for many words, and there is also a time for sleep," Manius wryly whispered, after reviving one last time.

He passed shortly afterwards. Some people die with a shocked expression on their face, as though the inevitable still takes them by surprise. Skin can be like cheap leather, or ashen or translucent. A mouth can be comically contorted, in agony or in a silent, primal scream. Raging against death, or life. Manius appeared at peace however, which is more than could be said for his friend, who remained by his side, clutching his lifeless hand. Weeping.

Ravilla returned with a surgeon, but it was too late. The praetorian descended the stairs, his caligae seemingly soled with lead, and reported the news to his commanding officer. At first Vulso couldn't quite believe what he was hearing – and asked Ravilla if he was sure. He was. The world was somehow less noble and less courageous with Manius no longer being a part of it. Vulso stood dumbstruck for a period of time, before he cursed the gods and ordered one of his men to pour out a jug of wine and take it up to his grieving friend. All the wine in the world couldn't wash his sorrow away though, the soldier dolefully imagined.

## 22. Epilogue.

Granite coloured clouds marbled the sunless sky. The breeze whipped itself into a gust. Another storm was due to come in from the coast, Varro predicted. He sat out in his garden, in Arretium. The tint of the sky reminded him of the marble he used to mark the burial plot of his friend, a year ago. So much in life reminded him of Manius' death. It was the refrain, or Chorus, to his existence. Not a day went by when Varro didn't think about his companion. But it was a good thing to remember him. Honour him. Raise a cup to him. Varro sometimes felt that, without his grief and guilt, he would be nothing.

His hair was mottled with grey patches. Dark rings, like bruises, circled his bloodshot eyes. Varro finished the dregs of his wine and poured himself another measure. A wax tablet lay on his potbelly, as he reclined on his favourite chair. Varro had spent part of the afternoon making notes for his next play. He only composed tragedies nowadays. His heart wasn't in writing any comedies. Try as he might, he couldn't think of, or believe in, any happy endings.

"I am just going to put the baby down for his nap," Lucilla called out, from the house. "I'll try to catch up on some sleep too."

"That's fine," Varro replied, half-hearing his wife. He envied how much the baby could sleep. Be dead to the world.

The baby.

The day after Manius died – was killed – Varro ignored Agrippa's orders to return to Rome and rode back to Arretium. He desperately needed to see Lucilla – and he also wanted to be the one to tell Camilla about her husband's passing. As much as he dreaded the scene of conveying the news to her, Varro didn't experience any sense of relief when he realised that he would be spared the difficult encounter.

The emotionally and physically exhausted agent reached home. He was met by Lucilla. Her eyes were puffy - and her face was pale. She could barely speak, from her sore throat and bouts of sobbing. She buried her head in his chest and told him her news. Camilla had died, just after giving birth to her son. When she asked where Manius was, Varro told his wife his news.

But the baby survived. *Manius Appius Varro.* It was the easiest decision he ever had to make in his life, to adopt the child. It was bittersweet, to say the least, to bring up his dead friend's son. The infant brought Lucilla a boundless amount of joy, albeit she sometimes felt twinges of guilt. The baby was a wondrous gift, which had come at a terrible price.

If only Varro could have been just half as content as his wife. He drank heavily. He slept fitfully. Nightmares forced him to relive Manius' death, over and over. During his waking hours he was haunted by a thousand "what ifs". He blamed an army of people for his friend's death. Caesar. Agrippa. Pulcher. Vulso. Maecenas. Stolo. But most of the time Varro blamed himself.

He would walk and swim alone in the morning, while Lucilla attended to the baby. The clouds which hung over him never showed any sign of dissipating. Work and his family helped. But not enough. His sorrow was the only thing which seemed real. Guilt followed him around, like a shadow. He was married to it, as much as he was married to Lucilla.

They barely made love anymore. But Lucilla was patient, understanding. And he remained faithful. Manius wouldn't have approved if he took a mistress, now that he was a father, he believed.

"I know that I have not been at my best of late," Varro said, with habitual understatement, shortly after Manius passed. "But I'm still aware that you're the best thing in my life, Lucilla. I love you, thankfully more than I hate myself. Whenever you catch me in a gloom, and I seem distant, just come up to me and hold my hand or kiss me. And hopefully I won't be in such a gloom," he added, with a faltering smile.

To help lift him out of his gloom Lucilla arranged with Fronto for Viola to come and live at the villa. The sweet mongrel could sometimes be as mournful as her new master, as she pined for her old one, but Varro could never be wholly unhappy in her company.

Fronto passed six months after Manius, dying in his sleep. Varro never got to say goodbye properly, to tell him how much he loved him. But Varro knew Fronto was pleased that he finally had a child, of sorts, who could carry on the family name. The estate manager had never quite been the same, after learning of the bodyguard's death. Varro was always conscious of how much Fronto had been a surrogate father to him over the years. But he hadn't quite realised how much Manius had been a surrogate son to the old man. Part of Varro was envious of his fate, when he passed. He occasionally pictured Fronto and Manius sharing a jug of Falernian in the next life, waiting for him to join them.

Shortly before Fronto died he visited Arretium. The estate manager asked his master what he intended to do with the rest of his life. Varro shrugged his shoulders and replied that he would try to be a good man and a good father. To try to make Manius proud.

"Unfortunately, I fear I'm failing. I was a better agent than I am a father," he lamentably confessed. "I'm just a sad man, as opposed to a good man."

Perhaps life shouldn't be about rolling a boulder up and down a hill. Sisyphus should have given up before he started, Varro reasoned. Instead of admiring Hector as a tragic hero, should he not consider him a absurd figure, for continuing to fight a losing battle?

We men are wretched things.

Fronto wasn't the only visitor to call on the retired spy during the course of the past year. Agrippa visited and stayed one evening. The first thing he mentioned was that his visit was just a social call. The nobleman could continue to enjoy his retirement.

"You've already given enough to Rome. Too much."

"How is Caesar?" Varro asked, out of politeness rather than genuine concern.

"Caesar is Caesar," Agrippa answered, revealing everything and nothing.

Whether both men felt they were wiser or not, compared to when Agrippa had initially recruited Varro, they certainly felt wearier. The conversation was sometimes stilted, especially when they mentioned Manius, but the wine flowed.

As well as bringing a consignment of his friend's favourite vintage, Agrippa delivered the news that his daughter was going to be married. To Tiberius. Caesar had suggested the union. "It will be a good, political match," Agrippa asserted, trying as much to convince himself, as his friend, of his argument. Agrippa felt like he had given enough – too much – to Caesar and Rome as well. Varro had met Vipsania a few times. She was a beautiful, intelligent young woman. A credit to her father. Her mother's daughter.

"Tiberius should consider himself a lucky man," Varro remarked. He couldn't bring himself to say that Vipsania was as equally fortunate. He couldn't share the truth about his prospective son-in-law. The truth wouldn't do anyone any good. Varro had his own family to worry about. The truth could make a son fatherless, or a father childless.

Agrippa no longer wrote to him - or proposed another visit. Perhaps Varro was dead to the spymaster, now he was no longer an agent. Now he would no longer work for the glory of Rome.

Agrippa did furnish Vulso and Macer with ample leave though to visit their friend – although the archer suitably spent more of his leave time of late in the company of his new wife, the freedwoman Sabina.

If any of the visitors who came to the villa noticed the change when they crossed the threshold, they didn't mention anything. But, shortly after Manius died, Varro painted over the mosaic in the doorway, containing the quote from Aristotle:

"*It is during our darkest moments that we must focus to see the light.*"

Varro thought he would be deceiving his guests - giving them false hope - if he allowed the words to remain visible.


**End Note.**

I hope you have enjoyed the Spies of Rome series, despite or because of its rather sombre ending. I certainly enjoyed putting the plots and characters together, to the point where I nearly succumbed to the temptation of continuing the series.

I still might. Do get in touch should you want to see more Spies of Rome books. There is scope to cover some of the events and assignments which happened between the three novels. In the meantime, should it be of interest, you may wish to read *A Brief Affair*, a short story included in *Rubicon: A HWA Collection*, which features Rufus Varro.

Should you have a taste for reading more about the real history behind the period than I can recommend the following: *The Roman Revolution*, by Ronald Syme; *Dynasty*, by Tom Holland; *The Twelve Caesars*, by Suetonius.

In relation to some historical novelists you may wish to read, I can recommend Steven Saylor, Peter Tonkin and Nick Brown.

I have also written several other series set in Rome – including *Augustus: Son of Rome* and *Sword of Rome: The Complete Campaigns* – which touch upon some of the characters and events mentioned in Spies of Rome.

I will now be taking a break from writing about the era, in order to put together a series set during the First Crusade. Do please contact me however if you have enjoyed Spies of Rome, or any of my other books.

Richard Foreman.
richard@sharpebooks.com

\*

Printed in Great Britain
by Amazon

29211135R00253